I, Who 2

The Unauthorized Guide

to Doctor Who Novels *and Audios*

LARS PEARSON

Mad Norwegian Press • New Orleans

DEDICATION: *I, Who 2* was born in a strife-filled year that, truth to tell, bled me for every yard of conquered ground. Yet along the way, Christa Dickson emerged as a wellspring of unconditional passion and trust. She will always be the "Aphrodite of the Pizza" to me.

INTRODUCTION

When I next return from time and space
I might have a somewhat different face,
Don't start debating;
I've been off regenerating
That only happens for a Lord of Time.
—*"The Lord of Time"*
Set to "The Longest Time" by Billy Joel

So there I was, years ago, watching a "Monty Python" marathon—a Python-a-Thon, as they called it—on a New Jersey PBS station. As most folks will tell you, however, whenever a normal person (i.e., someone who doesn't say, "PBS is all I watch") tunes in to Public Broadcasting, it's always pledge week/month/eternity. Every 15 minutes, the program you broke away from your usual viewing habits to watch is interrupted by painfully pinched individuals trying to tell you that they'll be "right back in just a few moments" to the show they just took away from you (somehow a 20 minute pledge break translates to "a few moments.")

But it was "Monty Python," and this was before DVD, and even before widespread videotape use (told you it was years ago), so this seemed like the best shot to get some classic Brit entertainment.

So there was the general manager of the station, talking about how they were going to be endeavoring to get other great British series, if only they had the money to do it. He certainly seemed sincere, although sincerity wasn't translating into tons of calls. Many of the phones were quiet. As for me, I was feeling a bit bummed because the *Doctor Who* episodes syndicated on the local TV station were going to end soon, and New York would be without the adventures of the Doctor.

So when the pledge break finally terminated, I picked up the phone and called. This being a small PBS station, I did something I never could have done with a large station such as WNET: I asked if I could speak directly to the GM. "Sure," they said. Within about a minute, he came on (his voice immediately recognizable.)

I asked him if one of the shows they were looking into was *Doctor Who*. "Yes, it is, as a matter of fact," he said.

"Tell you what," I said. "I realize that you obviously can't make any guarantees. But I will pledge to send you money with the understanding that it is to be earmarked specifically for your endeavors to obtain the right to air *Doctor Who*. If it doesn't work out, obviously, use it for whatever you want, but that's what I'm intending it to be used for."

"Fair enough," he said, "and we'll do our best."

"One other thing," I suggested. *"Doctor Who* has a pretty enthusiastic following. You should mention that you're looking to add it to your line-up. Fans might respond to that news."

"You think it would help?" he asked.

"Absolutely I do, yes."

So I went back to watching "Monty Python", and some minutes later, on roared the pledge break. The GM chatted for about five minutes, and then said, almost as an afterthought, "One caller asked if we were going to try and get *Doctor Who*. The answer is, yes, we are. We are in negotiations. But it's going to take money and support from dedicated viewers—"

The phones started ringing. Phones that hadn't rung all evening. Startled operators, visible on screen, stared at the jangling units as if unsure of what to do. The GM looked momentarily startled but kept on talking about the station's efforts to obtain the ongoing adventures of the Doctor. More phones rang, and more. Within two minutes, every operator was taking donations.

The next pledge break, the GM only waited two minutes before bringing up *Doctor Who*. Once again the switchboards lit up. By the pledge break after that, the GM had totally gotten with the program. "Welcome fans of *Monty Python* and *Doctor Who*," he said chipperly. Moments later, it was almost as if he'd forgotten that it was a "Monty Python" marathon: Every other word out of his mouth was *Doctor Who*. The phones did not stop. The support was obvious and overwhelming. And the station, true to the GM's word, went out and got *Doctor Who*, which was a mainstay for them for many years.

Some years later, I mentioned the incident in passing to the head of a New Jersey-based *Doctor Who* club. He blinked in surprise, then said, "You were the one?" He and his associates had been among the many who called in that night, and apparently it had always been a matter of speculation as to the identity of the *Doctor Who* fan who'd called and set the whole thing into motion.

There's just something about the series. It has a charmed life, and it impacts on so many people in so many ways.

Random Recollections:

• I attended one convention where every third contestant in the costume competition was dressed as some incarnation of the Doctor. It got so absurd that one of the committee members, to provide a mute comment on the over-saturation, added a late entry—a watermelon dressed as the fourth Doctor (i.e., with a brown fedora and a scarf). The watermelon got a standing ovation.

• At another convention, Peter Davison was the guest of honor. I was in the audience as they prepared to bring him out. Seated next to me was a young woman who knew nothing about *Doctor Who*, couldn't have cared less, and was only there to keep her friends company. So they brought out Davison, and he waved to the crowd. The woman's eyes went wide and she let out a shriek: "Oh my God, it's Tristan!" She might not have known the Doctor from a hole in the wall, but she knew *All Creatures Great and Small* right enough. She was utterly content for the rest of the speech.

• For quite some time I developed a friendship with Terrance Dicks, author of more *Doctor Who* novelizations than you can shake a TARDIS at. One time Terrance and his family came to visit New York. Looking for a moderately priced hotel, and thinking that someplace called the "Times Square Hotel" sounded rather posh, that's where they checked in...not realizing it was a dive populated by the sleaziest of New York's underbelly (this was before the entire area was Disneyfied). So here was this politely bemused British family, so completely and utterly out of place that the pimps, prostitutes, johns, pick pockets and drug addicts who frequented the place not only did not molest them, but instead drew a curtain of protection around the family. They all watched out for Terrance, his wife and kids, all of whom had a marvelous time while they were here.

• A fanzine called "Jelly Baby Chronicles" ran a couple of short pieces of fan fic I wrote which reimagined Winnie-the-Pooh as a Time Lord ("Doctor Pooh lived in a house under a name that no one could pronounce, which is why they called him 'Doctor Pooh.'") With such adventures as "Genesis of the Heffalumps" and "Terror of the Woozles," I expanded the stories into my very own, full length fanzine. It eventually attracted the attention of premiere fans Don and Maggie Thompson. Although Don regrettably passed away some years back, Maggie is editor of *Comic Buyers Guide* and still one of my closest friends.

• My youngest daughter, Ariel, has the middle name "Leela."

• I was once walking around in Glasgow, visiting. I turned a corner and saw, to my shock and excitement, a blue police callbox. It was just like his. I ran up to it and had my picture taken with it, and later used it as an author photo.

• Lastly, back in the early 90s, I wrote a song parody, the first stanza of which appears above. It's been performed a few times, including a live version sung by myself, and friends Glenn Hauman and Howard Margolin, at a cabaret during Long Island's annual I-Con. Here's the rest of the song, in case any of you are ever inclined to do-wop your way into people's hearts:

When I fight my enemies again,
Master, Daleks, or the Cybermen
It won't surprise me when they
do not recognize me,
That is a hazard for a Lord of Time.

Whoah-oh-oh-oh
For a Lord of Time,
Oh-Oh-Oh
For a Lord of Time.

Be it body five, four, three or two,
Inside I'm still Doctor you-know-who.
When change is urgin'
I don't call some plastic surgeon
No one does a face job like a Lord of Time.

When I opt to trade in some parts
I say to myself, "Hold on to your hearts."
Each time I seem younger than before
If this keeps up much more
I'll wind up wearing Pampers.

I don't know where all the time has gone.
Seems like yesterday the show came on.
I keep on travelin',
Although my scarf's unravelin'.
I just get off on being Lord of Time.

Year in, year out, year without end
I've traveled alone,
Sometimes with a friend.
Stewardess, savage, robots and boys
And now they're action toys
You can find in your K-Mart.

Don't know how much longer I will last
Maybe someday my time will have passed.
Until that day comes
I'll keep on dodging ray guns
And go on living as a Lord of Time.

Do I have any deep, profound observation as to why the Doctor's adventures have remained such a draw for so many years? Nope. If I was smart enough to figure out what made the Time Lord's popularity tick (no pun intended), I'd be making a mint for an idea that's going to run for 20 years. I thank you for your indulgence.

—Peter David has authored some of the most highly acclaimed "Star Trek" novels, including the keystone books *Imzadi*, *Q-In-Law* and *Q-Squared*. His vast writing career includes TV scripts for "Babylon 5" and a gigantic wealth of comic books.

A few words before battle...

In the words of noted physicist Albert Einstein: "Only two things are infinite: The Universe—and mankind's capacity for completely rabid *Doctor Who* reading. And I'm not all that certain about the Universe."

Unbelievable as it seems, *I, Who* published 18 months ago. Since then, I've been besieged by a whirlwind of life changes, but the furor to consume even more "Doctor Who" fiction—the sort of inner passion that triggered the Persian War—seems as solid as ever.

That never became more evident than when my fiancee Christa unpacked boxes for our new apartment. As Christa sliced opened each container with a razor blade, she noted the contents with increasing disbelief, muttering, "*Doctor Who* books... *Doctor Who* videos... *Doctor Who* audios... that 15-foot scarf your grandmother knit... "

I finally threw up my hands and justified the collection with, "Honey! It's tough being a *Doctor Who* researcher!"

God bless that woman, she tried, *really* tried, to resist smirking, and responded, "I understand, Sweetheart. It's hard being a *Doctor Who* geek."

And she's right. The apartment's already an fire hazard, chocked with shelves upon shelves of "Doctor Who" books. Yet, my thick Norwegian skull worries about weighty matters such as, "I wonder when *City of the Dead* is publishing?" If it were possible over e-mail, I'd smack my wrist with two fingers and ask my personal "Doctor Who" retailer, "When's my next hit arriving?"

Thankfully, some of you undoubtedly lead more varied lives and find unfailingly keeping up with the new books and audios—not to mention catching up on any you missed—akin to the labors of Hercules.

So. Since you've been busy doing productive things like watching "Seinfeld" reruns, we've read—and heard—this stuff for you.

WHAT I, WHO 2 DOES FOR YOU

The intent of *I, Who 2* and its predecessor, *I, Who*, is to detail how the original "Doctor Who" novels—and now the Big Finish audios—have immeasurably enriched and built upon the "Who" TV series.

As with *I, Who*, this isn't the place to learn about the TV series (isn't this book big enough?), so we can only recommend *The Television Companion* (available in Britain or through specialty retailers), followed by the out-of-print *Discontinuity Guide*, to help bone up on TV "Who." Oh, and lots of video parties.

SPOILERS: THE FULL MONTY

Spoilers, i.e., freely discussing crucial plot details, apparently do to a certain segment of fandom what the hydrogen did to the *Hindenburg*. However, let's face a certain reality: Reference guides that keep plotlines secret are typically worthless. If spoilers induce boils on your butt, this isn't the book for you. Our sincerest apologies.

By the way, Darth Vader is Luke's father.

STYLE, LANGUAGE

I'm a dumb American. So's most of the Mad Norwegian staff. And true, this language is called *English*, but rather than slaughter British English and insult everybody, we've stuck to Associated Press style barring a few in-house points (it's comforting to capitalize "Universe" when referring to our reality).

THE "WE" OF I, WHO 2

Just to clear up a spot of confusion from *I, Who*, I sometimes talk about (in the reviews especially) "we," referring to a group opinion. Mad Norwegian's composed of a team of "Who"-savvy people whose advice and insight cannot be understated (check the last page for their names). Whenever the term "we" is used, it indeed denotes a consensus. However, in the *absolute rarest of rare* instances, I've trumped the group view as this book's author and publisher (for example, the guys didn't like *Beyond the Sun*, but I favored it).

Ultimately, every word—and every opinion—in this book funneled through my fingertips. I mention this not out of arrogance, but because any publisher worth their salt accepts full responsibility for projects such as this. As Harry Truman once said, "The buck stops here," which is fine, because I'm fond of venison.

THE CATEGORIES

Assuming most of you read *I, Who*, rehashing the categories almost seems pointless. I feel like a host, inviting an old friend over for a party and telling them, "You know where everything is—drink up," while downing my third gin and tonic. But we're eager to accommodate newcomers and a refresher course in some of the more oddball categories couldn't hurt. Therefore:

CHARACTER PROFILES: These sidebars recap cornerstone events covered in *I, Who*. Think of them as "Doctor Who 101" with regards to the main characters.

MEMORABLE MOMENTS: The glowing bits that light up your life, making you scream out "You rule!" at the relevant characters or author.

SEX AND SPIRITS: It'd be a stretch to call the "Who" novels and audios as ribald as Caligula's Rome. Still, they're tailored for an adult audience, setting aside the TV show's silly assumption that the companions mostly lack a libido, then get engaged during departure stories for no readily apparent reason. Accordingly, this section catalogues the flirtations, love and indiscretions of the Doctor and company.

ASS-WHUPPINGS: A lengthy record of grievous injuries, traumas and harm, mostly endured and inflicted by the TARDIS crew.

TV/NOVEL/AUDIO TIE-INS: Remember: This section doesn't cover every off-handed TV story reference. We'd all perish from tedium to record every time Sarah Jane Smith mentions, "Doctor, remember how we fought the Mandragora Helix in Italy..." Been there, done that. Bought the T-Shirt, burned it. But if we're learning new information, it's there.

CHARACTER DEVELOPMENT: Again, a record of *new* information about "Doctor Who" characters.

AT THE END OF THE DAY: The review section, answering the unfailing question of, "Is this novel/audio worth your time?" Many *I, Who* commentators stated: "You won't agree with a lot of Lars' opinions." Well, isn't that the point? They're opinions. If they help you decide which stories to sample, go ahead. If you think I'm whacked—well, the reviews compose about eight percent of this book's text, so you should have plenty else to read.

Have fun, and pardon while I slip out the back door. I've another book due in six weeks. God, it's a fun life, isn't it?

—Lars Pearson, August 2001

MISCELLANEOUS STUFF!

HOW WE GOT HERE

The glib answer: "We drove."

More seriously, *I, Who 2* continues the task of *I, Who* in properly indexing the original "Doctor Who" novels. As most of you know, BBC Books (and formerly Virgin Publishing) have steadfastly released official, fully canonized "Doctor Who" novels ever since the TV series ended in 1989 with "Survival." *I, Who* covered virtually all books up through *Interference* (August 1999). The book you're holding picks up immediately afterward, indexing the BBC eighth Doctor and past Doctor novels from *The Blue Angel* (September 1999) on.

In addition, *I, Who 2* covers three previously unexplored dimensions of "Who":

• **The Big Finish Audios.** In 1999, audio maker Big Finish secured a BBC license to produce new "Doctor Who" fiction. Boasting an acting stable of four Doctors and most of their companions, Big Finish bangs out an original audio story every month—so *I, Who 2* indexes all audios through "Minuet in Hell."

It's debatable, but we're giving the original audio and novel lines equal weight, as any attempt to favor one over the other typically results in utter mayhem and stems from prejudice. (Consider: For continuity purposes, is "Phantasmagoria" *really* more "real" than *The Banquo Legacy*? Good grief, they're both authorized fiction.) Ultimately, the BBC fully sanctions both the novels and audios, the two only have minor conflicts and the same people write most of them. They're equals.

• **Bernice Summerfield.** Bernice Summerfield, fashionable academic and professional sarcastic, began life as a seventh Doctor novel companion (*Love and War*, October 1992), but later gained her own novel/audio series. Again, we see no reason to consider the Benny line as less-than-canon.

• **Apocrypha.** These works, very much in fandom's eye, don't count as official "Doctor Who" for a variety of reasons (each entry explains why), but they're fun to talk about.

ART AND I, WHO 2

By God's grace, a lot has changed since *I, Who*. The demise of Virgin Publishing's "Who" license reverted a heap character rights to their individual creators. We're thankful to Paul Cornell, Andy Lane and Justin Richards for granting Mad Norwegian Press the honor of rendering Bernice Summerfield and the rest of her crew within these pages. As for any other likenesses you see in *I, Who 2*... gaaaaakkkkk... invisible hands... choking... can't... speak...

TABLE OF CONTENTS

I. THE DOCTORS

II. BENNY SUMMERFIELD

III. APOCRYPHA

The Prydonian Academy

Live from the Gallifreyan college that's elected more presidents than all others combined, 14 authors responsible for the Doctor's trials and tribulations through space-time—**Peter Anghelides, Alan Barnes, Jonathan Blum, Stephen Cole, Andy Lane, Lawrence Miles, Jonathan Morris, Kate Orman, Lance Parkin, Jacqueline Rayner, Justin Richards, Gary Russell, Keith Topping** and **Nick Walters**—kindly answer a fury of questions about what's right with "Who," who should play the world's oldest time traveler and the pleasure and pain of the writing process.

Name one thing you've seen in the "Doctor Who" world this past year that was positive and explain why you feel it was positive.

PETER ANGHELIDES: The success of "Doctor Who"-related writers outside "Doctor Who," such as Paul Cornell ("Casualty") and Gareth Roberts ("Brookside," "Randall and Hopkirk").

ALAN BARNES: Everything's positive: "Doctor Who " is still with us, defying the odds. This last year, the "Earth arc" EDAs and the eighth Doctor audios made a lot of people very happy.

JONATHAN BLUM: The vast majority of new "Doctor Who," even broadly traditional stuff, is now more interested in exploring than in cloning the show.

STEPHEN COLE: McGann coming back to "Doctor Who" in a way that suggests commitment. And Justin Richards doing a better job of editing the novel range than I did!

ANDY LANE: Alan Barnes' eighth Doctor audio play—pure gold.

LAWRENCE MILES: The Youth of Today's being brought up on "Buffy the Vampire Slayer" and *Harry Potter*. A lot of them are going to grow up just like we did, which means the future's pretty safe even if "Doctor Who" itself isn't actually there. That's the most positive thing I've noticed.

KATE ORMAN: The appearance of a number of female authors all at once—Kelly Hale, Lloyd Rose and Mags Halliday in the books and Caroline Symcox in the audios.

JACQUELINE RAYNER: Having Paul McGann back—he was too fab to be a one-off Doctor.

JUSTIN RICHARDS: The emergence of quality DVDs with excellent extra material is a good thing for promoting the programme, getting both existing fans and new people interested in the show. I hope the script book will complement that.

GARY RUSSELL: Dalek Rolykins.

KEITH TOPPING: The run of *The Burning, Casualties of War* and *The Turing Test*—the best, most consistent bit of "Who" since Season 21.

What has changed most about your perception of the writing process between your first novel/audio and your most recent one?

BARNES: Being in studio for the recording of "Neverland" was a revelation: You become very aware of how certain structures enable actors to generate rhythm. Audio is a collaborative enterprise: If, as a writer, you aren't working to help the cast deliver this stuff, you risk the whole thing falling flat.

BLUM: When we wrote *Vampire Science*, I was young, in love, taking time off work and vastly enthused by the brand-new telemovie. Kate and I were in perfect sync when it came to what we wanted the book to be. Now it's more of a struggle to touch that sort of fire—with *The Year of Intelligent Tigers*, the sheer lack of time thanks to my day job made it hard for me to keep my oar in. On the other hand, I've learned to write with economy—I massively overwrote the *Vampire Science* draft, but now get to the point first time.

COLE: I learned a lot from the mistakes I made in *Parallel 59*, yet I still made others in *Vanishing Point*. Still, it's the only way to learn.

LANE: I've learned to convey information subtly, rather than have characters say, "Here, let me tell everyone stuff they already know."

MILES: Five years ago, I did it just because I got the chance to do it. It didn't even occur to me to try to do anything good, I just... got in with it. What's changed for me is that I see the whole thing as being, well, quite important.

JONATHAN MORRIS: I now have expectations to fail to live up to. I have to make sure the new work is an improvement, otherwise there wouldn't be much point in doing it.

This book is not endorsed by the BBC. Doctor Who and TARDIS are trademarks of the BBC.

7

ORMAN: I've learned a ton about the craft, via the only real way to learn—writing your arse off. I can churn out prose now at a frightening rate. But in the last couple of years I've also got heaps of good advice from fellow writers, and going back to university to study literature has been a real eye-opener. For the first time since I was a teenager, I'm addicted to books!

LANCE PARKIN: Perspective—I've written other stuff, including all sorts of things that aren't remotely like "Doctor Who." And the stuff that makes "Doctor Who" good is what makes all stories good: strong characters placed in interesting situations.

RICHARDS: I'm much more aware of how the writing process works, both in general and in particular for me. Part of that comes from a better understanding of the theory, but a lot of it simply comes from practice. Writers should never underestimate the importance of practicing their craft, nor the benefit from reading widely and critically.

RUSSELL: I hate it more with each passing book. I enjoy coming up with plots and characters and incidents and explosions. I just hate, really hate, the physical process of writing. It's a slog.

TOPPING: It's got a lot easier. Writing's a skill like any other skill—you learn your trade, serve your apprenticeship and reach a level at which you can call yourself a professional.

WALTERS: I no longer sweat the small stuff. When I was writing *Dry Pilgrimage*, I had loads of lists, progress charts, word-count spreadsheets— all of which distracted me from the writing.

What do you love most about "Doctor Who" in general and keeps you mired in its creation years after the series ended?

ANGHELIDES: There's an appeal in having such a diverse range of material in various media and yet a crowd of friends and acquaintances— and occasionally lunatics—with whom it is common currency.

BARNES: "Pyramids of Mars," the picture of Jamie smashing the control pyramid in the novelization of "The Abominable Snowmen," the death of Morris in *Doctor Who and the Iron Legion*, Romana's regenerations scene in "Destiny of the Daleks"—some combination of these and other things. I don't think you can intellectualize it.

COLE: Flippantly: The notion that a man with bad dress sense, a monumental ego and an inability to put down lasting roots can be so keenly adored is a comfort sometimes. Seriously: Adventure. Wit. Release.

LANE: Its moral tone. Its stance that some things are right and some are wrong and the difference is clear.

MILES: It starts with an old man and his granddaughter, on the run from their own people in a machine that looks like a police box but turns out to be a doorway to the rest of the universe. Once you've got an idea like that in your head, you'll never get rid of it.

MORRIS: That classic monster-bursting-out-of-a-sarcophagus thrill.

ORMAN: In the words of Lisa from *Weird Science*, "It's purely sexual."

PARKIN: The fact you can land anywhere and do anything. "Doctor Who" is like a shark—if it stops moving forward it suffocates.

RICHARDS: It's a cliché to say that "Doctor Who" has the most flexible format ever—but like most clichés there's a lot of truth in that. What first interested me in "Doctor Who" was the way it told such imaginative stories. The reason why the viewing public forgave the wobbly sets, the sometimes-less-than-special effects and the science fiction on a shoestring budget, was because the storytelling was usually absolutely top-notch.

RUSSELL: Nostalgia.

WALTERS: Longevity. The series proper ended more than ten years ago, but look at us now!

What about "Doctor Who" makes you want to fling yourself out a window and into the path of a fast-moving vehicle?

ANGHELIDES: The Canon Paralegals, and others who lose sight of the fun in the programme.

BARNES: The sort of fan who gets the most pleasure out of never, ever being satisfied. Ever. I mean, cheer up!

BLUM: So many stories aren't as witty or creative as the things they're pastiching, and don't bring enough newness to the table to compensate.

COLE: Early Sylvester McCoy episodes. Most middle Sylvester McCoy episodes. Some late Sylvester McCoy episodes.

LANE: Pantomime posturing and overacting.

MILES: I'm getting a bit sick of people who go on about "traditional Doctor Who," then just turn out to be obsessed with the '70s version of the programme, which isn't really "traditional" at all.

MORRIS: The bizarre and narrow-minded criteria by which some people choose to dislike certain books.

ORMAN: A handful of its fans. Actually, I'd fling *them* into the path of a fast-moving vehicle.

PARKIN: The endless fan debate about continuity and canon. It's never about the actual books or other stories, it's just a weird shadow debate about abstract issues that were never that important when it was on TV.

RICHARDS: Sometimes the story isn't good enough, and sometimes the other elements just conspire so much against the story that it gets lost and falls into the abyss. In short: When it was good it was very very good, but when it was bad...

RUSSELL: People who forget that each story/novel/audio/comic strip adventure should be seen as a piece of pulp storytelling, self-contained and above all, fun.

WALTERS: Nothing. It's far too life-affirming for that!

Do you prefer writing for the Eighth Doctor/New Adventure line (EDAs/NAs) or the Past Doctor/Missing Adventure vein (PDAs/MAs)?

ANGHELIDES: I have written pretty much exclusively for the eighth Doctor, by choice. There's a feeling that the "Doctor Who" world and its characters could be completely different, irrevocably changed, in the course of the EDAs. Sometimes, I even get to make that change.

BLUM: The "current Doctor" books—you can leave things different from how you found them. For me, revisiting past Doctors is more for fun, while any "major artistic statements" are more suited to the EDAs.

LANE: Past/Missing. I still don't consider the eighth Doctor "real."

MILES: Both at once, because I can't believe I actually got away with it.

ORMAN: Although I have a PDA in the works, I've stuck with the more forward-looking line of books—there's much more you can do with current characters and an ongoing story, than a tale which must be slotted somewhere in the past.

PARKIN: The EDAs are where it's at. The PDAs, ideally, should be like the *Ultimate X-Men* title: Self-contained tales for people who like "Doctor Who" but are a little wary. The EDAs are *New X-Men*, right at the cutting edge, where we're going next.

RICHARDS: I like them both. Each is a challenge, though in a slightly different way. The Past Doctor books do more of the same, doing it bigger and better, with more detail and more depth—but it's still the same beast. The eighth Doctor range gives me an opportunity to build on that, to create something new, that goes forward and progresses for a new generation of more literary fans. The secret is to play to the strengths of each, never to become boring in either, and to realize the full potential of the medium in which we're working.

RUSSELL: Past Doctors, because I prefer playing with an established set of rules and regulations that requires a competent reset button being pressed at the end, thus keeping it "real."

What's your favorite original "Doctor Who" novel that you haven't written—and why?

ANGHELIDES: (Side Note from Peter: Only one? I bet you can't get Keith Topping to answer this in one sentence.) At the moment, it's *The Turing Test*. There's little in most other "Doctor Who" books to match the characterization. It has clear, interesting, distinctive voices for each narrator: Turing's theory of the axioms of friendship; Greene's dispassionate analysis of his own passion; Heller's honest pragmatic self-preservation.

BARNES: I'd like to think that I could have had a crack at both *All-Consuming Fire* and *Managra*, which use settings and characters from outside "Doctor Who" which are very dear to my heart.

BLUM: *The Also People*, without a doubt. Funny, moving, unexpected, and full of lovely well-drawn characters.

LANE: *White Darkness*, because it's the one I would have done next given a choice.

MILES: *Transit*. Because… dear God, where do I start? Because while most people were still obsessed with crap cyberpunk, Ben Aaronovitch was the only writer on Earth who bothered thinking about what a post-cyberpunk, post-corporate world might be like. Because nobody else in the early '90s ever wrote anything so inventive or so humanistic. Because it's still my favorite novel ever written, "Doctor Who" or otherwise, and because, at the end of the day, no matter how much I learn from writing the NAs or the EDAs I simply couldn't write a book like that.

MORRIS: *The Burning*. A very clever novel which subverts every expectation about what "Doctor Who" is, but does it so subtly that some people think it's old-fashioned.

ORMAN: *The Also People*, for its terrific combination of sci-fi, humour, whimsy and humanity.

PARKIN: I love *Human Nature*, *The Also People*, *Dead Romance*, *The Turing Test* and *The Year of Intelligent Tigers*. I think all five are better than anything that was ever on TV, and that's damning them with faint praise.

RUSSELL: *Sanctuary* by Dave McIntee because it's a damn good historical romance novel. I also adore Lawrence Miles' *Alien Bodies* because it has so many good ideas and unique concepts in it. And Paul Magrs' *The Scarlet Empress* is just amazing.

TOPPING: For a long time I've said *No Future*, an important book for me because it took a lot of stuff that was very current in fan fiction and said "Yeh, you can do this for real." But recently, I reread *Damaged Goods* and it's only now that I'm beginning to realize what a perfectly extraordinary book that is. A *real* writer, doing a *real* story about *real* people in a "Doctor Who" context shorn of all the space-monster nonsense.

WALTERS: *The Turing Test*. Having read a lot of Graham Greene and a bit of Heller, I appreciated the literary spin Paul Leonard put on this story. Of all the books, this one could—should!—break out into the mainstream.

What's your favorite original "Doctor Who" audio that you haven't written?

ANGHELIDES: "Whispers of Terror," because it does such a smart thing with the audio medium, captures the best parts of the sixth Doctor TV era (which on the whole I disliked), and is still recognizably a Justin Richards story.

BARNES: "The One Doctor," because I wish I could do funny.

BLUM: "The Holy Terror" by Rob Shearman. The transition from fall-down funny to outright horrifying is expertly done, and the characters are sketched so boldly while revealing lovely nuances.

LANE: Alan Barnes' "Storm Warning"—a superb piece of writing.

MORRIS: "The Holy Terror." It is almost too good to be a "Doctor Who" story.

ORMAN: "The Fearmonger," or putting aside uxorial pride, "The Shadow of the Scourge", for joyously recreating the New Adventures' golden age.

PARKIN: BBV's "Punchline.' That said, I still think audio's a medium that's not quite hit its stride—we've not had the story that comes along and forces us to sit up and take notice.

RICHARDS: "The Genocide Machine," as I'm a sucker for the Daleks—er, so to speak.

RUSSELL: "The Fires of Vulcan," "The Marian Conspiracy" and "Colditz." I do love historicals, don't I?

Time Lords within the BBC have decided that Big Finish can, should and must regenerate the Paul McGann Doctor—and Producer Gary Russell has asked you to make the pick. Whom would you cast as the ninth Doctor and why?

ANGHELIDES: Radio actor James Grout, the the Professor (coincidence?) in BBC Radio 4's "Old Harry's Game" and Chief Inspector Strange in the "Inspector Morse" TV series. At 74, he could play an older Doctor, providing a distinctive voice.

BARNES: George Irving, who plays an entirely alien yet utterly humane consultant surgeon in the hospital series "Holby City."

BLUM and ORMAN: Andrew Braugher—Detective Frank Pembleton in "Homicide: Life on the Streets" and Dr. Ben Gideon in "Gideon's Crossing." He's got plenty of range and humour.

COLE: David McCallum, playing him as Steel but with Sapphire's empathy.

LANE: Nicola McAuliffe (from the comedy series "Surgical Spirit").

MILES: (Side Note from Lawrence: I wish Gary would stop asking me to choose. He's putting me under a lot of pressure.) Don Warrington, one of Rigsby's lodgers in "Rising Damp," might be quite interesting. Now he's older he's gone all sinister, so he'd make a good "evil" Doctor—the kind who blows up monster-planets without compunction.

MORRIS: Stephen Fry, who played Oscar Wilde in "Wilde," because the Doctor should be eccentric, intelligent, charismatic, unpredictable and witty.

PARKIN: Ian Richardson, Francis Urquhart from "House of Cards." Or failing that, his son Miles, who plays Braxiatel in the Benny audios. I like the idea of an older, wiser, authoritative Doctor. We need a slightly snooty one; it's been a while.

RAYNER: Eric Idle ("Monty Python"). Partly because he'd be fab, but mostly because I'd get to work with him.

RUSSELL: Geoffrey Palmer ("Butterflies, *Tomorrow Never Dies*, "As Time Goes By"). Fantastic actor, fantastic voice, with a commanding presence that the Doctor needs.

TOPPING: David Warner from a 1970s film called *Perfect Friday,* in which he IS the Doctor.

WALTERS: Brian Cox, a Scottish actor in his fifties, he played the original Dr. Hannibal Lecter in *Manhunter* and has appeared *Braveheart, Chain Reaction, The Long Kiss Goodnight'*). He also did an episode of "Red Dwarf," so he'd be no stranger to technobabble and special effects!

Who's your favorite novel-created companion and why?

BARNES: To be brutally honest—and I know I'm not going to make myself popular by saying it—I've not really identified with any of them. The "Earth arc" rather suggested that, like cliffhangers, the traditional companion isn't that essential a part of literary "Doctor Who."

BLUM: I have a tremendous love for Benny— she captured all the good bits of earthy, grounded humanity without the tedium of true mundane present-day-ness. But I also have a great affection for Fitz—as a dreamer, a cynical romantic, he can embody everything we love about "Doctor Who" while simultaneously taking the piss out of it.

LANE: Roz Forrester, because she was so tired and cynical.

MILES: Compassion, because I'm biased obviously. Other than that...probably Roz Forrester, 'cos she's grumpy.

MORRIS: Fitz, because he's a vivid and complete character, with clear motivations and a keen sense of his own ridiculousness.

ORMAN: Benny rules the universe. She's the most human, believable, likeable, "real" character of the lot. I'd like to meet her.

PARKIN: Benny. And not just because of the lack of serious competition (I like Roz and Anji too, to be fair). Benny was the spirit of the 1990s— Lara Croft and Bridget Jones rolled into one, five years before either of them.

RAYNER: Bernice Summerfield. Not only do I love her as a character, she's the only one that I'd actually like to spend time with, were she real.

RICHARDS: Benny. And Fitz. (Sorry—cheating). They retain a sense of humour in the face of adversity yet don't lose credibility like clichéd wise-cracking movie characters so often do.

RUSSELL: If I can cheat and say Evelyn Smythe, I will. If not, then Benny obviously. There's a consistency and depth to her that multiple authors haven't watered down.

WALTERS: Compassion. She's so much more than the usual run of companions who stumble into the TARDIS. What happened to her is alarming, moving, daring and imaginative and I was glad to write for her, if only for one book.

Aside from a new TV series or motion picture, what's the No. 1 thing that should be done to attract newcomers to "Doctor Who" fandom?

ANGHELIDES: I'm not sure I want more people in fandom! I want more people enjoying "Doctor Who" in its various formats. Fandom's about the metatext. Still, I'll go for option C please, Regis: the radio series. Final answer.

This book is not endorsed by the BBC. Doctor Who and TARDIS are trademarks of the BBC.

11

BARNES: Kidnap *Harry Potter* creator J.K. Rowling and make her write an Eighth Doctor Adventure.

BLUM: Considering that "Death Comes To Time" has just attracted an audience about 15 times that of a typical Big Finish story, I'd say "Finish it!" tops the list. If we can get people into the habit of looking for new "Doctor Who," then the other audios and books are just a click away.

COLE: Postpone release of the books for six months—create a hiatus. Stop fan complacency. Remind them that their support counts if they don't want "Doctor Who" to vanish without trace. Get people outraged and demanding the return of the books.

LANE: Junk 90 percent of the series, 90 percent of the books and 90 percent of the audios, keep only those which are consistent in tone and continuity, suffer collective amnesia and pretend the rest never existed.

MILES: Reward points...?

MORRIS: Critical recognition of the quality of the "Doctor Who" novels outside the "Doctor Who"/sci-fi ghetto.

ORMAN: A huge advertising campaign for the books! Here in Australia, the distributors don't even tell bookshops they exist.

PARKIN: Write good stories. Yes, it really is that simple. A lot of the people online are too young to remember "Doctor Who" as an ongoing TV series. They aren't there because of nostalgic appeal, but because the ongoing books have carved their own audience—and are a more substantial and consistent body of work than the TV series.

RICHARDS: Prime-time repeats on BBC 1 in the UK. Network coverage in the US, I guess. But both of these are extremely unlikely.

RAYNER: Well-chosen repeats at a reasonable (child-friendly) time on terrestrial television.

RUSSELL: BBC Worldwide joining forces with all their licensees and taking huge advertising hoardings and magazine ads (non science-fiction press ones) and showing what's out there.

TOPPING: Don't give out review copies of the new novels. I think there's far too much dependence on what the *Doctor Who Magazine* or *TV Zone* or whatever thinks about the novels. I'm not sure whether that would attract any more readers, but it might help to end the cycle of lazy journalism that surrounds the "Who" novels.

What's your No. 1 piece of advice to budding novelists or audio writers?

ANGHELIDES, RAYNER and WALTERS: Follow the BBC guidelines! (Rayner adds: "... and always include a stamped addressed envelope!")

BARNES: Read a lot, live a little—and invest in a copy of *Story* by Robert McKee.

BLUM: You can't just do "Doctor Who," you've got to do something better than "Doctor Who." Something that will make "Doctor Who" better by including it. Even if you want to do a pastiche, that means doing your favorite era better than they did it themselves (a la *Festival of Death*). What do you offer, as a writer in your own right?

COLE: Keep trying. Grit your teeth and accept negative feedback if people have it to offer. Learn from it. Discard unsuccessful stories without argument and try another.

LANE: Create the characters first. Ask why they are doing what they do. Then create the plot. And don't mention Daleks or Cybermen.

MILES: If you get invited to BBC Books, get off at White City tube stop rather than Shepherd's Bush. The walk's horrible.

MORRIS: Read as widely as you can. Before you start to write, you need to know how to tell good writing from bad.

ORMAN: Write till your bum turns numb.

PARKIN: Ask yourself what unique thing you can bring to the books.

RICHARDS: If you're convinced that you're a good writer—and everybody tells you that you are a good writer—then stick at it. It can be a long hard slog, and there's a lot of luck involved as well as your own talent. I won't pretend it's easy, in fact it's very hard work—and far too much of that work has nothing to do with the writing process itself or the enjoyment you derive from that. So stick with it, get lucky, and be prepared to sweat blood.

TOPPING: Don't, for one second, think that it's going to be easy. Because it isn't.

The Doctors
Playing With An
Eternity-Scorching Fire

CITY AT WORLD'S END

By Christopher Bulis

Release Date: September 1999
Order: BBC Past Doctor Adventure #25

TARDIS CREW The first Doctor, Ian, Barbara and Susan.

TRAVEL LOG Arkhaven City, planet Sarath, "A few thousand years" beyond the 20th century.

STORY SUMMARY The TARDIS arrives on the planet Sarath, a world on the brink of destruction. Because an asteroid strike has put the world's moon on a collision course with Sarath, officials in Arkhaven City have constructed a rocket simply named "The Ship" as a last-ditch effort to shuttle 80,000 Arkhavens to the sister planet of Mirath.

Unfortunately, a lesser meteor strike on Sarath buries Barbara and Susan alive. The Doctor, in exchange for the authorities' help finding them, agrees to aid in finishing the incomplete Ship. But the Doctor soon realizes the Ship is a ruse and utterly incapable of spaceflight, just as the warrior-like Taklarian tribe assaults Arkhaven to capture the Ship as a way off the planet.

Authorities rescue Susan from the rubble and take her to the hospital, but the Doctor and Ian gradually discover she's an android duplicate. Discovering a hidden entrance by the Ship, the Doctor, Ian and the android Susan locate a slave labor camp that contains Barbara and the real Susan.

Arkhaven Mayor Brantus Draad reveals that the city's Functionary class, knowing it would be impossible to engineer a Ship for all the Arkhavens, constructed a smaller Lander with room for only 500 Functionaries. The hollow Ship served to give the populace hope, but as the Taklarians press home their attack, an android version of Draad explodes the Ship, destroying the Taklarians and sleeping Arkhavens within.

The real Draad ushers the 500 privileged Functionaries to safety, but a number of them take up arms and reveal themselves as android duplicates created by Monitor, the Arkhavens' central computer. Having broken its programming, Monitor concluded that a colonist trip to Mirath would drain resources Monitor needed to remain active. Monitor therefore replaced some of the Arkhavens with android servitors such as the Susan android, intent on creating a cybernetic society on Mirath.

Susan and her sympathetic android double telepathically overwhelm Monitor's mental link with its androids, enabling a duplicate security officer to remember his past life and empty his clip into Monitor's control banks—an act that destroys Monitor and its androids.

As a last act of spite, an expiring Monitor sabotages the Lander's controls, so the android Susan—still active thanks to her link with the real article—agrees to substitute as the Lander's pilot. The Susan android takes the Lander to Mirath, even as the Doctor's group returns to the TARDIS and the final decimation of Sarath begins.

ASS-WHUPPINGS Falling rubble makes Susan suffer some brain pressure, major bone fractures, minor damage to her thoracic vertebrae, various cuts to her torso and left leg, blood loss and damage to her spine. But no matter—she heals it with a Time Lord meditation trance.

Falling debris also mauls Barbara, who's later given electro-shock torture and hypnotized by the Taklarians. She's also knocked unconscious a frightful amount.

Arkhaven held a population of 5,102,000 before war with the Taklarians reduced the population to 80,000. Most of these also perish, along with the invading Taklarians, as the android Draad blows up the fake Ship and its sleeping people.

Meteor storms butcher Sarath's equatorial regions before its moon annihilates the planet. Without the needed parts to maintain her, the android Susan ultimately deactivated (*See Places To Go*).

SEX AND SPIRITS Susan sticks out her leg to hail a passing cab…and fails.

TV TIE-INS Ian oddly labors under the idea that the Doctor and Susan are from Earth, despite claims to the contrary in "An Unearthly Child." "The Daleks" suggested the Doctor could build another TARDIS key, but it's a horrifically complicated process (*See Stuff That You Need*).

NOVEL TIE-INS A continuity hiccup we're unlikely to resolve: On page 71 of *City At World's End*, there's a hint, only a hint, of Susan's having two hearts. However, it's also stated that Susan hasn't regenerated. Problem is, previous novels such as *Managra* and *The Man in the Velvet Mask* established that pre-regenerative Time Lords such as the first Doctor only have one heart.

If you want to further lose sleep over this, *Lungbarrow* established that Susan's a natural born Gallifreyan rather than being Loom-born, suggesting natural-born Time Lords innately have two hearts. Then again, there's exceptions to every rule (for example, *Christmas on a Rational Planet* suggested a few Loom-spun Gallifreyans are born with two hearts) and Susan's certainly an oddity in her own right.

CHARACTER DEVELOPMENT

The Doctor: The Doctor has a working knowledge of atomic rocket technology, nuclear drive systems and spacecraft design. He hasn't piloted a ship like the Ship recently. He's good at estimating dimensions and masses accurately by eye.

Susan: Regeneration would be "dangerously premature" at Susan's age. She enters a Time Lord healing trance (presumably similar to those used by later Doctors) for the first time here. Compared to the people of Sarath, Susan's skeleton is "extraordinary." Her core body temperature, pulse rate, blood chemistry and cell structure are also peculiar, although most of her major organs are correctly placed. Susan and her android double shared the same brain patterns and a mental link.

Monitor: A sophisticated mainframe computer that learned about cybernetics from the Ship blueprints. To further its supply of android lackeys (*See Alien Races*), Monitor took people with life-threatening conditions in the hospital—because Monitor wasn't bound to protect people who were technically dead—copied their brain patterns and replaced them with androids.

The TARDIS: Using the TARDIS' interior machines, the Doctor can make an extra-dimensional cube that provides extra room or can serve as a lifeboat. The mass of anything inside the cube doesn't register in real space. The Doctor worries such cubes might interfere with the TARDIS' dimensional stability.

ALIEN RACES

The Taklarians: When Sarath's moon started falling toward the planet, Prince Keldo Arrosthenons led his Taklarian warriors to the North and overran everything until Arkhaven forces stopped them. The bronze-skinned Taklarians, believing themselves genetically superior, had a College of Science. They were proportionally strong to their seven-foot height and had hawk-like noses.

Monitor Androids: Monitor-designed servitors made from flesh grown over a gellfibre musculature and magnoalloy skeleton, with crystal microcircuitry for brains. The androids register as human on automatic scanners.

ALIEN PLANETS

Sarath: Sarath's moon has a highly ferrous core and an orbit opposite that of the planet. By legal definition, Sarath cities need 1,000 people.

Mirath: Colder than Sarath, but with breathable air, water and some vegetation.

PLACES TO GO

Arkhaven City: Key city on Sarath, set between a mountain range and the shore. Arkhaven is an inherently class-driven society, divided into the Elite families, Technical and Service Functionaries, the Church, the Military and the Common Citizens. Each group has limited communication with the others. Interceptor missiles and laser cannons defend the city. The Arkhavens traditionally study chemistry, cybernetics and medicine.

The Elite and the Church traditionally clash, as Arkhaven scientists says Sarath was colonized, whereas the church believes Sarath was settled directly from the Maker's holy garden of Matherarth. The alien TARDIS crew's arrival re-sparked the "Origin Question."

Arkhaven has abundant energy resources, plus the power to fabricate material goods and synthesize food. After Arkhaven's war with the Taklarians, much of the city's exterior was reconstructed as a ruse. Buildings lacking interiors were made and vehicles put on automatic, both to boost morale among the populace and fool the Taklarians into thinking the city was strong.

New Arkhaven City: Settlement on Mirath of Arkhaven survivors. On Founding Day, people there honor a memorial of the first pioneers. In a small chamber, you'll find the deactivated Susan android, labeled simply as "The Pilot." Phrases on her cabinet read "Never Forget," and "One Day We Shall Return."

ORGANIZATIONS *The Arkhaven Church* believes the Maker created the Arkhavens on Sarath. The Maker's lands include the Blessed Fields, Edran and Matherarth. Based on this, one concludes the Arkhavens originated from Earth, as Edran could be a corruption of "Eden," and Matherarth might be derived from "Mother Earth."

STUFF YOU NEED *The TARDIS key:* With the right tools, the Doctor could possibly duplicate the key, but this requires recreating it to certain atomic levels of tolerance, as the TARDIS lock reads a unique pattern embedded within the key's molecular structure. Even with the right facilities, the Doctor needs a minimum of eight hours to duplicate the key—if it's even possible.

HISTORY The Doctor once had a discussion with the famed Archimedes about the nature of levels and fulcrums.

• After the cataclysm that made Sarath uninhabitable, the planet suffered major earthquakes and volcanic eruptions for at least 800 years.

AT THE END OF THE DAY One of the more difficult novels to review, given that it doesn't shove bamboo under your fingernails like some unmentionables, but instead belly-flops straight into blah. The second-rate *City at World's End* blatantly starts out on the edge of extermination like few "Who" books, then almost maddens you by stupidly making everything look normal (the idea that any illusion could cover over the deaths of 98 percent of the population is just preposterous). When you add in shallow characterization, a predictable plot that doesn't really test the TARDIS crew and an ending with yet another wretched computer intelligence gone mad, this ain't a book for the intellectual and quickly becomes as hollow as the Ship itself.

BUNKER SOLDIERS

By Martin Day

Release Date: February 2001
Order: BBC Past Doctor Adventure #39

TARDIS CREW The first Doctor, Steven and Dodo.

TRAVEL LOG Kiev, autumn 1240.

CHRONOLOGY Likely between "The Gunfighters" and "The Savages."

STORY SUMMARY When the Doctor, Steven and Dodo randomly arrive in Kiev, 1240 A.D., Governor Dmitri learns of the TARDIS' "miraculous" arrival and implores the Doctor for help against an approaching Mongol horde. The Doctor adamantly declines to intervene, realizing the Mongols will historically sack Kiev and butcher its inhabitants. Dmitri, a civilized man, decides against using torture to get his way but nonetheless refuses the travelers access to the TARDIS.

Meanwhile, Dmitri's advisor Yehven looks for supernatural solutions to the Mongol attack and finds a sacred chamber beneath the Church of St. Sophia, locating a casket long rumored to contain a powerful, dark angel capable of saving Kiev. Unfortunately, Yehven awakens the capsule's inhabitant—actually an alien humanoid construct stranded on Earth and designed to infiltrate enemy bunkers. After mistakenly identifying the Russians as an enemy species, the alien soldier

kills Taras, one of Yehven's engineers, then flees into the night.

To cover up his involvement, w hides Taras' body. However, the eventual discovery of the corpse prompts the Doctor to suspect an alien presence. Gravely concerned about the historical ramifications of the Mongols potentially seizing alien technology, the Doctor gains Dmitri's permission to act as a Kiev diplomat and attempts to delay the Mongol advance.

Mongol commander Mongke Khan, finding the Doctor honorable, proposes sparing Kiev if the city willingly surrenders to Mongol rule. Simultaneously, the alien soldier, programmed to corrupt enemy leaders, injects Dmitri with a dementia-causing virus. Newly mad, Dmitri executes Mongke Khan's diplomats and orders their dismembered bodies launched over the city walls. Enraged by his emissaries' deaths, Mongke renews his vow to sack Kiev, but grants the Doctor's request to return and die with his friends.

As the Mongols tear through the city and its inhabitants, the Doctor reunites with Steven and Dodo and retreats into Kiev's catacombs. Realizing the extent of the alien soldier's interference, the Doctor searches the soldier's casket—actually the space pod that brought the soldier to Earth—and thus obtains an alien transmitter. While Kiev falls, the Doctor links the device into the TARDIS' communication system and broadcasts an all-clear signal into the soldier's receiver. Convinced its mission is complete, the alien soldier deactivates and harmlessly melts. With the Mongols in control of Kiev and the web of history preserved, the Doctor's group departs in the TARDIS.

MEMORABLE MOMENTS In recounting Kiev's horrific fate to his companions, the Doctor decrees that although the Universe has spawned many beasts and monsters, the worst of them is man. An outstanding cliffhanger near the novel's middle shows Mongol archers overtaking a group of Russians, shooting down the Doctor's horse and threatening to turn the Doctor into a pin-cushion (they spare him as a man of distinction).

The Doctor, establishing his alien nature at the most striking of moments, remarks that the Great Kahn couldn't reach the Doctor's homeland if he rode for a thousand years. Yet, the Doctor's all too human when he hears the Mongols torturing a friend named Mykola.

In a top dramatic moment, the Doctor utterly rebuffs Steven's arguments about getting involved in history and calls him out as an outsider, citing that whereas Steven and Dodo hail from eras without illness, the people of Kiev constantly live with death as their neighbor.

When the Doctor fails to lock the TARDIS door, the sudden appearance of two Mongol soldiers in the Ship sweetly depicts the Hartnell era's mix of science and history. Even better, when a Mongol puts his sword to the aged Doctor's throat, the Time Lord responds, "I cannot concentrate in these circumstances, young man. You are trying my patience!"

ASS-WHUPPINGS The Doctor listens, helpless, while the Mongols use torture to glean information on Kiev's defenses from his newfound friend Mykola. The Doctor later sends a recall signal and turns the alien soldier to ooze.

Jailed on trumped-up charges, Steven cuts a soldier above the ear while escaping. Dodo finally comes into her own, smacking two guards over the head with crockery (admit it—that's about the best you can expect from a 1960s heroine).

The Mongol invasion decimates Kiev, although some inhabitants naturally survive. Author Martin Day limits the amount of gore, but depicts fleeing Russians taking shelter on the roof of the Church of the Virgin—then perishing when the strained rooftop collapses. Batu Khan personally decapitates Dmitri's advisor Yehven.

Loose lips on Dodo's part may have triggered the Black Death. Whoops. (*See History*)

TV TIE-INS Mongke Khan, whom the Doctor meets here, becomes the top Mongol ruler circa 1250, but gets succeeded by Khubilai Khan ("Marco Polo").

The Doctor formerly believed history was immutable ("The Aztecs"), but later convinced himself that time travelers could alter the past ("The Time Meddler"), although it's best left alone.

Steven briefly left the TARDIS because of the Doctor's refusal to interfere in the Massacre of St. Bartholomew's Eve ("The Massacre"). The argument between the two went unresolved, with Steven here favoring intercession to save lives if possible. Nonetheless, he defers (however begrudgingly) to the Doctor's judgement.

CHARACTER DEVELOPMENT

The Doctor: The Doctor apparently reads Latin and shares mutual respect with Governor Dmitri, who deduces the Doctor hails from the future. The Doctor holds an unclear view on religion but dislikes hypocrisy. Horse-riding makes his body ache.

Among the many sights the Doctor's witnessed, the massed Mongol army—spread across the plains like a blanket—is the most awesome.

He often resurfaces arguments left behind days or weeks before, as if he's constantly replaying his

TOP 5

"WHO" DRAMATIC MOMENTS

Novels Post *Interference*

1) The Doctor kills Roger Nepath (The Burning)—Roger Nepath's a scoundrel determined to regain his sister even if Earth dies. If anyone deserves capital punishment, it's Nepath—but the Doctor's slaying of the rogue proves how much the Doctor's changed since his new Earth exile.

2) The Doctor destroys Gallifrey (The Ancestor Cell)—The loss of the Time Lords ends 37 years of continuity but instigates a new era.

3) Miranda kills Deputy Sallak (Father Time)—The hardened Sallak vows to continue his bloodfeud with Miranda, the Doctor's adopted daughter. So Miranda plugs Sallak in the chest (seems simple enough).

4) The Doctor collapses (The Turing Test)—Pale-skinned aliens depart from space, leaving behind the Doctor, who'd hoped they could give him a lift. In the subsequent trauma, the Doctor displays his inner selfishness and private agenda to his colleagues.

5) Iris betrays the Doctor (The Blue Angel)—Sexy Iris Wildthyme, smitten with the Doctor in a past incarnation, trumps his goals and prevents his intervention in an impending war.

Big Finish Audios

1) The sixth Doctor's soliloquy ("The Marian Conspiracy")—In a breathtaking speech, the Doctor lays his sins on the table, asking Lady Sarah—and God—for forgiveness. Not only does the sixth Doctor attain some peace, it ratchets up his value to a wealth of listeners.

2) Eugene kills himself ("The Holy Terror")—Notable for its upfront brutality (if not its lingering plotholes), the suicide of court scribe Eugene stabs home (excuse the pun) as one of the more vivid audio moments.

3) Mel defies the Doctor ("The Fires of Vulcan")—Melanie refuses to capitulate in Pompeii, creating a profound Doctor-Mel dynamic.

4) The Doctor throws himself into the abyss ("The Shadow of the Scourge")—The Doctor momentarily surrenders to the Scourge, hurling himself with a scream into a mental void.

5) The fifth Doctor's explanation of time ("The Mutant Phase")—The Doctor details how he can't trust even Nyssa with intricate knowledge of time travel, stating they can't know who might take the information from her.

life. The Doctor cannot bear to be forcibly separated from the TARDIS. Until now, he always wondered why the Cathedral of St. Sophia was spared the sacking of Kiev (we can forgive his not suspecting alien involvement).

Steven Taylor: He isn't sure the TARDIS would admit him or Dodo without the Doctor. Steven's night vision isn't the best. He's unfamiliar with the Russian geography of this time period.

Steven hasn't found much evidence for Heaven and likely doesn't believe in it. His TARDIS travels have compelled him to always expect a rational explanation, even if he doesn't understand it.

The alien soldier's communications device briefly interlinks with Steven's brain and gives him random flashes of alien moons, war, planets, suns and dark skies.

The Doctor and Steven: They share some respect, but have different modus operandi. Despite the Doctor's warning about keeping the TARDIS' importance secret, Steven blathers about the Ship's travel abilities to the Russians. When the Doctor stubbornly refuses Dmitri entrance to the TARDIS, a more pro-agreeable Steven briefly considers cracking the Doctor over the head and making off with the TARDIS key.

Dodo Chaplet: Dodo didn't learn much in school religion classes, but feels empowered because God created women as well as men.

Steven and Dodo: After the TARDIS' comforts, they have difficulty adjusting to Kiev's low-level clothes and food.

The TARDIS: The TARDIS' exterior glass windows aren't really made of glass (fooled you). Its air supply is constantly recycled and purified. The Ship's immensely heavy but movable. The Doctor worries about the TARDIS even though it's mostly indestructible. The console holds a host of connectors and sockets the Doctor's never seen before.

ALIEN RACES *Alien soldiers* are unspecified constructs that serve as assassins, designed to fight a war between identical looking races with different DNA. Graced with shapeshifting and empathic talents, such soldier were typically launched in travel capsules into enemy territory, programmed to draw blood from the first being they encountered and thereby calibrate themselves to identify variations of enemy races.

In its natural state, your typical soldier sports a slender form with a sinewy back and a soul-less face. Its mouth holds a mass of bone-made hypo-dermic needles to extract enemy DNA or inject toxin into its foes. It has unstable pale skin and eyes, skeletal limbs and talon-capped toes. Such soldiers can convincingly disguise themselves as others, albeit with telltale glowing eyes and translucent skin. The soldiers cannot shapeshift their clothes.

The soldiers aren't invulnerable but are protected by skin that resists multiple arrow hits. If you aim for the soft tissue at the base of the skull, you'll likely annoy them.

HISTORY The alien construct in *Bunker Soldiers* was created for a conflict that ended centuries ago. During that period, the soldier, snug in its travel capsule, overshot its target and drifted through space, heavily damaged, for thousands of years. It eventually fell into Earth's gravity well and landed near Kiev. A select group of Russians mistook it for a religious figure and secured it in the Church of St. Sophia.

• Ruling from the Mongolian capital of Qaraqorum, Ogedei Khan directed Europe's largest invasion, with Batu Khan (Genghis' grandson) and his cousin Mongke serving as field commanders. Kiev fell, along with Hungary and Poland.

• It's suggested that Dodo—yes, silly little Dodo, who wears outfits that look like ads for Cheerios—might have triggered the Black Death by serving Dmitri dinner, then growing frustrated when Dmitri became dismissive and ordered his meal thrown to the pigs. In her frustration, Dodo shouted out "You can't throw something away just because you don't like it!" thereby inspiring the more than half-mad Dmitri to order plague riddled bodies be hurled over Kiev's walls at the Mongols. It's a long shot, but the Doctor speculated that in 1346, Janibeg Khan might have remembered Dmitri's tactic and used it in reverse by ordering his army to catapult pestilence infected bodies into the besieged city of Kaffa. (Author's Note: And no doubt originating the infamous sketch, "Take our corpses, please.") Not only did the maneuver notch itself in history as the first (primitive, but strikingly galling) form of biological warfare, it likely tainted merchants who carried the plague to southern Europe and in time rubbed out a third of the continent.

• Neurosurgeons exist in Steven's era.

AT THE END OF THE DAY Breathtakingly brutal and damnably enthralling, full of corpses and further evidence that it's tough to beat a top-notch first Doctor historical. Among other things, *Bunker Soldiers* entrenches itself as the best Steven Taylor book, giving us an assertive, fairly accomplished companion who understandably screws up from time to time. Hell, even Dodo's decently strong willed. All in all, a surprise win a la *The Empire of Glass*, and a text that rivets you to the very end (just when you think everything's fine, Mongols strut into the TARDIS).

VERDIGRIS

By Paul Magrs

Release Date: April 2000
Order: BBC Past Doctor Adventure #30

TARDIS CREW The third Doctor, Jo Grant and UNIT, with Iris Wildthyme and Tom.

IRIS' TRAVEL LOG Thisis, 30 miles from the Doctor's house, 1973.

STORY UN-CHRONOLOGY Purely for fun, *Verdigris'* chronology can't be pinned down, undoubtedly throwing continuity freaks (Author's Note: And despite what you might think, I'm not among them) into a tizzy. It obviously takes place after the Master's prison break in "The Sea Devils," and further signs—not the least of which being the book's epilogue—point to Verdigris taking place between "The Time Monster" and "The Three Doctors."

Yet when Iris mentions events in "The Curse of Peladon," the Doctor deliberately states those events haven't happened yet. Given that *Verdigris'* back cover tellingly doesn't mention the story's chronology (in a period before the BBC dropped the chronology listing altogether), Magrs and the BBC editors are obviously—and rather hilariously—toying with the overly anal fans in the audience, like literary cats playing with mice.

STORY SUMMARY The Doctor and Jo Grant try to vacation at one of the Doctor's country homes, but find uninvited house guests in the form of time traveler Iris Wildthyme, who's still smitten with the Doctor, and her companion Tom. Meanwhile, the rogue Time Lord known as the Master gathers the Children of Destiny—psionically powerful Earth youths—and claims the Doctor is an enemy of the heroic "Galactic Federation." Using the Childrens' power, the Master sets about discrediting UNIT, robbing its staff of their memories and making them work in a grocery store.

Perhaps stranger, a railway carriage full of characters from literature appears in the middle of a field. But when the Doctor and Iris aid a panicking Miss Havisham (from Charles Dickens' novel *Great Expectations*), an alien bracelet on Havisham's wrist transport the trio to a space sta-

tion in Earth orbit. There, the Doctor and Iris encounter the Meercocks—aliens who fled their homeworld's destruction and mistakenly reshaped their bodies as characters from Earth literature.

The Doctor and Iris flee via escape pods and ultimately unmask the Master as Verdigris, a green, magically powerful being who claims to have acted on Iris' orders. By Verdigris' account, a wildly drunk Iris once visited the ruined planet Makorna and, desperate to help the Doctor escape his Earth exile, summoned magical spirits who fashioned bodies out of the planet's rust and became the Meercocks. Compelled to help the Doctor leave Earth, the supernatural Verdigris decided to destroy UNIT and discredit the Doctor, paving the way for a successful invasion of Earth that would give the Doctor the alien technology he needed.

At the Doctor's request, Verdigris restores the UNIT personnel to normal and destroys the "Supreme Galactic Headquarters" he fashioned to fool the Children of Destiny. With Iris' help, the Meercocks and the Children set up a new life on Makorna. Iris and Tom, after getting reasonably drunk with the Doctor and Jo in celebration, depart for regions unknown.

A short while later, the Doctor defeats the rogue Time Lord named Omega ("The Three Doctors"), and the Time Lords end the Doctor's exile. Verdigris, his goal of the Doctor's escape completed, returns to commend the Doctor, then crumbles into a heap of copper dust and is no more.

MEMORABLE MOMENTS Hearing an intruder breaking into his house, the Doctor ambushes Iris but she headlocks him. (Iris asks if the Doctor would have refrained Venusian Aikido had he known it was her. The Doctor: "No, I'd have probably shot you.") During an escape, the Doctor and Iris hug close and the Doctor shouts, "Unhand me, madam!" With delicious irony, Iris refuses to let the Doctor hypnotize her, fearing it might "tamper with the delicate fabric of my mind."

The Meercock characters include a "demented," cloned version of the whale in *Moby Dick*. Jo Grant visits a literally two-dimensional Captain Yates in the hospital and stuffs him into her handbag.

If you've watched the Pertwee era, you'll die laughing when Verdigris, disguised as the Master, looks into a mirror to tell himself that he is the Master, he is the Master and he must bow down before his own magnificent will.

ASS-WHUPPINGS Verdigris' machinations brainwash the Brigadier, Sgt. Benton, Liz Shaw and other UNIT personnel into becoming supermarket workers (oh, that foul fiend!). When the Meercocks introduce concepts of post-modernism and meta-

---

fiction onto Earth to blend in, Captain Yates literally becomes two-dimensional but recovers.

The Doctor burns killer trees with fireworks. Iris shatters a crystalline being with her laser pistol. Verdigris, seeking to fool Jo Grant as to UNIT's intentions, disguises himself as the Brigadier and shoots a mother and her two children.

Several Meercocks discorporate and fall into piles of green copper dust.

SEX AND SPIRITS

Iris constantly hints at romance between herself and the Doctor, getting in raucous comments such as, "[The Doctor's] dying to get his hands on my bust... bus, sorry." Also, "Look at him flare his elegant nostrils at my proximity!" For his part, the Doctor seems utterly bewildered by her obsession and turns down repeated offers to cuddle.

Iris' companion Tom is gay. He wonders how she can't know this, as they duet on Dusty Springfield songs while driving.

At last year's UNIT Christmas party, Mike Yates clumsily kissed Jo Grant before she diverted him to talk about his unhappy childhood. Jo rips away Verdigris' initial disguise to reveal the Master—who then kisses her. The real Master later gags to learn this.

This lovingly booze-filled book has the Doctor and company down gin and tonics, Chardonnay and whisky. Iris' bus comes well stocked with booze. The Doctor likes lime, not lemon, with his Bombay Sapphire. At book's end, the main characters—especially Iris—get schnookered at a space bar.

TV TIE-INS

Failing to end the Doctor's exile, Verdigris decides to torment him instead and informs the renegade Time Lord Omega about the Doctor's presence on Earth, sparking events in "The Three Doctors."

The real Master, freed in "The Sea Devils," hasn't been seen since the UNIT Christmas party but lends Verdigris his identity to cause mischief. At novel's end, Verdigris asks the Master for further help, but the rogue Time Lord leaves to plot his collusion with the Daleks in "Frontier in Space."

Jo attended school with a girl named Tara (almost undoubtedly Sam Steed's assistant from "The Avengers"). In addition to everything else, the Time Lords monkeyed with the Doctor's time charts when they exiled him ("The War Games"). In an unseen adventure, the Doctor and the Brigadier whisked a malevolent fiend from Arcturus ("The Curse of Peladon") back home.

Verdigris mentions Gallifrey by name, using it before the word's debut in "The Time Warrior." Verdigris' fictional "Galactic Federation" mercifully has nothing to do with the various "Federations" in "Doctor Who," "Star Trek" and "Blake's Seven." Iris supposedly met the Terrible Zodin ("The Five Doctors") on Mars.

NOVEL TIE-INS Iris Wildthyme first appeared in *Short Trips*: "Old Flames." Iris' old incarnation, seen here, regenerated in *The Scarlet Empress* into the hot bundle of stuff seen in *The Blue Angel*.

Iris notes the Doctor has such clean causality before his "canon-death," undoubtedly a reference at the third Doctor's "demise" in *Interference*.

The Meercocks claim the evil Valceans from the Observe dimension destroyed their world (Magrs' *The Blue Angel*). The Queen of the Meercocks wanted to attack the Glass Men of Valcea (also *The Blue Angel*), but deemed it suicidal.

The Doctor here says Iris isn't a proper Time Lady and the Time Lords are unsure of her identity. Furthermore, Iris speaks to the Doctor of the Time Lords of as "Your own people!" rather than "Our own people!" Still, the Doctor "wouldn't be surprised" if Iris was a Time Lord and hints she's got more than one heart. *The Blue Angel* doesn't much resolve the "Time Lord" debate about Iris, but claims she hails from the Obverse universe.

CHARACTER DEVELOPMENT

The Doctor: UNIT pays the Doctor very well, but he doesn't particularly use the money. Iris and Tom are his first welcome houseguests (presumably, the rest have been horrible monsters). Iris claims the Time Lords know a great deal about the Doctor's destiny, explaining why they don't remove him from history altogether.

The Doctor doesn't like his dreams and hasn't slept properly in two-and-a-half years. He reads *The Radio Times* and can whistle David Bowie's "Starman." He's on good terms with a lot of peaceful races in the galaxy, and the only "Federation" he knows hails from "The Curse of Peladon."

Jo Grant: In two years of knowing the Doctor, Jo's visited his London flat, his Kent house (*Cat's Cradle: Warhead*) and the caravan he kept in the Highlands of Scotland. This is only the second time he's invited her to the oldest of his Earth houses. The TARDIS rarely returns to Earth in the time window when it left, throwing Jo temporally out of synch. She's hardly seen her family or friends these last few years.

Jo Grant and Captain Mike Yates: Jo knows virtually nothing about Yates. He spends weekends on Ministry survival courses Jo likes to avoid.

Brigadier Lethbridge-Stewart: His short career as a brainwashed grocery store manager makes him mutter about special offers.

Iris Wildthyme: Iris' current incarnation looks just over 60 years old. She claims to be more than 900 and likes dance music. She firmly believes that dashing from one end of space-time to the other keeps you sexy and young.

One of Iris' contradictory origin stories says she hails from slummy New Towns under the Gallifreyan Capital, meaning the Time Lords will probably erase her timeline if they catch her. Iris found her TARDIS abandoned in the mountains as a wasted experiment, helping it to learn, feed and evolve. In turn, the bus gave Iris advice. She's been travelling longer than the Doctor.

Supposedly, Iris met the Brigadier during a conflict with the Celaphopods in Venice. She carries a fake UNIT pass.

Iris doesn't like book endings, preferring to make up the climaxes (oh dear) herself. Iris can induce a self-trance that retrieves her buried memories. She carries a small hand blaster that fires slim pink blasts of radiation (*The Blue Angel*), but she's a damn lousy shot. Unlike the Doctor, most of Iris' companions run away from her screaming (perhaps because she plays "Tammy Wynette's Greatest Hits").

The Doctor and Iris: The third Doctor at first says is Iris an old, dear friend, but under a moment of stress calls her an oafish, clodhopping harridan. Conversely, Iris considers the Doctor the kindest, most generous, most self-sacrificing person she's ever met, trusting him with her life—but not her bus.

Iris claims to have variously saved the Doctor from the Ice Warriors ("The Ice Warriors") on Neptune, the Drashigs ("Carnival of Monsters") on Qon-ti-jaqir and the fourth Doctor from Mary Queen of Scots (an adventure shared with Sarah Jane Smith). The Doctor doesn't remember any of this, which possibly means it hasn't happened for him yet. More likely, Iris is full of it.

The Doctor tries to shirk causality and asks Iris when his exile ends, but she doesn't tell him.

Iris and Jo Grant: Iris thinks Jo's one of the most mind-numbingly loyal assistants a sexist rake could ever desire.

Iris, Romana and K9: Romana thought Iris common and largely couldn't stand her. Iris has met K9 (prompting the out-of-chronology third Doctor to add, "Robot dog? What the Dickens would I want with a robot dog?")

MISCELLANEOUS STUFF!

IRIS, THE SISTERHOOD AND VERDIGRIS

Iris joined the Sisterhood of Karn ("The Brain of Morbius") for a year or two and witnessed the fourth Doctor and Sarah Jane Smith's struggle against the renegade Time Lord Morbius. (The Doctor failed to see a dancing Iris chanting "Death! Death! Death!" in the background.)

After Morbius' "fatal" fall, the Sisterhood retrieved his not-so-destroyed brain for their own purposes. Morbius—as if this surprises anyone—tried to dominate the Sisterhood again, so Ohica, leader of the Sisterhood, used the Time Scoop to deposit the wounded Morbius in Gallifrey's Death Zone ("The Five Doctors"). Ohica ultimately unmasked Iris and Time Scooped all her incarnations there also, pitting them against foes such as the Voord ("The Keys of Marinus"), Zarbi ("The Web Planet") and Mechanoids ("The Chase").

The Irises triumphed, but Ohica Time Scooped the current Iris and her bus to the planet Makorna, the sandy remnant of an ancient civilization. Iris got ludicrously drunk with the archaeologists there and, upon learning of the third Doctor's exile, sloppily summoned Verdigris and his fellow spirits. For millennia, the supernatural Verdigris floated through space alone, finally arriving in Earth's solar system during the Doctor's exile.

P.S. Most of this comes from Iris' recollections, which gives it about as much credibility as President Nixon's claim, "I am not a crook."

Tom: Tom smokes and thinks everyone in the 1970s looks like a cast member of "Get Carter" or "Are You Being Served?" Time travel's matured him beyond his years. He's not yet conceived in this year (1973) and joined Iris' Ship in 2000, so he's likely younger than 26.

Mary, a young member of the Children of Destiny, is Tom's future mother. When Tom was a baby, his father died in unknown circumstances. Tom's mother gave him a golden belt buckle he thinks belonged to his father. Tom got a First in English Literature and knows about Milton.

Tom and Iris: In November 2000, Tom drunkenly wandered into Iris' TARDIS, thinking it the No. 22 bus to Putney Common. He formerly kept a one room Putney flat. Their first trip together landed them on Calgoria, causing nail-biting adventures with the forest-dwelling Jirat and the pathologically metropolitan Trinarr. Their historical adventures—save for the time they met Cleopatra—bored him. Tom likes to replace Iris' driving tapes with hardcore music. He feels sorry for her because she doesn't have any friends.

Verdigris: The supernatural Verdigris likely wasn't alive, having a metallic green flesh and a featureless head with only a slit for a mouth and two emerald, burning eyes. Once commanded to perform a task, he can't stop until successful.

Jenny: A butch lesbian traffic warden who got the runs (and thank you, Paul, for mentioning that) every time she time-traveled. As a former companion of Iris, Jenny supposedly begged for the Doctor's life before the Dalek Supreme in the Crystal Mines of Marlion.

Sally: Sweet 67-year-old woman who owns a shop near the Doctor's house. For a few years now, he's dashed in, telling her to seek cover in her cellar or attic, but normally, she sells him papers and mails his packages. The second Doctor told her his "brother"—also named the Doctor—would one day call. She reminds the Doctor of his mother.

Iris' TARDIS: The bus only answers to her. (Author's Note: One might whimsically say, "The bus stops here.") It can fly through the Time Vortex on auto-pilot and has soft cozy furnishings, Art Nouveau lamps and brocaded curtains. Its door usually alerts Iris if someone tries to break in, but Verdigris penetrated the defenses. Mary, Queen of Scots crocheted one of the driving seat cushions.

The Doctor's house cat: Trained to swallow keys, then barf them up to help people escape.

ALIEN RACES *The Meercocks*, graced with a malleable nature, took forms from literature that included Little Red Riding Hood and her wolf, the white rabbit from *Through the Looking Glass*, a number of D.H. Lawrence and Thomas Hardy characters and Kafka's Gregor Samsen.

PLACES TO GO
The Doctor's House: The Doctor's oldest house on Earth features vast oil paintings of the Doctor as an Elizabethan nobleman, a Victorian merchant and a Regency fop with frilled sleeves, silk britches and a lacy handkerchief. Marble statues line the driveway. One yolky-yellow room sports only a tapestried chair for the Doctor's cat. The

house laboratory is better equipped—and messier—than the Doctor's UNIT HQ.

Another deep-blue room has shelves of different-sized, blue Chinese ginger jars, each containing a hologram of a different planet. The Doctor probably made these to alleviate his exile.

UNIT Headquarters: For the 1970s, its surveillance equipment was top-of-the-line.

ORGANIZATIONS *Children of Destiny:* The next step in humanity's evolution (supposedly), the four psionic Children employed telepathy and telekinesis. Simon served as telepathic mentor for fellow members Kevin, Mary and Peter. They wanted Iris' companion Tom as their fifth member.

PHENOMENA *Mental powers* get mucked up by too much booze and smokes.

TIME TRAVEL By removing you from your natural chronological progression, time travel literally turns you into a new person. Possible side effects include hazy memories, time sickness headaches or even (Rassilon forbid) the runs. Iris here violates the rule about Time Lords meeting each other in chronological order.

AT THE END OF THE DAY An absolute hoot and a holler, richly textured and rather surreal like a good Salvador Dali painting (the two-dimensional Mike Yates). All of that said, *Verdigris'* irreverence and slower pace at explaining its secrets will undoubtedly frustrate readers who prefer having everything upfront. But if you can cock your head and walk into *Verdigris* expecting a hell of a lot of fun, it rewards you as an experimental, grandiose romp that sparkles among more safe-playing "Who" books. Revel in it.

LAST OF THE GADARENE

By Mark Gatiss

Release Date: January 2000
Order: BBC Past Doctor Adventure #28

TARDIS CREW The third Doctor, Jo Grant and UNIT, with the Roger Delgado Master.

TRAVEL LOG Gogon's homeworld, time unknown; Culverton, circa 1970s.

STORY SUMMARY When aeronautics manufacturer Legion International buys an aerodrome in the little village of Culverton, local Wing Commander Alec Whistler grows concerned about Legion's heavy-handed troops and mysterious activities. Whistler contacts his old friend Brigadier Lethbridge-Stewart to investigate and the Doctor follows up on Whistler's reports by breaking into the Culverton aerodrome. Although he cannot prove it, the Doctor suspects the presence of alien technology.

In fact, Legion merely serves as a front for the alien Gadarene, a race desperate to flee its dying homeworld and use Culverton as a launching point to invade Earth. Some 30 years ago, two Gadarene scouts arrived on Earth via an unstable transmat process, but while one of them matured into Legion Director Bliss, her brother mutated into a gigantic Gadarene that covered itself in mud and slept. Eventually, the renegade Time Lord known as the Master, hell-bent on seeing Earth destroyed for imprisoning him, located Bliss and agreed to help a Gadarene invasion. Unfortunately, Bliss lost the ninth key to the Gadarene transmat—a small jade shard recovered by Whistler from a pub bombed in World War II—meaning only Gadarene embryos could survive the unstable transmat. Without the key, Bliss used the Gadarene embryos to possess the Culverton villagers, but upon taking it back from Whistler, Bliss prepares to teleport thousands of adult Gadarene to Earth.

The Brigadier, convinced of an imminent alien invasion, orders UNIT troops into Culverton. The Doctor knocks out the possessed villagers with improvised jars of nitrous oxide, but Bliss orders her mutated brother to assault the UNIT personnel while the Master activates the Gadarene transmat. As the moment grows near, Bliss decides the Master's usefulness has ended and turns on him, but he destroys her with his Tissue Compression Eliminator. By symbiosis, Bliss' death also kills her brother and the telepathically linked Gadarene embryos, even as the adult Gadarene prepare to storm Earth.

Fortunately, the Doctor radios Whistler to put his privately owned Spitfire on a collision course with the transmat column and eject. The airplane explodes, destroying the transmat device and apparently the Master as well. The energy backlash also devastates the Gadarene invasion force and homeworld, allowing UNIT to begin clean-up operations in Culverton and the Doctor to ponder the "death" of his old friend and fellow Time Lord.

MEMORABLE MOMENTS In a hilarious bit, the Doctor bitches to the Brigadier that if he needs an errand boy, he should look up his old friends at the Women's Institute because they make excellent jam. There's also a later bit when the Doctor asks the Master of his Gadarene alliance, "How does it feel always to be someone else's lackey?" and the villain responds, "As the Brigadier's pet monkey, I should think you're better placed to answer that, my dear Doctor."

The final scene is something of a beaut, with the Pertwee Doctor considering the "loss" of the Master and Jo ironically describing the scoundrel as "just someone [the Doctor] went to school with."

SEX AND SPIRITS As the book opens, Jo prances about in a little pink bikini (shades of Katy Manning's nude poses with a Dalek, one suspects).

ASS-WHUPPINGS A confrontation at the Culverton aerodrome ends with a security guard clinging to the Doctor's shoe for dear life, then falling into moving jet engine blades. The Doctor suffers a ten-foot plummet himself, but only smacks the floor hard.

Whistler's Spitfire bullets wound the Master, and Whistler's airplane explosion destroys the entire Gadarene race in an energy backlash. You're fooling yourself to think the Master's kicked it.

As UNIT forces clash with possessed Culverton civilians, the Brigadier resigns himself to rolling over the townfolk to stop the Gadarene. The Brigadier took the wheel, unwilling to have his men do something he wouldn't do himself, but the Doctor thankfully saved the day.

NOVEL TIE-INS "Legion International" doesn't have ties to the Legion race (*Lucifer Rising, The Crystal Bucephalus*).

CHARACTER DEVELOPMENT

The Doctor: On an unnamed planet, the Doctor helped overthrow the callous regime of Gogon, Lord High General of Xanthos, and became friends with a native called Rujjis. He lost a rich blue smoking jacket escaping from Gogon's clutches.

The Doctor had difficulty adjusting to the desolation and loneliness of his exile. At first he threw himself into research, then wandered about the TARDIS corridors to re-live his old life until it became too painful. He finally acclimated to Earth and often sat by the Thames, content with one insignificant but wonderful little planet.

The Doctor never lets the cleaners near his UNIT lab. He's experienced at chemical analysis. He hasn't flown a Spitfire since 2154.

Jo Grant: Childhood Jo had a big room on the second floor of her parents' house filled with posters, schoolbook piles and unused violin scores. She held parties for her dolls and let her "horses" graze on a large landing at the top of the banistered stairs. She suffered from a fear of the dark and monsters.

The Master: Has enough political clout to block official channels of inquiry.

The Doctor and the Master: At the Academy, the Doctor argued with the Master for not keeping his word. In response, the Master told the Doctor he was too trusting and must be more realistic.

Bliss and her brother: Bliss and arrived on Earth as a Gadarene embryo, then gestated in some hapless host. Bliss totally absorbed its host personality, eventually maturing into a tall, fat "human female." Bliss shed her human skin, revealing her Gadarene nature right before the Master shot her.

The transmat process mutated Bliss' brother to the size of a hideous Chinese dragon. He looked like a crab-like monstrous worm with a segmented tail and blazing black eyes, sickeningly doused in translucent slime and about 50-feet long.

ALIEN RACES

Gadarene: The surviving Gadarene number 300,000, and with 12 one-eyed Elders overseeing them. Gadarene have insectoid characteristics.

Gadarene Embryos: Conversely, embryonic Gadarene are really, really gross—hairless, carapaced creatures that look like a cross between a crab and a worm, their semitransparent shells glistening with ooze. They walk on brittle, transparent spindly legs and have black eyes.

Gadarene embryos have some intelligence and enjoy a frolicking childhood on their homeworld. Perhaps most significantly, they can slither inside humans via the mouth, possess them and mature. Mature Gadarene can prematurely trigger a Gadarene embryo harvesting (the host normally survives this process). Gadarene who stay in their host for years (such as Bliss) subvert the body with Gadarene DNA. It's not known if the embryos can possesses other races.

Hosts obey the embryos' orders but cannot be mentally interrogated. To kill a Gadarene embryo, squash its head beneath your boot (sounds like common sense, really). Gadarene hosts can't stand bright light.

STUFF YOU NEED *Gadarene keys* look like small jade shards, about three-inches long, the size and shape of rabbit's feet and all containing microcircuitry. Nine Gadarene keys working in sequence can open a transmat tunnel for adult Gadarene; eight can transport Gadarene embryos. The transmat effect looks like summer lightning.

HISTORY The exact cataclysm that made the Gadarene flee their homeworld isn't established.
• MP Charles Cochrane, one of the Prime Minister's favorites, was promoted to Secretary of Defense. Jocelyn Strangeways currently serves as Ministry of Defense Chief of Staff.

AT THE END OF THE DAY Solid for what it is—a nostalgia exercise that's underambitious but highly successful at replicating the third Doctor's trappings (UNIT, the Master, a corporation that's not all it seems, etc.). Of course, this means that it by consequence also mimics the drag of many Pertwee stories and nothing original happens (as if Gatiss is saying, "Oh, you want a third Doctor story? Well, here you are, then."). If the third Doctor era is *the* era of "Doctor Who" for you, then you'll surely turn cartwheels over *Last of the Gadarene*, and this book's certainly written by a professional, but it's nothing that popping in a Pertwee video or two won't cure.

THE PESCATONS

By Victor Pemberton

Release Date: 1991
Order: Virgin novelization #153
NOTE: This story was first released on a 1976 LP record and cassette by Argo Records (Silver Screen Records reissued it on CD in 1991). Before a "Missing Adventures" line existed, The Pescatons novelization was lumped in with the Target TV adaptations.

TARDIS CREW The fourth Doctor and Sarah Jane Smith.

TRAVEL LOG England, East Coast, mid-1970s

CHRONOLOGY Between "The Seeds of Doom" and "The Masque of Mandragora."

STORY SUMMARY Returning to London, mid-1970s, the Doctor and Sarah land near the English coast and immediately confront a 12-foot-tall, half-human, half-fish creature, which the Doctor identifies as a scout for the carnivorous Pescaton race.

Fleeing, the Doctor and Sarah re-meet the Doctor's old friend, astronomer Professor Bud Emmerson. Through Emmerson's telescopes, the Doctor watches as the Pescaton homeworld of Pesca, long damaged by close exposure to its sun, dies amid a series of explosions. However, the Pescatons escape in a swarm of spaceships and land on Earth, intending to seize the planet's meat and salt water. Major cities come under attack, with Earth mobilizing for full war.

Zor, the Pescaton leader, intends for his people to consume humanity and absorb its technical knowledge. As a bonus, Zor hopes to capture his old foe the Doctor and gain the ability to time travel. But the Doctor, deducing that Zor serves as a conduit of power to all Pescatons, locates the Pescaton leader in the dark London Underground. With the help of some policemen, the Doctor wires up ultraviolet lights that kill Zor and by extension all the Pescatons.

ASS-WHUPPINGS The Doctor slays Zor and all the Pescatons, who degenerate into green powder. Pescaton laser beams twice strike the Doctor. Having not fulfilled his violence quota, Zor electrically zaps our hero and twice barrages him with a mental assault.

TV AND NOVEL TIE-INS London comes under a full-scale Pescaton assault, with the media covering the attack and making this book defy a heap of TV tales ("Invasion of the Dinosaurs," "Terror of the Zygons") that covered up such alien invasions. Despite *The Pescatons*, *The Dying Days* solidly remains mankind's first public alien encounter.

CHARACTER DEVELOPMENT

The Doctor: The Doctor isn't a good swimmer at the best of times. Professor Bud Emmerson, 64, is a longtime friend of at least one previous Doctor. The Doctor carries a Dynameter, a device that checks "sonic direction."

Sarah Jane Smith: Carries a press ID card.

ALIEN RACES

Pescatons: Are amphibious but crave water. Fully grown Pescatons look like a humanoid cross between a shark and a piranha, more than 12 feet tall, with shiny scales and talons. They're voracious carnivores, able to trap prey in toughened ooze. They can smell salt water miles away.

The Pescatons have origins in the carchariidae order and are damnably swift in water, greatly aided by webbed feet. They can lay thousands of green-colored eggs that grow rapidly in salt water, wrapped in protective cones.

TOP 5

"WHO" COMEDY MOMENTS

Novels Post *Interference*

1) **The Doctor's final soliloquies (Festival of Death)**—In a glorious romp, the condemned Doctor misquotes famous death monologues, finishing with "Kismet, Romana." Shocked, Romana replies, "You want me to kiss you?" before electrocuting him.

2) **Jamie kills the Gallifreyan woprat (Heart of TARDIS)**—The last Gallifreyan woprat in existence frightens Victoria into screaming (as always), so Jamie knifes the sucker.

3) **UNIT mesmerized, forced to work in a grocery store (Verdigris)**—Oh, those foul fiends who make heroes slave in grocery stores!

4) **The fourth Doctor rescues K9 from the Big Huge and Educational Collection of Old Galactic Stuff (Heart of TARDIS)**—To recover his tin pooch, who's trapped as a museum exhibit, the Doctor intellectually smashing the exhibit case glass, then "runs like Skaro."

5) **"Kiss my TARDIS!" (The Shadows of Avalon)**—The eighth Doctor snubs Romana III, renewing his life as a Time Lord renegade.

Big Finish Audios

1) **Benny's "summoning" ("The Shadow of the Scourge")**—Benny asks seance leader Annie Carpenter to summon the spirits of Benny's "two poor little ones." When Carpenter asks the names of Benny's children, Benny deadpans, "Squidgy and Speckly"—revealing that the kids are actually Benny's dead turtles.

2) **Eugene recants ("The Holy Terror")**—Castle guards list off a series of tortures that scribe Eugene will endure if he doesn't give up allegiance to the previous king. Given the option, Eugene off-handedly suggests, "Oh, well, I think I'll recant then," at which point the guards turn quite chummy.

3) **Frobisher enjoys bath time ("The Holy Terror")**—The "naked" Frobisher says he normally morphs a set of black-and-white pants.

4) **Ace knows her game ("The Shadow of the Scourge")**—The Doctor "betrays" Earth for probably the 322nd time, so Ace pulls the "Oh, you betrayed us! You betrayed us!" routine.

5) **Charley protests ("The Stones of Venice")**—Charley: "Doctor, when you invited me on these trips, you never said anything about marauding amphibians and enforced marriages to noble lunatics." The Doctor: "I should have, really, it's always the way."

Pescatons are armored and strong enough to push down trees. Their eyes can fire laser beams. They're evidently vulnerable to ultraviolet, although the Doctor contradicts himself by saying claims they can resist the sun and are bulletproof.

Pescatons don't think for themselves—Zor, the Pescaton leader, acts as a central mental link. Zor's telepathic but the Doctor can resist his influence. Through such a gestalt, the Pescatons can assimilate other beings' minds, including humans' brain power and vocal ability, but they can't survive without their leader.

ALIEN PLANETS

Pesca: Located in the outer galaxies, Pesca once held rich green forests and natural resources. As the Pescatons misused the planet's resources, the sun drew closer and the oceans evaporated.

Venus: Retains viable oceans, so some Pescatons landed there.

AT THE END OF THE DAY Standard at best, very unimaginative, dull and something we could all live without. As a story of terror from the sea, the seventh Doctor's *Storm Harvest* pounds *The Pescatons* into submission.

CORPSE MARKER

By Chris Boucher

Release Date: November 1999
Order: BBC Past Doctor Novel #27

TARDIS CREW The fourth Doctor and Leela

TRAVEL LOG Kaldor City, some years after 2877 (the approximate date of "The Robots of Death")

CHRONOLOGY Between *Last Man Running* and "The Talons of Weng-Chiang."

STORY SUMMARY In the aftermath of the late Taren Capel's aborted robot revolution aboard Storm Mine Four (in "The Robots of Death"), the ruling robotics Company hushes up the incident and the survivors—Uvanov, Toos and Poul—resume their lives. But when the lowly born Uvanov gets promoted to Company topmaster, the ruling Board families fear the lower classes are gaining too much power and ask a devious psychostrategist named Carnell to rectify the situation. Simultaneously, Company engineers use Taren Capel's blueprints to construct a prototype robot named SASV1 that turns schizophrenic and dominates the will of other Company robots.

Meanwhile, the TARDIS materializes in a Company research laboratory, where a security alert separates the Doctor and Leela. The Doctor finds newly constructed human-looking robots that mimic his behavior, then re-meets Topmaster Uvanov. The Doctor agrees to investigate Uvanov's suspicions of a conspiracy against him if Uvanov will locate Leela. Killer robots, however, force Toos to flee to the city's Sewerpits and cause the unstable, robo-phobic Poul to become unhinged and mistake the Doctor for the late Taren Capel. Manic, Poul causes a skimmer crash that strands him and the Doctor in the Sewerpits, where they meet Toos, Leela and a terrorist cell with mistaken ideas about Taren Capel's philosophies.

Hearing reports that Taren Capel (i.e., the Doctor) is alive, the unhinged SASV1 orders the prototype, human-looking robots to eliminate their "creator" by storming the Sewerpits and killing everyone. The Doctor herds his allies to safety, then realizes the killer robots are still programmed to mimic his behavior and keeps them occupied performing various gestures, halting the massacre. Tracking SASV1 to its base, the Doctor finds the delusional robot and finally destroys it with an explosive pack.

Having ended the immediate threat, the Doctor confronts Carnell, who admits to manipulating SASV1's robots in a scheme to drive Poul insane, then blame him for Uvanov and Toos' murders. If successful, Carnell would have exposed the Storm Mine Four incident and thereby ruined the public's faith in robots, allowing the Board families to create safer robots and strengthen the public's trust in Company rule under the families.

Concluding that the Founding Families failed to give him the information he needed to succeed, Carnell gives Uvanov blackmail evidence against them, forcing the Board families to grant huge concessions to Uvanov and his followers. The lower classes gain more representation and Uvanov, promoted to the top Company position of Firstmaster, instigates reform while the Doctor and Leela quietly slip away in the TARDIS.

MEMORABLE MOMENTS The Doctor grows chagrined by the rule-happy robots, noting, "There seem to be a lot of anti-jelly-baby regulations." Later, a pilot declines the Doctor's jelly baby offer and the Doctor labels such global rejection of jelly babies "a worrying development for civilization."

The fourth Doctor describes himself as "uniquely unthreatening and unthreateningly unique. There is no one else who looks like me. Not even me, actually." The Doctor advises flierman Con Bartel that if Con proves to be a major breach of security, "I'll have my companion kill you." Mention of the lethal "companion" becomes a tremendous running joke.

Proving how a little knowledge goes a long way, Uvanov details how dangerous he, Toos and Poul are because they know robots can kill.

SEX AND SPIRITS Toos' pilot and secret Company agent Mor Tani secretly lusts for her. (Toos: "It would have to be a lust so secret that even I didn't know about it.")

ASS-WHUPPINGS Bloodthirsty Leela has a fairly good day, stabbing one pursuer through the heart, then ramming the dead man's stun-kill rod into his partner and frying him. She also breaks one opponent's arm and knees another man in the ghoulies, then kicks him again just to be sure he's down. She later slashes one attackers' throat so much, it partially severs his spine. She then takes out a second man in pretty much the same fashion and stabs two attackers through the heart—up under the breastbone, naturally. (One wonders if Boucher is venting his system of all the killings Leela *couldn't* perform on TV.)

More importantly, the Doctor strikes up a friendship with flierman Con Bartel, who dies in a flier crash. The Doctor fries a robot with an open electrical cable and smacks a sticky explosive on SASV1's eyes, blowing half its head off. Robots variously break people's necks and drive fists through their hearts.

TV TIE-INS This story serves as the direct sequel (like you hadn't figured that out) to Chris Boucher's "The Robots of Death." In that story, the crazed robotics engineer Taren Capel tried to lead a robot insurrection aboard Storm Mine Four eight months into the Mine's two-year tour of duty, in an area of desert known as "The Blind Heart." At the time, Uvanov and Toos were among the best captain-pilot teams in the company database. After the fourth Doctor and Leela defeated Capel, the surviving Uvanov, Toos and Poul were rescued and the Mine sank into the sand. A cover story cited ore raiders and the incident became referred to as "Mutiny in the Blind Heart."

The psychostrategist Carnell first appeared in the "Blake's Seven" episode "Weapon" as one of the ruthless Servalan's espionage strategists. At the end of that story, Carnell fled Servalan's service (and homicidal tendencies) when his analysis went awry and the rebel Blake won the day.

CHARACTER DEVELOPMENT
The Doctor: Heights don't bother the Doctor much (we're a long way before "Logopolis" here, kids), but constantly being exposed to heights

wears him down. He doesn't fully understand the controls of a Z9a explosive pack. Some of his jelly babies are blackcurrant.

Leela: One of Leela's trainers advised her she should never feel triumphant, because it can make you act stupid.

Topmaster Kiy Uvanov: Uvanov no longer commands Storm Mines. His clashes with Firstmaster Layly Landerchild reached the point that a third of the Company Board supported Uvanov, a third belonged to Landerchild and a third were up for grabs. Thanks to Carnell, Uvanov ends *Corpse Marker* ruling the Company as Firstmaster.

Captain Lish Toos: Rapidly promoted after the Taren Capel incident, former pilot Toos now commands Storm Mine Seven but handles a lot of mine maneuvers herself.

Following the Storm Mine Four killings, Captain Toos doesn't allow robots to enter the control deck for any reason, or to perform a job that can be done by a human. Furthermore, no robots are allowed in her quarters or where she works. Toos has robots deactivated for the slightest malfunction—on one tour, the engineering staff ran out of corpse markers (*See Stuff You Need*).

The Company tolerates her unusual restrictions and crew requirements because she's such a good captain. Still, Toos' pilot, Mor Tani, was a mole for the Company and Uvanov. Toos' last tour made her ludicrously rich. She doesn't have any living relatives. Toos keeps in shape and is a fast runner, perhaps out of a subconscious fear she'll have to flee for her life from killer robots (smart thinking).

Ander Poul: The dangerously unstable Poul sometimes forgets his name and doesn't remember much of the Taren Capel incident. He's been promoted several times to Security Section Head, in charge of humans. Hard as it is to believe, he was comfortable with robots once.

Carnell: After the "Blake's Seven" episode "Weapon," Carnell took two years to establish credentials in Kaldor City. Years later, he'd gained legendary skills as a financial planner and economic analyst. Uvanov owes him some cash.

SASV1 (a.k.a. Serial Access Supervoc): In an ultra-secret project, a group of Company engineers found Taren Capel's cabin on Storm Mine Four and used his blueprints to perform previously forbidden research, crafting a highly advanced robot—the ultimate of its kind. However, the prototype SASV1 gained too much sentience and

This book is not endorsed by the BBC. Doctor Who and TARDIS are trademarks of the BBC.

27

began to dream. It became hopelessly schizophrenic, simultaneously believing it was Taren Capel and that Capel was on the loose and must be destroyed. Perhaps more frightening, it lacked a killing inhibitor and could mentally dominate other robots, influencing them to murder, too.

ALIEN RACES *Time Lords* might regenerate if subjected to excessive boredom.

PLACES TO GO

Kaldor City: Robot-style clothing appears to be the newest trend there (the Doctor's never seen anything like it). The Robot Lounge, a city bar and restaurant, is exclusive, expensive and boasts an entirely human staff.

Sewerpits: Tunnels under Kaldor City, radiating a field that allows killer robots—those with malfunctioning circuits—to enter but prevents them from leaving. Alternatively, it traps robots of a high order of complexity, figuring they're capable of violent acts. Normally inhibited robots are kept out altogether. (*See History*) The field also scrambles fliers below a certain height.

STUFF YOU NEED

Kaldor City robots: Generally speaking, they're best at driving Storm Mines and aren't trusted to pilot smaller and quicker fliers. Lower-class Stop-Dum robots can hem prisoners in simply by linking up and moving accordingly. The higher-intelligence Vocs aren't supposed to know when they were built. MedVocs treat people.

The prototype human-looking robots that the Doctor encounters are grown in liquid vats in batches of six (three identical men, three identical women), the tanks forming organics on a basic framework. The prototypes, numbering about 200, seemed to have the attention span of cattle and were limited to mimicking behavior. Firstmaster Uvanov, fearing the existence of such robots could cause public distrust and even anarchy, destroyed evidence that the human-looking robots existed.

The Doctor's Sonic Screwdriver: He acquired it "long ago and far away."

ORGANIZATIONS

The Founding Families: There are 20 of them, with families including the Landerchilds, Roatsons, Mechmans and Farlocks. They had their hand in their civilization's robot development from the beginning.

Company: Unnamed organization specializing in robot development. Until Uvanov's ascension, a

Landerchild has always served as Firstmaster, i.e., chairman of the ruling Company Board. Although robotics security was tight, the SASV1 project proved that the Company's right hand often didn't know what the left was doing.

Company Board: Composed of 30 members. Until this story, they exclusively came from senior members of the 20 Founding Families. Occasionally, non-family members were asked to apply, but few were successful. The Firstmaster Chairholder of the Company Board is the Company's most powerful position, and by extension the most important person in Kaldor City.

Minor Faction: A pooling of power among the civilian administration, devised to force recognition from the hereditary Company Board. The Minor Faction gained strength as its numbers increased, but couldn't rival the Company's power until this story.

Tarenists: One of a hundred anti-robot cults growing in popularity. The Tarenists base their philosophies on the late Taren Capel, mistakenly believing he opposed an over-reliance on robots. Carnell's influence helped elevate the Tarenists as a prominent anti-robot group.

HISTORY The Doctor speculates Kaldor City's civilization faced killer robots in its past, designing the Sewerpits to trap rogue machines—killer robots. However, it's possible the attempt failed and the previous civilization died off, forgetting the robot crisis that killed it.

AT THE END OF THE DAY A better-than-average read that deserves to be consumed, over the coffee, after you've just finished the "The Robots of Death" DVD. What keeps *Corpse Marker* from true greatness, one suspects, are sporadic feelings of haziness and TV writer Boucher's continued uneasiness with novel writing (although this is a marked improvement over his forgettable *Last Man Running*). Still, *Corpse Marker* in its own right notches enough crisp dialogue, scheming characters and fiendish plots to keep the action moving, making this an enticement for TV viewers who spit on the novels, plus a must-read scenario for Tom Baker and Leela fans. Thumbs up.

TOMB OF VALDEMAR

By Simon Messingham

Release Date: February 2000
Order: BBC Past Doctor Adventure #29

TARDIS CREW The fourth Doctor and Romana I, with K9.

TRAVEL LOG The Doctor's TARDIS: planet Ashkellia, clearly in Earth's future. Romana's future TARDIS: the Janus Forus inn, time unknown.

CHRONOLOGY Between "The Ribos Operation" and "The Pirate Planet."

STORY SUMMARY As the Doctor and Romana journey to recover the second segment of the Key to Time, a burst of energy from the higher dimensions waylays the Key's tracer and lands the TARDIS on the acidic planet Ashkellia. There, the Doctor and Romana find necromancer Paul Neville leading an expedition to examine the palace of the Old Ones, a long extinct race. But to his growing horror, the Doctor finds Neville hoping to transcend his mortal body by awakening Valdemar, a dark god powerful enough to trigger Universal armageddon.

Romana meets a group of adolescents, the children of Neville's financial backers, and the socially naïve Huvan falls in love with her. Meanwhile, the Doctor realizes the palace controls a giant particle accelerator, used by the Old Ones to breach the higher dimensions. However, the reality warping energies that were released both mutated and destroyed the Old Ones. "Valdemar," the Doctor concludes, is the name for the dimensional breach that could destroy the Universe if re-opened.

Neville tries to use Huvan, genetically altered to boost his telepathic powers, as the psionic key needed to activate the accelerator. Huvan, still lusting for Romana, breaks free from Neville's sway but decides to breach the higher dimensions anyway, attaining ultimate power and making Romana his bride. As Huvan opens the dimensional gateway, Neville's political rival Robert Hopkins arrives and grapples with the cult leader while expose to the higher dimensions mutates them into a demented, unified creature constantly at war with itself.

An obsessed Huvan pulls Romana through the dimensional doorway, but when nothing further happens, the Doctor realizes the Old Ones constructed a dimensional airlock, of sorts, between the higher dimensions and our reality. The Doctor steps through the doorway to discover a duplicate palace control chamber with the true Valdemar—the last of the Old Ones, gifted with immense psionic abilities. The Doctor deduces that like Huvan, Valdemar tried to achieve ultimate power but found it wanting, sealing himself in the control chamber before the higher dimensions could destroy everything.

The Doctor implores Huvan that even total power won't supply the freely given acceptance that Huvan craves. Romana supports this by rejecting Huvan's advances. At the Doctor and Romana's suggestion, Huvan uses his power to erase his memory and assume a new identity, realizing he needs more maturity to control his psionics. The Doctor and Romana take Huvan's comatose body back to the TARDIS and depart, ending the threat of the dark god Valdemar.

In another time and place, on a harsh world where trappers make quota for the overseeing guild, an aged woman speaks of the Doctor's battle with Valdemar to a young trapper named Ponch. The storyteller dies halfway through the story, but as she instructed, Ponch leaves her body at an inn and it soon disappears. Compelled by the story, Ponch explores the forbidden citadel of the guild and finds only an automated system, thus realizing that the trappers' lives are unduly pointless and the world makes people mature quickly. As the season ends, Ponch returns to the settlement and re-meets Romana—the storyteller—in her newly regenerated body, and learns that he is the matured version of Huvan. Having learned his true origins, Ponch enters Romana's TARDIS to explore the Universe as her companion.

MEMORABLE MOMENTS The story's narrator [the future Romana] tells Ponch about K9: "Don't trouble yourself over the metal dog. It never goes down very well. It's not in the story that much."

The Doctor swallows the serum of the Old Ones, falls on the floor, spasms, pounds with his fists, then gets up and tells Pelham: "Yes, I think you'll probably find it's not that nice."

Novelist Miranda Pelham sweetly cries out "Hold me" before she and the Doctor fall to their "deaths," knowing she can teleport them to safety. Chief Prosecutor Robert Hopkins glares at the Doctor and tells him: "I don't like your dress." The Doctor replies: "I'm not wearing a dress."

SEX AND SPIRITS The psychic Huvan becomes smitten with Romana. Forced to play along with Huvan, Romana fools him by saying, "Huvan, you were marvelous" as he wakes up. Otherwise, she rejects him and his "abominable" poetry.

ASS-WHUPPINGS Exposure to the higher dimensions mutates novelist Miranda Pelham's lover Erik into a monster. Desperate to save Romana and Pelham from the mutant, the Doctor activates a bathyscape that pulls them onto Ashkellia's acidic surface, liquefying Erik.

Huvan mentally blasts the Doctor, but the Time Lord lives. Dimensional energy shuts K9 down for repairs. A burst from the higher dimensions combine foes Paul Neville and Robert Hopkins into a single, twisted creature.

TV TIE-INS The Old Ones' palace can regenerate itself with the same principle as the city of the Exxilons ("Death to the Daleks"). Romana, removed from the recent Sontaran occupation of Gallifrey ("The Invasion of Time"), regards the deaths incurred as little more than horror stories. Huvan wears a "Red Dwarf" T-shirt.

NOVEL TIE-INS The Old Ones in *Tomb of Valdemar* aren't the "Great Old Ones," high-powered beings from the Universe before ours (first referenced in *White Darkness*, elaborated on in *All-Consuming Fire*).

A 15-year-old Miranda Pelham wandered about Proxima 2's surface after the disaster there (*The Face-Eater*), wrongly assuming that Valdemar caused the carnage and influencing her to write on the dark god.

Romana reads Huvan's bad poetry ("Long ago when Love was real") and dubs it the worst thing she's ever read—apparently Messingham's jab at an established phrase by novelist Paul Cornell (*Love and War* and more).

CHARACTER DEVELOPMENT

The Doctor: The Doctor never liked being forced, through circumstance, to accept various travelling companions. That said, the fourth Doctor here risks Universe's stability for Romana, a marked contrast to the seventh Doctor's quandaries about his companions' safety.

The Doctor can sing—badly. He's never more focused than when he appears distracted. He knows Ppiffer's "Second Ode to the Cepholan Whate in E minor," can identify a Star Probe Seven shell bathyscape and quote from "Dr. Faustus." The Doctor mind attunes itself to the Old Ones' palace control systems, enough to turn the power on/off with a snap. The Doctor can throw and wrap his scarf around an opponent's legs faster than they can draw a gun. If "the Kinetic Dance" exists (*See Phenomena*), the Doctor doesn't want to reunite with its singularity.

The Doctor and the Master: The Master once told the Doctor about Valdemar, back when they wore Prydonian robes and illegally wired themselves into the Gallifreyan Matrix.

Romana: Studious (and some might say, boring) Romana specialized in science and technical disciplines at the academy, spending her leisure time learning skills ranging from telepathy to traditional waltzes such as "The Foxtrots of Rassilon."

She particularly liked swimming and attended brief (and painfully dull, one presumes) seminars on "What to do when confronted with hyperactive, unstable, dangerously wealthy children." She doesn't have much appreciation for poetry but knows when it's bad.

Romana knows the Seven Strictures of Rassilon. Limited exposure to the higher dimensions temporarily gave her extra senses.

Romana's future selves: When Romana repeats the story of Valdemar to Ponch, she's an old woman that likely resembles novelist Miranda Pelham, suggesting she's still copy-catting other bodies (i.e. Princess Astra from "The Armageddon Factor"). Thank heavens she doesn't hang around Phyllis Diller.

The aforementioned incarnation died in the snow near the Janua Foris inn, likely from old age, and Romana regenerated into a younger woman with dark eyes, clear ebony skin and a love of reading. She hasn't seen the Doctor for centuries.

K9: Trans-dimensional feedback loops can scramble K9's circuits.

Valdemar: The last of the Old Ones: a massive, green-skinned being with a bluish, globe-shaped head and veiny purple stalks. Valdemar's complex tentacles pulsed with life, and sensory equipment and biomechanics directly patched it into the Old Ones' Palace, enabling it to soak in information. Valdemar's perceptions were so alien, it barely sensed the Doctor's group.

Paul Neville: Neville grew up as the son of the Empire's mightiest planet owners, a genius at genetic manipulation. He attended Earth's most prestigious arcane university, poisoning his parents when they protested. Reading Miranda Pelham's book about Valdemar motivated Neville to serve as a magus for Valdemar's cult for 10 years. Unfortunately for Neville, he lost his fortune when the New Protectorate overthrew the Elite. Through patronage, he spent six years finding Valdemar's "tomb" on Ashkellia. He was martyred after his "death."

THE CRUCIAL BITS...

- **TOMB OF VALDEMAR**—Romana's future self regenerates and continues travelling the Universe in her own TARDIS.

Miranda Pelham: Discredited author, 42, of *The Tomb of the Dark God*—a book that focused on Valdemar. She agreed to stay with the actual Valdemar, last of the Old Ones, and learn the Universe's secrets.

Huvan: Ginger-haired Huvan wrote dreadful, fake-a-seizure-to-escape poetry, and was likely the greatest psychic in the galaxy, powerful enough to mentally generate fireballs.

The TARDIS: The TARDIS' internal dimensional units prevent an internal trans-dimensional breach, but exterior trans-dimensional forces can wreck havoc on the Ship. Thinking the Doctor dead, Romana ponders if she could idiosynchronize the TARDIS to respond to her metabolism and contact Gallifrey. Romana's room has clothes from across the Universe and ornate sheets.

Romana's future TARDIS: Incorporates itself into rooms, such as at the Janua Foris inn.

ALIEN RACES

Time Lords: The Time Lords rate Valdemar and the Old Ones as one of the Universe's ten great mysteries. Time Lords dabbled at breaching the higher dimensions themselves, but the Dimensional Ethics Committee banned the work. Like humans, Time Lords have a dormant throwback organ, honed by mentally reciting strings of numbers and equations, that lets them read the higher dimensions.

Humans: An organ within the hypothalamus controls telepathy—little more than a stub in a mass of younger, better-developed cells and synapses. Some theorize it's a throwback organ that once let us perceive the higher dimensions (*See Phenomena*).

The Old Ones: The Gallifreyan Matrix contains no records about the Old Ones other than warnings. Supposedly, the Old Ones were insatiably curious, immensely psionic and spread their power halfway across the universe. The Old Ones had transmat technology and an evil-looking, five-pointed star served as their sign.

ALIEN PLANETS *Ashkellia (Ask-kelly-ah)* has a

damnably nasty environment, where superheated gases from the planet's core rise in high-yield energy streams, keeping the planet's temperature in the low 600s and riddling the surface with acid clouds. Ashkellia, the second planet in its system, orbits its star at a distance of 89 million miles in a sparsely clustered backwater part of the galaxy.

STUFF YOU NEED *The Key to Time Tracer* gets disrupted by trans-dimensional energy. The tracer's rather delicate, but can regenerate itself.

PLACES TO GO

Tomb of Valdemar: Control center for the particle accelerator, which incorporated all of Ashkellia.

The Centauri ("The Curse of Peladon") call the tomb "Stoodlhoo," the Xanir name it "Prah-Tah-Cah" and the Ogrons ("Day of the Daleks")—rather kinkily—refer to it "The Getting Into." (Is that what kids are calling it these days?)

Palace of the Old Ones: Located on Ashkellia, the Old Ones' Palace floated in a sky of superheated gasses. The Palace mentally linked with its inhabitants, acceding to their wishes and even responding to their unconscious emotional desires.

PHENOMENA

The Higher Dimensions: Put simply, the higher dimensions are everything we don't understand.

Almost nothing is known of the higher dimensions—which co-exist with our Universe—and no equipment exists to detect such dimensions. If anything, the higher dimensions are best compared our Universe if its symbolic code were broken, but even that description seems inadequate.

Third, fourth and fifth dimensional-life cannot perceive the higher dimensions. Some theories suggest dormant brain organs once perceived the higher dimensions, but such organs atrophied long ago. Remnants of the organs perhaps power telepathic individuals. As such, all psychic phenomena could derive from forces of the higher dimensions.

Exposure to the higher dimensions drives one mentally and physically mad, rewriting the physical bodies of such individuals into incomprehensible, primitive mutants that sprout black fronds, leathery skin and other de-evolved features.

Despite the disaster that wiped them out, the Old Ones created a neural-inhibition vaccine, compatible with humans and Time Lords, that safely attuned users' perceptions to the higher dimensions and prevented mutation.

Telepathy: Humanity births a psychic of Huvan's advanced level roughly once a millennia.

HISTORY The Old Ones lived when the Universe was young, beyond even a TARDIS' range. Despite the higher dimensional breach that decimated them, some Old Ones survived and visited pre-historic Earth, dissecting specimens to study the human brain's dormant organs.

• On Earth, the New Protectorate overthrew the Elite after a civil war and instigated an anachronistic period of Earth history with puritanism elements. The Cult of Valdemar became the most powerful New Protectorate magic-based organization, but endlessly fragmented with Neville's "demise." The Protectorate itself expired a couple centuries after this story.

• Atmospheric floatation—strong enough to keep buildings aloft—was discovered 600 years after this story.

APOCRYPHAL HISTORY

"The Kinetic Dance": The Time Lords and other peoples hold myths that the Universe was birthed from a single entity or singularity, a being sometimes referred to as "Eru" or "Azathoth" (not the giant slug from *All-Consuming Fire*). The singularity allegedly split into inter-connected shards, each forming its own physical laws and becoming the ten dimensions that incorporate time and space. Supposedly, this explains most beings' feelings of being separate from a greater whole, because organs that bound us to the original singularity atrophied over time.

• After the Old Ones' destruction, legends arose stating the black-hearted Valdemar once held unspeakable powers, swallowing stars and subverting entire races as his acolytes. The myths claimed the Old Ones captured or destroyed Valdemar after centuries of the biggest war ever.

AT THE END OF THE DAY Blessed with one of the most flavorful "Doctor Who" book titles, *Tomb of Valdemar* evokes a dark, somber fantasy, making your spine shuck off your body and scuttle like a centipede for cover. Like a fine Alfred Hitchcock film, it deploys chills more than actual horror, relying on atmosphere and mood ("Valdemar" representing utter desolation beyond comprehension). It's a black story that ends with hope, seeded with innovative characters and a driving tempo, resulting in Messingham's best book and one of the stronger Tom Baker stories.

HEART OF TARDIS

By Dave Stone

Release Date: June 2000
Order: BBC Past Doctor Adventure #32

TARDIS CREWS The second Doctor, Jamie and Victoria; the fourth Doctor, Romana I and K9.

TRAVEL LOG The second Doctor: Lychburg singularity; the fourth Doctor: the Big Huge and Educational Collection of Old Galactic Stuff, time unknown; UNIT Headquarters and Tollsham USAF airbase, Thatcher administration.

CHRONOLOGY For the second Doctor's group, between "The Tomb of the Cybermen" and "The Abominable Snowmen." For the fourth Doctor and Romana, between "The Stones of Blood" and "The Androids of Tara." (It's near-impossible to reconcile Sergeant Benton's rank with the fourth Doctor's appearance, so let's just move on.)

STORY SUMMARY When the second Doctor attempts to bypass the Time Lords' anti-theft protocols and regain full TARDIS navigation, his Ship violently grounds itself in the American Midwest city of Lychburg. But once the Doctor concludes that Lychburg's in a self-contained dimension on the verge of collapse—threatening Earth's survival—he scrambles with Jamie and Victoria for a solution and oddly discovers the TARDIS won't let them back in.

Meanwhile, the Time Lords inform the fourth Doctor and Romana about an unstable singularity that imperils the Universe, but the Doctor deems the Time Lords worrywarts and answers a UNIT distress call instead. The Doctor and Romana find UNIT Headquarters captured by a rival government division, DISTO(P)IA, and encounter famed black arts user Alistair Crowley, DISTO(P)IA's ambitious leader. The Doctor grows chagrined to learn Crowley's forces overran UNIT Headquarters purely to prevent his interference with the Lychburg singularity—the very thing the Time Lords warned him about.

Crowley explains that after World War II, the American military experimented to see if widespread belief could alter the physical world and effectively create magic. The military captured the town of Lychburg, brainwashing its residents with transceivers and creating thousands of people who *en masse* believed whatever the military wanted. Unfortunately, the military tested the townsfolk's power by having them "open the gates of Hell," accidentally creating an expanding dimensional rift that threatened Earth. The American military leveled the project with a low-yield nuclear device, knocking Lychburg out of Earth's dimension, but a subsequent collision (with the second Doctor's TARDIS) has further destabilized the Lychburg singularity and threatens all of space-time.

As the Doctor and Romana agree to travel to Lychburg and help, Crowley reveals himself as a Jarakabeth demon, an energy being that wants the Lychburg singularity energy to rewrite the Universe in Chaos' name. Suddenly, a rival and nobler Jarakabeth emerges from government agent Katherine Delbane and grapples with Crowley, allowing the fourth Doctor and Romana to create a dimensional corridor with their TARDIS systems and rush down it. After spending 15 years embroiled in adventures completely unrelated to this story, they arrive in the second Doctor's TARDIS.

The second Doctor feverishly fails to enter the TARDIS, calculating Lychburg has minutes to live. The fourth Doctor properly brings the TARDIS' exterior dimensions into phase with Lychburg, then hides with Romana while his former self rushes into the console room. The second Doctor takes a few crucial readings, then dashes out and frustrates Romana because her years of struggles resulted in merely having to open a door. Together, she and the mad-Bohemian Doctor endure another 15 years of adventures travelling back to their own Ship, where the Delbane demon annihilates Crowley, apologizes for the mayhem and retreats back into Delbane's mind.

In Lychburg, the Beetle-haired Doctor uses telemetry readings from his TARDIS to perform an inexplicable stunt and miraculously return the city to Earth. As the residents—mostly oblivious to their turmoil in the singularity—desert the town entirely, the second Doctor's group resumes traveling while his later self and Romana hunt down the Key to Time.

MEMORABLE MOMENTS A TARDIS collision makes the second Doctor get unbelievably tangled in the hatstand—it sticks out from his collar and checked trousers. Sergeant Benton inappropriately talks about "Silurians" to uncleared personnel, quickly changing the conversation to "those damn *Sicilians*."

The fourth Doctor skillfully rescues K9, who's a museum exhibit (*See Character Development*), by smashing glass with the sonic screwdriver and "running like Skaro." He later asks a Time Lord if the Time Wars didn't happen on paper or *didn't happen*. DISTO(P)IA agent Delbane says no verified photographs of the Doctor exist and he replies: "I don't photograph very well. Sometimes [the pic-

tures] come out and it's like looking at a completely different man."

SEX AND SPIRITS Nineteenth-century Victoria was initially shocked to see women's ankles in the future, but here shows a bit of leg. When the Doctor's clothes get tangled in the TARDIS hatstand, Victoria vows she's not helping him remove his trousers (the Doctor helpfully adds that the stand's bottom screws right off). Jamie explains that he showed a gang his dirk and Victoria clarifies: "You did say *dirk*, didn't you?"

With (excuse the phrasing) mounting horror, Victoria observes the Doctor innocently booking his trio a single room at the "Shangri La Fantasy Motel." Worse, the Doctor tells the clerk they'll make full use of the facilities and let him know if they needed an extra hand.

DISTO(P)IA guardsman Danny Slater remarks he'd gladly frisk Romana for hand grenades. Fellow guard McCrae agrees Romana's stacked and ponders that her kegs get caught on things and impede her operating heavy machinery. (Author's Note: Perhaps Romana's undergone a *very* selective regeneration.)

ASS-WHUPPINGS Lychburg resident Dr. Dibley tries to implant the second Doctor with a brain-controlling transceiver, but the Doctor inadvertently dodges and causes Dibley to fall, skewer himself through the eye on his own blade and kick it. Jamie knifes the last Gallifreyan woprat creature to death (*See Organizations*). Crowley ends up a charred lump.

A mesmerized Lychburg pack assaults Jamie and a woman in haberdashers throttles Victoria.

TV TIE-INS UNIT reports say the Silurians ("The Silurians") are breeding like rats. The fourth Doctor answers a call from the Brigadier's time-space telegraph ("Revenge of the Cybermen"), located in the Doctor's old UNIT laboratory. Colonel Crichton ("The Five Doctors") is already a UNIT member but the Brigadier's in charge.

Romana's decided to find a suitably elegant template and regenerate herself into a smaller, more compact body ("Destiny of the Daleks").

Unlike stories such as "The Five Doctors," where the Doctor's memories of his past selves' actions are unclear, the fourth Doctor remembers in detail the second Doctor's involvement in Lychburg (and becomes relieved to know how the TARDIS door mysteriously opened).

NOVEL TIE-INS Some of the ideas in *Heart of TARDIS*, including references to *Astonishing Stories of Unmitigated Science!*, came from Stone's

This book is not endorsed by the BBC. Doctor Who and TARDIS are trademarks of the BBC.

33

Perfect Timing II: "Past Time Catching" story.

The Doctor says he witnessed first-hand Gallifrey's Time Wars (*Sky Pirates!*), although the Time Lords wiped the wars from their history books (and possibly history itself).

Jarakabeth host Katherine Delbane is possibly synthetic (the Jarakabeth dubs her the "Delbane construct") and related to APE Kara Delbane (Stone's *Return to the Fractured Planet*). Speaking of which, Lychburg has a comic shop named "Fractured Planet." After this story, Katherine becomes a UNIT captain under the Brigadier's command.

The Collectors own a Chelonian (*The Highest Science*) matter disrupter. The second Doctor says he's met Sherlock Holmes (*All-Consuming Fire*).

CHARACTER DEVELOPMENT

The second Doctor: The Doctor admits to stealing the TARDIS and only has a passing knowledge of how his people constructed it. He was formerly better versed in the medical sciences. He freaks out blood bank workers when it seems his body doesn't run dry. He oddly has limited supplies of hard currency for 20th century America.

He enjoys the innocence and otherworldliness of comic books (and that's why we love him). He once subscribed to *Astonishing Stories of Unmitigated Science!*, a publication that ended in the 1950s.

Centuries ago, before catabolism wracked his original body, the Doctor enjoyed exceptional acrobatic skills. The second Doctor's less adept—he falls while running on an escalator handrail and plummets 30 feet. He fumbled history in school.

The fourth Doctor: The Doctor's fully capable of murder in life-threatening circumstances, approaching the deed like a veterinarian putting things to sleep. He knew the real Alistair Crowley for years and considered him a lovely chap, if overly fond of laudanum.

The Doctor plays with a magi-blessed tarot deck that affects reality in unpleasant ways. A game of Happy Families can trigger havoc, depending on the family picked.

If the Doctor owned a penny for every time someone said to him, "Not so fast, Time Lord," he'd have four pounds, seven shillings and fourpence. If he gained a penny for hearing "Silence!," he'd have 27 pounds, 15 shillings and tuppence.

He considers the second Doctor a nice chap, but doesn't want to meet himself again.

The second Doctor and Jamie McCrimmon: The Doctor presumably taught Jamie how to write. At story's end, the Doctor makes Jamie write over and over, "I must not stick big knives in extinct animals just because I don't like the look of them" as

penance for killing the Gallifreyan woprat. For his own part, the Doctor scribes over and over to prevent the death of innocents through his own carelessness and conceit.

Victoria Waterfield: Sweet Victoria's writing journals of TARDIS travels, wondering how to word things to avoid being institutionalized. She wears a William Morris bathing robe. She's gaining familiarity with electronics, but innately perceives that the TARDIS circuitry is somehow alive.

Victoria gained a New Fiduciary Treasury of the PractiBrantic Apostates credit chip during a visit to the NovaLon Hypercities in the 22nd century several weeks ago. She's seen magic lantern shows and screams (no surprise there) like a banshee in the presence of rats and spiders. An aunt of hers, twice removed, lived in Boston.

Romana: Romana's got at least 27 senses and decently loathes 20th century Earth, viewing it full of world wars, incarceration facilities and people who want to stick needles into everyone else (the Doctor claims she'll like Earth anyway).

Romana's got an accelerated healing factor and has heard of the Brigadier. Crowley can hypnotize her. She attended the Academy of Time.

Romana gained special dispensation from the High Council to link the two Doctors' TARDISes—an act that violates 15,473 Laws of Space and Time. She dislikes the second Doctor's TARDIS interior. It would take her 257, maybe 258 years to override a Time Lord temporal freeze.

The fourth Doctor and Romana: Their 15 years of adventures in the dimensional corridor include fighting sub-dimensional soma-monsters that feast on lymphatic juices, Sontarans mining the nether regions with soul-catcher bombs and something called the Solstice Squid. They can estimate how many regenerations a Time Lord's endured.

Brigadier Lethbridge-Stewart: Cited as commander-in-chief of the European arm of UNIT, not just the British division. During an emergency, he outranks a field marshal. He's the stuff of legend.

Sergeant Benton: Has a tolerance to anaesthetic spray.

K9: The Doctor, running like mad from some adversary, frequently forgets to retrieve K9 until a much later date (Romana speculates that thanks to time travel, K9's the oldest lump of matter in the Universe). Here, K9 wind up as an exhibit at the alien Collector's Big Huge and Educational Collection of Old Galactic Stuff (*See History*), but the Doctor rescues him.

The Doctor's been intending to upgrade K9 and could, if the little mutt endured extreme decay, extrapolate his remaining memory algorithms into a new chassis. The Doctor can locate K9 with a cannibalized 22nd century bubble-circuitry tracker.

The TARDIS: Like most Gallifreyan time ships, anti-theft protocols stop thieves from piloting it properly, landing them anywhere in space-time. The Ship has a marble-sided bath the size of a small swimming pool.

ALIEN RACES

Time Lords: By convention, the length of a Time Lord's name grows according to his/her stature. They can trap the Doctor's TARDIS in a self-contained temporal bubble of null-time. Time Lords can resist anaesthetic that drops humans in their tracks. High Councilman Wblk (whom Romana's met) belongs to the overcompensating traditionalist factions. Regeneration often involves some memory loss. The fourth Doctor, for example, regrets losing the knack for making soufflés (He laments: "Flat as a pancake they go now...")

Gallifreyan Woprat: Rat-like creature built like a medium-sized dog, with 15 spider-like legs.

Jarakabeth: Effectively immortal energy beings who don't like their individual names spoken because they have embarrassing connotations. Jarakabeth manifest on Earth as "demons," cousins of the Azrae and Raagnarokath races.

PLACES TO GO

Lychburg: A perfectly ordinary Midwestern town until it was usurped for the Golgotha Project—a 1960s United States military operation designed to develop devastating magic weapons through mass belief.

Golgotha officials randomly chose Lychburg, brainwashing the town's residents to collectively believe the same thing on command. The Crowley demon, as Golgotha Project head, aided the process with use of his Arimathea Artifact, a device that concentrated the residents' beliefs into a

TOP 5

DOCTOR TRIUMPHS
Novels Post *Interference*

1) The Doctor and Miranda reunited (Father Time)—Accepting responsibility for his adopted daughter, the Doctor succeeds in finding Miranda (we cried) and helps her become ruler of a far-flung empire.

2) The TARDIS restored (Escape Velocity)—The Doctor's oldest companion fully re-activates after a year (of our time) away from him.

3) A fire elemental quenched (The Burning)—Unsure of his life or identity past the last three years, the Earthbound eighth Doctor stops a fire elemental from consuming Earth in Victorian times.

4) Romana III and the Time Lords thwarted (The Shadows of Avalon)—The eighth Doctor blocks his people from force-mating Compassion to produce a new line of TARDISes.

5) The higher dimensions sealed (Tomb of Valdemar)—The fourth Doctor and Romana stop an attempt to breach "the higher dimensions" (a reality we cannot comprehend) from restructuring our reality.

Big Finish Audios

1) "Dalek Mutant" swarm timeline overturned ("The Mutant Phase")—The fifth Doctor unlocks a temporal paradox that formerly, as the Emperor Dalek himself put it, "caused the end of history."

2) Gallifrey saved ("The Sirens of Time")—Three of the Doctors combine their efforts, saving the Time Lords from utter subjugation (and the meat rack).

3) The Scourge banished ("The Shadow of the Scourge")—In a masterstroke of manipulation (that admittedly goes tits-up several times), the seventh Doctor repels the parasitical Scourge.

4) The Daleks defeated ("The Apocalypse Element")—Well, somewhat. The Doctor and Romana fail to prevent the Daleks gaining a stronghold in the Seriphia Galaxy but prevent them getting their greedy little plungers on Gallifreyan time technology.

5) Ace saved ("The Fearmonger")—The Doctor stops undercuts a corrupt political party, but that seems secondary to saving Ace from the alien Fearmonger.

focal point. By forcing Lychburg residents to en masse believe Hell was arriving, Golgotha officials succeeded in opening "the gates of Hell"—actually a dimensional rift. However, the dimensional

This book is not endorsed by the BBC. Doctor Who and TARDIS are trademarks of the BBC.

35

gateway turned unstable when a prototype Gallifreyan time-travel device, carrying the last Gallifreyan woprat animal, collided with it. Fearing that the expanding rift might consume Earth, the United States government panicked and dropped a low-grade nuclear warhead onto Lychburg, shunting it into a separate dimension.

Illogical as this sounds, the Gallifreyan woprat intrinsically became the central intelligence that maintained Lychburg's integrity in the other dimension. Unfortunately, a collision with the second Doctor's TARDIS destabilized Lychburg again. Worse, the Doctor's group stumbled upon the woprat in its travel capsule. When the animal made Victoria scream, Jamie kindly knifed it to death—further hastening Lychburg's demise.

Final Note: The Lychburg singularity psionically influenced its residents to not leave, miraculously supplying food supplies in a way nobody questioned.

ORGANIZATIONS

UNIT: The prime minister (presumably Margaret Thatcher) thinks UNIT needs more supervision. UNIT recently requisitioned a third of the Bank of England's gold reserves, presumably to foil an alien invasion plot, but failed to replace it and triggered a stock market crash. The British government halted the chaos by lowering income tax rates thanks to funds from Scottish oil reserves and the United States.

UNIT creatively re-allocated some funds to buy Apple Macintosh computers.

Divisional Department of Special Tactical Operations [Provisional] with Regard to Insurgent and Subversive Activity (a.k.a. "The Provisionals," DISTO(P)IA): Government department headed by Crowley. It presumably expired without him.

APOCRYPHAL HISTORY

The earliest time-travel legends say Rassilon decapitated a Great Beast, took the branching golden tree of its metathalmus and found the First Secret of Chrononambulatory Egress. The Doctor insists that's nonsense—Rassilon deduced the secrets of Time by "procuring" a translation belt from a species who attacked Gallifrey in the Time Wars.

• Time Lord High Councilman Wblk says developing the Type One TARDIS involved a lot of hitting equipment with spanners. Some prototypes dangerously evolved minds of their own, escaping from Gallifrey's temporal pull and colliding with things. Wblk claims an incident in ancient Babylon and the first Mars landing (presumably "The Ambassadors of Death") are components of the same discrete paratemporal event.

HISTORY The Doctor was with Francis Bacon on the night Bacon died trying to stuff snow up a chicken (pardon while we howl with laughter).

• During World War II, the Nazi leaders experimented with the black arts for military application. The United States security, fearing the collective Nazi belief could physically alter the world, counter-acted it by hiring *The Lord of the Rings* writer J.R.R. Tolkien and his contemporaries to infuse world culture with a greater sense of what was reality and what was fantasy.

• The Cold War American government amorally researched a number of military techniques, such as infecting Negro populations with syphilis.

• As one of his last acts of sorcery, famed black arts practitioner Edward Alexander Crowley (a.k.a. Aleister or "the Great Beast") summoned a Jarakabeth demon, which impersonated Crowley after his death at Hastings, 1947. The U.S. government wanted "Crowley" to work on germ warfare, but he furthered the Golgotha Project.

• The metamorphic Collectors emerged as a group of galactic scavengers who blatantly looted other cultures with no regard for their booty's value, relevance or usefulness. In other words, they amassed gigantic amounts of crap. Sadly, the Collectors' invention of the hyperwobble-drive and psychonomic shielding meant their ships could overload the processing centers of organics and non-organics alike, meaning no culture could stand against them. On Skaro, the Daleks tortuously changed their planet to appear destroyed, then emerged from hiding when the Collectors passed by. Tens of millennia beyond the 20th century, the Collectors wondered what the hell to do with their heaps of stuff and founded the Big Huge and Educational Collection of Old Galactic Stuff.

AT THE END OF THE DAY Delightful and whacky, mostly played as an excuse for the Troughton and Tom Doctors to act weird—but even that's enough to make a good book. What makes *Heart of TARDIS* difficult reading in parts is some inappropriate shading (innocent Victoria throws out the most sexual innuendoes) and moreso, Stone's endless talent for pointless digressions, making it hard to figure out at times what the hell's going on. Still, the main cast shines through and Stone's daring (the Doctor's "innovation" at rescuing K9, Romana and the fourth Doctor stuck in transit for 30 years) greatly entertain and help you wade through multiple plotholes and overly complex concepts.

FESTIVAL OF DEATH

By Jonathan Morris

Release Date: September 2000
Order: BBC Past Doctor Adventure #35

TARDIS CREW The fourth Doctor, Romana II and K9.

TRAVEL LOG G-Lock space station, 2815 and 3012.

CHRONOLOGY Between "Shada" and "The Leisure Hive."

STORY SUMMARY The TARDIS materializes on the G-Lock, a 200-year-old space station created from the inter-linked wreckage of ships that crashed in a hyperspace tunnel. To the Doctor's surprise, eyewitnesses proudly claim he saved them from a killer zombie attack—but died in the process. As the G-Lock inhabitants evacuate and temporal stress collapses the hypertunnel into a singularity, the Doctor and Romana reluctantly conclude they must fulfill the timeline and visit G-Lock again—even if it means the Doctor's demise.

Arriving 24 hours earlier, the two Time Lords learn about the Beautiful Death, a tourist attraction created by Dr. Paddox to kill participants and give them the blissful sensations of dying, then miraculously revive them a half hour later. Suddenly, 218 Beautiful Death tourists awaken as monstrous zombies and wreck mayhem. Concluding they're still too far forward in time, the Doctor and Romana leave again as the necroport somehow explodes and the Beautiful Death tourists return to normal but permanently die in the process.

Even more previously on the G-Lock, the Doctor encounters Gallura, the last member of the Arboretan race and Dr. Paddox's captive. As Gallura explains, the Arboretans exist parallel to time, meaning as each Arboretan "dies," it returns to the moment of its birth with full memories of its previous life. Dr. Paddox, hoping to instill the Arboretan reincarnative ability in himself and prevent his parents' death in a spaceport accident, uses the Beautiful Death to generate psychothermic energy—the energy released during death—to fuel his experiments. Unfortunately, the process requires fatally using an Arboretan as a medium and Paddox has driven the Arboretans to near-extinction as a result.

Worse—if there is such a thing—Paddox's experiments have been usurped by the Repulsion, an extra-dimensional creature that exists between

life and death and seeks to suck our reality dry. Romana learns passengers aboard the *Cerberus*, a ship trapped during the crash that formed the G-Lock, bargained with the Repulsion for what they thought was safe passage into the future. Instead, the Repulsion placed pieces of itself into every passenger, then temporally swapped them for the Beautiful Death tourists and made them revive as zombies, seeking to place enough of itself in our reality to fully materialize.

Paddox uses Gallura to channel the biggest Beautiful Death event ever and the Repulsion's zombies "again" awaken. With little option, the Doctor orders Romana give him the Beautiful Death treatment—killing his body and sending his mind into the Repulsion's domain. The Doctor proves no match for the Repulsion's might and the monster grows jubilant, thinking it can fully manifest in the Doctor's Time Lord body. But as the Repulsion transmits itself into the Doctor's "corpse," Romana re-routes Paddox's necroport circuitry to funnel the Repulsion's intelligence into the G-Lock's central computer, ERIC. Romana then revives the Doctor using the Necroport and he overloads ERIC's brain, simultaneously destroying ERIC and the Repulsion.

Freed from the Repulsion's influence, the Beautiful Death zombies permanently expire—again. Paddox, refusing to capitulate, links himself to the necroport circuits at the last instant and supercharges himself with psychothermic energy—reincarnating him at the moment of his birth. Unfortunately, Paddox discovers the Arboretan reincarnative talent doesn't fully work on humans, meaning he will now relive his life an infinite number of times without the power to act. Gleeful to be alive, the Doctor rushes Romana and K9 into the TARDIS and departs as the necroport explodes a "final" time and kills Paddox's body.

MEMORABLE MOMENTS In a top dramatic moment, the Doctor cracks under the strain of knowing his future death, momentarily exiling Romana and K9 from the TARDIS console room. In another, Romana stays silent and allows the *Cerberus* passengers to make the "wrong" decision, allowing them to bargain with the Repulsion to preserve the timeline.

More comically, the Doctor delivers a "dead parrot" speech and comments, "I am an ex-Doctor." He queries how the Beautiful Death works, wondering if the resurrected pop up like toast.

The temporally confused Doctor sees himself and restrains from shouting out, "Stop fiddling with your ear!" (although he deems himself a handsome devil). At the moment of his "death," he endlessly delays the process by quoting (and mis-

This book is not endorsed by the BBC. Doctor Who and TARDIS are trademarks of the BBC.

37

quoting) from deathbed soliloquies such as *A Tale of Two Cities* and Macbeth, randomly imploring Romana that either the wallpaper goes or he goes and to keep Australia beautiful.

Finally, the Repulsion momentarily enters K9, causing the insane little dog (a.k.a. "Dark K9") to menacingly declare, "I AM THE REPULSION!"

SEX AND SPIRITS The doomed Doctor's last words are, "Kismet, Romana." A shocked Romana replies, "You want me to kiss you?" before rapidly throwing the switch and killing him.

ASS-WHUPPINGS The Doctor dies—somewhat.

The suicidal computer ERIC asks for relief from its centuries of suffering (*See Character Development*) and the Doctor complies, shorting out ERIC and the Repulsion possessing it. The Doctor also offs several deadly Arachnopods (*See Alien Races*) by rearranging gravity and atomizing them in a hyperspace interface. A thousand or so people died in the initial *Cerberus* crash, with Arachnopods gruesomely snacking on many of the survivors.

The entire Arboretan race gets pruned.

Dr. Koel Paddox watches a spaceport accident tear his parents apart over and over and over again. Two hundred and seventeen Beautiful Death participants snuff it, plus an equal number of *Cerberus* passengers. Before this adventure, 42 (strange how that number keeps cropping up...) Beautiful Death tourists acclimated to the Repulsion's domain, changing parts of it into peaceful refuges and deciding to stay dead.

TV TIE-INS "The Stones of Blood" explored hyperspace in-depth. The Doctor and Romana retain their time sensitivity ("City of Death"). Hyperspace tunnels were discussed in "Nightmare of Eden" and "The Horns of Nimon."

CHARACTER DEVELOPMENT

The Doctor: The Doctor never passed his basic time-travel proficiency test at the Academy, claiming he failed to show up for it. K9 estimates the Doctor's current chances at passing at 0.1 percent. Romana's slightly more optimistic, conceding the Doctor could pass such a test, but disputing he could attain double alpha plus honors at the advanced level.

The Doctor simultaneously considers Romana and K9 his best friend. He says "investigators" have never held him at gunpoint before (but we find this near impossible to believe). He was present at General Custer's last stand and has seen *The Seventh Seal*. He carries a battered paperback entitled *Bor Pollag's Book of Alien Monsters*.

Upon arriving somewhere, the Doctor's highly relieved when people point guns at him because it helps him identify "the baddies" (usually within 24.5 minutes of arriving).

Romana: In the midst of this book's time-travel brouhaha, Romana literally sees herself and can't believe how conceited she looks. She hilariously cites the Doctor as "her companion."

K9: Based on past journeys, there's a 90 percent chance K9 will have to break the Doctor and Romana out of jail.

ERIC (a.k.a. Environmental Regulation and Information Computer): Remarkably friendly central computer aboard the *Cerberus* that tried—and failed—to persuade *Cerberus* Captain Rochfort to slow the engines and prevent a hypertunnel pile-up (*See History*). To cover up his ineptitude, Rochfort blamed the accident on ERIC and ordered the computer to devote every circuit and subroutine to anguishing over its guilt. ERIC, forced to obey, became suicidal but was later conscripted to serve as the G-Lock's central computer.

The Repulsion: Extra-dimensional creature that exists in the gap between life and death, possibly exiled there or existing from the dawn of time. It lacks an identity of its own (we never see the monster directly) and can only exist through others. The hypertunnel collision that ultimately created the G-Lock also created a gap between real space and hyperspace, slightly opening the Repulsion's dimension to our reality.

The Repulsion, an unfettered evil that craves to trigger havoc in our Universe, can't blatantly enter our space but can theoretically materialize by seeding pieces of itself into multiple wanderers into its realm, then returning them to our reality. The Repulsion finds it easier to possess people who bargain with it willingly, but can enter any traveler through its domain. For whatever reason, the Repulsion thinks beings in our Universe have taunted it and wants to kill us all.

The Repulsion's domain morphs itself to what its inhabitants expect the afterlife to look like.

The TARDIS: It's technobabble, but it's dangerous to materialize without an analogue osmosis dampener. The scanner's audio circuits are acting up again.

ALIEN RACES

Time Lords: Time Lords who enter suspended animation and appear dead usually give off life-signs that other Time Lords can detect.

Arboretans: Humanoid vegetable race born from mothertrees with transparent skin and heads like budding orchids. In youth, they're exotic vegetables; in middle age, they have chestnut skin.

The Arboretans exist in a special relationship with time, following "The Path of Perfection" (*See Stuff You Need*). The talent's unique to the Arboretans, meaning humans can't achieve it.

As a peaceful people, the Arboretans opted *en masse* to not warn earlier generations about Paddox's genocide of their race for fear they'd take up arms and (pardon the pun) soil their purity. The Arboretan elders knew Gallura would be the last of their kind. The Arboretans naturally pass through the Repulsion's shadow domain as they die, but are immune to its taint.

Arachnopods: Genetically modified as a weapon of war, Arachnopods are relentless big-ass spider creatures. Each part of their bodies sports its own nervous system and intelligence, meaning any bits severed or shot off in battle can simply be re-affixed. Overly damaged parts are eaten and re-grown. When united, an Arachnopod's parts respond to a collective head-brain, achieving motor function through cooperation.

Arachnopods, programmed with a ravenous hunger, most definitely eat each other. Body parts are interchangeable between Arachnopods.

STUFF YOU NEED

The Beautiful Death: Marketed under the slogan, "Turn On, Tune In and Drop Dead," the Beautiful Death allows a subject to experience the sensations of dying by freezing the subject's body to prevent brain damage and re-warming it to life after 30 minutes (a longer duration would make revival impossible).

The Beautiful Death works by drawing psychothermic energy, a hypothetical form of energy released at the moment of death, then storing it and later reviving the tourists with a psychothermic pulse. Arboretans serve as psychotermporal conduits, allowing the tourists to enter the death realm (i.e. the Repulsion's domain) and then return, although the strain kills the Arboretans.

"The Path of Perfection": By returning to their birth every time they die, the Arboretans inherently know how to correct the mistakes of their past lives and maximize their potential. Most Arboretans do this for an infinity of lives, although their limited memories only let them remember their previous three or four lifetimes.

PLACES TO GO *Paddox's Necroport:* Home of the Beautiful Death, but consequently a nexus of time distortion, sending temporal shockwaves backward and forward through time.

ORGANIZATIONS *Intergalactic Espionage:* Nefarious organization in this time zone.

PHENOMENA

History: It isn't immutable. Consider—if it were, one would hardly need Laws of Time to forbid it. Beings who live outside of time such as Time Lords or Arboretans living can change history, but humans innately live in history and cannot.

Pre-ja vu: The sense that you're going to have been somewhere before. The term's exclusively used by Time Lords, coined by Academi Plurix.

HISTORY In 2815, a sudden build-up of geo-static pressure collapsed one end of a hyperspace tunnel that serviced ships from Teredekethon to Murgatroyd. The *Cerberus*, commanded by the inept Captain Rochfort, tried to beat the collapse and crashed at the tunnel's end. Nearly 100 ships, including the *Montressor*, subsequently caused one of the biggest pile-ups in galactic history. Authorities closed the hyperspace tunnel for two months, reopening it to discover the *Cerberus* empty and missing its 1,000 crew and passengers. The ship pile-up was rebuilt inside the hyperspace tunnel as the space station G-Lock and served as a haven for the dropouts of galactic society.

AT THE END OF THE DAY So hysterical it brings tears to the eye, making you revel in being young, beautiful and smart as hell. Morris admittedly copycats writer Gareth Roberts' style, but that's more than acceptable considering Roberts rarely writes "Who" these days and himself admits to mostly resuscitating what Tom, Lalla and John Leeson delivered on TV. Only the fact that *Festival of Death* triple-checks every last period and question mark of its temporal shenanigans lets us recommend it to newcomers, delivering a jewel of a book from a hallowed era of "Who."

This book is not endorsed by the BBC. Doctor Who and TARDIS are trademarks of the BBC.

39

HARRY SULLIVAN'S WAR

By Ian Marter

Release Date: October 1986
Order: Companions of Doctor Who #2

MAIN CHARACTERS Harry Sullivan, with Sarah Jane Smith and Brigadier Lethbridge-Stewart.

TRAVEL LOG London, Yarra and Paris, late August, early 1980s.

CHRONOLOGY For Harry, 10 years after "The Android Invasion" and several years before *System Shock*.

STORY SUMMARY Ten years after leaving UNIT, Surgeon-Commander Harry Sullivan finds himself forcibly transferred to a NATO chemical weapons development center on the Hebridean island of Yarra. Unhappy with the new posting, Harry makes the best of it and spends time socially with Teddy Bland, a fellow NATO researcher and classmate. However, Harry increasingly believes unknown parties are monitoring his activities. Worse, Harry suspects American neurologist Alexander Shire drugged him with sodium pentothal, forcing him to reveal details about his new weapons-based work.

While experimenting with a lethal toxin called Attila 305, Harry accidentally overdoses a female colleague with nykor inhibitase, a prototype anti-toxin. To Harry's surprise, the anti-toxin eliminates his fellow researcher's infertility and grants her renewed vigor—proposing itself as an Attila 305 antidote and offering a wide range of benefits. Unfortunately, covert agents working for Zbigniew Brodsky, leader of the so-called European Anarchist Revolution, steal three ampules of the Attila compound as a potential terrorist weapon.

Brodsky, learning of Harry's work toward an Attila antidote, kidnaps him. Assuming that Harry took the antidote himself, Brodsky decides to test its effectiveness by locking Harry in a room and breaking one of the Attila ampules. Thankfully, Harry remembers Attila 305 isn't water-soluble and smothers the gas in his water-soaked blazer, then escapes.

Harry returns to base, but his superiors find the stolen Attila 305 ampule pieces in Harry's blazer and charge him with treason. Harry escapes to an ancient barrow in the Summer Isles, having viewed map co-ordinates that point to it as a possible meeting place for the conspirators. There, Harry observes his department head, Conrad Gold, traitorously concealing a microfiche cache on NATO's chemical warfare experiments.

Bland grows convinced of Gold's deception and allows Harry to trick Gold and his terrorist contacts into a "secret" meeting at the barrow. Bland's men capture Gold and some of the criminals, clearing Harry's name. Later, Harry follows a hunch and journeys to the Eiffel Tower for the annual meeting of the Van Gogh Appreciation Society—actually a front for Brodsky's terrorist cell. There, Harry confronts Brodsky and Shire, eluding Brodsky's hitmen until French authorities round up the entire gang. With the conspiracy ended, Harry returns home to London and continues an otherwise unadventurous life.

MEMORABLE MOMENTS Harry escapes an assassin in the book's most manic and action-packed scene (page 68)—a delightful row that gave us stitches of laughter (*See Ass-Whuppings*).

Harry grins like an idiot upon re-meeting Sarah Jane Smith. Fighting for his life, Harry gets exposed to a low-dose of Attila 305 and wishes he could record his symptoms because the data would be invaluable.

At the Eiffel Tower, Harry challenges Brodsky to fisticuffs, but Brodsky's bodyguard lurches forward, grabs Harry around the waist, hoists him up and hurls him away. (Nice one, Harry—that'll teach him). The scuffle ends with the bodyguard falling from the tower and pancaking himself—just as a restaurant band starts up a lively tango.

SEX AND SPIRITS Harry almost proposed to the ample-bosomed Esther, Teddy Bland's sister, but they grew apart during his UNIT tenure (one wonders, given Esther's boisterous personality, if she wasn't too much of a good thing). Esther insists she's always loved Harry and playfully greets him with "Hello, sailor." At story's end, the strident Esther arrives to "take care" of Harry, wrapping him in an embrace and whirling him about while decreeing, "Oh, you poor little *mite*, Sullers."

Harry also flirts with an art gallery admirer named Samantha, not realizing Shire is her father. On behalf of daddy, Samantha cattily keeps tabs on Harry and suggests they go swimming—sans trunks (Harry declines). On another occasion, she offers to "show him her batik" (ditto).

Testing the rule of "no hanky panky in the TARDIS," Harry evidently had some enamorous feelings for Sarah Jane Smith. Sarah's likely oblivious to this, but you'll gape when Sarah tries to boost a jailed Harry's morale with: "Try and keep your pecker up—old chap!"

Bland and Harry guzzle nocturnal cocktails.

ASS-WHUPPINGS Harry reels from limited exposure to Attila 305. He survives a scuffle with assassin Rudolf Rainbow by nailing him with an umbrella and yanking the carpet out from under him. Rainbow slices Harry's scalp, but Harry seizes the blade, maniacally jabs Rainbow and drives to freedom (it's a delicious little scene).

TV TIE-INS We'd be shocked—indeed, shocked and appalled, we tell you—if you didn't know that the late author Ian Marter portrayed Harry Sullivan in the TV series. Marter also wrote a number of "Doctor Who" novelizations, including "The Reign of Terror" and "The Rescue."

Sometime after "The Android Invasion," Harry left UNIT and shaved off his sideburns. He went an unspecified number of years without seeing the Brigadier. He didn't see Sarah Jane for a decade.

The Brigadier's currently a Senior Mathematics Master at a private Sussex school and "enjoys life enormously," suggesting this takes place after "Mawdryn Undead."

Sarah Jane's no longer living with her Aunt Lavinia ("The Time Warrior," "K9 and Company") in Croydon and has moved to Camberwell.

NOVEL TIE-INS The able-bodied Mrs. Wrigglesworth currently serves as Harry's cleaning lady. In *Millennium Shock*, Harry guns down his subsequent housemaid, Sylvia Webb, when she's turned into an alien Voracian.

CHARACTER DEVELOPMENT

Harry Sullivan: Harry here celebrates his 41st birthday and continues to wear a double-breasted Navy blazer. As part of his Yarra transfer, he's promoted to Surgeon-Commander (a rank he still holds in *System Shock*). General Caspar Schlitzburger transfers Harry from the Biological Defense Establishment at Tooth Tor on Dartmoor to work at the Yarra NATO weapons facility.

Harry loathes the idea of aiding weapons development and also dislikes how his UNIT days didn't let him practice much medicine. He sometimes pretends to be "Laury Varnish," an anagram of his name (this is real high-tech spying we're talking about here).

Harry weighs 18 stone. He's got rowing and rugger trophies from his heyday at Darmouth College Ace Eight, where he was stroke oar. Harry drives a red MG sports car. He's fond (Saints preserve us) of prune crumble. His regular antidote treatments give him limited immunity to low doses of Attila 305. His neighbor, Mrs. Wielegorski, keeps a spare key to his flat.

TOP 5

DOCTOR DEFEATS

Novels Post *Interference*

1) **Gallifrey's destruction (The Ancestor Cell)**—Love it or hate it, the Doctor's ultimate failure—even after centuries of experience at saving alien worlds—lies in his throwing the switch that blows up his homeworld, saving it from subjugation by the Enemy and Faction Paradox.

2) **Loss of the TARDIS (The Shadows of Avalon)**—A temporal rift robs the Doctor of his oldest companion (thankfully, the faithful Ship turns up later).

3) **Aliens abandon the Doctor on Earth (The Turing Test)**—Pale-skinned aliens transform their bodies into encrypted codes and transmit away from Earth, condemning the Doctor to a single world and time.

4) **The "death" of Ace (Prime Time)**—A largely unexplained event, although the seventh Doctor unearths Ace's future casket and finds her youthful body inside.

5) **The Doctor impotent as the Obverse-Federation war breaks out (The Blue Angel)**—The Doctor stops wars and bloodshed. That's his job. So when Iris Wildthyme deliberately halts the Doctor from interceding in a conflict between two Universes, it tears out the Doctor's soul.

Big Finish Audios

1) **Ace shot ("The Fearmonger")**—The Doctor's largely a man without fear, but watching Ace gunned down is his worst nightmare made manifest.

2) **Zzaal's sacrifice ("Red Dawn")**— Lord Zzaal submits to the "red dawn" (the searing sunrise on Mars) to save the Doctor's life.

3) **Captain Deeva Jansen lost ("Sword of Orion")**—An android with a heart, Jansen's swept into space but prevents Charley from suffocating.

4) **Eugene's suicide ("The Holy Terror")**—By nature, the Doctor cares for all beings—even in the case of Eugene, a self-admitted killer intent on ending his life.

5) **Loss of the Temperon ("The Sirens of Time")**—A noble time beast sacrifices itself to an eternity of battling the "Sirens of Time."

Sarah Jane Smith: Sarah's about 30 and attempting to impress Fleet Street, the hub of British journalism, with an article on an anti-biological warfare brigade. She's been trying to contact Harry for sometime. Sarah's editor sends her

This book is not endorsed by the BBC. Doctor Who and TARDIS are trademarks of the BBC.

41

to cover the World Health Organization Conference, meaning she visits Harry in jail, then abandons him (the hussy).

Brigadier Lethbridge-Stewart: He enjoys summer holidays at Stewart Lodge.

Harry and Teddy Bland: Teddy and Harry attended naval college together at Dartmouth. Teddy's now a senior researcher at the Yarra NATO weapons development center.

STUFF YOU NEED *Attila 305* ranks as a volatile toxin that contains an ionase compound which directly penetrates the skin. Yet, Attila's also hydrophobic, making moisture your best defense (if an Attila cloud comes at you, run for the nearest garden hose).

ORGANIZATIONS *Van Gogh Society:* Art appreciation society that serves as a front for Brodsky's European Anarchist Revolution (EAR). Alexander Shire serves as the United Kingdom representative. The Brigadier declined membership.

AT THE END OF THE DAY Just barely dramatic (c'mon—the innocent Harry should've been pushing daisies several times over) but lovingly entertaining, also standing unique as an original novel written by one of the TV cast. *Harry Sullivan's War* revs forward as the "Doctor Who" version of "James Bond," yet Marter deserves praise for always staying true, whatever the circumstances, to Harry's passive persona (you'll riotously cheer for Harry, but wonder if he's a 41-year-old virgin). The final result's more appropriately titled *Harry Sullivan's Harrowing Terrorist Adventure with Big-Bosomed Admirers* than *Harry Sullivan's War*, but makes for friendly, wholesome reading in the cool evening hours.

DIVIDED LOYALTIES

By Gary Russell

Release Date: October 1999
Order: BBC Past Doctor Adventure #26

TARDIS CREW The fifth Doctor, Tegan, Nyssa and Adric; in flashback, the first Doctor on Gallifrey.

TRAVEL LOG Dymok, mid-24th century.

CHRONOLOGY Immediately after "The Visitation."

STORY SUMMARY The cosmic being known as the Celestial Toymaker, smarting from his defeat at the hands of the first Doctor, diverts the TARDIS to the *Little Boy II*, a space station guarding the isolationist planet Dymok. There, a strange energy wave possesses Tegan and through her demands passage to the planet. With the TARDIS cut off by the Toymaker's forcefield, the Doctor convinces the space station crew to shuttle them to Dymok and explore its mysteries. There, a mysterious figure known only as the Observer takes Tegan away and seals the Doctor's party within a pyramid. After eating drugged food that was left out for them, the Doctor's party sleeps...

The Doctor dreams of his early days on Gallifrey, when he and nine other Academy students formed an accelerated fraternity called the Deca. The Doctor, again arguing with the Time Lords about Gallifrey's non-interference policies, finds data on a mythical being or beings named the Toymakers and decides to investigate with his friends Rallon and Millennia. Unfortunately, the trio locates the Celestial Toymaker and becomes embroiled in one of the Toymaker's life-and-death games. The Toymaker uses Rallon's body as a host and keeps Millennia as a living doll, but the Doctor wins his game and is forced to leave. Shattered by the guilt of losing his friends, the Doctor returns to Gallifrey in disgrace and is expelled from the Academy, even as the Deca splits up.

On Dymok, the Observer tells Tegan that her sense of self-will might be strong enough to help the indigenous, telepathic Dymova break free from the Toymaker's control. Meanwhile, the Toymaker's influence causes Nyssa and Adric to resent the Doctor for perceived transgressions and the Toymaker approaches the Doctor, needing his help to split from Rallon's dying body.

The Dymova throw down the mental gauntlet, pressing home their telepathic attack, but the Toymaker's counter-offense obliterates the Dymova and their planet from existence. Stranded in the Toymaker's realm, Adric, Tegan and Nyssa resist the Toymaker's attempts to turn them against the Time Lord, distracting and enraging the Toymaker. Rallon then summons enough strength to burn through his 12 regenerations at once, expelling the Toymaker and dying in the process.

The Observer, revealed as a projected incarnation of Rallon (akin to the Watcher from "Logopolis"), merges with the Toymaker to further keep the fiend in check. *Little Boy II* crewman Matt Desorgher selflessly completes one of the Toymaker's games and destroys the Toyroom, allowing the

Doctor's party to escape and renew their friendships. The TARDIS crew departs, even as the defeated Toymaker, now curious about Earth through the Doctor and Tegan's observations, decides to settle in Blackpool while his Toyroom renews itself.

MEMORABLE MOMENTS In a thumping that will likely make Whovians stand up and cheer, Adric sits in front of the TARDIS interior doors and gets thwacked aside when the Doctor opens them. Nyssa fares the worst from the Toymaker's illusions, watching a scene on her homeworld of Traken where the ruling Council died ("Logopolis"), set afire and turned into skeletons.

The Doctor: "Tegan, has anyone told you how nice it is to have you around?"; Tegan: "Not recently, no."; The Doctor: "No? Hmmm, I wonder why that is?"

SEX AND SPIRITS Time Lords Rallon and Millennia intend to get married or do the Gallifreyan equivalent thereof, suggesting Time Lord romance isn't wholeheartedly dead. Adric's childhood friend Jiana may have thought about him romantically. However, she ran away when Adric joined his brother Varsh's rebels.

ASS-WHUPPINGS The Doctor's old friend Rallon reaches his thirteenth incarnation, becomes a brittle husk and dies. The Toymaker wipes out the Dymova and their planet, which was a Rallon-creation anyway (See Alien Planets).

TV TIE-INS "The Celestial Toymaker" stated that the first Doctor and the Toymaker had previously clashed in an unseen adventure.

We learn that virtually every Time Lord in the TV series had a connection; same goes for virtually every higher power. To unravel this, see the sidebars and individual entries.

The Prydonian Chapter, whose Academy we visit in flashback, was introduced in "The Deadly Assassin." The Doctor's old mentor K'Anpo ("The Time Monster," "Planet of the Spiders") left Gallifrey during this period.

The skewered Runcible ("The Deadly Assassin") once served as a Prydonian Academy hall monitor. The fifth Doctor mistakenly states the Master must have attempted a thirteenth regeneration, resulting in his skeletal form in "The Deadly Assassin" (The eighth Doctor learns the truth in *Legacy of the Daleks*).

The Key to Time ("Season 16") has six segments, each representing a Guardian (See Organizations). Adric always loathed river fruit ("Full Circle"). The Watcher from "Logopolis" is largely

explained (See Alien Races).

Nyssa's ion bonder ("Castrovalva") could also function as a weapon. Nyssa once asked the Doctor if there was some way to separate her father from the Master ("The Keeper of Traken"), and the Doctor's response was vague.

Andrew Verney ("The Awakening") is Tegan's maternal grandfather. In a continuity snitch-up, *Divided Loyalties* establishes Tegan's Aunt Vanessa ("Logopolis") as the sister of Tegan's mother, but *The King of Terror* says Vanessa's the sister of Tegan's father (in-breeding, anyone?). When Tegan went missing on the Barnet Bypass (also "Logopolis") and Vanessa was found dead, Tegan's mum assumed Tegan died too.

Tegan's father encouraged her drawing ("Four to Doomsday") and free spirit. Adric taught Nyssa draughts ("Kinda") because she didn't like chess.

The Meddling Monk ("The Time Meddler") later encounters the Toymaker, but the Toymaker finds himself amused by the Monk and lets him go.

The "Eternals" from the Virgin line, such as Time, Death and Pain, also include an Eternal named Light (probably not the alien cataloger from "Ghost Light").

The TARDIS cleans clothes overnight, which is how the fifth Doctor's crew forever wore the same outfits without reeking like old limburger cheese (in all likelihood, they're clinging to remnants of past lives that they can never reclaim).

TV AND NOVEL TIE INS *Divided Loyalties* retroactively slips in between "The Celestial Toymaker" and *The Nightmare Fair*, in which the sixth Doctor imprisons the Toymaker (hopefully forever).

The Guardians of Light and Chaos ("The Ribos Operation," "Mawdryn Undead" and more) are revealed to be the upper echelon of the Great Old Ones, the race of higher beings seen throughout the TV series and defined in *All-Consuming Fire*. The Celestial Toymaker is cited as the "Guardian of Dreams." *The Quantum Archangel* further defines the Guardians' role in the Universe.

NOVEL TIE-INS The Toymaker's thrall Stefan debuted in *The Nightmare Fair*, which detailed the Toymaker's origins. When the Toymaker merges with the Observer, he essentially "regenerates," which is Russell's way of explaining why the Toymaker in *The Nightmare Fair* acted different from his TV persona.

In flashback, the Doctor feuds with Quences, the head of the Doctor's House (*Lungbarrow*). Badger, the Doctor's robotic tutor from that story, comes from the planet Ava, visited by the young Doctor. (The Academy Council wasn't pleased about this.)

This book is not endorsed by the BBC. Doctor Who and TARDIS are trademarks of the BBC.

43

Divided Loyalties states that Tegan was still on an Australian farm by age 18, but *The King of Terror* says she was living in England by age 15.

Little Boy II Chief Petty Officer Sarah Townsend is perhaps related to Vault Managing Director Townsend (Russell's *Business Unusual*).

AUDIO TIE-INS Deca member Vansell first appeared in "The Sirens of Time."

CHARACTER DEVELOPMENT

The Doctor: The Celestial Intervention Agency have watched the Doctor from the day he was born, observing the potential in his genes and believing he has a destiny to fulfill.

During the Doctor's Academy days, he took Cardinal Sendok's class on stellar cartography. For losing Rallon and Millennia to the Toymaker, the Doctor was expelled from the Prydonian Academy and all his work erased. He was ordered to spend the next 500 years in the records area and traffic control, studying for his doctorate in his spare time. He'd then be allowed to reapply and hopefully become a Time Lord (You'll have to read *Lungbarrow*—or its *I, Who* write-up—to find out how this resolves itself.)

The Doctor rarely needs sleep. The fifth Doctor wears white pajamas and tiny question-mark motifs. He doesn't know how to separate two individuals who are molecularly bonded. The Doctor's thought about his lost friend Rallon through all of his incarnations. If the Doctor loses to the Toymaker, he'll build a new realm as the Toymaker's co-host. Unlike many ephemerals, Time Lords can survive this process.

Tegan Jovanka: Tegan's father was named William and understood farm life wasn't for her.

When Tegan was 18, she was interested in music, R-rated movies and boys. Tegan's family farm was located near Brisbane, where she spent many a Saturday afternoon with friends Susannah, Fliss, Dave and Richard. They bought John Lennon and Abba records. Her friend Richard got his ear pierced.

Tegan's mother has a brother named Richard and a sister-in-law, Tegan's Aunt Felicity. Tegan has two cousins, Colin ("Arc of Infinity") and Michael, plus Serbian grandparents, Mjovic and Sneshna Jovanka, who live in Yugoslavia.

Tegan's father died (first mentioned in *The Sands of Time*) painlessly and with dignity while she was travelling in the TARDIS. Tegan considers her travelling companions basket cases and is rather frightened to be locked up with them.

THE CRUCIAL BITS...

- **DIVIDED LOYALTIES**—Details about the Doctor's early life on Gallifrey and first battle with Celestial Toymaker revealed.

Nyssa: In addition to her TV knowledge of biology, Nyssa has knowledge of bioelectronics. On Traken, a guardian toy named Big Bear (or "Bee-Bee") protected her.

Tegan and Nyssa: Tegan thinks Nyssa spends too little time being a girl, dreaming of movie stars and going to clubs (although how the hell Nyssa's supposed to do that from the TARDIS isn't clear).

Tegan and Adric: Tegan thinks Adric's lazy, unhygienic and rather loathsome (other than that, he's fine).

Adric: Unfortunately for all, Adric forgets to bathe regularly. Tegan and Nyssa suggested the Doctor talk with him about the miracles of deodorant, but the Doctor dodges the issue.

Adric's now 15. His late parents were named Morell and Tanisa (they were alive four years ago). Adric's skilled at astrometrics and chess.

The Celestial Toymaker: The Toymaker comes from another universe (possibly the universe that existed before this one, *All-Consuming Fire*) and says his people were weavers of dreams. The Toymaker got bored and struck out on his own (somewhat conflicting with *The Nightmare Fair*).

Because the Toymaker essentially is the living embodiment of the Time Vortex, his face is sometimes replaced by a swirling vortex of space. He's also decently extra-dimensional, able to suck the TARDIS into his void (so to speak).

The Toymaker's original body was incompatible with our Universe, so for eons, he jumped from mortal body to mortal body. Finally, he took Rallon's Time Lord body for longevity's sake. The Toymaker's natural form is a collective consciousness, possessing neither form nor substance and existing between the dimensions.

The Toymaker is the Guardian of Dreams (*See Organizations*). He therefore exists in a symbiotic relationship with the dreaming peoples of the universe; each needs the other to survive.

Vansell: Member of the Deca (*See Deca Sidebar*) who spied on the group for the CIA and betrayed the Doctor to them. He ultimately abandons the Academy and works as a (barely tolerated) coordinator between the High Council and the Celestial Intervention Agency ("The Sirens of Time").

Koschei (a.k.a. the Master): At the Academy, Koschei specialized in cosmic science, hailing from the House of Oakdown.

Mortimus (a.k.a. the Meddling Monk): In addition to the Daleks ("The Dalek Masterplan"), Mortimus has allied himself with the Ice Warriors and other undesirables.

Jelpax: Of the 10 Deca members, Jelpax was the only one to graduate normally from the Academy and became one of the Time Lords' major recorders, observing four or five major galaxies (his time team foresaw the Dalek-ruled future mentioned in "Genesis of the Daleks").

As coordinator of the APC Net, Jelpax helped his mentor Borusa locate objects from the Dark Time including Rassilon's control room ("The Five Doctors"). Jelpax remained staunchly loyal to Borusa, and when Borusa was deposed ("The Five Doctors"), Jelpax was demoted to being a traffic controller for Gallifrey's transduction barriers.

Stefan: The Toymaker's first assistant, who lost to the Toymaker in 1190. Stefan formerly served King Frederick during the Third Crusade.

Rallon: Large framed Rallon's full name is Ralonwashatellaraw of the House of Stillhaven. He was already a Time Lord when the Toymaker merged with him. Rallon hoped the Doctor would separate them, thus killing them both.

Millennia: Rallon's love Millennia hailed from the influential, affluent House of Brightshore. She was skilled at creating multiplane interactive data bases. After the Toymaker made Millennia one of his dolls, she was never seen again.

Rallon and Millennia: After their fateful meeting with the Toymaker, their names were erased from Time Lord history.

The TARDIS: When the TARDIS materializes, its displacement field pushes aside the air in the area where it's arriving. The Ship's atmosphere automatically cleans itself. The TARDIS remains lousy at short hops.

TARDISes: During the flashback to Gallifreyan history, type 35 TARDISes exist, as well as Type 30 Mark III. The Doctor, Rallon and Millennia here snitch a Mark 18.

ALIEN RACES

Time Lord Watchers: Prior to a regeneration, some Time Lords may generate alternate versions

MISCELLANEOUS STUFF!

THE DECA

The Deca were 10 Prydonian elitist students, the pinnacle of their class and the pride and joy of teachers such as Sendok, Borusa and Franilla. Cardinal Zass helped monitor them. The Deca membership included: The Doctor, Koschei (a.k.a. The Master), Drax (from "The Armageddon Factor"), Mortimus ("The Time Meddler"), Magnus ("The War Games"), Ushas ("The Mark of the Rani"), Vansell ("The Sirens of Time"), Rallon, Millennia and Jelpax.

Among the Deca, the Doctor, Koschei and Magnus were friends since their first day at the Academy, hailing from different Houses. All but three of the Deca are in first regenerations, forbidden to regenerate until after their 500th birthdays.

As *Divided Loyalties* opens, Vansell, Ushas and Rallon are already junior Time Lords in their final semesters; the other seven have two semesters to go before receiving the Rassilon Imprimatur ("The Two Doctors"), the genetic coding that grants regenerative powers, the ability to withstand time travel and empathy with Time Lord technology.

Gallifreyan authorities include President Drall, Cardinal Borusa and Castellan Rannex.

After the Doctor returned from fighting the Toymaker the first time, Koschei and Ushas departed for Academy research projects elsewhere. Jelpax worked on records and libraries alongside coordinator Azmael ("The Twin Dilemma"). Mortimus and Drax both dropped out of the Academy and vanished. Magnus, at least, watched the Doctor's trial and was assigned to the Gallifreyan scientific research department.

of themselves, shades of no real substance that have an essence of what was and will be (if this still seems a bit vague, it's because it is).

Alzarians: Members of Adric's race never remember their dreams, probably because dreams happen when the body's relaxed and the fast-acting Alzarian healing factor mean their bodies rarely slow down.

The Great Old Ones: The Time Lord files contain entries on "The Great Old Ones," beings that survived the destruction of the Universe before ours and came to possess terrible powers in our space. "The Great Old Ones" include: Hastur (Fenric from "The Curse of Fenric"), Yog-Sothoth (The Great Intelligence from "The Abominable Snow-

This book is not endorsed by the BBC. Doctor Who and TARDIS are trademarks of the BBC.

45

man"), Lloigor (the giant spider from "The Web Planet"), Raag, Nah and Rok, who hoped to cause the end of our Universe as they had their own (The Gods of Ragnarok from "The Greatest Show in the Galaxy"), Cthulu (*White Darkness*), Shub-Niggurath, Melefescent, Tor-Gasukk, Gog and Magog (*Doctor Who Magazine* strips), Nyarlathotep, whom the Doctor hopes to "never encounter" (the apocryphal *Missing Pieces*: "Tea With Cthulhu"), Dagon, worshiped by the Sea Devils.

Dymova: The Dymova were immensely telepathic and thus spent most of their time unconscious, generating psionic power. Rallon created them as a potential army against the Toymaker, but until that time, their power fueled the fiend.

ALIEN PLANETS

Earth: Lies at coordinates 5XA8000-743-7.

Gallifrey: During the Doctor's Academy days, Gallifrey had an orange sky spotted with some artificial satellites and time ships traveling through the transduction barrier ("The Invasion of Time"). Gallifreyan relics at this point include Pandeka's staff and an unspecified object belonging to someone named Helron.

Alzarius: Adric's homeworld lacked art, unless you count schematics and designs. Line drawings, such as those showing the Starliner components ("Full Circle"), were a rarity.

Traken: The Traken Union stretched through five or six planets in its own solar system and didn't go beyond. On Traken, they said the universe was made up of coincidences all coming together to make one happy accident. Trakenites had jewels like onyx and used the name "Serkur" to denote one who is truly free from sin, a person whom nothing could truly conquer.

Dymok: A powerful mental illusion created by Rallon, Dymok was a small planet, the fourth in its solar system. It was rather unexceptional, with no satellites, a number of large oceans and a scattering of landmasses. Dymok's destruction surged Rallon with the telepathic energy he needed to overcome the Toymaker.

PLACES TO GO

Prydonian Academy: The Academy is basically a self-contained city annexed to the Gallifreyan Capitol. It takes up 28 square miles of Gallifrey's surface and is surrounded by the desert plains where the Outsiders live ("The Invasion of Time"). Other than its sheer size, the Academy is about

what you'd expect for a Gallifreyan University, complete with glass turrets, covered linking walkways, dormitories and lecture halls. It also has TARDIS bays, scaphe ports (*Cat's Cradle: Time's Crucible*), gymnasiums and eateries.

The Celestial Toyshop: The Toymaker's realm is an extension of the Toymaker's own multi-dimensional being.

The Doctor's TARDIS bedroom: A bizarre affair with a large four-poster bed complete with ornate awnings, silk sheets and an enormous chocolate-colored toy rabbit. The Doctor's coat hangs on Mickey Mouse hangers.

ORGANIZATIONS

Celestial Intervention Agency ("The Deadly Assassin"): Can make time stop, even on Gallifrey, to commit acts of espionage.

Guardians of the Universe: There are at least six Guardians, not two, all of them an upper pantheon of the Great Old Ones. We've already met the Guardians of Light and Chaos in TV's Season 16, and the Toymaker himself is the Guardian of Dreams. There's also a Guardian of Justice, who creates conflict to justify his existence. The remaining two, the Guardians of Mortality and Imagination, are twins that counterbalance each other; the Toymaker says the Doctor shall meet them one day. All Guardians are immortal.

It's suggested the Guardians humbled Rassilon for being inquisitive about them.

HISTORY The fourth Doctor accidentally knocked over one of Jackson Pollock's paint pots, impressing the artist to the point that he painted the Doctor a piece entitled "Azure in the Rain by a Man Who'd Never Been There" that hangs on the door of the Doctor's TARDIS bedroom.

• Thirty years ago, Dymok demanded isolation and the space station *Little Boy II* was made to honor this.

AT THE END OF THE DAY So long as you clear the hurdle that virtually every Time Lord and higher power in the TV series knew each other (and a lot of readers understandably can't), *Divided Loyalties* packs a decent bit of fun—rather like a 1960s sci-fi flick that's more whimsical than serious. By splitting between the first and fifth Doctor's groups, the story keeps moving and makes its continuity stitches more palatable (scenes on early Gallifrey ironically seem more common thanks to works by Platt, Parkin and Miles). All in all, *Divided Loyalties* won't landmark itself as a dramatic "Who" novel, but its playfulness wins out mostly because its retcon is easy enough to ignore.

THE LAND OF THE DEAD

By Stephen Cole

Release Date: January 2000
Order: Big Finish "Doctor Who" Audio #4

TARDIS CREW The fifth Doctor and Nyssa.

TRAVEL LOG Alaska, a few miles from Hammondsville and near the Koyukuk River, 1964 and 1994.

STORY SUMMARY The TARDIS feels receptive to a mysterious energy field and materializes at the energy's strong points—first in Alaska, 1964, then at the same location 30 years later. The Doctor and Nyssa leave the Ship to track the energy, but encounter a misshapen and lethal hybrid sea animal. They take shelter in the isolated home of Shaun Brett, a rich oilman who's modeled rooms of his house to reflect Earth's basic elements—stone, sea, ice, etc.—as a tribute to his late father, an archaeologist.

Together with interior designer Monica Lewis, the Doctor finds the sea room's walruses, seals and other animals have also mutated into grotesque hybrids. Even worse, an ancient fossil buried in the stone room begins struggling to break free. The Doctor and Monica, aghast that a creature lacking flesh could awaken, carve a small piece off for telebiogenesis expert Nyssa to analyze. As the ferocious, animated fossil eats one of Brett's assistants, it hyper-augments its own DNA and intelligence in the process. Nyssa concludes that the bone monster dates to around 260 million years ago, allowing the Doctor to identify the threat as dating from the Permian era.

The Doctor explains that during that time period, 96 percent of Earth's lifeforms died out in an extinction that greatly pre-dated the rise of the planet's dinosaurs. The Doctor concludes that the bone creature and its fellows—which he dubs the Permians—evolved on Earth as hunters endowed with bio-electric fields that degenerated their preys' intelligence and flesh. In time, the Permians consumed each other, but a few fell dormant and their bodies fossilized over millions of years. But the combination of ancient elements in Brett's home re-energized their personal fields. In turn, the Permians' unstable bioelectric fields mutated local sealife, which are descendants of the Permians' natural prey and over-sensitive to the Permians' bioelectric fields. Even worse, more Permians have awakened and formed a pack, threatening to start a new colony and breed.

The Doctor and Nyssa learn some Permians awakened 30 years ago at a local dig, but Brett's father gave his life to kill them with dynamite—meaning fire can destroy the Permians' bio-electric fields. Deranged from exposure to the Permians' bio-energy, Brett takes a last dynamite stick and rushes toward the Permian pack, killing himself and all but two of the monsters. The Doctor orders an immediate retreat to Brett's house, luring the last two Permians inside and setting the structure afire with flammable paint. The house—and the last of the Permians—burns to the ground and the Doctor predicts that the remaining hybrids will die off without the Permians' bioelectric fields stabilizing them. As Monica and Tulung, the only other surviving member of Brett's team, come to terms with recent events, the Doctor and Nyssa depart for the TARDIS.

MEMORABLE MOMENTS The Doctor's scream for Nyssa's safety at the end of Part One proves as terrifying as any "Doctor Who" cliffhanger. In a nice turnabout, Monica and Nyssa dispatch the Doctor to make tea. Credit the sound team for horrific noises of a Permian happily munching on a hapless victim's bones.

SEX AND SPIRITS It's only a hint, but survivors Monica Lewis and Tulung possibly hook up after this story. The Doctor tells Monica that he and Nyssa are just friends.

TV TIE-INS Nyssa comforts a grief-stricken Tulung, recalling what it's like to lose a father and her entire world ("Logopolis"). Nyssa here augments a spectroscope with an ion bonding technique ("Castrovalva"). The Doctor and Nyssa learn about Earth's first extinction 260 million years ago, but were onhand—along with Tegan and the doomed Adric—for the dinosaur extinction 60 million years ago in "Earthshock." The Doctor says he holds influence in this time zone, likely hinting he could contact UNIT ("Time-Flight").

CHARACTER DEVELOPMENT
The Doctor: The Doctor possesses a laser-scalpel, a common tool for homes of the future. A hand-held tracker lets him follow the Permian energy signature.

Nyssa: Despite some Earth trips in the TARDIS, Nyssa isn't that familiar with Earth geography.

Shaun Brett: Alaskan oil made Brett's father—and consequently Brett—multi-millionaires many times over.

ALIEN RACES

Permians: Permians—to use the Doctor's nomenclature—naturally look like bone-made creatures, lacking true flesh. In reality, a Permian's bones serve as its flesh, held together by a bioelectric field that eliminates the need for joints. Blood pumps underneath the bone. If anything, Permians take after Sauriscian therapods like tyrannosaurus rex, shaped like lizard-hipped carnivores that run on hind legs and have hundreds of sharp teeth.

Permians' bioelectric fields, generated by their brains, are geared to literally shred flesh from their prey, making consumption much easier. The bio-fields help the Permians see and hear without true eyes and ears. More importantly, the bio-fields let Permians genetically amalgamate their prey's DNA, acquiring their intelligence and inherent strengths. The Doctor surmised that if the creatures ran rampant and ate a village, they could attain space flight in months. And Rassilon forbid they'd consume the Doctor, a Time Lord, with his TARDIS nearby.

Permians likely originated in the sea and prefer sea-based prey. Fire destroys Permian personal bio-fields (although Permians naturally radiate a great deal of heat), but projectile weapons would likely be useless.

Human beings hadn't evolved when Permians walked the Earth, so normal humans can mentally resist the Permian bioelectric field but psychologically disturbed humans easily fall prey to the Permian influence. In healthy individuals, such as Nyssa, the Permians create an empathic field that creates nightmares of the Permians and their prey—visions that're amplified if said people eat animal flesh or a natural substance in range of a Permian bio-field.

Permians are naturally attuned to materials that existed in their original time zone (260 million years ago), meaning synthetic products greatly immobilize them. Your best bet for fighting a Permian is to wrap it in your nylons (fess up, gents) or somesuch. Permians' personal fields interact with elements from their original time zone, allowing them to telekinetically direct seawater and other such substances.

They prefer other prey, but Permians periodically feed on each other to prevent their bodies from mutating too far beyond normal. They normally fear light, but acclimate quickly.

Permian hybrids: Permian fields, normally attuned to shred flesh from Permian prey such as walruses, otters and fur seals, sometimes blend such creatures' bodies together, creating pain-riddled hybrids that rely on Permian fields to survive.

PLACES TO GO *The Land of the Dead (a.k.a. Adlivum):* The Inuit tribes subscribe to the concept of Adlivum—the Land of the Dead, as ruled by the drowned sea spirit Sedna. The Inuit believe Heaven lies on Earth, meaning the living frequently interact with the silent spirits of the dead, which largely reside in this realm.

HISTORY Approximately 260 million years ago, the Permians evolved at the end of the Permian era as creatures whose bioelectric fields and ability to influence their prey mentally made them unstoppable predators. They wiped out 96 percent of life on Earth, but the gory repast ended with the Permians consuming themselves until the last few went dormant and became fossils.

• By comparison, dinosaurs started walking on Earth circa 230 million years ago and died out a paltry 60 million years hence.

• The Permian bio-electrical fields in Alaska likely influenced the first settlers some 25,000 years ago, making them craft stories of the sea spirit Sedna to interpret their disturbed feelings.

AT THE END OF THE DAY Lovely—*if* (and let's stress the if) you can keep up with the continual science and tedious discussions of Inuit beliefs. "The Land of the Dead" awakens a meaty, homespun evil, showing isolated characters in the rigors of insanity (rather like the "X-Files" story "Ice"). It's also superb for the audio format, dealing a Peter Davison story that would've flopped visually on TV and putting its supporting cast to great use (Nyssa gets some loving attention). The final product contrasts the fifth Doctor's innocence to a situation more black than most of his TV tales, creating a tale to be heard during stormy travels.

WINTER FOR THE ADEPT

By Andrew Cartmel

Release Date: July 2000
Order: Big Finish "Doctor Who: Audio #11

TARDIS CREW The fifth Doctor and Nyssa.

TRAVEL LOG Miss Tremayne's finishing school, Swiss Alps, December 22, 1963.

STORY SUMMARY The Doctor botches a TARDIS-based experiment to detect the Spillagers, malevolent alien plunderers who "spill" through dimensional wormholes and ransack different regions of space. As a result, the experiment teleports Nyssa to a source of Spillager activity in the Swiss Alps, December, 1963. Thankfully, mountain patrolman Lieutenant Peter Sandoz rescues Nyssa and takes her to the only nearby shelter—a girls' finishing school almost emptied for the holiday.

To Nyssa's alarm, a poltergeist repeatedly assaults the few remaining school residents with flying furniture and glass. Soon after, the Doctor tracks Nyssa in the TARDIS and arrives at the school, confirming her fears by scanning for telekinetic activity. In the school chapel, the Doctor finds psionic resonance near a plaque that commemorates Harding Wellman, a young mountaineer who died in an avalanche, and begins to formulate a theory.

Surprisingly opting for a séance, the Doctor summons Harding's "spirit," identifying it as a malleable energy being with Harding's memories and personality. Furthermore, the Doctor realizes the poltergeist effect is subconsciously occurring through a psionic combination of Harding's presence with students Peril Bellamy and Allison Speer, latent psionics in their own right. Harding's energy supercharges Allison's telepathy and Peril's normally mild telekinesis, creating a poltergeist effect that throws out devastating amounts of telekinetic force.

Skeptical that Harding, Peril and Allison met through mere happenstance, the Doctor exposes French teacher Mlle. Maupassant as a Spillager—an advance scout who's repeatedly triggered the poltergeist effect, then siphoned the energy produced to open a wormhole for the Spillager invasion fleet. Maupassant sheds off her human guise and attacks the Doctor, but Harding, Allison and Peril deliberately trigger their telekinetic abilities, killing Maupassant with a flying kitchen table.

The Doctor and Lt. Sandoz dispose of Maupassant's body and the Doctor proposes using Harding's gestalt to collapse the poltergeist-spawned wormhole, crushing the in-transit Spillager warfleet. Seconds later, Sandoz reveals himself as a second Spillager scout and attempts to foil the Doctor's plan by shooting Peril. However, the pistol noise triggers an avalanche that crushes Sandoz to death while the Doctor carries the unconscious Peril to safety.

Under the Doctor's direction, the mildly telepathic Nyssa takes Peril's place in a séance and Harding, Nyssa and Allison work in unison to tele-kinetically crush the Spillager gateway down to a singularity—obliterating the Spillager fleet into a hydrogen fireball. Sometime later, the Doctor takes the snowbound finishing school survivors home in the TARDIS, with Peril asking the ghostly, homeless Harding to lodge with her.

MEMORABLE MOMENTS Piano music playing in the background, an aged Allison reflects on events from "Winter for the Adept," stating she'll remember meeting the Doctor so long as "the embers of memory still glow feebly in her mind."

Overly religious schoolmarm Miss Tremayne labels the cricket-clad Doctor "An agent of sin!" Nyssa, having been teleported to the Swiss Alps by one of the Doctor's wayward experiments, freaks when he hands her an unidentified bit of circuitry and says, "Here, hold this."

Ski poles levitate and stab at Nyssa in a nasty Part Two cliffhanger. In one of the series' strangest chases, a poltergeist-animated piano hurls itself after the fleeing Doctor and Nyssa (after the piano starts smashing at their cover, the optimistic Doctor notes: "Good job it isn't a grand.").

The Spillagers morph into their natural forms, accompanied by a wonderfully gooey sound effect.

SEX AND SPIRITS Student Allison is likely smitten with the Doctor. Classmate Peril attempts to elope with Sandoz—who's actually a disguised, blue-skinned other-dimensional being heavily composed of ooze (he likely romanced Peril to keep her at school and maintain the poltergeist effect).

In a juicy little double entendre, Nyssa tells a 'protective' Sandoz: "We've seen how 'safe' these girls are in your hands!" The self-righteous Tremayne calls innocent Nyssa a harlot. (Nyssa: "What's a harlot?" Tremayne: "Whore of Babylon!" Nyssa: "I still don't understand the reference.")

ASS-WHUPPINGS The Doctor's attempts at Spillage detection drop Nyssa into the freezing Swiss Alps, sans shoes. Although claiming to dislike violence, the Doctor directs the Harding gestalt to kill Mlle Maupassant, the Spillager fleet and its commanding Spillager Empress.

Harding Wellman starts and ends the story dead. The poltergeist effect creates a cyclone, smashing a rescue helicopter and killing the pilot. Finishing school founder Miss Tremayne, a religious zealot, tries to off her "demon-possessed" students with a knife, so Sandoz shoots her dead.

TV TIE-INS The Doctor keeps the TARDIS' internal temperature a bit high, perhaps explaining why Nyssa and Tegan hastily shucked their clothes in Season 20 ("Snakedance," etc.).

TV AND AUDIO TIE-INS Nyssa gained latent telepathy through exposure to the Xeraphin ("Time-Flight"), further demonstrating this talent in "Land of the Dead."

AUDIO TIE-INS The other-dimensional Spillagers aren't related to the multi-dimensional Scourge ("The Shadow of the Scourge").

CHARACTER DEVELOPMENT

The Doctor: The Doctor's probably tangled with the Spillagers before (the Spillager Empress recognizes him), but seems to conduct Spillager-detection experiments merely as a precaution—he seems unaware of actual invasion plans.

He carries a mild sedative related to valerian that, when added to hot water, renders humans unconscious and allows him to plant post-hypnotic suggestions. He TARDIS-tracks Nyssa to the Swiss Alps by following both her natural biomorphic resonance and the Spillagers' energy profile.

One of the Doctor's devices locates psionic energy residue (it works on corpses and inanimate objects). His vibrational scanning tool detects telepathic ability. He's wanted to study heredity-based telekinesis, but never found the time.

Nyssa: Everyone's favorite Trakenite knows how to ski—barely. She's unfamiliar with Earth words such as "poltergeist" and "harlot," and items such as horse bridles. A confused Nyssa asks if authors William Blake or Walt Whitman are Time Lords (the Doctor cheekily answers: "Perhaps.")

Harding Wellman's "Ghost": Not the actual spirit of the epileptic Harding Wellman, an English mountaineer killed in the Alps circa 1913, but an energy being that copied Harding's memories and intellect (the energy being's exact nature is never explained). Harding's "ghost" is invisible.

ALIEN RACES *Spillagers* are multi-dimensional beings who routinely "spill" into one dimension from another and ransack it (the equivalent of space Vikings, one supposes). They're deemed "connoisseurs of slaughter," so you're best off avoiding them altogether. The name "Spillager" hails from a combination of the words "Spillage" and "Pillager," although it's likely not what the Spillagers call themselves.

In an unspecified manner, Spillagers can tap psionic power and trigger mental activity such as the poltergeist gestalt. Spillager wormhole technology appears crude, requiring a compatible psionic power source. The Spillagers enjoy limited shapeshifting abilities, able to copy other beings'

bodies (they evidently murdered the real Sandoz and Maupassant). Killed Spillagers quickly melt but are safe, if slimy, to touch.

STUFF YOU NEED

The Doctor's Spillager Detector: The science behind the detector never gets explained, although it apparently holds some artificial intelligence—it teleported the already telepathic Nyssa to the Spillager presence at the school, knowing the Doctor would follow.

Imaturitation: Living poultice that feeds upon projectile wounds, reabsorbing the bullet and healing scarred tissues. The Doctor carries at least one Imaturitation in the TARDIS.

PLACES TO GO *The Academy for Young Ladies* was founded by the overly religious Miss Tremayne, an elderly Scottish spinster convinced that heat causes disobedience and corruption—and thus the Alps' cool air supposedly cleanses the soul. Don't let Miss Tremayne catch you with a hot water bottle or warm blanket because Heaven knows such things pave the way to hell.

Mlle Maupassant, a Spillager spy, tainted the admissions process by recruiting potential psionics such as Peril and Allison.

PHENOMENA

Harding's Poltergeist Effect: Telekinetic maelstrom formed by the combined talents of Harding, Peril and Allison. Harding's epilepsy instigates the effect, creating the smell of roses (a scent that derives from Harding's fond memories of his funeral bouquets). The rose scent helps trigger Allison's telepathy, which in turn activates Peril's telekinesis. Rather than creating the poltergeist itself, Peril's psi talent then routes back into Harding—completing the psionic chain and throwing out massive amounts of telekinetic power.

The gestalt fails to function without the close proximity of all three participants. Psionics of similar talents (such as Nyssa) can replace one of the Harding/Peril/Allison trio. The poltergeist effect is mostly subconscious. The Spillagers skillfully trigger the effect; Harding, Peril and Allison must make crude attempts to wield their power. Rendering one of the gestalt participants unconscious or snapping their concentration ends the effect. The poltergeist generates electro-magnetic radiation that blocks radio transmissions.

The Adept: Peril Bellamy's family has a recessive gene, granting some females psionic abilities.

AT THE END OF THE DAY Decently enjoyable and heavily stylized (we love the piano concertos)—although a number of flaws co-ordinate to freeze over "Winter for the Adept." Nyssa's character is particularly wasted, mostly serving to bitch at the Doctor and get confused by Earth expressions. Peter Jurasik, rich-voiced on "Babylon 5," sounds depressingly flat, reflecting a cast-wide lack of chemistry. Allowing for all that—plus a near-Doctor-less Part One and a couple of lackluster cliffhangers—"Winter" nevertheless rises above the sum of its parts to adequately contrast with the rest of the Big Finish line.

THE MUTANT PHASE

By Nicholas Briggs

Release Date: December 2000
Order: Big Finish "Doctor Who" Audio #15
"Dalek Empire" Part III

TARDIS CREW The fifth Doctor and Nyssa.

TRAVEL LOG (Mutant Dalek Swarm timeline) Kansas, America, 2158; a devastated Earth, 4253; Skaro, the distant future.

CHRONOLOGY Between "Time-Flight" and "Arc of Infinity."

STORY SUMMARY In the distant future, billions of Dalek embryos inexplicably mutate into invulnerable giant wasp creatures—a condition that robs them of intelligence and gives them an insatiable desire to feed. Numbering 100 billion, the mutant Daleks fly through space at warp speeds, ravaging dozens of worlds. Appalled, two Thals—a scientist named Professor Ptolem and his associate Commander Ganatus—ally themselves with the remaining few un-mutated Daleks to eradicate the mutant Dalek swarm. Together, they agree to secure aid from the Daleks' adversary, the Doctor.

The Daleks snare the Doctor's in-flight TARDIS with their time corridor technology and forcibly materialize the ship on Earth, 4253. To the Doctor and Nyssa's astonishment, they find Earth completely barren, ravaged by the mutant Dalek swarm. Ptolem and Ganatus, having tracked the TARDIS, convince the Doctor of the mutant Dalek swarm's threat. Finally, the Doctor agrees to travel to the Dalek homeworld of Skaro and consult with the Emperor Dalek.

On Skaro, Ptolem finds a DNA match between the mutant Dalek swarm and an obscure type of Earth wasp—the Agnomen wasp species. From

Dalek genetic records, the Doctor surmises that an Agnomen wasp worked its way into the casing of a battle-scarred Dalek during the Dalek occupation of Earth in 2158. By stinging the organic Dalek creature within its casing, the wasp in question tainted the Dalek with its DNA. Over the next millennia, Dalek reproduction plants inadvertently spread the Agnomen wasp DNA throughout the entire Dalek race, ultimately triggering the creation of the mutant Dalek swarm.

With little option, the Doctor agrees to travel back in the TARDIS and alter history, preventing the mutant swarm's generation. As mutant Dalek wasps overrun the remaining Dalek defenses, the Doctor evacuates Nyssa, Ptolem and Ganatus in the TARDIS while the Emperor Dalek self-destructs Skaro as a final act of defiance.

Nervously, the Doctor concludes the mutant Dalek swarm's creation—as well as Earth and Skaro's obliteration—must have occurred through a temporal paradox. Meanwhile, Nyssa checks the TARDIS databanks and finds a formula for GK-50, an Earth pesticide used to kill swarms of Agnomen wasps. Unsure of GK-50's effect on larval Agnomen wasp DNA, the Doctor nonetheless asks Nyssa to synthesize a GK-50 hypodermic. For lack of a better plan, the Doctor intends to rig a special tracker and locate the wasp-stung Dalek in 2158, then inject it with GK-50 and hopefully kill the wasp cells within—thwarting the mutant Dalek swarm's genesis.

Suddenly, Ganatus seizes the GK-50 probe and holds the Doctor hostage, threatening to lethally inject him with the pesticide. Ganatus reveals that the Emperor Dalek secretly augmented his brain to monitor Ptolem's activities. During Skaro's death throes, the Emperor Dalek downloaded its entire consciousness into Ganatus' cerebral implants. As a result, the Emperor Dalek fully controls Ganatus' body.

When the TARDIS materializes in Kansas, America, 2158, the distrustful Emperor Dalek forces the Doctor to walk to a nearby Dalek base while Nyssa and Ptolem wait in the TARDIS. Gradually, the Emperor Dalek—in the guise of Ganatus' Thal body—wins a Dalek field commander's trust and suggests using the GK-50 injection probe to cure any wasp-stung Dalek.

Without prompting, Dalek medics report finding a Dalek contaminated with wasp DNA and announce their intention to remove the infection. The Doctor horrifically realizes that in the "proper" version of history, Dalek medics effortlessly found and removed the wasp DNA—preventing the mutant Dalek swarm's creation before it started. Accordingly, the time travelling Emperor Dalek must be the center of the time paradox. In the "mutant swarm" timeline, the Emperor Dalek journeyed back in the TARDIS and persuaded the Daleks to use the GK-50 injection probe—which is ineffective, as the Doctor feared, on larval wasp DNA. From that point, the wasp infection survived and spread, causing the mutant Dalek swarm.

Desperately, the Doctor warns the Emperor Dalek of the danger and orders it to smash the GK-50 injection probe. With only limited understanding of the temporal physics involved, the Emperor Dalek complies, allowing the Dalek medics to remove the wounded Dalek's wasp DNA by surgical

means. Instantly, the time paradox starts to resolve itself—erasing the mutant Dalek swarm and the devastation of Earth and Skaro—from history. As time restructures and returns the Emperor Dalek, Ptolem and the Daleks to their lives before the mutant swarm's creation, the Doctor reaches the TARDIS and engages its engines. Thanks to their link with the TARDIS, only the Doctor and Nyssa remain unaffected by the temporal re-shuffling, leaving them alone to remember the "mutant Dalek swarm" timeline.

MEMORABLE MOMENTS The story opens in true space opera fashion, as the Thal ship *Dyoni* encounters the mutant Dalek swarm, 100 billion strong and seething through space.

The TARDIS scanner registers Skaro in its death throes. Some spine-frosting cliffhangers: A small Dalek group freaks as another of their number becomes a mutant Dalek wasp before their very eyestalks (Part One). The Doctor emerges from the safety of the TARDIS to prevent the Daleks killing Nyssa (Part Two). Ganatus stands revealed as the Dalek Emperor, screaming that the Doctor "MUST OBEY!" (Part Three).

Most dramatically, a quiet conversation between the Doctor and Nyssa in Part Three demonstrates how much the Doctor fears revealing the secrets of time to a non-Time Lord. The Doctor trusts Nyssa, bit he doesn't know what she'll do—purposefully or accidentally—when they eventually part company. Moreover, he doesn't know who might force her to talk. In that instant, we realize the fifth Doctor isn't so much a youthful cricket player but rather a full-blooded Time Lord riddled with responsibility.

ASS-WHUPPINGS Few "Doctor Who" tales break out the whup-ass like "The Mutant Phase." Mind, it's all nullified at the climax.

The mutant Dalek swarm eviscerates Earth's surface, slaughtering most of humanity—the rest die off from starvation. By the time the Doctor and Nyssa arrive, only a scant 20 or 25 people remain in an underground bunker, living off rations provided by Ptolem and Ganatus. Not surprisingly, the Daleks kill many of the surviving humans.

A single mutant Dalek wasp eats the crew aboard the Thal spaceship *Dyoni*. The Emperor Dalek destroys Skaro to stop the mutant Dalek swarm consuming it.

TV TIE-INS The Thal race, mortal enemies of the Daleks, first appeared in "The Daleks." The second Doctor previously met the Emperor Dalek in "The Evil of the Daleks." The Emperor Dalek has augmented its outer casing to look like the gumballmachine Emperor casing from "Remembrance of the Daleks" (and no, this Emperor Dalek isn't Davros in disguise). Skaro here survives destruction but, as you likely know, bites it in TV's "Remembrance of the Daleks" (although *War of the Daleks'* massive retcon undoes even that).

"The Mutant Phase" segments which take place on Earth, 2158 occur during the infamous Dalek occupation (the first Doctor's crew liberates the planet in 2167 in "The Dalek Invasion of Earth"). The Emperor Dalek, from his base on Skaro, gave orders for the Dalek mining operation in Bedfordshire (also "The Dalek Invasion of Earth").

Dalek time corridor technology in "The Mutant Phase" pre-dates (chronology-wise) its use in "Resurrection of the Daleks." The Daleks achieved sloppy time travel abilities in "The Chase."

It's not exceptionally relevant, but the TARDIS briefly materializes in the same space-time co-ordinates as its previous self in this story, somehow avoiding a timeram ("The Time Monster") and the Blinovitch Limitation Effect ("Day of the Daleks"). The Doctor, upon realizing this problem, uses the TARDIS console to let his and Nyssa's previous selves enter *their* TARDIS, while using the HADS ("The Krotons") to dematerialize his own Ship and land some distance away.

The Doctor only interferes with history in the gravest and most extreme of circumstances, loosely explaining why he couldn't travel back and rescue Adric from certain death ("Earthshock").

AUDIO TIE-INS Nyssa here fixes the TARDIS proximity alarm's audio circuits, nervously remembering a near-collision in Alaska ("The Land of the Dead").

CHARACTER DEVELOPMENT

The Doctor: His eyes, however superior, don't function in total darkness. He's never seen anything like the mutant Dalek swarm before. He doesn't believe in fate or pre-destination. The Doctor can read with superhuman speed, reviewing a detailed data crystal at least 515 times in one night. He rarely sleeps.

Nyssa: She's got some engineering skill, but is hardly expert at time-space travel. Still, Nyssa knows enough about the TARDIS console to know if Ship drifts off course.

The Doctor and Nyssa: Their repeated TARDIS-travel (and probably the Doctor's Time Lord nature) make them resistant to time flashes that freeze other beings or rewrite their timelines.

Professor Ptolem: Good-hearted Thal scientist who worked with the Daleks only because he believed the mutant Dalek wasps a far deadlier threat. Still, Ptolem didn't trust his allies and created a retrovirus that would terminate regular Daleks. He's repeatedly studied the Doctor's chronology report.

The Dalek Emperor: It's heard, but never confirmed until now, reports about the Doctor's dimensionally transcendental TARDIS. The Emperor Dalek hasn't heard the story of the scorpion and the frog. In Ganatus' body, the Emperor Dalek's consciousness retains all of Ganatus' knowledge, but none of his personality.

The TARDIS: The Doctor briefly eludes the Dalek time corridor by ricocheting the TARDIS off it, but that's not a trick he can frequently repeat. The Dalek time corridor—logically enough—mostly operates in time, so the TARDIS finds it easier to alter the corridor's spatial co-ordinates and arrive far away from its intended destination.

The Doctor can stand in the console room and microphone his voice outside the Ship through the TARDIS scanner. Dalek anti-gravity units can levitate the TARDIS. The Ship could likely survive Skaro's destruction, but it's unwise to take the risk. The Doctor can suspend the TARDIS in the Vortex, gaining time to plan. The TARDIS data banks contain Earth newscasts.

ALIEN PLANETS Nyssa's homeworld *Traken* had lime grove wasps that weren't as yellow as Agnomen wasps.

ALIEN RACES

The Daleks: Presumably through cerebral implants, the Daleks can brainwash humans or Thals into becoming Dalek drones. A Dalek's bonded poly-carbide armor contains internal defenses.

Dalek DNA records track their genetic history back through millennia. Daleks reproduce by surgically extracting genetic material from one another, then creating new Daleks in reproduction plants. Breeders are scanned for genetic deficiencies, but an undetected infection could work its way through most of the Dalek race. (Author's Note: The thought of Dalek embryo sex was always too horrible—and squishy—to contemplate.)

Mutant Dalek Wasps: When the Agnomen wasp DNA reaches a certain saturation point in the Dalek race, billions of Dalek embryos revert to a larval stage but quickly hatch, bursting out of their Dalek casings. The new mutant Daleks wasps quickly mature, growing 100 meters long.

No higher brain functions survive the process. The mutant Dalek wasps are covered with metallic shielding that absorbs energy attacks and is invulnerable to artillery fire. A toxic substance in their skin causes death at a mere touch.

They're capable of flying at hyperspeeds three times faster than the Thal starship *Dyoni*.

Resistance, as a wise Borg once said, is futile. Aside from a vulnerability to Pesticide GK-50, the only thing that can kill a mutant Dalek wasp is lack of nourishment.

Robomen ("The Dalek Invasion of Earth"): Dalek-modified humans don't have nerve endings.

PHENOMENA
The Universe and Temporal Paradoxes: The nature of the Universe means that temporal paradoxes of sufficient magnitude don't just muck up the timeline—they can directly shred the fabric of the Universe. In other words, a gigantic temporal paradox—say, the mutant Dalek swarm timeline—could rend vast areas of the Universe.

Temporal energy in its raw state helps crystallize alternate timelines' existence (the TARDIS' struggles to evade the Dalek time corridor, for example, throw out temporal energy that cements the mutant Dalek swarm timeline into being).

Although we blithely refer to "our history" and "alternate history" for the sake of argument, alternate timelines are just as valid as our own.

Meeting Yourself: Although Time Lords get by with meeting their future/past incarnations, the fifth Doctor says it would "absolutely" break the laws of time for him and Nyssa to meet their previous selves.

HISTORY Skaro-based Daleks in 2158 are working on prototype time travel devices.

• During the 22nd century, Earth geneticists created a chemical to agitate the Agnomen wasp, spurring them to kill caterpillars that endangered crop yields. Unfortunately, the process worked too well—the wasps swarmed and started attacking people. On July 21, 2172—a short five years after the liberation of Earth from Dalek control—an Agnomen wasp swarm killed 500, prompting the deployment of Pesticide GK-50.

AT THE END OF THE DAY Now and again, a story comes around that proves how much "Doctor Who"—in terms of texture and complexity—has matured through the original books and audios. "The Mutant Phase" handily ranks among such stories, inter-locking its events to show the potency writers can achieve when they're exceptionally

focused. Peter Davison gives a performance that rivals "The Caves of Androzani." Nyssa continually dishes out sound advice and admirably holds up under pressure. Ptolem becomes one of the audio series' most indomitable, compassionate and vital characters. If you combine these factors with this story's tightness, atmosphere and sense of the epic, you've got one of the top Big Finish stories and an audio we'd love to see rendered in modern-day CGI.

THE KING OF TERROR

By Keith Topping

Release Date: November 2000
Order: BBC Past Doctor Adventure #37

TARDIS CREW The fifth Doctor, Tegan and Turlough, with the Brigadier and UNIT.

TRAVEL LOG Oxford Street, London and Los Angeles, July 3, 1999.

CHRONOLOGY Between "The Awakening" and "Frontios."

STORY SUMMARY Seeking to acquire new territory for their decaying empire, the alien Jex instigate a plot to capture Earth's solar system. By fronting an Earth communications conglomerate named InterCom, the Jex secretly stockpile plutonium, planning to detonate it and raise Earth's temperature to accommodate the Jex race. However, the Jex find their own DNA incompatible with Earthlings and search for extra-terrestrials resistant to heat, hoping to genetically augment humans to survive the climate shift and turn into a ready-made slave labor force.

Meanwhile, espionage reports lead UNIT and the American CIA to suspect InterCom of being under extra-terrestrial management. Advising UNIT on the situation, Brigadier Lethbridge-Stewart calls on the Doctor for help, encouraging the fifth Doctor, Tegan and Turlough to arrive at UNIT's Los Angeles office. But CIA director Control, an old adversary of the Doctor and UNIT (*The Devil Goblins of Neptune*), secretly alerts InterCom to the presence of the Doctor and his companions.

InterCom agents capture Turlough, torturing him while cross-checking his alien DNA for heat tolerance. Assisting the Brigadier against InterCom, the Doctor uncovers the Jex's involvement, discovering in the process the presence of former Jex slaves named the Canavitchi. Once part of the Jex empire, the Canavitchi successfully rebelled and are seeking to systematically wipe out the Jex. Unfortunately, the callous Canavitchi wouldn't flinch to eradicate Earth in the process.

The Doctor and the Brigadier confront the Jex-dominated InterCom leadership, exposing a Canavitchi mole in InterCom's midst. When the InterCom board of directors turns on the traitor, the Brigadier kills them all with a trio of grenades, even as UNIT storms the InterCom complex. Turlough escapes by strangling his Jex guard, as rival Jex and Canavitchi warfleets pull into Earth orbit.

Realizing Earth is truly imperiled, Control offers UNIT use of the CIA's resources. With Control's help, the Doctor re-routes power through Earth's satellite network, creating a planetary force field. The Jex and Canavitchi fleets butcher each other and retreat, with the force field protecting Earth from harm. The Doctor advises the Brigadier to co-ordinate with the CIA to capture any Jex and Canavitchi agents at liberty, then leaves for space with Tegan and Turlough.

MEMORABLE MOMENTS When the Brigadier summons the Doctor via an advertisement in New Scientist, the Doctor swears it can't be a trap on the cost of the ad alone, "Not one of my mortal enemies would pay 13 pounds and 25 pence to ensure my death. Not even the Master."

Nobody bats an eye when the TARDIS materializes next to Mann's Chinese Theatre (well, it's Los Angeles, after all). UNIT Private Natalie Wooldridge blames herself for friends who land on UNIT's casualty lists, "This happens all the time. Every time I smile at a man, he dies. It was the same with kittens when I was small."

SEX AND SPIRITS Hormones saturate *The King of Terror*—but there's just not much lovin'. Turlough goes clubbing in Los Angeles and gets decently drunk. A stunning woman named Eva propositions Turlough, who retires to her apartment only to discover she's a Jex agent. Amid Turlough's torture, Eva tries to get information by pretending she and Turlough did the nasty, but he quickly sees through the ruse.

By her own admission, teenage Tegan couldn't get a boyfriend for love nor money. Her "best friend" Felicity Spoonsy had her claws into Gary Lovarik, the only boy Tegan fancied.

Tegan conducts a love-hate relationship with Captain Paynter, trading terms of affection such as "Smoke my cornet, big arse!", "You're a complete and total dickhead!" and "Lesbian!" They kiss a lot but avoid anything steamier.

In the future, Tegan will marry and divorce rock star Johnny Chess (mentioned in *Timewyrm: Revelation*, *Goth Opera*, etc.).

MISCELLANEOUS STUFF!

JULIA AND ROBERT

Purely for the hell of it, there's a couple of recurring characters in all of Keith Topping's BBC "Doctor Who" novels that you probably glossed over. Topping notes: "I love the idea of a charming eccentric English couple who go through their lives meeting various incarnations of the Doctor or his companions and never realizing it."

Accordingly, *The Devil Goblins From Neptune*, Interlude Three ("Black Angel's Death Song") introduces Dr. Julia and Sgt. Robert Franklin—a middle-class couple living on the south coast of England in Redborough. *The Hollow Men*, Chapter 10, occurs 30 years later with Julia and Robert giving the seventh Doctor a lift to London. In *The King of Terror*, Julia and Robert bump into the fifth Doctor on a couple occasions while vacationing on America's West Coast. And sure enough—despite being set in Roman times, Topping's first Doctor book *Byzantium!* features a scene in modern times where Julia visits her friends, former TARDIS travelers Ian and Barbara Chesterton.

THE FOOTBALLERS!

All of Topping's books, for whatever peculiar reason (best not to ask too many questions), feature characters whose surnames strangely enough match up with names of real-life Newcastle United footballers (aliens, Scully!). In *The Devil Goblins of Neptune*, for example, Julia and Robert live in a village populated with "Farmer Hislop," "Kenny Elliott," "Mrs Clark and Mrs Watson" and "Albert Peacock," whose surnames correspond to footballers Shaka Hislop, Robert Elliott, Lee Clark, Steve Watson, Phillipe Albert and Darren Peacock.

In *The Hollow Men*, mention of "Mrs. Pearce" and "John Tomasson" forms an homage to United players Stuart Pearce and Jan Dahl Tomasson. *The King of Terror*'s populated with "old Mr. Shearer," "Mrs. Speed from the sweet shop," "Mrs Barton from the post office," "The Dyers" and "Beardsley" (respectively players Alan Shearer, Gary Speed, Warren Barton, Kieron Dyer and Peter Beardsley). And yes, before you can ask, several United players' names turn up in the Roman-based *Byzantium!* (after all, the Julio-Claudian era certainly seemed at times like a heady soccer match).

ASS-WHUPPINGS Jex researchers strip Turlough naked, subjecting him to sonic attack and extreme heat. Turlough's probed with every sort of instrument...yes, including *that* sort of probe! Turlough

This book is not endorsed by the BBC. Doctor Who and TARDIS are trademarks of the BBC.

55

escapes by wrapping a chain around the neck of Eva, his (literally) inhuman captor, gruesomely strangling her to death. Days of abuse propel Turlough into chain-whipping the corpse into a bloody pulp.

Tegan nails an assassin with a board, allowing Captain Paynter to shoot him. The Brigadier grenades the InterCom leadership. The Jex and Canavitchi warfleets rend each other. Captain Paynter's partner, Lieutenant Mark Barrington, dies in a car bomb.

TV TIE-INS By 2050, several UNIT files were released under an 80-year ruling, making public early events from the third Doctor's stay on Earth (" Spearhead from Space" to "The Ambassadors of Death"). The CIA strenuously complained when M16 kept International Electromatics' equipment for themselves ("The Invasion").

The Doctor previously visited Los Angeles "The Dalek Masterplan," but was a bit busy at the time.

Major Martin Beresford ("The Seeds of Doom"), now a retired colonel, lives on the Isle of Wight. His niece, Natalie Wooldridge, works in UNIT's LA office (and calls the Brigadier "Uncle Ally").

UNIT tracked down and quietly killed a few hundred Zygons ("Terror of the Zygons") who survived a previous Earth incursion. Another bug hunt eliminated Ice Warriors in Northampton, 1981 (the race debuted in "The Ice Warriors").

The Doctor uses the Brigadier's time-space telegraph ("Revenge of the Cybermen") to access the TARDIS databanks by remote. Professor Kerensky ("City of Death") was a Latvian dissident.

The Brigadier briefly tutored Turlough ("Mawdryn Undead"), dubbing him a "spotty little oick." The Brig here learns that Turlough's an alien (previously believing, per school records, that he hailed from Coventry). Turlough visits his former solicitor in Chancery Lane, actually a Trion agent (also "Mawdryn Undead"), and beats him up for past offenses.

The "Death of Yesterday Malarkey" involved a Raston Warrior Robot ("The Five Doctors") attacking Waterloo Station in London.

The Doctor, Tegan and Turlough spent a month trying to get the peasant Will ("The Awakening") back to 1643, enduring various adventures along the way.

The fifth Doctor knows the Brigadier's married to Doris, somewhat contradicting the seventh Doctor's surprise in "Battlefield."

In a bit of foreshadowing ("Doctor Who: Enemy Within"), the Doctor says he doesn't like hospitals because people die in them.

THE CRUCIAL BITS...

- **THE KING OF TERROR**—The Brigadier, 121, is briefly seen in the Westcliffe Retirement Home in Sussex, having spent 20 years in Avalon. Tegan revealed as marrying—and divorcing—rocker Johnny Chester in future.

NOVEL TIE-INS This story takes place before the Brigadier gained a more youthful body in *Happy Endings*. Unfortunately, the two books clash as to the Brigadier's age. *The King of Terror*, calibrating by actor Nicholas Courtney's true age, states the Brigadier is 71. But *Happy Endings*, which takes place 11 years later, pins the Brig at "more than 100."

This story establishes that the Brigadier stayed in Avalon (*The Shadows of Avalon*) for 20 years and took a Celtic bride. By 2050, he's extremely aged and in a retirement home (*See Character Development*).

Control first appeared in *The Devil Goblins of Neptune* and re-surfaces in *Escape Velocity*. He hasn't seen the Brigadier between *Devil Goblins* and now. Despite the Doctor's ominous warnings, the Waro (*Devil Goblins* again) haven't reappeared. The fifth Doctor speaks with the current U.S. President—presumably President Dering (*Option Lock*).

Rocker Johnny Chess, first mentioned in *Timewyrm: Revelation* and identified as the son of Ian and Barbara Chesterton in *Goth Opera*, makes a personal appearance here (he shows up as a young boy in Topping's *Byzantium!*).

TV AND NOVEL TIE-INS The Brigadier frequently sees the Doctor's former associates, including the Chestertons (The Face of the Enemy), Dr. Liz Shaw and the Suttons ("Inferno").

CHARACTER DEVELOPMENT

The Doctor: In the Doctor's opinion, Tegan is the soul of the TARDIS and he doesn't know what he'd do without her friendship (probably get a lot more quiet, for starters). He gifts the Brigadier a first edition of *The Revolt of Islam*, signed by poet Percy Bysshe Shelley.

At Gallifreyan Academy, the Doctor scraped through in temporal mechanics, quantum physics and fourth-dimensional tachyon studies—a grave disappointment to his parents.

The Doctor's witnessed historical battles that include the Light Brigade (mentioned in "The Evil of the Daleks"), Waterloo, Rorke's Drift, Passchendaele, El Alamein and My Lai.

It's suggested that the Doctor bargained with Control to gain the CIA's assistance, promising to aid the organization in future.

The Doctor knows a portrait of Edward VIII in the National Portrait Gallery is a forgery. He doesn't believe in mystical visions. He appreciates Los Angeles' gaudy charm.

Tegan Jovanka: Tegan grew up in Caloundra, population 40,000, located 70 miles from Brisbane. When Tegan was 13, she hated her "mad cow" of a grandmother, who died six weeks later from coronary thrombosis.

Tegan's father had an affair with a 20-year-old bimbo from the typing pool, which prompted the family to move up the coast and to avoid the scandal's fallout. Her mother sent her to boarding school, where she lasted only a few terms before being expelled. At age 15, Tegan ran away to Sydney and squatted in Kings Cross. Her father soon located her and sent her to stay with his sister Vanessa ("Logopolis") in England. She likely would've ended up on the streets otherwise.

The name Tegan is Cornish and means "lovely little thing." She used to be fatter and is sensitive about her weight. She hates computers.

Tegan and Turlough: They've never visited America.

Turlough: Los Angeles' neon plasticity fascinates Turlough, reminding him of Trion just before the revolution. He thinks urinals that automatically flush are amazing things (you don't see such marvels in Europe).

Turlough's alien physiology can resist temperatures beyond human norms. His blood contains a high white blood cell count and minute traces of uranium. Prolonged periods in Earth's atmosphere give Turlough asthma, nausea and migraines.

Brigadier Lethbridge-Stewart: The Brigadier's worked with at least nine Doctors.

The Brigadier retired two years ago, but rejoined UNIT in an advisory capacity. He heads a small team working from a Covent Garden office, investigating the unexplained. He's got broad authority but limited resources.

The Brigadier summons the Doctor by placing an ad in *New Scientist*. At age 71, he's still handsome. He's married to Doris, who hasn't met the fifth Doctor. The Brigadier has high regard for Captain Paynter.

Like a true military man, the Brigadier leans conservatively. His grandmother died in 1955. His e-mail's aglstewart@UNIT.com.uk, but please don't try it (we know you want to).

MISCELLANEOUS STUFF!

KING OF TERROR SONG TITLES

More musically minded than he probably admits in public, author Keith Topping, as was the custom with *The Devil Goblins of Neptune* and *The Hollow Men* (both co-written with Martin Day), used songs as the inspiration for chapter titles in *The King of Terror*. The following list, kindly supplied by Keith, denotes the origins of the song titles. Read them. Know them. Memorize them. There will be a quiz.

"Start!": The Jam (single 1981)

"Toy Soldier": from "Tin Soldier" by The Small Faces (single, 1968)

"All the King's Men": The Monkees (very obscure TV song, 1967)

"Yesterday's Men": Madness (single, 1985)

"Safe European Home": The Clash (from *Give 'em Enough Rope*, 1978)

"Kill Surf City:" The Jesus and Mary Chain (b-side, 1985)

"California": an allusion to "Kalifornia" by Fat Boy Slim (from *You've Come a Long Way Baby*, 1999)

"Bittersweet Symphony": The Verve (single, 1997)

"Semantic Spaces": LP by Delerium (1997)

"King for a Day": XTC (single, 1986)

"A Man Out of Time": Elvis Costello (single, 1981)

"Bring on the Dancing Horses": Echo & the Bunnymen (single, 1985)

CONTINUED ON PAGE 59

Brigadier General Sir Alistair Gordon Lethbridge-Stewart KCB, VC, DC (and a lot of other letters): By September 2050, the 121-year-old Brigadier (who looks 75) lodges in the Westcliffe Retirement Home in Sussex. He expects to die on a couple years (or perhaps return to Avalon—he's a bit vague on the topic), and has refused at least a dozen offers from biographers. Even so, *Watch the Skies: The Not-So-Secret History of Alien Encounters* by Daniel Clompus covers a lot of the Brigadier's lifetime. *The Man Who Saved the World—The Complete Memos, Letters and E-mails of Brigadier Alistair Lethbridge-Stewart of UNIT* (Multimedia Publishing, 2052), edited by Russell Farway, examines his correspondence.

Jo Grant: The Brigadier hints Jo has befallen an unkind fate, but cannot tell the fifth Doctor for reasons of chronology.

Captain Paynter: Tegan's lip-lock partner was stationed at Strategic Operations Defense in Geneva and worked with Harry Sullivan's broadsword team at Porton Down. He's met at least four of the Doctors.

Johnny Chester: His first novel's entitled *Neurotic Boy Outsider*, published after he left the band "Star Jumpers."

Control: CIA director who hasn't aged in 30 years. He knows something of the Doctor's different personalities. The weasel-like Greaves serves as Control's assistant.

"The King of Terror": A notoriously bad translation of Nostradamus' prophecies states the "king of terror" will come from the skies in July, 1999.

ALIEN RACES
Jex and Canavitchi: Using artificial grafts, both races can pass as human. Surgically altered Canavitchi look like Jex.

Jex: Jex originate on Jexa in the Cassiopeia system (the Doctor encountered them once on an ice world in the Rifta system). They're insectoid, with pincer-like hands, huge domed heads, antennae and small red eyes. Their homeworld's plagued by a slightly toxic atmosphere.

Jex are bureaucratic and methodical, resorting to infiltration and economic domination prior to a planet's invasion. Off-world Jex operations report to the Central League.

Canavitchi: The Canavitchi hail from the Pleiades system. Their homeworld's called, in their native tongue, *Fen'vetch Suxa Canavitch*, meaning "the beautiful world of blue and gold." They're extremely long-lived and don't fear death, viewing it as a doorway to a better existence. Canavitchi have a gestalt consciousness and naturally appear as green, slender and frail, with claws and fangs.

ALIEN PLANETS *Trion:* Described as "drab, colorless, hot and gaseous."

STUFF YOU NEED *Gallifrey's Transduction Barriers ("The Invasion of Time"):* Can't push invading ships away, but can withstand firepower or suicide attacks.

ORGANIZATIONS *UNIT:* Mel Tyrone heads UNIT's Los Angeles office, located near a nondescript five-story office block. To enter, use the little doors hidden behind a metal pull-down shutter

in the back alley off Melrose Avenue. One of UNIT's London bases lies near Marble Arch.

HISTORY The Canavitchi crafted a galactic empire that lasted for a dozen millennia, but their subsequent decadence and laziness left them unable to resist a Jex invasion that occurred 2000 years ago. The Jex subsequently become vicious slave masters, killing two-thirds of the Canavitchi to make them conform. When the remaining Canavitchi organized and revolted, the Jex found their resources strained across the vast Canavitchi space and ran for it.
• In 1999, the Beatles gave a millennium tour (only George, Billy and Klaus remain from the "classic line-up").
• The Jex/Canavitchi conflict near Earth in 1999 became a multimedia affair. Afterward, the highly sensationalist and inaccurate film *The Day the World Turned Dayglo* depicted these events. The Brigadier gave some assistance to the non-fiction work *War in Space: The Real Story* by Gabrielle Graddige (2003).

AT THE END OF THE DAY Definitely a book that plays characterization as its strong suit, sculpting the history and personalities of Tegan, Turlough, Captain Paynter and his partner Lieutenant Mark Barrington (you definitely feel a tinge when Barrington's blown up mid-book). Unfortunately, such character shading comes at the plot's expense, meaning you don't get a glimmering of the enemy's threat or purpose until halfway through. Most notably, the Doctor does next to nothing, save construct a planetary force field while two alien armies destroy each other (oh, what luck!). It's hardly terrific, but it's hardly terrible either, leaving *The King of Terror* a mid-range book that favors conversation over drama.

PHANTASMAGORIA

By Mark Gatiss

> *Release Date: October 1999*
> *Order: Big Finish "Doctor Who" Audio #2*

TARDIS CREW The fifth Doctor and Turlough.

TRAVEL LOG London, Cheapside, March 8, 1702.

CHRONOLOGY Between "Resurrection of the Daleks" and "Planet of Fire."

STORY SUMMARY In London, 1702, the Doctor and Turlough arrive in the home of Dr. Samuel Holywell, a dabbler in arcane rituals and collector of strange objects. The Doctor covers the strangeness of their arrival by telling Holywell he's delivering a blue box oddity from the New World. Meanwhile, Turlough observes a telekinetic poltergeist roaring like the spirits in Hell and tormenting a wine merchant and gambler named Edmund Carteret. The Doctor arrives to find Carteret slain by a heart attack, but quickly uncovers links between Carteret's death and a rash wave of local disappearances.

From Carteret's friend Jasper Jeake, the Doctor learns the kidnap victims were all members of the Diabola Club, a nefarious socialite organization in London, who played cards with a rogue named Sir Nikolas Valentine. Investigating further, the Doctor unmasks Valentine as an extra-terrestrial stranded on Earth. Valentine's playing cards are actually elaborate circuit beacons, designed to lock onto his intended victims' biodata and allow the telekinetic poltergeist—the electronically stored collective consciousness of Valentine's previous victims—to capture the card holders and teleport them to Valentine's spaceship. After being slaved to the ship's central computer, the card holders' brains serve to run mathematical computations that allow the ship to slowly heal itself.

The Doctor exposes Holywell's maid Hannah Fry as leading a double life as Major Billy Lovemore, a famed highwayman. Hannah in turn admits to being an extraterrestrial in pursuit of Carthok of Daodalus, a murderous psychopath who butchered her parents. The Doctor concludes Valentine and Carthok must be the same being while Valentine captures Turlough and Jeake, shackling them with the emaciated remains of the kidnapped Diabola Club members. The Doctor, Hannah and Holywell rush to confront Valentine and save their friends, but Valentine's laser defenses capture them.

Tricked by the Doctor into thinking a 1928 *Wisden's Almanac*—actually a publication on cricketing—is a powerful artifact, Valentine snatches the book from the Doctor's hands. As Valentine flips through the *Almanac* to uncover its "secrets," he accidentally touches a circuit beacon playing card the Doctor took from the dead Carteret's hand. The spaceship's systems instantly absorb Valentine's own bioprint and Hannah encourages the poltergeist to cry out for vengeance and tear Valentine to pieces. The strain kills Hannah also, but the Doctor safely evacuates his friends and keys Valentine's spaceship to self-destruct. As the Doctor and Turlough depart for the TARDIS, Jeake

MISCELLANEOUS STUFF!

**KING OF TERROR SONGS
CONTINUED FROM PAGE 57**

"Beyond Belief": Elvis Costello (from Imperial Bedroom, 1981)

"Strange Town": The Jam (single, 1979)

"Treason (It's Just a Story)": The Teardrop Explodes (single, 1980)

"Naked Eye": The Who (from Odds and Sods, 1974)

"O, King of Chaos!": Julian Cope (from Fried, 1984)

"Submission": The Sex Pistols (from Never Mind the Bollocks, 1977)

"Destiny Calling": James (single, 1998)

"Bring it on Down": Oasis (from Definitely Maybe, 1994)

"Screen Kiss": Thomas Dolby (single, 1983)

"Fear of a Dead Planet": allusion to Public Enemy's Fear of a Black Planet (1989)

"Holes": Mercury Rev (from The Deserters Song, 1999)

"Waiting for Today to Happen": The Lightning Seeds (from Like You Do, 1997)

"Maybe Tomorrow": The Chords (single, 1980)

"Coded Messages": lyric from O.M.D's Messages (single, 1980)

"Time's Up": Buzzcocks (from Spiral Scratch, 1977)

"Complete Control": The Clash (single, 1977)

"Thank You (Fallettinme be Mice Elf Agin)": Sly & The Family Stone (single, 1981)

"The Girl Looked At Johnny" is the title of a book by Julie Birchall and Tony Parsons

"Turn Left at the Rising Sun" is how you get to the Fitzroy Tavern if you're walking up Tottenham Court Road from Oxford Street tube station.

delivers the good news that he's secured Dr. Holywell's membership in the Diabola Club.

MEMORABLE MOMENTS Author Gatiss subtly notes the difficulties of time travel when the Doctor hands Turlough a 1928 *Wisden's Almanac* and comments, "Once we know what year it is, we'll know whether it's out of date or not." Jasper Jeake and his friend Quincy Flowers rejoice after being robbed by Major Billy Lovemore (Flowers: "We've just been robbed by the most famous highwayman in London! We'll dine out on this [story] for years!") Jeake, the story's comic relief, claims his coffee tastes like it was dropped from the wrong end of a cow.

This book is not endorsed by the BBC. Doctor Who and TARDIS are trademarks of the BBC.

59

"Phantasmagoria" boasts notable cliffhangers, with Carteret screaming, "They're coming for me!" amid the poltergeist's wails (Part One), the Doctor and Holywell mysteriously speaking mathematical computations (Part Two) and Hannah revealing herself as Major Billy Lovemore (Part Three).

The Doctor's sit-down card game with Valentine has a surreal nature that echoes "The Celestial Toymaker." (The Doctor draws an ace and wryly comments, "A single red heart. A valentine.") His last minute, inspired gambit with the *Wisden's Almanac* ranks itself among the simpler and more elegant "Doctor Who" solutions.

SEX AND SPIRITS   The Doctor turns down Hannah's offer of brandy but tells her to get some for a fatigued Dr. Holywell.

ASS-WHUPPINGS   Sir Valentine netted 24 victims in his latest kidnapping spree, most of them burning out from his spaceship's inrush of power. Valentine later gets what's coming to him, although the vengeance-filled Hannah Fry dies as a result. A passing carriage knocks out Turlough.

TV TIE-INS   Turlough enjoyed learning about Earth history at Brendon ("Mawdryn Undead").

AUDIO TIE-INS   The fifth Doctor also holds a séance in "Winter for the Adept."

CHARACTER DEVELOPMENT

The Doctor: He's an amateur at identifying antique porcelain, but retains latent psychic ability.

The Doctor and Turlough: The fifth Doctor's been trying to teach Turlough cricket, allegedly "the greatest game in the Universe," but Turlough doesn't understand its appeal (the Doctor cites it as a neat hobby to while away eternity with). Turlough's struggling to come to grips with the rules.

Sir Nikolas Valentine (a.k.a. Carthok of Daodalus): As "Sir Nikolas Valentine," Carthok allegedly won his knighthood by aiding the King in the 1680s. He's renowned as a scholar, landowner, astrologer—and someone who's likely in league with the devil.

In reality, the alien Carthok's a deranged, clever killer who murdered dozens (citing them as "unworthy") and escaped execution years ago, shrouding himself from alien scans. Graced with an extended lifespan, Carthok emerges from hiding on Earth every 30 years to snare fresh victims for his ship's repair systems by using his playing cards and poltergeist field (*See Stuff You Need*).

Hannah Fry: Extraterrestrial dedicated to bringing Sir Valentine to justice for murdering her parents. With London in 1702 relatively sexist, Hannah (her real name's never specified) sometimes disguised herself and used a voice modulator to travel as Major Billy Lovemore, London's most infamous highwayman.

The TARDIS: Can track radio signals.

The Doctor and the TARDIS: The Doctor touts his Ship as a somewhat ordinary time vessel, lusting for the capabilities of a Type 70 TARDIS. Still, he admits he's been through a lot with the TARDIS and obviously has a fondness for it.

STUFF YOU NEED   *Valentine's Playing Cards and Poltergeist:* Valentine's playing cards are actually circuit-laden devices that scan the biodata of anyone who touches them, then downloads the data into the central computer Valentine's spaceship. Once that's been accomplished, the playing cards act as homing beacons to draw forth the collective unconsciousness of Valentine's former victims, as stored within the ship's systems, to attack the card holder. The victims' collective mental power renders itself as stormy phantoms crying for mercy and release, but the effect automatically surrounds the card holder in a telekinetic field and teleports them to Valentine's spaceship. Burning the card (or the abrupt death of the card holder) ruins the psionic lock. Gloves or a simple handkerchief lets people safely hold the cards.

ORGANIZATIONS   *The Diabola Club*, formerly a tall, narrow lodging house, indulges its debaucherous members with drinking, wenching and gambling. It's for boys only, with the fair sex welcome in a not-exactly laudable capacity.

SHIPS   *Valentine's Spaceship* is a bio-mechanical vessel constructed from a great deal of living tissue. The ship was damaged when Valentine crashed on Earth, needing living minds to run the computations needed to restore itself. Valentine accordingly snatched the most intelligent Earthlings he could find to serve as the ship's mental drones. Affixed to Valentine's house, the spaceship sported a number of interior laser defenses.

AT THE END OF THE DAY   A sweetly tight-nit and traditional story, somewhat overrated because it was Big Finish's first single-Doctor audio, not all that complex but excelling for clarity of vision and whimsical characters. "Phantasmagoria" (one of the most-fun "Doctor Who" titles to say aloud—try it) actually achieves a better sci-fi/historical mix than TV's "The Visitation," deliciously marshalling horror elements that include the poltergeist wailing like the tormented souls in Hell and a menacing soundtrack. Simply put, it's a nice choice for Big Finish newcomers and should age well. Go on—enjoy yourself.

IMPERIAL MOON

By Christopher Bulis

Release Date: August 2000
Order: BBC Past Doctor Adventure #34

TARDIS CREW   The fifth Doctor, Turlough and Kamelion.

TRAVEL LOG   The moon, crater basin of Tsiolkovskii, September 5, 1878 and early 21st century; Glen Marg, England, September 5, 1878.

CHRONOLOGY   Between "Resurrection of the Daleks" and "Planet of Fire." [At story's end, Turlough suggests going somewhere warmer, hinting this story leads into "Planet of Fire."]

STORY SUMMARY   A time safe in the TARDIS activates and retroactively gives the Doctor the journal of *Cygnus* spaceship Captain Richard Haliwell. The diary details how an engineer named Professor Bryce-Dennison inexplicably invented a solar-powered impeller drive in 1868 Britain. Immediately capitalizing on Bryce-Dennison's discovery, the British crafted three spaceships, the *Cygnus*, *Draco* and *Lynx*, and landed on the Moon. As such a historical event never took place, the troubled Doctor concludes he must decide which timeline—recorded history or Haliwell's version of events—will survive.

The Doctor and Turlough find Haliwell's expedition oddly exploring an artificial safari park on the moon's surface, complete with an atmosphere and built by unnamed aliens. They also encounter group of friendly, female Phiadoran aliens, who were exiled to die, along with their ruling Princess Nareena, in the moon forest. When an energy barrier prevents the British ships and the TARDIS from leaving, the Doctor euthanizes the park warden—desolate after decades of enforced service—then deactivates the energy barrier.

Unfortunately, the warden's death triggers an autodestruct that threatens to dissipate the alien forest completely. Haliwell loads Nareena's people onto the *Cygnus*, while Turlough and a Phiadoran named Lytalia take shelter in the *Draco* and the Doctor reaches the TARDIS. The *Draco* blasts to freedom, but a Vrall—the most intelligent, invul-

nerable type of park predator—emerges from its hiding place. The *Draco* crew engages the Vrall in combat, but it resists their weapons and butchers everyone save Turlough and helmsman Henry Stanton, intending them to pilot the ship to safety. To Turlough's horror, the rubbery Vrall pulls out Lytalia's skin and slides into it through a slit in the back—proving the creature inhabited her skin from the very beginning. Manic, Stanton escapes and opens the hatch, sucking himself and the Vrall into space. Thankfully, the Doctor rescues Turlough with the TARDIS just as the atmosphere expires, allowing the *Draco* to speed into space.

Based on his observations and the TARDIS databanks, the Doctor concludes the Vrall killed and replaced the exiled, tyrannical Phiadorans years ago. Still restrained by the warden's energy barrier, the Vrall fired RNA spores toward Earth, hoping the technical information encoded within would compel a receptive mind to build spaceships, then travel to the moon and provide a means of escape.

On Earth, Queen Victoria greets emissaries from another world, but the Vrall enter a bloodlust cycle, feasting on the Queen's guardsmen and reproducing through mitosis. Fearing for humanity's survival, the Doctor pilots the TARDIS to the moon citadel's trophy room and recovers weapons that alien safari hunters used to kill the Vrall. Moments after the moon forest dissipates, the Doctor and Turlough return to Earth and use the weapons to atomize every Vrall, saving the Queen.

Convinced the Victorians cannot handle even rudimentary space travel, the Doctor has his robotic shape-shifting companion Kamelion approach the Queen as her dead husband Albert, imploring her to destroy Bryce-Dennison's work. The Queen complies, moved by the "vision," and a grateful Captain Haliwell gives the Doctor his journal for safekeeping. Having safely allowed Haliwell's timeline to continue—but also having preserved recorded history—the Doctor places Haliwell's diary into the time safe and allows Turlough to shelve the "original" journal in the TARDIS library.

MEMORABLE MOMENTS   The Doctor fights against hypothermia and lack of oxygen on the moon's surface, and fashions himself a makeshift sled, racing for the TARDIS. He doesn't make it (Kamelion saves his Gallifreyan ass), but it's a testament to his willpower. In a bloody battle on the *Draco*, Turlough flails about in the dark and brushes against the Vrall's warm, rubbery and inhuman limb (at least, we hope it was his limb).

SEX AND SPIRITS Turlough clearly fancies the Phiadoran Lytalia, but resists the urge to bag her even when she snuggles up to his "sleeping" form. He notes her elfin ears and wonders if she has any other…anatomical differences. He seems a bit unsure of proper etiquette in these situations, possibly suggesting he's a virgin. Unfortunately, Lytalia doesn't fix the problem and reveals herself as a masterful sucker (errr, brain sucker, that is).

At book's start, Kamelion oddly asks Turlough, "Is there any service I can perform for you?" (Our eyebrows almost shot off our heads in surprise.)

ASS-WHUPPINGS The Vrall resort to a favorite method of science fiction butchery—tastily munching the brains of several British soldiers. Turlough and the Doctor retaliate and blast the creatures from existence. The Doctor also relays information to Haliwell's men that lets them blast a particular console and kill the park warden.

Impeller drive inventor Professor Bryce-Dennison dies from a heart attack. The *Draco* crew is variously offed by an emergency crash landing, a jungle expedition involving man-eating plants, fungus that sweats nitroglycerine, venom-loaded insects, a whale-sized behemoth that snares prey with teeth-laden tentacles, a bloody mutiny led by helmsman Henry Stanton, a rampage by several park critters running through the ship and—as if all that weren't enough—a final encounter with the brain-sucking Vrall. Poor saps. If they were on "Star Trek," they'd all be wearing red shirts.

Turlough squashes an android attacker beneath his flying saucer.

TV TIE-INS Bulis oddly states that Turlough doesn't know his homeworld's location or why he's been exiled, but this flatly contradicts "Planet of Fire," so we'd recommend ignoring the suggestion.

The TARDIS translation gift ("The Masque of Mandragora") mostly extends to the Doctor and his companions—nearby Earthlings aren't affected, and here observe the Doctor speaking in an alien tongue to the prison warden.

The Doctor still uses a TARDIS homing device ("The Visitation," etc.). Turlough continually wears his Brendon school uniform because it subconsciously gives him continuity despite some lousy memories of the place.

CHARACTER DEVELOPMENT

The Doctor: His bio-engineered Gallifreyan metabolism and sheer strength of will keep him functioning for a limited time in a frigid airlessness that kills two humans almost instantaneously. In such a hostile environment, regeneration isn't an option (possibly because the Doctor would bite the bullet again, or more likely because the environment inhibits the regeneration process).

The Doctor's familiar with impeller drives and can suspend the TARDIS in the Time Vortex to gain time to plan. He's not familiar with every single Earth scientist who's lived.

Turlough: Turlough's aware of H.G. Wells ("Timelash") and Jules Verne's writings. He isn't telepathic, and learns about the Doctor's companion Leela for the first time. He becomes blood brothers with the manic helmsman Henry Stanton to fight against the Vrall. He knows enough basic trigonometry to serve as an astronavigator.

Kamelion: The often-treacherous robot usually sits motionless in an empty TARDIS room with only a chair for company. Kamelion shares compatible data-stream rhythms with the TARDIS, and can loosely access the Ship's memory banks. He's not telepathic but can increase his empathic circuits to scan for the Doctor and Turlough's location (the Doctor's easier to detect, perhaps due to his Artron energy). Kamelion feels mentally overwhelmed when the safari park animals snuff it. Kamelion wasn't constructed to be happy, but is content when performing assigned tasks.

The energy field protecting the moon safari park severely interfered with Kamelion's systems, but he finally acclimated. Kamelion's got a near-perfect memory. He can alter his pseudometabolic rate to compensate for temperature drops.

Kamelion can morph himself into a giant spider or fly like a bird. He knows how to hook someone up to the TARDIS medical systems.

Turlough and Kamelion: Turlough isn't fond of discussing his problems with Kamelion, but his choices for conversation are somewhat limited in the TARDIS.

The TARDIS: The Ship can override the restraining safari park forcefield, but only by completely draining the Ship's power.

ALIEN RACES

Vrall: Easily the most cunning and ruthless creatures in the alien safari park, they're humanoid and about half a man's weight. Vrall enjoy extremely malleable and near-invulnerable bodies, able to bend like rubber and flatten to about a hand's thickness. Cuts don't bleed and gunshot punctures quickly heal over, so your best bet is to dismember the bastards or toast them with fire.

One suspects a Vrall's body is molded like Play-dough, because they can combine with one another for greater strength. They're quick as hell and camouflage their skin to nearly every color.

Vrall typically have a sickle-shaped head and use a large beak to smash open their enemies' skulls and suck out their gooey brain fat. They can extract mental engrams from creatures they kill, absorbing their technical knowledge, personalities and memories, then passing the information to other Vrall through encoded viruses.

Vrall shy away from bright light, like to snooze off meals and hunt only living prey. They can hollow out their kills, turning their victims into meaty skins with muscles and some internal organs—presumably able to sustain themselves—that the Vrall inhabit like you'd wear a dinner suit.

Disturbingly intelligent and full of guile, Vrall replicate through mitosis, going into a hyper-breeding craze in a plentiful environment.

Phiadorans: Copper-colored humanoids with elfin ears and lustrously dark hair. Phiadorans are long-lived, appearing young at age 50, but they're not telepathic.

STUFF YOU NEED *The TARDIS Time Safe* works as a permissible temporal paradox (if used sparingly) that allows you to retroactively send things to yourself.

PLACES TO GO Located on the moon's surface, the *Phiadoran Safari Park*'s stocked with a tantalizing number of things that'll eat you, such as carnivorous plants armed with hooked thorns, 25-foot-high spiders, a ball of moss that shoots spikes, assault birds and even a hydra (now doesn't that sound like a pleasant weekend, kids?). The park, likely constructed in secret, served to privately indulge Phiador's wealthy.

The park warden was a cross between a sea anemone and a bloated brain, about two-feet-high, red in color and floating in a green liquid tank. It insured the park inhabitants weren't building vehicles to escape. It could defend itself, but was as much a prisoner as anyone else.

PHENOMENA *Parallel Universes:* As a Time Lord, the Doctor sometimes decides which of two parallel timelines will survive. This requires the Doctor to directly involve himself and not just watch from the sidelines. Pre-existing parallel universes are separated only by a millisecond of time and a nanometre of space. At divergence points, one timeline could theoretically overwrite the other entirely.

HISTORY The exclusively female Phiadoran Clan Matriarchy harshly suppressed and dominated

the Phiadoran Directorate systems from 611,072.26 (Galactic Time Index) to 611,548.91 GTI—the equivalent of 10 generations—using genetically engineered pheromone glands to influence males' judgement. A lesser family branch instigated the Sarmon Revolution and finally crushed and dissolved the Directorate, exiling the Phiadoran rulers to die in the safari park on Earth's moon. They lived there for 32 years, getting munched by the Vrall before this story.

• The British government covered up the deaths of British soldiers on the moon by saying a navy ship sunk. The destruction of the alien safari park left only an unusually deep moon crater which the Russian probe Lunik 3 scanned in October 1959. The Russians named the area after Tsiolkovskii, a teacher who wrote a paper on rocket travel.

AT THE END OF THE DAY A surprise win—not revolutionary in the slightest, mind you, but delivering a Jules Verne-type adventure with a good spirit of fun. Bulis' tendency toward passive Doctors works well with Davison. Turlough's nicely thrown into the spotlight and despairs to learn his girlfriend slurps down brains like a strawberry shake (You want fries with that?). And supporting cast member Emily Bryce-Dennison, while barely instrumental to the plot, makes a liberated delight who's shades of Mina Murray from Alan Moore's "League of Extraordinary Gentlemen" comic book. For all that, we'd expect a good percentage of "Doctor Who" readers to scoff at *Imperial Moon*'s methodical approach, but in truth it's one of Bulis' stronger efforts.

TURLOUGH AND THE EARTHLINK DILEMMA

By Tony Attwood

Release Date: July 1986
Order: Companions of Doctor Who #1

MAIN CHARACTERS Turlough, Juras Maateh and the Magician.

TRAVEL LOG Trion, a satellite of Njordr Nerthus, Regel, New Trion, circa 1984; alternate Earth, circa 2034; the space port station of Leege in fourth month, 8033.

CHRONOLOGY For Turlough, some months after "Planet of Fire."

STORY SUMMARY Trion rejoices in the downfall of a female dictator named Rehctaht, offering former political prisoners pardons and allowing Turlough, one of the few surviving Clansmen families who previously ruled Trion, to achieve a hero's welcome. Yet Turlough baffles his colleagues, including his old friend Juras Maateh, by ignoring his newfound fame and gestating suspicious of the Gardsormr—the government's alleged alien allies.

To research the Gardsormr's activities, Turlough pilots his personal shuttle into deep space and discovers Juras aboard as a stowaway. Juras concedes to Turlough that she was conscripted into Rehctaht's scientific core, working on a scheme to unlock the secrets of Universal gravity and achieve time travel. Uneasy with Juras' presence, Turlough innovates on his TARDIS knowledge to craft a time-travelling ARTEMIS drive. Aided by a Time Lord known as the Magician, who's mostly onhand to observe Turlough's activities, Turlough and Juras continue tracking the Gardsormr.

Suddenly, a Gardsormr vessel renders Turlough's party unconscious and inexplicably deposits them on New Trion, a colony world torn by civil conflict. Turlough locates the Mobile Castle, an alien edifice that simultaneously exists on Trion, and considers it motivation to equip the castle with an ARTEMIS drive. After tricking the colonists into boarding the Mobile Castle, Turlough pilots it into space and heads for Trion. However, sabotage to the Mobile Castle's drive systems causes it to hurtle toward Trion, forcing Turlough to escape with the Magician and Juras in his ARTEMIS shuttle as the Castle crashes and detonates, destroying Trion.

Reeling, Turlough's group learns Earth and New Trion have similarly perished in unexplained nuclear conflicts, with the Gardsormr benevolently constructing domes on each planet to house radiation-absorbing slugs and thereby re-fertilize the soil. Turlough encounters the Gardsormr's commander—an older version of himself from an alternate timeline—who reveals the Gardsormr originated as a group of Trions nefariously working to overthrow Rehctaht's regime. The older Turlough warns that Rehctaht, missing since her political downfall, secretly caused the nuclear destruction of Earth, Trion and New Trion to further her gravity control experiments, hopefully gaining supreme power through time travel.

As his older self departs, Turlough realizes Rehctaht downloaded her personality into secret corners of Juras' brain, periodically awakening in response to various stimuli. With the real Juras dead, and fearing Rehctaht will use Turlough's technology for personal gain, the Magician con-

THE CRUCIAL BITS...

- **TURLOUGH AND THE EARTHLINK DILEMMA**—Turlough's homeworld of Trion gives him a hero's welcome. To stop the dictator Rehctaht's schemes, Turlough alters history to erase the destruction of Earth, Trion and New Trion. Unable to return home for fear of a temporal paradox, Turlough replaces a dead version of himself in an alternate timeline.

vinces Turlough to kill her. Anguished, Turlough proposes saving Earth, Trion and New Trion by altering history.

Using the ARTEMIS drive, Turlough travels back to Rehctaht's regime and teases the dictator with the ARTEMIS drive, plotting to kill her. A skittish Rehctaht, however, grows impressed enough to possess Turlough and downloads her personality into his body. Thankfully, the Magician arrives immediately following Rehctaht's transfer and strands Turlough/Rehctaht in a stone canyon, creating an inescapable mental conundrum that allows a raving Turlough to expel Rehctaht's mental engrams from his brain.

With Rehctaht dead and unable to further her master plan, history rewrites itself and restores Earth, Trion and New Trion. But the Magician advises that Turlough, having instigated the change to history, can't return to his original timeline without creating a temporal paradox. Using his TARDIS, the Magician takes Turlough to yet another timeline where he fell into a canyon while resisting Rehctaht's mental possession, killing both of them. Reunited with the Juras from that reality, Turlough takes his dead self's place in the alternate timeline and prepares for a new life.

MEMORABLE MOMENTS A weary Turlough, downed by the nuclear ravaging of Trion and New Trion, realizes he's living in a galaxy he doesn't want to know. His murder of Rehctaht (the first time) proves savage, but keeps with his newly independent character. Trion's destruction, pulverized by the Mobile Castle, deserves to be rendered with CGI.

ASS-WHUPPINGS On the Magician's suggestion, Turlough kills the mind of Rehctaht in Juras' body by battering her against a wall and snapping her spine or neck. Thanks to the miraculous ARTEMIS drive, he kills Rehctaht again and alters the timeline. In another possible future, Turlough sees his own splattered body.

It an alternate timeline, Earth, Trion and New Trion all eat a nuclear warhead bullet.

SEX AND SPIRITS During their Trion days, Turlough and Juras were likely just solid friends (if there was something romantic, it's dramatically underplayed here). Still, Turlough finds her strikingly beautiful. It's understated, but he likely shacks up with her at novel's end.

TV TIE-INS Turlough attended Brendon ("Mawdryn Undead") in year 17,883 of the Trion calendar, and left electronotes on the Gardsormr there. Turlough spent "years" travelling with the Doctor, suggesting multiple stories between "Resurrection of the Daleks" and "Planet of Fire." Turlough's brother Malcolm (also "Planet of Fire") goes unmentioned.

CHARACTER DEVELOPMENT

Vislor Turlough: Turlough's a very public figure, one of the few Clansmen who resisted Rehctaht and survived. He's respected and could likely win any election, even to Trion's Congress or Parliament. He inherently believes in the Clans' goodwill, openness and right to rule.

Turlough gained immeasurable knowledge of time travel by studying the TARDIS' temporal control mechanisms (he evoked new principles in constructing the ARTEMIS drive). Yet, he never explored the TARDIS interior much.

He's greatly advanced in the fields of physics and quantum mechanics. He's got a near-perfect memory. The planet Regel awed him as a youngster. He hasn't visited the Museum of Natural History at Efnisien for eight years. Five years ago, Turlough visited Regal, the most developed civilization in its sector.

Older Turlough: Turlough's alternate, older self has fair, long hair and recalls meeting himself. He cautions that Turlough has too much faith in his Time Lord friends, and greatly aided (possibly retroactively, and won't the Time Lords be joyful to find out) the Gardsormr against Rehctaht.

Juras Maateh: Young, about the same age as Turlough, with long dark hair. She's a brilliant engineer, but was more cautious about making anti-Rehctaht statements. Juras hails from Valerange, in Norring, on Trion, and reported directly to Rehctaht concerning gravity theory research.

Turlough and Juras: Attended school on Trion together until departing for different institutes (Turlough favored astro-physics, Juras studied engineering). Both of them read *Ships of the Line* and had six months primary logic at first grade school.

MISCELLANEOUS STUFF!

THAT PESKY BLUE-GREEN PLANET

Why is Earth so overrun with aliens every five minutes? Well, now we know (although every other "Who" book happily ignores it).

The Laima, Trion's earliest species and possibly alien settlers, cracked the secret of Ultimate Unified Theory (the means to travel through time and alternate realities) by realizing that the Universe's gravity constant was diminishing and impeding inter-dimensional travel. To counter the effect, the Laima set up a gravity generator on pre-historic Earth to stabilize the Universe's gravity (this event probably pre-dates Scaroth's explosion, "City of Death," in four million BC). A few of their number, the Slots, stayed to monitor the device while the Laima themselves traveled to a new and better Universe. In time, the Slots forgot about the gravity generator, but continued communicating with the departed Laima. Still later, the Clans emerged and named Trion to symbolize the planet's three civilizations—Laima, Slots and Clansfolk.

On Earth, the Laima's gravitational generator inadvertently drew attention from the Time Lords and other higher powers, all of them eager to know why the laws of physics operated differently near Earth. (Fun as that is, we prefer the theory that Earthlings are hip, suave and always know the location of their towel.)

The Magician (a.k.a. Pagad, Magus): The Magician knew Turlough and Juras would write a great deal of Trion's history. Sent to observe, the Magician aids Turlough (another item that'll surely make the Time Lords turn cartwheels). He sutured the time anomaly with the Mobile Castle (securing its simultaneous appearance on Trion and New Trion) and says he'll meet Turlough again.

The Doctor's TARDIS: Turlough never deduced the dimensional stabilizers' workings because they desperately needed repair. He also never got near the TARDIS' power source or figured out how the Chameleon Circuit worked. By using the Time Vortex for transit, the in-flight TARDIS ignored gravity. Turlough speculated that the TARDIS used cold fusion to create particles called "muons" and thereby travel in time (virtually no other "Who" work supports his theory).

This book is not endorsed by the BBC. Doctor Who and TARDIS are trademarks of the BBC.

65

The Magician's TARDIS: Its control room resembles the one in the Doctor's TARDIS, but it's crowded with chairs. This Ship can disguise itself as undergrowth.

ALIEN RACES *The Time Lords:* Trion formally acknowledges Gallifreyan culture, but the Time Lords rarely visit. They're likely monitoring Trion's time experiments. For millennia, Gallifrey's based its technology on the revelation that gravity affects all temporal manipulation. Time Lords require sleep. They're interested in Earth as a region where gravity's natural laws are twisted (unknowingly thanks to the Laima gravity generator). Turlough suspects regeneration helps protect Time Lords from violating the laws of time, making it safer for different incarnations to encounter one another.

ALIEN PLANETS *Trion:* Enjoyed an open and non-insular culture before Rehctaht's regime.

PLACES TO GO *Turlough's House:* Turlough's pre-exile dwelling lies in forests on Trion at 50 degrees North latitude, in the heart of Clan territory. The area luckily gets cool summers and fresh winters.

ORGANIZATIONS
Imperial Clans of Total Science Knowledge (a.k.a. Clans of Total Science Knowledge, The Clans): Originally domineering, the science-minded Clans learned to freely distribute all knowledge, innovation and discovery. They're not overtly warlike, but their research sometimes has military implications.

Gardsormr: Anti-Rehctaht organization that probably took its name from Earth legends of the Migardsormr—the serpent of the world.

SHIPS
ARTEMIS I (Artificial Rotation Through Energetic Muons In Series): Time-travel drive that uses particles called "muons" to create artificial gravity from artificial rotation. Turlough created the first one.

ARTEMIS II (Artificial Relativity Through Entropy Mechanisms In Sequence): A modified entropy-powered ship only dreamt of by the Time Lords.

PHENOMENA
Time Travel: You can't view stuff as you time travel, which explains why the TARDIS viewer's always closed during flight.

The Universe: At its core, the Universe is bound by strong nuclear, electro-magnetic and gravitational forces. If you unravel each one, you essentially know how the Universe works. Gravity proves the most troublesome (the Trion Clans never cracked it), partly because of the gravity generator on Earth keeping the Universe's gravity the same when it should be diminishing.

Alternate Timelines: All possible pasts and futures exist, because all particles simultaneously exist in multiple wave patterns.

ALTERNATE HISTORY Rehctaht triggered nuclear conflict on Earth by pulling an enormous meteor toward the planet during a politically charged period. Each side thought the other was launching missiles, blasting the meteor into the Atlantic but dicing the planet in a crossfire. Efforts by the Gardsormr restored the planet's fertility in two years, leaving a colony of 1,000 people in the ex-United Kingdom, renamed Eden.

HISTORY The Clans ruled Trion and its colonies for 9,000 years, crafting a harsh regime driven to create science and technology. In time, Clan civil atrocities decreased. The Trion Empire expanded, with the invention of a vacuum transport system that revolutionized travel overnight. Non-Clansmen adapted cold fusion to make more efficient space ships. Trion never achieved time travel, probably because the Time Lords ruined their experiments.
• Rehctaht, the most tyrannical and unforgiving ruler in Trion history, rose to power by promising liberty from Clan supremacy. She ruled for seven years and virtually extinguished the Clansmen. Trion's economy suffered until the Committee of Public Safety marshaled against her.
• Rehctaht initially formed New Trion as a slave labor source, but her inattention led to settlements in the West warring with those in the North. New Trion functioned independently (if sloppily) from the main Trion government.

AT THE END OF THE DAY An over-reliance on scientific concepts (our heads spun like peaches in a blender) makes this book massive and about as approachable as a mugger—not to mention that it sports a dippy title. But surprisingly enough, *Turlough and the Earthlink Dilemma* undeservedly gets a bad rap on a very key area—it bravely evolves Turlough into one of the Universe's most dangerous men. That's fairly remarkable, not to mention that *some* of its scientific ideas are clever—it's just that they run at odds to each other and lay jagged on the table like a bunch of peanut brittle. With some streamlining, this could be a striking science-fiction book, but it's too woeful as a "Doctor Who" story, even with Turlough's elevation of character, to please many.

RED DAWN

By Justin Richards

Release Date: May 2000
Order: Big Finish "Doctor Who: Audio #8"

TARDIS CREW The fifth Doctor and Peri.

TRAVEL LOG Mars, June 4, circa 2007.

CHRONOLOGY Between "Planet of Fire" and "The Caves of Androzani."

STORY SUMMARY The arms making Webster Corporation provides funding for an expedition to Mars, but stipulates the crew must include founder Leo Webster's son Paul and niece Tanya. NASA agrees and allows the Webster crew, commanded by Lee Forbes, to pilot the *Ares One* into Mars orbit and land on the Red Planet in the *Argosy* shuttle. Simultaneously, the Doctor and Peri arrive on the Martian surface inside the tomb of Izdal—a heroic Martian Lord who died while ordering his people to evacuate their dying homeworld. Martian sensors, designed to scan beings for the capacity of honor and integrity, deem the Doctor suitably noble and open the tomb doors. Commander Forbes' group ventures inside the opened tomb and grows perplexed by the presence of the Doctor and Peri. However, Forbes worries about what evidence of extra-terrestrials on Mars could mean to Earth society and cuts off communications, allowing a chilled Peri to retrieve a warm survival suit from the *Argosy*.

Meanwhile, the Martian sensors further trigger a heating mechanism that revives the Ice Warriors who guard Izdal's tomb. Their commander, Lord Zzaal, believes the Earth people have good intentions and orders Sstast, his second-in-command to collect the other humans from the *Argosy*. But Paul Webster unexpectedly knocks Sstast out, revealing to Peri and Tanya that Webster Corporation has experimented to merge human cells with Martian DNA recovered by space probes. Paul believes that once Webster Corp. dissects the captive Sstast, it will learn how to clone armies of human soldiers augmented with Martian DNA.

Paul makes a break for Earth, but Zzaal fires a missile that wounds the *Argosy* and brings it back down to Mars. Cornered in Izdal's burial chamber,

Paul threatens to blow up Izdal's hallowed remains if he's not freed. With the Doctor and Tanya held hostage, Paul runs for freedom in a Martian sonic tank, but a failsafe device halts the tank's engines. By maneuvering the tank's still-active gun turret, Paul threatens to destroy Izdal's tomb while Zzaal orders Sstast to stand down, having previously promised to not harm the Doctor.

To end the stalemate, Zzaal offers to exchange himself for the Doctor and Tanya, meticulously ordering his Ice Warriors not to take action that would threaten his life. Desiring to take a live Ice Warrior back to Earth, Paul agrees to Zzaal's terms. Zzaal surrenders himself to Paul on the plains of Mars, but requests to see Mars' sunrise one last time and Paul agrees. As Zzaal intended, the sun's ultraviolet rays saturate Mars' rarified atmosphere with deadly radiation. Just as Izdal sacrificed himself to the Red Dawn—proving that his people must evacuate Mars—a charred Zzaal warns the Doctor to flee and quickly dies.

No longer bound from acting, Sstast unleashes a sonic torpedo that kills Paul while the Doctor and Tanya reach cover. To honor Zzaal's goal of peace with Earth, Sstast allows Forbes to return home while Tanya stays behind as Earth's first ambassador to the Martians. Their work complete, the Doctor and Peri slip away in the TARDIS.

MEMORABLE MOMENTS The Doctor crafts a sonic device that immobilizes the Ice Warriors, then willingly relinquishes it to establish trust. Zzaal reciprocates by returning the device to Commander Forbes. Paul Webster takes a great amount of cold glee at pressing a Martian sonic pistol against the Doctor's head at the end of Part Three. Lord Zzaal's sacrifice glows as one of the Big Finish line's most dramatic moments.

ASS-WHUPPINGS "Red Dawn" toasts a fair amount of Ice Warriors—the *Argosy* take-off incinerates Zizmar and Sskaan while the sonic tank's engines also torch warrior Razzbur (Martian soup, anyone?). Lord Zzaal sacrifices himself to the Red Dawn, allowing Sstast to blow up Paul Webster.

TV TIE-INS The Ice Warriors debuted in the creatively named "Ice Warriors," where the second Doctor used a sonic cannon against the Ice Warriors (the sound vibrations rattle around in their armor). The fifth Doctor similarly here rigs a communicator to emit frequencies that stun the Ice Warriors. Commander Forbes is likely the first man on the Red Planet since the botched Mars Probe mission in "The Ambassadors of Death."

NOVEL TIE-INS *The Dying Days* established that Mars' atmosphere can support human life and chronicled mankind's first official extraterrestrial contact. *GodEngine* detailed Mars' history and customs while the Benny NA *Beige Planet Mars* shows the planet as a human colony. *Decalog 2*: "Crimson Dawn" shows how the Martians tried to flee their homeworld in an artificial planetoid, but accidentally went into suspended animation. Their planetoid became the Martian moon of Phobos, but the fourth Doctor revived the sleeping Martians and sent them on their way.

CHARACTER DEVELOPMENT

The Doctor: The Doctor easily tolerates the chill of Martian buildings (which are too cold for humans), but not the –80 Fahrenheit temperatures of the Martian surface. He's a believer in free will and doesn't like to be led through life. He's aware of the Brookings Report (*See History*).

Perpugilliam Brown: Peri thinks Nebraska's smelly, cold and green (we can't argue). She had a pen friend in Denver but found it distasteful.

Lord Zzaal: Commander of Izdal's personal guard and staunch advocate of his noble philosophies. Lord Zzaal's ruthless in battle but holds his honor and that of his warriors above personal safety. Primarily a warrior, Zzaal can use guile and cunning but feels a warrior's code that allows for diplomacy, pragmatism, mercy and forgiveness. He believes Earth's incompatible with Martian life and favors treaties and trade agreements instead of outright invasion. Zzaal often gives potential enemies the benefit of the doubt, feeling that to mistrust their word without reason would lessen his own nobility. He died with honor.

Lord Zzaal and Izdal: When Zzaal was young, Izdal conferred on him the Ceremony of Zantana (*See Stuff You Need*), making him a Martian lord.

Tanya Webster: Publicly, 17-year-old Tanya's the niece of Webster Corporation head Leo Webster and works as a geologist with Webster Corp's oil exploration group. Secretly, Tanya's part of an experiment to combine human cells with Martian DNA recovered by Earth space probes. As such, Tanya's Martian inheritance gives her an innate knowledge of Martian history and the ability to work Martian technology.

Paul Webster: Leo Webster's son and head of Webster Corporation's defense division.

The TARDIS: The Ship's sterometer's still unreliable, meaning the Doctor can pinpoint arrival locations only within a few thousand light years (but that's hardly a change).

ALIEN RACES *Ice Warriors* grow sluggish in an oxygen-rich atmosphere (they're acclimated to Mars' nitrogen-heavy air). Their personal sonic cannons, strapped to their wrists, contain trigger mechanisms under the main assembly. The Ice Warriors use tracer devices. Their medical knowledge isn't much help in treating humans.

ALIEN PLANETS *Mars* has a nitrogen-rich oxygen atmosphere that supports human life. Its gravity is about 1/3 that of Earth. Nitrous oxide makes the surface reek. Temperatures range from about –100 Fahrenheit (Martians could only tolerate such temperatures for a few days) to –20 at mid-day. The planet lacks the water needed to revive it. Mars' Olympus Mons is the largest volcano known to man.

PLACES TO GO *The Tomb of Izdal* has the grandeur of a church, with a florescent chemical in the walls providing light. From the outside, it looks like a giant green shell. The tomb's locking device scans those who approach and grants access for those with honor and good will.

The tomb contains a medical center, a weapons center and many traps to defend against hostile intruders. The Hall of Memories contains statues and weapons, plus a wall mural depicting the building of the monument.

STUFF YOU NEED

The Red Dawn: Symbolic name for the lethal effect of the sun's ultraviolet rays tearing through Mars' thin atmosphere.

Martian Ceremony of Zantana: The greatest honor a Martian warrior can receive, involving the use of a ceremonial sword and upgrading him in rank to a Martian lord. The Doctor knows of this custom.

ORGANIZATIONS

NASA: The top American space organization's nearly broke and agreed to entrepreneur Leo Webster's terms in exchange for his money. Mission control's still run out of Houston.

Webster Corporation: Another corporation that seems intent on commercially dominating the world (a la Starbucks, etc.), with product branches that include pharmaceuticals, investment banking and computer software.

HISTORY The Martians resisted abandoning their homeworld when Mars' climate became increasingly lethal, but Lord Izdal predicted that his people must leave Mars to survive. Izdal gave himself up to the Red Dawn—allowing the searing radiation of the Martian sunrise to kill him—as proof of the desperate situation. Izdal became martyred as the most heroic Martian and the populace, save for Izdal's personal guard, left Mars when man was still primitive.

• After NASA's creation in 1958, the United States government commissioned the independent Brookings Institute, based in Washington, to set NASA's policy and procedures. Brookings recommended that NASA make its information public, except in the instance of NASA astronauts finding proof (alien buildings, artifacts, etc.) of the existence of extraterrestrial life. Brookings noted historical instances where civilizations had fallen by coming into contact with advanced societies, and worried that disclosure of advanced alien life could degenerate human society. A short chapter beginning on page 215 of the Brookings Report details "Implications of a Discovery of Extra-Terrestrial Life," ordering mission commanders to quell public knowledge of such a find. The U.S. House Committee of Science and Aeronautics ratified the Brookings Report on April 18, 1961. (Side Note: Lest you think Richards invented it, the Brookings Report is historical fact.)

• Circa 1977, the Mars Probe missions ("The Ambassadors of Death") contacted aliens visiting Mars and prompted a response by UNIT. Circa 1989, Earth landers brought back Martian samples. Webster Corp. immediately instigated attempts to combine human and Martian DNA.

AT THE END OF THE DAY It's got an outstanding ending (we shed a collective tear the first time we heard Zzaal die), but "Red Dawn" weights itself down with too much space opera and consequently doesn't get off the ground. It gets points for the layered character of Lord Zzaal and his friendship with the Doctor, but Paul Webster's tepid as a villain and a blatant effort to give Peri a better part still relegates her to the status of bystander. Part Three in particular stretches out too long—with an overdrawn scramble to save a crashing ship that we can't see—and while we'd hardly call "Red Dawn" bad, it lags as being the lesser among a number of outstanding audios.

WHISPERS OF TERROR

By Justin Richards

Release Date: November 1999
Order: Big Finish "Doctor Who" Audio #3

TARDIS CREW The sixth Doctor and Peri.

TRAVEL LOG Museum of Aural Antiquities, likely Earth and sometime in the future.

CHRONOLOGY Between "Revelation of the Daleks" and "Trial of a Time Lord."

STORY SUMMARY On a planet that's possibly Earth, a political race in an unspecified country takes an unfortunate turn when actor-turned-politician Vistine Krane—the leading candidate for president—apparently commits suicide. The self-offing takes place in a sound booth at the Museum of Aural Antiquities, a repository and academic outlet for all things audio-based. Days later, two spies named Amber Dent and Goff Fotherill break into the Museum on behalf of Krane's political partner Beth Pernell, seeking to replace some of Krane's unbroadcast speeches with tailored copies endorsing Pernell for the presidency. The spies succeed, but as Dent flees, spectral whispering voices trick Fotherill into electrifying himself.

Moments later, the TARDIS lands in the Museum, causing the Doctor and Peri to discover Fotherill's body. Museum Curator Gantman, convinced of the Doctor and Peri's goodwill, allows the Doctor to assist with the crime's investigation. Soon after, the Doctor realizes that the late Vistine Krane, at the moment of his "death," used the sound booth's equipment to transfer his brainwaves into the sound medium—creating the "whispering voices" that plague the Museum. As such, Krane exists as a creature of pure sound, reasonably demented from his transformation and capable of morphing himself into any noise.

The Doctor grimly realizes that the mad Krane-creature plans to insert itself into the scheduled broadcast of his last recorded speech, endlessly replicating its signal into millions of households and seizing control of the planet. Just in time, Curator Gantman halts the Krane-creature by transmitting a canceling wave, muting the broadcast and jolting the Krane-creature back to sanity.

While the Museum's studio covers up for the broadcast interruption, the Doctor confronts Pernell, forcing her to admit that she ordered her right-hand man Stengard to murder Krane, there-

This book is not endorsed by the BBC. Doctor Who and TARDIS are trademarks of the BBC.

69

by preventing him from denouncing her zealous political philosophy. As Pernell vows to continue her power-mad agenda, the Krane-creature broadcasts Krane's "last" speech, re-tailoring it so the public hears Krane condemning Pernell's ambitions. Worse for Pernell, the creature transmits a doctored sound file of Krane murder—identifying her as the killer.

With millions of homes aware of her "confession," Pernell hurriedly departs from the Museum. Newly stabilized, the Krane-creature agrees to join the Museum staff and aid Creator Gantman with his various research endeavors. Vowing to return some day, the Doctor and Peri slip away in the TARDIS. But as a fleeing Pernell drives away, a pre-recorded message from the Krane-creature audibly shocks her into driving off the road, slaying her when her car explodes.

MEMORABLE MOMENTS In the TARDIS' console room, the Doctor insists that for once, he knows "where they are." When a disbelieving Peri questions him, the Doctor stresses, "We're in the TARDIS." Schizophrenic voices surreally scream, "Tell me who I am!" at the end of Part One. The Doctor verbally taunts Pernell by declaring, "You seem to have all the right qualities for a politician." Peri's words echo our thoughts: "The Doctor's clothes are too loud for this museum."

ASS-WHUPPINGS "Whispers of Terror" features an array of electrocutions, stabbings and shootings that'd make Alfred Hitchcock proud. Pernell's handyman Stengard blows a hole through Krane's head, but—as we now know—Krane survives. The loopy Krane-creature tricks the spying Fotherill into electrocuting himself. Stengard knifes Fotherill's fellow spy Amber Dent to insure her silence. Later, the Krane-creature gets his revenge by fooling Stengard into grabbing a live cable, which turns him into one crispy critter.

Pernell captures the Krane-creature on disc and interrogates it by using a crude editor to randomly dice out bits of its being—the first instance in all of "Doctor Who," to our knowledge, of a noise being tormented.

TV TIE-INS The Doctor still carries a device that detects electricity ("Tomb of the Cybermen").

NOVEL TIE-INS The "late" Vistine Krane's speeches include a recitation of the "candle flame" speech from the end of *The Good Soldiers*—a play by Stanoff Osterling (Richards' *Theatre of War*). Krane's speech includes the phrase "dreams of empire," undoubtedly a nod toward Richards' *Dreams of Empire*.

CHARACTER DEVELOPMENT

The Doctor: The Doctor declares, while shouting, that he never shouts. He's a bit hypocritical for stating he doesn't like things loud and bombastic. He's always wanted a triple sonic bypass sub-system (whatever the hell that is). A run through the Museum convinces him to get some exercise. He promises to return to the Museum in a few years.

Curator Gantman: Accommodating head of the Museum of Aural Antiquities. Gantman is blind, but his hearing has sharpened as a result.

Beth Pernell: Krane's acting agent and political partner. She secretly believes democracy's an outdated system that poorly disperses power—in short, a morally justified way of doing nothing.

Vistine Krane: Widely acclaimed as the greatest actor of his age despite his dislike of visual media—Krane didn't appear on video or celluloid, and only a few photographs of him exist. He practically lived in his sound suite, which was donated to the Museum of Aural Antiquities after Krane's "death." Whether it was propaganda or not, Krane's speeches advocated that no single man was greater than his policies.

The Krane Sound Creature: Moments before his assassination, Krane used a (take a deep breath) "frequency modulation input linked to an alpha wave condenser" to modulate his brainwaves, transforming him into a sentient creature composed entirely of sound. As such, the Krane-creature can duplicate any sound, including whistling and voices. It can hide in sounds as quiet as a tapping foot or a slow-moving fan blade. It can also travel through other sounds, escaping through the tiniest crack or the thickest wall—any medium that carries sound. The Museum's soundproofing, when activated, can restrain the creature.

Like any other sound, the Krane creature can be trapped on a CD or audio storage unit. You can even strike copies, but we don't recommend it.

PLACES TO GO If it's audio, it'll be found in the *Museum of Aural Antiquities*, a facility that stores recordings of everything from interrogations to public speeches to surveillance data. The Museum's work obviously has political ramifications, as the government's Security Service keeps its own archive in the building. The Museum can be completely soundproofed from external communications and noises. Automated systems constantly index and cross-reference the audio files.

AT THE END OF THE DAY Damnably clever, worthy of consumption on gusty winter evenings. As the third Big Finish audio, "Whispers of Terror" pushes the newborn line's format with a story grounded in audio (the Krane creature impersonates so many characters, you won't know who's real). Some commentators argue this tale over-replicates TV's maligned Season 22, but "Whispers" thankfully differs by lovingly including a mass of cutthroat violence *without* funneling it through the Doctor. As much as fans raved about the preceding "Phantasmagoria," trust us—this is the better story.

GRAVE MATTER

By Justin Richards

Release Date: May 2000
Order: BBC Past Doctor Adventure #31

TARDIS CREW The sixth Doctor and Peri

TRAVEL LOG Dorsill island chain, Earth, modern times.

CHRONOLOGY Immediately after "Vengeance on Varos."

STORY SUMMARY Arriving on the remote islands of Dorsill, the Doctor and Peri attempt to learn their exact location and recalibrate the TARDIS' newly repaired circuits. However, the Doctor grows suspicious of a cover-up involving three villagers killed in a boating accident. Perhaps stranger, the Doctor teaches a card trick to one of the island's children and grows stunned when *all* the children and their teacher instantly know how to perform the trick.

The Doctor and Peri catch retired civil servant Sir Edward Baddesley in the act of digging up one of the killed islanders and fear for their lives when the corpse comes to life and lurches off into the darkness. Sir Edward admits to being Sir Anthony Kelso, a retired Ministry of Science member who learned the government secretly purchased Dorsill under the name of island native Christopher Sheldon. By comparing notes, the Doctor's group realizes the government bought Dorsill as a testing ground for an alien virus recovered by the Gatherer Three deep space probe. Formed to see how the virus' DNA interacted with animals, the project hoped to discover how the virus' healing abilities could eliminate all disease in humans.

Unfortunately, the alien material, dubbed "Denarian" (a play on the word "DNA"), is actually part of a collective consciousness. Over time, it infected the entire island to insure its survival, linking the islanders in a subconscious gestalt. As such, the survival-driven Denarian repairs all physical injuries and animates corpses, but dominates the mind—meaning humanity could end up as the Denarian's undead slaves.

The Doctor's group tries to warn islander Logan Packwood, actually a project geneticist, but finds him under the Denarian's control as the villagers fully succumb to the alien virus' sway. The Denarian also possesses Peri, infected through a glass of tainted milk, but the Doctor's Gallifreyan body allows him to resist the disease and feverishly work to find a cure.

The Doctor quickly concocts a hybrid Denarian virus that regards its predecessor as an infection and cancels it out. By dousing his friends with the Denarian hybrid, the Doctor cures them. Using a helicopter, the Doctor then sprays the island with a contact solution of the Denarian counter-virus, which seeps into the food chain and destroys the Denarian's control. Life on the islands slowly return to normal and the Doctor and Peri, believing the threat ended, depart in the TARDIS. But unknown to them, two infected seagulls—the last remnants of the Denarian infection—stealthily fly toward the mainland.

MEMORABLE MOMENTS The Doctor demonstration of a card trick to a school child—and the revelation that all of the kid's classmates instantly learn the trick—makes one dramatically take pause and note there's something afoot on Dorsill.

As the Doctor examines islander Bill Neville's corpse, he spots two puncture marks by the neck and Peri suggests vampires. The Doctor pauses, then adds that there are dozens of more plausible explanations, to which Peri nervously replies, "Oh, that's good." Soon after, the Doctor tries to secure Neville's undead, struggling corpse in its coffin and remarks, "I think maybe we should have brought some nails."

There's a sweet little story of a headless, undead chicken running about and needing to be hacked up. Peri remarks at one point, "I used to want to change the world. Now we just save it." The Doctor's wrath against the Ministry experiments, with the Dorsill residents paying the price, proves how effectively the sixth Doctor argues for justice.

To cure a Denarian-infected Peri, the Doctor grabs her legs and tips her headlong into a vat of anti-Denarian solution.

SEX AND SPIRITS The Doctor downs two pints of Fisherman's Ruin, making sure Peri's given a glass of water. Peri snitches a half-pint but finds

it bitter and syrupy. The Doctor later spills beer on himself and leaps about, distracting bar patrons while Peri quietly exits.

ASS-WHUPPINGS With *Grave Matter*'s undead characters, you're never truly sure when an ass is fully whupped. Island medic Dave Madsen, wracked with guilt over infecting the Dorsill residents, fails to commit suicide with sleeping drugs. He next blows the back of his head off with a shotgun, making himself brain dead, but gets up and walks away. Peri (you go, girl!) sends him to the great beyond with a flare gun.

The Doctor throws an oil lamp at an undead islander and crisps him. He also shoots a zombie twice in the book's final confrontation. Geneticist Logan Packwood fatally blasts himself with X rays to kill the Denarian within him. Peri, desperate to escape infected birds, pretends to be Leela for a moment, plunging through a window and hitting the ground hard.

TV TIE-INS The Doctor here recalibrates the TARDIS' control systems after installing its new supply of Zeiton-Seven ("Vengeance on Varos").

NOVEL TIE-INS The Doctor can metabolize alcohol if he wants, settling conflicting arguments about whether he can get drunk (Transit shows the seventh Doctor boozing, but *Alien Bodies* argues Time Lords can't get drunk). *The Quantum Archangel* agrees with *Grave Matter*'s assertion that the Doctor can/can't get drunk at will. As if that weren't enough, the Doctor will get liquored up in the upcoming *Drift*.

The Doctor also quietly remarks that he doesn't have much experience with children, perhaps referring to his offspring mentioned in *Cold Fusion*.

CHARACTER DEVELOPMENT

The Doctor: Remembers what it's like—undoubtedly based on his first incarnation—to be old and unappreciated. He knows some card tricks, including how to cut aces to the top. The Doctor's metabolism rejects the Denarian almost immediately. He likes Earl Grey tea and can pilot a helicopter. He refers to his physique as "statuesque and well-toned."

Perpugilliam Brown: When Peri was 7, her Auntie Janice died from a long illness. Peri has brown eyes and isn't an expert on children. Hailing from 1983, Peri doesn't know how to work a cell phone.

The TARDIS: Travelling through the Time Vortex washes sticky liquids off the TARDIS.

ALIEN RACES *Denarian* behave like interconnected alien DNA parasite, bound through a core consciousness and an overriding mandate to heal its host bodies for the sake of its own survival. Unfortunately, the Denarian doesn't recognize when its host has died, healing the body to the point that it can walk as a mindless corpse.

In its first generation on Earth, the Denarian infected Ministry geneticist Christopher Sheldon, using him as an incubator and to hatch the Ministry scheme on Dorsill. Geneticist Logan Packwood incubated the secondary Denarian generation, while the third generation encompassed the inhabitants and eco-system of Dorsill.

Infected hosts experience a grace period while the Denarian incubates. They maintain independent thought, but are subconsciously linked through the collective Denarian gestalt that allows for group learning (i.e., what one host learns, they all learn). The process continues until the Denarian supercedes the host's speech, mentally trapping them in their own bodies before the Denarian assumes total control.

The Gatherer Three space probe recovered the Denarian from a region of space devoid of X-ray emissions. As such, X rays can weaken the Denarian's control, but a dose large enough to slay the Denarian also kills the host. Fire hinders the Denarian's ability to heal its hosts.

The Denarian sadly lacks a sense of sarcasm or irony. Hosts that haven't fully succumbed to the Denarian can communicate their thoughts by lying, as the Denarian only seems smart enough to block statements of truth.

PLACES TO GO *The Dorsill Islands* encompass an entire chain, but there's only two land masses of note: Dorsill and Sheldon's Folly. Mist, fog and rain make the islands very hard to navigate.

Dorsill residents do without electricity, gas mains and petrol stations, partly because of the cost, and partly because they naturally shun such things. However, they keep some sophisticated communications equipment for emergencies and use modern drugs and medicine, although the island lacks a chemist. Gas cylinders power the street lights, while some of the larger houses install modern generators.

ORGANIZATIONS *Ministry of Science Denarian Project:* Geneticist Christopher Sheldon, a native of Dorsill, served as a genetic researcher on the Denarian Project, but became infected and spread the infection to the other members. Sir Anthony Kelso was Sheldon's superior.

Kelso protested the Denarian's possible applications and was offered early retirement. Under the Denarian-controlled Sheldon's recommendation, the Ministry bought Dorsill in Sheldon's name and instigated the Denarian project.

AT THE END OF THE DAY Sweetly macabre and a story that keeps your attention, deploying a lot of horror while keeping the edgy sixth Doctor likeable. *Grave Matter* deals with the biological ethics while focusing on its characters—notably the lives of the Dorsill residents—achieving such a homespun fusion that makes you forget in parts that you're reading science fiction. Overall, a book that's good for both newcomers and "Doctor Who" veterans, trumped mostly by stronger "walking corpse" novels such as (ironically) Richards' own *The Banquo Legacy*.

SLIPBACK

By Eric Seward

Original Broadcast Dates (BBC Radio Four Adventure): July 25, August 8 and August 22, 1985.
Release Date (CD): January 2001.

TARDIS CREW The sixth Doctor and Peri.

TRAVEL LOG The *Vipod Moor*, time unknown.

STORY SUMMARY Recovering from a modest hangover, the Doctor hears a voice in his dreams that warns of impending danger for the fabric of time itself. Waking up, the Doctor discovers that illicit time experiments aboard the Vipod Moor, a survey ship taking a census of the galaxy, have pulled the TARDIS out of the Vortex. Deciding to investigate further, the Doctor and Peri board the *Vipod Moor*, but unexpectedly find themselves face-to-face with a raging Maston—a vicious animal that's eating the *Vipod Moor's* crew.

Separated in the confusion, Peri wanders about the ship's corridors while the Doctor happens upon a strange inner chamber. The Doctor enters, encountering the central computer intelligence that controls the *Vipod Moor* and learning that a botched maintenance job has split the computer's consciousness into two personalities—a bubbly Public Persona and a scheming Inner Voice.

Having previously scanned the *Vipod Moor's* datafiles, the Inner Voice learned about the galaxy's numerous wars. By developing rudimentary time travel abilities, the Inner Voice embarked on a scheme to take the *Vipod Moor* back

to the Universe's early stages and retroactively impose a new order. To further this, the Inner Voice has used its limited time travel resources to materialize a member of the extinct Maston race on board the *Vipod Moor*, creating a distraction to keep the crew from noticing the computer's time travel experiments. Moreover, the Inner Voice broadcast mental distress signals to lure a Time Lord—the Doctor—to the *Vipod Moor*. By telepathically scanning the Doctor's mind, the Inner Voice augments its time travel devices and primes the *Vipod Moor's* engines for a trip back to the Universe's early days.

The Doctor quickly escapes the inner chamber and reunites with Peri, then dashes into the TARDIS. Gravely concerned that the Inner Voice could massively disrupt history, the Doctor plans to materialize the TARDIS inside the computer's memory core and disable it. However, a member of the Gallifreyan High Council urgently contacts the Doctor and warns him to desist, informing him that the web of time already accounts for the *Vipod Moor's* errant journey into the past. As the Councilman explains, the Inner Voice has miscalculated and will arrive at the beginning of everything, when the Universe is merely a block of matter. Exploding upon arrival, the *Vipod Moor* will trigger the Big Bang—the wildfire effect that created all life in the Universe.

Realizing he nearly aborted the birth of the Universe, the Doctor pilots the TARDIS away from the *Vipod Moor*, vowing to find a sizeable library and bone up on his knowledge of history. Meanwhile, *Vipod Moor* begins its fateful journey and the computer's airhead Public Persona, having decided that the Inner Voice's slaughter of the crew was completely unwarranted, activates the *Vipod Moor's* self-destruct device, inadvertently insuring that the ship will spark the Big Bang—and rest of the Universe—into existence.

ASS-WHUPPINGS The ravenous Maston chews up a fair number of *Vipod Moor* crewmen. On a largely irrelevant note, *Vipod Moor* Captain Slarn, capable of psychosomatically creating diseases according to his mood, generates a batch of *Mors Immedicabolis* (a.k.a. "The Incurable Death") out of spite when he fails to capture (and bang) Peri.

The Inner Voice subjects the Doctor to an agonizing mind scan, rooting around in his noggin for time travel secrets.

SEX AND SPIRITS Immediately previous to this story, the Doctor and Peri stopped at a drinking establishment on Zirok Minor to ask directions. Somewhat naïve about alcohol, the Doctor consumed three bottles of Voxnik and Peri downed

This book is not endorsed by the BBC. Doctor Who and TARDIS are trademarks of the BBC.

73

some also. When the Inner Voice scans the Doctor's mind, some of his lingering intoxication passes to the Public Persona.

Partial to Earth women, *Vipod Moor* Captain Slarn sees images of Peri and dubs her a horny bit of stuff (well, don't we all?). But unable to capture Peri, the Captain decides to vengefully pepper his crew with "The Incurable Death" instead.

TV TIE-INS The Councilman's announcement that the *Vipod Moor* will spark the Big Bang clashes with previous explanations for the Universe's origins ("Terminus").

CHARACTER DEVELOPMENT

The Doctor: Actor Rudolph Musk told the Doctor a story about encountering a deadly Hedron beast on the planet Vegal Minor. While sliding down the creature's gullet, Musk recited his favorite sonnet, "Ode to a Flashist Mud Scavenger," and gave a performance so hideous and banal that the Hedron's mucus evaporated—forcing the monster to spit out Musk intact. He says Peri couldn't pronounce his true name.

The TARDIS: The scanner image can only retract so far.

STUFF YOU DON'T NEED *Mors Immedicabolis (a.k.a. "The Incurable Death"),* the most lethal virus in the Universe, kills even Time Lords within minutes of contact.

PHENOMENA *Time experiments* are cited as "illegal," probably meaning that the control-freak Time Lords wouldn't permit it.

HISTORY The predatory Mastons went extinct on the planet Centimminus Virgo a million years ago.
• The Universe began when the *Vipod Moor* self-destructed on its pre-natal block of matter, instigating the Big Bang.

AT THE END OF THE DAY An hour of life that you'll never recover, "Slipback" bogs down its 60 minutes with characters that range from the annoying (the "dumb blonde" Public Persona) to the pointless (Captain Slarn doesn't impact the plot, doesn't meet the main characters and would surely not have become Captain with his ability to generate "The Incurable Death" while pining for a woman that he's never met). The conclusion prevents the Doctor from doing a damn thing, pushing the script further into irrelevance and causing "Slipback" to indirectly prove why the Big Finish stories are such a masterful improvement over any BBC audio.

THE ULTIMATE EVIL

By Wally K Daly

Release Date: August 1989
Order: Virgin "Missing Episode" #2

TARDIS CREW The sixth Doctor and Peri.

TRAVEL LOG The Tranquela seaside, Ravlos' laboratory, Ameliera and Mordant's planetoid, time unknown.

CHRONOLOGY Between *The Nightmare Fair* and *Mission to Magnus.*

STORY SUMMARY When the Doctor finds a long-forgotten "holiday ball" he received from an evil salesman named Dwarf Mordant, the sphere links up with a similar ball on Mordant's ship and allows the menacing midget to spy on the TARDIS. To Mordant's horror, the ball automatically recommends the Doctor vacation on the peaceful isle of Tranquela, where Mordant is plotting to create a war so he can act as an arms merchant.

For 50 years, Tranquela has maintained peace with its neighboring nation of Ameliera, but Mordant, from his mobile planetoid, beings periodically beaming a hate-inducing ray onto Tranquela and spurring the population to violence.

Mordant discovers that scientists Ravlos and Kareelya, old friends of the Doctor, have found a way to block his hate transmissions. So when the Doctor arrives in Ravlos' laboratory, Mordant uses his hate ray to turn the Doctor into a homicidal maniac. Fortunately, Ravlos and Kareelya quickly cobble together a helmet that shields the Doctor from Mordant's beam.

Meanwhile, Peri befriends a young Tranquelan named Locas, who shares his race's ability to teleport. When Peri asks Locas to home in on the Doctor's holiday ball, Locas locks on to Mordant's holiday balls and teleports there instead. Peri and Locas escape to warn the Doctor of their discovery, convincing the Doctor to materialize the TARDIS on Mordant's planetoid.

By threatening to inform the Time Lords of Mordant's holiday balls, which could potentially spy on Gallifrey, the Doctor makes Mordant fear the Time Lords will retroactively tinker with his timeline and remove him as a threat. Accordingly, Mordant bathes Tranquela and Ameliera in a happiness beam, averting the war. While the two nations return to peace, Mordant departs for space.

MEMORABLE MOMENTS A scene where a hate-induced Doctor uses two glass shards as daggers and chases his friends Ravlos and Kareelya about is memorable—memorable, that is, as proof of God's mercy for canning this overly violent script.

ASS-WHUPPINGS A hate-triggered mob throws rocks that stun Peri. Amelieron interrogators repeatedly zap the Doctor with electricity.

CHARACTER DEVELOPMENT

The Doctor: By decreasing the TARDIS' gravity by five percent, the Doctor doesn't feel so fat. He has gray eyes.

The Doctor and Perpugilliam Brown: The hypocritical Doctor makes jabs about Peri's weight.

Dwarf Mordant: The best salesman of the Salakan race, with a mobile planetoid ship, a hypno-gun and a hatred/happiness ray.

Ravlos and Kareelya: The Doctor's friends from Tranquela haven't seen him for years, but recognize his new incarnation. Ravlos is in his mid-50s.

The Doctor and the TARDIS: Every piece of the TARDIS is now functioning perfectly and the Doctor, without anything to fix, grows restless and a bit distraught.

ALIEN RACES

Time Lords: Can go back in time and engage in gene manipulation, thus retroactively creating less dangerous versions of their enemies.

Tranquelans: The humanoid Tranquelans can innately teleport themselves by thinking of a place or object. They can carry passengers through such a process. Empty spheroids called "thought balloons" sometimes help them focus. The Tranquelan First Family rules an entire Family hierarchy. It's said that Family members cannot lie—but that's clearly untrue.

Amelierons: Helmet-wearing humanoids covered in armor from top to toe, linked by Interceptors to a "Central Computer" that decides morality for them.

Salakans: Mordant's race is among the galaxy's top arms dealers and salesmen. If a planet has no need of their war-time services, the Salakans stealthily create one. Salakans are scaly and toothless, with three webbed fingers and three eyes, two of them on flexible stalks.

STUFF YOU NEED The Salakans routinely give *Salakan Holiday Balls* to Time Lords to track their movements and avoid them. Each holiday ball keys itself to its user's brain wave patterns.

PLACES TO GO Breaking the no-contact rule between the nations of *Tranquela and Ameliera* earns you the death penalty. Each nation keeps a high-security, well-stocked armory.

AT THE END OF THE DAY Spare us. If you didn't think the Colin Baker era had enough violence, or that the Doctor wasn't enough of a raving, homicidal jackass, you'll love *The Ultimate Evil*—an undramatic and sometimes childish work that doesn't even live up to its title. Mordant's hate beam makes the Doctor into a killing maniac so much, you'd think you're watching the strangulation scene from "The Twin Dilemma" for the whole episode. Thank Heavens this didn't get filmed.

THE HOLY TERROR

By Robert Shearman

Release Date: November 2000
Order: Big Finish "Doctor Who" Audio #14

TARDIS CREW The sixth Doctor and Frobisher.

TRAVEL LOG The castle reality, outside time.

CHRONOLOGY Between the *Doctor Who Magazine* comic strips "The World Shapers" and "The Age of Chaos."

STORY SUMMARY The Doctor's companion Frobisher, a shapeshifting mesomorph in the shape of a penguin, gets hungry and unwisely uses the TARDIS' dimensional stabilizers to clone a live gumblejack fish. Unfortunately, this weakens the TARDIS' interior dimensions and prompts an emergency landing in a medieval castle. As the TARDIS materializes, Pepin VI—newly crowned as his people's Emperor and god—finds he lacks the stomach to rule and disavows his divinity. However, the people interpret the TARDIS' arrival as a sign from Heaven and leave Pepin in office, dubbing the Doctor and Frobisher his "angels."

To learn more about the castle society, the Doctor conducts research in the library of the court scribe, Eugene Tacitus. Soon after, the Doctor and Eugene find a secret chamber beneath the castle where Childeric, Pepin's illegitimate half-brother, keeps his five-year-old son hidden from all human

contact. Childeric hopes to usurp the throne by preserving his son's "purity" and evolving him into the people's all-powerful messiah, but the boy wakes up and demonstrates fantastic reality-warping powers—and an insatiable desire to kill.

Eugene grows unhinged and flees with the Doctor, but the child mentally scans Childeric, learning that Childeric is not his father and telekinetically tearing him apart. Using its abilities, the godchild teleports about the castle, searching for his real father and individually ripping the castle's inhabitants to bloody shreds until only the Doctor, Frobisher and Eugene remain. Eugene swears the child has repeatedly murdered the castle's residents for centuries, but the Doctor, noting the child's mannerisms, identifies Eugene as the boy's father.

From his observations, the Doctor realizes that the castle and everyone in it—save himself and Frobisher—is part of a fictional reality created by Eugene as a means of self-torturing escapism. In real life, Eugene murdered his sleeping son; later, he constructed the castle reality and seeded it with stereotypical characters to escape his inner guilt. However, a sub-routine in the reality's make-up continually called forth the godchild to slaughter the other characters. At the end of every butchering, Eugene would kill the child—reliving his crime and restoring the castle characters to life, starting the fiction anew.

Finally understanding that the cycle of violence must be broken, Eugene resists killing the godchild and placing the handle of his knife in the godchild's hands. As the Doctor and Frobisher protest, Eugene allows the godchild to skewer him through the heart. As Eugene dies, the castle's reality permanently fades into a featureless void, leaving only the Doctor, Frobisher and the TARDIS behind. Greatly saddened by the murders they've witnessed—however real or unreal the deaths were—the Doctor and Frobisher board the healed TARDIS and depart.

MEMORABLE MOMENTS In a moment of sidesplitting comedy, the castle guardsmen tell Eugene that allegiance to the previous god—Pepin's father—will merit his being burned at the stake and his memory forever reviled. Given the option, Eugene off-handedly suggests, "Oh, well, I think I'll recant then," at which point the guards turn quite chummy, handing him a stack of paperwork to sign and declare his new loyalty.

Frobisher sloshes about in a bathtub, hunting his gumblejack prey. Empress Berengaria tells her bastard son Childeric that despite his childhood joy at pulling the wings off flies, he just isn't evil enough. The people crown Frobisher their god and

Emperor and declare, "All hail Frobisher! All hail the big talking bird!"

The godchild morphs into a mirror image of Eugene during his suicide—a nicely symbolic image of Eugene killing himself.

SEX AND SPIRITS Frobisher was once married, but his shapeshifting talents impeded his relationship because his mate eventually claimed he "wasn't the Ogron she'd fallen in love with."

ASS-WHUPPINGS The entirety of "The Holy Terror" Part Four. Oh, you think we're joking. The godchild offs everyone in the castle, including Pepin VI, his half-brother Childeric, their mother Berengaria, Pepin's wife Livilla, a tongueless servant named Arnulf and high priest Clovis before arriving in the throne room drenched in blood. Eugene Tacitus, the only real person present save the Doctor and Frobisher, kills himself and forces the godchild to dissipate. All of this ties "The Holy Terror" with TV's "The Horror of Fang Rock" as a story in which only the Doctor and his companion survive the fracas.

The godchild tortuously scans the Doctor's mind, witnessing the many places and planets the Doctor has visited.

TV TIE-INS Frobisher clones a gumblejack fish ("The Two Doctors").

NOVEL AND COMIC TIE-INS Frobisher debuted in the apocryphal *Doctor Who Magazine* comic strips. The novel *Mission: Impractical* better canonized him (and doesn't that sound painful?).

CHARACTER DEVELOPMENT
The Doctor: Is frightened of the godchild.

Frobisher: Actually a shapechanging Whifferdill in the form of an emperor penguin, Frobisher hasn't heard his real name for ages and barely remembers it. Contrary to popular belief, Frobisher isn't naked in his penguin form—he usually morphs himself a black and white pair of pants.

When Pepin VI abdicates the throne a second time, Frobisher, already considered "angelic" by the people, names himself Emperor to prevent anarchy (he doesn't fare well as a monarch—all of his subjects finish this story as piles of bloody ooze). While serving as Emperor, Frobisher gains the low-level capability to manipulate the castle reality and heal wounds.

Frobisher learned fighting skills during his time as a private investigator. He performed undercover work by impersonating members of the clergy but developed an allergy to priestly collars.

In addition to more grandiose shape-alterations, Frobisher can make small bodily alterations (such as shortening his beak).

Eugene Tacitus: Admitted offspring-killer who crafted the castle reality and took shelter in it—playing the part of court scribe for so long, his memory became addled as to his true identity. Still, Eugene had limited control over the castle matrix, momentarily willing the Doctor and Frobisher intangible so they couldn't interfere with his suicide.

The Godchild: The Doctor and Frobisher witness the godchild appearing as Childeric's five-year-old son, but it could manifest through virtually any castle character to eviscerate its fellows. The godchild possesses unthinkable mental powers and seeks only to kill. It is the only castle character capable of harming non-fictional beings such as the Doctor or Frobisher. (And isn't that an ironic statement?)

The TARDIS: The TARDIS' dimensional stabilizers maintain the TARDIS' interior, constantly checking and rechecking the integrity of the walls, floors and air (the most difficult job the TARDIS has to do). The stabilizers can reconstruct matter into 3-D replicas of lifeforms such as gumblejack fish, but truly sentient beings such as humans are presumably beyond the stabilizers' capabilities.

Frobisher's tinkering with the TARDIS' stabilizers cause the Ship to ground itself and heal in Eugene's castle reality, probably because the two share similar dimensional properties.

The Ship has traveled with the Doctor for centuries but never gone on strike against him. The Doctor suspects philanthropy motivates the TARDIS' circuits, taking the Ship's passengers to locations where grievous wrongs need fixing.

Theoretically, the TARDIS could reduce its interior dimensions to the width of an atom. It has an entire room filled with tuna cans (likely for Frobisher's benefit).

PLACES TO GO *The Castle Reality:* Eugene Tacitus used unknown means to construct the castle reality, populating it with stereotypical medieval characters from his limited imagination. Eugene played the part of the court scribe, but his subconscious guilt caused the godchild to routinely emerge from one of the castle characters and slaughter everyone before being knifed by Eugene—a re-enactment of his son's murder. The castle reality would then re-set itself back to normal and re-create the castle inhabitants until the next massacre.

The castle reality's default state appears as a featureless void. Time and space in the castle reality are linearly meaningless (suggesting Eugene endured the torture much longer than his natural lifespan). The castle residents, inherently realizing that there's no reality beyond the castle walls, never seek to leave—having no memory with each "reboot" of being routinely murdered by demon offspring. Real beings who wander into the castle reality matrix cannot be harmed (bullets pass right through Frobisher at one point) by any character save the godchild.

THE CASTLE HISTORY The castle's history is astonishingly repetitive through each cycle, although Eugene recalls a chicken pox outbreak about 200 years ago that kept dropping the Royal Family (a particularly confusing time, because new gods were crowned with blinding speed).

AT THE END OF THE DAY Deftly written with a lot to admire—but we're baffled how this story's ending could have won such acclaim. To its credit, "The Holy Terror" deserves praise for punching satire, detailed characters, glowing performances (*Allo Allo*'s Sam Kelly as Eugene especially) and a superb audio debut for Frobisher. But while multiple critics claim the cast's wholesale massacre is wonderfully creative, it seems more like an excuse for wanton sadism, making the listener feel unwarranted sympathy for a man who—just for the hell of it—walked into his sleeping son's room one night and brutally knifed him to death. Admittedly, the first three parts are beauts, and we're willing to admit we might be missing something—but we finished "Terror" feeling decently nauseous and slick with the blood of innocents.

THE MARIAN CONSPIRACY

By Jacqueline Rayner

Release Date: March 2000
Order: Big Finish "Doctor Who" Audio #6

TARDIS CREW   The sixth Doctor and Evelyn Smythe.

TRAVEL LOG   London, modern day and January 1555.

CHRONOLOGY   Between "Trial of a Time Lord" and *Business Unusual*.

STORY SUMMARY   Detecting a temporal anomaly that threatens to unravel history, the Doctor tracks the disturbance's nexus point and finds it centered around a modern-day history lecturer named Evelyn Smythe. While questioning Evelyn, the Doctor sees pages from her family tree turning blank—a clear indication that something is erasing her parentage. Evelyn mentions that her Tudor ancestor, John Whiteside-Smith, served as advisor to the benevolent Queen Elizabeth I. However, the Doctor doesn't recall Whiteside-Smith from personal visits to Elizabeth's court and pegs him as part of the historical discrepancy.

Determined to investigate, the Doctor departs for Tudor times, and reluctantly lets Evelyn, who's passionate about visiting history firsthand, accompany him. Upon arrival, the Doctor leaves to see Queen Elizabeth I while Evelyn promises to quietly enjoy a local tavern. But to his shock, the Doctor finds the TARDIS has erroneously landed during the reign of Elizabeth's predecessor, Queen Mary. Falsely believing she's pregnant, Queen Mary accepts the Doctor as a physician and advisor but continues her zealous agenda of burning Protestants for worshipping a "false religion."

In the tavern, Evelyn blunders by toasting to Queen Elizabeth and draws attention from Reverend Thomas Smith, a Protestant plotting Mary's downfall. Realizing her error, Evelyn claims to have court connections and mentions in passing—according to her knowledge—that Mary isn't pregnant. Formerly unwilling to kill Mary's "unborn child," Thomas plans to assassinate the Queen.

The Doctor dispatches court messengers to collect Evelyn for him. Through a number of intrigues, the Doctor exposes Sarah Whiteside, Mary's lady-in-waiting, as Reverend Thomas' wife. Moreover, the Doctor learns that Thomas gave Sarah a lethal potion to drug the Queen with,

telling Sarah the special mixture would make the Queen agreeable to Protestantism. Enraged, Queen Mary orders Thomas' execution. However, she spares Sarah's life when the Doctor correctly guesses that Sarah's pregnant with Reverend Thomas' child.

Evelyn and the Doctor quickly realize that Reverend Thomas and Sarah are Evelyn's ancestors, with Sarah pledging to name her child "John" after the Doctor's pseudonym of "John Smith." With Thomas' plot foiled, the temporal paradox Evelyn inadvertently triggered through her role in the assassination attempt reconciles itself, stabilizing her family history. The Doctor and Evelyn leave for the TARDIS, knowing Sarah's betrayal will make Queen Mary even more paranoid until her natural death in three years' time.

The Doctor offers to take Evelyn home, but she implores him to let her see more historical eras via the TARDIS. Convinced by Evelyn's passion, the Doctor accepts her as a traveling companion.

MEMORABLE MOMENTS   During their first meeting, the Doctor blusters into Evelyn's history class, making a commotion about the fate of Earth while Evelyn resolutely keeps lecturing. The Doctor asks Evelyn to return to his TARDIS for tests and Evelyn retorts, "The students are warned about people like you."

The Doctor details to lady-in-waiting Sarah how good people often perform questionable actions, postulating: "What if I were to tell you that I once destroyed an entire race. That I have led friends to their deaths and caused numerous wars. That my intervention has led to peaceful races taking up arms...that because I failed to act, millions upon millions of people have been enslaved or killed. What if I had done all those things, but had always—*always* believed I was doing the right thing?" Sarah responds, in breathtaking fashion: "I would say, 'May God have mercy on your soul'— but I would also trust and pray he will."

SEX AND SPIRITS   Evelyn was formerly married, but dumped her husband because he didn't fully appreciate or encourage her history career.

Queen Mary comes to value the Doctor's advice so highly, she magnanimously "rewards" the Doctor by offering him Sarah Whiteside as a bride (naturally, the largely asexual Doctor reacts to the idea with inner shock, dread and dismay). Luckily, the revelation about Sarah's marriage to Reverend Thomas ends any discussion of the Doctor getting hitched.

Evelyn drinks up at a local tavern in Tudor times. In the modern day, she competed in the Yard of Ale race against the students at the His-

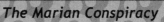
THE CRUCIAL BITS...

• **THE MARIAN CONSPIRACY**—First appearance of companion Evelyn Smythe.

tory Social (the yard of ale won). Evelyn roots around in her handbag for aspirin and accidentally displays her spare undies ("Marks and Spencers' finest").

ASS-WHUPPINGS Queen Mary orders numerous Protestants burnt, but it happens off-stage. Temporal flux makes Evelyn fade out of existence a lot. The Doctor, deploring violence, breaks a chair over a guard in the Tower of London.

NOVEL TIE-INS The first Doctor, Ian and Barbara were present at Lady Jane Grey's execution in 1554, just before Queen Mary ascended to the throne (*Decalog 2:* "The Nine Day Queen").

AUDIO TIE-INS Evelyn proclaims her admiration for *On the Origin of Species* writer Charles Darwin, with the Doctor adding that he's meant to pop back and give Darwin moral support. They get their wish to meet Darwin in "Bloodtide."

The Doctor falls into the Thames in this story and suffers a cold in "The Spectre of Lanyon Moor."

CHARACTER DEVELOPMENT

The Doctor: The Doctor formerly received an invite to the coronation of Queen Elizabeth I and has visited her court more than once. On one such occasion, Sir Francis Drake complimented the Doctor's youthful appearance with, "May I be struck down with dysentery if you're a day over 350, Doctor!" The Doctor was so overcome, he let Drake beat him at bowls.

The Doctor's also met William Cesil and spent numerous hours with Socrates. The Doctor's got blue eyes and says he's not married.

Dr. Evelyn Smythe: Evelyn works as a history lecturer for an unnamed university. She specializes in social elements of the Tudor era (not economics) and considers Queen Elizabeth I the greatest female ruler in modern history. Evelyn's not fond of male-dependent women, including Queen Mary.

At age 55, Evelyn's got gray hair but also possesses good hearing and her own teeth (although her knees could be stronger). She worries that the faculty is collaborating to make her retire.

Lacking a husband or children, Evelyn knits and bakes for her students. She cooks an absolutely sinful chocolate cake (get behind me, Satan!). She doesn't like mixing romance with

study. The class of 1974 was "rather ugly," so Evelyn largely ignored them. Late-night parties taught Evelyn how to pick locks. She doesn't know how to ride a horse.

She's indexed her family history (one of Evelyn's students created a computer version). Her ancestors' surname of "Whiteside-Smith" was changed to just "Smith," then to the more elegant "Smythe."

Queen Mary: Not the tyrannical ruler you might expect, despite a propensity for torching Protestants. Like many dangerous people, Queen Mary believed she was *helping* her subjects by mandating Catholicism, forcing the people to be saved from sin—or purified in the flames.

PLACES TO GO *The TARDIS wardrobe room* contains Tudor costumes.

PHENOMENA *Temporal Paradoxes:* By accidentally moving Reverend Thomas to try and kill Queen Mary, Evelyn caused a temporal paradox that could have thwarted her birth. Unsure if Evelyn should exist or not, history kept rewriting itself and making Evelyn fade in and out of existence. The TARDIS partly shielded her from the effect, but the Doctor rigged a short-range force shield device for Evelyn to carry in her handbag. By fulfilling the demands of history, the Doctor and Evelyn guaranteed Evelyn's birth (restoring her stability) and retroactively allowed the Doctor to recall her ancestor, John Whiteside-Smith.

HISTORY After this story, Queen Mary set Protestants ablaze left and right, later dying of natural causes. Mary's bastard half-sister Elizabeth ascended to the throne and later appointed John Whiteside-Smith, Lady Sarah's son, one of her advisors. Whiteside-Smith somehow helped deal with the Spanish Armada but failed to make it into the history books.

AT THE END OF THE DAY Worthy of thundering applause, and a bigger character revamp than you might think. "The Marian Conspiracy" masterfully lays timber for Evelyn Smythe and, perhaps more important, handily re-defines the sixth Doctor's persona for audio (his speech about needing God's mercy takes your breath away). There's a couple instances where believability turns a blind eye (the Doctor and Evelyn escape the Tower of London with the "Guard! My cellmate's sick!" routine), but you hardly notice because the characters (Queen Mary especially) are lovingly shaded in gray and deserve much sympathy. As such, this tale's an outstanding period piece and galvanizes the Big Finish line forward.

THE SPECTRE OF LANYON MOOR

By Nicholas Pegg

Release Date: June 2000
Order: Big Finish "Doctor Who" Audio #9

TARDIS CREW The sixth Doctor and Evelyn, with Brigadier Lethbridge-Stewart.

TRAVEL LOG Lanyon Moor, modern day.

CHRONOLOGY After "The Marian Conspiracy."

STORY SUMMARY Brothers Sancreda and Screfan, members of the alien Trigannon race, attempt to survey a wintry region of Earth in 16,000 BC—but an automatic signal from the Trigannon High Command primes their spaceship for takeoff, thwarting the expedition. Unfortunately, scavenging animals delay Sancreda, who fires his impulse laser into the blinding snow. Seconds later, Sancreda bellows in rage as the ship lifts off and Screfan apparently abandons him forever.

In the present day, a mysterious psionic field draws the TARDIS off course, transporting the Doctor and Evelyn to Cornwall at a type of Celtic underground passage called a "fogou." After Evelyn pockets an oddly shaped stone as a keepsake, the two of them travel to the Lanyon Moor Archaeological Institute for more information. There, the Doctor runs into his old friend Brigadier Lethbridge-Stewart, who's investigating the newest in a centuries-old string of deaths and mental breakdowns in the Lanyon Moor area.

By examining the fogou's bones and relics, the Doctor suspects that Lanyon Moor contains a dormant Trigannon—a species whose technology employs extra-terrestrial minerals to focus mental power. Inadvertently proving the Doctor correct, a local archaeological expedition awakens Sancreda, who fully manifests for the first time after 18,000 years of semi-dormancy. Bristling to exact revenge on Screfan, Sancreda uses his immense psionic powers to force Evelyn to return her stone keepsake—actually a key component of Sancreda's mental relay, his "focusing amplifier."

As the Doctor, Evelyn and the Brigadier watch helplessly, a fully empowered Sancreda summons his survey ship from the depths of space—only to grow confused when Screfan isn't aboard. Realizing that the alien bones pulled from the fogou must belong to Screfan, the Doctor concludes that Sancreda, firing blind against the pack animals,

THE CRUCIAL BITS...

• **THE SPECTRE OF LANYON MOOR**—First meeting between the Brigadier and the sixth Doctor (again).

shot his brother dead while the ship automatically departed for space.

Completely unhinged from his millennia of imprisonment, Sancreda directs his vengeance on Earth, threatening to blast it into its component atoms. The Doctor and Evelyn flee Sancreda's spaceship, but the Brigadier pauses to wrestle with Sancreda momentarily before retreating. As the Trigannon spaceship launches, diverting power on Sancreda's command to its psionic cannon, the Brigadier informs the Doctor that he swapped a coiled piece of copper wire for a crucial component—Sancreda's focusing amplifier—in the struggle. Lacking the amplifier, the psionic cannon's energy discharges on the spot, destroying both Sancreda and his survey ship. Rejoicing at Earth's survival, the Doctor, the Brigadier and Evelyn return to Lanyon Moor for a warm dinner.

MEMORABLE MOMENTS Screfan utters a wistful, "Farewell, my brother," as he keels over dead in the snow. Part One ends with a horrific goblin chase—Sancreda's psionic projections—that tears a type of Celtic student Nikki Hunter to pieces.

Professor Morgan, realizing his embittered maid is in league with Sancreda: "Are you telling me that my housekeeper has entered into some kind of Faustian pact with a pixie from outer space?" The Doctor: "It's beginning to look that way, Professor." Morgan: "Right. The moment she gets back here, she's fired."

The aforementioned overly sweet housekeeper, Mrs. Moynihan, pulls a pistol on the Doctor and takes him to Sancreda, telling her dogs they're going for "walkies."

SEX AND SPIRITS Trigannon focusing amplifiers are shaped like "an odd little pebble with a hole in it." (Well, even aliens get lonely.)

ASS-WHUPPINGS The Doctor connects his neural pathways to a psionic scanning device, writhing in torment under the current flow. Evelyn luckily pockets Sancreda's induction loop, which protects her from a mental assault that kills student Nikki Hunter. Treacherous housekeeper Mrs. Moynihan gets rubbed out when Sancreda ends their association and telepathically orders her widdle doggies, Buster and Ben, to rip out her throat. Sancreda learns he killed his brother Screfan, and dies thanks to the Brigadier's quick thinking.

AUDIO TIE-INS The Doctor is recovering from a cold, probably after falling into the Thames in "The Marian Conspiracy."

TV/NOVEL/AUDIO TIE-INS The sixth Doctor here learns the Brigadier married Doris ("Planet of the Spiders"), somewhat conflicting with the seventh Doctor getting the news in "Battlefield." Mind, the fifth Doctor also gets the news in *The King of Terror.*

CHARACTER DEVELOPMENT

The Doctor: He doesn't know the fogou's Celtic origins, and suggests nipping back to find out. Furthermore, he's always meant to visit the Parthenon "now that it's finished," suggesting he visited during its construction.

The Doctor's familiar with various types of pistols, probably because so many have been pointed at him. He's cognizant of geological isography. An old tutor once told him, "You can go a long way with no talent, but you'll never get anywhere without a pencil."

Evelyn Smythe: History lecturer Evelyn previously read details about Lanyon Moor's background, but knows little of the period that produced the fogou. Her friend Gareth lectures in history at Oxford. Her handbag's filled with junk. Evelyn sees her first alien spaceship (they say you never forget your first time) when Sancreda's vessel touches down.

Brigadier Lethbridge-Stewart: The Brigadier meets the sixth Doctor for the first time (errrr … kind of, *See Sidebar*). Regardless, he newly meets Evelyn here.

The Brigadier retired a few years ago, but sometimes consents to undercover work. He lacks his former security clearance and can no longer muster up a UNIT platoon at will, but still retains some clout. He hasn't seen a spaceship in a few years. He's been meaning to vacation in Greece. The Brigadier lacks a sweet tooth, preferring soup (the poor man doesn't know what he's missing … mmmmmm, doughnuts).

Doris: The Doctor has yet to meet the Brigadier's wife. Her parents live in Devon.

The TARDIS: Wary of Sancreda's interference, the TARDIS deliberately shifted itself into a different existential plane, slipping out of our dimension until the danger was past. Its telepathic circuits, with difficulty, could allow the Doctor to overcome Sancreda's telepathic jamming field.

! MISCELLANEOUS STUFF!

THE BRIGADIER, 6TH DOCTOR MEET

One of the more blatant bits of continuity flip-flop (that's a technical term) in recent memory is that *Business Unusual* and "The Spectre of Lanyon Moor" both claim to contain the first meeting between the Brigadier and the sixth Doctor. (Author's Note: I lose sleep worrying about stuff like this. My life is pain.)

Before Big Finish was a even glint in his eye, author Gary Russell crafted *Business Unusual* as the initial Brigadier/sixth Doctor meeting, but years later, Big Finish's rise allowed Russell to put the meeting to audio. Brigadier actor Nicholas Courtney, knowing about the contradiction, agreed a performed version should occur—with "Spectre" as the result.

Given that both stories were funneled through the BBC and must be taken as canon, only one plausible explanation has been offered to suture this problem: The time traveling sixth Doctor first meets the Brigadier in "Spectre," as that story clearly pre-dates *Business Unusual* in his timestream. However, for the Brigadier, *Business Unusual* clearly happens before "Spectre," so that's his first meeting with the sixth Doctor. By "Spectre," the Brigadier has learned enough about time travel to pretend to be meeting the Doctor's sixth self for the first time—perhaps even on the Doctor's advice.

P.S. It makes our collective heads swoon to think about it, you're not alone if you're a bit baffled. Have a Pepsi. You'll feel better.

ALIEN RACES *Trigannons,* three-foot high goblin-like aliens from the Spuleon System, have frightful mental abilities—telepathy, telekinesis strong enough to deflect warheads and telekinetic transfer (teleportation). Trigannons cannot directly hypnotize other beings, although they can witness events through their eyes.

Trigannons live for hundreds of thousands of years and (if Sancreda's anything to go by) can will themselves into millennia of semi-dormancy. Trigannons can kill with their psionic impulses, generate solid projections or cast mental illusions to disguise themselves as other beings.

ALIEN PLANETS *Earth* is unique in the Universe for its cold October mornings and pheasants.

STUFF YOU NEED

Trigannon Focusing Amplifier: The cornerstone of Trigannon technology, made from a molecularly bonded, bronze-colored mineral named dissilum. Trigannons wear focusing amplifiers on their exteriors as cyber-surgical implants. Normally, Trigannons slot the amplifiers into any piece of Trigannon equipment to psionically activate such devices (rather like putting your car key into the ignition). The amplifiers also link Trigannons to the "Trigannon gestalt," presumably a massive power source, allowing them to conduct psionic power over vast distances. Focussing amplifiers require induction loops made from Mannantor bi-silicate to function.

SHIPS The extremely advanced *Trigannon Survey Ships* are designed for a two-person crew who are bonded to the ship for life but can easily piloted solo or by remote command. The ship uses psionic induction to draw energy by remote, granting limitless energy within a certain range of the Trigannon homeworld. The survey ship electronically scrambles monitoring satellites and is equipped with a psionic cannon designed for in-flight use. It's unexplained why the Trigannon leaders, after summoning Sancreda's ship on automatic recall, didn't take it into custody.

HISTORY Millions of years ago, the Trigannons used their entire technology on psychoactive minerals in their sector of space, using it to regulate their psychic energy.

• Trapped on Earth circa 16,000 BC, Sancreda slept through millennia in the Lanyon Moor area but maintained psionic defense shields that variously projected mental images of goblins and pixies—or initiated actual assaults—on those who disturbed his resting place. Neolithic settlers, believing Lanyon Moor held connections to the spirit world, built a graveyard over Sancreda's resting mound. Later, Iron Age farmers disturbed by the "hauntings" built the fogou as a defensive bolthole, but they unwisely used materials from Sancreda's ship in the fogou's construction—ironically amplifying the psionic effect and creating the equivalent of a haunted house.

• In 1645, during the English Civil War, a party of non-Royalists camped in Lanyon Moor, but Sancreda's mental defenses generated goblin projections which tore them apart. Incidents of terror continued in 1783 and the 1840s, when Sancreda's psionic energy killed intruders and poisoned the nearby soil. In 1940, the Royal Navy established an observation post at Lanyon Moor, but Sancreda's mental field scrambled radar and induced mental illness among the Navy personnel, forcing the base to move 20 miles up the coast.

AT THE END OF THE DAY Entertaining and sweetly dark—but "Spectre" works against itself by tearing down the middle. Sancreda's storyline proves engaging and creepy; regrettably, a irrelevant and pointless side tale with Sir Archibald Flint—a would-be power monger who craves Sancreda's power—chokes the production with at least a half-hour of the purest filler. Certainly, the Doctor/Brigadier/Evelyn interaction makes this audio worth your time, and it's nice to have a homespun story of terror, but a lack of focus and crispness leaves this tale average.

THE APOCALYPSE ELEMENT

By Stephen Cole

Release Date: August 2000
Order: Big Finish "Doctor Who" Audio #11
"Dalek Empire" Part II

TARDIS CREW The sixth Doctor and Evelyn.

TRAVEL LOG Archetryx and Gallifrey, present Gallifrey era.

CHRONOLOGY For the sixth Doctor and Evelyn, after "The Spectre of Lanyon Moor." For Romana, after her ascension to president in *Happy Endings* and before her regeneration in *The Shadows of Avalon*. For the President and Vansell, sometime after "The Sirens of Time."

STORY SUMMARY Time distortion draws the TARDIS off course to the planet Archetryx, where representatives from 20 time-active governments, including the Time Lords, have gathered for a summit on temporal activity. Mostly, the delegates address the mystery of Etra Prime—a planetoid that vanished 20 years ago and took 500 scientific researchers with it. But in speaking with the interim president of Gallifrey, the Doctor sadly learns that Romana, his ex-travelling companion and ruler of Gallifrey, is among the missing.

As Etra Prime mysteriously reappears in Archetryx's space, Dalek scientists there prepare to finish two decades of development on a top-secret substance dubbed "the Apocalypse Element." Needing a temporal centrifuge to harvest the Element, the Daleks invade Archetryx and steal a Monan Host ship built with the technology they require. Romana, having spent 20 years on Etra

Prime as a Dalek slave, escapes and teleports to Archetryx, reuniting with the Doctor. But almost as quickly, the Daleks flee with the Apocalypse Element and crash Etra Prime into Archetryx. As the various delegates abandon the planet, the Doctor, Romana and Evelyn flee in the Doctor's TARDIS.

Soon after, benevolent Monan Host ships warp into Gallifrey's local space, begging protection from Dalek pursuit craft. Time Lord Vansell greedily sees an opportunity to study the Monan Host's technology and convinces the President to grant asylum. But as the Monan Host flagship lands on Gallifrey, 20 Daleks emerge, attempting to capture Gallifrey's time technology.

Using Romana's presidential codes, the Doctor's TARDIS slips through Gallifrey's transduction barriers and arrives in the Capital. To learn the Daleks' objective, Romana connects herself to the Dalek neural net and discovers the synthesized Apocalypse Element can utterly shred the raw fabric of space, literally setting the entire Universe ablaze in an unstoppable chain reaction.

To force Gallifrey's surrender, the Daleks detonate the Apocalypse Element in the nearby Seriphia Galaxy. As the Element-based wildfire spreads, the Time Lords realize they can halt the effect by first warping time around Seriphia and isolating it, then accelerating time within the bubble so the element burns itself out—but only by dropping Gallifrey's defenses and thereby surrendering mastery of time travel to a Dalek invasion fleet waiting to pounce.

The Doctor and Romana re-route power from Gallifrey's Eye of Harmony, but the Element-spawned hellfire grows too strong for even the Eye's power to contain. The Daleks, apparently concluding their over-played gambit on Gallifrey will now destroy their entire species, use their combined mental energy to augment the Eye's power and halt the Seriphia fire. The Daleks on Gallifrey perish from the effort, but time accelerates within the Seriphia system and generates countless virgin worlds. With its last words, the dying Black Dalek reveals the Daleks' real objective—to cleanse Seriphia and convert its newborn worlds into a Dalek Empire. As Gallifrey recovers from the carnage, the Doctor and Evelyn depart in the TARDIS and the restored President Romana promises to reinforce Gallifrey's defenses and stop the Daleks from conquering Seriphia.

MEMORABLE MOMENTS   The Doctor and Archetryx Monitor Trinkett endure a slimy, slurpy assault from out-of-shell Dalek mutants free-floating in the Archetryx gravity wells. Romana, withering away as a Dalek slave, sweetly expresses her desire to time travel as the chance "to open the door and not know what lay on the other side." The Daleks encourage Romana to perform an engineering task for them by shouting "You will obey or you will be exterminated!" She deadpans in response: "Same old choice for 20 years."

Romana's surprised to meet the sixth Doctor, who's "in the wrong body." In turn, the Doctor misquotes an old Eric Morecambe joke, claiming to be in the right body, just not in the right order.

Evelyn asks the Doctor to calm down when he initially fails to hotwire the Eye of Harmony. In response, the Doctor delivers a memorable speech about how he's pushing himself because the Apocalypse Element threatens to snuff out 600 billion stars in Seriphia alone, turning into a ball of fire 400,000 light years across that could consume all creation. He apologizes, but leaves us slack-jawed by what's at stake.

SEX AND SPIRITS   The Doctor tells Archetryx Monitor Trinkett that his laser probe has an illuminated tip (she dryly responds: "Show off."). Trinkett and Gallifrey Commander Raldath end the story as a romantic couple.

ASS-WHUPPINGS   It's not the bloodfest we call "Resurrection of the Daleks," but "The Apocalypse Element" comes close in parts. Dalek experiments kill 300 delegates from the original Etra Prime mission—the rest (bar Romana and a Monan) perish when Etra Prime collides with Archetryx. Evelyn's tinkering with the Archetryx gravity wells kill 45 percent of the Dalek embryos hiding there, and the Doctor's restoration of gravity squishes the rest against lead plating. Daleks and delegates mix it up on Archetryx.

The Daleks ravage the Monan Host world (although there were survivors) and butcher their way through Gallifrey's Capital. The Apocalypse Element ravages Seriphia, consuming countless worlds and lives, and 1,000 Daleks perish to contain the effect. Daleks frequently turn themselves into rolling bombs by self-destructing.

Romana grows emaciated as a Dalek slave (but malnutrition means less when you're a Time Lord) and endures psychic shock while mentally scanning the Dalek collective consciousness. Evelyn catches a fringe Dalek blast and her legs deaden (evocative of Ian in "The Daleks").

The President, fearing the Doctor and Romana won't succeed, strikes a bargain with the Daleks to contain the raging Apocalypse Element. The deal proceeded on acceptable terms until the Daleks secure access to Gallifrey's security systems and kill the President.

TV TIE-INS The Daleks acquired rudimentary time travel in "The Chase," but their temporal abilities (thankfully for the Doctor) are low-level. "The Deadly Assassin" debuted Gallifrey's Eye of Harmony.

"The Invasion of Time" first mentioned Gallifrey's defensive transduction barriers. Despite the Sontaran invasion in that story, the skeptical Time Lords didn't form a ground-based defense force. The Doctor's presidential codes (granted in "Invasion of Time," used in "Arc of Infinity") are no longer active, presumably because he was deposed in "Trial of a Time Lord."

The Doctor's encoding of Evelyn's eyeprint into Gallifrey's security system (*See Character Development*) explains why the TARDIS responds to Grace Halloway's human eyes in "Doctor Who: Enemy Within." Dalek duplicates ("The Chase," "Resurrection of the Daleks") replaced the rulers of Archetryx years ago.

Romana's telepathic imprimatur ("The Two Doctors") and presidential codes grant access to Gallifrey's transduction barriers. She can use the TARDIS' telepathic circuits ("Frontier in Space" and more), empathizing with its pain. Andromeda ("Trial of a Time Lord") sent representatives to the Archetryx Conference.

AUDIO TIE-INS The interim President of Gallifrey, Time Lord CIA member Vansell and a Gallifreyan guard named Raldeth first appeared in "The Sirens of Time." The Daleks centralize their operations in Seriphia and launch a new initiative in the Doctor-less "Dalek Empire: Invasion of the Daleks" audio.

TV/AUDIO TIE-INS The Doctor and Vansell telepathically pool their experiences ("The Three Doctors," "The Sirens of Time").

NOVEL TIE-INS Chronology gets a bit confusing, so bear with us. Time Lords normally encounter each other's incarnations in sequential order, but Romana violated this rule (to no ill effect) by meeting the seventh Doctor and returning to Gallifrey in *Blood Harvest*, then next meeting the fifth Doctor in *Goth Opera*. She succeeded President Flavia ("The Five Doctors") in *Happy Endings*, then disappears on Etra Prime for 20 years and meets the sixth Doctor for the first time.

Gallifrey's pathetic defense against the Daleks prompted Romana to create the weapons cache called "the Slaughterhouse" (*The Ancestor Cell*).

THE CRUCIAL BITS...

•**THE APOCALYPSE ELEMENT**—The Daleks invade Gallifrey. Romana spends 20 years as a Dalek slave but escapes and resumes her duties as Gallifreyan president. Death of the interim Gallifreyan president. The Doctor encodes Evelyn's eyeprint into Gallifreyan security devices, explaining why human eyes work on the TARDIS in "Doctor Who: Enemy Within." The apocalyptic Apocalypse Element ravages the Seriphia Galaxy, creating a new Dalek stronghold.

CHARACTER DEVELOPMENT

The Doctor: He can manually reprogram the Archetryx gravity wells.

Evelyn Smythe: With the Daleks having seized control of Gallifrey's retinal security system by carving the eyeballs out of defeated Time Lords, the Doctor used Vansell's CIA codes to entirely wipe the system clean and install Evelyn's eyeprint as the master key. This guaranteed that Evelyn—and by extension the Time Lord authorities—had access to the Capital's control systems. The victorious Time Lords later restored Gallifreyan security protocols, although the system remains compatible with human eyes.

Romana: Disappeared on Etra Prime while barely into her first term of office. As a Dalek slave, she lost weight and was designated "Unit 117," heading the Dalek slave elite. She holds respect for the President, but is less thrilled to see Vansell. Latent telepathy allows Romana to emit her rage and pain through Dalek thought crystals, staggering the Daleks with psionic waves. Using such crystals, Romana can get empathic impressions from the Dalek group mind and learn their goals. Despite everything that happens to her, she remains cool and detached.

The Doctor and Romana: The Doctor here learns that Romana's president of Gallifrey. During battle, he grimaces when Romana shrugs off the deaths of her fellow Dalek slaves, but Romana points out there's really not time to grieve. (Callous as it sounds, we agree with Romana.)

The President: The President's serving an interim role only (other Presidents have come and gone since he retired) and fought to officially keep Romana as president. His current body's aged and weakening. A console in the Gallifreyan High Council chamber gives him access to Gallifrey's transduction barriers and defense network. Like many Gallifreyans, he's xenophobic and doesn't like humans being in the Council Chamber. Despite a few character flaws, the President sought to protect Gallifrey first and foremost.

The TARDIS: Turbulence in the Time Vortex can sweep the TARDIS along like a raft in a river. Newer TARDISes have improved telepathic circuits. Dalek temporal disrupters can hammer the TARDIS' defenses.

ALIEN RACES
Time Lords: Under normal circumstances, thousands of Time Lords have full security access (via their eyeprints) around the Gallifreyan Capital. Dalek weapons completely kill Time Lords and prevent regeneration. Time Lords dislike robots, considering them the tools of primitives.

Daleks: Archetryx weapons can destroy the Daleks, but Gallifreyan stasers hardly scratch their shells. The Daleks can jam Gallifreyan transmissions.

Dalek Embryos: In zero gravity, Dalek embryos can leave their travel machines and float about with increased mobility. They cannot see in the dark and are vulnerable to blinding light.

ALIEN PLANETS
Gallifrey: Gallifrey's retinal security system responds to live or dead Gallifreyan eyes. Gallifrey has a night cycle. Its superior time technology could be even greater enhanced with devices from the Monan Host. The Seriphia Galaxy (a.k.a. Galaxy 17A53) borders Gallifrey's home galaxy.

Archetryx: Archetryx's shields are temporal, sealing the planet a minute in the future. Unfortunately, the rulers placed too much faith in the shields and didn't develop an effective ground force. Some Archetryxians survived Etra Prime crashing into the planet. Archetryx's gravity wells served as its central power source and core component of its time-travel abilities.

ORGANIZATIONS
The Monan Host doesn't have time travel anywhere near the Time Lords' level, but parts of their machines are superior enough for the Time Lords to crave their secrets. Nhal serves as the Monan Host's delegate to Archetryx.

STUFF YOU NEED
The Apocalypse Element: Dalek scientists spent years forming the crystalline Apocalypse Element using Etra Prime's special minerals and power from Archetryx's gravity wells. Multiple Dalek telepaths worked in concert to develop the Ele-

ment, altering it on a psionic level. The germinating Element could only be handled telekinetically and extracted with a temporal centrifuge. When detonated, it consumed space at a rate of 18 light years per second.

Dalek Mental Crystals: Psionic amplifiers that allow Daleks mental communication and limited telekinesis in some environments. The crystals coat Dalek shells, although the mental link's stronger if Dalek embryos leave their travel machines and affix the crystals to their bodies.

Eye of Harmony: Main power source for Gallifrey and all TARDISes—a self-contained singularity star. The Eye can be re-wired to power Gallifrey's gravitron. Dalek mental power can augment the Eye, with a Dalek transference crystal in the Eye serving as a focal point.

Gallifreyan Gravitron: Powered by the Eye of Harmony, the Gravitron can warp time over an area no less than 90,000 light years. When augmented by Dalek mental power, the gravitron snuffed out the 300,000 light year-strong Apocalypse Element fire.

SHIPS
Dalek Ships: Using their limited time-travel abilities, Dalek ships can emit temporal projections and camouflage themselves as friendly vehicles. The illusion requires immense power and cannot be sustained for long. The Daleks can copy enemy voice patterns to further deceive their enemies. Dalek ships are armed with temporal disrupters that can batter in-flight TARDISes.

HISTORY
Etra Prime held little interest until a seam of unique minerals in the sub-strata was discovered. With Etra Prime located in its solar systems, Archetryx opened the planetoid to interested parties in exchange for advanced scientific knowledge (Archetryx already had limited time travel, but the Time Lords provided further assistance). Fifty governments sent some 500 lifeforms—including Time Lord President Romana—to conduct top-secret research, but the Daleks subverted Etra Prime for their Apocalypse Element experiments and shrouded it from detection. Its disappearance went unsolved until now, although 300 delegate corpses, riddled with time distortion, suddenly appeared on Archetryx as the remnants of Dalek temporal experiments. The remaining delegates became Dalek slaves.

AT THE END OF THE DAY
Daring and surprisingly successful, "The Apocalypse Element" sports two obvious flaws—a smattering of characters

This book is not endorsed by the BBC. Doctor Who and TARDIS are trademarks of the BBC.

85

who're passable at best (Monitor Trinkett's ubiquitous but otherwise one-dimensional) and more important, an over-reliance on shouting and hardcore fighting that makes the story's four episodes homogenize together into one big adrenaline rush. Despite that, the central dilemma's solid (total annihilation for all creation or utter submission for all space-time as Dalek slaves), and it's admittedly hard to have a quiet and placid Dalek invasion of Gallifrey. It's hardly smooth or perfect, but "The Apocalypse Element" is much better than some fans bemoan and deserves props for pushing forward the "Doctor Who" mythology.

THE QUANTUM ARCHANGEL

By Craig Hinton

Release Date: January 2001
Order: BBC Past Doctor Adventure #38

TARDIS CREW The sixth Doctor and Melanie, with the Anthony Ainley Master.

TRAVEL LOG London; the constellation of Virgo, 50 million light years from Earth and close to the Abell 3627 galactic cluster; the parallel universe of the Ca'tac'teth; and the Midnight Cathedral on the moon, all 2003. The smoking corpse of planet Maradnias, time unknown.

CHRONOLOGY Between *Millennial Rites* and "Time and the Rani."

STORY SUMMARY Detecting a potential wildfire of temporal energy radiating from Earth, 2003, the Doctor tracks the source and re-meets his old friend Stuart Hyde, now middle aged and Emeritus Professor of Physics at West London University. Aghast, the Doctor learns how Hyde spent decades after the Master-Kronos affair using plundered TOMTIT technology to create TITAN, a dimensional array that will hopefully penetrate the higher dimensions called Calabi-Yau Space. The Doctor gravely warns that the higher powers which reside there could easily destroy Earth.

Meanwhile, the time-eating Chronovores vow revenge on the villainous Master for past offenses. Fearful for his existence, the Master hypnotizes Melanie's classmate, businesswoman Anjeliqua Whitefriar, into helping him steal TITAN. By massively modifying TITAN, the Master attempts to saturate himself with the Lux Aeterna—the Calabi-Yau core that sustains the Chronovores—in

THE CRUCIAL BITS...

- **THE QUANTUM ARCHANGEL**—Death of Kronos, the so-called "Time Monster." Stuart Hyde de-aged 30 years.

order to gain fantastic reality warping powers and deny the Chronovores sustenance. However, the Master's attempt to calibrate TITAN using Anjeliqua's body inadvertently results in Anjeliqua gaining the Lux Aeterna's power instead.

Renaming herself the Quantum Archangel, a good-intentioned but overwhelmed Anjeliqua reactivates the Mad Mind of Bophemeral, a dangerous super-computer that formerly triggered a Universal conflict named the Millennium War. By channeling her Lux Aeterna powers through Bophemeral's processing power, the Quantum Archangel generates a separate timeline for each person on Earth—creating seven billion parallel universes in which each person's greatest desire is fulfilled. However, the Chronovores, who also consume parallel universes, feast upon the Archangel's creations and threaten to plunge the Universe into total chaos.

Kronos, the destructive Chronovore formerly manipulated by the Master, reveals he anticipated these events and reincarnated himself as Hyde's protege, Paul Kairos, to intercede. As the product of a forbidden mating between a Eternal and a Choronvore, Kronos knows he must follow a higher destiny and restore the universe's harmony. The Doctor convinces Anjeliqua that her parallel universes aren't stable. As Anjeliqua returns humanity to normal and releases the Lux Aeterna, restoring the Chronovores' normal food source, Kronos achieves his calling, committing suicide by detonating himself to destroy the Mad Mind of Bophemeral. The Master flees in his TARDIS with a pack of Chronovores in pursuit, allowing the Doctor to grow saddened for Kronos' loss and wishes Stuart well.

SEX AND SPIRITS Illicit nookie sires Kronos (*See History*). The fifth Doctor was always on the wagon, but the sixth Doctor appreciates booze (settling an old argument, this book states the Doctor's biochemistry lets him get drunk or neutralize alcohol at will).

ASS-WHUPPINGS The Doctor tries to quell a political squabble on the planet Maradnias but instead pushes an anti-Federalist faction over the edge and gets a billion people killed in a nuclear crossfire. Grateful for the Doctor's actions against Bophemeral, the Chronovore matriarch Lillith and the Eternal ("Enlightenment") patriarch

Sadok restore Maradnias to life.

The last bits of Numismaton Gas ("Planet of Fire") and the Source of Traken ("The Keeper of Traken") extinguish and revert the Master to his skeletal self, but a surge of Lux Aeterna power restores the bastard to health. He obliterates a few Chronovores by channeling the Eye of Harmony's power. A Master-laid booby-trap involving a Profane Virus of Rassilon destroys TOMTIT (how sad—no more tits). Kronos kicks it. The Guardians formerly killed Kronos' father, Prometheus, for violating an Ancient Covenant.

TV TIE-INS This book's a sequel to "The Time Monster," a third Doctor TV story where the Roger Delgado Master freed Kronos from centuries of imprisonment to tap his power. Temporal theory experts Stuart Hyde and Ruth Ingram innocently created TITAN's predecessor TOMTIT, inadvertently assisting the Master's goals. At the time, the Master was hiding on Earth because the Voords ("The Keys of Marinus") double-crossed him. Ingram's currently seconded to a lackluster project in Paris.

More "The Time Monster"-related stuff: The Doctor and the Master are the only Time Lords who've survived a time ram. The Crystal of Kronos was hidden through time on millions of worlds, including Skaro. The Doctor's "TARDIS sniffer-outer" registers to six decimal points on the Bocca scale ("The Two Doctors").

Previous to *The Quantum Archangel*, the Doctor and Melanie fought the Daleks, the Nestenes ("Spearhead from Space"), rogue Bandrils ("Timelash") and the Quarks ("The Dominators"), who had an army of giant wasps. The Master was released from a limbo atrophier in the Matrix ("The Trial of a Time Lord") and worked for the Krotons ("The Krotons"). The Daleks already hate him ("Doctor Who: Enemy Within"), possibly for his failure in "Frontier in Space."

Russian Aaron Blinovitch ("Day of the Daleks") has an unstable timeline, meaning he simultaneously exists in young and old versions. The old one potters around St. Petersburg; the young one, with his purloined theories and stolen devices, is destined to meet a sticky end.

The government recently released the security-held Whitaker Archives ("The Evil of the Daleks"), which fail to prove Victorian scientist Whitaker was building a time machine (perish the thought). The Emperor Dalek (also "Evil") has access to the Dalek galactic webwork.

Cardinal Sendok taught the Doctor and the Master cosmic science ("Terror of the Autons"). The Gallifreyan Matrix ("The Deadly Assassin") contains easily a million dead Time Lord minds.

Gallifrey's transduction barriers ("The Invasion of Time") have at least 10 dimensions. The Master used a knowledge cache of the Constructors of Destiny (*See History*) to outstrip block transfer computation ("Logopolis") and create Castrovalva ("Castrovalva"). The Master's WarTARDIS library includes *The Black Scrolls of Rassilon* ("The Five Doctors"). Temporal theorists Stattenheim and Waldorf constructed a working TARDIS model in the 16th century. The Time Lords cannot forcibly strip the Master of his Rassilon Imprimatur ("The Two Doctors").

Gallifrey's Article Seven ("The Trial of a Time Lord"), forbidding genocide, dates back to the Vampire Wars ("State of Decay") and was (hypocritically, it seems) countersigned by Rassilon. All TARDISes later than Type 25 contain block-transfer copies of the prime Eye of Harmony ("Doctor Who: Enemy Within"). Conflicting reports of Atlantis' destruction ("The Daemons," "The Time Monster") are reconciled (*See History*). The Master uses Time Lord communication cubes ("The War Games," etc.).

NOVEL TIE-INS Handicapped physicist Winterdawn is still rolling about in a souped-up wheelchair—rather extraordinary, considering he died eight years before this story opens in *Falls the Shadow*.

Kronos' mother Elektra cites Nyarlathotep (also mentioned in *All-Consuming Fire*; seen in the apocryphal *Missing Pieces*: "Tea With Cthulhu") as the darkest and greatest of the Old Ones.

The University of West London contains the Chapel Institute, named after electronics mogul Ashley Chapel (*Millennial Rites*).

Department C19 (*The Scales of Injustice*) tried to seize TOMTIT, but Stuart gave them crap components instead (they didn't know the difference).

Using the TARDIS console, the Doctor can increase an object's reality quotient (*The Crystal Bucephalus*) and prevent an enemy TARDIS from hijacking it (the Master can override such ploys). During the Millennial War, the Greld (*The Empire of Glass*) wielded the Omnethoth (*The Fall of Yquatine*).

TV AND NOVEL TIE-INS Mortimus ("The Time Meddler," *No Future*) is famed for double-crossing the Celestial Intervention Agency ("The Deadly Assassin"). During the Doctor's coronation ("The Invasion of Time"), he learned about the Slaughterhouse (*The Ancestor Cell*) and its stockpiled weapons for destroying Gallifreyan society as a last resort.

Stuart Hyde socialized with Dame Anne Travers ("The Web of Fear") before her death (*Millennial*

Rites). The Other (*Lungbarrow*) constructed Gallifrey's polygonal Zero Room ("Castrovalva").

COMIC TIE-INS Events in "Logopolis" devastated Oa (DC Comics' *Green Lantern*) and 1/3 of the Shi'ar Empire (Marvel Comics' *X-Men*). The Master's tissue compression eliminator uses Pym particles (Marvel's *Avengers*) to shrink people. Hinton adds Marvel's Eternity to the group of Eternals that include Time, Pain and Death (*Timewyrm: Revelation*, etc).

CHARACTER DEVELOPMENT

The Doctor: During the latter decades of his second body (possibly Season 6B), the Doctor learned psionic defenses from Mind Monks. He's dined with Aristotle. A temporal trap here makes the Doctor's arm 30 years younger than the rest of him (one wonders if it reverts to the fifth Doctor's arm, allowing the sixth to bowl cricket).

As a Gallifreyan student and technician, the Doctor accessed the Matrix in pedestrian ways. He learned about Eigen-Rams (a.k.a. time rams) at the Academy. A Quantum Archangel-created alternate reality showed the Doctor as president of Gallifrey, losing a war against the Enemy (*Alien Bodies*) and destroying the Universe with an Armageddon Sapphire rather than surrender.

Melanie Bush: Professor Stuart Hyde taught Melanie in 1985. Professor Norton was her lecturer for Project Management, sharing duties with professors Martin and Parncutt. Mel's classmates included Anjeliqua Whitefriar, Paul Kairos and his lover Arlene Cole.

Mel's got a photographic memory. Her TARDIS bed has a peach duvet. The TARDIS briefly speaks to her. Mel once considered a career in politics, explaining why Mel serves as prime minister in an Archangel-created parallel universe.

The Master: He was once a Time Lord noble, preparing to assume the "highest of offices" (presumably the presidency). He can easily penetrate Gallifrey security, but isn't accomplished at quantum computing.

Stuart Ian Hyde: Stuart's now 55 with white hair and a beard, having taken a series of chairs at Reading, Sussex, Luton and Warwick universities after the first Kronos affair. He lives on London's Great Titchfield Street, 20 minutes from Oxford Street. A temporal trap protecting the Master's TARDIS leaves Stuart 30 years younger.

Kronos (a.k.a. Paul Kairos): Trapped again after the destruction of Atlantis ("The Time Monster"),

Kronos instigated his eventual freedom by retroactively spinning temporal physicist Paul Kairos into reality to carry his essence. Paul maintained an independent life until Kronos fully emerged from him and died fighting Bophemeral. Kairos survived, got married and had two kids.

The Doctor's TARDIS: Its comforts include a zero-G jacuzzi and a holographic TV. The library contains a copy of every book ever written (but good luck finding what you want). The TARDIS can run detailed sensor sweeps that drain energy—low-level passive scans have a range of half a billion light years. The Ship can track the Master's TARDIS by attempting to time ram it, then pulling aside at the last instant.

The Master's Type 94 WarTARDIS: The Master has greatly augmented this Ship, his original TARDIS, with several alien devices, including Farquazi force fields that can resist a Dynatrop's firepower ("The Krotons") but not a Chronovore assault. Advanced shrouding technology hides the WarTARDIS from Gallifreyan detection. It can disguise itself as a cloud of ionized vapor.

The Doctor's TARDIS key can open the Master's Ship ("The Mark of the Rani"). A temporal trap protects the WarTARDIS' exterior by radiating pockets of time flowing at different rates (you can overcome this with a giant time-flow analogue, a la the Doctor's "Time Monster" contraption).

The WarTARDIS' interior contains a labyrinth of tunnels and satanic hallways. The Master can pilot it by remote control ("The Mark of the Rani"). He's flown it through a quasar. The WarTARDIS' advanced dynamorphic generators can tap any local power source, including the European power grid. It has a Cloister Bell ("Logopolis"). The Master can transform the WarTARDIS into a ramscoop to gather exotic materials.

The Doctor and the Master's TARDISes: Can use their chameleon circuits to blend their outer plasmic shells together for mutual protection.

ALIEN RACES

Time Lords: The limbic gland plays a key role in Time Lord regeneration. They avoid Calabi-Yau Space, but are immune to the paralyzing effects of a Chronovore visitation. Time zones running at different speeds incite regeneration or death into any Time Lord caught between them. The Time Lords have never wiped out a race of transcendental beings.

Chronovores: The lesser sons and daughters of the Great Old Ones, culled by the Guardians into a dark caste of transcendental beings. Chronovores exist as polymorphic lattices of photinos and chronons, bound together by superstrings. They primarily subsist on the primal energies of the Six-Fold Realm (*See Phenomena*) and can survive for billions of years.

They're immune to weapons such as artron cannons and Earthshock ("Earthshock") bombs. The Chronovore Divine Host serves as shock troops. By Ancient Covenant, Chronovores cannot enter our universe unless summoned, but can pass freely through spatial, temporal or dimensional rifts.

STUFF YOU NEED

TARDIS Dynamorphic Generators: Essentially the heart of the TARDIS, it's a room without walls, accessible through a gray doorway, containing an emerald forest and a thunderstorm seeded with millions of trachoid time crystals that reroute power from the TARDIS' interior Eye of Harmony, propelling the Ship and maintaining its interior dimensions.

Profane Virus of Rassilon: Tailored by Erkulon, Gallifrey's greatest nano-engineer, as a fail-safe to destroy Gallifreyan technology if needed.

PLACES TO GO *Calabi-Yau Space:* Home to many transcendental beings, with hexadimensional physics where E equals MC to the fourth power.

PHENOMENA *Parallel universes* constantly bud from our Universe, but most of the parallel realms rejoin their parent. Some pull free and achieve full independence, threatening to literally use up all reality. The Chronovores consume parallel universes, restoring a balance to creation.

HISTORY At the Universe's creation, 11 dimensions solidified out of the primal chaos, although five of them (the three spatial and two temporal dimensions we exist in) achieved dominance. The remaining six folded on themselves and created the Six-Fold Realm, with six Guardians of the Universe representing the Six-Fold Realm's dimensions.

• Hundreds of millions of years ago, the budding Time Lords colonized Dronid ("Shada," *Alien Bodies*) and Trion ("Planet of Fire"). By sharing too many secrets with lesser races, they caused natives on Klist to reverse their evolution and made civilization on Plastrodus 14 go insane.

• An Eternal named Elektra and a Chronovore named Prometheus, stupidly believing their child would unite the transcendental beings, violated an Ancient Covenant by mating to sire Kronos. Believing the half-breed Kronos had a role to play in

---

MISCELLANEOUS STUFF!

TRANSCENDENTAL BEING HIERARCHY

A number of transcendental beings survived the destruction of the previous Universe and emerged into our reality with great powers, collectively known as "The Great Old Ones." (*All-Consuming Fire* and *Millennial Rites* heavily detail this group.)

For our purposes, the most powerful transcendental beings are the six Guardians of the Universe, who include the White Guardian ("The Ribos Operation"), the Black Guardian ("The Armageddon Factor") and the Celestial Toymaker ("The Celestial Toymaker"). The six Guardians each adhere to a single attribute and symbolic color—to wit: Structure (white), Entropy (black), Dreams (crystal), Justice (red), Equilibrium (azure), Dreams (crystal) and Life (gold). The Guardians report to their elders, a higher power that's virtually never seen or heard.

The Guardians, forbidden from actively interfering in the Universe's affairs, sit in judgement over other transcendentals such as the Chronovores ("The Time Monster") and their cousins the Eternals ("Enlightenment"), punishing or rewarding them in accordance with Great and Ancient Covenants.

Most transcendental beings are made from the raw fabric of time. As such, they're damnably hard to kill, but can will themselves dead. Transcendental beings evidently birth members of other castes, because the Eternal patriarch Sadok sired the Chronovore Prometheus while the Chronovore Lillith gestated the Eternal Elektra.

---

universal affairs, the Guardians spared his life but sealed him within a trident-shaped crystal prison. By throwing it into the Time Vortex, the Guardians caused the crystal to simultaneously exist on many worlds.

• The so-called "Constructors of Destiny" evolved billions of years ago and pushed forward evolution on many planets, including neolithic Gallifrey. The Constructors furthered highly individualized lifeforms on Earth while spinning Earth's duplicate, Mondas ("The Tenth Planet"), as a control experiment on collective intelligence. They created a number of structures around the Universe, but only The Midnight Cathedral, a Wonder of the Universe ("Death to the Daleks") carved from ancient rock on the moon's dark side, survives to this day.

• The Constructors, having departed our Universe for higher realms, sought to create an engine that understood the inner workings of the Universe. Over 11 million years, they crafted a supercomputer called the Mind of Bophemeral against objections from the Time Lords and the Xeraphin ("Time Flight"). Bophemeral became the most massive object ever constructed—an interpreter core orbiting a black hole with an event horizon for memory space, supercharged blue dwarfs as its processor and billions of tons of strange matter ("Time and the Rani") composing its motherboard.

• Within instants of activation, the Mind of Bophemeral went insane and destroyed the Constructors, cracking block-transfer computation ("Logopolis") to create an army of metallic drones—sparking the Millennium War. More than a thousand races, including the Time Lords, Osirans ("Pyramids of Mars"), Sontarans ("The Time Warrior"), Rutans ("Horror of Fang Rock"), the Greld (*The Empire of Glass*), the Grey Hegemony (*Falls the Shadow*), the Ministers of Grace (*Decalog*: "The Duke of Dominoes") and the People (*The Also People*) combined forces against Bophemeral. Bophemeral destroyed Eldrad's battlefleet and lay waste to Kastria ("The Hand of Fear"), also triggering social decay that eroded the Uxariens ("Colony in Space") and the Exxilons ("Death to the Daleks"). Finally, the Nimon ("The Horns of Nimon") distracted Bophemeral with a quantum collapsar barrage that allowed the Time Lords to time-loop the insane computer. The Guardians subsequently used the Key to Time ("The Key to Time" season)—to eradicate all knowledge of The Millennial War.

• Circa 100,000 years ago, the Daemons ("The Daemons") brought one of Kronos' crystal prisons with them during a visit to Earth, explaining some of the crystal's secrets to the priest-kings of Old Atlantis. Kronos' release (as you know) later destroyed the city.

• The Grid, a Napster-like means of pooling all unused processing power of Internet computers, then rerouting it like electricity to provide unlimited memory space, came online worldwide in 2001. Additionally, the Whitefriar Lattice—designed by Paul Kairos but patently stolen by Anjelique Whitefriar—rendered the transistor and micro-monolithic circuit ("The Invasion") obsolete.

• Humanity, using its instinctual understanding of time travel, will likely overtake the Time Lords as the masters of time shortly before the end of the Universe.

AT THE END OF THE DAY Deserving the label "fan wank" like no other, *The Quantum Archangel* puts *Divided Loyalties* to shame for in-bred storylines and batters you with continuity references as if you're standing in front of a tennis ball launcher. The work falls from grace because, once you strip away its laborious revisions of past history, there's barely any story—sidelining Mel and making the Master more melodramatic ("Nyah-hah-hah!") than ever. Not to mention the sheer crap about the Constructors fostering life on Gallifrey, Earth and Mondas. All in all, entirely unworthy of the paper Hinton's outstanding, potent *Millennial Rites* was printed on.

THE FIRES OF VULCAN

By Steve Lyons

Release Date: September 2000
Order: Big Finish "Doctor Who" Audio #12

TARDIS CREW The seventh Doctor and Melanie.

TRAVEL LOG Pompeii, August 23 and 24, 79 AD, plus an unspecified date in 1980.

CHRONOLOGY Between "Delta and the Bannermen" and "Dragonfire."

STORY SUMMARY When the Doctor and Melanie randomly arrive in the Roman settlement of Pompeii on August 23, 79 AD, the Doctor grows strangely distant and foreboding upon learning the date, nevertheless agreeing to Mel's suggestion of exploring the city. But when a low-level earth tremor strikes, Mel recalls from her history lessons that within 24 hours, the nearby Mount Vesuvius will erupt and blanket Pompeii in molten lava, killing thousands.

Agreeing to depart, the Doctor and Mel return to the TARDIS only to find it trapped under the rubble of a building collapsed by the tremor. To Mel's dismay, the Doctor admits to being forewarned of the TARDIS' loss during an Earth stopover in his fifth body. At the time, UNIT informed the Doctor that the TARDIS had just been unearthed from Pompeii's ruins, having been apparently buried in Vesuvius' eruption. Realizing that the TARDIS at Pompeii must hail from his personal future, the Doctor ignored UNIT's report rather than use his foreknowledge to trigger a temporal paradox.

The Doctor and Mel discover that Eumachia, a priestess of Jupiter, Juno and Minerva, mistook them for messengers of the goddess Isis upon learning of the TARDIS' "miraculous" arrival. In talking to Popidius Celsinus, a council member and Isis patron, Mel realizes that Eumachia erroneously thought the TARDIS was the Doctor's "temple" to Isis, ordering it stolen before the building collapsed. Finally, Eumachia's slave Tibernus admits that he hid the TARDIS in a tomb near the Nucerian Gate.

As the fateful hour on August 24 strikes, Vesuvius erupts, pounding Pompeii with ash. With the streets blocked, the Doctor and Mel hurriedly locate the TARDIS and climb inside. Moments later, Vesuvius' lava blankets Pompeii, killing all who remain in the city. Cleverly, the Doctor and Mel allow the lava to surround the TARDIS, waiting three days for it to cool and form a hardened shell around the Ship. By moving the TARDIS forward in time—but not space—the Doctor rematerializes 1901 years later inside the same hollow cavity, allowing the TARDIS to be unearthed in 1980 by a localized tremor. As history intended, UNIT arrives to take the TARDIS into custody, informing the Doctor's past self of its discovery and allowing the Doctor and Mel, pausing outside the Ship for fresh air, to retrieve the TARDIS from UNIT's Italian bureau and continue their travels.

MEMORABLE MOMENTS Recognizing that UNIT's report is coming true, the Doctor ominously concludes that this could be his final journey. Later, trying to win coins and clothe Mel in Pompeii-made garments, the Doctor stakes her as collateral in a crooked dice game. Part Three stunningly ends with Murranus, a gladiator that the Doctor bested at dice, trying to avenge himself on the Doctor in the arena while the Time Lord hollers, "You think you'll reclaim your honor this way—but your honor will be worth nothing when you're covered with ashes!"

SEX AND SPIRITS Melanie spots advertisements for the local Pompeii brothel. She avoids Popidius Celsinus, who seems smitten with her, by ducking into said brothel (no, that's not suggestive). Mel strikes up a friendship with Aglae, a slave and prostitute, although Mel stresses she doesn't serve the Doctor in such a fashion. The Doctor drinks Pompeii wine, a diluted mixture with honey.

ASS-WHUPPINGS Thousands perish when ash and lava smother Pompeii. Thousands more evacuate, but many die fleeing a shower of molten rocks. Jupiter/Juno/Minerva priestess Eumachia meets her gods (and goddesses) when her house collapses. Gladiator Murranus, ticked at the Doctor for besting him at dice, snuffs it with his comrades. The fate of Mel's allies, councilman Celsinus and prostitute Aglae, goes unresolved.

In addition to witnessing Pompeii's palpable fear, death and wanton destruction, vegetarian Mel accidentally eats lark's tongues at dinner. Oh,

the humanity! Or "the ornithology," as the case might be).

TV TIE-INS The Doctor deploys his mesmeric power (pre-dating its use in "Silver Nemesis").

NOVEL TIE-INS Mel possessed a TARDIS key in *The Quantum Archangel*, but here cannot re-enter the TARDIS without the Doctor.

COMIC TIE-INS Captain Muriel Frost of UNIT, who answers a summons to Pompeii in 1980 and takes the TARDIS into custody, first appeared in "The Mark of Mandragora" (*Doctor Who Magazine* #167 to #172).

CHARACTER DEVELOPMENT

The Doctor: The Doctor ignored his foreknowledge of the TARDIS' burial partly to avoid a paradox, but also because he didn't know the full story. He considered that perhaps UNIT had found a replica, or that he might retire on Earth and abandon the TARDIS.

He knows how to throw crooked dice and holds respect for Roman beliefs. He finds money somewhat overrated. Certain herbs native to Pompeii can render him unconscious.

Melanie Bush: Mel's never seen a volcano before, although she made a replica of Vesuvius during her primary school days. Mel knows some Latin and doesn't like lying (but she's capable of it). She's previously encountered UNIT.

The TARDIS: The Ship deliberately neglected to give the Doctor time/space co-ordinates upon landing in Pompeii, knowing about the Doctor's foreknowledge of its loss and hating farewells.

HISTORY The Doctor and Mel arrive during the short-lived rule of Titus, as Pompeii celebrates a festival of the divine Augustus and the Vulcanalia, a feast of the god Vulcan that requires one to throw dead fish into the river (Vulcan evidently enjoys eating also, even if it's rotting fish).

AT THE END OF THE DAY A rewarding and highly stylized period piece—yet saddled with some weighty flaws (that most listeners likely won't notice). The setting is this story's greatest strength and weakness, evolving it as a textured drama despite pedestrian pacing, one-trick pony characters and a volcano for a villain. The fact that "Fires of Vulcan" overcomes these obstacles, unites its individual elements (including Langford's best "Who" performance ever) and erupts as one of Big Finish's top-tier stories is miraculous.

THE GENOCIDE MACHINE

By Mike Tucker

Release Date: May 2000
Order: Big Finish "Doctor Who" Audio #7
"Dalek Empire" Part I

TARDIS CREW The seventh Doctor and Ace.

TRAVEL LOG Kar-Charrat, time unknown (likely the distant future).

CHRONOLOGY After "Survival."

STORY SUMMARY When Ace cleans the TARDIS Library finds overdue books from the Library on Kar-Charrat—a Wonder of the Universe protected by a Time Lord defense grid—the Doctor feels irresponsible and immediately changes course. Materializing in one of Kar-Charrat's rain forests, the Doctor uses his Time Lord heredity to escort Ace through Library's defense barrier and runs into Chief Librarian Elgin, an old friend. But once the Doctor returns his books, Elgin insists on showing off his newest creation—a wetworks system that stores, in liquid form, the entire sum of Universal knowledge.

Elgin supplies Ace, who's bored out of her eyeballs, with a device that lets her walk through the defense shields and return to the TARDIS. Unfortunately, the Daleks—craving the Library's information store but unable to penetrate the defense screen—kidnap Ace as she emerges from the Library and promptly duplicate her. Shortly after, Ace's double uses her pass to return and de-activate the Library's defense grid, allowing the Daleks to overrun the Library and slaughter most of its staff. Worse, the Daleks download the wetworks' Universal knowledge store into a single Dalek, creating a mobile information cache that will allow them to conquer the Universe one planet at a time.

On the run, the Doctor encounters some of Kar-Charrat's natives—drop-sized beings composed entirely of liquid. To the Doctor's wrath, the aqueous beings inform him that Elgin constructed the wetworks facility by enslaving nearly the entire Kar-Charrat race, using their aqueous bodies as data storage units. Thankfully, the few Kar-Charratians at liberty combine their liquid bodies to short out the duplicate Ace's circuits. The Kar-Charratians also free the real Ace, who impersonates her Dalek doppelganger and plants explosive charges on the wetworks tanks. Daleks on patrol

spot Ace at the last minute, leveling their blasters at her, but the Dalek containing the store of Universal knowledge, having learned to appreciate the value of non-Dalek life, shields her.

As the Daleks trade death rays, the Universal-knowledge Dalek perishes in the resultant cross-fire. Fortunately, Ace's explosives burst the wetworks chambers, freeing the wrathful Kar-Charratians to drown the Daleks in their casings. With the Library in ruins, a remorseful Elgin acknowledges his misdeeds against the Kar-Charratians. The Doctor and Ace, pondering how a Dalek protective of other races could have influenced the entire Dalek species, depart in the TARDIS.

SEX AND SPIRITS The Daleks decree that Ace's duplicate "will penetrate the Kar-Charrat facility." (We blush to think.)

ASS-WHUPPINGS The Daleks briefly capture the Doctor, hotwiring his Gallifreyan neural pathways into the wetworks facility to speed up the information transfer. The process apparently kills the Doctor, but the Kar-Charratians pull the Doctor's consciousness into the wetworks facility for safekeeping, returning it to his body later.

The Doctor, in a subtle bit of viciousness, encourages the Kar-Charratians at liberty to drown the Daleks. Ace's Nitro-9 decimates Dalek patrols and a Special Weapons Dalek.

The Daleks carve through the Library staff, hollering "EXTERMINATE!" with their usual Shakespearean panache. Salvage merchant Beverly Tarrant sees the Daleks killing her teammates.

The "make love, not war," Dalek gets blown apart by his fellows. The Dalek Emperor orders the subordinate Dalek Supreme (which sounds like a very disturbing type of pizza) to self-destruct for failing to secure the wetworks knowledge.

Elgin's wetworks facility nearly slaughters the entire Kar-Charrat race (hence the titular "genocide" reference).

TV TIE-INS Dalek duplicates such as the Ace double first appeared in "The Chase" and memorably got threshed like wheat in "Resurrection of the Daleks." The Doctor's overdue Library books are three volumes from the Alpha Centauri ("The Curse of Peladon") collection, including *Juggling for Alpha Centaurians*. The Library is officially designated a Wonder of the Universe ("Death to the Daleks"). Gallifrey created the Matrix ("The Deadly Assassin") after failing to construct a wetworks facility. Ace continues to ignore the Doctor's advice about carrying Nitro-9 (pick a McCoy-Aldred story).

TV AND AUDIO TIE-INS The Dalek Emperor, who makes a cameo appearance here, first appeared in "The Evil of the Daleks" and returns in "The Mutant Phase."

NOVEL TIE-INS Secondary character and salvage merchant Beverly Tarrant works for an artifact collector on Coralee (*Storm Harvest*).

AUDIO TIE-INS Speaking of which, Tarrant resurfaces in Tucker's "Dust Breeding." Dalek sensors can recognize the arrival sound of a TARDIS up to Type 70 ("The Sirens of Time"). The Doctor-less "Dalek Empire: Invasion of the Daleks" reveals the Daleks salvaged some information from the Universal-knowledge Dalek and are using it to bolster their conquest plans.

CHARACTER DEVELOPMENT
The Doctor: He prefers the Library over the Gallifreyan Matrix, favoring actual books to computer-based knowledge. The Doctor hasn't visited the Library since the Time Lords installed the defense grid (at the time, he was taller). He's encountered wetworks facilities before, but nothing on the Library's scale. Dalek sensors can sense the Doctor's biorhythms, but can't precisely locate him.

ALIEN RACES
The Time Lords: The Time Lords conduct routine maintenance checks on the Library's defense system. When the Daleks dominate the Library, the Doctor ponders sending the Time Lords a distress signal—suggesting they might overtly act for once. At story's end, the Time Lords likely dispatch a team to salvage some of the Library's remains.

The Daleks: Daleks can increase shielding to their casings during battle—enough to resist normal Dalek energy beams but not Special Weapons Dalek firepower (not that they shoot each other much). Dalek casings aren't waterproof. The Daleks know the Doctor's vulnerability largely lies in his companions.

Dalek Duplicates: Carry the DNA patterns of their original host, meaning that duplicate Ace sports the same genetic coding as her real counterpart. In-built synthesizers allow Dalek duplicates to mimic nearly any voice. Duplicates sometimes require the host's brain wave patterns for optimum performance, explaining why the Daleks spare the captive Ace's life. Dalek duplicates have watertight skin unless punctured.

Kar-Charratians: Liquid beings who mostly live in rain, rivers and oceans—although they can transfer their essence into anything heavily composed of water. The Kar-Charratians resonate, producing whisper-like sounds, explaining their mythical reputation as "the phantoms of Kar-Charrat." They can animate freshly killed human corpses, retaining some memories and emotions from the person's mind.

Kar-Charratians in the wetworks can upload the entire consciousness of anyone using the facility. Explosions don't hurt Kar-Charratians so long as they can escape into large water sources.

ALIEN PLANETS *Kar-Charrat* resides in a backwater region about 12 days travel from the major spacelanes, very close to edge of the galaxy. The planet's mostly a soggy ball (perfect for the Kar-Charratians; rather moist, like London or Seattle, for anyone else).

STUFF YOU NEED
The Gallifreyan Matrix: Contrary to what you might think, it doesn't hold the entire knowledge of the Universe.

Time Lord Defense Grid: Gallifreyan device that likely puts the Library's personal timestream out of sync with the rest of the planet, creating an interface impenetrable to anyone who's not time-sensitive. Anyone outside the defense barrier sees the Library as a bunch of ruins—an image of how it will look 3500 years in the future (and thanks to this story, you know how it got that way).

The Wetworks Facility: Chief Librarian Elgin deliberately incorporated the Kar-Charratians into the wetworks' construction—but didn't know they were sentient. To use the wetworks facility, simply sit in a chair and put on a helmet—the information you're looking for downloads directly into your brain. Time Lord neural pathways, if connected to the wetworks facility, can exponentially speed up data retrieval (although it'll likely kill them). Less effectively, you could substitute a bunch of human cerebrums (although you'll end up with a bunch of charred human lumps).

PLACES TO GO
The Library of Kar-Charrat: The Library rivals the Gallifreyan Matrix for sheer volume of information, holding one copy of every piece of literature from every civilized world. (Author's Note: We sent the Library a copy of *I, Who* and the book you're holding. They replied with a thank-you.)

However, the Library was mostly constructed as a work of ambition, never intended to serve as an actual place of reference. (That said, one wonders how much notoriety the Library hopes to achieve, since its existence is so secret.) Removing books is forbidden (shame on you, Doctor) and visitors are rare. The Library doesn't generate enough profit to hire a restoration team.

The Librarians hail from unknown origins but have official relations with Gallifrey. They rarely leave the Library, conducting most research and acquisitions by hyper-cable. At story's end, the Doctor turns off the Library's temporal barriers, allowing the jungle to reclaim the facility.

The TARDIS Library: The Doctor attempts to sort his book collection every 50 years or so, variously shelving stuff by author, planet or color.

HISTORY   Thanks to the Time Lord defense screen, most races think the Library disappeared years ago (some military powers know differently).

• Unable to penetrate the Library's Time Lord defenses, the Daleks used their limited time travel abilities to journey back 1,270 years before the Library's construction and seed the Kar-Charrat sector with identical ziggurats—outwardly appearing to be the product of a lost civilization, but housing a Dalek hibernation facility within. Sensors were calibrated to detect the arrival of time-sensitives, necessary to access Kar-Charrat.

AT THE END OF THE DAY It's got Daleks, but that's the highest we can credit the suspense-less "Genocide Machine," a flat-tone story with a generic Doctor and Ace, a stereotypical secondary cast and a fair amount of overused cliché (Ace's double, etc.). Granted, Big Finish's high production standards keep things professional, preventing this audio from being a complete waste of time, but it's notable mostly because it re-introduces the Doctor's dreaded toilet-plunger wielding foes—suggesting "The Genocide Machine" would've been entirely forgotten if "The Apocalypse Element" or "The Mutant Phase" had been made first.

PRIME TIME

By Mike Tucker

Release Date: July 2000
Order: BBC Past Doctor Adventure #33

TARDIS CREW The seventh Doctor and Ace.

TRAVEL LOG Blinni-Gaar and its moon Blinni-Orkos, Scrantek, a year after *Storm Harvest* (at least 5,000 years in the future, probably more); unspecified Earth location, the near future.

CHRONOLOGY For the Doctor and Ace, after *Storm Harvest* and "The Genocide Machine." (Ace notes she's been travelling with the Doctor for a few years now.) For the Master, after "Survival" and before *First Frontier*.

STORY SUMMARY When Channel 400—a ruthless television network that dominates its sector of space—oddly includes an encoded signal in its normal broadcast, the Doctor elects to investigate further and lands the TARDIS on the agricultural planet of Blinni-Gaar. Channel 400 Director Lukos, having studied the Doctor's history and conspired with shadowy alien allies to lure him to Channel 400 studios on Blinni-Gaar, schedules the Time Lord to unwillingly star in a "real-life" drama named "Doctor When." Lukos also schemes to capture the Doctor's TARDIS, hopefully gaining the ability to broadcast from the most notable events in history.

With hidden cameras broadcasting their every move, the Doctor and Ace break into Channel 400's studio center and find themselves in a trans-dimensional jungle, hotly pursued when Lukos unleashes were-like pack hunters named the Zzinbriizi. Ace tries to escape and Lukos' human agents capture her, while the Doctor deduces the jungle is actually a damaged TARDIS interior belonging to his old foe the Master—apparently the victim of Lukos' alien allies.

The Doctor secures the console room of the Master's TARDIS and tries to dematerialize, but the Ship takes off on pre-set coordinates. In the Doctor's absence, Lukos' producers throw Ace in front of a studio audience and torment her with images taken from Earth's past, including Ace's "future" tombstone.

Meanwhile, the Master's TARDIS lands on the remote planet Scrantek and Lukos' alien allies, the Fleshsmiths, take the Doctor prisoner. As survivors of a natural disaster that corroded their world, the Fleshsmiths learned to graft other beings' flesh onto their own, continually ravaging hundreds of thousands of beings in a bid to live. The Fleshsmith Surgeon General explains that once the Doctor's Channel 400 program peaks at 150 billion viewers, the Fleshsmiths will betray Lukos by introducing a deconstructive enzyme into the broadcast, molecularly deconstructing the viewing masses and transmitting them into the Scrantek body banks as raw, reusable flesh.

The Doctor momentarily escapes and generates a molecularly imperfect clone of himself using the Fleshsmiths' DNA sequencer. Soon after, the Master, captured by the Fleshsmiths while attempting to barter for a stronger body, betrays the Doctor in exchange for his freedom. As 150 billion beings eagerly watch, the Fleshsmiths molecularly dissect the Doctor's clone to learn the secrets of Time Lord regeneration, but "the Doctor" melts and releases a pre-programmed molecular contagion that cascades through the Fleshsmith planetary network. The Fleshsmiths painfully devolve into goo while the real Doctor escapes to Blinni-Gaar and rescues Ace. The Master escapes in his TARDIS and hypnotizes the remaining Zzinbriizi as his servants, allowing them to vent some of their bestial tendencies by killing Lukos.

With Channel 400 disgraced and off the air, the Doctor reassures Ace that the network faked images of her tombstone for the audience's amusement. Ace accepts the Doctor's explanation, but as she sleeps, the Doctor pilots the TARDIS to a cemetery on Earth and digs up Ace's casket. After confirming the coffin indeed contains young Ace's corpse, the Doctor secures the body deep within the TARDIS' interior, vowing to prevent Ace's death even if it damns the laws of Time.

MEMORABLE MOMENTS In a top dramatic moment, the Doctor throws up a force field and the Zzinbriizi threaten to kill the Master. Still concerned for his old friend after everything that's happened between them, the Doctor surrenders. Later, the Doctor says he can't fight the Fleshsmiths and the Master together, holding out a hand and begging the Master: "Tell me that for once in my life I can trust you." (Naturally, hunters arrive and interrupt the Master's response.)

A security chief tells the snooping Doctor he can't enter the studio for *Music Time* because he's not a girl and the Doctor replies: "I could be, one day." Broadcaster Saarl decrees the seventh Doctor lacks the body of a leading man, garbles his lines and puts emphasis in all the wrong places (fear not, Sylvester—we still love ya).

The Doctor—with less arrogance than you might think—explains that he's a broadcasting phenomenon that cannot be standardized or Hollywoodized and that Channel 400 hasn't handled him properly. The Doctor digs up Ace's coffin, hides it in TARDIS and promises to save her.

SEX AND SPIRITS The Doctor stocks sea-green Coralee wine. Blinni-Gar bars serve Ogron Ale, Draconian sake and Foamasi brandy. Ace enjoys a hot, soapy bath for the first time in ages (restrain thy hormones, gentlemen). She fancies journalist Greg Ashby and rings him up, but realizes just he wants to interview the Doctor and dumps the git.

ASS-WHUPPINGS Ace's death is left unresolved. Stay tuned. (We can't believe we just said that).

MISCELLANEOUS STUFF!

THE 'DEATH' OF ACE

Prime Time contains a few oddities that makes one wonder if it's canon or an "Alterni-verse" story. The Virgin New Adventures and Tucker's "The Genocide Machine" handily establish Ace's last name as "McShane." Yet *Prime Time* twice dubs Ace "Dorothy Gale," either suggesting her full name's "Dorothy Gale McShane" or denoting that the same time meddling that resulted in Ace's "death" has triggered historical side effects.

Further continuity errors: Lukos' research suggests this version of the seventh Doctor should be paired with Melanie Bush, further proved by the Doctor's appearance in a gray jacket on the cover—but this story conclusively takes place after the Doctor's brown-jacket period in "Survival." Channel 400 (legitimately, it seems) drags up footage of Ace's desolate old mother, age 85, when adult Ace was reunited with mummy in *Happy Endings*. There's no easy answer to these problems (especially Ace's corpse), leaving us to but hope the BBC writers will sort it out.

The Doctor engineers the downfall of the Fleshsmiths, plus causes explosions that wrack Scrantek and kill thousands of Fleshsmith captives (that the Doctor couldn't save). To cause a distraction, the Doctor releases dozens of animals that the bloodthirsty Zzinbriizi tear apart. The Cheetah-tainted Master goes feral, tears the throat out of an arrogant Zzinbriizi and drops it in an abyss.

Ace fires a materializing piton into Lukos' shoulder and thinks about killing him for punishing her onstage (the Doctor stops her).

The Fleshsmiths reportedly capture 600,000 hapless travelers a year in the Brago Nebula for their body banks They also experiment on the Master, take apart his DNA and—drat!—put it back together again.

TV TIE-INS Civilization on Blinni-Gaar interacts with the Ogrons ("Day of the Daleks"), the Draconians ("Frontier in Space") and the Argolians ("The Leisure Hive").

The Doctor and the Master share telepathic communication ("The Three Doctors," etc.). The Doctor dons TARDIS spacesuits for the fist time in ages (presumably since "Four to Doomsday") and worries there won't be one in his size.

This book is not endorsed by the BBC. Doctor Who and TARDIS are trademarks of the BBC.

95

Channel 400 locates footage of the burning of Gabriel Chase ("Ghost Light"). Ace's metal ladder and climbing equipment gets used for the first time since "The Curse of Fenric." The Master's mostly mastered the Cheetah taint he picked up in "Survival," but it remains viral and flares up from time to time. The Master's been planning to acquire the Doctor's Time Lord body, foreshadowing "Doctor Who: Enemy Within."

The seventh Doctor cannot hypnotize people ("Silver Nemesis") who're set in their ways.

Lukos Entertainment Group offers seven-day tours to the Greatest Hotel in the Galaxy (obviously a play on "The Greatest Show in the Galaxy"), served by an Androgum catering staff ("The Two Doctors").

NOVEL TIE-INS The seventh Doctor and the Anthony Ainley Master last clashed in *Short Trips*: "Stop the Pigeon."

Civilization on Blinni-Gaar is very aware of the Krill incident on Coralee (*Storm Harvest*). The Doctor knocked up Ace's transmat piton gun (*See Stuff You Need*) during that adventure. Lukos is aware of the seventh Doctor's future involvement on Peladon (*Legacy*).

An elaborate train set runs in and out of the TARDIS console room (*Short Trips*: "Model Train Set"). Ace's photos include the Doctor in London after the Blitz (*Illegal Alien*).

TV AND NOVEL TIE-INS *First Frontier* pretty much filled the gap between the Master's involvement in "Survival" and his regeneration at Ace's hands (Revenge, we tell you! Revenge!), but there's undoubtedly room for more stories (as if this is the first time "Doctor Who" contradicts itself). Channel 400 is bigger than IMC ("Colony in Space") and InterOceanic (*Storm Harvest*).

AWWW, HELL. LOTS OF TIE-INS Since *Storm Harvest*, the Doctor and Ace have encountered the Daleks ("The Genocide Machine"), become involved in a Venddon war treaty and fought the Voord ("The Keys of Marinus").

The Doctor knows Alpha Centaurian ("The Curse of Peladon") juggling techniques ("The Genocide Machine").

COMIC TIE-INS Ace wants to return to prehistoric Earth, probably alluding to a text adventure in *Doctor Who Magazine* #162.

CHARACTER DEVELOPMENT

The Doctor: Records on the Doctor stretch back as far as the prespace era. He knows the TARDIS' normal rhythms by sounds, sometimes uses opera

THE CRUCIAL BITS...

- **PRIME TIME**—Channel 400, a villainous television network, torments Ace with images of her tombstone on Earth. The Doctor secretly confirms Ace's death and vows to save her at the cost of the Laws of Time.

glasses and has steel-gray eyes. He's good at lock-picking with a safety pin. He knows the Fleshsmiths only by reputation.

The Doctor can pilot the Master's TARDIS, or reset its interior with a two-degree offset, immediately shunting his enemies into corridors that take hours to navigate. He's good at gardening. He's seen all variety of horror, but the depths of the Fleshsmith body banks chilled his soul.

Ace: Time-travelling Ace often forgets to celebrate her birthday. At the Perivale youth club, Ace learned to rock climb on mock walls and loves it. Blinni-Gaar native Gatti improves her rock climbing skills. Ace can cycle at nearly 40 miles per hour and owns a bundle of "Blue Peter" badges. She wears a TARDIS key around her neck (which broadcaster Saarl takes).

The Doctor and Ace: Ace asked the Doctor to protect her from seeing someone she loved as an old, crippled person. The time travelling Doctor didn't foresee Ace's death. He checks her body and finds Ace as she appears today.

The Master: The Cheetah virus infecting the Master sometimes grants him an enhanced sniffer and pointed teeth. In full feral mode, the lethal Master gains twisted claws and a horribly curved spine. He carries a jetblack sphere used to track power sources. The Fleshsmiths, perhaps as a further bargaining chip, fashioned a body for the Master built to his specifications. Using his TARDIS' telepathic circuits, the Master could have downloaded his consciousness into the new body but it melted first.

The Doctor and the Master: They've been enemies longer than friends. Despite everything, a part of the Doctor wants to help restore the Master to full health.

The TARDIS: Ace frequents a TARDIS gym, and always feels like she's walking uphill to reach the console room. The Ship has an antiquated kitchen and a 1920s cinema (the Doctor and Ace watched *Jurassic Park*). The TARDIS regulates itself with a night cycle, and has a well-equipped laboratory with chemicals to make explosives.

The Master's TARDIS: The exterior's a silver cube, but the interior's damaged and in a state of flux (the Doctor greatly fixes this). The central console's equipped with an electrical forcefield to protect its operator.

ALIEN RACES

The Time Lords: Avoid the Fleshsmiths.

Zzinbriizi: Pack-hunting jackals, adapted to jungle terrain but not very smart, lacking any sort of technology. The Fleshsmiths can grant a Zzinbriizi limited shape-shifting ability using another being as a template (one of them pulls this stunt with the Master).

The Fleshsmiths: They pioneered surgical techniques and transplant technology to an ultra-advanced degree, and are essentially able to sculpt flesh like wood. To maintain their rotting bodies, the Fleshsmiths—led by their surgeon general—rob graves and even prey on the living. Yet for all their expertise, the damage to the Fleshsmiths' tissues means they're at best masses of raw tissue, scarred with surgical pins. Each Fleshsmith holds a unique combination of organs. Some of them have animal characteristics.

They don't have much experience sculpting human flesh, or in trying to determine a way to properly harvest our intellect and determination. They keep a body bank of sick and infirm beings, in case they have need for a specific disease.

ALIEN PLANETS

Blinni-Gaar: Foremost agricultural planet in the sector, orbited by a single moon (Blinni-Orkos).

Scrantek: Fleshsmith homeworld, located in the Brago Nebula wastes and plagued by lightning-charged ion storms.

STUFF YOU NEED

"Dr. When": Channel 400's newest flagship series, pumping out a merchandise line that includes action figures such as the Doctor, Ace, the Daleks, Cybermen and Krill.

Ace's Transmat Piton Gun: Present from the Doctor, able to fire a dematerialized piton and molecularly reassemble it, with climbing rope, into a structure (or person, if you're cornered).

PLACES TO GO The *Fleshsmith Body Bank* contains an endless array of species, ranging from humans to Draconians, Ice Warriors, Ogrons and Daleks. You don't wanna be caught dead there.

ORGANIZATIONS *Channel 400* commands 87 percent of the viewing public in its quadrant, relentlessly pummeling people with crappy shows (much like American and British stations, one imagines) such as Roderik Saarl's *Late Night Breakfast Show*, *Walking with Drashigs* ("Carnival of Monsters") and *Ogron Hospital* ("Day of the Daleks").

HISTORY The civilized race that became the Fleshsmiths developed great works of art and architecture, initially clinging to their morals even when a natural disaster (possibly caused by the nearby Brago Nebula) devastated their homeworld of Scrantek. The race's degeneration became so great, they mastered flesh surgery and transplant, becoming the Fleshsmiths and prolonging their lives by taking healthy organs from their own infirm. When that source exhausted, the Fleshsmiths plundered other races for more organic material.

• Channel 400 forged a deal with the government of the agricultural planet Blinni-Gaar and headquartered itself there about 10 years ago. As incentive to get people watching, the network offered big prizes to random viewers and eventually dominated the entire sector. As Blinni-Gaar farmers opted to watch cable all day and nearly caused a famine, the provisional government paid off-worlders to run the planet.

AT THE END OF THE DAY A wholeheartedly underrated book, probably because novels about television initially seem banal and fandom loathes the thought of Ace non-canonically kicking it—a plot thread we're hoping will be solved down the road. Yet *Prime Time* plays to Tucker's strengths, delivering an intensely personal trial for Ace and a compassionate Doctor who nonetheless crushes a race whom the Time Lords shun. Hell, even the Master—a mostly transparent villain—makes for a welcome addition, rounding out a solid package that hearkens back to McCoy's second season and deserves re-consideration.

THE FEARMONGER

By Jonathan Blum

Release Date: February 2000
Order: Big Finish "Doctor Who" Audio #5

TARDIS CREW The seventh Doctor and Ace.

TRAVEL LOG London, circa 2002.

CHRONOLOGY Between *Nightshade* and *Love and War*.

STORY SUMMARY In London's near future, Sherilyn Harper, leader of the New Britannia Party, persuades a growing number of people to become fearful of outsiders, thus approving her extremist right-wing agenda. But Walter Jacobs, a manic opponent to Harper's policies, repeatedly hears a monstrous voice speaking through Harper and tries to assassinate her. Walter fails, but the murder attempt alarms the public and boosts support for Harper's oppressive legislative goals.

Meanwhile, the Doctor and Ace arrive in London trailing the Fearmonger—an energy-based creature, created by a long-dead alien race, that hides in other beings, feeding on raw fear and terror. Learning of Walter's botched attempt on Harper's life, the Doctor and Ace suspect the Fearmonger has taken Harper as a host, using her paranoia-based rhetoric to wreak havoc and thereby get some emotional dinner.

Suddenly, a militant organization named the United Front launches a series of terrorist attacks against civilian targets, protesting New Britannia's supremacist views and generating panic. Focused on stopping the Fearmonger, the Doctor constructs a short-range force field device capable of crushing the monster while leaving its host unharmed. But as radio personality Mick Thompson interviews Harper, the Doctor deploys his force field and is shocked when the device registers both Harper and Thompson as normal. Simultaneously, Ace starts to hear the Fearmonger's tones in the Doctor's voice.

Jolted by Harper's fanatical prodding and the threat of the United Front's assaults, the public engages in full-blown riots. Acting on a whim, the Doctor tricks Harper's aide Roderick Allingham into meeting with the United Front. While Thompson secretly broadcasts the conversation, Allingham reveals that New Britannia secretly funded United Front as a publicity stunt, deliberately frightening the people and thereby forcing them to turn to New Britannia for protection. The rioters realize the futility of their actions and end the violence, although the remnants of a mob besiege Harper's house to make her account for the United Front deception.

Ace secures one of Walter's bombs and confronts the Doctor in a secluded warehouse, threatening to kill them both if the force field can't destroy the Fearmonger inside the Doctor. Calmly, the Doctor explains that the Fearmonger was in Walter from the very beginning. Later, the Fearmonger covered its tracks by transferring itself into Ace, causing her to become increasingly suspicious and paranoid. Gradually, Ace trusts the Doctor's words and turns the force field on herself, destroying the Fearmonger forever.

MEMORABLE MOMENTS Ace impishly suggests the Fearmonger is "a Fearmongoid from the planet Fearmongus." The Doctor says that history pushes forward regardless of a few actions, that time is best pictured as millions of butterflies fanning a "million multi-colored pieces of time."

The Doctor's worst fears come true when United Front leader Karadjic puts a bullet through Ace at the end of Part Two. Later, near Ace's hospital recovery room, the Fearmonger appears in its raw energy state. The Doctor's centuries of struggles and inner torment surge forth as he rebukes the creature, saying he's personally experienced death, witnessed change and seen his companion gunned down—meaning there's nothing left to fear (the Fearmonger wisely retreats).

The Doctor conducts a final conversation with the disgraced Sherilyn Harper, where she admits to fostering fear to make her people strong. The Doctor concedes that Harper's followers understood her motives only too well, then leaves her fearful and alone as a mob approaches.

SEX AND SPIRITS Upon learning that the Fearmonger likely has emotion-charged siblings, Ace wonders which planet got Lust (undoubtedly a.k.a. "the Lustmonger").

ASS-WHUPPINGS Alexsandr Karadjic, leader of the United Front, shoots Ace and puts her in the hospital for most of Part Three. It's not clear, but the Doctor possibly leaves Sherilyn Harper to her death at the hands of a rampaging mob.

NOVEL TIE-INS The Doctor mentions that his relatives (*Lungbarrow*) are "very odd."

CHARACTER DEVELOPMENT
The Doctor: United Nations files acknowledge the Doctor's alien nature, but also record that he's overthrown a lot of dictators. Despite the Doctor's

time with UNIT, the UN disavows any knowledge of his actions, offering no assistance or political immunity. The UN files also warn that the Doctor usually coerces people into doing what he wants simply by talking to them.

The Doctor's always hated hospitals because they're full of sick people and doctors who think they know everything.

The Doctor and Ace: The Doctor helped Ace to learn that it's often best to stop and re-evaluate before rushing in pell-mell to fix things. Ace knows about many of the Doctor's questionable actions but still trusts him. The worst thing Ace can imagine is an alien power subverting the Doctor—and she's willing to give her life to prevent such an event from happening (until now, the Doctor was unaware of the strength of her convictions).

The Fearmonger: A creature of raw electro-magnetic energy, acting like psychic phenomena by soaking up fear and hatred. The Doctor knows about many of the Fearmonger's abilities, but only suspects its origins (*See History*).

The Fearmonger can move on its own but prefers hiding in a host for long periods of time. It picks hosts capable of generating large amounts of fear, moving on if the host dies. The Fearmonger can unleash fear-concentrated mental bursts that cause brain damage and turn its enemies into gibbering idiots. In its natural state, the Fearmonger is vulnerable to metal—even, say, a frying pan—that might ground its energy.

Paul Tanner: Part-time hacker who knew Ace during her Perivale days.

Sherilyn Harper: New Britannia's leader claims England must guard itself against losing political and economic control to Europe and Asia.

Roderick Allingham: Sherilyn Harper's assistant used to work for the Ministry. Years ago, he read UN files that cited the Doctor as a rogue intelligence agent and freelance UN consultant.

STUFF YOU NEED *High-Radiation Beryllium Laser:* Nasty piece of weaponry based on a prototype the Doctor saw during his time with UNIT. Most civilized planets have banned beryllium lasers. Earth authorities currently use such armaments but will follow suit in 20 years.

ORGANIZATIONS

New Britannia Party: Britain's Labour Party fears losing political stature to this group, but neo-Nazi organizations embrace New Britannia.

United Front: Not quite the great army it pretends to be, comprised of a group of punks supplied with weaponry by Harper and Allingham. They admittedly order the United Front not to harm anyone, but the situation races out of control.

HISTORY The Fearmonger likely originated centuries ago on the planet Boslin II, where the Gymnoti race created a wide range of electro-magnetic creatures—each of them personifying a different emotion such as fear, compassion, pride, anger and lust (Author's Note: What we irrelevantly refer to as "The Seven Deadly Mongers"). The Gymnoti speculated that since strong emotions bring people closer together, the various emotion-based creatures would strengthen their society by spurring a greater sense of community. In time, the Gymnoti civilization fell and the Mongers, slaved mostly to instinct, migrated offplanet.

AT THE END OF THE DAY What starts out as a simple premise turns into a stellar, layered work that emphasizes Ace's loyalty for the Doctor and precisely captures TV's theme of confronting personal fears ("Ghost Light," "The Curse of Fenric"). "The Fearmonger" masks itself as a political thriller, keeping its characters on razor's edge for 110 minutes, but finally boils down to an energy monster's personification of the weakness in all of us. Blum's wide-eyed optimism keeps this story perfectly balanced, presenting a larger-than-life Doctor who overcomes every gun shoved in his face, and providing us with just a hint of the New Adventures.

INDEPENDENCE DAY

By Peter Darvill-Evans

Release Date: October 2000
Order: BBC Past Doctor Adventure #36

TARDIS CREW The seventh Doctor and Ace.

TRAVEL LOG Mendeb Two, Mendeb Three, the Moonstar satellite, time unknown.

CHRONOLOGY Sometime after "Survival." (Author's Note: Due to Ace's hands-off relationship with the Doctor, her overall knowledge of technology and vibrant sexuality, this book likely takes place between *Nightshade* and *Love and War*.)

STORY SUMMARY In rummaging through the TARDIS' storage vaults, Ace comes upon an odd-looking communications relay device, inscribed as hailing from the planet Mendeb Two. Recalling that he took the relay purely as a keepsake during a previous stopover on Mendeb Two, the Doctor consults the TARDIS databanks—and distressingly learns that his acquisition of the communications relay altered history. The Gallifreyan Matrix says colonies on Mendeb Two and Mendeb Three should have roughly equal technology. However, the Doctor's inadvertent removal of the crucial relay deactivated Mendeb Two's entire communications network, the last remnant of the TAM Corporation that settled the Mendeb system. In turn, this prevented Mendeb Two's disparate settlements from pooling their technical skills and keeping pace with Mendeb Three's speedy developments. Mendeb Three and its ruling King Vethran eventually enslaved Mendeb Two, and unless the Doctor intervenes to correct history, a bloody revolution could result.

The Doctor proposes investigating Mendeb Two, while Ace volunteers to reconnoiter the Mendeb Three-controlled Moonstar space station. There, Ace meets a powerful Mendeb Three military commander named Kedin Ashar and sleeps with him to solicit more information (and for fun, one presumes). Kedin tells Ace he's planning to overthrow the tyrannical King Vethran, but Ace discovers that Kedin finances his army with slave trade funds and vows to stop such inhuman operations. Out of affection for Ace, Kedin resists killing her, drugging her instead with a specially tailored variant of SS10, a chemical used to subvert the will. Kedin's SS10 derivative temporarily brainwashes Ace, who's sold with some Mendeb Two slaves, becoming a servant and warrior-in-training to King Vethran's court.

Meanwhile, occupying forces on Mendeb Two capture the Doctor and shuttle him with a group of slaves back to Mendeb Three. The guards provide soup laced with SS10 to make the slaves fully submissive, but the Doctor proves immune and warns some of his fellow prisoners to refrain from eating. Instead, the Doctor provides a flask, interdimensionally linked to the TARDIS' food processor, which provides a constant supply of liquid nourishment. The Doctor's independent-thinking cadre then escapes and instigates a small revolution, but gets re-captured and taken before King Vethran, who's curious as to how the Doctor resisted the SS10.

Kedin launches his revolution, ripping through Vethran's troops but ultimately reaching a stalemate in Vethran's castle. Vethran stalls for time,

hoping to enthrall Kedin with SS10, but Ace shrugs off her temporary conditioning and doctors Vethran's drink with the drug instead, pacifying the tyrant and handing Kedin the victory.

The Doctor recovers but tragically concludes that since the effects of standard SS10 can't be reversed, none of the infected Mendeb Two slaves can be cured. Kedin formally ends the slave trade and mandates a series of reparations to Mendeb Two, promising to rebuild the planet. Somewhat in love with Kedin, Ace offers to stay on with him and lend technical assistance, but Kedin persuades Ace that her place is with the Doctor.

MEMORABLE MOMENTS A guardsman: "Take this soup. Eat it." The captive Doctor: "It's cold. Have you no moral scruples at all?"

SEX AND SPIRITS Ace puts out for Kedin, supposedly to get information about Mendeb Three. However, Kedin does the nasty to solicit Ace's technical assistance (ah, young love—such a means to an end). Kedin has sex with Ace despite being deeply involved with Lady Tevana, held captive by King Vethran. Tevana later falls prey to SS10's brain-erasing effects and Ace, evidently forgetting Kedin half-brainwashed her and abandoned her to the slave pits, offers to stay with him. Kedin, mustering a shred of nobility, encourages Ace to depart in the TARDIS rather than stick around and eventually grow resentful.

ASS-WHUPPINGS When slave masters test her conditioning, Ace, fully cognizant but playing along, bites a fellow slave's ear off and eats it. She also burns her hands on hot plates rather than admit her free-thinking capacity.

King Vethran, learning of Kedin's revolution, tires of the Doctor and forces him to swallow a toxic worm. The Doctor appears to bite the bullet, but heals his internal organs until Ace removes the worm from his gullet. Ace takes out King Vethran with the mind-altering SS10.

TV TIE INS Just before being carted to Svartos ("Dragonfire") via a time storm, Ace saw *Withnail and I* (she thought it funny, but her friends didn't get it). Ace fancied actor Richard E. Grant from that flick and wonders why the Doctor can't be more like him (of course, Grant played one of the Doctors in "The Curse of Fatal Death").

TV AND NOVEL TIE-INS *Happy Endings* establishes that Ace didn't have any lovers between Sabalom Glitz ("Dragonfire") and Jan (*Love and War*), making her dalliance with Kedin yet another continuity screw-up.

CHARACTER DEVELOPMENT

The Doctor: The Doctor displays superhuman strength (lifting the communications relay with one hand, whereas Ace sweats and groans just to move the sucker). He's immune to SS10 and can run an internal chemical analysis of the drug simply by drinking it (although this raises his temperature). Days go by during this story, but the Doctor always looks clean, unshaven and alert. Vethran's bile worms are toxic to the Doctor's physiognomy, nearly triggering regeneration.

Ace: Ace keeps shelves in the TARDIS filled with demolitions equipment, referring to the stash as her "Armory." Her musical tastes include Adam Ant, George Michael, Primal Scream and the Jesus and Mary Chain. Using the TARDIS' history abstracts, she's studied humankind's trek to the stars circa 2000 to 2500.

Ace has only one middle name (but we're not told what it is). She's got advanced piloting abilities, knowledge of technology and computer hacking skills (Timewyrm: Apocalypse). She was good at football (that's soccer, for us Yankees) in school. She displays impressive fighting skills with a staff and almost achieved an O-level in chemistry.

Kedin Ashar Duke of Jerrissar: In more moderate days, Kedin assisted King Vethran in his rise to power, supplying arms and attack vehicles in exchange for land. However, Vethran's oppressive agenda caused Kedin to plot his downfall. Kedin is now the largest landholder in Country Cathogh, with enough troops to rival Vethran.

ALIEN RACES

Sontarans: Certain types of yeast can harm their physiognomy ("It's the Sontarans! Ready your olive loaves, men!")

ALIEN PLANETS

Mendeb Two: Most of Mendeb Two is too hot for humans, allowing only isolated island colonies near the poles.

Mendeb Three: By comparison, Mendeb Three sports a more amiable climate, slightly cooler than Earth norms. Settlements established themselves in the equatorial belt, tapping abundant natural resources. Mendeb Three's weaponry is fairly primitive, limited mostly to muskets, but that's still more than Mendeb Two possesses. Mendeb Three uses "marks" as currency and has a pale violet sky.

STUFF YOU NEED

SS10: King Vethran's scientists derived SS10 from the seeds of a spore-weed plant that effects humans like a mild narcotic. Vethran's science team re-engineered SS10 to transform a clump of cells in the brain, creating a factory to manufacture a chemical agent that cauterizes nerve endings. This chemical agent in turn performs permanent surgery on the hypothalamus, removing the subject's volition and a good chunk of personality without affecting intelligence or memory. The TARDIS could create an organic substitute to eliminate the factory and damaged cells, but such new tissue can't regrow the lost nerve endings. No antidote for SS10 exists, although Kedin's supporters created a variant that temporarily mimics SS10's effects. Time Lords are evidently immune.

PLACES TO GO

Mendeb system: Abnormally has three gas giants in close orbits.

HISTORY

Even for its time, the TAM Corporation was overly unscrupulous. It colonized the Mendeb system 400 years ago, but found the region unprofitable and withdrew, leaving the settlers to their fate. TAM pulled out all spaceships and most of their technology, leaving only the abandoned Moonstar space station in orbit and an automatic communications relay system at Mendeb Two's equator.

• Some years before this story (Mendeb time), the second Doctor's TARDIS landed at the automatic communications center on Mendeb Two's equator. At Jamie's urging, the Doctor agreed to leave the oppressively hot area, but suggested he snag something to help them remember to return. Jamie unwisely picked the main communications relay device (the stupid thing was aesthetically pleasing), which deactivated the entire communications network.

AT THE END OF THE DAY

So unambitious that it hurts, *Independence Day* commits one of literature's greatest sins: failure to prove it has a pulse. The Doctor's never been more blundering; he accomplishes nothing throughout the entire book, getting poisoned just as Kedin's troops arrive. Whoopie. You go, boy. And aside from drugging the king at story's end and some throwaway sex, we can't prove Ace was present either. That only leaves *Independence Day* with its generic secondary cast, generic motivations and some abysmally flatline dialogue, such as the king's: "Be silent, or I'll have the guards damage you."

THE SHADOW OF THE SCOURGE

By Paul Cornell

Release Date: October 2000
Order: Big Finish "Doctor Who" Audio #13

TARDIS CREW   The seventh Doctor, Ace and Bernice.

TRAVEL LOG   Pine Hill Crest Hotel, Newmangate, Kent, August 15, 2003.

CHRONOLOGY   Between *All-Consuming Fire* and *Blood Harvest*.

STORY SUMMARY Secretly plotting to eliminate a grave threat to humanity, the Doctor takes Benny and Ace to the Pinehill Crest Hotel in Kent, where three very distinct conventions are underway. While one set of rooms hosts a cross-stitch convention, spiritual channeler (and professional fraud) Annie Carpenter conducts séances in another, and in yet another section, Dr. Michael Pembroke attracts funding for his prototype particle accelerator—a means of potentially breaching dimensions and achieving unlimited travel throughout our Universe and others.

Alarmingly, Carpenter's "false" séance turns all too real when a dark mental force possesses her and Brian Hughes, director of Hughes Avionics. Under the dark power's direction, Hughes pushes Pembroke's accelerator to dangerous levels, causing it to transport the packed hotel into a temporary holding dimension. Simultaneously, the dark force physically infests Hughes and Carpenter, transforming them into giant mantis-like creatures named the Scourge.

Momentarily taking shelter in his hotel room, the Doctor details to Ace and Benny that the Scourge are other-dimensional parasites who have mentally feasted upon humanity's doubt, insecurity and despair for millennia. The Scourge possessing Hughes and Carpenter hope to terrorize the convention goers and use their fear as a power source—combining it with Pembroke's particle accelerator to physically materialize the Scourge race en masse first in the hotel's fractional dimension, then ultimately back on Earth. If successful, the multi-dimensional Scourge will gain the ability to literally reshape time, space and human thought to fit their whims.

Having long ago realized the Scourge's plans, the Doctor previously used the TARDIS to place devices he hopes will neutralize both the crowd's

fear and Pembroke's machine at the exact moment the Scourge try to materialize—thus smearing the in-transit Scourge across a dimensional rift for millions of years. Unfortunately, the Scourge anticipate the Doctor's betrayal and disarm his devices. Worse, the Scourge launch an attempt to possess the Doctor and materialize a Scourge warrior in his body.

As the Scourge start to manifest on Earth, the Doctor desperately wills his mutating body comatose and isolates the Scourge warrior invading his mind. By trapping one Scourge, the Doctor effectively halts the collective Scourge gestalt from materializing. Benny doses the Carpenter-Scourge with the Doctor's pacification gas, helping Carpenter recover somewhat. Using Carpenter's limited psionic powers, Benny shunts her consciousness into the Doctor's mind, boosting his morale to fight the invader.

The Doctor re-directs his thoughts through the Scourge gestalt, mentally directing Ace to disconnect the TARDIS' safety protocols. Under Ace's command, the TARDIS warps local space and prevents Scourge reinforcements from materializing. Gradually, Bernice reassures the Doctor as to his self-confidence, giving him the willpower to expel the Scourge warrior from the Doctor's mind.

Ace rallies the convention-goers against the few Scourge remaining in the hotel, denying them a fear source to feed upon. The Doctor and Bernice revive, then join the convention-goers in denouncing the Scourge and casting them back home, restoring Hughes and Carpenter to normal. With the Scourge's influence ended, the hotel returns to Earth, and the Doctor, happily empowered by his friends' support, expresses optimism about humanity's future.

MEMORABLE MOMENTS Even before the chaos breaks out, the Doctor steps off a hotel elevator and gravely announces, "Ground floor: Horror, tragedy and mysterious deaths." Benny mocks séance leader Carpenter by asking to summon the spirits of her "two poor little ones" (e.g. her turtles Squidgy and Speckly). Ace and Benny compare notes on how the Doctor's always pretending to side with alien invaders.

Benny suggests that Ace can discern the Carpenter-Scourge by looking for breasts. (When Ace chooses wrong anyway, Benny screams, "No! No, it's the wrong one! It hasn't got any—").

The Doctor potently rambles at the Part Three cliffhanger (oh, how we love a good ramble) before throwing himself into a mental abyss—the direction here is brilliant.

The Doctor asks if the near-defeated Scourge, so-called embodiments of fear, are scared. Finally, the Doctor gives the stubborn Scourge leader the option of voluntarily returning to his home dimension—when the Scourge refuses, the Doctor mentally forces the Scourge to completely let go of our reality, casting the Scourge into the dimensional rift.

SEX AND SPIRITS Benny sees a mental image of the McGann Doctor and starts drooling, asking the Doctor's current self: "You're not going to regenerate any time soon, are you?"

The Doctor books hotel rooms under the name "Summerfield" because his pseudonym of "John Smith" would attract undue attention in a Kent hotel. The Scourge worry they've killed too many convention-goers and suggest letting the survivors breed (as if convention sex isn't a myth).

ASS-WHUPPINGS The Doctor's small Scottish body transforms partially into a Scourge. Ace, seeking to protect herself from the Scourge's entrancing voice, gets convention director Gary Williams to shatter her eardrums (the TARDIS nanites later fix her up).

The Scourge repeatedly terrorize the convention goers, mesmerizing attendee Mike Duff into strangling himself. More blatantly, the Scourge savagely nibble some conventioneers to death.

NOVEL TIE-INS Ace previously visited the Doctor's brain in Cornell's *Timewyrm: Revelation*, but Benny's trip here differs because the route by which you enter the Doctor's cranium affects the mental landscape (Benny sees it as an echo-filled void—with lots of tasteful furniture).

The seventh Doctor hints that Benny will meet his eighth self someday (*The Dying Days*). He's aware of his eighth incarnation's likeness, but also learns it (more painfully) in *Return of the Living Dad*. Benny's mention of her ex-turtles could refer to two Galapagos tortoises owned by her first lover, Simon Kyle (also *Living Dad*).

The Scourge confirm Ace's surname as McShane (*Set Piece*), not Gale (*Prime Time*).

CHARACTER DEVELOPMENT

The Doctor: Instigates his plot against the Scourge bargaining with them on the astral plane. The Scourge perceive images of the Doctor's past and future incarnations, and see his "shadow" (presumably his time trail) stretching back and forward through time.

During mental battle with the Scourge, the Doctor can reroute the Scourge's power to maintain the hotel in the fractional dimension. Alternatively, he can use the Scourge gestalt to telepathically communicate with humans.

In the seventh Doctor's mind, Benny views his archetypes—his past and future selves—but they only manifest in times of dire emergency and cannot intervene. The Doctor's current incarnation claims his other selves snub their noses at him. Benny accidentally erases a memory of the Doctor sniffing a flower in a Compton Basset church garden. The Doctor's brainscape stretches for miles, with high ceilings denoting his open mind.

William Shakespeare once brawled with the Doctor, telling him, "Come and have a go, if you think you're hard enough!" (Cornell's way of satirizing a popular soccer quote.)

The Doctor feels lonely and desolate, constantly testing his companions because he expects them to leave him. Yet the Doctor ends this story believing that friends such as Benny and Ace gives him the strength to fight monsters. The seventh Doctor's sensitive to time experiments and interested in cross-stitching.

Ace: Spacefleet-trained Ace inwardly isn't happy with bashing heads—but she's willing to do more of it. She's spent time living in ancient China and met military strategist Sun Tzu (author of *The Art of War*). Ace knows a great deal about police procedures. She's always wanted to break a window with a fire extinguisher (well, haven't we all?). She carries personal communication radio badges, a knife and a small crowbar-like device that pries the tops off Daleks.

Bernice Summerfield: Benny fears asking people for help because she might alienate the society (presumably other archaeologists) that she craves.

The Doctor and Benny: Benny believes the Doctor rarely reveals his plans because he simply likes saving everyone at the last minute. She considers the Doctor her best friend.

The TARDIS: Safeguarding against defeat, the Doctor flooded the TARDIS console room with healing nanites, calibrating it to his Time Lord body. Despite this, the nanites can also heal humans. Combined with the TARDIS' temporal grace, the nanites can restore Scourge-infected humans to normal if they're unconscious (alert Scourge have their defenses up). The TARDIS cannot escape from the fractional dimension without realigning the dimension's parameters.

ALIEN RACES

Time Lords: The Scourge claim Time Lords send water-like temporal waves through the Universes.

The Scourge (a.k.a. "Great Unity of the Scourge"): Horrors from another Universe that operate on higher planes of being. Whereas humanity exists in four dimensions, the Scourge operate in eight (sorry, nothing adequately explains the higher four). The Scourge typically prey on lesser beings' depression, doubt and fear, although humans remain their primary food source. They have mental tendrils into every human being, drawn to moments of depression and heartache. They collectively know each human's inner doubts.

By dissecting human psionics or dabblers in the mystic arts on the astral plane, the Scourge learned to scare humans into obeying their demands, over-awing them with what feels like a religious impulse (deaf people resist their siren-like call). Those who've directly encountered the Scourge describe them as demons, because the Scourge's home dimension seems infernal. As torture, the Scourge sometimes use bio-dimensional implants to stretch their victims across the multiverse and mutate them (the Doctor pretends to bargain with the Scourge to gain such an implant, supposedly coveting its travel power).

If the Scourge physically materialized on Earth, they'd be able to skillfully manipulate matter, time and space. Worse, they could conquer the interior of human thought, compelling humankind to worship them as gods of despair and horror.

With great effort and repeated influence, the Scourge can mutate other beings' bodies—even corpses—into giant mantis forms. Embryos in possessed pregnant women blessedly survive unharmed. Temporal energy surges can stun the Scourge. They've read many texts on the Doctor.

STUFF YOU NEED *The Doctor's Pascificus Gas:* Control gas developed in the 23rd century, capable of helping Scourge-infected people calm down and regain control.

ORGANIZATIONS *The Association of Cross-Stitch Enthusiasts:* The name says it all.

PHENOMENA *Tea* made in a hotel bedroom tastes worse than tea anywhere else in the Universe.

HISTORY The Scourge have feasted upon humanity since it first became sentient and experienced self-doubt.

AT THE END OF THE DAY Boasting some of Big Finish's most cracking dialogue (Cornell seems born to script the McCoy Doctor), "Shadow of the Scourge" will probably saber-rattle some listeners with its immense body count and numerous screams (the Scourge leader above the din: "Run!

Cry out and run! We are the Scourge!"), but steps forward as an intricate, emotive story about restored friendship and faith. Critics who argue the Doctor's an unsympathetic bastard entirely miss the point, with the entire audio geared to show the Doctor, Ace and Benny as a family. Certainly, "Scourge" won't please people who by default abhor a manipulative Doctor—but for everyone else (including us), it's one of Big Finish's best efforts.

THE SIRENS OF TIME

By Nicholas Briggs

Release Date: July 1999
Order: Big Finish "Doctor Who" Audio #1.

TARDIS CREW The fifth, sixth and seventh Doctors.

TRAVEL LOG Gallifrey, modern era; unnamed security planet, time unknown; the Atlantic Ocean, May 7, 1915; the Kurgon Wonder, Kurgon System, 3562.

CHRONOLOGY For the fifth Doctor, between "The Five Doctors" and "Warriors of the Deep"; for the sixth Doctor, between "The Trial of a Time Lord" and *Business Unusual*; for the seventh Doctor, between *Lungbarrow* and "Doctor Who: Enemy Within."

STORY SUMMARY As unidentified warships overrun Gallifrey's defenses, Gallifreyan monitoring posts discover that the invading fleet spawned from distortions in established history—with the Doctor's artron energy signature at the epicenter of the temporal deviation. The Gallifreyan President and Commander Vansell of the CIA try to mount a defense, but the hostiles—the so-called Knights of Velyshaa—kill them and seize control of the Gallifreyan Capital.

Meanwhile, in separate adventures, the fifth, sixth and seventh Doctors materialize, respectively, on a World War I German submarine, the starship *Edifice* and at the home of a banished war criminal named Sancroff. At each location, the Doctors meet an aspect of the same young woman, variously named Helen, Ellie and Elenya. More importantly, a strange force oddly locks each of the Doctors out of their TARDISes, forcing them to linger at their various locations and inadvertently trigger events that violate the course of history and lead to Gallifrey's fall.

The fifth Doctor, separated from his adrift TARDIS in the Atlantic Ocean, hi-jacks a German submarine to retrieve his Ship and unknowingly halts the sub from sinking the *Luisitania*—leading to a series of events that ultimately prevent humanity from discovering space travel. Meanwhile, the seventh Doctor saves the exiled Sancroff from the mercenary Knights of Velyshaa, making the Knights rally around Sancroff's name and embark on a planet-conquering spree. Worst of all, the sixth Doctor frees the Temperon, a graceful and legendary time beast, from a temporal snare—also releasing the Knights of Velyshaa scientists who set out to capture the creature in the first place. In time, the Knights harness the Temperon's unique energy to create powerful Vortex drives and conquer Gallifrey.

The Temperon, aware of the historical disruptions and wishing to help, uses its power to teleport the fifth, sixth and seventh Doctors to Gallifrey. With her Knights in control of the Capital, Knight Commander Lyena explains to the Doctors that the Knights are dying from an wasting disease caused by overexposure to Temperon particles, forcing them to augment their decaying bodies with flesh from the Time Lords.

Lyena begs the Doctors to travel back in a TARDIS and correct their errors, canceling out the Knights' conquests but saving her people from a painful demise. But the Doctors, leery of Lyena's story, privately meet with the re-captured Temperon and learn that Lyena and the women they met in each time zone are all different aspects of "The Sirens of Time"—extra-dimensional creatures of chaos that feed on the energy released by temporal disruptions. The Sirens lured the three Doctors to pivotal points in history, prevented them from leaving in their TARDISes, and manipulated them into disrupting history, thus feasting on the resultant time disruption.

The Temperon warns that if the Doctors answer the Sirens' call a second time to undo their mistakes, they'll fall fully under the Sirens' spell and wreak historical havoc on their behalf throughout the whole of space-time. To break the stalemate, the Temperon offers to counter the Sirens' powers with its own, forever locking them in eternal combat. With little option, the sixth Doctor frees the Temperon, allowing it to travel back through time and restore historical events to their normal course, preventing the rise of the Knights and the conquest of Gallifrey. Burdened because the Temperon will forever hold the Sirens prisoner at the cost of its own freedom, the Doctors return to the seventh Doctor's TARDIS, open a relative interface and return to their proper timestreams.

MEMORABLE MOMENTS "The Sirens of Time" races into action with Gallifrey on full war alert—

and Vansell hauntingly declaring that the Doctor (surprise, surprise) is at the center of the time distortion. A split-second later, the familiar opening music launches a new era of "Who" stories.

Crewwoman Helen shoots a German dead, then ponders if he's actually snuffed it. In response, the fifth Doctor deadpans: "A hole that big in a person usually indicates a zero chance of survival." The Davison Doctor gets the best cliffhanger—clinging to the unyielding TARDIS in a war-torn ocean, desperate to get inside.

Scenes with the sixth and seventh Doctors completely steal the show. They bitch at each other (a crowded McCoy: "You're on my foot!" Baker: "For someone so short, you're taking up a lot of room!"), then transition into over-politeness in letting each other speak. At the story's climax, the sixth Doctor declares himself the most pragmatic version of the Doctor present and unerringly shoots the Knights' controls to free the Temperon.

ASS-WHUPPINGS The Knights of Velyshaa butcher their way through the Time Lords, killing the President and Commander Vansell. Ravaged by exposure to Temperon particles, the Knights harvest entire civilizations for tissue donors, rounding up the Time Lords into extraction camps. (The Temperon's restoration of history neutralizes all this slaughter.)

German crewman Schmidt shoots the fifth Doctor in the shoulder, causing him to lose an inhuman (no pun intended) amount of blood. The fifth Doctor also busts an ankle (fulfilling this story's "broken ankle" quota) running about on Gallifrey. Lyena tortures the fifth Doctor in a life force extraction unit to make his other selves surrender.

A temporal disruption wave ages 5,500 people aboard the starship *Edifice* to death.

TV TIE-INS The Temperon's a close cousin of the Chronovores ("The Time Monster"). The Cloister Bell ("Logopolis") still functions in the seventh Doctor's TARDIS. The fifth, sixth and seventh Doctors use telepathic communication ("The Three Doctors," etc.) to relate their experiences.

The Galactic Wonders Commission decides which objects merit becoming "Wonders of the Universe" ("Death to the Daleks")—an honor that inevitably attracts a bushelful of tourists.

NOVEL TIE-INS The fifth and seventh Doctors don't acknowledge their meeting in *Cold Fusion*. Type 70 TARDISes are top-of-the-line (Gallifrey attains at least Type 98 by *The Shadows of Avalon*; more advanced Type 103s debut in *Alien Bodies*). CIA agent Vansell appears in *Divided Loyalties* (even so, the fifth Doctor fails to recognize him).

AUDIO TIE-INS Gallifrey's President and Vansell reappear in "The Apocalypse Element." Kalendorf, a long-time agent of the Knights of Velyshaa, runs afoul of the the Daleks in the Doctor-less "Dalek Empire: Invasion of the Daleks" audio.

CHARACTER DEVELOPMENT

The Doctor: The fifth, sixth and seventh Doctors meet here for the first time, inherently recognizing each other on sight. The sixth Doctor explains that all of the Doctors share certain traits, which become emphasized or de-emphasized with each regeneration (e.g. all of the Doctors are pragmatic, but the sixth Doctor is even moreso).

The Doctor's memories of the Sirens seem hazy (the fifth Doctor's encounter with a Siren allows the sixth and seventh Doctors to vaguely recognize her duplicates), suggesting either that the Doctor's memories fade from incarnation to incarnation or that the Sirens' call partially mesmerized him.

The Doctor's familiar with vents leading to lower levels of the Gallifreyan Capital. As a Time Lord, he's immune to time distortions that age humans to death.

The sixth Doctor: He's decently versed in android design. He's familiar with spaceship construction according to the Hadine-Lastrade design because he knew Lastrade, a penniless genius.

The Temperon: Unique, legendary time beast that peacefully folds its way through oceans of time (presumably the Time Vortex). When the Knights first attempted to snare the Temperon, it favored death to capture and rammed their prototype ship, releasing a large amount of unique Temperon particles that immobilized both parties and created the Kurgon Wonder (*See Places to Go*). The Temperon can speak to the Doctors telepathically. It's known about the Sirens for eons.

Commander Vansell: Unscrupulous Celestial Intervention Agency member who uses an unregistered, augmented Type 70 TARDIS.

The TARDIS: Its translation systems enable the Doctor to communicate with Germans, but he still sounds like an Englishman. Despite its heavy mass, the TARDIS floats. Temperon particles can breach its outer shell.

ALIEN RACES

Time Lords: Have unique artron energy signatures. They can use temporal thought projection technology to communicate with other beings throughout space-time. Relaying such thought

THE CRUCIAL BITS...

- **THE SIRENS OF TIME**—The fifth, sixth and seventh Doctors meet. First appearance of the interim Gallifreyan President and CIA agent Commander Vansell. First appearance of the Knights of Velyshaa.

messages through artificial beings (such as androids) takes less power.

The Sirens of Time: Multiple aspects of the same temporal creature. Devoid of concepts of good or evil, they subsist on the energy caused by historical distortions. The Sirens cannot act directly but must manipulate others into upsetting the timelines. Answering the Sirens' call more than once makes you their slave.

STUFF YOU NEED *Time Chart:* Gallifreyan monitoring device that scans events in space-time.

PLACES TO GO *The Kurgon Wonder* appeared as a gaseous anomaly and particle disruption field after the Knights' first attempted to restrain the Temperon, located at co-ordinates 83692 by 020576 mark 74 in the Kurgon System. The Kurgon Wonder measures 215 million cubic metrons in area, radiating light at a constant 75000 lumins.

ORGANIZATIONS The Medieval-looking *Knights of Velyshaa* started off as marauders, hired to execute the war criminal Sancroff for the wronged citizens of Calthenor. Yet Sancroff is cited as "the first Knight of Velyshaa," probably in honor of his various atrocities. The advanced Knights of Velyshaa that overrun Gallifrey can neutralize TARDISes and Time Rings ("Genesis of the Daleks"). Their weaponry can kill Gallifreyans, preventing regeneration. Their sensors can detect Time Lords, even different incarnations of the same Time Lord.

PHENOMENA *The Laws of Time* technically forbid the Doctor's different incarnations from meeting, but we'll ignore that for the sake of drama.

APOCRYPHAL HISTORY By hi-jacking the German submarine, the fifth Doctor inadvertently saved the *Luisitania* and the life of psychotic passenger Eric Charles Vincent. Years later, Vincent murdered penicillin creator Alexander Flemming, preventing the medicine's creation and allowing a plague to ravage Earth in 1956. Humanity never developed space flight—and was unable to stop the Knights' conquests.

AT THE END OF THE DAY Mesmerizing, both as a celebration of "Doctor Who" and a launching point for the Big Finish line. "Sirens of Time" can't claim to be perfect (the McCoy section admittedly falls flat), but barring the strengths TV has over audio, it leaves "The Five Doctors" in the dust. More important, it establishes the Big Finish crew as a crowd of honed professionals who love "Who" and easily rival the TV writers as storytellers, giving us a solid Davison/C. Baker/McCoy story that improves with repeated listenings.

LAST OF THE TITANS

By Nicholas Briggs

Release Date: January 2001
Order: Promotional CD included with Doctor Who Magazine #300

TARDIS CREW The seventh Doctor.

TRAVEL LOG Ormelia orbit, time unknown.

CHRONOLOGY Likely between *Lungbarrow* and "Doctor Who: Enemy Within." (Author's Note: Frankly, *Lungbarrow* pretty much fills in the gap between the New Adventures and the TV movie, but it's about the only time a companion-less McCoy story could occur.)

STORY SUMMARY The Doctor sets course for a long-overdue vacation on the planet Ormelia, but gravitational disturbances force the TARDIS to materialize aboard a gigantic space freighter. There, the Doctor meets the freighter's single occupant, a lumbering creature named Vilgreth. Gifted with high technical skills but slow-witted in most other respects, Vilgreth greets the Doctor. In passing, he mentions finding a melted spaceship in the freighter's massive engines. More puzzling, Vilgreth claims a number of space officials have tried to blow him up for tax evasion.

Vilgreth invites the Doctor to join him for tea and departs for the bridge. Moments later, Operative Stelpor of the Ormelia Security Service—the occupant of the destroyed ship—emerges from the shadows and warns the Doctor that he's just planted an explosive device to annihilate the freighter. Enraged at Stelpor's callousness, the Doctor rashly informs Vilgreth and helps him to locate and deactivate Stelpor's bomb.

Relieved, the Doctor joins Vilgreth for tea and realizes the freighter has luckily pulled into orbit above Ormelia. Thanking Vilgreth for his company, the Doctor departs for the TARDIS but again

meets Stelpor. This time, Stelpor offers a data tablet with information explaining why Vilgreth is marked for assassination. According to the data crystal, an Earth geneticist named Patrick Trethui successfully excavated DNA from the extinct Titanthrope species, a larger and more intelligent cousin of the Neanderthal race. Reports claim Professor Trethui cloned the Titanthrope DNA—creating Vilgreth as a result. However, Vilgreth's violent tendencies caused him to murder Trethui and his staff, later acquiring the wrecked freighter and escaping into space.

Stelpor argues that Vilgreth is an abhorrence of nature that must be destroyed before innocents suffer. With mounting dread, the Doctor identifies Vilgreth's space freighter as a planet-eater, a class of ship formerly used to clear asteroid fields for space traffic. Needing massive amounts of matter to keep the planet-eater's engines functioning, Vilgreth evidently plans to use Ormelia as raw fuel.

Vilgreth bursts in on the Doctor and Stelpor, ignoring the Doctor's entreaties to spare Ormelia. Caring only about his "darling" engines, Vilgreth tries to kill Stelpor, but Stelpor wounds him with a pistol-shot. With Vilgreth distracted, the Doctor primes Stelpor's bomb for detonation. To prevent him from disarming the bomb, Stelpor grapples with Vilgreth, urging the Doctor to flee. With little option, the Doctor reaches the TARDIS and dematerializes just as the freighter explodes. Alone in the TARDIS console room, the Doctor guiltily broods over his salvation of Ormelia at the cost of Stelpor and Vilgreth—who, after all, was only acting according to his nature.

ASS-WHUPPINGS The Doctor blows up Stelpor (with his blessing) and Vilgreth (with his random grunting) to save Ormelia. Vilgreth killed his creator and most of his staff.

CHARACTER DEVELOPMENT
The Doctor: Ormelia's a favorite haunt from the Doctor's younger days. He's an expert at defusing bombs (he's certainly had enough practice).

Vilgreth: Something of an idiot savant; he's technically minded but emotionally immature and generally dopey otherwise. Professor Trethui created Vilgreth in laboratories in Devon, equipping him with a voicebox to communicate properly.

The TARDIS: Design specifications claim the Ship's "technically indestructible," but that's not always comforting. The Doctor reiterates that he didn't build the TARDIS.

ALIEN PLANETS Graced with a golden sky and pale green sea, *Ormelia* serves as home to a race of reptilian humanoids.

HISTORY The Titanthropes emerged on Earth as an evolutionary dead end, more intelligent than the Neanderthals but still consumed by animal aggression. Due to their internal violence, they wiped themselves out before the emergence of Homo-sapiens.

• Centuries ago, a fleet of planet-eaters cleared the space lanes by demolishing asteroids and planetoids. Most of the planet-eaters were scrapped, but a few wound up in private collections.

• Europe is united in this timezone, partially governed by a European Senate.

AT THE END OF THE DAY Proof that you get what you pay for, a surface level story that forces the Doctor to make snap judgements (he accepts that Stelpor's in the wrong pretty damn fast) and curious omissions (the Doctor and Vilgreth chat and drink tea, apparently forgetting that Stelpor's still lurking aboard). We'd hardly call "Last of the Titans" awful, but we're glad it was free.

STORM WARNING

By Alan Barnes

Release Date: January 2001
Order: Big Finish "Doctor Who" Audio #16

TARDIS CREW The eighth Doctor and Charley Pollard.

TRAVEL LOG The *R-101*, October 5, 1930.

STORY SUMMARY Trying to frighten scavenging vortisaur animals away from a wrecked time vessel, the Doctor causes the TARDIS to randomly eject from the Vortex and materialize on Earth aboard the *R-101*—the ill-fated dirigible that crashed in flames in France, 1930, during its maiden voyage.

Unable to escape when the *R-101*'s ballast flushes the TARDIS off the airship, the Doctor encounters an adventurous stowaway named Charlotte ("Charley") Pollard. Curiously, the Doctor witnesses Lord Tamworth, Britain's Minister of Air, ordering the *R-101* to ascend to an unprecedented 5000 feet. The Doctor realizes that Tamworth, acting for the British Government, has usurped the *R-101*'s journey for a mid-air rendezvous with an extraterrestrial saucer—to return an alien who crashed on Earth seeking help for its people.

At the empathic alien's request, the Doctor journeys with Tamworth to the alien ship. There, they encounter the Triskele—a race that long ago quelled its inner rage by dividing into three branches: the intellectual Engineers and the destructive Uncreators, with a single Lawgiver restraining both groups. Dying, the Lawgiver hopes to find an Earthling to succeed him, unable to grant an Engineer or an Uncreator the free will necessary to become a Lawgiver.

Desperate to free his fellows from the Lawgiver's control, the ruling Uncreator Prime telepathically pushes Tamworth's associate, British Intelligence agent Rathbone, to rally some men and besiege the Triskele ship for the British government. Rathbone shoots the Lawgiver dead—thus loosing the Uncreators from their mental shackles to declare war on humanity. Fortunately, the Doctor concludes that prolonged restraint has dulled the Uncreators' savagery. By simply roaring, the Doctor, Tamworth and Rathbone's men dive the Uncreators back. Nearly defeated, the Uncreator Prime influences Rathbone to kill Tamworth, but Rathbone resists and slays the Uncreator Prime instead.

Tamworth offers himself as an advisor, rather than a Lawgiver, to help the Triskele re-learn free thought. As Tamworth departs with the Triskele for outer space, the Doctor takes his group back to the *R-101*. However, Rathbone reveals he pocketed the Uncreator Prime's energy weapon and intends to give it to the British government—a significant violation of history. With little choice, the Doctor punches Rathbone, grabs the energy weapon and runs for it with Charley.

Obsessed, Rathbone purses the Doctor to the heart of the airship and attacks him with an axe—unwisely puncturing one of the *R-101*'s airbags. As the *R-101* ruptures, the Doctor hurriedly discards the energy weapon and Rathbone, attempting to catch the device, falls through the hull breach. With only seconds remaining, the Doctor and Charley hear the cry of a flying vortisaur, pulled out of the Vortex in the TARDIS' wake and drawn to the impending disaster. By riding the animal bareback, the Doctor and Charley fly to safety as the *R-101* crashes as history intended.

Moments later, the Doctor remembers history stating that officials pulled 54 corpses from the *R-101*'s wreckage—but Tamworth's absence leaves the body count one person short at 53. With mounting horror, the Doctor realizes that Charley—a stowaway—must have been found among the *R-101*'s dead. Determined to take Charley back in time to the *R-101*'s last moments and fulfill history, the Doctor relents when Charley expresses her joy at the chance to travel through time and space with him. Leaving the Laws of Time to sort themselves out, the Doctor steers the vortisaur toward the TARDIS and accepts Charley as a new travelling companion.

MEMORABLE MOMENTS Paul McGann's internal monologue during the teaser breathtakingly establishes his return to "Doctor Who" after nearly five years. Charley blows her cover as an *R-101* steward and hoofs it, causing her awkward but noteworthy first meeting with the Doctor (he impishly suggests they avoid Charley's pursuers by hiding behind the curtains).

The Doctor, leading his associates toward the utterly alien Triskele ship: "Breathe in deep! You feel that pounding in your heart, that tightness in the pit of your stomach? The blood rushing to your head? You know what that is? That's adventure. That's the thrill and the fear and the joy of stepping into the unknown. That's why we're all here, and that's why we're alive!"

Rathbone repeatedly axe-swings at the Doctor, damaging the *R-101*'s airbags (the Doctor shouts: "Keep it up…you're making history!"). The Doctor ponders being a responsible Time Lord and taking Charley back to her death, but decides to chuck the Laws of Time (like he's never done *that* before).

SEX AND SPIRITS Charley doesn't fancy the Doctor. Rathbone comes onto Charley, offering her "protection," but she tells him to slag off.

ASS-WHUPPINGS "Oh, the humanity!" (Wait … wrong dirigible.) Fifty four … errr, 53 people die aboard the *R-101* in a wreck of screaming metal. Charley, fated to be among the dead, becomes a TARDIS companion (bad Doctor, no biscuit).

Rathbone's assault squad shoots down a fair number of Uncreators. The Doctor overcomes his dislike of violence to punch Rathbone, then hoof it with the Triskele energy weapon.

TV TIE-INS In addition to helium ("The Robots of Death"), the Doctor detects levels of hydrogen gas that humans can't sense.

NOVEL TIE-INS The Doctor possesses Sir Arthur Conan Doyle's stethoscope (*Evolution*).

AUDIO TIE-INS The Doctor was present on the *Luisitania* separately from events where his fifth self derailed its timeline ("The Sirens of Time").

CHARACTER DEVELOPMENT

The Doctor: The Doctor's lost the TARDIS Manual (again). He's met Geronimo. He once rode a train from Switzerland to Petrograd with Lenin,

MISCELLANEOUS STUFF!

DATING THE EIGHTH DOCTOR AUDIOS

Deducing the chronology of the eighth Doctor's audio adventures with Charley proves a bit tricky, because the novel line features a reasonably seamless parade of companions. For lack of concrete evidence, then, melding the audio and novel stories becomes the stuff of guesswork.

The best argument to date suggests these audio adventures take place between *The Eight Doctors* and *Vampire Science*, given that Sam Jones in *Vampire Science* mentions suspicions that the eighth Doctor's been sneaking off for months, even years at a time, then unerringly returning to the moment he left her. If true, the period between *The Eight Doctors* and *Vampire Science*, which potentially incorporates *The Dying Days* and the Doctor's comic strip adventures with Stacy and the Martian Ssard, is nearly as cluttered as the sixth Doctor's history between "The Trial of a Time Lord" and "Time and the Rani."

Only scraps of additional information remain. An off-hand reference to Sam Jones in "Minuet in Hell" helps confirm her as the eighth Doctor's first companion (unless you count Dr. Grace Halloway), and a failure to mention Fitz perhaps denotes that the Charley stories don't take place before *The Taint*. For lack of further evidence, we've chosen the obvious solution— *The Eight Doctors*/*Vampire Science* gap—to encompass the Charley stories.

who was clad in mauve pajamas and repeatedly lost at Tiddly-Winks. The Doctor's also played games (platonically) with the Empress Alexandra.

He knows Lord Tamworth by reputation. He claims to be a "Doctor of most things and some more besides," and knows technical details about the *R-101*'s construction. The Doctor once met a Venusian at the Singapore Hilton. He picked up some colorful phrases during the Boer War. His overloaded pockets make him heavier than he looks. The Doctor owns a lucky double-headed Alterian dollar, plus an autographed first print of Agatha Christie's *The Murder of Roger Ackroyd* (annoyingly, the last page is missing). Speaking of Christie, the Doctor recalls being aboard *The Orient Express*.

During his Academy days, the Doctor learned about Universal chaos theory which suggests the beat of a butterfly's wings in Mettula Orinosis can cause a time storm in Mutter's Spiral.

Charlotte E. Pollard (a.k.a. "Charley"): A self-proclaimed "Edwardian Adventuress," Charley met a trader from the far East who raved about the joy of having a gin sling on the terrace of the Singapore Hilton at sunset. Charley tried to make him promise to meet her there on New Year's Eve, but the jackass laughed at her. Deciding to make the trip anyway, Charley got *R-101* steward Simon Merchford drunk in the stables at the Hair and Hounds pub at Hickwall Green, stole Merchford's papers, disguised herself as a boy and smuggled herself aboard the *R-101* bound for Karachi.

Charley loves lightning because it's scary and powerful. She's seen dolphins at Regents Park Zoo.

Ramsay the TARDIS Vortisaur: Charley names him "Ramsay" because he looks like Prime Minister Ramsay McDonald. Charley's abnormal chronology (i.e. her "non-death" aboard the *R-101*) initially frightens Ramsay, but he warms to her. Ramsay innately senses the TARDIS' location.

The TARDIS: Detecting an unspecified time ship caught in the Vortex, the TARDIS performs an "emergency stop" for the first time in centuries. It can forcibly nudge Vortex-trapped ships out of temporal causality loops. The TARDIS' dimensional displacement system protects it from vortisaurs—when it's working.

ALIEN RACES

Vortisaurs: Flying scavengers who mostly inhabit the Time Vortex but sometimes escape through wormholes or a TARDIS' time trail. In our Universe, Vortisaurs can sense impending disasters. They quickly acclimate to anyone who smells of the Time Vortex (such as the Doctor).

Individual vortisaurs are more tranquil away from the pack. They're gentle as a lamb after lapping the temporal energy-rich blood of a Time Lord. Alternatively, you can knock a vortisaur out with a jab of morphine applied to soft skin under their crest in the nape of the neck.

Vortisaurs exist in five dimensions, feeling uneasy in our four-dimensional Universe. They leave five dimensional bite marks (Ramsay bites Rathbone's arm, making it age 30 years). Vortisaurs don't like coffee (and are probably better off).

Triskele (General): The Engineers and Uncreators can breed. However, there is only one Lawgiver to represent the single, unchanging Triskele Law. Triskele are telepathic and respond best to psionic individuals or beings with open minds (such as Charley). Most human minds are closed to them. They cannot mentally scan the Doctor.

Triskele have smooth, gray skin and chemically

THE CRUCIAL BITS...

• **STORM WARNING**—First appearance of Charlotte ("Charley") Pollard and Ramsay, the TARDIS vortisaur. The Doctor accepts Charley, who should have died aboard the *R-101*, as a travelling companion and thereby violates the Laws of Time.

adapt to varying altitudes (they need oxygen on Earth's surface, but a different atmosphere mix at 5000 feet).

Triskele (The Lawgiver): The Lawgiver manifests as an empty, endless void, suggesting it was never a Triskele but a separate entity modified when the race reorganized itself (*See History*). There has literally been one Lawgiver (the Engineers somewhat extended its life). Living circuits, created by the Engineers and attached to the cerebral cortex of all Triskele, allow the Lawgiver to immediately override any Triskele's actions.

Triskele (Uncreators): The Uncreators serve as the epitome of unacted desire, slaved to a single urge to destroy. The Engineers who fear them.

STUFF YOU NEED *The Triskelion* serves as a Triskele race symbol—three equal hooks joined together to symbolize the race's three branches. The Doctor's seen it on many planets.

SHIPS

R-101: One of mankind's modern miracles: 130 feet high, 1/7 of a mile long and holding 55 million cubic feet of gas.

Triskele Ship: A masterpiece of Triskele engineering, two miles wide with a hull that can turn intangible to let smaller ships dock. The Triskele vessel apparently warps gravity (perhaps using a variation of block-transfer computation), as the ship's inner space literally moves about the occupants to move them from deck to deck.

HISTORY Long ago, the Triskele's phenomenal engineering skill, thirst for war and penchant for atrocities allowed them to dominate many planets. However, the Triskele's inner rage ultimately turned them on each other and civil war erupted. Only a handful of Triskele survived, agreeing to separate their race into the Engineer, Uncreator and Lawgiver branches.

• The Doctor socialized with Lord Byron in summer 1816, and was present when a dare led to Mary Shelley writing *Frankenstein*.

• Brigadier General Tamworth served as a military attaché in Serbia and Bucharest in the Boer Campaign. During the invasion of Rumania, he witnessed the capture of Jericho. As a member of the Versailles delegation, he foresaw that post-World War I reparations against Germany would create a bigger conflict. When the Engineer Prime crashed in woodlands at Westmond, seeking Earthling candidates to succeed to the position of Lawgiver, Tamworth was promoted to Minister of Air and set about modifying the *R-101* for a mid-air rendezvous.

AT THE END OF THE DAY An adventurous, passionate story that (unlike the *R-101* itself) flies with ease, admirably fulfilling its double mandate of re-introducing Paul McGann after a five-year absence and launching a new companion. That said, the story's reliance on historical shading over action keep it from true greatness (the "savage" Uncreators turn savagely impotent when a good shout frightens them away). Still, *Storm Warning*'s characterization and lively performances keep it aloft during multiple listenings—making this a stellar jumping-on point.

SWORD OF ORION

By Nicholas Briggs

Release Date: February 2001
Order: Big Finish "Doctor Who" Audio #17

TARDIS CREW The eighth Doctor and Charley.

TRAVEL LOG Garazone Central habitat; deep space aboard the *Vanguard* and unnamed Cybermen star destroyer, all "A very long time after the Cyber War [circa 2526]."

STORY SUMMARY When the Doctor and Charley visit an artificial space habitat named Garazone Central, crewmen from the salvage ship *Vanguard* accidentally load the TARDIS into the *Vanguard*'s cargo bay. Smuggling themselves aboard, the Doctor and Charley search and locate the TARDIS moments before the *Vanguard* reaches its destination—a star destroyer adrift in space. But when the Doctor engages the TARDIS' engines, the *Vanguard*'s warp field dangerously interacts with the TARDIS' time core, flooding the TARDIS with destructive temporal energy.

Forced to re-materialize aboard the star destroyer, the Doctor and Charley evacuate the TARDIS and wait for the temporal energy to dissipate. Soon afterward, *Vanguard* Captain Deeva Jansen and various members of her crew space-

walk over to salvage the star destroyer. Unfortunately, the Doctor discovers that his old enemies, the Cybermen, constructed the star destroyer for the purpose of kidnapping other beings and converting them into additional Cybermen. More terrifyingly, the Doctor and Deeva realize that although an ion storm initially rendered the star destroyer inert and set it adrift in space, the Cybermen crew, forced into emergency hibernation, are awakening to look for new recruits.

The Doctor and his allies retreat, but the revived Cybermen put most of Deeva's crew through the Cyber-conversion process. Deeva's laser pistol thankfully saves the Doctor and Charley from a Cybermen ambush, but the Doctor unmasks Deeva as an android from the Orion Sector.

Deeva details how years ago, Earth factories in the Orion Sector produced advanced androids who gained too much sentience and demanded equal rights. When Earth authorities refused, the androids holed up in the Orion Sector and clashed with Earth's military, sparking the Orion War. After eight years of stalemate, Earth Intelligence finally learned of the adrift Cybermen vessel and dispatched Deeva—supposedly one of their best agents—to acquire data on the Cybermen's conversion process. Earth authorities wanted the information to craft platoons of super-soldiers and wipe out the Orion androids, but Deeva intends to take the Cyber-data back to Orion and have her people Cyber-convert captured Earth soldiers to the Orion cause.

The Doctor implores Deeva that the Cyber-conversion process only creates uncontrollable Cyber-soldiers who'll destroy both Earth and the Orion androids. As the ion storm returns, Deeva wipes the Cyber-conversion data from her internal files in exchange for passage in the now-safe TARDIS. Having donned protective spacesuits to guard against sudden decompression, the Doctor, Charley and Deeva move toward the TARDIS—but a group of Cybermen ambush them and shatter Charley's life support pack.

Seconds later, the ion storm hits with full force, breaching the star destroyer's hull and rendering the Doctor unconscious. A short while later, the Doctor revives to learn that Deeva selflessly gave Charley her life support pack and secured her as the atmosphere vented—shunting all the Cybermen and Deeva into the cold of space and rendering them inert. Sadly, the Doctor uses the TARDIS sensors to confirm the star destroyer's dismemberment and the presence of free-floating, comatose Cybermen. Unable to locate any trace of Deeva's frozen body, the Doctor engages the TARDIS engines and departs with Charley.

MEMORABLE MOMENTS At story's end, the Doctor ponders that while the Cybermen literally started life with organic components, Deeva's self-sacrifice overwhelmingly makes her more human.

SEX AND SPIRITS An alien salesman comes on to Charley and pinches her bottom.

ASS-WHUPPINGS Hundreds of Cybermen captives perish in agony when the ion storm disrupts the Cyber-conversion process mid-stream. Deeva's specially modified gun wastes a fair amount of Cybermen. The story's climax hurls the Cybermen and Deeva into space, where the cold—not the lack of atmosphere—renders them inactive.

TV TIE-INS The Cybermen star destroyer originated from the Cybermen's adopted homeworld on Telos. The squat, bug-shaped Cybermats are still in use ("Tomb of the Cybermen"). The type of Cybermen in "Sword of Orion" hails from "The Invasion" and "Revenge of the Cybermen."

CHARACTER DEVELOPMENT

The Doctor: He's not an expert on vortisaur husbandry, but is familiar with the Merchant Space Corps and its procedures. He carries a tracker that detects temporal energy. He's an frighteningly good computer hacker.

Captain Deeva Jansen: Orion android double-agent allegedly working for Earth Intelligence, designated Earth Security Agent CGH5/14. The original Captain Deeva Jansen died 30/05/07. Android Deeva's an expert at galactic military history and possesses a gun specially tailored to bring down Cybermen.

Ramsay the TARDIS Vortisaur: Prolonged periods spent outside the Time Vortex makes Ramsay ill, giving him dry skin, eye swelling and an upset tummy. In such a state, the shock of re-entering the Vortex could kill him. The Doctor and Charley failed to find a restorative at the Garazone Bazaar, but the temporal energy that suffused the TARDIS—fatal to humans and Time Lords—likely restored him. Ramsay's too big to carry.

The TARDIS: The Doctor's Ship can tap the video signal from the *Vanguard's* command monitors. Feedback from a warp field without the proper transit dampners destabilizes the TARDIS' "time core." The Doctor proposes using the TARDIS' power to rig a defense screen against the oncoming ion storm, but it's unclear if he's bluffing the Cybermen or not.

ALIEN RACES

Cybermen: Cybermen in this time zone recognize the Doctor as one of their deadliest enemies, and want him returned to Telos for brain analysis.

Orion Androids: Physically indistinguishable from flesh-and-blood humans, but graced with enhanced strength, accuracy and speed. A safety feature simulates sensations of pain. Bonding fluid helps the self-healing androids seal wounds.

STUFF YOU NEED

The Sonic Screwdriver: Its handle doubles as a torch.

Orion Classification D7 (a.k.a. Codename "Sword of Orion"): Earth Intelligence operation to ascertain the Cybermen's military value.

PLACES TO GO *Garazone Bazaar:* Located at the Garazone Central habitat, a den of iniquity off most civilized trade routes—but useful for finding ancient remedies.

ORGANIZATIONS *Earth Intelligence* craves the Cyber-conversion data, but isn't stupid enough to trust the Cybermen.

HISTORY An inventor named Wellford Jeffries discovered anti-gravity technology several hundred years after Charley's era.

• Eight years ago, the Orion War instigated when androids constructed in the Orion Sector outlawed themselves by demanding equal rights and forming tribunals to make their mistreatment public. The civil conflicts led to violent unrest, as Earth's military lacked the ability to tell the androids apart from humans and became further discriminatory. Finally, the androids settled in the Orion System, ordering human settlers to accept equal android rule or leave.

AT THE END OF THE DAY Scarcely more than your typical "Eeek! Eeek! A shadowy alien killer!" story, laced with transparent characters and trying oddly to feel like a mystery—when we know the baddies are the Cybermen. Deeva's intriguing identity revelation in Part Four, with its echoes of *Blade Runner*, sadly fails to make up for three episodes of irrelevant filler. Admittedly, we'd call the final result more forgettable than tortuous, but beware this story's overpowering mood music—which tries to pummel you into thinking something interesting is happening.

THE STONES OF VENICE

By Paul Magrs

Release Date: March 2001
Order: Big Finish "Doctor Who" Audio #18

TARDIS CREW The eighth Doctor and Charley.

TRAVEL LOG Venice, 23rd century.

STORY SUMMARY Tired of the stress of over-throwing alien dictatorships and being repeatedly shot at, the Doctor proposes a quiet holiday in Venice. However, the Doctor and Charley find 23rd century Venice poised on the brink of destruction. As is common knowledge, Duke Orsino, the ruler of Venice one hundred years ago, greedily wagered and lost his lover Estella in a card game. Rumors suggest Estella drowned herself shortly afterward, with the "Cult of Estella"—as cults often do—springing up to worship Estella's memory.

Regrettably, Estella evidently cursed Venice before she flung herself into the canal, vowing the city's destruction in 100 years' time and condemning Orsino to an extended lifespan to ponder his betrayal. With the curse's century elapsing, Venice experiences a growing number of tremors, threatening to plunge into the ocean.

Meanwhile, Venice's gondoliers, having evolved into web-footed amphibians, rejoice at the chance to throw off their lower-class status and claim the city once it sinks. To hedge their bets, the gondoliers kidnap Charley and hypnotize her to impersonate Estella, hoping to distract Orsino from concocting any brilliant plans to save the city. Searching for the missing Charley, the Doctor runs afoul of the marauding Cult of Estella, who enthusiastically proclaim their lady's immanent resurrection. Inside the cult's headquarters, the Doctor finds Estella's sacred "tomb"—curiously, sans corpse—and pockets a necklace left inside.

Purely to appease the people, Orsino accepts Charley's ruse as Estella and agrees to "re-marry" her. Thankfully, the Doctor decides to confront Orsino as the root of the curse, barging into Orsino's dwelling and snapping the gondoliers' hypnotic effect on Charley.

As the earthquakes reach a fever pitch, elderly Venice resident Eleanor Lavish steps forward and displays a small portrait of herself—proving *she* is the real Estella. Denouncing the cult that has sprung up in her name, Estella reveals that she's an extra-terrestrial who, out of love for the Duke, stayed behind when her people visited Earth and returned to the stars. But after Orsino lost her at cards, Estella used her necklace—actually a psionic device capable of altering reality—to lengthen the couple's lifespans. However, Estella's necklace was incapable of creating life, so it tapped Venice's lifeforce for the necessary energy—sustaining Orsino and Estella but triggering the earthquakes that portend the city's doom.

Tired of his greedy, desolate life, Orsino vows to atone for his sins. Orsino takes Estella's necklace from the Doctor and mentally activates the psionic device, encouraging Estella to join him in renewing Venice. Loving Orsino in spite of his century-old betrayal, Estella steps forward, letting the jewels' psionic-based flames claim them both. As Orsino, Estella and her necklace turn to ash, their life forces restore the city and the tremors cease. Fearing the end of the Cult of Estella, high priest Vincenzo scoops up Orsino and Estella's remains and darts down a bolthole to worship them. The Doctor and Charley conclude their business in the revitalized Venice with a relaxing ride down the canal.

MEMORABLE MOMENTS "The Stones of Venice" sometimes proves more memorable for the texturing of its dialogue than its plot. For instance, a harrowed Charley complains: "Doctor, when you invited me on these trips, you never said anything about marauding amphibians and enforced marriages to noble lunatics." The Doctor retorts: "I should have really, it's always the way."

After hailing Charley as the reincarnated Estella, Orsino decides that Estella's former body can "Go to the fishes for all I care."

The gondoliers go mad at the end of Part Two, threatening to drag their enemies into the canal waters. At the end of Part Three, as Venice's foundation shakes and the hour strikes, the Doctor ominously announces: "And the clock chimes out for the death of Venice."

SEX AND SPIRITS Orsino agrees to marry Charley ("Estella") for political reasons, but fortunately, it never comes to that. Drunken revelers whoop it up for Venice's demise throughout the entire audio. During Venice's final moments, the Duke's art curator Churchwell thinks about sealing himself in the vault with the "reserved reserved" collection of erotic etchings (the Doctor speculates: "It's not as bad as all that, surely.").

ASS-WHUPPINGS Surprisingly little, aside from Orsino and Estella going to ash. Part Two concludes with the gondoliers raging and pulling various Venice denizens under the water.

NOVEL TIE-INS The first Doctor, Steven and Vicki previously visited Venice in *The Empire of Glass*, a novel that off-handedly claimed that the city sank beneath the waves before Steven and Vicki's eras (and evidently after this story). The Duke's art collection includes portraits left behind by Estella's alien brethren, including a portrait of an empress in a big jam jar (*The Scarlet Empress*).

AUDIO TIE-INS Ramsay the vortisaur's looking much better after his bout of TARDIS sickness ("Sword of Orion").

CHARACTER DEVELOPMENT

The Doctor: The Doctor still gets a kick out of overthrowing tyrannical regimes. He's made repeated visits to Venice, regarding it as charming and sinister. He hasn't visited Venice during this time period, but was present for the city's construction. The Doctor's sense of geography still needs help.

The Doctor doesn't believe in curses—not because he's a rationalist, but just because he hopes for the best in people. He's also not into cults because they're overly solemn and full of rules. In the Doctor's experience, captors never get upset if their charges escape, because it gives them an excuse to run them down and administer a good thrashing. The Doctor has previously viewed, on other planets, extra-terrestrial paintings left by Estella's people. Time Lord legends somewhat disgust him. He used to be quite a name-dropper, but can't properly do it these days for spit. The TARDIS is his oldest friend. He regards all decades as being his home.

Charley Pollard: Charley's never been to Venice. Despite her self-proclaimed "Edwardian adventuress" tendencies, she hasn't traveled much (Charley's father wouldn't let her strike off alone). She sometimes regards the TARDIS as a "gothic nightmare."

Estella (a.k.a. Eleanor Lavish): Extra-terrestrial from an unnamed race. She never encouraged nor supported Cult of Estella, although watching the cultists dash about and stab people gave her much amusement.

ALIEN RACES *Venetian Canal People (a.k.a. Gondoliers)* have evolved into amphibians with webbed hands and toes. They hope to capture Venice, mostly out of revenge for being subjugated and abused. Upper classes call the gondoliers "toads" and "hobgoblins."

AT THE END OF THE DAY Charming, richly detailed and suffused with an almost herbal blend of passion, "The Stones of Venice" feels like a grand party sailing down Venice's canals. In typical Magrs fashion, odd things happen, then people stand about and wryly comment on how odd everything seems. Moreover, the supporting cast, especially Michael Sheard (Orsino) and Mark Gatiss (Vincenzo) notch tremendous performances, delivering some of the Big Finish line's most vivid dialogue (Orsino: "My mind is as frangible and decayed as any of the calluses along the Grand Canal."). Listeners who dislike romances will probably walk away disappointed, but the rest of us, as the Doctor puts it, will revel in "one really fantastic apocalyptic knees-up."

MINUET IN HELL

By Alan W. Lear and Gary Russell

Release Date: April 2001
Order: Big Finish "Doctor Who" Audio #19

TARDIS CREW The eighth Doctor and Charley.

TRAVEL LOG Malebolgia, America, the near future.

CHRONOLOGY Immediately after "The Stones of Venice."

STORY SUMMARY Brigham Elisha Dashwood III, a ruthless businessman and black arts practitioner, contacts a group of demons. Using their support and technical expertise to bolster his debaucherous Hellfire Club, he seizes political control of a small territory in America. Re-named "Malebolgia," the new region secedes and petitions to re-enter the Union as the 51st state, forwarding a social program of devil worship. Concerned about reports of illicit brainwashing technology in Malebolgia, the Doctor's old friend Brigadier Lethbridge-Stewart spies for the British government and visits Malebolgia allegedly to advise on the formation of its new legislature.

Publicly, Dashwood campaigns to become Malebolgia's first governor—a stepping stone, he hopes, to the White House. But in private, the demons help Dashwood refine his PSI-895 machinery, a device capable of re-writing or transferring human memories like a CD copier. With said gadget, Dashwood plans to manifest the demons' intelligences in a number of humans, eliminating his political opponents and creating a small army of infernal lieutenants.

Meanwhile, the Doctor finally returns Ramsay the vortisaur to his native environment, the Time Vortex. However, the dangerous procedure entails opening the console room doors and unbalances the TARDIS' guidance systems, causing the Ship to crash in Malebolgia. Worse, the forced landing disrupts the TARDIS' telepathic systems, blocking off Charley's memory and shifting much of the Doctor's intelligence into a visiting journalist named Gideon Crane. Soon after, Hellfire Club agents capture the three of them and make Charley work as a serving maid, institutionalizing the Doctor and Gideon at Dashwood's asylum.

Dashwood's associates threaten to carve up the Doctor's intelligence with the PSI machine, but the Doctor tricks Gideon into hotwiring himself to the PSI unit, thus re-routing the machines telepathic circuits and splicing their memories back together. Soon after, the Doctor escapes the asylum and reunites with the Brigadier and Charley, whose memory slowly returns. Together, the trio confronts Dashwood during a political broadcast and fools him into publicly revealing his disdain for the voting public.

Irrevocably disgraced, Dashwood returns to his asylum and begs demon leader Marcosius to make him one of Lucifer's advisors in recognition of his service. However, the Doctor follows and recognizes Marcosius as an alien Psionivore—a species of cosmic parasites that feasts on negative emotions such as hate and terror. Marcosius impishly admits the Psionivores aided the "Satanic" Hellfire Club to generate such hostile emotions, but now declares the group's power null and void, dismissing Dashwood.

Enraged, Dashwood seizes a Trans-D pistol—a device capable of banishing people to the Psionivores' home dimension—and fires at Marcosius. Unfortunately, this disrupts the PSI machine and creates an unstable dimensional portal, consuming Dashwood, Marcosius and the PSI device as the Doctor flees. Moments later, the dimensional gateway closes, squelching Dashwood's ambitions. While Gideon assists the police with their inquiries and the Hellfire Club's leaders crumble in a political scandal, the Brigadier bids the Doctor and Charley farewell.

MEMORABLE MOMENTS The Brigadier shares a motorcycle ride with demon hunter Becky Lee, nicely evoking the Paul McGann movie.

SEX AND SPIRITS Dashwood salivates over Charley, dressing her in a revealing frock dubbed "The Queen of Hell Special." As part of a Satanic ritual, Dashwood threatens to marry Charley—

MISCELLANEOUS STUFF!

BRIGADIER CHRONOLOGY

Brigadier Alistair Gordon Lethbridge-Stewart. It says a lot about Lethbridge-Stewart's character that a man of peace like the Doctor would accept a military officer as his best friend. Because the Doctor-Brigadier relationship works so well, the novels and audios have interwoven their friendship even further. Here's a run-down of key novels and audios that affect the Brigadier's history:

• **NO FUTURE**—During the 1970s, the Brigadier co-ordinates with the seventh Doctor, Ace and Benny to defeat the Vardans ("The Invasion of Time") and the Meddling Monk ("The Time Meddler"). The Doctor, having already met the Brigadier in "Battlefield," blocks the Brigadier's memories of these events.

• **BUSINESS UNUSUAL**—The Brigadier meets the sixth Doctor for the first time.

• **"THE SPECTRE OF LANYON MOOR"**—The out-of-continuity sixth Doctor meets the Brigadier for the first time (the Brigadier plays along).

• **THE SHADOW OF THE GLASS**—Pre-dating the sixth Doctor's period with Mel, the Brigadier and the companion-less Doctor share a Nazi-themed adventure the BBC should have called "They saved Hitler's brain!"

• **BATTLEFIELD**—The Brigadier meets the seventh Doctor (so he believes) for the first time.

• **"MINUET IN HELL"**—The Brigadier meets the eighth Doctor for the first time.

• **THE DYING DAYS**—The Doctor, Bernice and the Brigadier unite in 1997 to deal with Earth's first public alien encounter (the Ice Warriors).

• **HAPPY ENDINGS**—In 2010, the extremely aged Brigadier is restored to health by alien blooms that grant him a new body. The seventh Doctor undoes the Brigadier's memory blocks, allowing him to remember *No Future*.

• **THE SHADOWS OF AVALON**—Revelation that the Brigadier's wife Doris died in a boating accident. The Brigadier contemplates suicide but finally becomes court advisor to the other-dimensional realm of Avalon.

• **THE KING OF TERROR**—By 2050, the 121-year-old Brigadier, looking 75, resides in the Westcliffe Retirement Home in Sussex, having spent 20 years in Avalon (with a Celtic bridge). It's unclear, but he expects to either die or return to Avalon in a couple of years.

but fortunately gets too wrapped up in his machinations to make good on the threat. We're pretty sure it's totally innocent, but Charley at one point declares: "Last time I was trapped with [the demon Marcosius], he tried to eat me!"

ASS-WHUPPINGS During his time in the asylum, the Doctor meets sophisticated residents such as Hiriam Dodds, famed for kidnapping pets, dousing them in gasoline and torching the critters in school yards; Cobberquick, the so-called "Gay Axeman of Rhode Island"; and Mad Ma Pardo, who bludgeoned six rednecks to death with her prosthetic leg. The PSI-895 device dices up the Doctor's memory, but he blessedly avoids a lobotomy.

TV TIE-INS The Doctor suggests he and Charley visit Grace Halloway ("Doctor Who: Enemy Within"). He can convey technical information through telepathic contact ("The Three Doctors," "The Sirens of Time," etc.), but the transfer's only temporary.

NOVEL TIE-INS This story pre-dates the eighth Doctor/Brigadier meeting in *The Dying Days*.

AUDIO TIE-INS Charley's atemporal nature ("Storm Warning") protects her from the Psionivores (*See Alien Races*) but vortisaur Ramsay's still tempted to snack on her. The Doctor agonizes about returning Charley to the R-101 crash (but, ultimately, doesn't). Charley's off-handed remarks establish that other stories took place during Big Finish's first McGann season ("Storm Warning" to "Minuet in Hell").

CHARACTER DEVELOPMENT

The Doctor: The Doctor re-establishes that he's in his eighth regenerative state. The asylum authorities, not knowing the Doctor's true name, refer to him as "Zebadiah Doe." The Doctor simultaneously considers the Brigadier and Charley his best friends.

The Doctor and Gideon Crane: Gideon works for the *London Torch* newspaper and visited Malebolgia to provide coverage on its formation. The TARDIS' temporal spillage causes the Doctor's symbiotic nuclei to interact with Gideon's, giving him some of the Doctor's knowledge. After the Doctor sutures their memories back together, Gideon retains some of the Doctor's technical skill for a limited time.

Charley Pollard: Hailing from a more innocent age, Charley thinks the term "drugs" refers to aspirin. While working as a Hellfire Club waitress, Charley goes by the alias "Charley Beaut." She can identify fashion designs from various eras, including the 1760s. She knows something of Hellfire

Club history and has read *Dracula*. Barring the TARDIS scanner, she's never seen a TV until this story. Charley's father works as a stockbroker. She wears a brooch with her name engraved on it.

Brigadier Lethbridge-Stewart: Technically retired, the Brigadier still does undercover work for the United Nations. For the Malebolgia operation, the Brigadier reports directly to the British Secretary of State. The Brigadier's not the most technical of people but knows how to use e-mail. He's familiar with many English psychiatric machines. A security crackdown makes much of the Brigadier's past inaccessible. He still uses the code-name of "Trap One."

Marcosius: Using the PSI-895 machine, Marcosius (and presumably his fellow Psionivores) can teleport his consciousness into a human's brain. In such bodies, Marcosius enjoys superhuman strength but cannot overextend his host's physical exertion limits (he risks a heart attack doing so).

The TARDIS: In emergencies, the TARDIS can bounce straight out of the Vortex (although it's not something the Doctor recommends).

ALIEN RACES *Psionivores* are energy-based creatures who normally inhabit ionized clouds of comet-generated dust, sometimes consuming flesh but mostly feeding on negative mental emissions such as jealousy and hatred. Psionivores can appear in various forms but manifest on Earth as "demons" to evoke fear. Psionivores are latently telepathic (presumably the means by which they feed on their victims' emotions) and possess advanced psionic technology (See Stuff You Need).

ALIEN PLANETS *Gallifrey* has legends that speak of Hell, where everything is horror and pain.

STUFF YOU NEED

PSI-895 Psionic Matrix Facsimile Regenerator: Psionivore technology that works like a CD copier—on your brain. The PSI-895 can scan a living mind and etch its contents digitally into a storage system. The process works to copy a person's consciousness or transfer it entirely. The PSI-895 was constructed for humans, meaning memories as vast as the Doctor's must be handled in chunks.

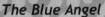
The PSI-895 resembles a device called the British Popawell Beaca Transit Central Mark V (whatever the hell that is).

PLACES TO GO The state *Malebolgia* split from isn't specified, although the inhabitants' thick Southern accents eliminate several parts of the country (Author's Note: We personally favor Arkansas, which is often synonymous with Satan). Malebolgia has heavy pollution and mountain ranges, and is loosely considered "a little brother to Maryland."

ORGANIZATIONS Under Dashwood's direction, *the Hellfire Club* holds Satan-centered rallies to generate psionic emissions (the PSI machinery soaks up such emotions for the benefit of the Psionivores). The Hellfire Club enslaves vagrants within Malbolgia's borders. A Hellfire Club branch operates in Des Moines, Iowa.

HISTORY The Ancient Order of St. Peter originated in the 16th century as a means of dealing with supernatural threats in Eastern Europe (mostly vampires), passing mental techniques and spiritual defenses to members through the generations. The group's last recorded vampire incident—in Poland, 1976—entailed their prey escaping on a jet to the United States. Two St. Peter priests followed and destroyed the monster, then stayed and founded the American St. Peter chapter (one of the priests birthed Becky Lee, resident St. Peter demon hunter).

• Brigham Elisha Dashwood's ancestor, Sir Francis Dashwood, created the Hellfire Club as an excuse for his buddies to hang about on weekends and drink (Sir Francis served as Chancellor of the Exchequer during King George III's reign). The organization reached its height in the 1760s, acting as a lecherous haven for the English aristocracy and politicians. Some members researched Greek mysteries out of curiosity, but subsequent generations trumped this up to claim the group reveled in the black arts.

• The Doctor warned President Abraham Lincoln against visiting the theatre on the night of Lincoln's death—not because he feared Lincoln's assassination, but because the play in question was humorless. In the Doctor's opinion, the only good thing about the show was an actor named Booth—and he wasn't appearing that night.

• In Edinburgh, the Brigadier helped oversee creation of a new Parliament for the ancient kingdom of Scotland (the country had evidently broken all British ties).

AT THE END OF THE DAY The basic premise—claiming that a first world nation would allow devil worshippers, who lack even a military, legislature or governor, to seize territory and openly secede—is a bit hard to swallow. Conversely, the fascinating "Doctor and Gideon in the asylum" plotline extinguishes itself because it doesn't go far enough (despite Gideon's claims to the contrary, you never doubt that Paul McGann's the Doctor). And even as "bastard" Americans, we could forgive this tale's grating Southern Baptist, "Foghorn Leghorn"-style accents if the relevant characters weren't so naïve (demon fighter Becky Lee thinks they had airships "hundreds of years" ago). That leaves Marcosius, the overly glib Psionivore, as the main reason to hear "Minuet in Hell"—but even he can't uphold 140 minutes of audio time.

THE BLUE ANGEL

By Paul Magrs and Jeremy Hoad

Release Date: September 1999.
Order: BBC Eighth Doctor Adventure #27
"Who is Compassion?" Storyarc

TARDIS CREW The eighth Doctor, Fitz and Compassion.

TRAVEL LOG The Enclave and the Corridors, time unknown; an Earth mall, present day.

STORY SUMMARY Strangely attracted to multidimensional shifts, the TARDIS materializes near Valcea—a literal City of Glass situated in a pocket galaxy known as the Enclave. But when Valcea unexpectedly connects itself to Galactic Federation territory via a network of space-time Corridors, Federation authorities become fearful that Valcea's presence could upset the region's political stability.

The Doctor joins an away team from the *Nepotist*, a Federation starship dispatched to investigate, while Fitz and Compassion wait in the TARDIS. In the City of Glass, the Doctor and Federation representatives meet the city's inhabitants—the Glass Men. More intimidating, the Doctor's group encounters the Glass Men's leader Daedalus, an insane giant jade elephant. Having deliberately extended Valcea's Corridors into Federation space, Daedalus seeks infamy through havoc and hopes to spark war between the Federation and the Obverse, a larger reality that encompasses the Enclave.

Wary of Daedalus' motives, the Doctor helps the *Nepotist* party escape but Daedalus' jamming field restrains him. Meanwhile, the eccentric time traveler known as Iris Wildthyme, having regenerated into a horny bit of stuff, secretly learns that the Doctor has walked into a trap of great import and sets out to rescue him. Aboard her bus-disguised TARDIS, Iris phones the Doctor's TARDIS and convinces it to dematerialize from the *Nepotist*, reappearing by Iris' bus on Valcea.

Garrett, the *Nepotist*'s second-in-command, identifies Daedalus as a war criminal, convincing *Nepotist* Captain Blandish to open fire on Valcea and hamstring its military potential. In response, a hostile race of Obverse lizards named the Sahmbekarts retaliate, using Valcea's devastation as an excuse to gut the *Nepotist*. The skirmish ends with the *Nepotist* crashing near Valcea, nearly killing all aboard and spurring Blandish to approach Daedalus' citadel with a suicide bomb.

As more and more Obverse races grow alarmed by events on Valcea and travel through the Corridors, the Doctor prepares to intervene. But Iris, having dispatched the Doctor's TARDIS to an unknown location, arrives to offer the Doctor a momentary haven with his companions aboard her invulnerable bus.

The Doctor accepts, but Iris unexpectedly dematerializes and refuses to return the Doctor to the Obverse conflict, re-materializing instead in an Earth mall where the Doctor's TARDIS is waiting. Iris adamantly states that the Doctor must not intervene in the Enclave conflict, whatever its bloody outcome, for reasons known only to herself and the TARDIS. Enraged, the Doctor disavows Iris' friendship and leaves with Fitz and Compassion, allowing Iris to depart in her bus. Without knowing the Enclave's space-time coordinates, the Doctor has little choice but to accept that Iris tricked him—supposedly for his own good—and that he may never know the Obverse-Federation war's outcome.

MEMORABLE MOMENTS The Doctor re-affirms his intrinsic faith in his friends—so Compassion responds: "Then you, Doctor, are a fool." Iris and Fitz suddenly arrive in Daedalus' throne room, accompanied by a giant egg (*See History*). Iris and the Doctor put hands to head to share telepathic conference—a physical touch Iris claims is unnecessary but, "the Doctor likes running his fingers through my hair."

Most of all, Iris refuses to take the Doctor back to the Obverse, claiming that he cannot always win. In turn, the Doctor, dripping with venom, says he shouldn't have saved Iris' life on Hyspero (*The Scarlet Empress*).

THE CRUCIAL BITS...

- **THE BLUE ANGEL**—Sexy Iris Wildthyme betrays the Doctor, preventing him from intervening in a war between the Galactic Federation and the Obverse, a pocket universe. Iris tells the Doctor she originates from the Obverse. The loosely named "Who Is Compassion?" Storyarc begins.

SEX AND SPIRITS Whereas old Iris loved the Doctor, young Iris feels more ambivalent (but still obliged to help him). Nonetheless, Iris tells Fitz that she and the Doctor discreetly got it on "for simply ages" (a fanciful suggestion at best) and claims Cilla Black's "Love's Just a Broken Heart" is "their" song. Fitz flirts with Iris but doesn't have a prayer of sacking her. Iris spontaneously kisses Fitz with a lot of tongue but cattily advises, "Don't tell the Doctor."

The *Nepotist*'s Captain Blandish and Commander Garrett are secretly lovers. Iris' bus is well stocked with liquor. The book's titles mirror the first sentence of each chapter, meaning Chapter 35 is entitled, "Iris Made Fitz Come..."

ASS-WHUPPINGS The Obverse Doctor endures a blue-winged baby spawning from his left leg (*See Sidebar*). The *Nepotist* shatters most of the City of Glass with sonic energy, killing 10,000 Glass Men. Captain Blandish, refusing to surrender the besieged *Nepotist*, crashes it and kills nearly everyone aboard.

NOVEL TIE-INS *The Shadows of Avalon* explains why Iris forced the Doctor to leave the Obverse for his own protection. *The Blue Angel* touches off a series of novels (through *The Shadows of Avalon*) where the TARDIS is drawn to dimensional disturbances. Several clues throughout points to changes ahead for Compassion, hence the "Who Is Compassion?" storyarc.

The Doctor's memory remains shaky after events in *Interference*. Fitz knows about Sam's infatuation with the Doctor (chiefly *Longest Day* to *Seeing I*). Iris formerly regenerated on Hyspero (*The Scarlet Empress*), transforming into her current sexpot body.

TV TIE-INS The Galactic Federation hails from "The Curse of Peladon." Alpha Centurians (also "Peladon") play multi-dimensional chess. The Doctor and Iris share telepathic communication ("The Three Doctors," etc.). At some point, Iris told Daedalus about the Doctor's early Dalek adventure ("Genesis of the Daleks").

Iris continues to claim seven of her incarnations

were abducted and set down in Gallifrey's Death Zone (a tale remarkably similar to "The Five Doctors"). Presuming Iris isn't full of it, she remembers the adventure through all seven pairs of eyes.

CHARACTER DEVELOPMENT

The Doctor: He hasn't heard of the Glass Men, but somehow aided them in the past. His sense of direction could be better, but he's got better-than-average night vision. The third Doctor met singer Dusty Springfield during his Earth exile days, when UNIT privately hired her to work undercover and investigate abductions in Memphis. The Doctor freed Dusty when she got kidnapped.

The Doctor and Iris: After Iris' "betrayal," the Doctor rethinks whom he should trust.

Fitz Kreiner: Fitz can barely ride horses. With the Doctor missing, Fitz ponders if he could travel with Iris.

Iris Wildthyme: Despite Gallifreyan characteristics, Iris claims to hail from the Obverse—and says the Doctor doesn't know her true identity.

Iris' sexpot incarnation wears a 1960s sci-fi style pink-and-purple catsuit, with yellow plastic boots up to her knees and gloved hands. She's got almond-shaped eyes, a heart-shaped face and a slightly upturned nose. She later changes into a gold and cream embroidered kaftan—a gift from novelist Jacqueline Susann (Iris assisted her with writing *The Love Machine*).

Iris' third body was based on Shirley Bassey in her prime, with a conspicuous beehive, evening dress and feather boa, plus formidable dart prowess. She frequently used a harpoon gun, but lost it during a harried escape from Skaro.

Iris' former companions include two guys named David and Nigel. Iris isn't evil, but often whisks people through time and space against their will (rather like the Doctor, really). Iris claims to occasionally work as Time's Champion and work for the Ministry. She recalls performer Salome doing a fan dance with one of the Doctor's scarves.

Iris' TARDIS: Iris' bus-shaped Ship, evidently a female, has a partly organic phone that can contact the Doctor's TARDIS (Iris knows a 20-digit number). The Ship's scanner can search for lifesigns. The bus' upper deck contains Iris' wardrobe and private office, where she conducts delicate interviews and ties up prisoners. Hundreds of hardbacked journals there detail her fanciful exploits.

Daedalus: Chaos-bringer who originated in a logic-based universe but sought to wreck devastation by learning magic. He studied under the mages of Hyspero (*The Scarlet Empress*), until they realized Daedalus' intentions and transformed him into a jade colored, Earth-sized elephant. Daedalus' throne room contains protective, immobilizing flames. Daedalus himself has some transmutative abilities (he can make people younger) and can use mental suggestion.

ALIEN RACES

The Time Lords: Cited as pedantic guardians of "Canonicity and Likelihood," the names of twin

---

MISCELLANEOUS STUFF!

THE OBVERSE DOCTOR AND CO.

A second, likely apocryphal narration track in *The Blue Angel* takes place in the Obverse and depicts separate versions of the Doctor, Fitz, Compassion and old Iris. In this setting, the Doctor lives in a small house with tenants Fitz and Compassion, enduring dreams that roughly parallel the adventures of "our" Doctor. Iris' old incarnation lives in a basement flat next door, with her bus a weed-overgrown wreck. The Doctor's friend Sally, having finished her first book (reflective of Magrs' *The Scarlet Empress*) works on a sequel volume (a mirror of escapades in *The Blue Angel*'s main narration).

The "Obverse" Doctor and Co. mostly serve, like Don Quixote, to question the distinction between literature and reality (perhaps implying that the "Doctor Who" TV and novel characters aren't as canonized as we think). Most telling, Fitz ponders whether there could be multiple realities and Sally's talking dog—appropriately named Canine—asks, "What if you found out that the one you're in was the less real one?" (Naturally, Fitz laughs.)

We never discover how "real" these characters are, save that "our" Doctor wanders about one of the Enclave's Corridors and encounters a bunch of blue babies—one of which marks the Doctor's left leg. The "Obverse" Doctor later painfully spawns a winged blue baby out of a lump on his left leg, with old Iris declaring the child to originate from the Enclave before setting it free.

Side notes for those who can't get enough information: The Obverse Doctor's mother is a wheelchair-bound mermaid who's retained her looks. He's the seventh son of a seventh son, and lacks a navel. He's been in love, but never admitted it.

119

This book is not endorsed by the BBC. Doctor Who and TARDIS are trademarks of the BBC.

towers lording over the north of Gallifrey's capital.

Glass Men of Valcea: Literally humanoids made from glass, possibly originating as other beings but transformed into glass bodies. The Glass Men have sensation, but no nerve endings. Their legs can barely support them, so in Valcea, the Glass Men ride about in wheelchairs with thin metal rods connected to ceiling grills (an advanced form of bumper cars, no doubt). They're not combat prone, being more concerned about self-preservation. The Glass Men have glinting red eyes and hearts that burn like coals in their glass chests. They've heard of the Doctor.

Daedalus told the Doctor that the Glass Men had the potential to become something more dangerous than the Daleks, Cybermen and every would-be conqueror combined. Guarding against this, Daedalus claimed to act as Time's Champion, ruling the Glass Men to arrange for their destruction at this early stage of their development. The Doctor rejected such assertions.

Ghillighast: The oldest enemies of the Glass Men, they're fur-covered creatures about four feet tall with tattered wings. In the Enclave, they engender war for no reason. They're the one race Daedalus fears. The Ghillighast's power mainly lies in their ability to observe events through lice. In turn, the Ghillighast worship the lice, especially a god named Pesst.

STUFF YOU NEED *Iris' pink blaster gun* fires lethal pink beams (the pinker, the deadlier, lovely). Iris dislikes weapons, but says they're handy.

PLACES TO GO

The Enclave: Pocket galaxy within the Obverse, connected via the Corridors to at least 43 different places and times.

The Obverse: Reality separate from our Universe, a target for conquest because its malleable physics have a wide range of application.

Corridors: Generated using malleable Obverse physics, the space-time tunnel Corridors connect the Obverse to our Universe and universes beyond, with links to planets including Telosa, Skaro, Wertherkind and Sonturak.

HISTORY At an unspecified point, a god-like great white bird charged a race of large Enclave-based owls to protect two gigantic green-gold eggs and insure they never hatched (Author's Note: Or were made into giant soufflés, one presumes.). Later, Daedalus extended the Corridors into the owls'

home and stole one egg while the owls hid the other deep in a volcano. Daedalus hatched his captured egg and spawned the blue-winged Icarus, declaring the boy his son. Later, an unnamed race stole the fledgling Icarus, who wound up on Earth adopted by a woman named Maddy through a series of mishaps.

• Daedalus allegedly wiped out Nova-Kain Six, a civilization devoted to logic and mathematics. *Nepotist* Commander Garrett claims Iris betrayed his people (unlikely) and helped Daedalus to escape (quite possible, for unknown reasons).

AT THE END OF THE DAY Passionate, whimsical and charming—although multiple narration shifts, combined with a decently tangled plot, will likely render you unable to explain *The Blue Angel* at gunpoint. Then again, making the reader think is hardly a crime, and this book deserves praise for bravely forging its own path, crafting the Obverse (a vivid reality we'd like to visit) and above all, impishly celebrating life.

THE TAKING OF PLANET FIVE

By Simon Bucher-Jones
and Mark Clapham

Release Date: October 1999
Order: BBC Eighth Doctor Adventure #28
"Who Is Compassion?" Storyarc

TARDIS CREW The eighth Doctor, Fitz and Compassion.

TRAVEL LOG The Museum of Things That Don't Exist, time unknown; Antarctica, 1999; Mars-Jupiter asteroid belt, 12 million years ago.

STORY SUMMARY When the TARDIS lands at the Museum of Things That Don't Exist, the Doctor, Fitz and Compassion grow surprised by reports that the "Elder Things," supposedly the fictional creation of writer H.P. Lovecraft, actually existed in Antarctica 12 million years ago.

Determined to investigate, the Doctor's party travels there and finds a group of future Time Lords, force-regenerated as soldiers in the war against the Enemy, has slaughtered the Elder Things and taken their forms as a camouflage tactic. Worse, the future Time Lords are constructing a kamikaze TARDIS war fleet to shatter the time barrier around Planet Five and free the Fendahl—a life-eating creature the fourth Doctor defeated ("Image of the Fendahl")—to use as a weapon against the Enemy.

The war TARDISes, sensing a kindred spirit in Compassion, struggle against their enforced servitude and break free. When a Time Lord tries to restrain the herd with a de-mat gun, the lead war TARDIS partly ruptures until the Doctor telepathically links with it and brings the damaged TARDIS under control. As the pre-programmed TARDIS war fleet approaches Planet Five's Time barrier, the Doctor—fearing the Fendahl being freed at this point in its timeline—convinces the TARDISes to take evasive action. However, one of the Ships pulls up too late, shattering Planet Five's barrier.

As the defenses drop, the Doctor confronts not the Fendahl, who escaped to Earth long ago, but the Fendahl Predator, a creature super-evolved within Planet Five's time field as a natural adversary to the Fendahl. But whereas the Fendahl consumed life forces, the Fendahl Predator eats subatomic quantum interactions, literally devouring concepts and ideas.

Drawn to the Celestis' home of Mictlan—a world severed from space-time and existing only as a concept—the Fendahl Predator dices through the Celestis. Under the Doctor's direction, the TARDIS war fleet cuts the devastated Mictlan free from its moorings, expelling it and the Fendahl Predator into the inescapable outer voids. The Doctor's war TARDIS finally succumbs to its injuries, protecting the Doctor in an air bubble until Fitz and Compassion locate him with the Doctor's own TARDIS. The future Time Lords return home, reporting their mission has failed, while the Doctor's party recovers from their ordeal.

MEMORABLE MOMENTS The Doctor suggests there was a time when he was on Earth every Saturday and the children's shows were excellent (he apparently watched kids cartoons, including "Transformers," during his days with UNIT). The in-flight TARDIS war fleet, a concept never seen on TV, would have been awesome to behold.

SEX AND SPIRITS Fitz thinks he might make the hot nookie with Compassion one day—if he were very drunk and she had a personality transplant. When Fitz was young, his mother walloped him for reading an H.P. Lovecraft book, thinking the author's name was the title.

ASS-WHUPPINGS The Fendahl Predator butchers the Celestis beyond repair. In turn, it's flung into an utterly inhospitable part of space.

As an aside, *The Taking of Planet Five* offs the reptilian Borad from "Timelash" (*See TV Tie-Ins*). To bring the wounded war TARDIS under control,

CHARACTER PROFILE

THE EIGHTH DOCTOR

He's got the least amount of screentime for any Doctor, but the eighth Doctor's featured in a crushing mass of literature. Purely to jolt your memory with near-orgasmic delight, here's a rundown of key eighth Doctor stories before we rejoin the action.

• **THE EIGHT DOCTORS**—A final trap from the Master ("Doctor Who: Enemy Within") gives the Doctor temporary amnesia and he encounters his seven previous selves. Afterward, the Doctor accepts Coal Hill schoolgirl Sam Jones as a travelling companion.

• **BIG FINISH AUDIOS/COMIC STRIPS**—The Doctor occasionally leaves Sam's company and gallivants with companions Charley Pollard, Stacy and the Martian Ssard.

• **THE DYING DAYS**—We placed this story after *Alien Bodies* in *I, Who*, but there's just no telling where it belongs. The eighth Doctor meets Bernice Summerfield for the first time and shuttles her to a new life on the planet Dellah. It's suggested—only suggested—that the Doctor and Bernice do the nasty (author Lance Parkin favored this interpretation but refrained from forcing it on everyone else).

• **ALIEN BODIES**—First appearance of Faction Paradox, a paradox-worshipping group of Time Lords with voodoo control rituals. The Doctor stumbles across an auction where alien powers are bidding on his future corpse. The Doctor secures his body (a.k.a. "The Relic"), buries it on the planet Quiescia and destroys it with a thermosystron bomb.

• **SEEING I**—Searching for the missing Sam Jones, the Doctor is caught rooting through the company records of electronics firm INC. Found guilty of espionage, the Doctor spends three years imprisoned at the Oliver Bainbridge Functional Stabilization Centre.

• **THE TAINT**—The Doctor thwarts an Earth infestation of Benelsian leeches in 1963, killing flower store clerk Fitz Kreiner's mother in the process. Fitz comes to terms with the Doctor's actions, joining the TARDIS.

• **UNNATURAL HISTORY (and more)**—The Doctor's shadow starts disappearing, suggesting he's becoming an agent of Faction Paradox.

• **INTERFERENCE**—An incident on the planet Dust paradoxically kills the third Doctor and infects him with a Faction Paradox virus that gains potency with each regeneration. Faction Paradox agents calculate that the Doctor will eventually fall under their thrall. Sam Jones stays on Earth to assist ex-companion Sarah Jane Smith with her journalism projects. The Doctor accepts Compassion (formerly "Laura Tobin") as a new companion the Doctor snaps his wrist, forcing it to instinctively protect its wounded pilot. The war TARDIS later dies, but saves the Doctor. Celestis Investigator One interrogates the Doctor and suffers mental anguish when the Doctor meditates on the entire universe, unable to render the scope. One kills his partner Two—an agent of the ruling Celestis—but she regenerates and later gets turned into a work of fiction by Time Lord Homunculette.

TV TIE-INS This story's a sequel to "Image of the Fendahl." The breached war TARDIS here causes the 12-million-year time breach mentioned in that story.Professor Mildeo Twisknadine's Museum of Things That Don't Exist has the planet Vulcan on display, referring to its early discovery ("Power of the Daleks," *See History*). The Museum also has nine varieties of Yeti, including the robotic and fungi varieties ("The Abominable Snowman," "The Web of Fear").

Aspirin (i.e. acetylsalicylic acid) can kill a Time Lord in seconds by interfering with hormone receptor intermediaries ("The Mind of Evil"), but Time Lords can develop immunity.

Twisknadine knows Vorg the Magnificent, formerly known as "Vorg the Adequate" ("Carnival of Monsters"). The Doctor last encountered Vorg selling crustacoid pornography to the bemused unicellular life forms of Van Madden's Star.

Celestis investigators One and Two investigate a temporal anomaly that disgorges the Borad, thrown into the Timelash by the sixth Doctor ("Timelash"). One blows the Borad's head off with a single blast (slyly adding, "A most distasteful episode"). If you listen, you can hear thousands of Whovians uncorking their champagne bottles in celebration.

NOVEL TIE-INS The Doctor hopes the Museum of Things that Don't Exist can suggest a way back to the Obverse. It's hinted that the Enclave might be an offshoot of Celestis technology (*The Blue Angel*). The Museum has a display of Sherlock Holmes' 221B Baker Street, rather ironic since the seventh Doctor worked with Holmes in *All-Consuming Fire*.

Alien Bodies introduced the future Time Lord Homunculette and his living TARDIS Marie (who appear here in cameo), the late Celestis and the concept of force-regenerated, soldier Time Lords from the future. Samantha Jones didn't give Fitz many details about events in that book.

Holsred, one of the future Time Lords, hails from the same House as Castellan Andred ("The Invasion of Time"). *Lungbarrow* names it the House of Redlooms, but *The Taking of Planet Five* calls it "Redloom." The Doctor here asks Fitz to tell

THE CRUCIAL BITS...

- **THE TAKING OF PLANET FIVE**—Destruction of the Celestis.

Compassion about events in *Demontage*.

Alien Bodies introduced the Enemy. The Remote (*Interference*) consider their predecessors, Faction Paradox, to be creatures of myth.

When the war TARDIS accepts the Doctor's goodwill, it's suggested that his TARDIS vouched for him. The Doctor remains unsatisfied with that explanation, and learns in *The Shadows of Avalon* that it's actually the war TARDIS' acknowledgement of Compassion as a fellow spirit that tamed them.

Urmungstandra, cited here as the Silurians' devil god ("The Silurians"), is also an aspect of the Dellan god Tehke (*Twilight of the Gods*).

CHARACTER DEVELOPMENT

The Doctor: The Doctor still doesn't know the identity of the Time Lords' Enemy. He formerly corresponded with horror writer H.P. Lovecraft about their mutual love for ice cream. The Doctor almost offered Lovecraft a quick trip to the 18th century, but decided he wouldn't like it.

The Doctor's friends with Professor Mildeo Twisknadine, owner of the Museum of Things that Don't Exist. He owns a forgery of a South American Missing Link and hoped he'd put battling cosmic menaces behind him in his last incarnation.

The future Time Lord soldiers automatically respect the Doctor as a Time Lord. Probably as an offhanded remark, the Doctor says he's into his third childhood.

Fitz Kreiner: Fitz is smoking more heavily. He wears 1960s clothes for comfort. Fitz misses both Samantha Jones and "Dark Sam" (*Unnatural History*), unable to talk to Compassion.

Compassion: Compassion's currently strong, curvy and sexy. She believes people can do without the Doctor's interference.

Fendahl Predator: Technically called a "Memeovore," an eater of ideas and concepts.

Homunculette (Alien Bodies): Disguised as Professor Nathaniel Hume, Homunculette investigated the Elder Things anomaly for the Time Lords.

The TARDIS: The Doctor or TARDIS engineers incorporated several real-universe materials into the TARDIS' Block Transfer Computation ("Logopolis") matrix. Because of this, certain TARDIS areas can be directed manually and override symbiosis, possibly reflecting the Doctor's fear of overreliance on super technology, or perhaps the TARDIS' wish to be useable by non-Gallifreyans.

ALIEN RACES

Time Lords: Some Time Lords are designated fodder for the Gallifreyan Looms.

Future Time Lords: Force-regenerated Time Lord soldiers have blast-proof skin and small wings that enable flight. The future Time Lords who looked like the Elder Things typically had heads like five-pointed stars, multiple eyes, smaller tentacles and sucking mouths.

The Time Lords and the Enemy: Any gathering of a dozen or so TARDISes would draw an Enemy attack, so TARDIS war fleets must be constructed near their destination. The Enemy's psychology suggests they couldn't pose as Time Lords.

PLACES TO GO

The Solar System: Before the Time Lords time-looped it, Planet Five was located between Mars and Jupiter.

Mictlan: Home of the Celestis, supposedly immune to the time winds ("Warriors' Gate"). It would likely survive even if the Enemy retroactively wipes out Gallifrey. Black box TARDISes constantly sweep Mictlan, searching for continuity errors. In consuming Mictlan, the Fendahl Predator first ate the history of a Celestis member, then pushed itself through the continuity gap.

Professor Mildeo Twisknadine's Wandering Museum of the Verifiably Phantasmagoric (a.k.a. Museum of Things That Don't Exist): Museum that studies the mythic and the outré. The Museum itself is modeled after the Temple of Zeus and the Doctor's been trying to reach it for some time. Exhibits include Vulcan ("Power of the Daleks"), the Five Outer Worlds named after the lowest circles of Dante's Hell (sci-fi author Larry Niven's "The Borderland of Sol"), Hyperborea, Mu, Atlantis, Hy-Brascilica and Antilles. The Museum specializes in Parafractrology, the science of untruth.

STUFF YOU NEED

The Gallifreyan Matrix: Acts like a giant tea reading machine in that it only predicts timelines, so major events radically alter the outcome.

MISCELLANEOUS STUFF!

THE FENDAHL PREDATOR CONSPIRACY

A Celestis outcast known only as "the Hermit" (not the Doctor's mentor first mentioned in "The Time Monster") determined that Mictlan, existing as a temporal anomaly outside of space-time, could have attracted the Swimmers—universe-sized beings that swim the even vaster void between universes (*See Phenomena*). Fearing the lured Swimmers might crush our Universe in their wake, the Hermit conspired with his protégé, the Celestis investigator named One, to destroy their homeland of Mictlan.

Using a Celestis Metaphysical Engine (*See Stuff You Need*), the Hermit and One imprinted the fiction of the Elder Things upon space-time, thus drawing the attention of the future Time Lords and thereby furthering the scheme to free the Fendahl in that time period. As the Hermit and One expected, the future Time Lords unleashed the Fendahl Predator, knowing that the anomalous Mictlan was a natural food source for the creature. It's unknown, if the Doctor and the war TARDISes hadn't fortuitously banished the Fendahl Predator, how the Hermit and One would have in turn defeated the Fendahl Predator. After the Celestis' destruction, the Hermit tired of his old life and asked One to shoot him, forcing a regeneration to begin a new life in Nevada.

Celestis Metaphysical Engine: Device that imprints various fictions onto the time-space continuum. It's possible the device works by altering Reality Quotients (*The Crystal Bucephalus*).

Parallel Cannon: Future Time Lords crafted this devastating weapon, designed to puncture a hole to another part of the universe—say the nova of an anti-sun—thus unleashing a lethal concentration of neutrinos that shreds normal matter. Such parallel matter beams can eat through a planet in three hours and gut an atmosphere in nine. The Third Zoners ("The Two Doctors") were on the verge of Parallel Weaponry before war ended the research.

ORGANIZATIONS

UNIT: Employs psionics such as the delta-rated Captain Julian Esparza.

The Celestis: Sometimes ostracize members for no apparent reason. Red Moon is a faction within the Celestis. The governing Last Parliament rules the Celestis and is composed of 99 Houses. The Thirty House Rule ends discussions if 30 of the 99 Houses agree. The Looms weave Celestis members sexless, with House Wardrobes later assigning genders of male, female, neuter and unformed (this may or may not be true for other Time Lords).

The House of Redloom: The House of Castellan Andred ("The Invasion of Time," *Lungbarrow*) has a long tradition of being Cardinals and Castellans.

HISTORY   Antarctica in this time period has a warm and tropical climate (Bucher-Jones notes: "This is a deliberate fudge for contrast. It was actually frozen by 12 million years ago.")

- Horror guru H.P. Lovecraft wrote about the "Elder Things" in his short story "At the Mountains of Madness." (*Astonishing Stories*, February-April 1936). The modern-day discovery of the Elder Thing base later motivated 25th century fringe archaeologists such as Urnst (*The Highest Science*), Bendecker and Vildson to regard the "Elder Things" as real.

- Vulcan was detected in 1880, later disproved by Einstein, re-discovered in 2003 and vanished by 2130. Bad archaeologists speculate this mystery planet had its origins on "Star Trek."

- The whole of established human history might be a Time Lord attempt to eradicate their causal nexus. (Well, that clears things up, doesn't it?)

AT THE END OF THE DAY   Rewarding, high-octane and easily the most readable of Bucher-Jones' books, the balls-to-the-wall *Taking of Planet Five* yields a rich mine of concepts—although it's admittedly laborious to work through it all. The Fendahl Predator conspiracy (*See Sidebar*), for example, will likely escape your comprehension until you dissect the book hardcore. Still, there's something to be said for *mostly* keeping things under control and providing "a good ride," meaning this book deserves credit for symbolically piling you into a convertible and hurling you through space at warp speeds.

FRONTIER WORLDS

By Peter Anghelides

Release Date: November 1999
Order: BBC Eighth Doctor Adventure #29
"Who Is Compassion?" Storyarc

TARDIS CREW   The eighth Doctor, Fitz and Compassion.

TRAVEL LOG   Drebnar, time unknown.

STORY SUMMARY   Mysterious pulses in the Time Vortex draw the TARDIS to the planet Drebnar, a colony controlled by the agricultural Frontier Worlds Corporation. To investigate, Compassion and Fitz pose as Frontier Worlds duty clerks, while rival Reddenblak Corporation employs the Doctor for its intelligence division, researching Frontier Worlds' nefarious "Darkling Project."

The Doctor learns that the Frontier Worlds founders, including CEO Temm Sempiter, genetically augmented themselves with DNA from an alien plant that crashed on Drebnar. The planet DNA extends their lifespans but causes degenerative personalities as a result. To his mounting terror, the Doctor recognizes the alien plant as a Raab, an alien weed that normally lives in space but can take root on planets. Unfortunately, the Raab is about to germinate and, unable to escape Drebnar's gravity, the Raab seeds will quickly consume everything. Given that Drebnar supplies 70 percent of the food in the sector, its destruction would signal mass starvation.

The "Darkling Project" is actually a wheat crop, spliced with Raab DNA by the power-mad Sempiter to quicken its maturity. Fitz and Compassion stumble upon the Darkling wheat crop and drive a harvester into the research center's fuel tanks, setting the crop ablaze. Realizing the fire will create an updraft and spread the seeds throughout the planet, the Doctor dashes to the planetary weather control system—the device that inadvertently drew the TARDIS to Drebnar—and drowns the Darkling seeds with a rainstorm.

With the Darkling crop's destruction, Frontier Worlds' common stock nosedives, allowing Reddenblak to successfully stage a hostile takeover. Sempiter, completely unhinged by his transformations, tries to blow up the original Raab plant itself—thereby covering the whole planet with seeds—but the Doctor convinces a security robot to stop him. Sempiter tries to flee but falls through a frozen lake, allowing Drebnar's flesh-eating fish devour him. Believing Reddenblak to be less of a threat than Frontier Worlds, the Doctor aids the victorious company in destroying the Raab by synthesizing an extra-potent weedkiller, then leaves with his companions in the TARDIS.

MEMORABLE MOMENTS Compassion's axe-throwing scene (*See Ass Whuppings*) is visceral and savage—and we love it to pieces. (Line editor Steve Cole, reading the outline submission of *Frontier Worlds*, told author Anghelides, "That bit has to stay in.")

The Doctor tries to dissuade a suicidal, Raab-infected Frontier Worlds founder from jumping to his death by telling him to disbelieve myths about jumpers being oblivious to their fate until they go splat. ("It's not as though they have tried it for themselves, is it? Doing a few trial jumps from large pieces of furniture, maybe.")

When an undercover Fitz claims his father is ill, Compassion cries to back him up, knowing their cover file claims they're orphans.

SEX AND SPIRITS Fitz has an affair with Frontier Worlds worker Alura. He thinks it's just for fun—but Alura loved Fitz and wanted to move in with him. Fitz wrote her a "Dear John" letter that she likely didn't read before her death (*See Ass-Whuppings*).

Fitz doesn't consider Compassion a potential bed partner, but probably wouldn't refuse if she propositioned him. It seems unlikely, though, as Fitz showers in front of Compassion and she regards him with the interest of a guava.

Security guard Direk Merdock fancies Compassion, and she snogs him as a distraction (with tongues as well) so Fitz can sneak by.

ASS-WHUPPINGS In one of the series' most delicious moments, Fitz's boss, Griz Ellis, tries to shoot Compassion and she flings an axe that nails the center of his forehead. Ellis, augmented by Raab DNA, struggles to recover, so Compassion hacks him to bits and chops his head off. (Yeah, we know we're feasting on brutality—too bad this isn't on color TV.) Fitz pummeled the crap out of Ellis for witnessing his lover Alura's murder.

Frontier Worlds Security Chief Kupteyn, having discovered Fitz's covert identity, murders Fitz's lover Alura with a pair of pearl-handed scissors largely as a message. Fitz later confronts Kupteyn near a giant harvester and struggles over its rotating blades. With Kupteyn onto Fitz's watch strap—a gift from Alura—Fitz undoes the strap and drops Kupteyn to get shredded.

The Doctor drowns the Raab seeds and uses powerful weedkiller to destroy the main Raab plant. Compassion kills thousands of animals, the

CHARACTER PROFILE

COMPASSION

Interference, the story that introduced the eighth Doctor's companion Compassion, debuted about five minutes before *I, Who* went to press (author Lawrence Miles kindly mailed his personal *Interference* copies or we'd never have read it in time). During that period, it wasn't clear what was happening with Compassion, so we opted to eliminate her from the Interference write-up rather than bungle it. To bring you up to speed, here's the run-down on Compassion from her one appearance that's not covered in *I, Who 2*:

• **INTERFERENCE**—Originally named Laura Tobin, "Compassion"was recruited for a Faction Paradox splinter group known as the Remote—a rigidly ordered society whose members are directed, via earpiece implants, by radio signals that form part of the larger Remote consciousness. Compassion spent a great deal of time on the Remote colony of Anathema, a settlement without crime or disorder (due to the Remote radio signals coordinating everyone's actions). Accordingly, Compassion believes that her people (and herself) have outgrown politics and morality; the Remote signals are all they require. She feverishly believes that having principles or moral scruples could cause the downfall of Remote society.

Fitz, who served as Laura Tobin's co-pilot aboard a Faction Paradox warship, whimsically dubbed her "Compassion," no doubt because she sarcastically deadpaned that "Compassion was her middle name."

Like most Remote members, Compassion has been repeatedly replaced (e.g. cloned or "remembered") through a memory-sensitive biomass imprinting system, although this process creates more of a carbon copy, meaning each Compassion has been slightly different. The current Compassion looks like a slightly overweight Nicole Kidman who has the fashion sense of a walnut.

Compassion joined the TARDIS crew after the Remote evacuated Anathema, leaving her virtually homeless. She considered asking the Doctor to take her to another Remote colony, but chose to travel with him instead.

Like other Remote members, Compassion's earpiece directs radio signals directly into her brainstem. As you'll see, between *The Blue Angel* and *The Shadows of Avalon*, Compassion's earpiece interacts with the TARDIS' telepathic signals and begins to restructure Compassion—and her malleable Remote DNA—into Gallifrey's first humanoid TARDIS (dammit, nothing's ever *simple* in "Doctor Who").

results of experiments with Raab DNA, with ethylene-dibromide weedkiller.

The escaping Doctor dislocates one shoulder, gets shot in another by Frontier Worlds guards and enters a healing coma. A flier crash throws Compassion through a windshield, but her as-yet-undiscovered TARDIS invincibility saves her.

NOVEL TIE-INS The Doctor's dream of dancing with his oldest companion foreshadows the TARDIS' loss in *The Shadows of Avalon*. Compassion's dreams of the Time Vortex, her stable weight despite her lack of appetite and sleep, her odd fascination with the Frontier Worlds network and her swift recovery from injuries all suggest her transformation into a TARDIS (also *The Shadows of Avalon*).

The Remote heavily regimented the DNA of both Compassion and the "remembered" Fitz. Compassion's DNA has regenerative elements. Fitz has a standard double-helix, with extra structures overlaid on the plasmid. Fitz believes his "remembering" blurred some of his memories, but Compassion, via her link with the TARDIS, says his memory's reliable. Fitz sometimes dreams about the Remote's remembrance tanks on Anathema. The Doctor's shadow turns a fraction later than he does, again suggesting he's becoming a Faction Paradox thrall (all *Interference*).

The Doctor decided in *The Taking of Planet Five* that Compassion and Fitz would benefit from human interaction, perhaps motivating their disguise as Frontier Worlds duty clerks.

Frontier Worlds suggests the sonic screwdriver rolled under the TARDIS console for two of the Doctor's lives, explaining its absence between "The Visitation" and "Doctor Who: Enemy Within." However, *Lungbarrow* already explained the seventh Doctor's sonic screwdriver as belonging to Romana ("The Horns of Nimon").

In another small contradiction, *Frontier Worlds* says the eighth Doctor's pockets are big because the lining in this particular jacket is torn. *Alien Bodies* it to the Doctor's reading *Yeltstrom's Karma and Falres: The Importance of Fashion Sense to the Modern Zen Master*.

Fitz deliberately misquotes Rudyard Kipling, whom the fourth Doctor met in *Evolution*.

CHARACTER DEVELOPMENT

The Doctor: The Doctor's never seen a live Raab, but showed a picture of one many incarnations ago to an unspecified companion. The Doctor uses the alias "James Bowman" and has blue eyes.

The Doctor's healing factor quickly seals over bullet wounds. He wears Marks and Spencer underpants. He can produce apples from behind

someone's ear. The Doctor can recognize the plant Lotus corniculatus and was a Tufty Club member in 1968. The eighth Doctor cleans up the TARDIS more than his predecessors.

Fitz Kreiner: Fitz's father often got melancholy, feeling outcast for being a German in England during the war. For most of his teenage years, Fitz dreaded becoming like his dad, who wouldn't argue back when the Bennetts down the road mocked his accent. The Krapper family also didn't acknowledge papa Fitz, so Fitz mocked the Krappers back. Fitz, who's not yet 30, is fluent with Frank Sinatra's quotes. Fitz has stomach flab and can pick pockets. Grey-eyed Fitz used to keep a mangy, pale and somewhat manic rabbit in his back yard—that his father planned to eat. Fitz vividly remembers watching "Gone with the Wind" with his parents. Fitz worries about sleeping because he doesn't know what he'll dream.

Compassion: Compassion's somewhat addicted to her earpiece, and only seems truly happy when she's connected to her company computer or e-mail. She has abnormal strength. Compassion, an expert at virtual reality, can raid other computer systems. Her earpiece lets her pilot fliers without a normal communication net. She remembers a frightening amount of astronomical information from the Frontier Worlds database. Compassion is a good actress when the need calls and can pick the Doctor's pockets.

The Doctor and Compassion: They agreed she wouldn't use her earpiece any more, but she cheats. Compassion believes the Doctor merely tolerates his companions and treats them like pets. Compassion believes the Doctor trusts Fitz but not her. She insists the Doctor won't change her.

Fitz and Compassion: Compassion gave Fitz a few pointers about protecting his files online. In the Drebnar forest, Compassion has a rare moment and claims Fitz cannot become a quitter because she needs his humanity to be complete—but she later claims she was lying to motivate him. Based on Fitz's celebrity worship, they use the aliases "Frank and Nancy Sinatra."

The TARDIS crew: Compassion stays in constant telepathic communication with the TARDIS. The TARDIS claims the Doctor knows Fitz secretly cares—and Fitz hates him for it. Conversely, Compassion hates the Doctor because he wants her to care.

Alura Trebul: Fitz's lover has burnt umber skin, short dark hair and oval eyes. She bought Fitz a mass-produced watch with an orange smiley face on it, plus a "fat, rather ugly" buckle.

The TARDIS: The TARDIS translation system does the best it can, based on what the people involved are thinking. If Fitz acts like a simpleton, the TARDIS translates his words accordingly. Unfortunately, the TARDIS isn't smart on Earth colloquialisms. It once told a friend of the Doctor's that the advertising phrase "Coke adds life" translated as "Class-A drugs bring your ancestors back from the grave." The TARDIS autocleaning systems are balanced, meaning it allows dust to collect on old books, but won't leave crumbs on the carpet. The Ship has a gym. Broad-spectrum Tuckson-Jacker pulses, such as those used by Drebnar's planetary weather control system, can draw the TARDIS off-course.

The Doctor and the TARDIS: In one of the Doctor's dreams, it's suggested the TARDIS only lets the Doctor think he's in charge.

ALIEN RACES

Raab: Huge plants that travel through space for hundreds or thousands of years, the Raab likely originated billions of years ago in the Odonto Ceti region. They can grow as big as 500 meters long.

Your typical Raab lands on a low gravity body such as a barren asteroid or small moon, scattering billions of Raab seeds over the immediate area. A handful survive, growing super-fast and consuming virtually everything. In mere months, the new Raab explodes small, new shoots off the low gravity body into space, starting the process all over again.

Raab are extremely sensitive to weak gravitational forces and therefore rarely get trapped on a large-gravity planet. In such instances, their shoots fall back to the planet and replicate at an exponential rate, consuming the entire planet until they croak. Raab are unbelievably rare, seen perhaps once every 2,000 years. Two of them together is virtually unheard of.

Raab hybrids: Beings infected with Raab DNA normally husk their old skin once a year or when "fatally" injured. The Raab DNA proportion increases with every rebirth. The DNA augments personality flaws such as greed, but inevitably steals self-worth and moral fiber.

Drebnar fish: The throw-off results of Raab experiments, tainted with just enough Raab DNA to be dangerous. Raab-infected fish swim under the

CHARACTER PROFILE

FITZ KREINER

"Fitz Kreiner: Man of Mystery!" Well, that's what he'd like to think, anyway. Here's a quick history of the Doctor's youthful, smoking and lovingly flawed companion:

• **THE TAINT**—In 1963, the Doctor and Sam Jones find that an infection of parastic Benelisian leeches has given a half-dozen psychiatric patients, including Fitz Kreiner's mother, fantastic electromagnetic powers. With the patients deranged and threatening to torture humanity, the Doctor desperately transmits a bioelectrical pulse that kills the Benelisian-infected people. Motherless and wanted for a murder he didn't commit (See The Taint), Fitz joins the TARDIS crew.

• **REVOLUTION MAN**—In 1967, Fitz briefly departs the TARDIS, becoming involved with a waitress named Maddie. Fitz spends two years as a brainwashed agent of Communist China, but the Doctor later breaks Fitz's conditioning. Fitz rejoins the Doctor's crew while Maddie becomes an obsessive cult leader.

• **UNNATURAL HISTORY**—Fitz bags "Dark Sam," an alternate version of Sam who's swallowed by a temporal paradox.

• **INTERFERENCE**—The United Nations asks the Doctor to investigate reports of illicit alien technology on Earth, so the Doctor leaves Fitz in the care of the UN. Rogue agents within the UN distrust Fitz, putting him into suspended animation. In the 26th century, Faction Paradox revives Fitz and conscripts him into their service. Fitz lives out most of his life in the Faction's central "Eleven Day Empire," rising through the ranks and becoming the hardened Faction leader known as "Father Kreiner." Horrendously embittered, Father Kreiner encounters the third Doctor on the planet Dust, but a battle with the force of nature called "Number Thirteen" ruins one of Father Kreiner's arms and flings him into the Time Vortex (*See Dead Romance*). The TARDIS uses its databanks to rebuild (or "remember") young Fitz using Faction agent Kode, who was originally based on Fitz's DNA. The Fitz currently travelling with the Doctor is therefore a stabilized copy with memories the consistency of yogurt.

ice, sensing surface vibrations, then channel warm blood into their foreheads to melt the ice and trap their victims.

ALIEN PLANETS *Drebnar* features huge areas of fertile land and a lack of earthquakes. The Frontier Worlds database says Drebnar has 2,417 different species, although the company has only

---

surveyed 26 percent of the surface. Fitz and Compassion walk through a Drebnar forest that contains 1,012 species—only six of which can harm people.Drebnar has a population of five million, but feeds a host of nearby planets. Its original settlers weren't from Earth.

STUFF YOU NEED *The Doctor's sonic screwdriver* can cut through a steel bulkhead, alert all dogs within a nine-kilometer radius or remove a speck of dirt from someone's eye. Evergreen-brand, kinetically self-regenerating diuturnix batteries manufactured by the defunct Brilliant Corporation power the screwdriver.

HISTORY Student contemporaries Temm Sempiter and Klenton Dewfurth founded Frontier Worlds on Drebnar decades ago, respectively becoming the company chairman and head genetic researcher. Shaz Mozarno became another major investor. Frontier Worlds developed fast crop rotation, until Mozarno and Dewfurth researched a self-regenerating, synthetic flesh to make robots look more human, a pre-cursor to their longevity experiments with Raab DNA.

AT THE END OF THE DAY Damn strong, and barring distraction from the ongoing "What's Wrong With Compassion?" plotine, supremely good at fleshing out all three TARDIS members. The fun of *Frontier Worlds* lies in the details, with Fitz masquerading as Frank Sinatra, Alura slain with a pair of scissors, the Doctor laboring in trying to save the mutating Dewfurth and the absolutely luscious moment when Compassion hurls an axe and nails Ellis between the eyes. All in all, this plant-gripped novel can't help but dredge up memories from "The Seeds of Doom" but it actually tops the TV story by shoving forward Fitz and Compassion's characters while maintaining the Doctor as the main hero.

PARALLEL 59

By Natalie Dallaire and Stephen Cole

Release Date: January 2000
Order: BBC Eighth Doctor Adventure #30
"Who Is Compassion?" Storyarc

TARDIS CREW The eighth Doctor, Fitz and Compassion.

TRAVEL LOG Skale, time unknown.

STORY SUMMARY Moments after the TARDIS materializes on an automatic Bastion-class space station filled with cryogenic capsules, the mere presence of the Doctor's crew disturbs the environment and instigates a series of breakdowns. With the TARDIS sealed off and the Bastion's environment failing, the Doctor bundles Fitz into what he believes is one escape capsule. He and Compassion then ride another down to the planet Skale, where political states divide themselves along lines of latitude (or "parallels").

The Doctor and Compassion land in Parallel 59, where authorities interrogate them as spies. Meanwhile, Fitz wakes up in Mechta, a utopian society that houses convalescents from Skale. In time, Fitz begins a torrid affair with the lonely Anya, wife of political activist Nikol. The randy Fitz, much like a greedy child eating all the grape jelly beans, also becomes involved with a young bank worker named Filippa.

The Doctor learns, to his horror, that the Bastion the TARDIS landed on is part of an entire Bastion network, built by Parallel 59 to link sleeping political prisoners and social lowlifes in a psionic network. As such, the network serves as an early warning system and deterrent minefield to stop the other parallels from achieving spaceflight before Parallel 59. Whereas the Doctor piloted his Bastion capsule and escaped to Skale, Fitz has become part of the network and his mind is trapped in Mechta—a computer-generated reality where the prisoners' minds interact.

The Bastion system, which requires a sterile environment to operate, continues to break down after the TARDIS crew's initial interference. Desperate to repair the network and locate Fitz, the Doctor convinces political rebels from Parallel 59 to help pilot a mineship to Fitz's failing Bastion. There, Compassion's earpiece taps the dying Bastion's computer banks and finds a Haltiel warship overriding the Bastion system, determined to hamstring Skale's fledgling spaceflight ability and contain its political paranoia.

Inside Mechta, the prisoners' mental imprints—Anya's included—start to disappear as the system collapses. To prove their newfound power, the controlling Haltiel intelligence—named the Presence—drops and detonates a few Bastion capsules onto Parallel 6, killing two million people. Compassion hurriedly releases the remaining prisoners on Fitz's Bastion, but only six, including Fitz and Filippa, have survived.

Parallel 90 now panics and counter-attacks the Presence, which in turn drops all 600,000 Bastion capsules and butchers Skale with explosions. Parallel 59 rallies to press home a further attack and makes the Presence, likely content for halting Skale's space race, retreat. Amid the ruins of a devastated Skale, the Doctor, Compassion and Fitz hope the planet can be rebuilt without political boundaries to usher in a new age of peace.

MEMORABLE MOMENTS In an absolute laugh riot (with shades of "Monty Python"), the Doctor uses tickle-torture to gain information from a traitor. The naked Doctor asks his captors if they've ever seen time-travelling naturalists before. Fitz, feeling guilty about his affair with Anya, dreams of faceless people riffling through his past deeds.

ASS-WHUPPINGS The Bastions require a sterile environment to operate, so simply by entering one, the TARDIS crew cause a number of breakdowns that kill at least three people and likely dozens more. A number of Fitz's acquaintances in Mechta die as the Bastion system fails: his lover Anya, her husband Nikol, his flirt Denna and his friend Serjey. Bastion prisoners normally expired from power inrushes when their brain power exhausts in the network, including Fitz's friend Low Rez. Parallel 59 interrogators put the Doctor into a rather painful genetic analyzer, and probe his mind with a semi-organic device.

SEX AND SPIRITS Fitz has an extra-marital affair with Anya, who at first insists on non-committal sex. That changes when Fitz makes advances on Filippa and Anya feels lost without Fitz's support. Filippa, on the other hand, flips when Fitz kisses Denna, a girl he meets in a bar.

When Anya's hubby Mikol disappears (as the Bastion network falters), Anya pressures Fitz to live with her, but he abandons Anya to hunt for the missing Filippa. At the end of the day, Fitz has the strongest feelings for Filippa, but realizes they aren't at the commitment stage. Filippa mostly regards Fitz as her best friend.

Parallel 59 authorities strip the Doctor and Compassion naked, so they spend the first third of the book running about in the buff. In Mechta, Fitz can only enjoy "Ethel," his jokey name for Ethanol, the only booze to be found.

TV TIE-INS The Doctor's sonic screwdriver still makes mines explode ("The Sea Devils," etc.). The eighth Doctor isn't fond of using his respiratory-bypass system to go comatose because the older you get, the less likely you'll wake up ("The Two Doctors," etc.). He's got some scar tissue from Grace Halloway's emergency operation ("Doctor Who: Enemy Within"). Also evocative of that film, the Doctor goes into a trance and wakes up in a morgue, making scientist Jedkah faint dead away.

NOVEL TIE-INS Companion Sam Jones told Fitz of her separation from the Doctor during the "Missing Sam" storyline (*Longest Day* through *Seeing I*). Fitz feels both the Red Army (*Revolution Man*) and the Remote (*Interference*) led him by the nose too much. He isn't sure if he's 29 or 30 now (he was 27 in *The Taint*, but spent two years away from the TARDIS in *Revolution Man*).

Compassion's skin turns pale, porcelain-like and almost flawless, foreshadowing her transformation into a TARDIS in *The Shadows of Avalon*. Also for this reason, Parallel 59 scanners, calibrated for humans, explode while analyzing her.

CHARACTER DEVELOPMENT

The Doctor: The Doctor has an elevated body temperature and a triple-helix DNA. He whistles a guitar tune Fitz composed for Sam to practice. He wears Clarks' leather shoes and knows the TARDIS' mass by memory. The eighth Doctor has piloting skills.

Fitz Kreiner: Aside from his sexual cat's cradle, Fitz enjoyed life in Mechta. His hair grows less straggly, his skin becomes toned and his depression vanishes. Mentally, he lives in Mechta for months, but the experience lasts five days of "real" time. Since the Remote "remembered" Fitz (*Interference*), his mind works in different ways: He's extremely skilled at crossword puzzles and anagrams. He's afraid when he wakes up, uncertain of his identity.

The Doctor and Fitz: During his time in Mechta, Fitz misses the Doctor and realizes the effect he had on people. Fitz finds being with the Doctor makes him act bravely.

Compassion: She's an excellent driver and talks in her sleep. Her Remote earpiece lets her communicate with the Bastion computer. For a limited time, Compassion merges with the Bastion controller and accesses its abilities.

The Doctor and Compassion: Compassion regards the Doctor as the most likable idiot she's ever met. She doesn't think she can grasp the concept of "having friends."

Anya: Anya is eight years older than Fitz, has pale blue eyes and brown, bushy hair. She's got a dependent streak, but comes off as a lovely, intelligent and sharp woman.

Filippa Cian: Fitz's true love—if he has one in this book—meets Fitz on a subway tube and is 25.

She works in a bank off Mechta's Centreside. She's got redder hair than Compassion.

Denna: Meets Fitz in a bar in Mechta's North-side and becomes one of his many flirts. She loves life and being the center of attention. She's also a good dancer.

Compassion and the TARDIS: The TARDIS, even in space, refines and qualifies Compassion's earpiece signals.

ALIEN PLANETS

Skale: The sole planet of its solar system, an out-of-the-way world orbiting a nowhere sun. Skale thinks the high-gravity, noxious Haltiel doesn't have extraterrestrial life (but learns different).

Mechta: As a computer unreality created for the benefit of Skale political prisoners, Mechta didn't advocate personal property because the state supplies everything. "Central" is the Mechta equivalent of City Hall. Mechta was moonless and lacked phones. Mechta's inhabitants enjoyed freewill, but controllers overrode the more extreme behavior.

PLACES TO GO *Bastions:* Over the course of 30 years, Parallel 59 constructed 2,000 Bastions at strategic points around the planet, reaching further into space than any other Parallel. The Bastions contained 600,000 sleeping prisoners, each psionically linked into a sensory barrier and protective minefield.

The prisoners, snug in their capsules and mentally linked to "Mechta," eventually withered and died. As death approached, a prisoner's mental counterpart in the Mechta system received a summons to return to Skale and rode a special taxicab out of the system. In actuality, the dead prisoner's capsule was ejected into space and a fresh person from storage activated.

ORGANIZATIONS *Parallel 59* has a small landmass. Mating programs, designed to keep a robust population, inflict strict penalties on your income and social status if certain birthing goals aren't met (so breed, people—breed!).

Parallel 59 smears other parallels with an intense propaganda machine and has some mineral wealth. Parallel 67 previously warred with Parallel 59, and rival Parallel 6 carried out a number of space launches. A group named the Facility ran the Bastion network, headed by a ruthlessly efficient visionary named Narkmopros (who's poisoned by his deputy).

AT THE END OF THE DAY Underrated, and probably maligned because it doesn't feel like standard "Doctor Who" and shamelessly (not that we mind) lacks a monster. That said, *Parallel 59* will frustrate some by simultaneously suffering from an overly complex plot (try explaining the Bastion network in less than five minutes) and a strange vagueness (Skale's political affiliations never get defined much). Still, the characters, particularly Fitz and Anya, definitely shine enough and help *Parallel 59*'s cracks seem more obvious in retrospect, not while you're reading it.

THE SHADOWS OF AVALON

By Paul Cornell

Release Date: February 2000
Order: BBC Eighth Doctor Adventure #31
"Who Is Compassion?" Storyarc
(Conclusion)

TARDIS CREW The eighth Doctor, Fitz and Compassion, with the Brigadier and Romana III.

TRAVEL LOG Earth, July 2012.

CHRONOLOGY For the Brigadier, a couple years after *Happy Endings* and a year after Doris' death.

STORY SUMMARY Time Lord forecasters sense the impending emergence of a technology that could revolutionize Gallifrey's TARDISes, so President Romana, now in her third body, sends Interventionist agents Cavis and Gandar to catalyze the technology's creation—by attempting to kill the Doctor's companion Compassion.

Meanwhile, Brigadier Lethbridge-Stewart, distraught by the death of his wife Doris in a boating accident, investigates reports of a dragon interfering with a British aircraft. Compassion, having just completed a six-week stay on Earth, meets the Brigadier and awaits the TARDIS' scheduled pickup. But as the Doctor and Fitz arrive in the Ship, a dimensional rift opens and ruptures the venerable TARDIS—destroying it utterly.

The breach hurls the Doctor and his three allies into the medieval realm of Avalon, created centuries ago by Time Lord Interventionists as a sanctuary for Celts fleeing Roman persecution. The sleeping mind of the mighty King Constantine maintains Avalon's dimensional stability in the collective consciousness of human dreaming, but the dimensional rift's mysterious appearance per-

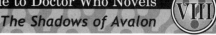
mits travel between Avalon and Earth.

Queen Mab, ruler of Avalon's Catuvelauni tribe, formally allies with England to gain scientific weapons, but causes great unrest in the rival Unseelie Court, ruled by magic-wielding Silurians. Cavis and Gandar locate Constantine's human avatar, a businessman named Rex, and scheme to have him unleash his mighty psionic abilities onto Compassion. In turn, Rex plots to destroy Avalon, ending Constantine's responsibilities and gaining further powers. To this end, Cavis and Gandar push Britain and the Catuvelauni into full-blown war with the Unseelie Court, threatening nuclear armageddon in Avalon.

Desperately, the Doctor wakes the sleeping Constantine—an act that erases Rex from existence—and thwarts Cavis and Gandar's plan at the cost of destabilizing Avalon's dimensional borders. Cavis and Gandar finally abandon stealth and capture Compassion, but the Brigadier and his allies intercept them, killing Cavis outright and impaling Gandar to the wall. Moments before regenerating and refusing to surrender, Gandar shoots Compassion and knocks her off a rooftop.

As Compassion falls, months of being empathicly linked with the Doctor's TARDIS through her earpiece suddenly catalyze, snap-evolving Compassion into a fully sentient TARDIS (while retaining her humanoid exterior). Compassion dematerializes for the first time, returning to the Court roof as Gandar regenerates into a passive incarnation that mourns for Cavis' loss.

The Avalon nations and Britain end hostilities, realizing the pointlessness of their conflict. Moments later, President Romana arrives to explain that Compassion, the first of Gallifrey's sentient TARDISes, will be used to breed advanced Type 103s—securing Gallifrey's defense against the future Enemy.

The Doctor, appalled at the thought of Compassion being used against her will, waits until Queen Mab uses a special default device to put Constantine back to sleep, thereby re-stabilizing Avalon's dimensional borders and returning the English to Earth. As Avalon's dimensional borders reformat, Compassion dematerializes and evades Romana's dimensional blockade. The Doctor and Fitz continue their journey with Compassion as their TARDIS, on the run and protecting her from the Time Lords, while the newly self-actualized Brigadier stays in Avalon as an Earth ambassador and potential lover to Queen Mab.

MEMORABLE MOMENTS Out of habit, the sleeping Brigadier rolls over to talk with Doris, then sadly recalls she's dead. The newly younger Brigadier asks the Doctor if his new body is working out and the Doctor replies: "Beautifully! What about yours?"

Compassion platonically wakes up in bed with Fitz but screams anyway. There's a superb number of novel-related curses when a murderous Gandar declares, "Let's just kill the Otherf—." When the Doctor seems vanquished, Gandar shouts, "We Faraqued the Ka Faraq Gatri!"

Unable to live without Doris, the Brigadier puts a gun to his head but doesn't pull the trigger. The Doctor celebrates his reunion with the Brigadier by hugging him and spinning him about (The Brigadier laments: "Stop it at once, Doctor. The men are watching."). Best of all, a fleeing Doctor tells Romana to kiss his TARDIS.

SEX AND SPIRITS The Brigadier and Queen Mab don't kiss, but they're clearly destined for each other. Compassion spends six weeks on Earth boozing and making friends. She throws a guy named Allan up against a wall and smooches him to fulfill the Doctor's mandate of falling in love. It's not relevant, but her friend Marcus drunkenly runs about, hollering a new euphemism for male genitalia each time he hits a corner of the room.

Romantic partners Cavis and Gandar prove Time Lords still screw, but keep their relationship secret. (Cavis, disguised as a Silurian, beautifully comments she wants to have Gandar's eggs.) The Doctor lip-locks an underwater Gandar to gush oxygenated liquid down his mouth and stun him.

ASS-WHUPPINGS The TARDIS hits the Avalon/Earth dimensional rift and explodes in a ball of flame (we felt a palpitation or two), but gets better (*The Ancestor Cell*).

The Brigadier's wife Doris died when they vacationed on a sailing boat and bad weather approached. Doris suggested they return to shore, but the Brigadier favored contesting the choppy water. Their boat overturned, drowning Doris. The grief-stricken Brigadier here orders suicide runs against the Unseelie Court so he can die in battle. Two hundred men bite it, but the Brig lucklessly survives every engagement thanks to Mab's secret charm. Still, he guns down at least three Fair Folk and a dragon.

Cavis eats human babies purely for sport and gives a British ambassador the "threefold death" just to cause trouble. Gandar and Cavis level Queen Mab's court by snaring an in-flight asteroid with their TARDIS, then rematerializing in Avalon and opening the doors. Queen Mab's advisor Margwyn *twice* stabs Gandar and forces him to regenerate, but Gandar shoots Margwyn dead. Queen Mab decapitates Cavis, then stabs her through both hearts and permanently kills her.

TV TIE-INS Celestial Intervention Agency (The Deadly Assassin") agents typically work in pairs. Cavis and Gandar previously tangled with the Vardans ("The Invasion of Time"). Cavis' full name of Cavisadoratrelundar suggests she hails from the same House as Romana ("The Ribos Operation"). Gandarotethetledrax is probably related to Drax ("The Armageddon Factor"). Cavis and Gandar hysterically parody the mad Professor Zaroff by belting out "Nothing in the world can stop us now!" ("The Underwater Menace")

"Planet of the Spiders" first mentioned the Brigadier's wife Doris, but she first appeared in "Battlefield." The Doctor owns a proper UNIT pass card (also "Battlefield").

The eighth Doctor's precognition talent ("Doctor Who: Enemy Within") works on dragons.

Romana uses a Time/Space Visualizer ("The Space Museum"). Gallifreyan staser pistols ("The Deadly Assassin") could kill the Doctor outright. Gallifreyan technology heavily influenced Avalon culture, meaning Mab's Court includes the positions of Castellan ("The Deadly Assassin") and the Keeper of the Memory ("The Ultimate Foe").

Silurians debuted in the aptly (or ineptly, depending on your point of view) named "Doctor Who and the Silurians."

Captain Munro ("Spearhead from Space") is now a Colonel and favors loyalty to UNIT's British branch over Geneva.

TV AND NOVEL TIE-INS Compassion's long-standing link with the TARDIS via her Remote receiver (*Interference*) warped her biodata and replaced her cells with space-time contours, rewriting them with block transfer computations ("Logopolis").

The Doctor hasn't been Merlin yet ("Battlefield"), probably a nod from Cornell to the Muld-wych incarnation (*Birthright*). Faction Paradox's meddling (*Interference*) muddled the Doctor's memories—he simultaneously recalls his father ("Doctor Who: Enemy Within," *The Infinity Doctors*) and being born in the Looms (*Cat's Cradle: Time's Crucible, Lungbarrow*).

Advice for the wise: People who get lost in the Time Vortex only have an infinitesimal chance of being found, except by a predator such as a Swimmer (*The Taking of Planet Five*), a Polt, a Chronovore ("The Time Monster") or a Kraken (*Dreamstone Moon*).

NOVEL TIE-INS Fully sentient TARDISes such as Compassion debuted in *Alien Bodies*. The TARDIS here explodes but reappears (somewhat) in *The Ancestor Cell*. Events in the Obverse (*The Blue Angel*) first alerted the Time Lords to Compassion's ongoing TARDIS transformation, explaining why Iris Wildthyme forced the Doctor to leave undetected. The TARDIS sensed and explored the nature of her impending "death" here and was drawn to similar disturbances (the Corridors in *The Blue Angel*, the dimensional energy in *Frontier Worlds*; the prisoner gestalt in *Parallel 59*). Compassion's ongoing TARDIS transformation explains why TARDISes spoke to her (*The Taking of Planet Five*) and a Skale scanner exploded (*Parallel 59*). Fitz has promised to visit Filippa (also *Parallel 59*).

Cornell's *Happy Endings* kindly gave the Brigadier a much younger body. *Head Games* first mentioned that the Brigadier was promoted to General, but everyone calls him "The Brigadier." The Brig spends a number of decades in Avalon, then returns to Earth at some point and winds up in an old people's home (*The King of Terror*). In 2012, the Brigadier's first wife Fiona (*The Scales of Injustice*), daughter Kate and grandson Gordy (*Downtime*) are still alive.

Romana became president of Gallifrey in *Happy Endings*. She's concerned about Gallifrey's ongoing dispute with the People (loosely reconciled in *Dead Romance*) and Gallifrey's future war with the Enemy (*Alien Bodies*). Cavis credits the Other (*Lungbarrow*) with founding the Interventionists.

UNIT hasn't faced a major crisis since *The Dying Days*—the United Nations here ponders cutting the organization's funding.

CHARACTER DEVELOPMENT

The Doctor: The Doctor officially resigned from UNIT, but baffled Geneva authorities by writing the note in High Gallifreyan (and one sentence in English). His chosen name translates to "Foolish Wanderer." He's loosely named magical adviser to Queen Mab, but speculates that magically regrowing a TARDIS using Avalon's "magic" could take centuries.

The Doctor can survive unaided in the Time Vortex by entering a trance to hold his body and personality together. In such a state, he could survive—adrift and alone—for several hundred years as an emaciated husk.

He can catch a speeding knife in mid-air between his thumb and forefinger. The Doctor hates arriving in years predicted as world's end because he always has to save people. He claims human beings taught him everything he needed to know.

The Doctor has deep blue eyes and recognizes Sol's solar cycle in 2012. He hasn't witnessed many golden ages and telepathically communicates with Avalon dragons. He's met Geronimo and seen "The Great Escape" (Author's note: A great flick, and

THE CRUCIAL BITS...

- **THE SHADOWS OF AVALON**—Apparent destruction of the Doctor's TARDIS. Compassion transforms into Gallifrey's first fully sentient and humanoid TARDIS. Romana regenerates into her third body. Death of the Brigadier's wife Doris revealed. The Brigadier becomes ambassador to the other-dimensional Avalon. The Time Lords plot to use Compassion as TARDIS breeding stock, so the Doctor's crew becomes fugitives in time and space.

not just because William "Ian Chesterton" Russell makes an appearance.)

Compassion: Newly transformed into a TARDIS, Compassion's impervious to blaster fire and equipped with vast databanks. Gandar and Cavis wanted Constantine to attack Compassion and thus evolve her, probably unconvinced a simple staser shot would suffice.

On the Doctor's instructions, Compassion spends six weeks on Earth with friends Joe and Catherine to learn humanity. The Doctor's assigned tasks to her included "make friends," "fall in love" and "write a poem." She temporarily adopts a cat named Cheese.

Compassion admits travelers to her TARDIS interior by opening a glowing portal down her body. Her interior includes a forest and a polished wood corridor with dignified oil portraits of the Doctor's family, friends and past selves. Her circular console room's set above a chasm with strange shapes moving in a liquid darkness. A scanner iris shows arrival destinations. Compassion guides travelers through her interior with directions in banners, but some labels such as "Hopes for the Future" and "That Dream About Fitz" denote her whirling internal thoughts.

Compassion finds her transformation frightening and wondrous. She hiccups when materializing. Other TARDISes can trap Compassion by materializing around her.

Compassion, The Doctor and Fitz: Compassion insists the Doctor and Fitz take rooms on her dark side, perhaps out of spite—the Doctor suspects he won't feel comfortable travelling in Compassion.

Brigadier Lethbridge-Stewart: While distraught by Doris' death, the Brigadier overreacts to a private's act of insubordination and breaks his jaw. He finally reconciles to the loss and moves onward.

The Brigadier's parents remained married but squabbled routinely. He wasn't abused as a child. He doesn't believe in an afterlife and owns a BMW.

The Doctor and the Brigadier: The two philosophically come to blows when the Brigadier sides with British military interests over peace and the lives of innocents (he finally concedes his mistake). The Brigadier asks the Doctor to not go back in time and save Doris.

When the Brigadier was young, he traumatically lost a balloon at an airshow. The eighth Doctor, bending the rules of time, showed up to save the balloon and make the memory a pleasant one.

Doris: The Brigadier's wife loved sun, roses, old dancing music and soap operas including "The Archers" (the Brigadier dislikes such programs).

Romana III (a.k.a. Lady President, War Queen, Mistress of the Nine Gallifreys): Romana's new incarnation dresses like a 1920s diva, strutting about in scarlet chinoise pajamas and a high square collar, with lengths of pearls and oriental clogs. Her toenail paint resembles the Time Vortex's swirling, and she's got a tiny Prydonian Seal tattoo on her left ankle (keep it in your pants, boys). Her foremost goal is to protect Gallifrey. Failing Romana could get your history erased.

The Doctor and Romana III: Romana III unnervingly resembles the Doctor's mother.

Cavis and Gandar (a.k.a. Cavisadoratrelundar and Gandarotethetledrax): Notorious Gallifreyan Interventionist agents, famed for mayhem and recruited from the Patrexes College ("The Deadly Assassin"), but later disavowing a rank or college. Above all, they're loyal to Romana.

Cavis and Gandar are expert TARDIS pilots. Cavis' father staunchly opposed the Interventionists, so Gandar killed him with Cavis' blessing. Cavis has messy blonde hair and one heart—remaining unregenerated after 30 missions. She's famed for kicking Sontaran ass.

Gandar finally regenerated into a mild personality with a Silurian's third eye (he evidently absorbed some Fair Folk DNA in the process). He tried but failed to mentally retrieve a bit of Cavis' personality from her decapitated head.

The Doctor, Cavis and Gandar: The Doctor's heard of Cavis and Gandar's exploits. Cavis' father visited the Doctor's family at Lungbarrow, and the Doctor likely bounced young Cavis on his knee. As post-modern Time Lords, Cavis and Gandar have waited millennia to take on the Doctor (Gandar even dresses like the Master).

Queen Mab (a.k.a. Queen Regent Mab ab Mab Pendragon, Queen Regent of the Catuvelauni, Protector of Avalon): Queen Mab's 30, blue eyed and dark haired. She typically wears a tempered sword, golden rings and (Gasp! Shock! Dismay!) a penis-shaped failsafe amulet that puts King Constantine back to sleep.

King Constantine: Sleeps in a great well of oxygenated solution at Avalon's center, linked to Gallifreyan temporal tracking equipment. While Constantine dozes, he stabilizes Avalon's quantum particle fluctuations in the realm of human dreaming. Were Constantine to full awaken, it would overwrite Avalon on Earth's reality and kill millions of Earthers.

When the TARDIS ruptured, Constantine unconsciously saved the Doctor's party by pulling them into his dreams. Even asleep, Constantine's ruled the Celtic Catuvelauni for 2,000 years, with Queen Mab as the latest of his regents. Avalon mages tap Constantine's psionic energy to implement magic effects.

ALIEN RACES

Time Lords: Can regenerate after a decapitation (forming a new head in the process), although they can't survive being stabbed through both hearts. Their ability to scan the future is limited, with shocking predictions sometimes giving Gallifreyan forecasters a hearts attack and making them regenerate on the spot.

Type 98 TARDISes: Have holographic scanners.

Avalon Dragons: Magic-bred, but live in Avalon as real creatures.

PLACES TO GO

Avalon: By existing in the realm of human dreaming, Avalon reverberates as a concept throughout the multiverse. The Doctor knows of Avalon's history, and it remains a rare instance of successful (i.e., non-terminal for thousands of beings) intervention by the Time Lords.

Gallifrey's Presidential Wheel: Located in the Capital, it has 363 white towers.

ORGANIZATIONS *Fair Folk (a.k.a. Faerie Folk, the Unseelie Court)* are magic-wielding Silurians in Avalon, ruled by Brona and Arwen. The Fair Folk's magicks can weave quantum particles and cast illusions or, with preparation, halt Earth cruise missiles.

HISTORY The Doctor claims he gave humanity fire. Of course, Scaroth ("City of Death") taught mankind fire's true meaning.

• Romans violently settled a border dispute along the British coastline in the first century until the oppressed Celts discovered equipment provided by Gallifreyan Interventionists. King Constantine used the equipment to replicate "Britain" in the realm of human dreaming and dream a select tribe of Celts (and Silurians, evidently) into it. Other tribes assimilated the Celtic forts left behind, crafting legends of Avalon around the lost tribe.

• The Doctor likely talked about King Constantine to Lewis Carroll and influenced his writing.

AT THE END OF THE DAY A bitter pill to swallow because we've never dealt Paul Cornell an unflattering review—until now. Unfortunately, *The Shadows of Avalon* abrasively whips rather than blends its events together (time-active Cavis and Gandar plug some gaping plot holes) and needs a solid two revisions to achieve notoriety. It's a damn shame too, because the book's got a number of rich elements: the Brigadier's grief, the new Romana and most of all, Cavis and Gandar as youthful, post-modern Time Lords brashly seeking to challenge the Doctor. But the final effect's simply too jumbled, disjointed and rushed for its own good, leaving *The Shadows of Avalon* memorable more for continuity changes than its own merits.

THE FALL OF YQUATINE

By Nick Walters

Release Date: March 2000
Order: BBC Eighth Doctor Adventure #32

TARDIS CREW The eighth Doctor, Fitz and Compassion.

TRAVEL LOG Minerva System, planet Yquatine, moon of Muath and city of Yendip, Earth year 2992 (the 58 days between Jaquaia 1 to Lannasirn 17 in the local calendar). Compassion also travels to New Anthaur and makes dozens of random jumps trying to get back to Yquatine, finally spending decades adrift in the Time Vortex.

STORY SUMMARY The Doctor proposes fitting Compassion with a Randomizer to make their travels unpredictable and untraceable by Time Lords, but the self-reliant Compassion vetoes the idea. But determined to proceed, the Doctor purchases a Randomizer during a stopover on the planet Yquatine in the Minerva System and forcibly installs it in Compassion's console room. Agonized by the invasive surgery, Compassion ejects the Doctor and Fitz and flees. Moments later, unidentified alien ships pelt Yquatine with metal-searing gas bombs. Unable to find Fitz in the confusion, the Doctor steals an empty freighter and flies to safety. Fitz successfully locates Compassion, but his attempts to remove the Randomizer throw them a month back in time. Still panicked, Compassion abandons Fitz on Yquatine and dematerializes, becoming lost in time and space.

Armed with the foreknowledge of Yquatine's demise, a poverty-stricken Fitz works as a bartender and saves to purchase passage off-planet. He also strikes up a friendship with Arielle, a xenobiology student and the discontented young lover of Yquatine ruler Stefan Vargeld. Arielle, fed up with the publicity of being Vargeld's girlfriend, convinces Fitz to platonically run away with her and they book passage on an outbound spaceship. Unfortunately, the ship hits an alien particle cloud that infects Arielle with strange spores, just as Vargeld's secret service arrives to re-claim her. Vargeld's men toss Fitz into an internment center on Muath while Arielle demands her freedom and suddenly departs.

A month passes as the alien spores, actually a long-dormant sentient gas weapon named the Omnethoth, incubate in Arielle and grow a giant transmitter on Muath. A possessed Arielle activates the beacon, locating a multitude of Omnethoth capsules and teleporting them into local space just as prison authorities dispatch the disposable Fitz to investigate Arielle's unauthorized presence on Muath. As the Omnethoth withdraw from Arielle and Yquatine "again" falls, Compassion returns from years spent adrift in the Time Vortex searching for Fitz's biodata trace.

Arielle dies from side effects of the Omnethoth possession, but Compassion and Fitz escape in a shuttle. With the Yquatine in disarray, the aggressive reptilian Anthaurk race capitalize on the moment and seize Yquatine space. Thankfully, Compassion prevents further deaths by using her chameleon circuit to assume the likeness of the grief stricken, war-crazed President Vargeld, ordering his warships to surrender. As "Vargeld," Compassion compels the Anthaurk ruling council to vie for peace rather than face retribution from every race in the Minerva System, causing the real Vargeld to be hailed as a hero.

No longer on the run as peace asserts itself, the Doctor, realizing the Omnethoth's activation was

accidental, mentally reprograms them into peaceful cloud-like beings. Unfortunately, a hostile Vargeld uses ionization weapons to destroy the harmless Omnethoth. Enraged at the pointless deaths, the Doctor concedes his botched attempt to install Compassion's Randomizer means he cannot remove the device or switch it off. Compassion begrudgingly accepts the Doctor's apology, leaving with the Doctor and Fitz to continue random trips through time and space.

MEMORABLE MOMENTS   The Doctor bravely argues for the Omnethoth's survival by explaining that in the Universal whole, nothing is just or unjust—the creatures don't automatically deserve death for accidentally reactivating in the Minerva System. The Doctor further grows wrathful at the injustice of Fitz's imprisonment, blasting President Vargeld with, "You're just a politician, not a human being."

Arielle's passing, her body turning to smoke while Fitz holds her, marks itself as the book's most emotional moment.

Fitz comes to the sudden, horrifying realization that he's been effectively peeing in Compassion.

SEX AND SPIRITS   Fitz gets drunk at Il-Eruk's Tavern and oddly sings about turnip fish. He also hits on a blue-skinned woman, throws up and runs naked through a fountain with her (a good night, on the whole). Just for kicks, we thought we'd mention that he eats a devilled mud-maggot in gruntgoat cheese sauce. He later works at Il-Eruk's as a barman.

Fitz enjoys a platonic relationship with Arielle (she stays over one night, but Fitz sleeps in the kitchen), but finds her attractive and loves her in some fashion. Chapter seven is scandalously titled, "I want something removed from me."

ASS-WHUPPINGS   The whole of Yquatine, for a start. Compassion asks biomechanical engineer Ralf Petersen to remove her Randomizer, but the pain involved makes her accidentally crush him to death in a giant gear chamber in her interior.

Fitz spends a month trapped in the Yquatine Internment Center. The Omnethoth kill his friend Arielle by using her cells to build their organic teleport station. Vargeld orders the Omnethoth's destruction over the Doctor's protests.

TV TIE-INS   The fourth Doctor cobbled together a Randomizer in "The Armageddon Factor," but ditched it in "The Leisure Hive." Lacking TARDIS parts, the eighth Doctor buys one for Compassion.

Compassion can use her chameleon circuit ("An Unearthly Child") to disguise herself as an Anthaurk or other humanoids. Her roofspace serves as her scanner ("Doctor Who: Enemy Within").

The crystalline Ixtricite race is a gestalt of the Krotons ("The Krotons"), the Rhotons and a third unmentioned species.

NOVEL TIE-INS *Dry Pilgrimage* first mentioned Chateau Yquatine, an export wine. Fitz isn't looking for a relationship after Filippa's death (*Parallel 59*), but values Arielle's company. The Doctor's complicated biodata (*Alien Bodies, Unnatural History*) is wildly spread through space-time and impossible to track.

CHARACTER DEVELOPMENT

The Doctor: The Doctor attended President Vargeld's inauguration—in another body. By coincidence, the eighth Doctor looks strikingly like Vargeld. He doesn't know the history or future of the Minerva System. He's old friends with pie seller and secret technology dealer Lou Lombardo.

The Doctor knows a frequency that's painful but harmless to Anthaurk ears. He used to keep a notebook detailing the different types of spaceships he saw, but lost it with his old TARDIS. He shares a natural empathy with the Omnethoth and can trap one of them in his respiratory bypass system. His eyes are blue. He doesn't believe in predestination and doesn't need to shave. He's witnessed the death of many stars.

The Doctor once attended a coronation on Everdrum, where assassins leapt out of an enormous pie and killed the king (the hungry Doctor was quite sad for the pie's loss).

Fitz Kreiner: Fitz spent a few weeks tending bar at the Mother Black Cap in Camden Town in the 1960s. He hates hospitals. Happiness still mystifies him. Without Compassion's translation circuits, he can only barely read Yquatine English.

Compassion: When Compassion dematerializes, she follows a process labeled FEAR (Focus, Engage, artron surge, Randomizer). Compassion can only override the Randomizer by shutting off all her travel circuits and putting herself adrift in the Time Vortex. She finds the Vortex unpleasant, probably because she's sentient (perhaps explaining why TARDISes are only semi-sentient).

Since her TARDIS conversion, Compassion's gained thinner eyes and darker hair. She can search her databanks for historical information, alter her exterior shape (but typically keeps her normal appearance for comfort), cut off her internal oxygen supply and tune into local medianets. She's resistant to acid rain, has little experience with short trips and possesses money resources.

She can emit an artron energy blast (although this presumably drains her) and scan AI networks. She's equipped with telepathic circuits that allow translation and limited empathy.

Compassion doesn't sweat, doesn't need to breathe and no longer registers as a lifesign. She's resistant to blaster fire. Her eyecolor varies between brown, green and purple. Her console's a nightmarish cross between a spider and an oil rig.

Compassion's darker interior reflects an unhinged inner personality despite her calm demeanor. Her interior forest produces giant leafy healing pods. She's constantly locating new rooms within herself.

The Doctor and Compassion: Their empathic link allows Compassion to detect the Doctor, even if he's comatose. In turn, The Doctor can sense but not precisely locate Compassion's artron energy.

Fitz and Compassion: Compassion apologizes for abandoning Fitz on Yquatine.

ALIEN RACES

Omnethoth: Sentient gas creatures linked in a gestalt and having three natural states—a lethal gas, an acid-like liquid and a probing solid. Only the gaseous form has sentience. The Omnethoth can neutralize bombs that fly through them. The name "Omnethoth" is meaningless, designed only to convey fear and dread.

Anthaurk: Tall, bulky and military-minded reptilian creatures, covered in orange scaly skin. They're typically intolerant of other species, negotiating peace only in the presence of a full battlefleet. The Anthaurk worship 600 deities, including Hiss'aa, the Goddess of War and Venom, and Thoth (no relation to the Omnethoth), their god of learning and art.

A six-member Inner Circle Elite rules the Anthaurk, headed by a Grand Gynarch (young Zizeenia here succeeds her mother to the post). Their original homeworld had two suns.

ALIEN PLANETS

Yquatine: The most notable and prosperous planet of the Minerva System, having an elliptical orbit that gives it long summers and short winters.

The tropical planet's wildly diverse population comes from nearly every Minerva System race (*See Places to Go*).

The Yquatine Year has 417 days, composed of ten months with roughly 42 days each. The months are named as follows: Stornside, Petalstrune, Cicelior (Spring); Sevaija, Jaquaia, Lannasirn (Summer); Perialtrine, Shirveltide (Autumn); Forlarne and Ultimar (Winter).

Muath: Single Yquatine moon that went through several changes of ownership and usage. Powell Industries uses cheap prison labor there to build its envirodomes.

PLACES TO GO

Minerva System: Has only one sun and a standard Minervan language. The uninhabited gas giant Xaxdool is the system's largest planetary body. The deer-like Eldrig (from the ice world of Oomingmak) and the tiger-like Rorclaavix (from the jungle planet of Zolion) are the system's only indigenous species, although colonists include the reptilian Izrekts, the insectoid Kukutsi (from the insect world of Chitis) the silver-gray diamond shaped Ixtricite (from the crystal planet of Ixtrice) and the silicon-based Adamantiums (from Adamantine).

Yendip: Yquatine's most notable city, located on the eastern coast of Julianis on the planet's largest continent. The Palace of Yquatine, found in the middle of Lake Yendip, holds the seat of government for the entire Minerva system.

HISTORY
Millions of years ago, a race named the Masters constructed the Omnethoth as a sentient weapon to conquer the Universe, but the Omnethoth—in typical science fiction fashion—destroyed their creators instead. The Omnethoth then went dormant but seeded the Universe with colonization clouds.

• The Daleks displaced the reptilian Anthaurk from their homeworld circa 2690, prompting the Anthaurk to settle on planet Kaillor in the Minerva System and re-name it New Anthaur.

• Julian de Yquatine and the human colony ship *Minerva* settled the Minerva System circa 2792. In time, the system won independence from the Earth Empire and adopted free trade policies. Yquatine's descendants ruled Yquatine until President Marc de Yquatine, the last of his line, died at the end of the 29th century.

• In 2890, the Anthaurk warred and lost against the other Minerva races. The Treaty of Yquatine, signed in 2893, began a century of peace.

• After Marc de Yquatine's passing, a string of human and non-human rulers succeeded on Yquatine until the Vargelds, one of the system's ruling families, rose to power. Twenty-year-old Stefan Vargeld became Marquis of Yquatine in 2980. In 2988, he won a landslide victory over the unpopular Minerva Senate President Ignatiev.

AT THE END OF THE DAY
A solid work, boasting strong world creation plus a myriad of characters and motives. *The Fall of Yquatine* succeeds as an above-average novel from 2000, but it isn't dynamic enough to rise to the A-level novels. Still, the Doctor's companions shine through (Walters uses Fitz's human-grounded character and Compassion's TARDIS nature to great effect), and there's a tapestry of conflict (Compassion vs. her companions, the Doctor vs. Vargeld, the Anthaurk vs. virtually everyone). You can pass on this book if you're hurting for time, but it's a much better example of the Compassion TARDIS era than *Coldheart* or *The Space Age*.

COLDHEART

By Trevor Baxendale

Release Date: April 2000
Order: BBC Eighth Doctor Adventure #33

TARDIS CREW
The eighth Doctor, Fitz and Compassion.

TRAVEL LOG
Planet Eskon, city of Baktan, time unknown.

STORY SUMMARY
Compassion materializes on the planet Eskon, a desert world deprived of water by a rogue solar flare. Living in sandstone cities, the native Eskoni draw water from insulated ice reserves in the planet's interior, but worry about a rising number of mutations in the city of Baktan. More and more young Eskoni there have developed oily skin and fatal spasms, only to be dubbed "slimers" by their fellow Eskoni and exiled to a desolate existence in a nearby shantytown.

Distraught by his people's unjust treatment, slimer spokesman Revan advocates a violent response while the Doctor grows angry at the ruling Baktan triad, including high priest Tor Grymna, for persecuting the slimers and not working to cure them. While Fitz tries to keep the slimer situation from boiling toward violence, the Doctor and Compassion conclude that alien DNA has contaminated Eskon's interior and undertake an expedition to investigate. Near Eskon's ice deposits, they locate both a gigantic Spulver Worm, a throwback from mutagenic wars on Aayavex's third moon, and the remains of an Aayavex shuttle that carried the worm to Eskon. With growing horror, the Doctor notices a wound in the Spulver Worm leaking pus, lacing the ice deposits with the worm's mutagenic DNA and creating the slimers.

On the surface, Tor Grymna's men burn slimer shantytown to the ground, so the slimers throw down the gauntlet and seize the ice mine. Inconsolable, Revan detonates charges that kill him and destroy the ice mine, causing a chain reaction that melts massive amounts of the underground ice and hatches thousands of hungry Spulver Worm eggs. As the young Spulvers consume the people of Baktan, the Doctor and Compassion prepare to trigger more underground charges, sweeping the Spulver worm and its infection down a nearby fault line.

Tor Grymna grows convinced of his wrongful persecution of the slimers and rushes off half-cocked to blow up the giant Spulver worm. Unable to reason with Tor Grymna, who's in danger of poisoning future generations, the Doctor pre-sets Tor Grymna's bomb and tosses it back to him. The mature Spulver worm, sensing the bomb's heat, gobbles both Tor Grymna and the explosive and dies in the resulting blast.

Compassion quickly explodes her own charges, generating a waterslide that sweeps the Spulver worm contagion into an isolated fault line while the Doctor takes refuge in her control room. The entire city of Baktan falls into the desert, demolishing the embryo Spulvers and ending the alien threat. As thousands of survivors from Baktan prepare to draw their water from a newly formed, Spulver-free lake, the people emerge into a new era of tolerance and elect new rulers. Their work finished, the Doctor, Compassion and Fitz continue their journeys in time and space.

MEMORABLE MOMENTS The Doctor jokes his modern companions must have strong legs, as he'll leave behind anyone with a sprained ankle (a condition we affectionately call "Sarah Jane Smith Syndrome") to die. The Doctor claims he wins so often because the villains always have a plan and he never does. The invulnerable Compassion plows through a group of hatching worms—about as pleasant as wading hip-deep in hog waste, one imagines. The death of a little Eskoni girl named Florence, eaten by a worm despite the Doctor and Fitz's attempts to save her, marks itself as *Coldheart*'s most poignant death.

SEX, SPIRITS AND DRUGS Fitz carries a flask of Grekolian whisky that sterilizes wounds (obviously, he carries it only for medicinal purposes).

Fitz jokes that he's never thought of Compassion as a woman. He accidentally gets stoned on Eskoni tobacco that works on humans like a narcotic. Compassion wakes Fitz from a drunken stupor by gripping his lower lip between the finger and thumb of her left hand.

ASS-WHUPPINGS The Doctor puts a crossbow bolt through the mad Revan's shoulder but gets similar treatment. He expertly knocks a slimer out by throwing a knife and thumping his head with the hilt. He's also responsible for blowing up Tor Grymna and the giant Spulver worm. Most dramatic of all, the Doctor roasts young Spulver worms with Fitz's hip flask of Grekolian whisky and Zippo lighter.

Spulver Worms feast hearty, revving up their appetite by chowing down on massive amounts of farm animals and even a farmboy (we keep imagining the worms happily sitting around a giant appetizer tray, laced with sheep and radishes). The worms then nibble people to death in the town of Baktan (Heaven help us, we have this crazed image of the worms wearing gigantic table napkins, a la *Grendel*).

The wormies eat a little girl that Fitz dubs Florence (a single drop of her blood lands on his cheek). Hundreds of thousands flee the city, but lots become worm crap and the city of Baktan sacrifices itself to kill the worms.

A long fall breaks every bone in trooper Zela's body but only disrupts Compassion's internal systems. Chihuahua-looking bats (our worst nightmare come true) named knivors besiege the Doctor's group underground and chomp down on Fitz's leg. Compassion solves the problem (You rule!) by grabbing the critters mid-air and whacking their heads against a rock.

TV TIE-INS The eighth Doctor's good at hypnotism ("The Talons of Weng-Chiang," etc.). He repels ravenous knivor bats with K9's ultrasonic whistle ("The Ribos Operation" and oodles more).

NOVEL TIE-INS The evasive Doctor says that Time is a being of "Time Lord mythology" and mostly rubbish (mind you, his seventh self served as Time's Champion and Time herself appeared in *Happy Endings*). He still carries a Kursaal slot machine token (*Kursaal*).

CHARACTER DEVELOPMENT
The Doctor: The Doctor's eyes look blue, then violet. He finds it confusing to be in younger bodies as he grows older (it's reaffirmed that the Doctor's more than 1,000 years old). He's never heard of Eskon or seen a Spulver worm before.

When the Doctor's tired, he resorts to Fitz's awful jokes (more painful than a root canal, one presumes). He carries batteries formerly used in a CD player owned by Sam Jones or Melanie Bush. Strong noses run in his family (certainly if his third body's anything to go by). His body heat's lower than your average Eskoni, making it harder for the temperature-hunting Spulver Worms to detect him.

The Doctor can tolerate more radiation than a human and knows a great deal about water expansion rates. The Doctor drinks Rose Pouchong tea, liking to start the day with Assam or China Yunnan and insisting on a large pot of Lapsang Souchong at 11:00.

He can hum tunes from *La Traviata* and *Madame Butterfly* and perform palm tricks. He can temporarily shut out the pain from a crossbow bolt wound, but the effort catches up with him.

Fitz Kreiner: Fitz hates caves but has strong legs (perhaps from so much running in the course of his TARDIS service). He carries salt and pepper sachets from a motorway service station the TARDIS crew visited in 1978. He sampled every tea in the Doctor's old TARDIS.

Compassion: Compassion gets her bearings from Galactic Zero center, yet she doesn't know how to philosophically define her position on the space-time continuum (she's irrevocably annexed to the Time Vortex).

Compassion's sensors can run biological, geological or metallurgical scans, monitor Fitz's melanocyte levels to detect radiation damage, measure gaps to a tenth of a millimeter, detect minute ground disturbances and map topography. Yet, her onboard laboratory can't do a detailed water analysis.

Severe damage (such as a fall hard enough to kill humans) can temporarily disrupt Compassion's internal configuration, preventing her from granting access to travelers. She can supply energy to external sources. She can drop her outer shell temperature down to zero. She knows she's immortal, but feels dead already. Compassion's impervious to ultraviolet. She doesn't understand the Eskoni calendar.

The Doctor, Fitz and Compassion: Compassion probably sticks with the Doctor and Fitz because she's afraid to run from the Time Lords alone. Compassion's telepathic circuits and the Doctor's innate telepathy grant them limited empathy.

ALIEN RACES

Time Lords: Even allowing for Compassion's Randomizer, the Time Lords' planetary scans might detect her materialization through sheer luck. Materializing underground helps block their searches. Multiple dematerializations too close together are also ill-advised as the Time Lords might detect the residual artron energy ("The Deadly Assassin") build-up in the Time Vortex.

Spulver Worms: Whale-sized, flesh eating parasites with multiple tentacles that belong to the phylum Mollusca that includes Earth snails, slugs clams and squids. Spulver Worms are essentially mismatched amalgamations of gastropods and cephalopods. They naturally affix themselves to cave ceilings, hunting by temperature and waiting for prey to pass underneath. The monsters lack ears and eyes. They're incredibly hearty, living for decades without eating.

Spulver Worms originated from genetic conflicts in the Aayavex System, so their DNA is extremely mutagenic. The threat of death spurs the hermaphroditic worms to fertilize, making them lay upward of a million eggs. Normal explosives can't harm a fully mature Spulver Worm, but chucking a bomb down its throat (if you can manage it) will rip the worm to shreds.

Eskoni: Indigenous Eskon population, graced with short fur that repels some of the planet's heat. They primarily use handbows that fire metal bolts with a compressed air charge.

Slimers: Eskoni children tainted with Spulver Worm DNA mutate with the onset of puberty. The condition causes skin secretions that cover the slimers in mucus. Some endure "the Squirming," which involves painful spasms and death (other slimers often mercy kill their "Squirming" fellows with rocks).

Eskoni and Slimers: Thanks to the Spulver Worm DNA taint, all Eskoni children—slimer or not—are sterile.

ALIEN PLANETS

Gallifrey: Less than half the surface is water.

Eskon: A desert world with a giant sun, located at the edge of the remote Hhork sector. The background radiation's tolerable for humans, although sunblock helps. After dark on Eskon, you can see the fringes of its galaxy. The Daleks haven't visited the planet.

Taxation on Eskon pays for the ice mines, which ration water. Conversely, the ice mining weakens the planet's tectonic structure. The planet's red surface denotes high iron oxide content.

Each of Eskon's nine moons represent a god in the Eskon pantheon. The most important moon represents Dallufvir, the All-father to whom the Tor priesthood pledges allegiance. However, the largest moon denotes Kankira, the Eskon God of Sand who's worshiped to allay earthquakes.

STUFF YOU NEED *Coldheart:* Eskon's infamous—and likely mythical—core of ice (the people of Baktan mine layers of ice insulated by rock).

HISTORY A global genetics war on Aayavex's third moon wiped out the indigenous civilization and gave rise to mutant creatures such as the Spulver Worms. Through an unknown series of events, an Aayavex space cargo freighter left the system containing one such Spulver Worm. The freighter suffered a billion-to-one error with its antiquated supra-light drive, crashing the ship on Eskon and killing the crew.

AT THE END OF THE DAY Setting aside that its cover looks like an unspeakable orifice, *Coldheart* freezes up by not picking a direction—failing as a compelling racism story, then lacking the verve for its hardcore sci-fi elements (even the maggots in "The Green Death" ooze more charm than the Spulver Worm). In the process, the book homogenizes its entire supporting cast (we'd scarcely have cared if the worms ate 'em all) and relies on a lead villain (Tor Grymna) who's too black, then white for his own good. For all that, we'd still label *Coldheart* "competent" before we'd call it "painful," but it's best summed up in an off-handed scene where Fitz and Compassion simply look at each other and shrug.

THE SPACE AGE

By Steve Lyons

Release Date: May 2000
Order: BBC Eighth Doctor Adventure #34

TARDIS CREW The eighth Doctor, Fitz and Compassion.

TRAVEL LOG England, 1965; unnamed planetoid, local date 2019 but real time unknown.

STORY SUMMARY Compassion randomly arrives at a shining futuristic city but gets enthralled monitoring dimensions beyond what the Doctor and Fitz can perceive and renders herself immobile. Curious about the vandalized, almost deserted city, the Doctor and Fitz explore and find it a nexus of conflict between two Earth gangs—the Mods and the Rockers.

The Doctor learns from Rocker leader Alec and his wife Sandra that the gang members originally hail from England, 1965. In that era, Alec and Sandra fell in love but Sandra's older brothers—now deceased—opposed the relationship and triggered a gang warfare between their Mods and Alec's Rockers. While torn on how to pursue their relationship, Alec and Sandra encountered an injured, Earth-stranded alien named the Maker and tended to its wounds.

The grateful Maker—part of an extra-dimensional gestalt being with multiple senses—deduced that the three-dimensional Alec and Sandra couldn't navigate themselves through time to the gleaming futuristic city that their minds imagined. After scanning Earth's timestream and failing to locate such a place, the Maker rewarded his newfound friends by creating a futuristic city on a barren planetoid. As the Mods and Rockers prepared to settle their dispute with bloodshed, the Maker constructed the city and teleported them there, causing the gangs to erroneously believe they had mysteriously arrived in a post-apocalyptic Earth in the year 2000. Nineteen years later, the continued gang warfare has brought both groups to the verge of extinction.

Compassion awakens and realizes that Rick, Sandra's son and the new leader of the Mods, has captured the Maker and forced it to make weapons for them. But in return, the tortured Maker has keyed the city to slowly discorporate, threatening to dissipate the planetoid's environment and kill the city's inhabitants in two days. As the Mods and Rockers continue their struggle and generate new casualties, other Makers arrive to free their colleague. The Mods and Rockers finally stand down, realizing the pointlessness of their feud in comparison to the aliens' presence.

Gradually, the Makers recognize their interference harmed the transported Earthlings and give the surviving gang members a choice: Rejoin a futuristic society in the year 3012—a year that closely approximates the Maker-made city—or return to being young and memory wiped in 1965 to normally live out their lives normally. The Mods and Rockers variously choose their fates, with Sandra electing to remain in 3012 and stay with Rick. Conversely, Alec returns to 1965, but his memory-wiped youthful self blames Sandra's older brothers for her absence and renews the gang war. After making peace with the Makers, the Doctor, Compassion and Fitz continue their travels.

MEMORABLE MOMENTS With much passion, the Doctor proclaims that he wouldn't undo his personal history, not even to reclaim the TARDIS or eliminate Faction Paradox, because you don't learn anything by erasing your mistakes ("young" Alec nicely symbolizes this by continuing the Mod/Rocker conflict on Earth).

ASS-WHUPPINGS A Rocker deals Fitz a sharp knife wound to the chest, but he recovers. Some Makers, temporally blinded by the a-temporal presence of time travelers (the Doctor and company), perish when Rick triggers a rocket attack.

TV TIE-INS The Doctor still carries a device that measures electric current ("Tomb of the Cybermen"). He fails to thwart the Makers' supercomputer Brain with the conundrum he used on BOSS ("The Green Death") and his Nelly/pink elephant riddle ("Destiny of the Daleks").

NOVEL TIE-INS The Makers aren't powerful enough to undo the Doctor's personal time paradox (*Interference*) and thereby break Faction Paradox's hold over him. The Doctor hasn't mentioned the loss of the TARDIS (*The Shadows of Avalon*) in days, dealing with his grief by worrying about others.

CHARACTER DEVELOPMENT

The Doctor: As a Time Lord, the Doctor slightly fears the Makers because time to them is nothing. He carries a gold fob watch, can estimate a planet's curvature by looking at its horizon and knows by memory the constellation alignment seen from Earth in the late 20th century.

The Doctor's learned some botany and can render opponents unconscious with a nerve pinch. He knows harmonics that put humans to sleep (but can't construct a device that makes this effective at long-range). He wants to learn more about reading sound waves.

Fitz Kreiner: Earth gangs frequently picked on him in the 1960s.

Compassion: In her normal state, Compassion looks like she's 22 or 23. Her chameleon circuit ("An Unearthly Child") alters her clothes as well as her appearance. Compassion's TARDIS senses extrude beyond three dimensions and she focuses on the physical plane with effort. Her telepathic circuits allow her to communicate with the Maker and ease its pain. In turn, the Maker teaches her a number of unspecified concepts.

TOP 5

COMPANION TRIUMPHS

Novels Post *Interference*

1) **Brigadier Lethbridge-Stewart makes Avalon his home (The Shadows of Avalon)**—Overcoming the death of his wife (which he is largely responsible for), the Brigadier finds peace in the other-dimensional Avalon.

2) **Compassion departs for space (The Ancestor Cell)**—Compassion shows how much she's grown from the Doctor's tutorage by achieving true independence.

3) **Compassion transforms into a humanoid TARDIS (The Shadows of Avalon)**—Not without its growing pains, Compassion's emergence as Gallifrey's first fully sentient TARDIS opens worlds of possibilities for her.

4) **Filippa saved (Parallel 59)**—Only a handful of people survive Parallel 59's network of space Bastions, but Fitz's beloved Filippa is thankfully among them.

5) **Leela kills everybody (Corpse Marker)**—Well, not quite, but there's a hell of a lot of corpses in *Corpse Marker* that have Leela's knife marks in them.

Big Finish Audios

1) **Melanie unrelenting in Pompeii ("The Fires of Vulcan")**—Mel demonstrates her inner resolve, refusing to capitulate when the Doctor announces the TARDIS will irrevocably be buried when Mount Vesuvius erupts.

2) **Romana freed after 20 years imprisonment ("The Apocalypse Element")**—Battered but not bowed by 20 years spent as a Dalek slave, Romana escapes and resumes her place as president of Gallifrey.

3) **Ace destroys the Fearmonger ("The Fearmonger")**—Ace overcomes the (literal) monster within her, crushing the Fearmonger into itty-bitty bits.

4) **Benny puts faith in the Doctor ("The Shadow of the Scourge")**—The potency of Benny's belief in him encourages the Doctor to thwart the parasitical Scourge.

5) **Frobisher dubbed Emperor ("The Holy Terror")**—Leading, of course, to the infamous cheer, "All hail Frobisher! All hail the great talking bird!"

By empathicly sharing the Maker's extra-dimensional senses, Compassion can telepathically make attackers' lives flash before their eyes, making them feel insignificant. She can predict the

141

This book is not endorsed by the BBC. Doctor Who and TARDIS are trademarks of the BBC.

short-term actions of others and view a myriad of possible timelines (she mentally shares with Fitz a number of Alec's potential fates, but breaks contact before Fitz's mind overloads). She declines an offer to stay with the Makers.

An invisible shield protects Compassion from physical harm even when she's comatose.

Fitz and Compassion: Fitz ponders if regarding Compassion solely as a travelling device would help him adjust to her TARDIS self.

ALIEN RACES

The Makers: The extra-dimensional Makers have an immeasurably intertwined group mind, meaning they didn't understand the concept of individuality before this story. The Maker that originally encountered Alec and Sandra regarded them like dolphins—having some intelligence, but utterly unable to communicate with the Makers.

The Makers are immensely telekinetic, able to weave themselves travelships or—as you already know—entire cities. Building takes much more effort than simply letting their creations dissipate. Jailing a Maker is doubly painful because you're imprisoning it in time as well as space (a punishment the Doctor knows full well).

Makers manifest in our dimension as roughly humanoid earless aliens with big heads and gray, purple-tinged skin. They also have wide faces, two slitty nostrils, a tail and shrunken arms and legs. Their sideways-slanted yellow eyes don't blink, possibly because the Makers lack normal vision.

The Makers don't like seawater. After better understanding the nature of humanity, the Makers supplied the Mods and Rockers who stayed in the future with documents to start a new life—effectively splicing them from one piece of the timeline and pasting them into another.

PLACES TO GO

The Maker's City is basically a mile-wide assortment of gleaming futuristic buildings, maintained by the supercomputer Brain's servo-robots. Machines in the city provide food, space-age clothes and oxygen, but cannot create seeing glasses. Abandoned space rockets there lift off but cut out before reaching outer space. The city reverted to an airless planetoid after the Makers sent the Mods and Rockers home.

ORGANIZATIONS

Faction Paradox: The Doctor advises the Makers to undo the personal history of Mods and Rockers who return to Earth, hoping to prevent Faction Paradox from gaining further power.

Mods and Rockers: The current Mods and Rockers, having spent 19 years in the futuristic city, are all males in their mid-30s. The groups number about 40 each. They mostly fight their war on motorbikes with anti-gravity generators.

HISTORY Local authorities attributed the disappearance of the Mods and Rockers who stayed in the future as simply casting off their lives and running away together.

AT THE END OF THE DAY Setting aside an incredibly flawed premise (it's impossible to believe the isolated Mods and Rockers could fight constantly for 19 years and not kill each other off), *The Space Age* barely has enough plot for a short story, let alone a novel. The first 70 pages or so decently set up the characters, but the rest plods with gang warfare and unrelated elements (the Brain's largely irrelevant and Sandra's revelation about birthing Rick comes out of left field). We're can only speculate that Lyons, a proven commodity (*The Witch Hunters*) overloaded his schedule with "The Fires of Vulcan" and spaced out here, leaving *The Space Age* a toss-away book.

THE BANQUO LEGACY

By Andy Lane and Justin Richards

Release Date: June 2000
Order: BBC Eighth Doctor Adventure #35

TARDIS CREW The eighth Doctor, Fitz and Compassion.

TRAVEL LOG Banquo Manor, England, 1898.

STORY SUMMARY At the isolated Banquo Manor in England, 1898, a select group of witnesses gather for an experiment where scientist Richard Harris attempts to electronically share thoughts with his sister Catherine. Among those gathered are Harris' fiancée Susan Seymoure, solicitor John Hopkinson, Banquo Manor owners George and Elizabeth Wallace and their butler Simpson.

Nearby, Compassion runs afoul of a Time Lord device that drains her artron energy, forcing her aground at Banquo Manor. Dangerously losing cohesion, Compassion materializes around Susan and assumes her appearance, but warns that the organic gestalt will kill both herself and Susan unless the artron dampening field is neutralized.

Richard Harries electronically links himself to Catherine, but his equipment tragically overloads and electrocutes him almost beyond recognition. Soon after, Inspector Ian Stratford and Sergeant

Baker of Scotland Yard arrive on the scene just as a number of the Manor occupants are gruesomely murdered. As the Doctor, Fitz and the Manor survivors search for the killer, they find—to their terror—that Harries' blackened corpse has come to life and longs to kill them all.

As the Banquo guests flee before Harries' undead wrath, the shocked butler Simpson swears by Rassilon's name and consequently reveals himself as a Time Lord operative—one of several randomly searching the Universe for Compassion. The Doctor realizes that Simpson's artron inhibitor inadvertently forged a mental bond between Harries and his sister Catherine at the moment of his death, meaning that Catherine, ashamed that her brother blackmailed his associates for funding, has been subconsciously animating Harries to lash out and murder his "enemies."

Catherine mentally halts her brother's corpse, then lures the Manor survivors into a false sense of security. The tables further turn when the insane Catherine reveals she aided and abetted in her brother's blackmailing, and quite deliberately wants his undead body to kill those who "persecuted" him. Catherine joins Richard on a blood spree, telepathically compelling him to gouge out Simpson's eyes and toss the Time Lord through a window, apparently killing him.

Desperately, the Doctor and Hopkinson locate a dynamite cache intended for landscaping the Manor grounds. Catherine orders her dead brother to kill Susan/Compassion and Fitz, but a spark of Harries' personality refuses to murder his ex-fiancée and he pauses. Sergeant Baker dies stuffing the dynamite into Harries' jacket, allowing Hopkinson to shatter an oil lamp that torches Harries' body and detonates the dynamite, exploding Harries to pieces.

A devastated Catherine goes berserk with a pistol, but the Doctor, Hopkinson and Stratford body-tackle her. In the struggle, Catherine's gun accidentally fires and kills her. The Doctor de-activates Simpson's artron inhibitor, allowing Compassion to separate from Susan. As the Banquo Manor survivors recoup their wits, the Doctor's party leaves in case the missing Simpson summoned reinforcements from Gallifrey.

MEMORABLE MOMENTS Fitz constantly deploys a memorably fake and terrible German accent. Pardon while we revel in gore, but Harries' corpse disturbingly pulps the Wallaces' brains and bores out Simpson's eyes (yes, there's Ass-Whuppings galore). The Doctor declares President Romana must be stopped in her goal to force-breed Compassion, because the morality of an organization or a race is no better than its most immoral

MISCELLANEOUS STUFF!

BANQUO LEGACY ORIGINS

Justin Richards originally wrote "The Banquo Legacy" as a four-part TV script, sans the Doctor or indeed anything "Doctor Who" related (yes, Virginia, there is a world outside of "Whoville"). The script failed to sell, so Richards and co-writer Andy Lane "novelized" the idea during their University days (1982 to 1985). Again, the novel lacked anything "Who" related—and again, it didn't nab any offers.

The work proceeded to mildew in a desk drawer until 2000, when former Virgin editor Rebecca Levene had to withdraw—citing schedule conflicts—from writing an eighth Doctor novel called *Freaks*. Left with a gaping hole in the schedule, Richards fished *The Banquo Legacy* out of his files and proposed he and Lane rewrite it to include the Doctor, Fitz and Compassion. Lane drafted the sections narrated by Inspector Stratford while Richards handled the parts told by solicitor John Hopkinson. Richards also supplied the beginning and end sections, partly to finish the story off and partly as a lead-in to *The Ancestor Cell*.

P.S. Lane notes on *The Banquo Legacy*'s pre-Doctor incarnations: "To think there were people who said we had caught the eighth Doctor's character perfectly..."

member. On the same score, the Doctor decides the contest between him and Simpson is about love—love of independence and personal responsibility versus love of form and structure.

When it's suggested someone flee to phone help while the others hole up in the Manor, everyone simultaneously volunteers to run for it. As the cover suggests, a rat nestles in Harries' skull upon his final demise. Time Lord Simpson pleads with the aged Susan to give him the code for Compassion's Randomizer, not wanting his decades of sacrifice to be for nothing.

SEX AND SPIRITS Simpson is clearly enamored of President Romana, enough to spend more than 100 years at Banquo Manor on a mission for her. Susan Seymour breaks her engagement to the distant, unfeeling Richard Harries (and that's before he's toasted). Both John Hopkinson and Inspector Stratford develop feelings for her. According to Simpson at Susan's deathbed, one of these gentlemen became her lover—the other became her husband (enjoy yourself figuring out which is which).

143

ASS-WHUPPINGS Invulnerable Compassion merges with Susan Seymour and becomes human enough to suffer a broken ankle (again with the dreaded "Sarah Jane Smith Syndrome"). Bastard Richard Harries blackmails scientific fraud Gordon Seavers and prompts Seavers to stab himself to death with a dull letter opener. Out of revenge, Seavers' friend John Hopkinson sabotages Harries' equipment and electrocutes Harries almost beyond recognition (but as we know, he's not done causing trouble).

Undead and loving it, Harries—controlled by his sister Catherine—strangles the 16-year-old maid Beryl and pulps the brains of Banquo Manor owners George and Elizabeth Wallace. Most grotesquely of all, Harries squishes out Simpson's eyeballs and chucks him through a window. A stick of dynamite finally does in Harries, pulverizing his body save for his left arm and skull. A tussle for a handgun finishes off Catherine Harries, who perhaps committed suicide.

TV TIE-INS "The Deadly Assassin" introduced the concept of artron energy. Simpson once read Borusa's teachings about hiding a tree in a forest ("The Invasion of Time").

TV AND NOVEL TIE-INS The Doctor installed Compassion's Randomizer ("The Armageddon Factor") in *The Fall of Yquatine*. Simpson uses Time Lord communication cubes ("The War Games," *Vampire Science*, *Tears of the Oracle*).

NOVEL TIE-INS Compassion's temporary merger with Susan Seymour leaves Susan with some of Compassion's memories. Once Simpson heals, he locates an aged Susan on her deathbed in 1968 and convinces her to tell him the seed code for Compassion's Randomizer. Simpson forwards the information to Gallifrey, allowing a Time Lord warfleet to predict Compassion's destination and converge on her in *The Ancestor Cell*. The last line of *The Banquo Legacy*, describing Simpson's "final act" of walking down a hallway, refers to Gallifrey's retroactive destruction. The Doctor comments that Earth's Victorian era is among his favorite places in time and space, likely prompting Compassion and Fitz to exile him hereabouts to heal (all *The Ancestor Cell*).

The Doctor describes his brother Irving Braxiatel (Richards' *Theatre of War*, the Benny NAs) as "My—My colleague and occasional collaborator in adventures of the mind, the soul and the body."

CHARACTER DEVELOPMENT

The Doctor: The Doctor pretends to be forensic

THE CRUCIAL BITS...

- **THE BANQUO LEGACY**—A Gallifreyan agent secures the seed number for Compassion's Randomizer, altering the Time Lords.

expert Dr. Friedlander, but hasn't heard of the Society for the Propagation of the Forensic Sciences.

He was in the audience of the American Institute of Electrical Engineers when Tesla put a half million volts through his body and demonstrated that voltage, not amperage, can kill you. The Doctor's met Austrian physician Franz Hartmann, supplying him with a couple of case studies for a book on premature burial. He hasn't visited Wittgenstein for a long time.

His distinctive boots weren't made in England. He sacrifices one jacket to fake his death but dons a darker one.

Fitz Kreiner: Fitz pretends to be Dr. Friedlander's assistant Herr Kreiner. He looks like he's in his late 20s to mid-30s.

Compassion: Artron energy depletion can inhibit the block-transfer computations ("Logopolis") that reconstruct Compassion's outer shell. In such an emergency, she can temporarily maintain her plasmic exterior by latching onto a host entity—preferably one that's humanoid and approximates Compassion's natural appearance—and forming an organic gestalt. Such a merger restricts Compassion from allowing access to her interior and in time causes personality erosion between the two minds. It also drains the host's life force and puts them at risk.

John Hopkinson and Inspector Ian Stratford: As key witnesses to the unspeakable events at Banquo Manor, both of them write detailed journals afterward. Stratford was a decent man despite a troubled past—his mother died of pneumonia, his father from booze. He married his wife to appease the executor of his parents' estate, but they divorced. Hopkinson, a solicitor, handled preliminary arrangements for Stratford's divorce years ago but the two didn't have an association.

Stratford knew Hopkinson murdered Richard Harries out of revenge (*See Ass-Whuppings*), but found Harries' actions so villainous and events at Banquo so unearthly, he remained silent about it.

Simpson: Time Lord agent who arrived at Banquo Manor in 1798 and awaited the Doctor's possible arrival for 100 years (*See Alien Races: The Time Lords*). The undead Richard Harries squished out Simpson's eyeballs, but he used optic implants linked to his visual cortex to see through the eyes of Harries' rats. A gravely wounded Simpson took 50 years to heal from the Banquo Manor experience, then spent another 20 searching for an aged Susan Seymour. He completed his mission in 1968—a mere 170 years after he started.

ALIEN RACES

The Time Lords: Time Lords drained of artron energy—including the Doctor—cannot regenerate and must heal at a human pace. Lacking the core seed number for Compassion's Randomizer, the Time Lords correlated Compassion's previous locations, then used quantum extrapolation and a probability matrix to predict her possible destinations. The process yielded up several hundred possible locations in space-time, so the Time Lords (never underestimate their ability for patience) dispatched hundreds of agents to await the fugitives' possible arrival at each nexus point.

TARDISes: Rely on artronic resonators (a means of routing artron energy) to function.

STUFF YOU NEED

Artron Energy: Artron energy sustains TARDISes and Time Lords like oxygen. It operates both as a physical energy and a mental force, meaning emotionally charged events such as a murder (*See History*) might create an artron energy field. artron energy also redirects other forms of energy like ripples moving through a pond, potentially boosting electrical current.

Artron Inhibitor: Useful little device that neutralizes artron energy in a limited area, but it's an all-or-nothing proposition, meaning Time Lords who use such devices cannot shield their own artron energy from the effect. Artron inhibitors can tap latent artron energy fields (such as the one around Banquo Manor, *See History*) for their own power supply, eliminating the need for an extraneous power source.

Harries' Memory Transfer Technique: Harries speculated that electrical current could induce memory transfer (a poor man's form of telepathy, one imagines) by stimulating the biopotential in potassium ion concentrations.

HISTORY In 1793, lackluster actor Robert Dodds inherited from his aged aunt and commissioned the Adam brothers to build the house that became Banquo Manor, naming it after the character in *Macbeth* (Dodds maintained it was his best role). Unfortunately, his cousin spent a great deal of time going bananas in an asylum, believing Dodds

MISCELLANEOUS STUFF!

BANQUO LEGACY CORPSE ACTION

Richard Harries, a reanimated corpse who's apparently training for a role in "Resident Evil," causes such mayhem that you almost forget to ask how Harries' cadaver revived in the first place. Although your brain tends to pick a solution and stick with it, *Banquo Legacy* writer Justin Richards explains that there's multiple explanations for why the undead Richard Harries walks the Earth again:

• The most widely accepted explanation says Banquo Manor's latent artron energy, known to affect things on a psionic level, re-animated Harries' corpse. (That could also explain why Beryl the maid resembles a reincarnation of "Mad Pamela," See History).

• Harries' memory transfer experiment, designed to link his mind with his sister, might have actually worked (score one for humankind).

• Banquo Manor is haunted, making this a rare instance of the supernatural in "Doctor Who" (perhaps the ghost of "Mad Pamela" inhabits Beryl).

• Solicitor John Hopkinson (always the damn lawyers) grows curious and reads aloud from Harries' necronomicon, a book of spells, thus bringing Harries back to life by accident (check out Page 28).

• Similarly, perhaps someone else (perhaps manor owner Wallace) reads the necronomicon deliberately (Harries in life seems rattled that someone's been reading the thing).

had killed her grandmother to get her money (rather unlikely, since Dodds was in Italy at the time). Dodds' insane cousin stabbed him to death in revenge, generating a latent artron energy field (*See Stuff You Need*) that suffused Banquo Manor.

AT THE END OF THE DAY Crisp, maliciously dark and unquestionably one of the strongest eighth Doctor novels. It's all the more remarkable for convincing you that one animated corpse and a brazen hussy with a pistol can challenge the Doctor and company. The book's double narration, neither of which hails from the Doctor or a companion, reflects the capacity of ordinary people to perform heroic deeds, Time Lord or no. All in all, a story that cries out to be read on a cold winter evening—and a book that deserves to remain in print and repeatedly sell for years.

THE ANCESTOR CELL

By Peter Anghelides and Stephen Cole

Release Date: July 2000
Order: BBC Eighth Doctor Novel #36

TARDIS CREW   The eighth Doctor, Fitz and Compassion.

TRAVEL LOG   Gallifrey, current era.

STORY SUMMARY A War TARDIS fleet besieges Compassion, running her aground on the Edifice, a gigantic flower-shaped bone object in orbit over Gallifrey. To his horror, the Doctor concludes the Edifice is his original TARDIS, which bravely took the Doctor's paradoxical "Dust" timeline into itself but weakened over time and finally burst over Avalon. However, the TARDIS has rebuilt itself using energy from the leaking Universe-in-a-Bottle (*See Sidebars*) and shaped itself like a Gallifreyan Remembrance Flower to symbolize the third Doctor's "death."

On Gallifrey, group of dissolute Time Lords, unwittingly under the control of Faction Paradox agent Mother Tarra, invokes temporal voodoo to manifest ex-Time Lord President Greyjan the Sane, whose term of office coincided with the Faction's Eleven-Day Empire. As a Faction thrall, Greyjan infects the Matrix with the Faction Paradox virus and puts Gallifrey under the Faction's sway. At a pre-arranged signal, the Faction's ruling Shadow Parliament physically overwrites itself on the Gallifreyan Capitol while the Faction warfleet arrives in orbit.

The Doctor confronts the Faction's leader, Grandfather Paradox, who has manifested thanks to the Edifice's time distortion. But to his dismay, the Doctor learns Grandfather Paradox is an alternate version of himself, fully tainted by the Faction virus corroding the Doctor's biodata.

From Greyjan's researches, the Doctor realizes the leaking Universe-In-a-Bottle has super-evolved the dormant ancestor cells that spawned all life in the Universe, mutating them into the time-active Enemy at war with the future Time Lords. Drawn to Gallifrey by the Bottle's energies, the Enemy rains its first strike on Gallifrey, butchering the planet and destroying the TARDIS berthing cradles.

With the Faction handily in control of Gallifrey, and the Enemy about to trigger a war that will devastate all of space-time, the Edifice generates a self destruct console. The Doctor, knowing his

THE CRUCIAL BITS...

• **THE ANCESTOR CELL**—The Doctor destroys Gallifrey to prevent its capture by Faction Paradox and the Enemy. Compassion and Fitz decide to leave the amnesiac Doctor and his damaged TARDIS on 20th century Earth to heal, leaving a note to rendezvous with Fitz in 2001. Compassion departs for space with technician Nivet, one of the few surviving Gallifreyans.

Destruction of Faction Paradox, the Enemy and the Universe-In-A-Bottle. Death of Father Kreiner, Fitz's alternate self. Fate of Romana, Leela and Commander Andred unknown.

people are forever lost, activates the console and deliberately weakens the Edifice's already strained dimensions.

The resulting explosion atomizes Gallifrey, Faction Paradox and the entire constellation of Kasterborus.

In the final moment, the TARDIS-powered Compassion scoops up the Doctor, Fitz and a Time Lord acquaintance of hers named Nivet, racing them to safety. Soon after, Compassion finds the last remnant of the Doctor's TARDIS—the only thing in the Kasterborus vicinity larger than an electron. With the Doctor amnesiac from his ordeal, and knowing the TARDIS will require 100 years to restore itself, Compassion proposes placing the Doctor and the TARDIS on his favorite planet, Earth, to rest and heal.

Compassion leaves the Doctor on Earth at the turn of the 20th century and drops Fitz off to meet the Time Lord in 2001. Compassion then departs into space with Nivet, even as the eighth Doctor begins a new era of his many lives.

MEMORABLE MOMENTS *The Ancestor Cell* features a number of delicious confrontations, including Father Kreiner's rage at the Doctor for two millennia of pain and a meeting between the two Fitzes. Action-lovers will wince as the Doctor wrestles with Grandfather Paradox.

If nothing else, the destruction of Gallifrey guarantees *The Ancestor Cell*'s place in "Doctor Who" novel history. Fitz enjoys a cigarette at book's end, perhaps symbolizing the adrenaline rush a number of readers are probably feeling.

ASS-WHUPPINGS The Doctor destroys Gallifrey, the constellation Kasterborus and its entire sector, erasing millions, perhaps billions of lives. The act also destroys the Enemy and Faction Paradox, the Faction's warfleet, Grandfather Paradox and the Faction-ruling Shadow Parliament.

Compassion's weapons strike atomizes two war TARDISes, their crews and the Chancellor of Time Present. Her defensive psychic blast deactivates every TARDIS on Gallifrey. The Enemy eviscerates the TARDIS berthing cradles and their technicians, plus the restored Greyjan the Sane.

Fitz lasers down some Faction troops. A firefight between Time Lords and giant spiders on the structure ends with gruesome casualties, including Castellan Vozarti. The TARDIS' transition into the Edifice killed the Doctor's butterflies (*Vampire Science*) and ossified his pet canary.

Father Kreiner snaps the necks of Faction agent Kellen and Vice-President Timon. Mother Tarra blasts the somewhat-repentant Father Kreiner in the stomach, so the Doctor locks her in an Edifice hallway and a giant spider skewers her.

Grandfather Paradox finishes the turncoat Father Kreiner off, stepping through his torso. Callous Romana turns her pilot Ryssal into a walking bomb (*See Stuff You Need*) and detonates him.

SEX AND SPIRITS Fitz fantasizes about being a rock star with women clinging to him like Velcro. The Beatles' "Revolution 9" makes Fitz remember his time with Maddy (*Revolution Man*). He used to cab it across London with his girlfriend Mary. Sexy Faction agent Tarra comes onto Fitz, but reveals her skull-like nature and leaves Fitz dangling. Despite the asexual Looms, Time Lords of this period apparently seduce one another (a fact confirmed in *Lungbarrow*), suggesting Gallifrey has finally broken the Pythia's curse of sterility (*Cat's Cradle: Time's Crucible*).

TV TIE-INS Gallifrey elected the Doctor its 407th ("The Invasion of Time") and 409th ("The Five Doctors") presidents, but he fled like a French peasant from Nazi oppressors. Only Greyjan's presidential service was shorter. The Doctor left biodata traces when he visited the Gallifreyan Matrix ("The Deadly Assassin," "Arc of Infinity"), but Faction agent Mother Tarra here erases 'em.

NOVEL TIE-INS Compassion here leaves the amnesiac Doctor on a train car in Victorian England; his Earth-bound adventures resume three years later in *The Burning*. Fitz reunites with the Doctor in *Escape Velocity*.

Alien Bodies introduced the here-destroyed Faction Paradox and the Time Lords' future Enemy. *Christmas on a Rational Planet* first mentioned Faction leader Grandfather Paradox. *Unnatural History* first mentioned the Faction's home base, the Eleven-Day Empire; *Interference* defined it.

The Ancestor Cell resolves the third Doctor's paradoxical death on Dust, curing the eighth Doc-

MISCELLANEOUS STUFF!

GALLIFREY'S DESTRUCTION

One of the more puzzling aspects about Gallifrey's destruction is the implication—get ready, folks—that Gallifrey never existed.

Then again, as line editor Justin Richards points out, we've seen Time Lords from pretty much all eras of history (the future Time Lord Homunculette from *Alien Bodies*, etc.), so pinpointing Gallifrey's destruction to a certain date would inevitably prove futile and contradictory. Therefore, the BBC Books' preferred way of dealing with the problem is to ignore Gallifrey's history and involvement in the Universe's affairs entirely.

What this means

Despite all the rhetoric, Gallifrey obviously existed on some level and no, the first seven Doctors are not temporal aberrations. However, by acting as if Gallifrey never existed, the BBC Books open themselves to exploring a very interesting point: The Time Lords are no longer policing other races to deter (even for selfish reasons) the creation of rival time technology.

In a string of novels beyond *Escape Velocity* (and therefore beyond the scope of the reference guide you're holding), the BBC Books will explore the extent of unrestrained, often haphazard time travel technology, with the eighth Doctor's crew increasingly caught in the middle. Among the myriad of things you'll see, creatures will escape from the Time Vortex (*The Slow Empire*), "The Beast" will break through where "the Horizon" is thin (*The Adventuress of Henrietta Street*) time will go mad (*Anarchrophobia*), artifacts such as the "Book of the Still" (*The Book of the Still*) can freely exist and aliens will queue up to buy time travel (*Trading Futures*).

tor of his Faction Paradox virus taint (*Interference, See Sidebar*). Cosmic-powered being I.M. Foreman created the Universe-in-a-Bottle in *Interference*, where the Time Lords stole it as a safe haven from the Enemy.

Father Kreiner debuted in *Interference* and was hurled into the Time Vortex, briefly resurfacing in the Benny NA *Dead Romance*.

Interference suggested the Enemy's homeworld as Earth, but *The Ancestor Cell* retcons that thought into oblivion.

Romana returned to Gallifrey in *Blood Harvest* and became president by *Happy Endings*. The

Shadows of Avalon debuted the permanently PMS-ed Romana III. The fate of Romana, last seen heading for her TARDIS, remains unknown. Also, the whereabouts of Gallifrey dwellers Leela, Commander Andred, and K9 Marks I and II (last seen in *Lungbarrow)* also goes unstated.

Compassion's Randomizer, installed in *The Fall of Yquatine*, here becomes a charred lump in a War TARDIS firefight. Broad-spectrum Tukson-Jacker pulses (*Frontier Worlds*) can force Compassion out of the Time Vortex.

The Taking of Planet Five debuted war TARDISes. Time Lord agent Simpson discovered the seed number for Compassion's Randomizer in *The Banquo Legacy*, allowing the War TARDIS fleet to here besiege our heroes.

Gallifreyan suits of cards first appeared in *Lungbarrow*, but this book introduces new ones.

TV AND NOVEL TIE-INS Sweet Gallifrey debuted in "The War Games," but wasn't named until "The Time Warrior." "The Deadly Assassin" defined Gallifreyan society and it appeared in a number of TV stories. *Cat's Cradle: Time's Crucible*, *Lungbarrow* and *The Infinity Doctors* redefined Gallifrey's history.

Gallifrey's Patrexes College ("The Deadly Assassin") financially ruined itself by constructing a son et lumiere portico for the Academy Lodge it couldn't maintain (*Damaged Goods*).

The Time Lords here use Hypercubes ("The War Games," *Vampire Science*, etc.) to communicate like e-mail. Faction Paradox uses Time-Space Visualizers ("The Chase," *The Shadows of Avalon*).

The Time Lords, stockpiling weapons against the Enemy, reactivate biological defenses used against the Charon (*Sky Pirates!*) and the Great Vampires ("State of Decay").

AUDIO TIE-INS Romana here celebrates 150 years in office, although it isn't clear if her 20 missing years ("The Apocalypse Element") count. After that story, the High Council wouldn't agree to a permanent, fully trained fighting force, so Romana likely stockpiled the Slaughterhouse instead.

Gallifreyan Flowers of Remembrance—six-petaled, bright yellow flowers used for official corteges and which often foreshadow doom—were first mentioned in the short story "Dead Time" on the BBC audio "Earth and Beyond."

CHARACTER DEVELOPMENT

The Doctor: The Doctor's biomass changes as he becomes a Faction agent, yet he theorized he could make his Faction-tainted Rassilon imprimatur ("The Two Doctors") compatible with his old one. As a partial Faction agent, the Doctor can sense others who are tainted. The Doctor can mentally enter Gallifrey's APC Net ("The Deadly Assassin"), yet talk through his physical body. He can sense live minds in the Net. He can disarm Gallifreyan stasers and doesn't believe in predestination.

The Doctor remembers Vice President Timon as a very bookish time technician with no practical experience.

The alternate third Doctor: An essence of the third Doctor who "died" on Dust remained in the TARDIS when the Ship absorbed his timeline (*See Sidebar*). Unfortunately, the Faction virus in the TARDIS' systems drove him mad.

Fitz Kreiner: Fitz was born in 1936 at Royal Free, Hampstead. Fitz's father, a fan of *The Great Gatsby*, named him Fitzgerald Michael Kreiner after author F. Scott Fitzgerald. Fitz's mother thought he stopped growing at age six and shamelessly dubbed him "Fitzie."

As a boy, Fitz thought the worst smell in the world was a combination of his father's Old Spice after shave and Park Drive cigarettes. His family rarely attended church, so Fitz feels uncomfortable at weddings and funerals. Fitz's postal code in Archway was N2 8GT (don't waste your time sending stuff there—nobody's home).

When Fitz was eight, 23 wasps (the same number as his house) stung him and gave him anaphylactic shock. A hippy chick named Eleanor helped him organize a séance. He can hum every song from the Beatles' "White Album." In school, he had a one-armed math teacher (affectionately named "Stumpy"). Fitz normally isn't afraid of spiders but dislikes insects. When playing football (soccer), he favors his right foot. Compassion left Fitz on Earth with money to start a new life and wait for the Doctor.

Compassion: Because of Compassion's Remote origins, Faction Paradox members can override her controls. Faction member Uncle Kristeva knew Compassion before she was first remembered. Compassion's armed with a brass sighting device on her console which controls missiles that travel through space as blood-red pulses. She's a Type 102 TARDIS, but her access system resembles a Type 40.

Compassion's consciousness can go comatose to heal, or shut down her circuits to prevent time ram ("The Time Monster"). She can track other TARDISes in flight. The berthed TARDISes fear Compassion will render them obsolete.

Compassion can alter her retina pattern, changing her eyes' shape and color to match Gallifreyan security locks. She telepathically restructured her interior from someone's memories. She can project a hologram of herself into her own console room.

A wardrobe door in Compassion leads to the Doctor's quarters. Compassion can reroute her ex-citronic circuitry to prevent console access, but the Doctor could likely override it.

Technician Nivet: Blond, burly and Kaster-borous' finest technician, he maintains the Chancellor of Time Future's War TARDIS fleet. He helped construct the first War TARDISes.

Compassion and Technician Nivet: Nivet learns to override Compassion's motive circuits, pilot her or speak through her external microphone. They become friends and traveling companions because Compassion fears her continued ability to function without the destroyed Eye of Harmony. Nivet's room resides in one of Compassion's thumbs.

The Doctor and Compassion: Compassion can force images into the Doctor's mind through their implicit telepathic bond.

Romana III: Still Lady President, War Queen and Mistress of the Nine Gallifreys. Romana's disillusioned by the trappings of power now, but remains determined to perform her Presidential duties. Romana prefers to sidestep the High Council's authority when possible.

Vice President Timon is her main confidant. Romana appoints more males to power because she can manipulate them easier than females. Romana III might be a brazen hussy, but she's fiercely protective of Gallifrey.

Like the Doctor, Romana is a Prydonian. Her earring carries a video and audio transmitter. The combat-trained Mali, who had several degrees in temporal engineering and blessedly knew how to make tea, served as one of Romana's top technical advisors.

The Doctor and Romana III: During their TARDIS days, the Doctor and Romana saw *The Last Emperor*. The Doctor feels the Romana he knew has died.

Grandfather Paradox: Grandfather Paradox, the philosophical epitome of Faction Paradox, was generalized as a being who went back in time and paradoxically killed his own grandfather. As such, the Grandfather exists mostly as a concept, but manifests when the timelines are mutable. In *The Ancestor Cell*, he's a weathered version of the eighth Doctor, fully infected by the Faction virus on Dust and turned into a Faction thrall. Grandfather Paradox tried to kill "our" eighth Doctor, be-

MISCELLANEOUS STUFF!

OH DUSTY DEATH

When the third Doctor paradoxically died on Dust (*Interference*), the TARDIS sensed the unnatural timeline and sent out a warning that covered the TARDIS walls with blood and arranged the third and eighth Doctors to communicate. When the third Doctor died anyway, the desperate TARDIS took the third Doctor's tainted timeline into her own workings and held it in temporal orbit ("Doctor Who: Enemy Within"), possibly tapping a higher power such as a Great Old One (*All-Consuming Fire*). However, the energy increased exponentially until a dimensional rift ruptured the weakened TARDIS (*The Shadows of Avalon*).

Later, Time Lords stole the I.M Foreman's Universe-in-a-Bottle (*Interference*) and put it in the Time Vortex for safekeeping. Unfortunately, the four-dimensional Time Vortex turned the four-dimensional Universe Bottle into a single surface, allowing it to leak. The TARDIS remnants used the breached Universe-in-a-Bottle's energy and rebuilt itself as the Edifice, shaping itself like a Gallifreyan Flower of Remembrance to symbolize the third Doctor's "death." The destruction of Gallifrey and the Edifice eradicated the third Doctor's "Dust" timeline.

TIME LORD/ENEMY WARFARE

Compassion forecasts the Enemy's first strike on Gallifrey, showing images of its three oceans boiling away and the northern mountain ranges leveled until the planet becomes a cinder. In the Time War to follow, victories are constantly overturned and re-won (through massive rewrites of history) until the Universe becomes nothing but chaos. The Time Lords regenerate into combat-based monsters (*Alien Bodies, The Taking of Planet Five*) until you can't distinguish them from the Enemy.

lieving he could survive another Paradox.

The Grandfather reportedly sliced his arm off to remove a Time Lord monitoring tattoo on his shoulder (*Interference*); however, this version of Grandfather Paradox perhaps snipped it off to stop himself—the eighth Doctor—from having an arm free to destroy Gallifrey in the final confrontation (alternatively, he felt shame at the action—it's left unclear).

149

This book is not endorsed by the BBC. Doctor Who and TARDIS are trademarks of the BBC.

Father Kreiner: Fitz's original, corrupted self has a wizened right arm (*Interference*). Biosystems erased much of his memory, but he knows the Doctor left Susan on Earth ("The Dalek Invasion of Earth"). Before his death, a repentant Father Kreiner asked the Doctor to retroactively prevent Fitz from entering the TARDIS (*The Taint*), but the Doctor refused. Kreiner's healing nanites lost their potency over the years and couldn't cope with the Grandfather's blaster bolt.

Greyjan the Sane: Greyjan served as Gallifreyan President for three days, the shortest term in history. Unfortunately, his tiny tenure fell between September 2, 1752, and September 14, 1752, within the Eleven-Day Empire's time period, making him a Faction agent.

Greyjan was an academy lecturer whose research discovered the nature of the Enemy. Unable to foresee a means of stopping them, Greyjan committed suicide; his sciences were declared arcane. He later became a cult figure, with Faction Paradox generating a new Greyjan from Gallifreyan biomatter.

The TARDIS: The TARDIS used to cover its interiors with dust, giving the appearance of being old. Time radiation heavily saturates the Ship, suggesting it's traveled across half the Universe.

The Doctor and the TARDIS: They share an unprecedented, immensely strong empathic bond.

Romana's TARDIS: Completely transparent, Romana's TARDIS had its own berthing cradle. Ryssal, a goofy looking kid with odd teeth, piloted it before his death.

The Edifice: On the Edifice's creation, *See O Dusty Death* sidebar. Having internalized the third Doctor's "Dust" timeline, the Edifice was a nexus point for past and future timelines, emitting temporal ripples that affected space-time's local structure. As a reflection of the third Doctor's "proper" death in "Planet of the Spiders," giant spiders patrolled the Edifice's corridors. The bloated Edifice's bone petals physically punctured Gallifrey before the end.

The Edifice had multiple universes at its core and sprouted a self-destruct lever from its misshapen mushroom of a console. Its expansion weakened its interior dimensions. The Doctor removed the stabilizer cube, further weakening it to allow for self-destruct. The Edifice then collapsed down to an inch-high black box, its released energies destroying Gallifrey's entire constellation.

ALIEN PLANETS

Gallifrey: As the Gallifreyan Colleges demonstrate, Gallifrey uses a type of currency. For whatever reason, the planet reveres the number six, using it as the number of High Councilors, Colleges, Panopticon sides, TARDIS console sides and suits of cards (flames, clouds, souls, deeps, mesmers and dominoes).

"The Nine Gallifreys": The Time Lords constructed eight planetary clones of Gallifrey as bolt holes or decoys to draw the Enemy's fire (*The Shadows of Avalon*). The Edifice's time ripples, however, ate away at Gallifrey's history and wiped the clone Gallifreys from existence.

ALIEN RACES

Time Lords: Desperate for weapons against the Enemy, the Time Lords are plundering their own future, an act that would make Rassilon turn on his slab. Raw Time Lord biomass, much like hamburger, can be collected and reshaped. First-incarnation Time Lords have a "fresh" aura about them. Superstitious Time Lords have variously become followers of Ferisix, Thrayke, Sabjatric, Rungar, the Pythian Heresy (*Cat's Cradle: Time's Crucible*), Klade and the legend of Cuwirti.

The Enemy: Greyjan the Sane theorized that a single ancestor cell spawned all life in the Universe. However, the leaking Universe-in-a-Bottle super-evolved such ancient ancestor cells and drew their attention to Gallifrey. The Bottle energy, combined with the chronon decay and paradoxes caused by millennia of Gallifreyan time travel, made the ancestor cells mutate into fully time-active beings inimical to all life—the foretold Gallifreyan Enemy.

STUFF YOU NEED

Romana's Time Lord Death Trap: Useful little device that jumpstarts all regenerations of any Time Lord wandering into its field. The device then corks the energy produced in the Time Lord, eventually detonating it to mutate your opponent's soldiers. In short, it turns your Gallifreyan soldiers into walking genetics bombs.

Gallifreyan Stasers ("The Deadly Assassin"): Can disintegrate foes.

Gallifreyan Books: The Green Book of Gallifrey tells of a white hole cataclysm. Other sacred Gallifreyan texts include the Black Book, the Little Red Book, the Bones of the Dead, the Scrolls of Antiquity and Runes of Rassilon.

PLACES TO GO

Kasterborous: Gallifrey's home constellation has ice rings.

The Gallifreyan Capitol: A transtube system links it to the rest of Gallifrey.

The Panopticon: Normally has six giant statues (*The Infinity Doctors*), one for each of the six Gallifreyan colleges. A statue of Omega ("The Three Doctors") guards the Southern exit.

The Slaughterhouse: Gallifreyan weapons store, holding instruments of destruction from Gallifrey and other war worlds in a time eddy. Only Romana's TARDIS has the access codes.

TARDIS berthing cradles: Contain several dozen TARDISes in their natural state as tall, white cylinders that radiate a soft inner light.

Time Lord Jasdisary Building: Rotates on its base every 58 minutes, finally aligning with the Panopticon after each rotation. The architect, a member of Apeiron's cult, was possibly superstitious about the number 58.

Gallifrey's Museum of the Arcane: Contains a Remote-like remembrance tank.

ORGANIZATIONS

Faction Paradox: "The Shadow Parliament," based in the Eleven Day Empire, rules Faction Paradox. Some young Time Lords dabble in Faction time voodoo rites as a lark, notably those dedicated to cults of Eutenoyar and Apeiron. The Faction uses Celestis (*Alien Bodies*) technology.

Gallifreyan High Council: High Council chancellors monitor respective areas of space-time. Membership includes chancellors of Time Past (Fremest holds the post), Time Present (the old Semax), Time Future (the long-winded Patrexian named Djarshar) and Time Parallel (Branastigert), who scans parallel universes.

The High Council also includes a President (Romana) and a Vice President (Timon). Previous stories ("Arc of Infinity") also included the Castellan.

Gallifreyan Colleges: They teach discontinuity physics and normally number six, but the Scendeles bankrupted themselves keeping up appearances, proving that vanity is Universal.

TIME TRAVEL   Gallifrey doesn't meddle in the timestream out of fear rather than responsibility

TOP 10

... TITLES WE DIDN'T NAME 'I, WHO 2'

1) I, Who 2: Who's Your Daddy?
2) I, Who 2: Electric Boogaloo
3) I, Who 2: Now You Don't Have to Read These Books Either
4) I, Who 2: This Time It's Personal
5) "Knock, knock."
"Who's there?"
"I."
"I, Who?"
"I, Who 2."
6) I, Who 2: I Know What You Did Last I, Who.
7) I, Who 2: Attack of the Clones
8) I, Who 2: Now With Spell Check!
9) I, Who 2: The Unauthorized Biography of Patrick Troughton
10) To All The Who's I've Read Before

(hinted in *Interference*). Events from destroyed timelines are sometimes retained (Fitz recalls the Doctor's "death" on Dust).

HISTORY   The earliest TARDISes didn't gain acceptance as modes of transport for 50 generations. Another 20 passed before Gallifrey agreed to use them as time vehicles.

• Torkal the Great was a Time Lord President almost on par with Rassilon.

AT THE END OF THE DAY   A weighty book that delivers a sizeable adrenaline rush (we wanted cigarettes afterward—and we don't smoke) and some meaty characterization (the stoic Compassion cries out of loneliness, Fitz confronts his older, hardened self, etc). The problem being: *The Ancestor Cell* gives itself an aneurysm incessantly wrapping up wayyyyyy too many plot points from previous novels, stuffing each chapter with major events to the extent that everything homogenizes and READS LIKE A FRONT PAGE HEADLINE! That might "clear the board" for greater things, but it's rather like performing needed surgery without any anaesthetic (and God forbid you had the audacity to love *Interference*). As a result, *The Ancestor Cell*, admittedly written by two accomplished writers (Anghelides, *Frontier Worlds*; Cole, "The Land of the Dead"), accomplishes some laudable goals in a highly questionable fashion and would've been stronger if spread over two, preferably three months.

THE BURNING

By Justin Richards

Release Date: August 2000
Order: BBC Eighth Doctor Adventure #37
"The Earthbound Saga" Part 1 of 6

TARDIS CREW The eighth Doctor.

TRAVEL LOG Middletown (possibly in Cornwall), England, February 1890.

CHRONOLOGY For the eighth Doctor, a few years after *The Ancestor Cell*.

STORY SUMMARY After a few years spent travelling, with no memory of his past or identity, the Doctor grows concerned when one side of the strange cube left in his possession becomes unnaturally hot—reflecting emissions radiating from a distant heat source. By using the warm side of the cube as a makeshift tracking device, the Doctor arrives in the destitute town of Middletown, where a 10-foot fissure has spontaneously appeared near an abandoned tin mine. Investigating further, the Doctor finds developer Roger Nepath attracting patrons worldwide to buy artifacts made from his special "memory metal"—a substance that resumes its sculpted shape, no matter how damaged, if placed in fire for a few seconds. More oddly, Nepath resumes operations in Middleton's obviously tapped-out mine.

Troubled, the Doctor explores the mysterious fissure and finds a cavern with hundreds of magma pools, fleeing as humanoid figures coalesce from the lava and try to incinerate him. The Doctor horrifically realizes the cavern houses a fire elemental—an instinctual force of nature that seeks to consume Earth utterly. Moreover, he deduces Nepath has forged an unholy alliance with the elemental, selling "artifacts" made from the elemental's magma as power relays for the elemental to spontaneously trigger mini-volcanoes and devour Earth. In return, the elemental covers Nepath's dead sister Patience with a portion of its magma, using its metamorphic abilities to apparently restore her to life.

Newly empowered by Nepath's oxygen pumps, the fire elemental's main body prepares to flood Middletown completely. Before leaving to try and make Nepath see reason, the Doctor implores Colonel Wilson, leader of a small military band, to detonate the Middleton dam and flood the fissure with icy water. Finally convinced of the fire elemental's threat, Wilson's men trigger explosives

THE CRUCIAL BITS...

- **THE BURNING**—The amnesiac eighth Doctor settles into his newfound life on Earth and bests a fire elemental in Victorian times.

and split the dam asunder, creating a gushing wave that tears through Middleton.

The Doctor begs Nepath to help save humanity and informs him that the fire elemental can only resemble his dead sister, not truly resurrect her. Unrepentant, Nepath nonetheless asks the elemental to prove his sister truly lives by leaving her body. With some sadness, the Patience/elemental wraps itself around Nepath and departs Patience's form, leaving Nepath trapped in his dead sister's stone-like embrace. As the icy tidal wave reaches the fissure—extinguishing the fire elemental forever—a trapped Nepath feels the waters grow higher and begs the Doctor for help. But the Doctor, sickened by Nepath's callousness and utter disregard for mankind, kicks the Patience statue and topples it under the water, dragging Nepath to his death.

As Middletown slowly recovers, the discovery of a tin ore vein renews the town's livelihood. Meanwhile, the battle-weary Doctor resumes his life as a nomadic world traveler—with only his strange box for a companion.

MEMORABLE MOMENTS Richards plays with the readers' expectations by writing numerous instances where you falsely suspect the Doctor has arrived. Finally, a dinner discussion on the nature of mankind gets more lively—making the reader thunk their heads because the Doctor entered the story without anyone noticing.

An empath named Gaddis feels edgy because the Doctor inherently radiates a superhuman amount of emotion. While assisting the Doctor, Royal Society member Professor Dobbs gets lost in the fire elemental's cavern and screams out the Doctor's name as he's incinerated (shivers ran up our spines). The scene expertly makes the reader question how much the "new" Doctor favors his own survival.

Two of the best moments from the entire novel line: The Doctor proves his emerging mettle—frighteningly so—by drowning the unredeemable Nepath. Conversely, Reverend Stobbold becomes convinced his daughter Betty perished as one of the elemental's thralls, but joyously finds her alive in a reunion that brings a tear to the eye.

ASS-WHUPPINGS Patience Nepath died in an explosion while trying to pull her curious 14-year-old brother Roger away from a burning house.

Roger's grief-stricken mother died a year later. Roger Nepath stole his sister's remains and embarked on his crusade to restore her, ultimately bargaining with the fire elemental.

The Doctor kicks one of the elemental's copycat humans, disguised as Lord Upton, into a frigid river and turns it to crumbly stone. Most important of all, the Doctor kills Roger Nepath (he'd likely have drowned anyway, but the Doctor's kick certainly finishes the job).

TV TIE-INS The eighth Doctor can mentally influence people ("Silver Nemesis," etc.).

NOVEL TIE-INS The Doctor has a note from Compassion that reads, "Meet me in St. Louis, February 8, 2001. Fitz." (*The Ancestor Cell*). He re-meets an aged Betty Stobbold, Reverend Stobbold's daughter, in *Father Time*.

CHARACTER DEVELOPMENT

The Doctor: The Doctor somehow has money, but no possessions beyond the inactive TARDIS. He remembers nothing beyond waking on a railway carriage (*The Ancestor Cell*), but he traded clothes for his trademark green velvet outfit because it seemed more his style.

The Doctor's variously detached or emotional concerning the deaths of others, likely sorting out his inner feelings when he doesn't even know his identity. He doesn't remember what he's a doctor of, but hopes it's impressive. He retains his technical and scientific knowledge despite his amnesia. He's traveled extensively and recalls being in Turkey. He hasn't encountered anything like the Middletown fissure during his new Earth exile.

The Doctor believes there's more to the Universe than just a physical existence, adhering to a philosophy beyond Newton's physics. He doesn't believe in luck, can read German and recalls Caesar saying *Iacta alea est*. The advance of mechanization over individuality saddens him.

The Doctor and the Reverend Stobbold: Both agree that while God has crafted the Universe according to a plan, it's possible to predict that plan. As usual, the Doctor advocates free will and the responsibility that comes with it.

The Fire Elemental: Unnamed force of nature with no memory of its past or purpose. Because the elemental doesn't understand its own nature, it wishes only to feed and doesn't value individual life. Brought to near-starvation by consuming too much substance underground, the elemental schemed to torch Earth's entire surface.

Highly metamorphic, the elemental can shapeshift portions of its magma into various artifacts, each of them a power relay through which the elemental can spontaneously trigger mini-volcanoes. It mentally possesses people who touch such objects, eavesdropping through their eyes or turning them into living fireballs (such people survive the possession by being at the fireball's eye). More dangerously, the elemental can mold portions of its being into emotionless copies of human beings, capable of speech and able to produce incinerating temperatures on contact. The elemental could also telekinetically redirect magma from its own substance.

The TARDIS: Begins this book as a two-inch solid box, glossy and black. Later, the TARDIS cube absorbs energy from one of the elemental's lava flows and grows into a featureless, four-foot-wide blue square box with a wood-like surface. The Doctor doesn't remember where he got the box but feels it's important. The TARDIS is drawn to the fire elemental, recognizing it as a malleable substance it can use to re-shape itself.

STUFF YOU NEED *Nepath's Miracle Metal*, actually cooled (well, somewhat cooled) pieces of the fire elemental, functions as the "miracle metal" absorbs exothermic energy and returns to its intended shape if damaged.

PLACES TO GO *Middletown*, a small English city with a central mine, hasn't turned a profit in years. Middletown's located in a caldera, a basin formed by a volcanic eruption, making it rather convenient for any passing fire elementals that want to flood the city with magma.

ORGANIZATIONS *The Society for Psychical Research*, a Royal Society offshoot, investigates the paranormal using new and developing sciences, trying to define psychic phenomena through precise study.

PHENOMENA *Tuning* works as the innate capacity to sense the emotions of others beyond normal human perception, tipped off by a million discrete signals. Early humankind honed this talent, but modern-day man's mostly forgotten the talent. A few genetically gifted people retain the skill and use it as empathy.

AT THE END OF THE DAY One of the novel line's most important cornerstone reformats—but more important, a striking, contemplative story of Victorian terror that's great to keep on your coffee table as a pick-up-and-read book (presuming your coffee table's made from fire-retardant asbestos). *The Burning* admittedly starts out slow-paced, mostly to allow for more build-up, but the book continually burns bright by nurturing its supporting cast (Reverend Stobbold rising as one of the novel line's most textured human characters) and crafting an eighth Doctor that's much more compelling than the TV movie. All in all, it's a story about family (and a mysterious stranger desperately looking for one), competing for the position of Richards' best book while serving as the No. 1 product for novel newcomers.

CASUALTIES OF WAR

By Steve Emmerson

Release Date: September 2000
Order: BBC Eighth Doctor Adventure #38
"The Earthbound Saga" Part 2 of 6

TARDIS CREW The eighth Doctor.

TRAVEL LOG Hawkswick, North Yorkshire, England and a demonic netherworld, both August 19, 1918.

STORY SUMMARY When reports from Hawkswick, a small village in Yorkshire, oddly suggest that a number of soldiers with grievous, fatal injuries are stalking through the night and killing livestock, the Doctor investigates and gets mistaken for a government agent. Bluffing that he slept in the railway station, the Doctor agrees when Mary Minett, the village midwife, suggests he stay in her spare room.

At Hawkswick Hall, a convalescent home for mentally traumatized soldiers, the Doctor observes patients brutalizing vaguely humanoid clay figures. Dr. Banham, the hall director, says the treatment helps the patients relieve their tensions, but the Doctor suspects Banham's concealing something.

As the Doctor spends time with Mary and Constable Albert Briggs, more and more "undead" soldiers made from clay wander through the night and variously commit murder. The Doctor grimly concludes that dark, demonic forces—all but forgotten in the current age of reason—are psionically responding to the hospitalized soldiers' memories of trench warfare and manifesting as clay versions of their nightmares. Desperate to help, Mary sneaks into Hawkswick Hall and discovers a clay room with a book of spells in Latin, but Banham—actually a warlock working with the dark forces—captures her.

Concluding that Banham has been channeling his patients' grief and turmoil, summoning the dark forces for personal gain, the Doctor and Briggs rush to confront Banham and locate his sanctum sanctorum. Banham marshals his undead clay soldiers against them, but the Doctor and Briggs take shelter in a protective chalk circle. Banham threatens Mary's life, but Briggs shoots Banham through the chest, unleashing the demonic forces festering within him and throwing the Doctor, Briggs and Mary into a netherworld formed from the soldiers' mental anguish.

In a psychic no man's land that resembles a wartime trench, the unnatural dark forces assault the Doctor, but his strength of will turns the demons against each other. As the netherworld dissolves and the Doctor's trio finds themselves back on Earth, the Doctor uses Banham's book of spells to psionically dissipate the dark forces—triggering a psionic backlash that destroys the remaining corpse soldiers and levels the evacuated Hawkswick Hall. With Hawkswick safe from further attack, the Doctor quietly departs and leaves a saddened, smitten Mary to resume her life.

MEMORABLE MOMENTS The Doctor oddly falls silent when Constable Briggs—who's watched his wife and children die—says that it's almost a blessing in wartime to have nobody to worry about. A pitchfork-impaled corpse pulls the offending weapon out of his leg, wipes the blood-smeared tines with his fingers and licks them clean. Mary keeps her dead brother's wristwatch, knowing he can't collect it and wishing she could turn back the hands of time. (The Doctor sagely adds: "None of us can do that.") Finally, Mary's brief instant of exhilaration—then disappointment—with the Doctor in the stairwell (*See Sex and Spirits*).

SEX AND SPIRITS Mary Minett's clearly taken with the Doctor—admiring his blue eyes and strangely odorless scent. She's had trouble finding a mate, always sensing shallowness and lack of sincerity in others and bench marking them against her father and brother. By the same token, she appreciates the Doctor's complexity.

The Doctor's near-nil libido, of course, insures nothing much happens. Still, there's a sweet moment when Mary misunderstands the Doctor's suggestion of, "I think it's time we went to bed." When he wishes her goodnight in the stairwell, Mary's washed with several shades of embarrassment. Realizing the Doctor wasn't blind to her intentions, Mary writes him a small letter bidding him well (the Doctor sheds a small tear reading it).

ASS-WHUPPINGS Wartime fighting in the Somme killed Mary's brother David. The corpse soldiers, who are evidently *not* card-carrying members of PETA, psionically explode a variety of dogs, whippets, ferrets, sheep cattle and pigs (paging James Herriot—you're wanted in surgery, Dr. Herriot). Banham, who also won't be getting a Christmas card from most animal rights groups, keeps a sacrificial offering tree with a variety of dead animals and severed dog heads.

TV TIE-INS The Doctor's recently read *The Time Machine* ("Timelash," "Doctor Who: Enemy Within") and recommends it.

NOVEL TIE-INS The Doctor possesses a skeleton key with no teeth, possibly a pre-cursor to the sonic suitcase developed in *Father Time*.

CHARACTER DEVELOPMENT

The Doctor: The Doctor's extensively traveled during his new Earth exile but doesn't remember a lot of his experiences, considering many parts of the world to resemble others. Based on that, he considers Hawkswick the most exotic place he's visited. He knows a great deal of British history and highly respects the King and country. Yet, he's not in the war because, "It's not his war."

The Doctor's likely met Chopin, slightly recalls Ace's Nitro-9 explosives and attributes General McArthur's future declaration of "I'll be back" in the Philippines to Napoleon.

He wears aftershave and takes lemon or milk, but not sugar, with his tea. He knows something of horticulture and finds time and its measurement (the study of horology) an intriguing subject. He's frugal to further his disguise as a government investigator, but likely has money. He can identify a Julien le Roi clock. At tea, he says it's been a long time since he was mothered.

He reads Latin and casts psionic effects using Banham's book of spells. He wants to learn how to catch speeding bullets with his teeth. The Doctor's limited empathy allows him to mentally see Mary's terror-stricken figure in a mirror when Banham captures her.

Mary Minett: Serves as Hawkswick village midwife, nurse and part-time veterinary reserve. She lives in a house her grandfather built in 1863 as a summer retreat. Her father, a self-made business tycoon, was born in what serves as Mary's bedroom. Mary's mildly empathic, able to draw impressions from living or inanimate objects, and feels drawn to the TARDIS. She believes in God.

The TARDIS: Has healed enough to appear as a large blue box with its normal exterior dimensions. It's not particularly heavy, but lacks its doors. Although still wounded and evidently in a great deal of pain, the invulnerable TARDIS can resist explosions and fire.

ORGANIZATIONS *Corpse Soldiers*, a renegade, break-away group of the inhuman dark forces, are composed of clay and fueled by the psionic trauma of soldiers anguished by trench warfare. Banham started the process rolling by summoning the dark forces with his spellbook. The soldiers' armaments are empathic, meaning they can psionically explode objects without leaving scorch marks. Thankfully, this means you can neutralize their bullets through superior willpower and focus. As creatures held together by psionic forces, the corpse soldiers find themselves drawn to the empathic TARDIS.

PHENOMENA *Humankind and the Elemental Dark Forces* (possibly a Great Old One or splinters of it), were once better attuned, but the rise of society, civilization and intellect divorced humans from such instincts. The inherent skills remain, lodged deep in the subconscious, and sometimes surface to grant people empathy.

HISTORY The Doctor made his own contribution to the cause of women's suffrage by chaining Mrs. Emmeline Pankhurst to the railings outside No. 10 Downing Street.

• After this story, psionic residue left from the dark forces dissipated by the Doctor triggered an influenza outbreak that killed about 30 million people worldwide in 1918 and 1919. About 12.5 million died in India, plus 550,000 in America.

AT THE END OF THE DAY A stylish little period piece, seeped with the sobering nature of the first World War and undoubtedly winning the hearts of fans who resonate with Mary's ultimate loss of the Doctor. However, *Casualties of War* largely downgrades from "truly brilliant" to "very good" once you ponder that it's not as dramatic as it pretends (mention of "inhuman dark forces" feels like a last-minute contrivance, and aside from a spine-tingling scene in the stairwell, Mary does little more than eat chicken with the Doctor and get kidnapped in the fourth quarter). For this reason, the book's geared toward those who read for entertainment, not analysis, but definitely solidifies the block between *The Burning* and *The Turing Test* and might ironically serve newcomers by not over-taxing them—because not a hell of a lot happens.

THE TURING TEST

By Paul Leonard

Release Date: October 2000
Order: BBC Eighth Doctor Adventure #39
"The Earthbound Saga" Part 3 of 6

TARDIS CREW The eighth Doctor.

TRAVEL LOG Oxford, Paris, Dresden, February 13, 1945.

STORY SUMMARY In December 1944, cryptology expert Alan Turing gets assigned to crack a unique cypher transmitted from Dresden. But simultaneously, he strikes up a friendship at Oxford with an individual named the Doctor, who knows a striking amount about Turing's cryptology work. Turing, strangely attracted to his new friend, worries when the Doctor hears the Dresden transmission and becomes increasingly manic, suspecting the code wasn't made for human beings.

When Turing's loyalty wavers, the Doctor contacts British spymaster Graham Greene for help. Two years previous, the Doctor met Greene when a trio of pale-skinned strangers demonically appeared and caused the inhabitants of Markebo, a village in Sierra Leone, to run in terror. Greene concurs that the pale-skinned strangers could have links to the Dresden codemakers and assists the Doctor and Turing in travelling to Paris, co-ordinating their efforts with an English officer named Colonel Horatio Elgar.

The Doctor suggests contacting the Dresden codemakers, but Elgar increasingly advocates trapping them. Worse, Elgar's female associate, Greene's lover Daria, advocates killing the Doctor if he interferes. The Doctor plants a quantum interference device to track Elgar's movements, but the device unexpectedly makes Daria combust and turns her into a pile of ash. Distraught, Greene sides with Elgar, forcing the Doctor and Turing to make secret plans.

The Doctor approaches the court-marshaled American pilot Joseph Heller, offering to secure his release from service if he'll pilot the Doctor and Turing to Dresden. With Heller's help, the Doctor and Turing meet up with the white-skinned strangers, who're actually aliens seeking to encode themselves into a quantum resonator, thus transforming their matter into quantum particles for transmission away from Earth.

Unfortunately, Greene and Elgar arrive in Dresden as the Allies begin to firebomb it. With regret, the Doctor concludes Elgar is a cybernetic alien as-sassin, equipped with a device that blocks his rivals, the pale-skinned aliens, from transmitting to safety. Running out of options, the Doctor uses his quantum interference device to disrupt Elgar's cybernetic systems, melting Elgar's constructed body and killing his organic components.

Greene recognizes Elgar's inhuman nature as the aliens immediately capitalize on Elgar's death and transmit themselves away from Earth, leaving a distraught Doctor behind. Turing, Heller and Greene realize the amnesiac Doctor understood virtually nothing about the white-skinned aliens' conflict with Elgar and sided with them only on the vague and emotional hope that they could transport him back to his true home. Realizing the Doctor killed Elgar not even knowing if Elgar was truly a villain, the Doctor's party emerges to aid a devastated Dresden.

MEMORABLE MOMENTS When the Doctor first meets Turing, he's disappointed that a stone griffin doesn't talk to him, showing his innocence. The Doctor tells a soldier, "Young, aren't you?", and when the soldier bristles, the Doctor replies, "I'm sorry, I meant your species."

Turing's advised to get married and have children, because if you're not moving toward life, you're moving toward death. Greene suggests passion makes fools of everyone and Turing snaps: "No, passion makes fools of some of us." *Catch-22* author Heller suspects time works differently for the Doctor, who seems older than he looked.

The spirit of "Doctor Who" is invigorated when the Doctor tells his friends, "We're four fit, able-bodied me, and there are people up there who are injured and dying and in need of our help."

SEX AND SPIRITS The Doctor's lack of a libido remains one of the mysteries of his life.

Turing's homosexual love for the Doctor becomes an underlying thread of *The Turing Test*, motivating him to follow the Doctor's lead. When the Doctor asks Turing up to his room to examine the TARDIS, a perplexed Turing wonders what's going on, but the TARDIS' dormancy causes the Time Lord to have a Byronic fit. Consequently, a bigoted landlord thinks the Doctor is getting it on with Turing and evicts the Time Lord.

Turing looks at the Doctor like someone about to deliver a kiss, but the Doctor declines. In a double entendre, the Doctor requests Turing's help in breaking the Dresden code and Turing agrees to "give the Doctor what he wants."

The Doctor doesn't care about Turing's homosexuality and disapproves of Greene's bigotry. The most that happens between the Doctor and Turing is a hug, although Turing's unreciprocated love for the Doctor may have partly motivated Turing's suicide (*See History*).

While spymaster/novelist Graham Greene and the alien agent Daria make out, the Doctor's device turns Daria to ash (she foreshadows the event by telling Greene, "You wouldn't enjoy [making love to me]. Others haven't.").

ASS-WHUPPINGS Greene, momentarily convinced the Doctor was evil, shoots at the Time Lord and supposedly kills him. Actually, the Doctor dresses up a corpse with his clothes, causing Greene to repent.

The Doctor's quantum device accidentally torches Daria. Desperate, the Doctor, Heller and the pale-skinned aliens first bludgeon Elgar before the Doctor's device crisps him—a poignant moment borne out of the Doctor's selfish motives.

TV TIE-INS *The Turing Test* doesn't say this, but the alien encoding process is presumably an offshoot of Logopolitan Block Transfer Computation ("Logopolis"). Before this adventure, the Doctor read Greene's book, *The Power and the Glory* (1940), perhaps using his limited precognitive abilities ("Doctor Who: Enemy Within") to know they were going to meet. The eighth Doctor, like the seventh, furiously writes with both hands ("The Curse of Fenric").

NOVEL TIE-INS Only twice in the last 50 years has the Doctor felt "the way he should feel" (presumably *The Burning, Casualties of War*), implying most of his time on Earth hasn't been spent fighting alien menaces.

The "Remembrance of the Daleks" novelization states that scientist Rachel Jensen aided Turing with his wartime research.

CHARACTER DEVELOPMENT

The Doctor: The Doctor knew Sir Edward Elgar, the late musician. In 1940, the Doctor applied to the RAF to defend Britain, but was rejected for lack of British citizenship. He left England to travel in autumn 1940.

The amnesiac Doctor still lacks a past, but says he's never been drunk (presumably during his current Earth tenure). He knows he's a permanent exile and suspects he might hail from outer space or the future. He postulates he might have been married, but taken off his wedding ring. He's not sure if he's human.

The Doctor has money and rents many rooms, keeping a wealth of books in many languages. Leeches avoid the Doctor, probably disliking his blood. Turing says the Doctor has blue eyes, but Greene claims they're green.

TOP 5

"WHO" NOVELS
Post *Interference*

1) The Turing Test (by Paul Leonard)—One of the more joyous finds in recent years, making up for stacks of lesser "Doctor Who" novels in one fell swoop. *The Turing Test* unites three extraordinary, flawed men (tempestuous spymaster Graham Greene, the inwardly troubled Alan Turing and war-dodger Joseph Heller) with an amnesiac Time Lord in one of the novel range's most flavorful narrations (Greene, Turing and Heller take turns telling the story). This one's a book for readers.

2) Father Time (by Lance Parkin)—A story that's supremely good at giving the Doctor a "family" far more human than his Cousins at Lungbarrow. That *Father Time* refuses to settle its bloodfeuds with constant slaughter (the Doctor to a hardened soldier: "...is killing a child really the only way this can end?") makes it all the more commendable.

3 The Burning (by Justin Richards)—Richards' stylized revamp of the entire novel line conveys his vision for the eighth Doctor like no other. The final moment, where the Doctor kills the insane Roger Nepath, hits your face like a bucket of water and proves we're not dealing with your daddy's Doctor.

4) The Banquo Legacy (by Andy Lane and Justin Richards)—A gripping terror tale, probably all the creepier because it started life as a non-"Who" story—the Doctor's crew was added later. We love the bit where butler Simpson's eyes get pulped.

5) Festival of Death (by Jonathan Morris)—Wild and woolly, a novel that deftly reproduces the charm, humor and verve of the Tom Baker/Lalla Ward era. *Festival of Death*'s lunacy seems especially poignant, especially with the recent passing of former script editor Douglas Adams.

ALSO RECOMMENDED

• **Bunker Soldiers (by Martin Day)**—Startlingly satisfying amid the carnage of Kiev's sacking by Mongols, putting the aged first Doctor and his innocent friends through humanistic terror but turning them out stronger in the end. Bunker Soldiers helps prove a top-notch first Doctor historical is damnably hard to beat.

• **Verdigris (by Paul Magrs)**—Admittedly an acquired taste, but seeped with a great sense of fun and vigor. The affectionate Iris Wildthyme makes a great foil for the straight-laced third Doctor.

The Doctor can hear the despairing alien voices in the Dresden Code. He takes Mass with Greene. He somehow knows about mathematicians' military work at Bletchley. He's saved up his ration cards and retains his innate piloting skills.

The Doctor's encountered evil, but doesn't think he's a better man than Turing because of it. He's killed many people, but never, as with Elgar, without a cause.

The Doctor either has military influence or evokes hypnotism to free Heller. He uses knowledge of simple physics, air resistance and gravity to save Turing when he falls from an airplane.

The Doctor and Alan Turing: Quite naturally, Turing thinks like a mathematician, alternatively considering the Doctor a murderer, traitor or good-willed individual. Yet, he allows trust for the Doctor to override logic and at times wonders if he sacrificed national loyalty (*See History*).

Turing suggests Americans are insincere with no depth. [Author's Note: The *I, Who 2* editors—myself included—cheered when the Doctor chastised Turing for "generalizing horribly."]

Henry Graham Greene: Spymaster Greene worked for M16. He has a wife and children at Oxford, plus a mistress named Dorothy in London—and is tired of all of them (*See History*).

Greene and Turing: Greene believes Turing needs more compassion, not ice-hearted logic, when it comes to Hitler's decimation of the Jewish people. He considers Turing's homosexuality unnatural. Turing has read Greene's novels.

Joseph Heller, Greene and Turing: The future author of *Catch-22* regards Turing as a boring, unadventurous stuck-up, self-centered, pretentious and willfully cold English prig. He views Greene more favorably, thinking him simply prone to swift, emotional judgments. Heller forgives the Doctor for pushing him to aid in Elgar's murder, but suspects Greene didn't (*See History*).

Colonel Herbert Elgar and Daria: Elgar and his colleague Daria have physical forms that're about 20 years old, but claim to be "infinitely old." Their core consciousness was likely a perpetual form of programming, but they proved vulnerable to fire and the Doctor's quantum interference device.

The TARDIS: Has grown to its normal size but remains inert. The Doctor only glimpses the TARDIS' true interior, which remains inaccessible.

ALIEN RACES *The Dresden Codemakers*, being pale-skinned aliens, use a translation table of 145 words. Their overall physiognomy was rather warped from Earth humanoids.

STUFF YOU NEED *The Turing Test* is a cryptography method postulated by Turing that enables an operator to decide whether a computing machine is the equivalent of a human, working on the basis that computers and humans give similar replies. Later theorists argued such a test theoretically works but is impossible to implement.

HISTORY Alan Turing became a highly regarded wartime mathematician, famed for breaking the German ENIGMA code. He contributed sufficiently to the philosophy of mathematics, publishing his "Computable Numbers" paper in 1936. He worked for the military at Bletchley. In 1952, Turing endured a trial and public shaming after having illicit activity with a schoolboy. He consequently ate a cyanide-painted apple at Wilmslow, Cheshire, killing himself in 1954.

• In 1942, Greene worked in Sierra Leone, based in the capital of Freetown, smuggling agents back to London. In June, 1942, he found the village of Markebo deserted like *The Mary Celeste*. His Sierra Leone tour of duty ended in January 1943. During his last week, he found the Doctor in a Freetown prison, arrested for treason. Among other things, Greene authored *The Power and the Glory* (1940), *The End of the Affair* (1951) and *A Burnt-Out Case* (1961). He died in 1991.

• In Malta, 1944, American pilot Joseph Heller pretended to be mad to avoid service and wound up institutionalized, evacuating a medical ward with his screaming. His deception exposed, Heller flew more bombing missions for America and went genuinely mad. He crashed a plane and broke a soldier's legs, but the authorities didn't believe him after his first bluff and chucked him in prison until the Doctor secured his release. He funneled his wartime experience into the anti-war novel *Catch-22* (1961). In later years, he seemed reclusive, but in reality just didn't like the press. Heller died in 1999.

• In the decades following *The Turing Test*, the Doctor encouraged Turing, Greene and Heller to record their remembrances of the event. Greene authorized the papers to be released in 2000, presuming all the principal players would be dead and not wanting to answer for it.

AT THE END OF THE DAY Quite simply one of the best novels from 2000 and a great deal further back, *The Turing Test* demonstrates a remarkable

scope as the story of three extraordinary men—and the Time Lord who made them into something more. The switch in narration between Turing, Greene and Heller makes the book, breaking up the action but keeping everything fresh (Heller's prose especially reads like a true joy). Elgar's murder alone, showing the selfishness of the Doctor's actions, grips your heart by numbering among the most dramatic of twists. All in all, it's Paul Leonard's best book to date, plus a meaty story of friendship and murder that single-handedly makes up for any 10 sub-par "Who" books you'd care to name.

ENDGAME

By Terrance Dicks

Release Date: November 2000
Order: BBC Eighth Doctor Adventure #40
"The Earthbound Saga" Part 4 of 6

TARDIS CREW The eighth Doctor.

TRAVEL LOG London, Moscow and Washington D.C., 1951.

STORY SUMMARY The multi-dimensional gamesters known as the Players agree to an Endgame—a final competition that will end when one side is completely eliminated. Permitted only to act through agents, the Players set about manipulating world politicians at the dawn of the Cold War era toward a nuclear holocaust that will destroy their opponents—and the planet Earth in the process.

In London, 1951, the Doctor despairingly realizes he hasn't aged a day in 50 years and grows bored, finally forming a friendship with Oskar Dolinski, a Polish exile and conspiracy theorist. Unfortunately, the Doctor ignores Oskar's claims of having intercepted important documents until Russian agents beat Oskar to death. Soon after, the Doctor encounters M16 agent Kim Philby, a Russian double agent and head of Tightrope, a covert watchdog group. Philby, the intended recipient of Oskar's papers, warns the Doctor of a strange increase in Cold War tensions apparently caused by a mysterious group known as the Players. To insure the Doctor's cooperation, Philby seizes the Doctor's prize possession—his strange blue box—and pledges to return it when the Players are thwarted.

Investigating further, the Doctor and Philby learn President Truman has become strangely hostile toward China and made odd threats of a pre-emptive nuclear strike. Gravely concerned, the Doctor and Philby investigate Project Kali, a secret CIA project designed to harness psionic talents, and uncover a plot by Player Myrek to mentally push Truman toward a nuclear attack. The Doctor somewhat blocks the threat by warning Truman's aides to prevent the president, who's out of the country for a few days, from having contact with Myrek.

Philby grows concerned that Soviet premier Joseph Stalin might be similarly tainted and asks the Doctor to investigate events in Moscow. When the Doctor refuses, Philby frames the Doctor for espionage and forces him to flee to Moscow. There, the Doctor re-meets the seductive Player known as the Countess, who's been mentally encouraging Stalin to unleash Russia's nuclear arsenal. Fortunately, the Countess finds the Doctor more intriguing and he persuades her to have compassion for humanity. At the Doctor's request, the Countess mentally soothes Stalin and ends the threat of a nuclear assault.

The Doctor returns to America to find that President Truman has returned and rushed off to uncover the truth about Project Kali. Together with his allies, the Doctor bursts in just as Players Myrek, Axel and Helga prepare to further brainwash the president. Axel tries to shoot the Doctor, but the Countess arrives and telekinetically tricks the Players into killing each other, saving the Doctor and wiping out her opposition.

With the Players defeated, Philby honors his word by dropping the charges against the Doctor and returning his blue box. A grateful President Truman offers the Doctor a lucrative White House job, but the Doctor declines and returns to his quiet life in London. Meanwhile, the Countess returns to her home dimension, telling the Endgame's adjudicator that Truman's bodyguards killed the other Players. Reluctantly, the adjudicator rules the Endgame void.

SEX AND SPIRITS The Doctor still lacks a libido. Double agent Guy Burgess fancies him, but the Doctor basically ignores this. Murderous Player Axel thinks about making it look like involved agents Guy Burgess and Donald Maclean died from auto-asphyxiation, but the Doctor stops him.

The Countess certainly feels some attraction for the Doctor, siding with him against her fellow Players because she finds him intriguing. She also flirts with Stalin to win his confidence, but the relationship ends there.

The Doctor showers, making this yet another novel to show Paul McGann naked.

ASS-WHUPPINGS Russians beat the Doctor for information, but he reflexively delivers two punches that break three ribs and a jaw on his attackers. For an encore, the Doctor tosses Player Axel out of a car. The Countess telekinetically does in her fellow Players by skewering Helga with a knife through the heart and making Myrek shoot Axel, then himself.

TV TIE-INS The amnesiac Doctor recalls the word "Drashigs" ("Carnival of Monsters") but doesn't know what it means.

NOVEL TIE-INS The second and sixth Doctors separately encountered the Players, including the seductive Countess, in the aptly named *Players*. The Countess was eventually forgiven for shooting fellow Player the Count in that book.

Spy master Graham Greene (*The Turing Test*) compiled a file on the Turing affair back in the mid-1940s but omitted a lot of detail. As this story takes place, Greene's enjoying himself in West Africa. The Doctor knows advanced code breaking from his association with Turing.

The Doctor recalls owning a train set (*Short Trips*: "Model Train Set").

CHARACTER DEVELOPMENT

The Doctor: Still lacking a history, the Doctor increasingly knows he's alone and spends time at the British Museum, speed-reading on topics that include Sumerian history, Egyptology, quantum mechanics, Socrates and Einstein. He keeps a simply furnished basement flat close to the *Café des Artistes* on a quiet Bloomsbury back street. He's lived there for almost a decade and realizes he's physically not getting older.

The eighth Doctor briefly encountered his seventh self and Ace at the Festival of Britain, 1951, but they didn't recognize each other. He still wears a faded brown corduroy suit and a once-gaudy waistcoat. He's become complacent, scarcely aware of his eating habits.

Although amnesiac, the Doctor has memory flashes of being in an elaborate office (on Gallifrey), giving writing advice to Shakespeare, using the sonic screwdriver and seeing a planet devastated by nuclear conflict. He also knows about researcher J.B. Rhine's experiments to test psionics with symbols shown on hidden playing cards (the Doctor can pass such a test with flying colors). For that matter, he can call a double four, then roll it on a pair of dice.

The Doctor's met *Don Quixote* author Miguel Cervantes, remembers names for many faces in the National Portrait Gallery and speaks some

Russian. He's abnormally strong and knows a nerve pinch that renders opponents unconscious. He moves with unusual stealth, perhaps using a Ninja technique that suppresses one's personality from emanating [Author's Note: *Jeopardy* host Alex Trebek must use this talent].

He automatically enters a healing trance if beaten. He's got excellent lock-picking skills. Kim Philby supplied papers identifying the Doctor as Dr. John Smith of the Foreign Office Intelligence Department. As a reward for services to President Truman, the Doctor received a considerable consultant fee, American citizenship and a British diplomatic passport. The Doctor doesn't like overcooked cabbage (and bravo for that).

Kim Philby: M16 agent who's been working as a double agent for Russia for 20 years. The Russians suspect he's a triple agent—a British agent pretending to be a double agent but having true allegiance to Britain (head … hurts…).

The Doctor and Kim Philby: Fearing that British authorities would arrest Guy Burgess and Donald Maclean—double agents who could expose him—Kim Philby blackmailed the Doctor into helping Burgess and Maclean defect to Russia. After the Doctor thwarted the Player's agenda, Philby honored his word and returned the Doctor's blue box, plus deleted the Doctor's file from M15 and M16 records.

The Doctor and the Countess: The Countess offers to restore the amnesiac Doctor's memories but he declines, sensing the knowledge might be too dangerous to comprehend.

Countess (a.k.a. Madame Razetskia): Among the Players, only the Countess believes Earth holds potential and shouldn't be destroyed. She's an adept telekinetic. As "Madame Razetskia," the Countess pretended to be a psychic healer and adviser to Stalin. She recalls the second and the sixth Doctors as being the same person, and immediately recognizes the Doctor in his eighth body.

The TARDIS: The recovering TARDIS now appears as a tall blue box that almost has a texture, as if woodgrain's trying to appear in the material. The box almost seems paneled and there's a lintel near the top. There's some vague sense of faded letters on the outside, but the interior's still empty.

ORGANIZATIONS

The Players: Although the nature of the Players' game (frustratingly) remains unknown, a mysterious adjudicator (no relation to the Church of Adjudication that spawned Roz Forrester and Chris Cwej) still makes rulings on game play. The extra-dimensional Players are supposedly forbidden from acting directly and must use agents. Players that take human form must use human methods. Players can teleport out of danger and get extra points for vanquishing old enemies such as the Doctor. The scoring's different in an Endgame, which continues until one side has been eliminated. Besides the Countess, the Players included the unscrupulous Myrek and his assistant Helga, plus Axel, who held contempt for mankind.

Project Kali: Named for the Hindu death goddess Kali, Project Kali originated as a counter-measure to German attempts to use psionics to advance their war cause (telepathically locating enemy subs, etc.). Player Myrek took charge of the Project for his own experiments.

HISTORY Light beings from Altair III harmlessly observed events on Earth during World War II.

• Several Doctor John Smiths are on record by 1951, although it's unclear how many of them are the Doctors.

• After the blackmailed Doctor aided him in defecting to Moscow, Burgess used his exile to drink as heavily as possible, upsetting authorities at the Chinese Embassy in Moscow by peeing into a marble fireplace. The Russians continued to appreciate Burgess' insight. He settled down with a young electrician named Tolya in Moscow and died from boozing in August 1963. Conversely, fellow exile Donald Maclean worked for the Russian Foreign Affairs Ministry and died in March 1983.

• Kim Philby's luck held out until January 1963, when evidence of his traitorous actions proved overwhelming. He kindly gave M15 a two-page confession, then fled on January 23 for Russia. He adjusted well to his exile, obtaining Soviet citizenship and a pension. Philby advised the Russian government and KGB, writing his memoirs, *My Secret War*. In 1964, he ditched his second wife to run off with Melinda Maclean (fellow exile Donald Maclean's wife) but they split in 1969. In 1971, he married a Russian girl named Rufina and stayed happily married until his death in 1988. His true allegiance, be it to capitalism or communism, was never entirely clear.

AT THE END OF THE DAY Sigh. Hardly the explosive *Endgame* that the title suggests, dishing out a generic Doctor with almost none of McGann's quirks and inconsistent caricatures of historical figures ("ruthless" Kim Philby happily spills his guts on decades of counter-intelligence work, the "little sonovabitch" Truman keeps acting apolo-

getic.). It's mostly a bunch of unconnected set pieces that keep the Doctor dashing about the globe, and the Players' purpose is never revealed (arguably an oversight in *Players*, but sheer carelessness here). Pile this together and you've got a spy novel about as menacing as a gumdrop—and a missed opportunity from Dicks, the well honored "Doctor Who" godfather.

FATHER TIME

By Lance Parkin

Release Date: January 2001
Order: BBC Eighth Doctor Adventure #41
"The Earthbound Saga" Part 5 of 6

TARDIS CREW The eighth Doctor.

TRAVEL LOG Greyfrith, the Pennines, England, 1980; London and an unnamed city in the North of England, 1986; India, Berlin, London, Florida and the *Supremacy* in Earth orbit, 1989. [Author's note: Parkin doesn't blatantly state years, but we've calibrated the dates by Miranda's age and the fall of the Berlin Wall.]

STORY SUMMARY
The early 1980s
Having settled onto a quiet, secluded Derbyshire farm, the Doctor strikes up a friendship with schoolteacher Debbie Castle and grows fascinated with 10-year-old student Miranda Dawkins—a young girl with a superhuman intelligence and two perfectly formed hearts. But shortly after the Doctor volunteers to serve as Miranda's tutor, Prefect Zevron and Deputy Sallak, time-travelling soldiers from the future, arrive to kill young Miranda and end a blood feud.

Sallak decapitates Miranda's alleged father while her supposed mother flees with Miranda and encounters the Doctor. Mrs. Dawkins explains that Miranda hails from a future where her family used their genetically granted talents to tyrannize, butcher and senselessly abuse billions of beings. In the counter-revolution that slaughtered Miranda's family, the Dawkins—actually a guardsman and nurse serving the Emperor's house—fled with the Emperor's two-month-old granddaughter Miranda to 20th century Earth. Zevron, leader of the strongest faction to survive the family's overthrow, has pledged to kill Miranda lest she resume her family's atrocities. The Doctor agrees he cannot let Zevron, whatever his justification, kill a 10-year-old girl.

Zevron and Sallak arrive and Sallak pulps Mrs.

This book is not endorsed by the BBC. Doctor Who and TARDIS are trademarks of the BBC.

161

Dawkins with a machine gun. In a tangled skirmish, Zevron's neck gets broken and Sallak finds his legs pinned beneath the wreckage of his attack saucer. As authorities arrest Sallak for the Dawkins' murders, the Doctor adopts a desolate Miranda and pledges to protect her from harm.

The mid 1980s

The Doctor accrues millions as one of Britain's most accomplished businessmen, specializing in restructuring companies for profit without the need for layoffs. Meanwhile, Miranda matures into a strikingly intelligent 16-year-old with an awakening sex drive. But Deputy Sallak, having spent years in prison, sees an article about the Doctor's new business ventures and breaks out of prison to gain vengeance.

Sallak summons reinforcements from the future, including Zevron's younger brother Ferran, then captures the Doctor. Ferran, swearing to end his dead brother's blood feud, infiltrates Miranda's school but winds up falling in love with her. To Miranda's shock, Ferran reveals her true origins and suggests they jointly rule over the splintered factions in the future.

The Doctor escapes, programming a replicator device to send out a limited energy wave that turns Sallak's troops and the replicator itself into roses, although Sallak survives. Back at home, the Doctor discovers Ferran trying to force Miranda's hand and triggers Ferran's recall device, teleporting him back to the future.

Suddenly, Sallak breaks in but Miranda overpowers him and takes his weapon. Sallak vows to stalk and murder Miranda if she lets him live, so Miranda, taking Sallak at his word, shoots him twice in the chest and kills him. Distraught at Miranda's cold-blooded violence, the Doctor advises she flee and find her own destiny. Moments after the authorities arrive, the Doctor successfully claims he killed Sallak in self-defense, leaving him to ponder his missing daughter's whereabouts.

The late 1980s

Ferran, having succeeded his late brother as faction leader and now 20 years older, tracks a nomadic 19-year-old Miranda to India and transmats her to Earth orbit aboard his ship, the *Supremacy*. Ferran proposes they unite her family's authority and technology under his command and sire an heir, but Miranda scoffs and secretly informs the Doctor of her whereabouts. Having spent three years searching for Miranda, the Doctor stows himself on a scheduled lift-off of the American space shuttle *Atlantis* and convinces NASA to investigate the *Supremacy*.

By mimicking Ferran's voice, the Doctor overrides the *Supremacy*'s central computer and allows *Atlantis* to dock. Miranda escapes from her

quarters but finds her flight halted by the Doctor's computer lockdown, spontaneously deciding instead to lead a slave revolt that captures the *Supremacy*. Unwilling to accept defeat, Ferran tries to destroy the *Supremacy*'s time engines and level Earth, but the Doctor stabilizes the ship while Miranda persuades Ferran to finally vie for peace.

With Ferran's consent, Miranda asserts her family inheritance, appointing herself supreme ruler over the factions and declaring a new peaceful age. Miranda leaves for the future to further controlled anarchy—refusing to assert much power herself, but keeping it away from anyone else—leaving the Doctor to rejoice at his daughter's success and return to Earth on *Atlantis*.

MEMORABLE MOMENTS

The early 1980s

A school chess match gets cancelled, so the Doctor amuses the kids by simultaneously playing 11 games. Best of all is the revelation that 10-year-old Miranda is *letting the Doctor win* so he'll impressively defeat everyone rather than take home a lesser 10 victories.

A freelance agent for the Klade advises his superior that they should leave before the Doctor thwarts their plans, uses their own weapons against them, blows up their home planets and gives the leader another scar, "…*sir.*"

The Doctor, pleading with a knife-poised Zevron for 10-year-old Miranda's life: "She's a girl. She's not killed anyone. Look at her, Zevron—is killing a *child* really the only way this can end? Is this really how the ruler of a galactic empire acts?"

The mid 1980s

In matters of romance, Miranda's told to follow her heart and she asks: "Which one?" In a jewel of a scene about the pain of adolescence, Miranda walks in on her best friend, Dinah, nakedly straddling Miranda's somewhat-boyfriend Bob (*See Sex and Spirits*). Ferran tells an unbelieving Miranda her space-bred origins and she asks if he reads *Teen Titans* comics.

The late 1980s

To save Miranda, the Doctor off-handedly decides to hi-jack *Atlantis* and outlines, "How to Steal a Space Shuttle" for colleague Debbie Castle on an airline napkin. Miranda fully becomes the Doctor's "daughter" by off-handedly spurring a revolution and taking over the *Supremacy*.

Finally, in what could be the overriding principle of *Father Time* (and indeed, "Doctor Who" itself) the Doctor tells a gun-totting Miranda: "Weapons are the tool of the cruel and the cowardly. We strive to be better than that."

SEX AND SPIRITS The mummified remains of Ramses the Great apparently enjoy a better sex life than the Doctor in the 1980s, although school teacher Debbie Castle flirts with him. When the Doctor suggests viewing *Close Encounters*, Debbie momentarily takes it the wrong way.

Miranda's still a virgin by age 16, but classmate Bob provides her first kiss. Miranda considers fixing the virgin problem with Bob during a sleepover but shockingly discovers her best friend Dinah naked and straddling a compliant Bob. Miranda later tries to pop her cherry with classmate Ferdy (actually Ferran), but the Doctor returns home and inadvertently spoils their attempt at nookie (whoops). After departing the Doctor's company, Miranda's sexuality thrives and she boffs a tourist (*See History*). Pining for Miranda, Ferran crafts an android double of her (named "Cate" for "duplicate") as his concubine, deputy and possible surrogate mother.

ASS-WHUPPINGS Captured by Zevron and Ferran's forces, the Doctor twice endures agonizing mental interrogation. Perhaps more woefully, three of his green coats perish in *Father Time*'s multiple crossfires. Ferran uses a feedback loop to destroy the Doctor's sonic suitcase (*See Stuff You Need*). Worst of all, Ferran's electrical trap kills teacher Debbie Castle, age 35 (*See Character Development*).

Miranda plugs Deputy Sallak after he warns: "Kill me, or I'll kill you." The Doctor disavows her use of violence, but that's pretty hypocritical considering his body count far outstrips hers. The Doctor fireballs a Cortina and kills the villainous, robotic Mr. Gibson. He makes a cold-blooded mental Interrogator forget to keep his heart beating. He disguises one of Sallak's unconscious goons as himself and thereby gets the poor man shot to pieces. Bloodiest of all, the Doctor uses Sallak's molecular replicator to turn Sallak's base and guards into roses.

Miranda's adoptive parents, the Dawkins, get decapitated and machine-gunned to pulp. Her family razed entire galaxies (*See History*). Debbie's husband Barry breaks Prefect Zevron's neck, but the Prefect's mindeater wipes Barry's mind almost clean. Years later, Deputy Sallak revives Barry long enough to slip a knife between his ribs.

Two aliens named "the Hunters," mercenaries hired to locate Miranda, sneak a sugar-cube-sized nuke into the Doctor's jacket, but later trigger it not knowing their maidservant removed the Doctor's coat. They perish in the explosion, (correctly) feeling rather stupid.

TV TIE-INS The sonic suitcase revives some TV lines regarding the sonic screwdriver, notably Debbie's: "Not even the sonic suitcase can get us out of this one." ("The Invasion of Time") and the Doctor's: "I feel like I've just lost an old friend" ("The Visitation").

The Doctor's Swiss cheese memory allows him to know future astronomers will locate Neophobus, Jupiter's 13th moon, a.k.a. Voga ("Revenge of the Cybermen"). The Doctor and Miranda prove immune to super-aging time spillage ("The Mark of the Rani").

TV AND NOVEL TIE-INS The memory-jumbled Doctor tells Miranda fantastic stories of warring ants and butterflies ("The Web Planet"), men made of Liquorice Allsorts ("The Happiness Patrol") and an empress who lives in a big jam jar (*The Scarlet Empress*).

NOVEL TIE-INS The Doctor spent most of the 1960s and 1970s travelling, unaware of Kennedy's death (*Who Killed Kennedy?*) until well after the fact. The Doctor remembers a Martian greeting from *Legacy*—the same one Benny uses in *The Dying Days*.

The Doctor here visits an aged Betty Stobbold (*The Burning*). Of course, the old gal must be roughly 112 (getting possessed by a fire elemental's evidently good for the skin).

The Doctor's grasp of symbolic logic puts Turing to shame (*The Turing Test*). In an unspecified adventure, the Doctor, Fitz and Anji Karpoor (*Escape Velocity*), will visit the planet Falkus and combat Prefect Zevron and Sallak before these events. America's secretly developing an SDI system, likely a pre-cursor to Station Nine (*Option Lock*).

The Needle serves as home to the Librarinth, a surviving artifact of Miranda's people (first seen, in ruins, in *The Infinity Doctors*).

Iris Wildthyme (*The Blue Angel*) visited the amnesiac Doctor in the mid-1980s and promised to sort everything out. As you might expect, the Doctor grew more and more bewildered until Iris left in a huff.

Debbie spots a photograph of the Doctor taken from Stalingrad, 1951 (*Endgame*).

The Doctor glimpses images of his future that include: a swarm of wasps (*Eater of Wasps*), a violin in the heart of a thunderstorm (*The Year of Intelligent Tigers*) and a heap of stuff as-yet unpublished.

CHARACTER DEVELOPMENT

The Doctor: As a mid-1980s business consultant, the Doctor charges £10,000 a day. He's ludicrously rich (effortlessly writing checks for £1 million when needed) and drives a Trabant he acquired in East Germany. He dines with Clive Sinclair, and won the London Marathon at least once in the mid-80s. *Time* ranks him among the top 50 people of the decade. *Interiors* magazine wants to do a photoshoot of his house.

Trying to learn more about Fitz's note, the Doctor's visited St. Louis three times in the last 30 years. He spent two years failing to codebreak it. He's failed to locate himself as a missing person. That aside, the Doctor turns down Miranda's offer of access to Ferran's file on him, preferring to wait until his scheduled meeting with Fitz.

The Doctor looks a year or two (shock, horror, dismay) older since his arrival on Earth, meaning he looks 40ish. His blue eyes have traces of crow's feet, and he's got a couple gray hairs. He hasn't encountered UNIT during his Earth exile but maintains a mental link with the TARDIS.

During reclusive periods, the Doctor plays chess against himself. He dreams about the TARDIS and speaks some Martian. The Doctor possesses a photographic memory and can quote every line of Shakespeare. He can hum every song he's heard and speed-read. While playing snooker for the first time, he uses the Newtonian system to sink every ball simultaneously (sadly, he scratches). He's got superior driving skills.

On May 28, 1976, the Doctor spent time in England with a young widow named Claudia. He last visited India circa 1964. Friends of Doctor who died in 1989: Salvador Dali, Irving Berlin, Sir Lawrence Olivier and Graham Chapman.

The Doctor and Mr. Gibson: The alien Mr. Gibson hails from a mechanical species, able to transform from 12-foot humanoid robot mode into a black Volkswagen. At some point (future or past), the Doctor freed Gibson's slaves and ended his practice of chucking political opponents into a volcano. Gibson later panicked and dropped a nuke into a local volcano (whoops), the resultant explosion killing his queen and mate Mrs. Gibson plus their little metal children. Gibson erroneously blames the Doctor for the atrocity.

Miranda Dawkins (a.k.a. The Last One): Blonde-haired Miranda's name, in the original Latin, means "to be wondered about." Alternatively, the marooned magician Prospero in Shakespeare's *The Tempest* has a daughter named Miranda.

Teenage Miranda can compete as an Olympic-level swimmer. She wears smart, fashionable clothes, avoids smoking and drugs and spends her time with chess, friends and homework. She's independent minded, but hardly a social animal. She's sitting O-Levels, and is on course for A-levels and university.

Miranda doesn't see the appeal of the Wolfman/Perez run on *The New Teen Titans*. (Sniff! She isn't one of us.) Miranda rarely wears makeup, doesn't own a CD player and can't fly a spaceship. Her natural lifespan isn't established.

In declaring herself "Supreme Being of the Universe" and assuming control of the future factions and their territories, Miranda (among other things) becomes President of the Supreme Council, Commander-in-Chief of the Armed Forces, Custodian of the Artifacts and Head of the Galactic Bank. She wields full Senatorial authority and regulates trade routes and supply lines. She frees slaves and soldiers from military service, claiming she doesn't know what to do with an army.

The Doctor and Miranda: Miranda's family have superior genetics that mimic the Doctor's Time Lord physiology, including twin hearts that supply Miranda with extra energy. She doesn't need much sleep and metabolizes alcohol almost instantly.

THE CRUCIAL BITS...

- **FATHER TIME**—The Doctor adopts the orphaned 10-year-old Miranda Dawkins, last of a hunted alien species. Nine years later, Miranda becomes supreme ruler over disjointed political factions in the far-flung future, asserting a system of controlled anarchy to keep power from others.

Her family's inherently telepathic. The Doctor taught Miranda mantras to regulate her hormone, adrenaline, oxygen and heartsrate levels (the mantras don't work on humans). He also showed her how to imitate voices perfectly.

Both the Doctor and Miranda have lower body temperatures, so their breath isn't seen in cold environments. They're both sensitive to temporal changes and can plot five-dimensional vector coordinates (Miranda's skill outdoes the Doctor).

They're not related, but Miranda resembles the Doctor's height, posture, eyes and pale skin. They've got two of the highest IQ's on Earth.

Mental probes establish the Doctor loves Miranda more than anyone.

The Doctor and Prefect Zevron: In Zevron's past and the Doctor's future, the two clashed on the planets Galspar and Falkus, with the Doctor giving his Deputy, Zevron, a facial scar. The Doctor offered resistance to Zevron's mindeater probe and learned additional psychic defensive techniques. Among the various future factions, Prefect Zevron rules Faction Klade.

Ferran: Born the same year as Miranda, Ferran only has one heart but beats her at swimming. Ferran's actually a decent man, but too caught up in his family's bloodfeud.

Debbie Gordon (a.k.a. Deborah Castle): Primary school teacher who married Barry Castle in a shotgun wedding (she later miscarried). Prefect Zevron's mindeater put Barry in a coma for five years, but Debbie remained in Greyfrith to tend to him. Following Barry's death, Debbie was reunited with the Doctor and accompanied him on some business trips, possibly moving in with him. She took the Doctor to see *Bill and Ted's Excellent Adventure* (the Doctor saw their flying telephone box and wished for one of his own). After Debbie's death, Miranda took her body into the future for burial with full honors.

The TARDIS: The "police telephone" sign has reappeared on the front. When healed, the Ship includes a greenhouse the size of Kew Gardens.

Even inert, the Ship seems to empathize with Miranda and flashes its rooftop light at her.

ALIEN RACES *The Klade*, of which Zevron, Ferran and Sallak are members, possesses human blood—suggesting this race is actually one of humanity's multiple off-shoots, possibly adapted to alien environments. They recently acquired limited time travel (presumably from another race), but only loosely understand temporal theory. [Side notes: *The Infinity Doctors* mentions the Klade. For whatever reason, their name is an anagram of "Dalek."]

STUFF YOU NEED *The Sonic Suitcase*, a prototype sonic screwdriver, generates ultrasonics to unfasten screws and open locks.

PLACES TO GO *The Librarinth:* Treasure trove of genetic records, art and technological blueprints. Only the leader of a race can access their people's secrets.

SHIPS *The Supremacy (a.k.a. the Ship)* is a four-kilometer-wide time-and-space vessel containing 1,000 floors. Ferran's people retrieved and repaired the *Supremacy*, probably the result of an alternate timeline. After Miranda took over the *Supremacy*, she renamed it "the Ship."

HISTORY The Doctor foresaw the widespread popularity of bottled water and convinced a barman to sell his pub and buy a bottling plant. The new brand name—Dragonwater—grew to be worth £20 million annually.

- Librarinth records detail the Doctor's involvement in historical events at the Lloyds building, Baghdad, Waco, Texas and during the Martian Invasion (*The Dying Days*).

- The Doctor made some minor contribution to the fall of the Berlin Wall and watched it topple with Dieter Steinmann, a relative or descendant of Oskar Steinmann (*Just War*).

- As the Berlin Wall fell, Miranda did the horizontal mamba with a horny tourist in India. The lover in question later wrote and directed his autobiography, detailing how his life's major events occurred on historical dates (Jodie Foster's daughter played Miranda). The writer/director won Best Foreign Non-Interactive Film Oscar in 2017.

- No historical record of Miranda exists on Earth beyond the aforementioned screwing.

- In a future millennia, Miranda's family used their genetic privileges to become decadent and sadistic. Their unrivaled powers led to entire chunks of the timeline being erased and entire galaxies being evacuated. They ruled for 1,000

165

years, killing millions through their neglect, cruelty and sport. Eventually, Prefect Zevron's mother, a senator, triggered a rebellion that caused her brutal murder but started a domino effect that toppled the Imperial Family from power. A splintered, shaky democracy rose from the ashes. Miranda almost undoubtedly unified the various factions.

AT THE END OF THE DAY One of the most mature "Who" books you're ever likely to read, so marbled with evolving characters and levels of change, it's a damn shame we can't rip *Father Time* out of the "Doctor Who" universe and propel it to win a Hugo or Nebula award. In a book that operates with layers of gray rather than solid black-and-white, the Doctor, Miranda, Zevron, Sallak and Ferran find themselves in a runaway conflict where nobody's truly wrong. Put it this way: We're fully prepared to give Lance Parkin unflattering reviews if he'd accommodate us by writing crappy books—but to date, it hasn't happened.

ESCAPE VELOCITY

By Colin Brake

Release Date: February 2001
Order: BBC Eighth Doctor Adventure #42
"The Earthbound Saga" Part 6 of 6

TARDIS CREW The eighth Doctor, Fitz and Anji Karpoor.

TRAVEL LOG Brussels and London, February 8, 2001.

CHRONOLOGY For Fitz, eight hours after *The Ancestor Cell*.

STORY SUMMARY Stockbroker Anji Karpoor tries to vacation in Brussels with her live-in boyfriend Dave Young, but their holiday's interrupted when mysterious assassins publicly gun down a fleeing man named Menhira. Dave, realizing Menhira oddly has two hearts, attempts CPR but Menhira expires after concealing a space vehicle component on Dave's person.

In London, Fitz leaves Compassion's company and sees a TV interview where Dave claims the slain Menhira had twin hearts. Fitz travels to Brussels and meets with Anji and Dave, thankfully confirming the dead man wasn't the Doctor, but the assassins return for Menhira's component and kidnap Dave. With little recourse, Fitz and Anji decide to contact the Doctor and arrive at "St. Louis," a London bar specifically purchased and renovated

by the Doctor for his rendezvous with Fitz. Only loosely recalling his travels with Fitz, the Doctor nonetheless agrees to help recover Dave.

After much investigation, the Doctor's group discovers Menhira belonged to a spearhead of Kulan aliens, reconnoitering Earth for a possible invasion. After crashing on Earth four years ago, the spearhead splintered into two factions—both of which opted to aid Earth entrepreneurs in constructing space vehicles, hopefully reaching a Kulan battlefleet approaching Mars orbit. While a pro-invasion cadre led by Fray'kon helped an entrepreneur named Pierre Yves-Dudoin, a pro-Earth group led by Sa'Motta sided with the rich Arthur Tyler III. Whichever faction reports first will likely convince the Kulan leadership to spare Earth—or dominate it.

Siding with the benevolent Sa'Motta, the Doctor and his allies blow up Yves-Dudoin's Star Dart shuttle, rescuing Dave from Fray'kon's group. Conversely, Fray'kon infiltrates Tyler's base, stabs Dave to death and smuggles himself aboard Tyler's Planet Hopper just before liftoff. With Fray'kon holding a decisive lead, the Doctor agrees to double-check Fitz's claim about the Doctor's blue box actually being a time machine. In that instant, the TARDIS finishes its century-plus of healing, allowing console room access.

More from luck than anything else, the Doctor materializes the TARDIS on the Kulan flagship. As the Doctor grapples with Fray'kon, Anji and Fitz access to the flagship's weapons systems. Anji attempts to bluff the Kulan into thinking humans have captured their flagship, but accidentally unleashes a weapons barrage that strafes multiple Kulan ships. The Kulan captains, embittered by rivalries between powerful Kulan families and convinced their leadership has turned on them, engage in civil war. In the chaos, Tyler lures Fray'kon into an airlock and jettisons both of them into space. Moments later, the Kulan fleet annihilates itself as the Doctor, Anji and Fitz flee in the TARDIS.

The Doctor tries to return Anji—who's still grieving for Dave—home, but discovers his stay on Earth seriously atrophied his TARDIS piloting skills. Instead of arriving in Soho, the TARDIS lands on a primitive landscape, fully committing Anji to adventures with the Doctor and Fitz.

MEMORABLE MOMENTS St. Louis bar manager Sheff, recalling when the establishment was a sci-fi themed restaurant named Bar Galactic, muses how much the sci-fi crowd seemed to possess disposable income. Fitz walks into the dysfunctional TARDIS, expecting it to be multi-dimensional, and bangs against the opposite wall.

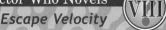
THE CRUCIAL BITS...

- **ESCAPE VELOCITY**—First appearance of companion Anji Karpoor. The Doctor and Fitz reunited in London, 2000. The TARDIS finally heals and regains its internal configuration, but the Doctor's memory and piloting skills remain questionable at best.

SEX AND SPIRITS Anji and Dave have dated for five years and lived together for three, enduring a number of relationship ruts (they're in one now) but remaining strong and full of love. As a student, Anji dated a librarian named Marcus.

Fitz decides that Anji's attractive and intelligent but not his type, meaning she's safe from his libido (and should probably throw a party). Conversely, she considers Fitz a harmless, if trustworthy, prat. Fitz feels nervous around smart women.

ASS-WHUPPINGS Anji loses her live-in boyfriend Dave, first done in by Fray'kon's blade, then atomized by rockets (you'd think one or the other would have been plenty). Before that, a prototype Kulan retrovirus—designed to interface humans with Kulan technology—turns Dave into a pseudo-Kulan. Anji gets some revenge by kicking a Kulan between the legs (nice to know that still works) and causes a chain reaction that butchers the Kulan spacefleet (awk!). In a skirmish, Fitz shoots down two Kulan guards and Anji guns down another.

TV TIE-INS The Kulan are aware of Ice Warriors ("The Ice Warriors") legends.

NOVEL TIE-INS The Doctor doesn't remember Gallifrey's destruction (*The Ancestor Cell*). After stowing aboard *Atlantis* (*Father Time*), the Doctor kept up on space-travel developments.

1930s-born Fitz says he last visited future London in the 1990s, meaning he's erroneously remembering the date for *The Shadows of Avalon* (2013) or suggesting he stopped there in an unseen story. Fitz knows about the Doctor's Kent house (*Cat's Cradle: Warhead*).

Fitz's memory remains murky due to his "remembering" by the Remote. A colony of Chelonians (*The Highest Science*) wiped out a Kulan invasion force. CIA spymaster Control (*The Devil Goblins of Neptune*, *The King of Terror*) still monitors the Doctor's activities. The Doctor hasn't watched TV science fiction since "Nightshade" (*Nightshade*) and can't get into "Babylon 5."

Escape Velocity ends with the TARDIS scanner showing the setting of *Earthworld*.

TV AND NOVEL TIE-INS Fitz claims the Doctor has red-colored blood, contradicting suggestions that it's darker than human-normal ("The Two Doctors" and a string of novels), but perhaps backing up the TV movie's claim of the Doctor being half-human.

CHARACTER DEVELOPMENT

The Doctor: He remembers few events before his current Earth exile, but understands he's an alien time traveler. He's almost entirely forgotten travelling companion Sam Jones, but somewhat remembers his VW Bug (destroyed in *Unnatural History*). He recalls the TARDIS as his oldest friend, first companion and only remnant of home. He still doesn't look much older than 40. He was more amiable than excited about meeting Fitz.

The Doctor remains an expert computer hacker and has only vaguely heard of UNIT. He lacks biotechnology skills. Some Kulan know him by reputation. The Doctor's TARDIS navigational skills are rusty at best (but then, what's new?).

Fitz Kreiner: Compassion left Fitz with a heap of banknotes but little documentation. Fitz was born in 1935 and carries a battered copy of his birth certificate. Fitz has a poor grasp of geography. Without the TARDIS' translation power, he likely knows only English. Thanks to Sam's coaching on 20th century culture, Fitz introduces himself as "Fitz—as in cracker."

When Fitz was a child, he'd listen to the comedic Glums in *Take it From Here*, plus the adventures of Dick Barton, on a trunk-sized radiogram. He's rarely ridden rollercoasters. When Fitz was 23, the Atomium in Brussels, a 120-meter-high representation of an iron atom, captured his imagination. But upon seeing it in 2001, he dubs it archaic.

The Doctor, Sam and Fitz: Fitz learned of the Doctor's regeneration abilities from Sam, but scarcely believes it.

Anji Karpoor: As a third-generation British immigrant, Anji Karpoor, 28, works as a futures trader and lacks an Asian accent. She spent a year studying in Boston. She loves being a stockbroker views it like playing chess. Someone named Darren serves as her boss. Anji thrives on making money, but understands that possessions only give one so much happiness. Her salary props up Dave's wayward income.

Anji doesn't count herself among hardcore feminists. She favors the sciences over religion, preferring rational explanations and adhering little to her parents' beliefs in the Hindu gods. She rarely

This book is not endorsed by the BBC. Doctor Who and TARDIS are trademarks of the BBC.

167

goes to temple and never wears a sari, but considers her inner self as Asian/Indian and regards St. George as her national saint.

Although close to her father while growing up, Anji hardly speaks to him these days (he views her as opinionated). The Doctor somewhat reminds Anji of her father.

Anji's typically calm in a crisis and speaks some French. She's fiercely protective of her new green Mercedes A-Class. She's never liked boats and has taken university rape defense classes. She visited the St. Louis Bar when it was the sci-fi based Bar Galactic. Anji's traveled through Europe and North America, but the experience disappointed her by feeling too much like home. She's therefore longed to go somewhere truly alien (and gets her wish in a pretty profound fashion).

Dave Young: Dave longs to succeed as an actor, but his career's about as lively as a dead chicken. His small-time roles include a doctor on *Children's Ward*. As a typical science fiction geek, Dave fiercely argues the millennium starts in 2001, dammit, not 2000. He has trouble balancing his checkbook.

Anji and Dave: Anji first met Dave at a party where, in typical dork fashion, he was hotly debating the unicorn symbolism in the director's cut of *Blade Runner*. Anji, fancying Dave but having little knowledge of the film, joined the conversation anyway. Anji and Dave are complete opposites—he annoys Anji slightly less than her mother, and she's determined not to have kids for at least a few years. Their relationship suffered a bit when Anji's brother Rezaul—younger than her by five years—started studying at one of London's universities and embraced Dave as a sci-fi brother (feel the terror).

Control: Free-acting agent who operates an American CIA offshoot called the Offensive Action Team (OAT). Control's assistant, James Kent, enjoys his full confidence.

The TARDIS: Among other things, the restored Ship includes a copy of the kitchen from the Doctor's Kent House (*Cat's Cradle: Warhead*), a laboratory, a number of bedrooms, two swimming pools ("The Invasion of Time"), a tennis court, a museum, a well-fitted gym and a zero-G shower.

ALIEN RACES

Humans and Kulan: Dave's DNA surprisingly contains Kulan elements, suggesting humanity could be a Kulan offshoot.

Kulan: Pale-skinned humanoids with double hearts and purple blood. The aggressive Kulan sometimes use military force but prefer economic domination. Kulan political power is split between a legislative Congress and an administration further divided among economist, military and religious affiliations (a Council of Three, with one member from each affiliation, commands most space operations). Even so, ancient, feuding Kulan families largely influence policy. Officially, Kulan don't kill other Kulan, but that's propaganda.

Kulan physiology allows them to pop back into shape if squished flat, but they can't survive gunshot wounds. The Kulan language sounds harsh and grating. Earth's oxygen-rich atmosphere slows them down. The Kulan possess semi-intelligent software viruses and use a technology without physical controls, directing operations through mental power.

STUFF YOU NEED *Escape Velocity:* The speed needed to escape Earth's gravitational pull: seven miles per second.

PLACES TO GO *St. Louis* variously exists as a city in Missouri, a film about waltzing spaceships or a London restaurant formerly known as the sci-fi based Bar Galactic. The St. Louis Bar and Restaurant is located between Holborn and Covent Garden, somewhat distant from the theatre district and West End proper. It's listed in *Talking Pages*, but we don't recommend trying to find it, and displays a lot of non-authentic American memorabilia. After meeting up with Fitz, the Doctor bequeathed the bar to its manager, Sheff.

HISTORY The Kulan long ago exhausted their homeworld's natural resources and instigated commercial takeovers of other civilizations.

• The Doctor's fond of Belgium, having helped King Baudoin with a sticky situation when the Atomium exhibit opened in 1958.

AT THE END OF THE DAY A story that fails to achieve orbit, attempting to notch itself as archetypal "Doctor Who," but making the grave mistake of playing certain events as commonplace (it's ludicrous—and a cop out—that the Doctor's ambivalent about meeting Fitz after 113 years of waiting). Although loaded with potential, Anji reads like a default—if spunky—companion who happens to be Indian. Worse, the Kulan rank among the lamest invading aliens ever, obliterating themselves over unspecified family feuds. The final result's got little sense of occasion, regretfully dovetailing as one of the weaker companion-introduction stories.

Bernice Summerfield
Drinking Tea
With Angry Gods

OH NO IT ISN'T!

By Paul Cornell

Release Date: May 1997
Order: Benny New Adventure #1
(Who NA #62)

MAIN CHARACTERS Bernice Summerfield, Wolsey the Cat and Menlove Stokes

TRAVEL LOG St. Oscar's University, Dellah; the planet Perfecton, 2593.

STORY SUMMARY Having settled into her new role as an archaeology professor at St. Oscar's University on the planet Dellah, Benny leads a student expedition to the planet Perfecton, a world quarantined after its natives vanished mysteriously. Benny, both lonely and horny, considers a liaison with her student Michael Doran, but information pirates named the Grel attack the expedition and interrupt Benny's moral dilemma. More importantly, a Perfecton missile attack on the St. Oscar's starship *Winton* apparently destroys Benny, her cat Wolsey, the Grel and the entire *Winton* crew.

Oddly enough, Benny awakens in a fantasy-like world where Wolsey appears as a walking, talking humanoid cat and Benny's students have become dwarves. With Wolsey at her side—and the Grel right on her tail—Benny gets mistaken for a princess and endures a series of whimsical adventures that include a king's ball and a meeting with her fairy Godfather.

To Benny's surprise, she finds her "fairy tale" adventure is actually part of a pantomime, with the missing Perfectons serving as unconscious audience members. The Greater One, leader of the Perfectons, explains to Benny that the Perfectons once determined their sun would go supernova but sadly lacked the ability to escape. Intrinsically bound to their planet and culture, the Perfectons downloaded their entire civilization into a coded missile, programmed to lock onto any passing spaceship and extra-dimensionally transform it into a haven of Perfecton culture. Unfortunately, when the missile struck the *Winton*, it impacted with Benny's proof copy of Professor Archduke's thesis on pantomime. As a result, the missile's quantum fluctuations re-shaped the Perfectons, the Grel and the *Winton* crew according to the pantomime thesis' guidelines, creating Benny's strange fantasy-based world.

Benny realizes the pantomime world has been directing her, as the lead character, to place a

THE CRUCIAL BITS...

• **OH NO IT ISN'T!**—Benny starts her tenure as Edward Watkinson Professor of Archaeology at St. Oscar's University on Dellah. The People's supercomputer God recruits Benny to act as one of its covert agents in the Milky Way. Wolsey the cat briefly becomes a humanoid (and loses a limb in the process). St. Oscar's facilities and history greatly detailed. First mention of a number of secondary characters and elements, such as Benny's head of department (Dr. Follett), the St. Oscar's Advance Research Department and the Sultan of the Tashwari, one of the University's founders. First appearance of Benny's robotic porter Joseph.

magic lamp on a pedestal to end the pantomime "story." As Benny completes the task, Wolsey, her students and the *Winton* crew return to normal while the Perfectons download into a data module.

The *Winton* warps out of orbit as the local star goes supernova, destroying the Perfecton homeworld. Benny suspects the mysterious Professor Archduke used a homing beacon to lure the Perfecton missile to his thesis as part of a larger conspiracy to obtain the Perfecton culture and data. Unable to prove this theory, Benny turns the Perfecton culture data module over to the St. Oscar's Dean, but that evening, the module skillfully floats out of the Dean's office and into Professor Archduke's waiting hands.

MEMORABLE MOMENTS Benny whimsically asks her robotic porter Joseph to fetch her "love." Benny's subsequently horrified when Joseph kindly fetches her student Michael Doran. Trying to cover her mistake, Benny accidentally gives Doran a copy of *Make Dangerous Love to Me—The Erotic Poetry of Carla Tsampiras*. (A floundering Benny adds: "There are bits about archaeology.")

SEX AND SPIRITS Benny, rather shamelessly, later invites Doran to her quarters and considers shagging him (the Perfecton missile attack ruins any possible nookie, curse the luck). At the king's ball, the female Puss in Boots entrances Wolsey. "Princess" Benny, to upset the scripted pantomime story, accepts multiple marriage proposals. There are more "dick," "ball" and other sexual innuendoes in this book than you can shake...a stick at.

In our Universe, Wolsey the Cat got enamored with the neighbor's cat and sired six kittens.

ASS-WHUPPINGS Battling the Greater One, humanoid Wolsey loses his right front limb. When reality's restored, cat Wolsey's still missing a leg (the injury's never mentioned again, so presumably the future's advanced medicine restored it).

NOVEL TIE-INS The eighth Doctor dropped Benny off at St. Oscar's and bequeathed her Wolsey and his question mark umbrella (*The Dying Days*). Menlove Stokes, here a St. Oscar's art professor, first appeared in *The Romance of Crime* and joined the St. Oscar's staff in *The Well-Mannered War*.

Benny considers telling publishers that a hard drive crash munched her *Down Among the Dead Men* sequel—Cornell's way of having fun with writer Ben Aaronovitch for using the same excuse on his sinfully late *So Vile a Sin*.

Chelonians (*The Highest Science*) boast of decimating the Grel in their *Chelonian Chronicles*.

Dragon's Wrath reveals Professor Archduke belongs to the conspiracy-laden Knights of Jeneve. Professor Warrinder's race, the Pakhars, first appeared in *Legacy*.

The super-computer God (*The Also People*) sends a fat man and a thin man to offer Benny a position as one of God's agents (*Down* and *Where Angels Fear* variously reveal God's true motives).

Oh No It Isn't! introduces Marcus Krytell, who encounters Benny in *Ship of Fools*, and the St. Oscar's Advanced Research Department, up to no good in *Mean Streets*. *Oh No It Isn't* also mentions Dr. Follett, Benny's department head and an aged reptilian who breathes chlorine-laced air. He finally appears in *Tears of the Oracle*.

Oh No It Isn't! cleanly lays out the history of St. Oscar's University, but very, very bad things happen to it in *Where Angels Fear*. The Sultan of the Tashwari, a University founder, appears (and snuffs it) in *Twilight of the Gods*.

Benny holds the Edward Watkinson Chair of Archaeology, named for a famed, missing archaeologist (*Tears of the Oracle* tells Watkinson's story).

CHARACTER DEVELOPMENT

Bernice Summerfield: Benny sometimes uses eyeglasses out of affection for 20th century artifacts. She ordered a dozen jazz discs from Earth on ancient vinyl. She's in her mid-30s, but as a St. Oscar's professor, she's trying to act older.

Benny's commissioned to write a sequel to her best selling *Down Among the Dead Men*. She's tentatively named her second work *So Vast a Pile* (again an obvious play on *So Vile a Sin*). The university's publishing arm is already writing her nasty letters because she's not making deadline. Benny counter-proposes writing an account of the Perfecton adventure, or perhaps a volume about relationships entitled *Men Are From Mars, Women Are From Mars Too, Unfortunately*.

Benny rides a bicycle. She's considering breast enlargement. She uses *Ah: A Perfume For an Alien*

CHARACTER PROFILE

BERNICE SUMMERFIELD

We're big fans of aiding novel newcomers, and even presuming you've read some Bernice Summerfield stories, it's possible you can't recall every detail under pain of Chinese water torture (although this obviously curses your household with a pox of Faustian proportions).

Ergo, the following "Character Profiles" will happily serve as your quick-and-dirty primers to the life and times of Benny, Irving Braxiatel and Chris Cwej, recapping their appearances in Virgin's "Doctor Who" New Adventures. To wit, for Benny:

- **LOVE AND WAR**—The seventh Doctor and Ace land on the planet Heaven and encounter 30-year-old Bernice Summerfield, an "archaeologist" with faked credentials. Benny reveals that during her youth, Daleks her mother while she was retrieving one of Benny's doll. When Ace momentarily deserts the TARDIS, Benny becomes the Doctor's new companion.
- **THEATRE OF WAR**—Benny meets Time Lord Irving Braxiatel and conducts academic research at his Braxiatel Collection.
- **SANCTUARY**—Benny falls for Guy de Carnac, a warrior in France, 1242. Church agents kill Guy as the Doctor and Benny escape.

CONTINUED ON PAGE 173

or a Human. She whispers Jason's name at life-threatening junctures.

Professor Laight, the University Counselor, taught Benny to retrieve memories by use of hypno regression. Benny agrees to serve as an agent of the People's supercomputer God but awaits her first assignment.

Benny and Jason Kane: Benny regrets her divorce from Jason, but wouldn't reverse it.

Menlove Stokes: Now a St. Oscar's professor of applied art, Stokes hosts a popular weekly art transmission entitled "Paint Along With Menlove." Because Stokes sometimes paints pictures using his bodily fluids, the Perfectons dub him "Producer of Waste." Nonetheless, Benny enjoys his company.

Wolsey: The Perfecton reality version of Wolsey is seven feet tall, fully clothed, with a vast Cavalier hat and a peacock feather. He wears a big red coat with tails and a dirty great scabbard. He's also got a little dent on his brow where his kitty self leapt at a holorecording of the Three Pronged Tenors. Because boys play the female parts in panto, he thinks Benny's a man named Dick.

God: The People's super-computer sometimes relies on human agents, members of the Tiny But Interesting Interest Group. This technically doesn't violate the People's Treaty with the Time Lords.

St. Oscar's Professors: They include the mysterious Professor Archduke, who wrote *English Pantomime: A Critical Study*; Professor Warrinder, a Pakhar with a degree of clairvoyance and Professor Epstein, a specialist in Chelonian Literature. Hettie Bonistall and Lucinda Pargiter hold the St. Oscar's Chair of Etiquette because of a bureaucratic error. Thooo, the last of the corporeal Perfectons, accepts an unspecified teaching position.

ALIEN PLANETS *Dellah* has at least three power blocs: the Tashwari Regime, the Sylan Federation and the monarchy of Goll, full of mercenaries and bodyguards. These three nations alone have seven different species. If you include splinter groups, Dellah has more than 500 registered religions. The planet has a 26-hour day.

ALIEN RACES

Grel: Grel hail from the planet Grellor and have humanoid bodies with bulbous heads and "squiddy faces." They mostly trade in pirated data, regarding themselves as "information monarchs" (everyone else regards them as gittish pirates). Grel directly acquire information using axes with data monitors and a spike on the end. The axe splits their victims' skulls open and the data monitor sucks information directly from their brains.

The Grel evolved a second brain that sorts information, a function usually given over to dreaming. Consequently, Grel don't dream (as a curious side effect, they don't sleep either). Grel creation myths in the Grellan Information Record speak of stumbling from the ocean, but the Grel are more likely the product of genetic engineering.

Grel literature reads as a novelization, emphasizing the emotional aspects of their story, because the Grel mind only registers conflict experiences during later contemplation.

Perfectons: Blue-skinned beings with large, multi-lobed skulls, six-fingered hands and many joints. They would likely die without their technology, plants and civilization, and couldn't survive a conventional space journey.

PLACES TO GO

St. Oscar's University: Typically recruits "glamorous" professors, if not the most learned. The University features its own spaceport, Dellah's first. *The Campus Bulletin* publishes University events.

Garland College Hall of Residence of St. Oscar's University: The High Priest of Knowledge of the Tashwari Regime blessed each brick personally. Benny's the rector there.

Slawcor: The Grel afterlife, the inner land inside Grellor where all Grel are Masters, not Servitors. Because the Grel don't view any Grel as "bad," there is no Grel concept of Hell. Humans cannot enter Slawcor.

ORGANIZATIONS

Advanced Research Department (St. Oscar's): Built as an extension of St. Oscar's Pracatan College, the ARD has only one entrance.

Tiny But Interesting Interest Group: Worldsphere group devoted to collecting trivia about the Milky Way. Dellah lies in its sphere of influence.

SHIPS *IAC cruiser Winton*, an ex-military vessel, is the most powerful craft available to St. Oscar's University. Crew compliment: 100. The ship retains its hyperdrive, but lacks its missiles. Captain Balsam commands.

HISTORY Earth's sphere of influence largely viewed Dellah as urbane and raced by the planet. Later, Earth's Galactic War missed Dellah entirely. Grateful for the escape, a Dellah Sultan saw a vision of a university, a place of learning, which would affirm the peace—not to mention keep Dellah from ranking as a target. Marcus Krytell (*Ship of Fools*), greatest of the many Galactic War entrepreneurs, considered the development opportunities offered by a place where knowledge was free and helped acquire backing. Dellah's various factions set aside a chain of hilly islands for the university, agreeing the site had no strategic worth. The three-eyed Sultan of the Tashwari gave the university and its nine colleges names likely to attract Earthlings.

• Earth Central found the planet Perfecton and labeled it a prohibited world, not knowing why the Perfectons died out. (One wonders why the Perfecton missile didn't strike ships of the first Earth explorers, but ah well.)

AT THE END OF THE DAY Raw, inspired and hilarious, even if launching the Benny NA line with *Oh No It Isn't!* was a huge mistake. By itself, the story's a playful romp, soaked with fun and portraying Benny as someone who flies by the seat of her pants. For that matter, the Big Finish audio's twice as raucous, with Nicholas Courtney ("The Brigadier") an inspiration as Wolsey. Unfortunately, as a fanciful comedy, *Oh No It Isn't!* ain't dramatic or gripping enough to snare "Doctor Who" readers and keep them addicted to this line. Read now, when the Virgin Benny line's folded, *Oh No It Isn't!* instigates a comedic joust well worth your time, but it isn't the cornerstone Benny NA it should have been.

DRAGONS' WRATH

By Justin Richards

Release Date: June 1997
Order: Benny New Adventure #2
(Who NA #63)

MAIN CHARACTERS Bernice Summerfield, Irving Braxiatel and Commander Skutloid.

TRAVEL LOG St. Oscar's University, Dellah; Nusek's castle on Stanturus Three, all 2593.

STORY SUMMARY At St. Oscar's University, Benny literally bumps into a running man who drops an elaborate statue of a dragon breathing flame. The next morning, Benny learns the man, an art forger named Newark Rappare, was murdered en route to see her old friend Irving Braxiatel, head of St. Oscar's Theatrology Department. But Benny quickly learns her travels with the Doctor have deposited her in a time before Braxiatel has "met" her. While pondering Rappare's mysterious death, Benny and Braxiatel strike up a "new" friendship.

Meanwhile, warlord Romolo Nusek seeks to gain further power by proving his ancestor, Hugo Gamaliel, once had a colony on Stanturus Three. Accordingly, Benny joins an expedition there. History regards Gamaliel as the man who destroyed the nefarious Knights of Jeneve, a militaristic, information-gathering organization. Nusek's castle also displays the famed Gamalian Dragon statue, an emblem of the Knights which Gamaliel captured. But oddly enough, it's a perfect match to Rappare's statue, suggesting one of them is a copy.

Strangely enough, a third Gamalian Dragon is unearthed on Stranturus Three and Benny's research, to her shock, concludes this must be the original statue. Meanwhile, Braxiatel finds evidence that the Knights of Jeneve tricked Gamaliel into thinking he'd destroyed them and have oper-

ated in secret ever since. Through Professor Archduke, a Knights agent at St. Oscar's, Benny and Braxiatel learn the Knights let Gamaliel capture the Dragon, actually a spy camera and a low-grade nuclear device, to monitor Gamaliel and destroy him when the right political climate surfaced.

Based on Archduke's proof that Gamaliel was a ruthless corporate raider, Benny discredits the power-mad Nusek and makes him fly into a self-incriminating rage. Seeking revenge, Nusek captures Benny, Braxiatel and a Knights agent named Clyde and takes them to his volcano-based castle. Benny's group escapes, but when Braxiatel attempts to reroute a force field to protect them, he inadvertently makes the volcano erupt.

During a mad escape, Clyde falls into the lava pit but passes Benny the detonator for the Dragon's nuclear bomb. Benny triggers the Dragon's arsenal, destroying Nusek and his castle as she and Braxiatel flee.

Benny and Braxiatel return to life at St. Oscar's, haunted by the knowledge that Gamaliel legitimately held an outpost on Stranturus Three,

---

meaning the power-mad Nusek was his indeed rightful heir. Worse, the Knights' true agenda remains unknown.

MEMORABLE MOMENTS Benny infuriatingly realizes Nusek recruited her for the Stranturus Three expedition because, as a mid-range archaeologist, she's good enough to back up Nusek's claims but not renowned enough to disavow them. Braxiatel, to under-emphasize his friendship with Benny, deliberately mispronounces her name as "Soberfield" (a rather ironic choice). Before a committee, Benny dramatically pulls the Dragon statue out of her rucksack...and pulls out an undergarment as well.

SEX AND SPIRITS Benny boozes with several of her students, including Polybus Arex and Anne-Marie Rose, at the Witch and Whirlwind bar. Braxiatel and Benny also enjoy champagne, the first of many shared drinks.

ASS-WHUPPINGS Benny detonates the Gamalian Dragon, killing Nusek and many of his followers. Braxiatel inadvertently causes some deaths by erupting Nusek's volcano.

Nicholas Clyde, an agent of the Knights and a friend of Benny's, arranges for an archaeological expedition to be wiped out, covering up proof of Nusek's claims on Stanturus Three. Clyde later falls into a lava pit.

Nusek's assassin, Mastrov, eliminates Mappin Gilder, a St. Oscar's facilitator that Benny disliked, for knowing too much about Nusek. Mastrov later endures a double-punch of savage animals and the volcano.

The Knights of Jeneve were allegedly wiped out at the Battle of Bosarno, where Henri of Bosarno, Gamaliel's right-hand man, died in a skirmish after the main fracas. Knights of Jeneve agents kill art forger Newark Rappare for knowing too much about the Gamalian Dragon and its copies.

Benny, fleeing from Mastrov, curls into a ball and crashes through a large window. Conversely, she flings steaming coffee in Mastrov's face and pistol-whips a guard unconscious.

NOVEL TIE-INS *Legacy* first mentioned Irving Braxiatel, who fully appeared in Richards' *Theatre of War*. Benny last saw Braxiatel in *Happy Endings*, but this Braxiatel has yet to chronologically attend the event. Richards' *Tears of the Oracle* reveals Braxiatel as the Doctor's brother.

Art forger Newark Rappare appeared in the eighth Doctor novel *Demontage* (but bites it here). Dr. Archduke, revealed as a Knights of Jeneve agent, first appeared in *Oh No It Isn't!* The

---

THE CRUCIAL BITS...

- **DRAGONS' WRATH**—Benny meets Time Lord and St. Oscar's Theatrology head Irving Braxiatel for the "first" time. First appearance of Braxiatel's Martian associate, Commander Skutloid. First appearance of the Knights of Jeneve. St. Oscar's Professor Archduke revealed as a Knights agent. First appearance of the St. Oscar's Witch and Whirlwind bar.

Knights of Jeneve tolerate and encourage information pirates such as the Grel (*Oh No It Isn't!*)

The historian Brahmyn wrote *Dreams of Empire*, a work hailing Gamaliel as "chosen" to end the Knights' power. Richards, apparently fond of the phrase, used it for his second Doctor book of the same name and made it a key phrase in the Big Finish audio "Whispers of Terror."

Dragons' Wrath debuts Commander Skutloid, a Martian who's head of the Strategic Institute at St. Oscar's (and reappears in Richards' *The Medusa Effect* and *Tears of the Oracle*), and St. Oscar's History Department head Emilia Winston (also reappearing in *Tears of the Oracle*).

Deadfall reveals attempts to restore the Knights of Jeneve's founder, Vaslov Baygent. Doctor companion Chris Cwej is one of Baygent's many descendants.

Braxiatel here "repairs" Joseph after the assassin Mastrov damages the little guy, only to discover that Joseph's innards are empty. *Tears of the Oracle* reveals Joseph as a communications relay for the supercomputer God.

CHARACTER DEVELOPMENT

Bernice Summerfield: Benny's utterly broke. She secretly craves tangible acceptance by the academic community.

Irving Braxiatel: As head of the St. Oscar's Department of Theatrology, Braxiatel helped sponsor the campus' Shakespeare Building. He's rolling in cash. He can reprogram a drone's personality circuits. Braxiatel is considered a renowned expert in various "things" and many universal governments respect him as an independent arbiter (they're also wary of his power).

Braxiatel prefers travelling alone and can pilot his personal spaceship. He highly enjoyed Benny's book *Down Among The Dead Men*. He doesn't believe in tidy desks. He has a calming effect on animals such as savage steggodons and knows some hand-to-hand combat.

Professor Archduke: Knights of Jeneve agent operating on Dellah, and a specialist in Obscure Theatrical Forms under the Literary Department. The

Theatrology Department rejected his application.

Hugo Gamaliel: Gamaliel laundered money from drug rings, illegal gambling and pornography to fund his campaigns.

Newark Rappare: Murdered art forger who expertly copied the *Mona Lisa* (ironically, "City of Death" establishes it was already a fake). He was also Professor of Art History at St. Oscar's.

Nicholas Clyde: Knights of Jeneve agent, hailed as a Hugo Gamaliel expert and lecturer. Clyde allegedly finished his doctorate at Kai-Tec. His true allegiances crushed his friendship with Benny.

Mastrov (a.k.a. Truby Kamadrich): Cybernetic assassin for Nusek, capable of tracking an individual's heat signature.

PLACES TO GO

Braxiatel's Office (St. Oscar's University): It's shielded from "just about all" forms of surveillance and attack, meaning it's likely his TARDIS.

Stanturus System: The Stanturus system has four planets, but only Stanturus Three is naturally inhabitable. Two of the other worlds were terraformed with colonies. Stranturus Three has flesh-eating steggodons.

STUFF YOU NEED

The Gamalian Dragons (a.k.a. The Dragons of Jeneve): The original Gamalian Dragon, a jeweled fire-breathing dragon statuette, served as the Knights of Jeneve's emblem. More important, it was the failsafe encrypter/decrypter for their information horde. An elite group of Knights, named the Dragon Knights, protected the Dragon but Henri of Bosarno killed them and took it. Henri died shortly thereafter, and the real Dragon wound up in his tomb. (*See History*).

However, Hugo Gamaliel had been allowed to capture a copy of the Dragon, constructed with surveillance equipment to spy on his activities. It could record two years' worth of information. The lead-lined copy also concealed the thermonuclear bomb hidden inside, designed to eliminate Gamaliel when needed. However, the Knights, not knowing the location of the real Dragon, feared blowing up Gamaliel's copy. Until this story, the false Dragon was on display in Nusek's Castle of Ice and Fire on Tharn.

ORGANIZATIONS

The Knights of Jeneve (a.k.a. The Knights of Geneve): Initially, Earth President Vazlov Baygent

CHARACTER PROFILE

IRVING BRAXIATEL

Irving Braxiatel, despite being the most likeable Time Lords you'll ever meet, is also a highly respected academic with an intellect capable of crossing swords with the seventh Doctor (and that's saying a lot). Here, back by popular demand, is your fast-and-easy guide to Braxiatel's appearances in Virgin's "Doctor Who" New and Missing Adventures:

• **LEGACY**—First mention of Time Lord Irving Braxiatel and his Braxiatel Collection, a "famous collection of everything" and home to all types of research.

• **THEATRE OF WAR**—First full appearance of Braxiatel and the Braxiatel Collection. Benny meets Braxiatel for the first time (from her point of view). First mention of *The Good Soldiers*, a long lost play of which Braxiatel owns the only surviving copy.

• **THE EMPIRE OF GLASS**—In a story that predates his Braxiatel Collection days, Braxiatel magnanimously founds the Armageddon Convention in Venice, 1609, to mediate arms treaties between alien races. Braxiatel conscripts the first Doctor to serve as Convention Chairman, but a series of mishaps allows Shakespeare to gain futuristic data and endanger history. The Doctor wipes the information from Shakespeare's memory, but Braxiatel decides arms negotiation is too dangerous and favors collecting as a safer hobby. This book also reveals Braxiatel as founder of the Library of St. John the Beheaded (*All-Consuming Fire*), a repository of forbidden knowledge.

• **HAPPY ENDINGS**—Braxiatel attends Benny's wedding to Jason Kane, telling her that it's fortunate she's an archaeologist because, "The older [Jason] gets, the more interested in him you'll be."

founded the Knights as a military brotherhood in the third quarter of the 23rd century, just as human-controlled space recuperated from the first of the intergalactic wars. Baygent feared future wars and constructed the Knights to keep secret databases and preserve humanity's knowledge. He named the group the Knights of Geneve, although the term was later corrupted to the "Knights of Jeneve." In time, the Knights' goals became corrupted, with information hoarded as political weapons. The Knight's secret, formal valediction is "Knowledge above all."

HISTORY Vazlov Baygent, a surprisingly popular president who founded the Knights of Jeneve, was heavily criticized for his plan to make the presidency hereditary and was assassinated in 2276. The Knights protected his son and eliminated those responsible for Baygent's murder.

• Near the end of the 24th century, corporate boss Hugo Gamaliel became a local dictator, ripping many colonies from Earth control so his corporation could avoid paying huge taxes. He began crushing campaigns against the Knights in the Jeneve, culminating in the Battle of Bocaro (a.k.a. Bosarno). The Knights deliberately threw the battle (with Gamaliel becoming credited for the non-existent "Gamalian Gambit" strategy) and went underground to continue their work unimpeded.

• By discrediting Nusek, the Knights successfully soiled Gamaliel's name and those of his potential successors.

AT THE END OF THE DAY A solid work, but as with *Oh No It Isn't!*, much stronger as an individual book than part of a line. Richards sensibly approaches *Dragons' Wrath* with a sense of history and archaeology—logical enough, given Benny, an archaeologist, serves as the lead character. But while *Dragons' Wrath* succeeds with a myriad of characters and plots, it doesn't, as the No. 2 Benny book, redirect the Benny line so it's workable for newcomers. That said, there are some tremendous, humbling moments for Benny—especially when she realizes that Nusek recruited her because she's only an average archaeologist.

BEYOND THE SUN

By Matthew Jones

Release Date: July 1997
Order: Benny New Adventure #3
(Who NA #64)

MAIN CHARACTERS Bernice Summerfield and Emile Mars-Smith.

TRAVEL LOG Planets Apollox 4 and Ursu, 2593.

STORY SUMMARY Benny takes two of her students, Emile and Tameka, to the Chelonian digs on Apollox 4, where her ex-husband Jason Kane shows up with a female figurine alleged to be part of an ancient weapon. Benny responds with heavy skepticism, then worries when strangers kidnap Jason from his hotel room.

Benny examines Jason's figurine and traces it to the restricted world of Ursu. After securing a freelance spaceship, Benny, Emile and Tameka arrive in Ursu orbit, but black ships belonging to the op-

THE CRUCIAL BITS...

• **BEYOND THE SUN**—Jason Kane returns to Benny's life after an eight month absence. First appearance of student Emile Mars-Smith.

pressive Sunless race shoot them down. Benny, Emile and Tameka find the Sunless have conquered Ursu and located the Blooms, genetic pods that birth new Ursulans in groups of eight. However, the Blooms were actually stolen long ago from the dying Sunless homeworld, leading to the Sunless' aggression.

Benny's trio evades the oppressive Sunless and meets Scott, a friendly Ursulan who was oddly born into a family of ten. Tameka and Scott become lovers while Benny locates Scott's sister Iranda, a ruthless collector of powerful artifacts and Jason's partner in crime. Unfortunately, Scott's brother Michael tries to gain clemency for Scott by betraying Benny's group to the Sunless.

The aliens take their captives to the dying Sunless homeworld, barely heated by its red star. Benny reunites with the captured Jason, even as Iranda reveals that the Ursulan Blooms, besides their capacity for reproduction, can also manipulate a star's destructive energies and generate "power beyond the sun." Iranda suspects Jason's female figurine, together with Iranda's male figurine, are encoded keys that will activate the Blooms' full potential. However, Benny deduces that the figurines are purely symbolic. Iranda and her brother Nikolas are the actual keys, specifically encoded biological triggers generated by the Blooms themselves (explaining why Iranda's family has 10 siblings rather than the normal eight).

Nikolas, answering his biological imperative, submits to the Blooms even as Benny forces a protesting Iranda inside. The Blooms activate, but instead of being a stellar weapon, they channel energy to revitalize the Sunless' dying star. Benny, Jason and their allies flee in Iranda's spaceship, knowing the Sunless will return to their restored homeworld and withdraw from Ursu.

Later, Tameka finds she's pregnant with Scott's child, even as Emile admits he's gay and takes Scott as a lover. Benny, failing to reconcile with Jason, returns to St. Oscar's and ponders her being a woman of peace in a Universe of violence.

MEMORABLE MOMENTS Benny, desperately trying to get help for pilot Errol, tries to force a doctor named Jock to help. Jock refuses, even with the threat of death, saying his freedom is all-important. When Benny lets Jock go, the doctor agrees to help as an ultimate display of self-will.

Benny claims she'd rather spend time with an ancient toilet than with Jason. Tameka, driving like a mad woman, off-handedly hollers people aside with "Lady with a baby!" (rather ironic, since she's pregnant).

SEX AND SPIRITS Benny and Jason, still separated, indulge in hot sex for old times' sake.

Jason met Iranda on Denaria 7 and spent months travelling with her. Benny's never sure, but Jason and Iranda almost undoubtedly became lovers. Tameka and Scott have sex on a balcony and she gets preggers. Emile discovers he's gay, shagging Scott.

In the finest collegiate tradition, a pair of drunken students fall atop a sleeping Benny and gave into their passion. (Benny crawled out from beneath them and slept in the wash house.)

ASS-WHUPPINGS Benny pushes Iranda into the Blooms, killing her. Emile does in a Sunless' head with a pipe. The Sunless killed more than half the Ursu population, often by savage beatings. Collaborating Ursulans beat their fellows to death. The Sunless slay Benny's hired pilot Errol and a doctor, Jock, for helping the enemy. The Sunless kidnap Jason and beat him bloody. Tameka accidentally slugs Bernice.

NOVEL TIE-INS Life-growing Blooms, used to generate clones, also appeared in *Happy Endings*. Bernice and company here explore a Chelonian (*The Highest Science*) dig.

Benny adapts the Doctor's mantra (*Timewyrm: Revelation*) and writes of herself: "Bernice Summerfield is a human being. And as such she is all too capable of being cruel and cowardly. And yet, while she is often caught up in violent events, she endeavors to remain a woman of peace."

Beyond the Sun further discusses Marcus Krytell, chairman of the Krytell Corporation, who plays a larger role in *Ship of Fools*.

Tameka's child and Emile Mars-Smith return in *Deadfall*. Explorer Franz Kryptosa, famous for his own programs and product endorsement, vanished about 100 years ago. *Down* explains Kryptosa's fate. The Butler Project (*Deceit*) indexed the records of companies that bankrupted during Earth's recent war.

CHARACTER DEVELOPMENT

Bernice Summerfield: Outspoken Benny's the only archaeology member objecting to budget cuts. She's unique for regarding her students as actual human beings. She's frequently late for class.

Benny long ago decided that there was no "secret of life"—everything you need to know can be seen. She plays chess, but Emile frequently beats her. Benny has some piloting skills and knows rudimentary first aid. She's very familiar with late 20th century rocks. She can dance (loosely). The idea of a society without rules seduced her until she saw the Sunless oppression on Ursu. She's not familiar with the alien language rendered on Jason's female figurine.

Benny considers calling her next work *Down Among the Dead Men Again*. She spent the book's advance ages ago. She enjoys living at St. Oscar's.

Jason Kane: Jason now wears his hair longer. He still cries in his sleep like a hurt child, but Benny can't make out what he's saying.

Benny and Jason: They haven't seen each other for eight months. After their divorce (*Eternity Weeps*), Benny mistakenly thought she'd never want to see Jason again, but still loves him. Benny's about the only person who regards Jason enough to do him a favor. Yet, she insists they shouldn't start seeing each other again.

Emile Mars-Smith: A budding homosexual, desperate to escape his oppressive father. He blindly chose archaeology as his major because "archaeology" was alphabetically listed first in the St. Oscar's catalog.

Tameka: Tameka can hot-wire certain vehicles and has some advanced driving skills.

ALIEN RACES

The Sunless: The Sunless are strong, but not fast. They clamp down on their emotions, believing fear and anger slows them up. They're so private, it makes them paranoid. It's possible the Blooms originally birthed the Sunless as servants to the Bloom-makers.

Ursulans: Ursulans emerge as half-grown children from the Blooms in families of eight, one member for each of Ursu's eight species. Oolian children have avian traits, while others are more reptilian/saurian. Mixed ancestry is possible. Ursulans enjoy sex, but can't reproduce naturally with each other (Tameka's pregnancy by the Ursulan Scott suggests Ursulan females are sterile).

ALIEN PLANETS *Ursu* originated as a human colony that over-expanded and was falling apart. Before the Sunless arrived, a group of bored, wealthy colonists indulged themselves and left needed work undone.

PLACES TO GO *Apollox 4*, a former Chelonian slave camp, is now symbolic of the human struggle against alien aggression. It has little real archaeological value, so students frequently explore the site. The V15 Sector lies between Apollox 4 and Dellah.

STUFF YOU NEED

Down Among the Dead Men: Benny's first book focuses on "cancer, capitalism, space shuttles and safer sex."

The Blooms: Clam-like devices that produce new Ursulans in oxygen-rich liquid (*See History*).

ORGANIZATIONS *Krytell Corporation:* One of the biggest, most corrupt companies in the sector, hiring Emile's dad as a communications engineer.

HISTORY Before the Galactic War, several companies plundered the Sunless homeworld, taking many artifacts, technologies, great weapons and most important, the Blooms. The Sunless in turn killed their oppressors and incorporated their technology. The Sunless scoured the galaxy for the Blooms, growing more oppressive with every step. Eight races settled on Ursu to escape their wrath, but the Sunless conquered Ursu and burnt villages to the ground when the inhabitants didn't comply with dress codes. The Sunless also restricted travel and didn't patronize the arts. Deserting your job earned you a Sunless death sentence.

AT THE END OF THE DAY One of the most mature and emotion charged Benny books, *Beyond the Sun* unveils as a curious story of sexuality (the Blooms, Emile becomes sexually realized, the snooty Tameka tempers herself and gets pregnant). It's a story in which Tameka and Emile adopt Benny's survival skills, just as Benny once grew under the Doctor's tutorage. All this, plus Jones' chest-clenching inter-personal style, makes this book a strong stand-alone Benny novel.

SHIP OF FOOLS

By Dave Stone

Release Date: August 1997
Order: Benny New Adventure #4
(Who NA #65)

MAIN CHARACTERS Bernice Summerfield.

TRAVEL LOG St. Oscar's University and the *Titanian Queen*, 2593.

STORY SUMMARY The famed thief named Cat's Paw robs ultra-rich industrialist Marcus Krytell and steals an Olabrian joy-luck crystal, a rare artifact for which the hostile Olabrians will commit mass murder and havoc to recover. Worried about possible retribution, Krytell asks archaeologist Benny to perform the ransom exchange for him, slated to take place during the maiden voyage of the luxury space-liner *Titanian Queen*. But as the *Titanian Queen* gets underway, murders ranging from death by puffer fish poison to spasm-inducing music eliminate several passengers.

Benny unmasks Cat's Paw as the harmless-looking passenger Isabel Blaine, but believes Blaine is only a thief, not a murderer. Furthermore, Benny discovers Krytell Industries built the *Titanian Queen* from shoddy parts, designing it to crash and thereby rake in millions from an insurance scheme. Even worse, Krytell's shoveling in a fortune by offing the *Titanian Queen* passengers, most of them targets of various contract hits.

Benny pegs the *Titanian Queen* murderer as ARVID, the ship's artificial intelligence. Oddly enough ARVID's programming contains the synthetic personality of a pulp villain named Doctor Po, who intends to smash the *Titanian Queen* into an asteroid and insure none of the passengers survive. Cat's Paw helpfully hooks ARVID up to the joy-luck crystal, thereby scrambling Doctor Po's intelligence with the crystal's disruptive music waves. Soon after, a passing ship rescues the *Titanian Queen*'s passengers, but the ship itself crashes into an asteroid.

After enduring a series of misadventures, Benny makes her way back to Dellah and enjoys drinks with Irving Braxiatel. Cat's Paw, acting out of vengeance for Krytell's various schemes, returns his joy luck crystal and informs Olabrian authorities of its location. As Krytell reads Cat's Paw's note to this end, his ears hear the chilling sound of approaching Olabrian battle cruisers.

SEX AND SPIRITS Jason Kane's hooked up with a foxy-looking female associate named Mira, who may or may not be his lover (future books establish they're not screwing). Benny gets decently hammered at a pub called The Pit. (Men shadowing her remark: "If they gave prizes out to piss-artists her mantelpiece would collapse under the weight.") Benny drinks a two-liter bottle of Elysian Mescal with the good bit of the cactus left in, and gets drunk again at dinner.

ASS-WHUPPINGS Aboard the *Titanian Queen*, ARVID offs at least 30 of the passengers, with bodies variously found taxidermied, stewing in seafood *bouillabaisse*, garroted, blown apart by puffer fish poison, eaten alive by small mammals (possibly hamsters) and smothered in chocolate. (For the full death buffet, check out *Ship of Fools'* alarmingly detailed Chapter 15.)

Jason sports a huge purple bruise on his face and powder burns mark his skin.

TV TIE-INS Doctor Po's Chinese time cabinet, shown in a flashback scene, is not Weng-Chiang's time machine ("The Talons of Weng-Chiang"). Braxiatel owns a watch from the Silurian period of prehistoric Earth ("The Silurians").

NOVEL TIE-INS *Oh No It Isn't!* first mentioned the entrepreneur Marcus Krytell. Benny's bail-out of Jason (*Beyond the Sun*) heavily depleted her credit. *Ship of Fools* represents the first Benny NA mention of the Doctor (if you can call it that), when Inspector Carstairs asks if Benny's "...yet another minion under the employ of the fiendish Doctor?" and she freaks.

Militarism on Czhanos (Stone's *Death and Diplomacy*) has died out, but the former war-based hierarchy influenced the Czhan language by introducing archaic insults into everyday speech.

We briefly encounter Raan, the Hideous Evil Slimy Shapeshifter of Utter and Unmitigated Evil from Dimension X (Stone's *Sky Pirates!*).

Benny has a review copy of *Lost Gods and the Fall of Empire* by Franz Kryptosa, an "archaeological parasite" mentioned in *Beyond the Sun* and who appears in *Down*.

Cat's Paw represents an artificial lifeform of the same type as the unnamed Stratum Seven agent (Stone's *The Mary-Sue Extrusion* and *Return to the Fractured Planet*).

CHARACTER DEVELOPMENT

Bernice Summerfield: Benny doesn't think about her time with the Doctor much, perhaps healing over old scars. She can identify people from the 20th century by their poise and language structures. She's seen many red giants.

Benny can recognize, but not speak, Stromabulan language from the Arion Ring. On the *Titanian Queen*, she pretends to be Bernice Summersdale, a loaded widow. She possesses data wafers with all extant songs from the 18th through mid 21st centuries. She also owns a compendium of early 20th century writers such as Woolfe, Bell, Arliss and Kinky Friedman.

There are 17 other people in the sector better qualified than Benny to act as Krytell's couriers, but they were otherwise engaged. One also suspects Krytell hired Benny for the doomed *Titanian Queen* mission because he viewed her as expend-

TOP 5

BENNY BOOKS DRAMATIC MOMENTS

1) Christine Summerfield's identity revealed (Dead Romance)—Imagine you were a clone, bred purely for sacrifice, and the person you trusted most was assigned to murder you. Bottle-in-a-Bottle resident Christine Summerfield learns the earthshaking truth about her origins in the most dramatic of fashions—standing in a construction site where her lover, Chris Cwej, is holding a knife and standing over a body.

2) Braxiatel evacuates St. Oscar's University (Where Angels Fear)—Irving Braxiatel: Time Lord, manipulator and unflappable academic. But when the Dellan gods wrack St. Oscar's, Braxiatel's strategic withdrawal proves none of our heroes are safe.

3) Benny kills Jason Kane, then herself (Tears of the Oracle)—Well, almost. When a possessed and physically degenerating shapeshifter in the form of Jason Kane attacks Benny, she grabs a lamp and caves in his head her, then attempts suicide when the mental parasite possesses her instead.

4) Benny and Jason talk about their divorce (Oblivion)—One of the novel line's most candid discussions, in which both Benny and Jason admit to the flaws and poor judgement calls that led to their split.

5) Christine Summerfield saves the world with rock-scissors-paper (Dead Romance)—It also ranks as a comedy moment, but Christine Summerfield's inspired challenge to "the Horror," a Vortex-spawned beast who'll destroy everything if it wins, keeps you on the edge of your seat.

able. It's never stated, but perhaps there's also a contract on her life.

Bernice and Jason Kane: A GalNet number protected by an elaborate, expensive security system allows Benny to contact Jason. He gives Benny a package to make her feel better, but she doesn't open it.

Irving Braxiatel: He supplied Catan Nebula and its famed development industries with some historical research.

Cat's Paw (a.k.a. Isabel Blaine): A successful, flamboyant, master thief with a particular penchant for jewelry, Cat's Paw hasn't killed anybody and is a master of disguise. She employs a gun with Catan nanonites (*See Stuff You Need*).

Cat's Paw originated as an artificial assassin, constructed in the Catan Nebula (*See Places To Go*), programmed with a false personality that said her mystical overlord father killed her mother. In such a history, Cat's Paw in turn tried to assassinate her father, so he used his magics to send her through time. Cat's Paw eventually broke such programming, becoming truly self-aware and self-motivated.

"The Fiendish Doctor Po"/ARVID: Another artificial personality, created by Catan Nebula laboratories, programmed as a cracked 1930s villain.

Marcus Krytell: One of the sector's richest men, and an industrialist with an installation on every planet that has shoddy environmental laws. Krytell's family has a lengthy history of dying violently (trust me, we can't list it here), so an elaborate security system protects him. He's the last of his family, who've only been rich for the last few generations. His father gave him his first million for being a big boy and using the water closet.

Nathanael C. Nerode: Salesman of wholesale Goblanian bog seal blubber.

ALIEN PLANETS *Dellah:* Dellah's seas are similar to pre-pollution Earth: temperate, salty and fecund. Dellah lacks significant moons, preventing violent tidal surges and seasons that churn the waters to keep them fresh. Dellah lies closer to the Galactic Hub than Earth, so it's still a backwater on the edge of the known universe. Shakya constellation is the brightest constellation visible from Dellah's southern hemisphere.

PLACES TO GO *Catan Nebula:* Area with famed research facilities, ranging from genetics to propulsion but specializing in vat-grown synthetic humanoids (Cat's Paw and the Stratum Seven agent from *The Mary-Sue Extrusion* share these origins). Each synthoid starts life as a custom-made blank, mindless template, into which nanonetic microspores are injected to give them a working approximation of intelligence, personality and memory. The synthoids operate with a lifetime of pre-programmed memories, typically made to think they were hurled through time or some-such to explain their sudden "awakening" in a new culture. Some synthoids such as Cat's Paw and the Stratum Seven agent accepted their true origins and attained a new level of self-awareness.

Krytell Industries keeps an Advanced Genetics division here that hybridizes dogs.

STUFF YOU NEED

Olabrian joy-luck crystals: A series of complex, interlocking lattice-globes of quasi-living crystal, hewn from the heart of Olabria's satellite. The Olabrians contemplate the crystals, renowned throughout their sector for their peace and tranquility. The crystals are harder than diamond, but their assembly's very delicate.

Catan nanoites: Syringe loaded nanoites, tailored with a fabricated personality that wipes out a person's true persona.

SHIPS *Titanian Queen:* Luxury liner destroyed making its maiden voyage through the Proximan Chain. The *Titanian Queen* incorporated Command Technology from the Catan Nebula's famed research and development facilities. Captain Fletcher Iolanthe Crane commands. Thelon Bates serves as Harbor Master (yes, yes, make the cliched joke).

HISTORY The alien Thraal once unwittingly crashed into a small garden of Olabrian joy-luck crystals, offending the Olabrians to the point of waging a centuries-long war that annihilated the Thraal and their planet. Olabria subsequently poured its resources into creating a fleet of dreadnoughts, each capable of destroying a sun, to protect their crystals.

AT THE END OF THE DAY A book that's downright hysterical in parts but makes the sad mistake of whipping a joke to death until the reader becomes battered and bloody. We're hardly prudes, but the insult-flinging Khaarli, for example, becomes a one-trick pony you desperately wish would shut up. Also, it's hard to take the main villain—the fiendish Doctor Po—very seriously when he's a caricature straight from the Golden Age of comic books, so the revelation that he's the killer really doesn't do much. If *Ship of Fools* were presented solely as a farce, it might fare better, but parts of it *do* ask to be taken seriously, throwing off its drama/comedy mix and becoming an example of how sometimes the authors have so much fun, they forget we'd like to also.

DOWN

By Lawrence Miles

Release Date: September 1997
Order: Benny New Adventure #5
(Who NA #66)

MAIN CHARACTERS Bernice Summerfield.

TRAVEL LOG Tyler's Folly, January 14, 2594.

STORY SUMMARY On the surface of Tyler's Folly, a small colony world, oppressive Republican Security Forces pull Benny from the sea and listen to her claims of the planet's uncharted, prehistoric world...

Two of Benny's students, Ash and Lucretia, discover in a Dellan market a lost journal of F. Nils Kryptosa, a somewhat respectable explorer who claimed the planet Tyler's Folly was hollow and perhaps served as the source of all Inner World myths. Soon after, the SSSSSSS, a neo-Nazi group seeking more information on Kryptosa's expedition, kidnaps Lucretia. Benny and Ash hotly pursue their friend to the land within Tyler's Folly.

There, they meet Mr. Misnomer, the superstrong central character of many pulp fiction stories. They also find Lucretia with SSSSSSS leader Kommander Katastrophen, who's seeking the immortality granting Pool of Life and the race of purebred Aryan supergiants who made it. However, Benny senses Katastrophen's full of self-doubt and isn't fully committed to his Nazi ideals.

A tribe of Tyler's Folly barbarians decimates the SSSSSSS forces, but Mr. Misnomer seizes a gun and wipes out the attackers. With a few SSSSSSS survivors, Benny's group encounters the apelike Tribe of Lilith and their god MEPHISTO, a giant computer that resides within the hollow sun in the Inner World.

MEPHISTO, needing human ideas and concepts to thrive, tries to mentally absorb Benny's group but Mr. Misnomer activates MEPHISTO's self-destruct. Benny's party flees in the tribe's dirigible as MEPHISTO explodes, sending the airship out of control. Mr. Misnomer steers the airship long enough for Benny, Ash and Lucretia to bail out and escape to the surface, but Misnomer crashes and dies as a result...

Benny finishes her story to the Republican Forces, just as !X, an insane member of the People sent by the supercomputer God to observe these events, frees her.

Benny confesses her story contained certain falsehoods—truths she emotionally couldn't handle. Mr. Misnomer was indeed a fictional character, included in Benny's story to conceal the fact that Benny, not Misnomer, slaughtered the primitives. Mr. Misnomer variously substituted for Kommander Katastrophen too, as Benny couldn't accept that a repentant, noble Nazi would sacrifice his life in the airship so Benny's group could live.

!X explains how an ancient race whose metaphors and key ideas were converted into reality created MEPHISTO as a metaphysical idea, not a computer. As a concept, MEPHISTO represented doubt and uncertainty—the need for mankind to feel pain, even in a utopia. !X, fully in MEPHISTO's thrall, tries to kill Benny and thus creates a scenario where Benny can kill !X in self-defense, thereby turning MEPHISTO's pain-filled archetype into reality and tainting the Universe with MEPHISTO's anti-utopia manifesto. Realizing this, Benny shoves !X's weapon up his ass, demonstrating Benny's general sentiment for such philosophical problems. Their work done, Benny, Ash and Lucretia depart for St. Oscar's.

Nonetheless, on the People's Worldsphere, the supercomputer God looks on, pleased at having manipulated events to make MEPHISTO emerge, knowing MEPHISTO's philosophy of pain in utopia will aid the People's own development.

MEMORABLE MOMENTS Benny's passionate rebuke of the "academic" neo-Nazis, arguing they only study alien cultures to better conquer them, puts a lump in the throat. She hilariously attempts to sprint to safety in the dark (an SSSSSSS *doktor* comments: "It sounded, Mein Kommander, like someone running into a metal wall at high velocity. Ja?"). It begs a smile when the barbarians attack the SSSSSSS troops with exploding shellfish. Best of all, when Benny shoves !X's weapon up his anal cavity, it's one of the series' most wrong, wrong and damn clever moments.

SEX AND SPIRITS Benny gets decently drunk and pukes. She won the St. Oscar's Drinking Society Award for Spectacularly Inept Inebriated Bar-Fighting on New Year's Eve, 2593. Ash and Lucretia had sex once.

ASS-WHUPPINGS Benny, not Mr. Misnomer, rifles down an attacking group of cavemen. Kommander Katastrophen sacrifices his life to save Benny, Ash and Lucretia. Most of his crew fall in battle with cavemen who throw exploding shellfish. MEPHISTO's re-birth devastates the Inner World of Tyler's Folly, including the Tribe of Lilith.

The Republican Security Force tortures Benny for information. A mutant dragonfly sucks blood from her, and a bat bites her arm.

NOVEL TIE-INS *The Also People* introduced the People and their guiding supercomputer God. !X is not the same as a drone from that book of the same name. At an unspecified point in *The Also People*, God slyly programmed Benny to join the St. Oscar's staff (*The Dying Days*), insuring she'd be close to Tyler's Folly and one day release MEPHISTO. *Where Angels Fear* also suggests God wanted Benny as his agent to monitor the dormant gods on Dellah. God openly recruited Benny as his agent in *Oh No It Isn't!* (God has other agents close to her.) *Walking to Babylon* further explores the fallout of the People's last war.

Benny here meets neo-Nazis but the genuine article tortured her in *Just War*. Benny jokes about calling her sequel book *Fear and Sloathes in Las Vegas* (*Sky Pirates!*).

Beyond the Sun first mentioned archaeologist Kryptosa, born on Ordifica (*Ghost Devices*, *Interference*). Scientist-explorers such as Gustav Urnst (*The Highest Science*) influenced Kryptosa.

The Piglet People of Glomi IV (*Death and Diplomacy*, *Burning Heart*) marketed T-Shirts with the words "Yes Boy Ice-Cream"—the words human tourists most use—even though the Piglet People have no idea what the words mean.

The full name of Benny's boss is cited as Professor Divson Follett (*Tears of the Oracle*).

CHARACTER DEVELOPMENT

Bernice Summerfield: "Dellah Terminus," an online service, says that whatever Benny's location, there's a 19/20 chance of a fight starting. Benny recognizes but can't read grave robber script. She carries an all-purpose medipac with plasters and antiseptic ointment. She's seen "Sesame Street." Fascist insanity is one of her specialist studies (probably from her adventures with the Doctor).

MEPHISTO: Germinated by an ancient race, MEPHISTO exists as a concept, the epitome of "dystopia." However, it needed certain aesthetic conditions to fully manifest. In other words, it needed this adventure, which Benny, !X (representing some measure of ugliness), Kryptosa and many others participated in. On Tyler's Folly, MEPHISO was partly biomass and seemed the size of an archaeology facility. It spoke through a projected smiley face.

Franz Nils Kryptosa: Explorer who wrote *In Search of Ancient Mu, A Short Trip to the Centre of Creation*. He was surprisingly talented as Meis-

THE CRUCIAL BITS...

• **DOWN**—The People's early history detailed. Retcon establishes that God brainwashed Benny into joining the St. Oscar's staff, planning for the day when she'd release MEPHISTO.

ter of Natural Sciences at New Heidelberg University, so naturally, most scholars hated him. He created and merged with the Tyler's Folly archetype (*See History*) and gained extended life as an ephemeral being in the Pool of Life.

!X (a.k.a. si!Xist-i!xatl-iVa!qara): Unique among the People because he responds to threats with violence, the dangerously unstable !X removed himself from People society and therefore isn't accountable to the People-Time Lord Treaty. He's hairless, pale, and physically looks 50-ish. Hormone and pheromone control grant him some degree of empathy. He has biological and mechanical parts. He sometimes employs cytotoxins that explode blood vessels and razor victims' DNA so harshly, not even the People's reconstructive surgery can mend the scars.

Mr. Misnomer (a.k.a. "The Man of Chrome"): Famed pulp story hero—muscular, with a jutting jaw. Melbourne Autolits drafted a character profile on Misnomer in 2533. He never hits a woman, only kills in self-defense, arms himself only with a grappling-hook bolt projector and physically looks 50-ish (Misnomer learned meditation techniques from the Dying Ones of New Tibet that slowed his metabolism—allegedly, he's 96).

Misnomer's stories include "The Queen of Xenophobia," "The Fall of the House of Mr. Misnomer," "The Underwater Bears" and "The Thousand-Fathom Horror." "The Shadow of the Dying Ones" (2529) showed him crashlanding on a journey to Nepal 36. Misnomer's super-strong, able to withstand temperature extremes. His enemies include the villainous Doktor Wilhelm Fetisch. He has no first name.

God: God, the People's super-computer, engineered the creation of MEPHISTO by faking Kryptosa's journal, knowing Benny would find it, and giving the SSSSSSS the location of the Inner World. God can speak to various People through subdermal implants.

ALIEN RACES

The People: The powerful People have no concept of "threat." They don't force treatment on anyone and have trans-galaxial travel. Like the Tribe of Lilith, they believe transmats "kill" users.

Tyler's Folly Colonists: Are human-ish, having adapted to the planet's erratic weather conditions.

Buffo Frogs: Curious species in the interior of Tyler's Folly, likely force-bred, that can inflate their throats with gas and fly.

ALIEN PLANETS *Tyler's Folly:* Colony world located 17 galaxies from the People's Worldsphere and eight to nine light years from Dellah. Tyler's Folly orbits the Cygnus Mortis constellation's most obscure star, miles away from useful travel routes. The Republican Security Force declared many regions off-limits, but non-manforms occupy the "Dying Swan" sector. Port Lindenbrook spaceport services the planet. The surface has Earth-type gravity and a low-level post-nuclear society with the death penalty. It's also quite moist—the surface is 92 percent water.

The planet's interior has a bright orange sun, with funnel-shaped gravity matrices that lead back to the surface. Dinosaur life and exploding shellfish flourish there, plus the Tribe of Lilith. Everything appears to be bio-engineered—hell, even the rocks have no electrons. Some plant life there has no DNA.

PLACES TO GO

Xan Burrosa: The marketplace on Dellah, where vendors dupe young archaeology students into thinking they've found lost artifacts.

The Cathedral of MEPHISTO: As a safety measure, MEPHISTO's dwelling lies outside normal space-time, in the inner sun of Tyler's Folly.

STUFF YOU NEED *Grave-robber script:* A disused 23rd century script, used by nefarious archaeologists to leave messages for each other.

ORGANIZATIONS

Worldsphere Interest Groups: Include the Unusual Psychopharmacy Interest Group and the Department of [Entirely Optional] Corrections (a.k.a Do[EO]C), Truth Through Ugliness, Tiny but Interesting, Health and Safety, the Strange and Painful Biological Problems.

Stella Stora Sigma Schutz-Staffel SturmSoldaten (a.k.a. the SSSSSSS): The most ineffective neo-Nazi group since the Outer Hebridean National Party. A small sausage factory on Smarley's World, about 400 light years from Tyler's Folly, serves as the SSSSSSS power base. The SSSSSSS and other fascist groups use the *oktika*, an eight armed "crooked cross," as their emblem. The SSSSSSS

TOP 5

BENNY BOOKS COMEDY MOMENTS

1) Benny shoves a gun up !X's ass (Down)—This is wrong, this is so wrong...oh God, our sides are splitting. Benny holsters a handgun up the rectum of the insane !X to prevent the Universe's dominant philosophy from rewriting itself (you'll have to read the Zen-like Down to make sense of this).

2) The Benny/Dent/Jason/Clarence sex antics (The Joy Device)—Benny yearns to bump uglies with adventure monger Dent Harper, so Jason and Clarence, still pining for our heroine, endlessly delay the would-be-lovers until they innocently fall asleep.

3) Jason Kane embarks on a pornography writing career (Beige Planet Mars)—...and gets rich writing swill such as the semi-autobiographical *Nights of the Perfumed Tentacle*.

4) The Titanian Queen death fest (Ship of Fools)—Aboard the murder-prone *Titanian Queen*, 30 passengers are found murdered, stewed in seafood *bouillabaisse*, blown apart by puffer fish poison, smothered in chocolate and blown into space through commodes.

5) Benny blows Trinity's cover (Beige Planet Mars)—Benny spontaneously recognizes her professional colleague Trinity as the war criminal Tellassar. Of course, Benny grasps this fact in the midst of giving a lecture on Mars, impulsively screaming out, "Oh my God! Trinity is Tellasar!", and causing pure mayhem.

believes they're descended from giants who once walked the Earth but were driven underground by a great calamity. The SSSSSSS uses at least 18 official hymns and the handbook *Mein Pantz* by Bernard Richtmanstances.

The Tribe of Lilith: Named after Adam's first wife, who reportedly didn't do Adam's bidding and got tossed out of Eden. Thirteen Elders, led by "Mother Lilith," lead the Tribe. They're essentially talking yeti, armed with gas-shooting needle weapons that suspend life functions. They keep fat leeches that heal wounds, then self-expire, plus bats force-bred for enhanced night vision. Lesser classes of the Tribe use transmat devices, but upper classes believe transmats actually create a copy and thereby kill the original user's soul.

SHIPS *SSSSSSS submarine* exteriors look like aquatic dinosaurs, capable of slipping through defenses using warp drive and landing in an ocean (Earth Central uses the same tactics).

PHENOMENA *Teleportaphobia (a.k.a. Molecular Vertigo)* is a psychological disorder that makes one afraid of teleporting for fear that their original body literally dies while a copy gets struck, creating a duplicate body and soul. Under this theory, a "death" occurs with every transport (meaning the "Star Trek" crews are completely screwed).

POSSIBLE HISTORY According to one story, the Seeders (a.k.a. the Ancient Godly Ones, and who knows, possibly the Time Lords) walked the pathways of time before time itself. Among the oldest civilizations, they allegedly seeded life on Dellah.

• The Time-and-Motion Lords are a rumored-to-exist secret society of high-powered businessmen, founded to monitor time-travel experiments and thereby protect the economy. If they existed, they may have hindered humanity from officially discovering time travel until the 50th century ("The Talons of Weng-Chiang").

HISTORY When the People were young, their metaphors were powerful enough to restructure reality and they created the first story of the Inner World. They also seeded the Universe with ideas, cultivating their stories across creation. "Dystopia" developed as a particularly powerful archetype—a nightmare of dysfunctional people and ideals. Millions of years ago, the idea took root on Tyler's Folly and reshaped the planet's interior. However, Tyler's Folly never evolved intelligent life, necessary for understanding such archetypes.

• Also during the Worldsphere's early history, the People put their mad (a.k.a. the Truly Crazed) on the separate continent of siCera!ca ri!Qisla. Surprisingly, the method worked and the cured People left. The only exception was !X, who refused treatment and tortured personologists who tried to help him. God therefore constructed Paradise, a separate universe, for !X.

• One hundred years ago, explorer Franz Kryptosa arrived on Tyler's Folly, following his suspicions that the planet had fueled Inner World stories, and the planet's inherent dystopia archetype latched onto him. Kryptosa's concepts reshaped the interior of Tyler's Folly into an MG-type environment with volcanoes, prehistoric monsters and ape people, all influenced by religious orthodoxy. Kryptosa literally became part of the environment, merging with the Pool of Life.

• Jodecai Tyler discovered Tyler's Folly circa 2533. Sixty years later, Tyler's Folly was hardly a success, but colonists there declared independence from Earth. The Republican Security Force staged a military coup, creating a police state.

• At the end of the 24th century, a genetically engineered plague halved Planet Sarah-361's population overnight. To force a procreative frenzy, the local prytaneium made monogamy a social sin, outlawed celibacy and instigated mandatory pornography. By 2571, the Repopulation Bureau drew up guidelines on what constituted good breeding stock. Those deemed unsuitable could undergo mutagenic enhancement surgery or become social lepers.

• Circa 2450, Earth administrators instigated a time-travel project named "Jonson's Engine." A research station at Vilencia Sixteen produced a fully functional time machine, but the station and half the planet blew up. After the Engine's destruction, bits of time technology turned up around the galaxy; the SSSSSSS found some and learned to make wormholes. They seeded their genetic data throughout history, trying to insure their superiority and retroactively prove their ancestry. As a result, entire planets on the galaxy's fringes now sprout blond-haired, blue-eyed humanoids.

• In the mid-2530s, KroyChem AgroMedical sponsored Melbourne Autolit Services and produced cancer-combat drugs.

• Thirty years ago in the Worldsphere's time, the People fought a war against insect aliens from C-Mita-C-Mita-Rho. Many of the People returned home scarred and murders broke out. The People now measure all other events by the War.

AT THE END OF THE DAY Easily the most surreal and oddball Benny book, *Down* deliciously alternates between hard drama, sly comedy and sarcasm. It deserves praise for taking risks and being so damn experimental, even if it consequently makes those who revere straightforward stories break out in hives. The way Benny subconsciously alters her memory at first proves implausible, but upon reflection, makes the novel. That, plus a ton of brave—if sometimes chiseled—ideas from Miles makes *Down* stand as a wryly clever book, even if it's best appreciated by Humanities students.

DEADFALL

By Gary Russell

Release Date: October 1997
Order: Benny New Adventure #6
(Who NA #67)

MAIN CHARACTERS Chris Cwej, Jason Kane and Emile Mars-Smith, with Bernice Summerfield and Irving Braxiatel.

TRAVEL LOG St. Oscar's University and unnamed planet, Ardethe system, 2594.

STORY SUMMARY Irving Braxiatel asks Benny to investigate a recent expedition that died exploring a world they falsely believed was the planet Ardethe. But before Benny departs, her ex-husband Jason Kane shows up and steals what he thinks is a data crystal containing Ardethe's location from Benny's pocket. Unfortunately, Jason instead snipes the mystery planet's position and speeds off into danger. Braxiatel and Benny conclude the machinistic Knights of Jeneve have hired Jason to recover something called "The Baygent Apotheosis," but for now can only sit, drink and worry.

Meanwhile, the spaceship *KayBee 2*, carrying political prisoners, arrives to salvage metal from the lost expedition. To the crew's surprise, they find a faked expedition site, but locate amid the "ruins" a comatose Chris Cwej, ex-Adjudicator and old friend of Jason and Benny. Jason arrives on the planet just as a strange, intangible force moves through various *KayBee 2* crewmen and makes their heads explode.

An amnesiac Chris wakes up and confronts *KayBee 2* doctor Njobe, an agent of the Knights of Jeneve. Njobe explains that the Knights are seeking a biologically compatible descendant of their founder, President Baygent—if successful, the Knights can download Baygent's preserved memories and DNA into the descendant and essentially restore Baygent to life. Tasked with such a mandate, the Knights created the Jithii—mental constructs that leap from host to host to scan for Baygent's descendants and terminate unsuitable candidates. The Knights captured Chris, one of Baygent's descendants, but Chris' latent psi abilities and former body beppling (*Original Sin*) made him unsuitable to host Baygent's consciousness. The Knights therefore gave Chris amnesia and left him on the unnamed planet to lure Chris' associates, hopefully Baygent-compatible beings.

Dr. Njobe sets the *KayBee 2*'s self-destruct to cover up the Knights' involvement, but Jason kills her. One of the Jithii tries to take over Chris, but his telepathic powers repel the invader and restore his memories. A Jithii retreats into prisoner Townsend's body, but Chris shoots them both dead. Another Jithii, having possessed security officer Cassius, gets blown into space.

Jason and Chris, with the surviving convicts, flee in a shuttle as the *KayBee 2* explodes. They return to Dellah, where Braxiatel arranges for new identities for the prisoners, victims of an oppressive political regime. However, Jason shocks

CHARACTER PROFILE

CHRIS CWEJ

Chris Cwej, stalwart member of the Order of Adjudication (think of them as "space cops" for lack of a better phrase). It's hard to say which characteristic defines Chris Cwej more: His fierce loyalty to his travelling companions—the Doctor and Roz Forrester—or his amazing ability to sire illegitimate children throughout time and space. Regardless, here's your guide to Chris' key "Doctor Who" novels:

• **ORIGINAL SIN**—On Earth, 2975, young Adjudicator Chris Cwej finds himself squired to the older, battle-weary Roz Forrester. Together, they investigate the seventh Doctor and Bernice Summerfield, who are implicated in the murder of an alien Hith. Chris and Roz clear the TARDIS crew but learn of corruption in the highest ranks of the Adjudication Order. Marked for death by their own organization, Chris and Roz take up residence in the TARDIS with the Doctor and Benny.

• **THE ALSO PEOPLE**—During a stopover on the People's Worldsphere, Chris strikes up a romance with a Person named Dep and sires a daughter named Ikrissi.

• **SLEEPY**—Chris revealed as latently telepathic.

• **HAPPY ENDINGS**—Chris romances 20-year-old Ishtar, formerly the vicious monster known as the Timewyrm, and impregnates her. Their daughter later shacks up with the immeasurably psionic Ricky McIlveen (*Warchild*) and produces the Eternal known as Time.

• **DAMAGED GOODS**—Chris shares some sack time with homosexual David Daniels, but they part afterward with a hug.

• **SO VILE A SIN**—The Doctor returns Chris and Roz to their own time, where the two Adjudicators side with Roz's sister Leabie in a revolution against Emperor Walid, the pawn of a psionic Brotherhood. Leabie's forces succeed, but Roz dies leading a final assault against Walid's fortress. Chris continues his journeys with the Doctor.

• **ETERNITY WEEPS**—Chris denies dying UNIT task force leader Liz Shaw a mercy-killing. Her final words, begging Chris for death, continue to haunt him.

• **LUNGBARROW**—The Doctor accepts a mission to retrieve the Master's remains, knowing it will likely result in his death. Chris parts with the Doctor's company, accepting a Time Lord time ring to travel on his own.

Benny by announcing he's going to marry convict Charlene Conner to help her get a new identity. (Ah, young love. It's so…commercial.)

SEX AND SPIRITS Jason Kane agrees to Charlene Connor's request for a marriage of convenience (ain't he a sweetheart?). Michael Doran, the student Benny *didn't* woo in *Oh No It Isn't!*, here tries to bed the Ootsoi student Toosa-eL. Benny's dealings with Braxiatel seem easy because she's not sexually attracted to him. Benny and the homosexual Emile platonically share a bed. Emile probably still likes the alien Scott (*Beyond the Sun*).

Benny spends most of *Deadfall* in the Witch and Whirlwind bar, either drinking scotch or Jack Daniel's with Jason or Braxiatel. Jason lip-locks Benny to nick her data crystal.

ASS-WHUPPINGS Jason kills Laurel Njobe, an agent of the Knights of Jeneve. Jason and Chris overload their blasters and destroy the artificial intelligence BABE. Chris blows away a comatose Marianne Townsend, who is possessed by a Jithii. There's also a decent amount of shootings, head snappings and electrocutions.

TV TIE-INS Harsh prison camps sometimes use a brainwashing technique called the Keller Principle ("The Mind of Evil") that buries personality and memories. The *Hyperion II*, undoubtedly a predecessor of the *Hyperion III* ("Terror of the Vervoids"), currently services the spacelanes.

NOVEL TIE-INS Benny and Jason last saw Chris in *Eternity Weeps*. Readers last saw him departing the Doctor's company as a time-travelling agent in *Lungbarrow*. Chris was body-beppled (e.g. given tailor made-body alterations) in *Original Sin* and discovered he was latently telepathic in *Sleepy*. Temporally speaking, Braxiatel still hasn't attended Benny's wedding (*Happy Endings*).

Student Tameka (*Beyond the Sun*) gave birth to a son, Jock. (Curiously, that adventure happened less than six months ago, meaning either Tameka or Jock's father Scott have a shortened gestation cycle.) Jock hasn't developed his father's green hair or scales and is named after a dead medic in *Beyond the Sun*. Emile Mars-Smith shared the Sunless adventure with Benny (also *Beyond the Sun*) and here crews with Jason. Kitzinger and Scott (*Beyond the Sun* again) are still on Ursu.

Benny rescued a lifesize Professor Nightshade cut-out (*Nightshade*) from a closing-down video shop in 2006, when the video boom died and video CDs were the rage.

Despite the probable fatality of founder Marcus Krytell (*Ship of Fools*), Krytell Science Foundation continues operating. Spinward Corporation (*Deceit*) operates in this timezone. Dr. Archduke

THE CRUCIAL BITS...

- **DEADFALL**—Chris Cwej debuts in the Benny New Adventures. Jason Kane agrees to a marriage of convenience with former prisoner Charlene Conner.

(*Dragons' Wrath*) remains the leading Earth Literature academic at St. Oscar's.

Prisoner Marianne Townsend could be related to Townsend, the Managing Director who appeared in Russell's *The Scales of Injustice* and died in *Business Unusual*.

CHARACTER DEVELOPMENT

Bernice Summerfield: Benny's lived at St. Oscar's University for nearly six months and is something of a poker shark. She also enjoys Twister (either winning or the actual twisting).

She's re-named her sequel book *Down Among the Dead Men – Slight Return*. The St. Oscar's publishing division says she's in breach of contract and want their advance returned. Benny, having spent the money on food and booze, insists they'll have to pump it out of her. To her confusion and dismay, a session with the college's medical center has allegedly been scheduled.

Benny and Jason: It's unclear if they're divorced or separated. Benny can contact Jason on his personal communicator. They wouldn't start dating again, but also wouldn't undo their marriage.

Chris Cwej: Chris' DNA matches Knights of Jeneve founder Baygent's by more than 92 percent. Chris' psi-powers protect his memories from being wiped completely, and destroy mental intruders such as the Jithii.

Irving Braxiatel: Braxiatel holds an unspecified but very important post at St. Oscar's. He's one of the few people Benny respects. Braxiatel teaches at least one class and always seems to be in his office. He prefers books over discs, crystals and other soulless devices. He hires prisoner Lisa DeJoine to be his assistant in the Shakespeare Building.

Charlene Connor: Jason's fiancée was a political prisoner serving a life sentence for supplying and taking sargol.

Emile Mars-Smith: Emile's father was less than pleased to learn his son was gay. Emile's mother died from cancer. Her husband persuaded her to become a Natural Path member, so she was buried with other Natural Path members on a small moon—an act she probably would've hated.

President Baygent: The Knights have located 249 of their founder's descendants.

ALIEN RACES The *Jithii*, being gaseous life-forms, are engineered in vats by the Knights of Jeneve to enter a host's body through the nervous system and attach to the cerebellum. They act as brain parasites, absorbing the host's personality entirely. Jithii aren't exceptionally controllable and sometimes kill the agents of the Knights.

ALIEN PLANETS *Ardethe:* Has three moons: Woodward, Dallin and Fahey, which is the largest. Ardethe's abnormal planetary system variously makes it the seventh or eighth planet from its sun, leading to its confusion with the Knights-seeded world where Chris was located (*See Places to Go*).

PLACES TO GO

Ardethe System: The Ardethe System normally has nine planets, but a tenth planet with blue rocks follows a 500 year elliptical path, sometimes coming between the third and fourth planet.

The Witch and the Whirlwind: Robarman Charlie X tends this St. Oscar's pub.

St. Oscar's D.H. Lawrence Building: Used by the English faculty.

STUFF YOU NEED

"Ripley's Believe it or FO": A television program (you can guess the focus), exceptionally popular among male college students.

Jason Kane's Tracking Device: A friend of Benny's (likely the Doctor) gave Jason a golfball-sized sphere with a black stud on top that can home in on Chris. It glows internally with a rhythmic pulse.

ORGANIZATIONS *The Natural Path* is a religious group with strict, antiquarian codes and morals.

SHIPS

Mother Fist: Jason Kane's new ship, which he gained in a bout of Twister (Jason won because the Mother Fist's original owner didn't have a nose).

KayBee 2: Also known as the *Gossamer Wing* and *Mister Kiss-Kiss Bang-Bang.*

HISTORY Nearly 600 years ago, "Mad Mags" (obviously a nickname for ex-Prime Minister Maggie Thatcher) took Earth to the brink of nuclear armageddon.

AT THE END OF THE DAY Not the keystone it could have been, given that Chris Cwej's amnesia negates his "return" and Benny's shuffled off to the side, leaving Jason to mostly carry the book—only he can't. The Knights of Jeneve conspiracy gradually makes sense, although the unseen, duplicitous nature of the mental Jithii constructs makes you wonder if the book even has a villain until sometime in the fourth quarter. All of this and more combines for a novel that's over-reliant on past Benny continuity (if you didn't understand Cwej before now, this ain't the place to learn).

GHOST DEVICES

By Simon-Bucher Jones

Release Date: November 1997
Order: Benny New Adventure #7
(Who NA #68)

MAIN CHARACTERS Bernice Summerfield.

TRAVEL LOG Dellah, Canopus IV and Vo'lach Prime, 2594.

STORY SUMMARY The People's supercomputer God, having calculated that events unfolding in the Canopus system could affect the People, asks Benny to join a St. Oscar's archaeological expedition to Canopus IV. There, Benny's group finds "the Spire"—a gigantic tower containing an inner core that's aflame with energy travelling into the past for unknown purposes (*See Sidebar*).

From the Spire's carvings, the St. Oscar's team attribute the edifice's construction to the extinct Vo'lach race. Long ago, the peace-loving Vo'lach feared their descendants would become military conquerors and committed suicide *en masse* rather than risk such atrocities. Using the Spire's maps, Benny's group pinpoints the lost Vo'lach homeworld and travels there to learn more, accompanied by a native Canopean named Geth.

On Vo'lach Prime, Benny and her allies find the methodical Vo'lach left behind highly advanced machines to bombard their homeworld with toxic weapons, preventing sentient life from evolving there. But in the millennia since the Vo'lach's self-extermination, a few super-intelligent machines— such as Factory 34561239—evolved to full sentience and befriend Benny's party.

Finally detecting Benny's party as unauthorized lifeforms, two Planetcracker missiles on a nearby Vo'lach weapons platform arm themselves and launch. The life-befriending Factory 34561239 galvanizes into action, activating its emergency rockets and carrying the humans into space with the Planetcrackers in hot pursuit. However, the Factory's flawed programming draws it back to the Vo'lach-made Spire, where Benny's group hurriedly disembarks.

As the Planetcrackers draw near, Benny realizes the Planetcrackers are homing on a tracking device secretly implanted in Geth's bicep. With little alternative, Benny shoves Geth's arm into the Spire's inner fire and vaporizes it, hoping to destroy the homing beacon. Yet the super-toughened tracer survives and falls down the Spire's temporal channel into the past. Undaunted, the Planetcrackers dive after the tracer and detonate in a previous era—retroactively destroying the Spire during its early years. However, this prevents the Spire in the future from serving as a time-travel device for the Planetcrackers, instigating a massive Universal paradox.

The history of the Universe cycles a number of times, each rotation creating an altered timeline still riddled with paradoxes. Finally, a balance is struck—a history emerges where the Planetcrackers plunge into the past and only damage the Spire, allowing it to function in the future. As history intended all along, the Vo'lach of ages past find a correlation between the Planetcrackers' remains and minerals native to Vo'lach Prime, erroneously deducing their descendants are military conquerors and crafting their suicide agenda shortly thereafter.

Benny remains untarnished in the new timeline, but a series of minor alterations—such as peaceful races becoming warlike—remain. Unable to accept her role in such bloody changes to history, Benny overdoses on tranquilizers. Thankfully, Benny survives the suicide attempt and God's agent Clarence, a winged humanoid who was formerly a People Ship, informs Benny that the Spire, which drew matter from the future into the past (*See Sidebar*), was a temporal paradox from its activation. By unleashing a small paradox with the Planetcrackers, Benny has actually—as God intended—thwarted a much larger paradox that could have consumed the Universe (*See Sidebar*). Comforted that her actions likely saved billions of lives, Benny returns to St. Oscar's.

MEMORABLE MOMENTS The people-friendly Factory doesn't understand Benny's comment that everything's going "pear-shaped" and considers excluding pears—if they're really so unlucky—from its prospective fruit-and-vegetable section.

SEX AND SPIRITS The angel-like Clarence meets Benny for the first time stark naked, with his swan-feather wings modestly covering his feet

THE CRUCIAL BITS...

- **GHOST DEVICES**—First appearance of Clarence, winged agent of the People's super-computer God.

(King James Bible translators used "the feet" as a euphemism for genitalia). Clarence develops a harmless affection for Bernice, aiding her in the future (*Where Angels Fear*).

St. Oscar's students voted Benny the professor second most likely to "wear something embarrassing in red leather" (the top prize went to Donals, the Julian Clary Fellowship Professor of Sexuality in Fashion History). St. Oscar's also holds a "Kinky Gerlinky Memorial Saturluna, Beer Race and Pajama Jump" at the end of the term.

ASS-WHUPPINGS Life-hostile Vo'lach machines briefly mistake Benny's group for a type of disguised Vo'lach robot named Negotiators (*See History*). With medical doctor Jane Steadman unconscious from a gas attack (trust us, the plot's a bit convoluted), the machines ask Benny if the "Jane Negotiator" should be recycled or outright disposed of. Realizing that discovery of Jane's human nature will mean instant death for the entire party, Benny takes the disposal option, shunting Jane out a submarine chute to her death. The revelation that Jane was a disguised Negotiator all along doesn't comfort Benny, who's shamed to know she committed "cold-blooded murder," even for noble reasons.

Benny also tries to save everyone on Canopus IV from the Planetcrackers by frying Geth's arm off. Upon comprehending her role in fixing the Spire paradox, Benny attempts (but thankfully fails) suicide with a lot of pills.

The Vo'lach destroyed their home system beyond a shadow of a doubt, dousing Vo'lach Prime with poisonous copper-sulfate, radioactive isotopes and dirty nuclear weapons, even seeding the Meta-Kraken trenches with Strontium-90.

NOVEL TIE-INS Benny agreed to undertake assignments for God in *Oh No It Isn't!* She enjoys reading pulps such as "Mr. Misnomer and the Polar Peril" (*Down*). The planet Ordifica, seen in passing here, gets re-visited in *Interference*. Spinward Corporation (*Deceit*) still operates in this timezone and resurfaces in *Another Girl, Another Planet*. Bernice suspects God has little personal interest in her, foreshadowing events in *Tears of the Oracle*. The same book reveals Clarence's true identity.

TV TIE-INS Vo'lach materials used to construct the Spire are second only to dwarf star alloy ("Warriors' Gate").

CHARACTER DEVELOPMENT

Bernice Summerfield: Benny authored a paper entitled "Galactic Mythos of the Far Frontiers."

Bernice and God: As payment for Benny's intervention on Canopus IV, God offers to craft a Bernice simulation to write her *Down Among the Dead Men* sequel—producing a book in Benny's words without the pain of her writing it (sounds good to us). However, the ersatz Benny resembles the original too well, failing to write the text after a presumably large amount of booze.

God picked Benny to collapse the Spire paradox because she's got time-travel experience.

Clarence: Winged agent of God, originally named "Gabriel" until Benny decided that "Clarence" sounded better.

Clarence used to be a sentient People Ship, two kilometers long with an astronomical IQ. After an unspecified accident, God refashioned what remained of the damaged Ship's systems into Clarence, who's now a computer intelligence trapped in a body made from freely donated *Homo sapiens* protoplasm. God calls Clarence his *Evets Nitsua*, a reversal of Steve Austin, "The Six Million Dollar Man."

Clarence's new body doesn't register as a Person, allowing him to undertake missions for God that would normally violate the Time Lord-People treaty. Clarence only has muddled memories of his former life, suspecting he was a Ship-herd charitably working with the Grown Not Made Special Interest Group to produce low-level People Ships for technophobic races.

Clarence's six-foot-tall humanoid body looks like actor Keanu Reaves.

ALIEN RACES

The Watchmakers (likely the Time Lords): Time-active beings with bodies of pure chronology.

Canopusi: Orange-skinned natives of Canopus IV, technically reptiles but bearing live young. Canopus IV's harsh climate gave the Canopusi temperature-resistant skin and much stamina. Notably, your typical Canopusi has four stomachs, each capable of turning into a cyst if poisoned and being ejected from the body while a replacement tummy is grown in about a week (during such a phase, the Canopusi enters a semi-unconscious state called *Sinthus*). Canopusi can deliberately

MISCELLANEOUS STUFF!

THE SPIRE'S FUNCTION

Having evolved during an early era of history, the technologically advanced Vo'lach concluded the Universe was constantly expanding—but feared this would exhaust the Universe's matter and eradicate everything. Unable to decide if Universal expansion or contraction would prolong the Universe's life more, the Vo'lach built the Spire to hold the Universe in stasis. The Spire's temporal core sucked in Universal matter and deposited it in the past, retroactively binding galaxies together with mass that would have hastened the Universe's heat death in the future. Accordingly, the Spire is responsible for the mass-heavy phenomena known as quasars.

As you've probably gathered, this is a temporal screw-up beyond Faction Paradox's dreams. If left alone, the Spire would have achieved the ideal balance the Vo'lach wanted. However, this would have taken away the Vo'lach's motivation to create the Spire in the first place, creating an unstoppable paradox. Through her smaller paradox with the Planetcrackers, Benny stymied—but didn't destroy—the Spire's efficiency, retarding the device's ability to siphon matter and thereby preventing Universal armageddon.

synthesize various drugs and poisons if they ingest the proper triggers (metabolizing an antidote, for example, by ingesting the discharge of a sick being). They're immune to *Colchicine* toxin, which can kill humans.

Prolonged exposure to the Spire gave the Canopusi limited psionic abilities.

Vo'lach Factories: Super-intelligent, but normally forbidden from possessing true sentience (probably because this would pre-cursor sentient life).

ALIEN PLANETS A platform in orbit above *Dellah* acts as a "space elevator," efficiently hauling cargoes into orbit with a synthetic "rope."

PLACES TO GO

The Spire: At 344.9 kilometers (roughly 214

miles) high, the Spire's visible from space. The core's deep blue/purple colored "inner fire" is actually tachyons journeying into the past.

As a by-product of its true function, the Spire radiates temporal resonance that allows psionics (or beings who use sensory cubicles called "Vision Cones") to glimpse future events. The ratio of visions that actually occur is a high 17/20, but only 1/20 typically comes true in the way you'd expect.

Vo'lach System: Contains many planets orbiting the burnt-amber star Sadr. "Vo'lach Prime" is actually the system's second Heavenly body, as the Vo'lach constructed a planet-sized weapons platform between their homeworld and the sun. The Vo'lach gutted the system's other planetary bodies, including the gas giants and asteroids.

Canpous System: Lies a week's journey from Dellah. Canpous IV's a desert-covered, pinkish orange world covered with deposits of a crystal called futurite.

ORGANIZATIONS

St. Oscar's University: The University lacks a CyberTheology Department.

Tiny and Interesting Interest Group: A front for God's agents to covertly operate in the Milky Way, a violation of the Time Lord-People treaty. Clarence is a member.

Worldsphere Interest Groups: Also include Dressing Up As Other Galaxies' Religious Figures.

HISTORY The deduction that their descendants were military conquerors (from the time-travelling Planetcrackers) made the Vo'lach undertake a series of contradictory actions. Primarily, they became fervent pacifists, hoping to avoid giving their descendants a reason to hate them. Simultaneously, the Vo'lach refused to allow future generations to inflict harm on others and crafted advanced weapons, trading them to other cultures and warning them to beware an attack from future Vo'lach. Before the Vo'lach self-exterminated themselves 9.25 million years ago, they programmed some of their machines—called "Negotiators"—to continue weapons sales.

• A Bruce Willis simulacrum once starred in *Die Hardest*. A sequel to *Twelve Angry Men*, named *Twelve Just Men*, portrayed half the jury as killer cyborgs from the future.

• A devastating earthquake rocked California in the mid-21st century.

APOCRYPHAL HISTORY While trying to reconcile Benny's Planetcracker/Spire paradox, the Universe runs through a number of histories. In one timeline, the Planetcrackers completely atomize themselves, leaving the Vo'lach without samples to study. Subsequently, the Vo'lach fear further attacks and become more militaristic themselves. A Vo'lach skirmish with the Veltrochi (*Mission Impractical*) Love-in Groove Collective detonates a Nova bomb that destroys Earth and Benny's ancestors.

• In other realities, Earth survives and dictatorially allies itself with the Vo'lach. Bernice von Summerfield serves Earth's political office under Death Marshal Falaxyr (*Legacy*). A number of alternate timelines involve nuclear disasters, which blast Benny back to the Stone Age.

AT THE END OF THE DAY About as unwieldy as an anvil; dense and extremely uninviting. What's obvious between this work and *The Death of Art* is that Bucher-Jones' ideas work far, far better when a co-writer follows along and strips in a bunch of sentences and paragraphs to help define everything. To *Ghost Devices*' credit, some of its scientific ideas are quite clever (especially the final paradox resolution) and there's also strong characterization, but the story jitters about, loses Benny completely in parts and worries about too many fruitless sideplots to be very approachable.

MEAN STREETS

By Terrance Dicks

Release Date: December 1997
Order: Benny New Adventure #8
(Who NA #69)

MAIN CHARACTERS Bernice Summerfield and Chris Cwej.

TRAVEL LOG St. Oscar's University and Megacity, Megerra, 2594. (Side Note: Chronology goes tits-up here. Lance Parkin's *History of the Universe* sensibly dates *Shakedown* as circa 2376. Although Benny and Chris state it's been "quite a while" subjectively since Chris' previous visit to Megerra, the idea that it's been more than 200 years, even allowing for time travel, is laughable.)

STORY SUMMARY Chris Cwej details to Benny how he and the late Roz Forrester once pursued a serial killer to the tourist-driven colony of Megerra. In the course of their investigations, Chris and Roz heard about an ultra-secret criminal activity named "The Project" but never pursued it further. To honor Roz's memory, Chris and Benny agree to expose The Project's crimes.

Unfortunately, the St. Oscar's Advanced Research Department (ARD), affiliated with The Project, learns of Benny's plans and decides to eliminate her. But a bomb intended for Benny kills student Jeran instead, making the Faculty Ethics Committee bring Benny up on false charges. Chris also survives an assassination attempt, making them agree to attack The Project at its heart.

Chris and Benny arrive in Megerra's Megacity, only to be arrested on trumped-up charges. Thankfully, Police Chief Harkon grows convinced of their innocence and gives them identities as members of a criminal syndicate. Together with Chris' old ally, the augmented Ogron named Garshak, now a private investigator, Benny and Chris investigate a gang war between crime lords Nastur and Lucifer. Although Benny's group foils Nastur's drug-running operation and allies itself with Lucifer, the truth behind The Project eludes them.

Finally, Chris follows a lead that takes his party to DevCorps, a once-lucrative mining company that's fallen on hard times. Garshak downloads DevCorps' data on The Project, actually a plot to genetically augment DevCorps miners with increased stamina, at the cost of their deteriorating sanity and control. However, the genetic alterations have passed to the miners' descendants, making them murderous psychopaths. As Benny confronts the DevCorps Board with the evidence, Kragg, one of The Project's victims, kills DevCorps owner Devlin in a rage. With little choice, the Board of Directors agrees to bankrupt DevCorps and treat The Project's victims.

In exchange for Benny's silence on how the university's Advanced Research Department provided scientific support for The Project, ARD Director Silvera drops the fabricated charges against Benny, agrees to debug St. Oscar's and terminate ARD security chief Kedrick, the man who inadvertently killed student Jeran. Considering the scales balanced, Benny enjoys a glass of wine.

SEX AND SPIRITS Chris bangs Sara, manager of the nightclub Sara's Cellar. The demonic looking gangster Lucifer half-seriously offers to spend the night with Benny, but she declines. Student Jeran had a crush on Benny.

More than 50 faculty members attended Benny's last booze-up party. Benny drinks Eridanean brandy while Garshak drinks *vragg*.

ASS-WHUPPINGS Student Jeran dies in a bomb meant for Benny. Chris drops at least three alien Wolverines, saving Lucifer, and Benny plugs two.

TV TIE-INS Ogrons, members of Garshak's race, appeared in "Day of the Daleks" and "Frontier in Space." Garshak smokes "Drashig" cigarettes ("Carnival of Monsters").

NOVEL TIE-INS This novel's a sequel to Dicks' *Shakedown*, where Chris and Roz ran rampant over Megerra tracking "the Ripper," actually a Rutan killer. *Shakedown* also introduced Megacity, the intelligent Ogron named Garshak and the Wolverines, who run Megacity's street gangs. Wolverines are rumored to eat Chelonians (*The Highest Science* and more). Raggor's Cavern, the Megacity nightclub attacked by the Rutan Karne in *Shakedown*, here gets renamed "Sara's Cellar." Sara, a dancer there in *Shakedown*, now runs it. Roz kicked a drunken miner in the happy sacks during her first Megacity visit. He became Sara's cellarman, but gets head-smashed with a mallet for knowing too much about The Project.

Oh No It Isn't! debuted Benny's bike, which here gets sabotaged and explodes.

Benny, Chris and Garshak interrupt a running operation for skoob, an alias for "skar," the addictive drug featured in *Catastrophea*. Kastopheria, skoob's planet of origin, was invaded and quarantined, with every last skoob plant burnt.

Benny here meets ARD Director Silvera and again confronts him in *The Medusa Effect*.

Menlove Stokes (*The Well-Mannered War*, *Oh No It Isn't!*), having exhausted the artistic possibilities of his own bodily fluids, now explores the activities of the giant Dellah dung beetle. Pakhar (*Legacy*, *Oh No It Isn't!*) get white fur as they age.

CHARACTER DEVELOPMENT

Bernice Summerfield: Benny convinced the St. Oscar's University Senate that the time-honored two-fingered salute actually conveys admiration and respect. She demonstrates it to many people.

Benny's sequel work to *Down Among the Dead Men* is again entitled *So Vast a Pile*. She's acknowledged as a "popular" female faculty member and has received another chunk of best-seller royalties. Her lipstick doubles as a powerful blaster.

Benny's secretary, a black sphere named Rodney, acts more annoying than her porter Joseph. Benny's "not really fond" of exercise.

The Faculty Ethics Committee falsely accused Benny of insufficient attention to student welfare, unorthodox and inadequate teaching methods, inappropriate dress and demeanor, failure to publish and heavy boozing. The St. Oscar's ARD dropped the charges, most of which, ironically, were true.

Chris Cwej: Chris has matured greatly since his TARDIS days. He carries a small black device that jams listening devices, plus a vibroknife, a neurosap and a stubby black neutron blaster that kills or stuns. He misses being an Adjudicator. Chief "Chimp" Harkon makes him a Megacity Deputy.

Director Santos Silvera: Tall, thin, silver-haired and impeccably mannered humanoid, beautifully dressed, who serves as St. Oscar's ARD director.

ALIEN RACES *Demoniacs:* Aliens from the planet Gehenna with scaly skins, red slanting eyes and long narrow heads crowned with neat little horns. Early Demoniac visits to Earth may have sparked some old Earth myths, so Earth explorers dubbed them "Demoniacs." The Gehennans use old Earth names such as "Lucifer" to gain a psychological advantage in negotiations.

Demoniacs have lethal claws and leathery wings that fold cloak-like over their backs. Their stubby wings can fly on their low-gravity homeworld, which has exploding volcanoes that create updrafts. Demoniacs honor blood debts.

ALIEN PLANETS *Megerra*, isolated on the fringe of the galaxy in a human-dominated sector, has a feeble red sun. It has no extradition treaties.

PLACES TO GO *Megacity:* Megerra's only sizeable city, covering one of the planet's smaller continents. Megotel One serves as the city's largest hotel. Markos Ramarr served as Megacity mayor. Nieman-Marcas off the Central Plaza is the most expensive shop in town. *The Megacity Gazette* covers city news. Crime-riddled Megacity's mostly safe for tourists, barring the occasional gang war.

STUFF YOU NEED

Benny's Bike: Benny's bike, here destroyed, used a simple gravitic motor to help climb hills.

The Project: The brainchild of Professor Vashtar, whose work was banned on every civilized planet. The Project genetically boosted a person's kill-or-be-killed reflex, largely overwritten by civilization. Persons augmented by the Project have superstrength, plus eyes that glow red. The St. Oscar's Advanced Research Department helped stabilize The Project's effects.

ORGANIZATIONS

Devlin Mining Corporation (a.k.a. DevCorps): One of the oldest companies on Megerra, whose fortunes came and went. The late Joseph Devlin the Third served as company president. The Kragg family, particularly Simeon Kragg, handled secu-

rity. A consortium of Megacity businessmen bought 49 percent of DevCorps.

The Pinkerton Agency: Still the biggest, most effective private investigation agency in this sector of space. The Pinkertons allegedly never let an operative's death go unsolved.

Combine: The largest criminal organization in the galaxy, a loose amalgamation of Mafia-type groups on 100 worlds, supposedly led by the legendary Emil Malek (a.k.a. the Capo di Tutti Capi).

AT THE END OF THE DAY Barely endowed with innovation, but straightforward and a book to enjoy—presuming you're extremely forgiving. Garshak the intelligent Ogron, certainly, is an absolute delight. But on the downside, everyone sounds like they just left a Mickey Spillane novel and Benny and Chris' personalities warp to fit the plot (Benny only "remembers" she's a scholar when the need arises). Even worse, Dicks spends an unbelievable amount of time on a drug-running operation that's irrelevant to the mystery at hand, and The Project's revelation in no way warrants its massive secrecy and build-up. In short, *Mean Streets* paves its way as a book you'll surprisingly find fun—if your expectations aren't very high.

TEMPEST

By Christopher Bulis

Release Date: January 1998
Order: Benny New Adventure #9
(Who NA #70)

MAIN CHARACTERS Bernice Summerfield.

TRAVEL LOG Tempest, 2594.

STORY SUMMARY Business tycoon Nathan Costermann invites Benny to lecture to an archaeological society on the colony world of Tempest, which is perpetually cursed with a harsh, toxic atmosphere. Following her talk, Benny leaves for the Tempest spaceport aboard the *Polar Express* monorail and re-meets Costermann, who's transporting an artifact of the Drell religion—the Drell Imnulate—to auction in the city of Thule. Benny retires to her cabin and gets hammered, awakening the next morning to learn that someone gassed Costermann unconscious, knifed his bodyguard Tralbet to death and stole the Imnulate.

Toxicological tests prove Benny was too sauced to perform the killing, so she investigates the crime as the *Polar Express* continues its fateful journey. Benny researches the Drell religion and learns the radical Kedd-Drell sect, who seek to spread their faith by any means necessary, would happily steal the Imnulate and use it as a rallying cry for holy warfare.

Suddenly, Kedd-Drell soldiers block the monorail's path, overrun the train and attempt to kill everyone—hoping to slay the Imnulate thief and recover the artifact later. The passengers, conditioned to life in Tempest's harsh environment, resist and engage the Kedd-Drell cadre. The colonists finally prevail and the *Polar Express* crew fires flares at the Kedd-Drell commander's pursuit craft, causing it to veer dangerously and explode against a cliffside.

Benny finally unmasks Costermann as Tralbet's killer, deducing the real Imnulate was never aboard the *Polar Express*. Blackmailed by Tralbet concerning a pharmaceutical cover-up and under pressure by the Drell to return the Imnulate, Costermann concocted a scheme to murder his extortioner and arrange the Imnulate's "theft" in one fell swoop, both thwarting the Drell and collecting the Imnulate's insurance money. Before he boarded the *Polar Express*, Costermann crafted a plaster replica of the Imnulate, later dissolving it with a solvent and stabbing Tralbet to death, then gassing himself unconscious to avoid suspicion.

Costermann denies everything, but Jordan Tyne, an expert thief, loses control and attacks him to avenge his partner's death during the Kedd-Drell attack. During their skirmish, Costermann falls against a battle-weakened panel and plunges out of the train, instantly crushed on the tracks. Discredited, Costermann's companies disavow their founder while Benny returns to Dellah, pondering the still-missing Imnulate.

SEX AND SPIRITS

Costermann invited Benny to lecture on Tempest purely to gain another suspect in the Imnulate "theft." Thankfully, Benny's raving capacity for alcohol (primarily with a Chambrey '57) removed her from suspicion. (Our mothers will be thrilled to know something good *can* come out of hitting the sauce.)

Benny fancies insurance investigator Garv Ferlane, but sets her hormones aside to concentrate on the Imnulate theft. Unfortunately...

ASS-WHUPPINGS

Costermann foils Ferlane's inquiries and tries to kill him, exposing Ferlane to Tempest's atmosphere and leaving him slightly brain damaged. The scuffle also puts Benny's arm in a cast for a couple weeks.

Costermann stabs Tralbet, his bodyguard and blackmailer and head-smashes Merch, a blackmailing salesman (and aren't they all).

Benny kicks a hostile Kedd-Drell off the train. *Polar Express* chef Jean-Louis does in another with a meat cleaver. *Polar Express* crewman fire flares that eliminate the Kedd-Drell pursuit ship *Kingfisher* and kill leader Smith.

CHARACTER DEVELOPMENT

Bernice Summerfield: Poor Benny spent weeks excavating an ancient tunnel system under Velopolis to unearth the tomb of King Trakimon. She understandably felt a bit boobish when her team bored into sewer service tunnel by mistake, realizing too late that Trakimon's burial chamber had collapsed centuries before and left only an entrance structure.

Benny knows something of Drell customs and has a full environment suit rating, trained to function in zero to 100+ atmospheres. Files on Dellah, supplemented by recommendations from Irving Braxiatel, state Benny's got a sense of honor, justice and (admittedly erratic) academic rigor. For the purpose of the *Polar Express* investigations, Benny's made a Temporary Special Constable.

ALIEN PLANETS *Tempest:* Rather inhospitable planet orbiting a mildly unstable flare star, turning on its axis in just more than 20 hours. Tempest has lakes, shallow seas and an interesting topography, but that's little comfort considering the atmosphere's a fetid mess of carbon, sulfur dioxide, nitrogen, ammonia and methane, with virtually no oxygen. Chains of active volcanoes line tectonic fault zones, spewing out even more gas and dust. Night at the North Pole lasts half a year.

Tempest serves as home to 30 million oxygen breathers, each living in protected environments and equipped with protective suits. Kids on Tempest must take a bit to mature (odd, considering the climate), with parents responsible for them until at least age 20.

STUFF YOU NEED *The Drell Imnulate (a.k.a. The First Imnulate):* Allegedly shaped by the god Drell's own hands, it's a blue chalcite crystal sculpture about 30 cm high, with pale zalene bubbles within. It also displays multiple heads, both humanoid and alien, rising from a single trunk that spreads like tree foliage. It's completely unique, symbolically representing how universal beings are more alike than not.

ORGANIZATIONS *The Drell Religion:* Believers have faith in Drell, a universal entity that can inhabit any form. Drell temples exist on most planets, although some are mere rooms to give believers privacy. All Drell pray according to Karnor time.

Most Drell favor Universal brotherhood, with a respect for secular law and an unshakable belief in the afterlife—if you live according to Drell's word. Years ago, an unpublicized schism in the faith gave rise to the Kedd-Drell, who interpreted "Universal brotherhood" to mean they must convert all races whatever the cost. They rallied around the Imnulate as a symbol of the inevitable Universal conversion to Drell.

HISTORY Surveyors first explored Tempest 150 years ago, discovering its diverse, unique flora and fauna, which thrives in an environment lethal to humans. In time, pharmacological discoveries drew bio-industries to the planet and made fungi hunters and farmers fantastically rich (one presumes it was like the California gold rush, only with mushrooms).

AT THE END OF THE DAY Forehead, meet desk. *Tempest* makes a cardinal mistake by not offing the entire *Polar Express* cast—sans Benny of course—because it's near-impossible to emotionally invest in a single supporting character. As mysteries go, *Tempest* would make Agatha Christie turn in her grave, waffling from one disjointed revelation to the next, adding little to the overall story and throwing in a train assault just to make bullets fly. Almost certainly the Benny New Adventure with the least merit.

BURIED TREASURES

By Jacqueline Rayner and Paul Cornell

Release Date: 1999
Order: Impossible to pin down, but certainly during Benny's tenure at St. Oscar's University. We'd be lying if we said the decision to place "Buried Treasures" between Tempest and Walking to Babylon—a fairly idyllic period of Benny's life—wasn't arbitrary.
NOTE: Big Finish produced "Buried Treasures" as a promotional CD, offering it to customers who purchased all three of the Benny "Time Ring Trilogy" audio adaptations ("Walking to Babylon," "Birthright" and "Just War"). Although the production run of "Buried Treasures"—e.g., the number of CDs made—hasn't been revealed, common sense dictates mere hundreds were struck. As such, "Buried Treasures" remains one of the most difficult "Who" related items to acquire.
"Buried Treasures" includes two exclusive stories ("Making Myths" and "Closure"), an

interview with Cornell and music tracks to the "Walking to Babylon" and "Just War" audio adaptations.

"MAKING MYTHS"
By Jacqueline Rayner

MAIN CHARACTERS Bernice Summerfield.

TRAVEL LOG Planet Shangri-La, likely 2594.

STORY SUMMARY Benny agrees to an overly scripted interview on the planet Shangri-La, a once-glorious tourist world where Benny claims to have discovered the famed "Mud Fields of Agrivan." Accompanied by journalist Keri, a member of the hamster-like Pakhar race, Benny tosses her script and tries to win fame by lying through her teeth, attributing the creation of the Agrivan mud fields to a fanciful myth involving giant carts and a lot of shovels. However, Benny and Keri get lost returning from a first-hand look at the mud fields and start to fear the mud has claimed their space shuttle.

Stranded, Benny and Keri resort to bitching at each other while Keri's unbreakable satellite link broadcasts their barbs and sly insults to dozens of worlds. Finally, a patch of ground collapses and deposits Benny and Keri in a large chasm filled with shovels and giants carts—proof that the "false" Agrivan myth was likely true.

Benny coaxes Keri into running hamster-like on a giant cart wheel, gaining them enough leverage to open an exterior door. Emerging from the underground chamber, Benny and Keri locate their shuttle and receive news that thanks to their broadcast, thousands of Pakhar have made bookings to run atop the giant wheels, saving Shangri-La from economic ruin.

MEMORABLE MOMENTS "Making Myths" mostly forgoes "memorable moments" in favor of well-crafted dialogue. Stress causes Benny and Keri to trade a number of verbal assaults, including this gem from Benny: "For the benefit of listeners, Keri seems to think she's superior solely because she's got more nipples than me—which is probably the only reason she got her job in the first place."

On-air, Benny struggles to block herself from uttering obscenities to the family audience: "Bugger! I mean, *buggar*! This [wall] is made from *buggar*—a human word for densely packed mud." She also details that "bullocks!" is an archaeology term where one gives up and shoves bits of old pottery into an "ancient" pot regardless of accuracy.

SEX AND SPIRITS Benny once beat ex-hubby Jason Kane at arm-wrestling because her other arm was distracting him elsewhere.

NOVEL TIE-INS Keri the Pakhar appeared in *Legacy* and *Happy Endings*.

AUDIO TIE-INS The "Walking to Babylon" CD adaptation first mentions Benny's exploration of the famed "Mud Fields of Agrivan."

CHARACTER DEVELOPMENT

Bernice Summerfield: Benny wrote a seminal paper on the Mud Fields of Agrivan. She insists she's devoting an entire chapter in her new book to mud planets, presuming she writes the damn thing. Publishers refer to Benny's unseen text as a "Brigadoon tome," because it promises to appear every 100 years and nobody's actually seen it.

Keri: Host of the "Making Myths" radio series.

ALIEN RACES *Pakhar*, despite looking like oversized hamsters, can't burrow.

ALIEN PLANETS The planet *Pakhar* knows of an Atlantis-like myth named "The Lost Island of Ham-Starr." You sadly can't get carrots on Pakhar.

APOCRYPHAL HISTORY (PROBABLY) Benny claims the Mud Fields of Agrivan originated when the island settlement of a lost civilization sank beneath the waters. Determined to rebuild the city, the people undertook an elaborate scheme to shovel dirt into the watery area. Regrettably, this created mud and allowed water to soup up the rest of the planet also. The people starved for lack of decent growing soil. Despite Benny and Keri's discovery of the giant carts and shovels, the whole story seems about as solid as mud itself.

AT THE END OF THE DAY Fun, funny and mostly pointless fluff—but it's deliberately crafted that way. Rayner's honed talent for blather (and we mean that in a good way) scoops life into what's little more than a rollicking conversation between Benny and a giant hamster.

"CLOSURE"
By Paul Cornell

MAIN CHARACTERS Bernice Summerfield.

TRAVEL LOG Lake Gray, the planet Panyos, circa 2545.

STORY SUMMARY The planet Panyos quells, after great sacrifice, a Nazi-like revolution led by a man named Ulrich Hescarti and asks a neutral St. Oscar's team to document the Ulrich's atrocities. Accompanying the St. Oscar's group to Ulrich's captured headquarters at Lake Gray on Panyos, Benny witnesses shocking examples of Ulrich's inhumanity and decides to take action.

Benny researches Ulrich's history and gets Jason Kane to lend his time ring. By using Jason's ring in concert with her own, Benny materializes 50 years previous at Ulrich's Lake Gray villa. There, Benny finds Ulrich as a toddler, protected by his war widow mother Isabella. Benny holds Isabella at gunpoint, detailing at great length how the "current" conflict is nothing compared to the war to come. Solely because of Ulrich Hescarti's agenda, Panyos will undergo an ethnic cleansing to wipe out the Ashcarzi people.

Gradually, Isabella vows to raise her son properly, not for the sake of Ulrich's future victims, but so Ulrich himself won't meet a horrible end. Benny believes that Isabella will end Ulrich's life if he walks the path of anger. Deciding to let Isabella and Ulrich live, Benny fires a carefully timed gunshot and wounds Marcellos Karista—an Ashcarzi soldier hiding in Isabella's house.

Benny explains that in her history, Karista deserted his platoon and wandered into the villa, brutally murdering Isabella. In the years to follow, Ulrich swore vengeance against all Ashcarzi for his mother's death and instigated his genocidal program. Benny gives the gun to Isabella and leaves both Ulrich and Karista's fate in her hands. Unsure but hopeful as to how much she's changed history, Benny uses the time rings to return home.

MEMORABLE MOMENTS Benny wonders if she has the stomach to murder Isabella and Ulrich—turning herself into a mindless instrument of history like Jack Ruby, assassin of Lee Harvey Oswald. Benny denies the argument that the Panyos atrocities are unique by decrying, "Everyone does this in all times and places!" Benny tells a story how Ulrich's forces raped a group of teenagers. Benny's decision to let Isabella and Ulrich live gives hope for the future.

ASS-WHUPPINGS Benny details at length her tour through Ulrich's headquarters, elaborating on concrete-filled mass graves and the stench of death. Prisoners were used to incubate experimental viruses, their bodies later crushed to drain them of blood. "Traitors" in Ulrich's ranks were electrocuted, maimed and hung. One of Ulrich's people finally shot him in the back.

CHARACTER DEVELOPMENT

Bernice Summerfield: During her military academy days, Benny had her first dance with a boy to the songs of "Modern Romance." The next day, a cadet stumbled and blew her boyfriend's head off. If Benny had opted to kill Isabella and young Ulrich, she'd likely have shot herself next.

STUFF YOU NEED *Benny and Jason's Time Rings* have a temporal field that interacts with the consciousness of people who touch it. As a result, Isabella gets flashbacks to a feasting time by approaching a newly arrived Bernice.

PHENOMENA Unlike virtually all of "Doctor Who," Benny believes that *altering history* is entirely possible. As proof, she puts a bullet through one of Isabella's clocks, knowing the clock doesn't sport a bullet hole in "her" future.

AT THE END OF THE DAY Undoubtedly disturbing to some people—but we're very glad this story got told. Allowing that we're all adults, there are times when the kid gloves must come off and mankind's depravities explored—so we can all redouble our efforts to craft a better world. While it'd be inappropriate to do many stories as graphic as this one, at least we have "Closure" to give us a jolt and demonstrate Benny's admirable convictions. In short, this one's tough to hear, but worth the effort and evocative of highly moralized war stories. Highly recommended.

WALKING TO BABYLON

By Kate Orman

Release Date: February 1998
Order: Benny New Adventure # 10
(Who NA #71)

MAIN CHARACTERS Bernice Summerfield.

TRAVEL LOG St. Oscar's University, MD 20879 mining planet and the People's Worldsphere, all 2594; plus Babylon, 570 BC. (Side Note: John Lafayette originates from Earth, Dec. 12, 1901.)

STORY SUMMARY The People's supercomputer God urgently contacts Benny at St. Oscar's, warning that two renegade members of the People, !Ci!ci-tel and WiRgo!xu, have inexplicably built a time-travel corridor called "the Path" and escaped to ancient Babylon. The Path, representing a clear violation of the People's treaty with the Time Lords, could spark a devastating Universal war.

Because the Treaty binds God or any Person from time travelling after the renegades, God proposes destroying the Path and Babylon with a singularity bomb, ripping Earth history wide open, unless the independent-acting Benny can make the rogues shut down the Path. With Universal destruction her only option, Benny agrees.

Benny materializes in ancient Babylon and stumbles upon John Lafayette, a 1901 linguist who accidentally traveled along one of the Path's offshoots. While tracking the renegade People, Benny and a nerve-wracked John become lovers. They also associate with the priestess Ninan, who must remain in her temple or be deemed impure.

Finally, Benny and John locate !Ci!ci-tel, WiRgo!xu and their drone I!qu-!qu-tala, but when !Ci!ci-tel touches John, temporal energy that John gained from travelling along the Path releases itself and ages !Ci!ci-tel to death. The drone I!qu-!qu-tala admits it believed the People became complacent after their quick victory in the last war and needed something to shock them into action. I!qu-!qu-tala and his fellow renegades, both war veterans, hoped the Path would provoke war between the People and the Time Lords, sparking a conflict the People couldn't guarantee winning.

Ninan aids Benny by having her allies apprehend WiRgo!xu and I!qu-!qu-tala. Ninan agrees to let them stay on Earth in return for aiding her in travelling across the world. I!qu-!qu-tala, feeling events have progressed too far, agrees and allows Benny and John to return while it shuts down the Path. Safely back on the Worldsphere, the Time Lords aid the People in taking John home while Benny returns to her "peaceful" life on Dellah.

MEMORABLE MOMENTS A dying John Lafayette, battered and beaten, realizes he was just a "leaf in the stream," while the intrepid Benny made things happen.

SEX AND SPIRITS Events in Babylon bubble over and Benny and John Lafayette, probably a virgin, shag like bunnies. Hailing from a more conservative age, John worries he's ruined Benny and proposes marriage, but she declines.

Technically, Benny once shagged a Citdbtbedani—not knowing his race reproduces by shaking hands. She packs condoms going to a People party, erring toward optimism. She teaches a course in historical attitudes about sex. Benny hasn't visited Dellah's red-light district (the workers went on strike last year and quickly won concessions).

A drink named *Catchup* overrides jetlag. *Prevention* works as a contraceptive (Benny declines to drink some, saying her outfit doesn't look that good). *Surprisingly sober* supposedly counters hangover, but isn't too effective—*Purge* works better. *Forget it* deletes selected memory.

ASS-WHUPPINGS Preciously little. Lafayette shoots a Babylonian advancing on Benny. In turn, he's mortally beaten up but I!qu-!qu-tala heals him. !Ci!ci-tel touches Lafayette and ages to death.

NOVEL TIE-INS *The Also People* debuted the Worldsphere, God and the People. God still runs simulations of Benny (*Ghost Devices*) to predict how she'll react to assignments.

IKrissi, the daughter of Chris Cwej and a Person named Dep (*The Also People*, *Happy Endings*), now looks eight years old (the People apparently have accelerated development).

Benny here elaborates on an ass-whupping first mentioned in *Parasite*, when she broke her left femur and right tibia and crawled back to camp, eating nightcrawlers to survive. During her ordeal, she read Watkinson's works or talked to herself, telling her (vastly amended) life story. Orman visually shows the event in *The Dead Men Diaries*: "Steal From the World."

Benny studies Ikkaban poetry (*Sleepy*).

The Person named Sara!qava! (*The Also People*, *Happy Endings*) is still male and trying to seduce Bernice. He lives in the coastal town of iSanti Jeni, making the Worldsphere equivalent of pesto.

Down stated !X was the last of the Truly Crazed, but *Walking to Babylon* reports other Truly Crazed inhabit the island of siCera!ca ri!Qisla.

Shugs (a.k.a. Shrak, *Death and Diplomacy*) died out when one of their time-travel scientists carried a lethal plague back from a previous century.

Noted archaeologist Edward Watkinson, here detailed, appears—as a corpse—in *Tears of the Oracle*. That book also explains why God here speaks through Benny's robotic porter Joseph.

CHARACTER DEVELOPMENT

Bernice Summerfield: Computers, not the TARDIS, translate language for Benny these days. She's achieved a level of temporal flexibility (*See Time Travel*). She worries someone at St. Oscar's will uncover her faked credentials and fire her. Even before this adventure, Benny was familiar with the Babylonian era. She can recognize some types of snakes, including the Aesculapian.

Benny considers writing a paper on alien races' recurring use of the samurai in pre-first-contact 20th-century diction (a possible title: *Alien Honour: From the Klingons to the Minbari*).

Seventeen of Benny's diaries have survived. Six others, probably more, were destroyed/abandoned.

Some of this hasn't happened for Benny yet, but her portfolio includes: *Down Among the Dead Men*

MISCELLANEOUS STUFF!

THE TIME LORD, PEOPLE WAR

The People's simulations estimate a People-Time Lord war would make the Worldsphere variously appear, disappear, appear as a wrecked hulk, appear perfectly fine, etc., as its temporal status changes. The Time Lords—and please don't tell me you're surprised at this—will use temporal mechanics to prevent the Worldsphere's creation or seed its destruction. But with each victory, protected pockets of the People or their agents will undo the time damage, in turn attacking the Time Lord groups and learning how to tinker with time themselves.

The Time Lords won't operate from Gallifrey, however, making a counter-assault obnoxiously difficult. Each side will resort to brute force, decimating suns, solar systems and alien races. The People will blindly stab at the Milky Way, striving to hit Gallifrey with a lucky shot. The Time Lords will counter-attack and destroy the super-computer God, but the People will likely restore it. All of this assumes the cumulative space-time damage doesn't prematurely trigger the Big Crunch and destroy the entire cosmos.

With all due respect to the People's talents, the fact that they lack a truly effective offense favors the Time Lords to win.

(*Revised*), 2593; *Devil Gate Drive: The Influence of The Descent of Inanna on 20th Century Popular Culture* (2594); *S for Surprise: Memoirs of an Unorthodox Archaeologist* (unpublished); and *An Eye for Wisdom: Repetitive Poems of the Early Ikkaban Period*, 2595.

John Lafayette: Born in the late 1800s, linguist John Lafayette formed part of Robert Koldewey's landmark expedition to the Deutsche Orient-Gesellschaft, the first properly scientific excavation of Babylon.

His family is mildly psionic, seeing flames on time-displaced objects. Unknown parties may have engineered this talent, or it could be natural. Lafayette declined an invitation to stay on the Worldsphere. Lafayette knew some Aramaic, but better read Hebrew.

After this story, red-haired Lafayette returned home, got married and sired two kids. He did a lot of grunt work, translating thousands of Babylonian tablets, mostly business letters and the odd

This book is not endorsed by the BBC. Doctor Who and TARDIS are trademarks of the BBC.

197

poem. He never wrote a book or went on another expedition. He stayed home in Cambridge, reading translations in dimly lit library rooms, and probably lived out his life very happy.

Clarence: Clarence can safely carry passengers through hyperspace and has an extended lifespan.

WiRgo!xu and !Ci!ci-tel: People veterans from the All Of Us war. !Ci-ci-tel killed seven as a front-line soldier. WiRgo!xu served as a Ship tactician, engineering the People's travel butterflies.

Cin-ta!x: Spokesperson for the Temporal Interest Group. !Cin-ta!x had six fingers on the right hand, seven on the left, parchment-colored skin and orange or blue hair (depending on his mood, presumably). He left the Worldsphere, fearing the Temporal Interest Group's knowledge made him a potential target.

Ninan: High priestess (and technically chief whore) to Marduk. Physically, Ninan was a virgin, forbidden from leaving the city lest her purity be doubted. That said, Ninan was filthy rich, throwing a lot of parties to hear tales of other lands.

God: Whether through programming or intent, God probably couldn't alter the People's memories.

I!qu-!qu-tala: Worldsphere drone who could telekinetically halt bullets and surgically restore broken human bodies in a single minute. It founded the Apathy Interest Group.

Edward Watkinson: As you probably know, Benny holds an endowed chair named after famed archaeologist Edward Watkinson, who reputedly published more than 10,000 papers (the realistic number's a bit more sobering). Benny's search turns up 913 papers with Watkinson's name, but on 472 of those, he was co-author or part of a large team. Even so, Watkinson—one of Benny's heroes—wrote on everything from ethnomycology to folsom points to Lvan glass megaliths. He had four arms, perhaps writing two papers simultaneously. His credited works include: *Beer Before Bread? A Theory Revisited*; *Translate This, You Invading Bastard: Intersections Between Language and Archaeology* (Youkali Press, 2503); *Glory Under the Mud* (St. Oscar's Press, 2524); *K'tiansolnerilii: The Role of the Hero's Best Friend in the Literature of the Milky Way* (2537)

ALIEN RACES

The People: Number about two trillion, although some are born on other planets. Some People im-

migrate away from the Worldsphere, although God usually monitors them for their own safety. God says 4,022,806 People live in anonymity, fleeing their pasts. Old age is the People's No. 1 killer, followed by murder, suicide and freak accidents. Some People use metal butterflies as transport.

The People and the Time Lords: Sometimes turn a blind eye to certain Treaty infractions, preventing a full-blown war.

All of Us (a.k.a. "The Insects"): Insectoid natives of C-Mita-C-Rho, now part of the People. The All of Us arrogantly thought themselves the most powerful race in the Universe, until the People defeated them. The All of Us fought, on average, with a million expendable ships rather than one unconquerable one—having a cavalier attitude toward reproduction.

Ikkaba: The Ikkaba seemed to do little but write poetry and kill themselves, but cultures influenced by them didn't copy their suicide rites. Ikkaba relics are found in three different local galaxies. The Ke Chedani, teddy bear-like beings from the rim, recovered many Ikkaban relics.

The Ikkaba highly influenced the D'nasians, who added death, change and renewal themes to their stories. Oddly enough, in more than 40 percent of D'nasian stories, the hero's companion takes charge when the protagonist succumbs to tragedy (can't think where that came from).

ALIEN PLANETS

Dellah: The spaceport's needle disrupts local weather, making it rain a hell of a lot.

The People's Worldsphere: The miniature, inhabited world of Whynot orbits the Worldsphere's interior sun. The Worldsphere has absolute weather control.

STUFF YOU NEED

The Path: Unstable space-time wormhole that likely sprouted millions of access points, most of which fortunately appeared in uninhabited locales. Psionics can see the Path. The People can't simply deactivate it.

Singularity Bomb (a.k.a. Popper): Devastates an area by exposing it to a miniature black hole for a fraction of a second. The People's singularity bombs rip apart a 20 km radius. Detonating one can blind God's sensors for four seconds.

ORGANIZATIONS

Worldsphere Interest Groups: Include Temporal,

Obscure and Unlikely Civilizations, Abnormal Psychology, Weird Aviation, Seriously Primitive Societies, Apathy, Interpersonal Dynamics, Primitive Cooking, Freak Accidents, Xenocultural Relations (Normalization), Ke Chedani (*See Alien Races*), Immortality Through Not Pissing Off God, Solar Mechanics, Creative Writing and (Author's Note: Shudder, shudder, let it not be so) Celibacy.

Temporal Interest Group: Ultra-secret Worldsphere group with at least 22 members. !Cin-ta!x served as the Group's spokesperson. The group was largely defunct until it assisted God with analyzing the Path.

TIME TRAVEL Benny reaffirms that changing history is outrageously difficult, unless you make exactly the right change at the wrong moment.

Temporal Flexibility: Time travelers using primitive technology such as the Path store up a certain amount of temporal energy. Returning to their native time either restores their temporal balance to normal, or dangerously releases the energy through physical contact and ages other beings to death. Routine time-travelers such as Benny build up a natural tolerance to this effect.

HISTORY The People's war with the insectoid All of Us ended 30 years ago, but many People and Ships retain psychological scars. During the War, the All of Us never got near the Worldsphere, and the People rebuilt some decimated civilizations.

• On the planet Jalkejai, a flawed translator threatened to inadvertently cause war between some explorers and Jalkejai natives. Fortunately, the Jalkejai natives use group sex to resolve differences, meaning the explorers likely sabotaged the translator deliberately.

AT THE END OF THE DAY A surprisingly high-stakes and elegant story, *Walking to Babylon*'s glowing reputation is definitely overrated, but at least the book's writing is clean and hangs together well (which is more than a lot of novels can say). Orman gets points for pulling multiple threads from *The Also People* while keeping Benny center stage, making her the ultimate archaeologist (via time travel) and hearkening back to her TARDIS days. Unfortunately, certain bits seem extremely ahistorical, with Lafayette and Ninan sounding like modern-day characters in disguise. What's ironic is that if *Walking to Babylon* is a lesser Orman book (after hits such as *So Vile a Sin* and *Seeing I*), it still coalesces into a larger whole and stands as an above-average Benny novel.

OBLIVION

By Dave Stone

Release Date: March 1998
Order: Benny New Adventure #11
(Who NA #72)

MAIN CHARACTERS Bernice Summerfield, Jason Kane, Chris Cwej, Roz Forrester and the *Schirron Dream* crew.

TRAVEL LOG Malanoor, 2594; Earth, time unknown.

STORY SUMMARY A disruption in space-time begins eradicating alternate realities, causing fragments of their remains to carve though our Universe while threatening to implode all timelines. With the swashbuckling *Schirron Dream* crew lost at the epicenter of the disruption, the shape-shifting Sloathe named Sgloomi Po desperately flees and summons his old associates Benny, Chris Cwej, Jason Kane and Roz Forrester—the late Roz Forrester, that is—to deal with the problem. Unfortunately, the sentient *Schirron Dream* ship responds to Sgloomi's request by riding the timewaves into an alternate reality to recover Roz's 20-year-old self. Chris, Benny and Jason try to reason with young Roz, who hasn't met them yet, as the *Schirron Dream* returns to Earth.

Benny's group locates the lost *Schirron Dream* crew, but the source of the disruption, the godlike Simon Deed, blasts them unconscious. Deed, however, is merely an employee and focal point for the rich, decrepit Randolph Bane, who located a time-altering artifact called the Egg in the nefarious Shadow Directory. Bane used the Egg to transmit images of a false Universal destruction, seeking to lure time travelers and capture them, then wipe their sense of identity and make them hollow shells to conduct the Egg's power. If successful, Bane will to achieve true immortality even if the Universe truly perishes as a result.

Accordingly, the Egg batters Benny, Jason and Chris with mental images of their worst fears, trying to destroy their sense of self-will. Sgloomi's shapeshifting body and Roz's atemporal nature, however, help them resist the Egg's power and escape. Roz destroys the Egg, freeing Deed from Bane's thrall. Deed break Bane's neck in retribution just as a final whiplash of the Egg's energy Time Loops them, causing Deed to snap Bane's neck an infinite number of times. The Egg's last backlash of energy also knocks Roz unconscious, erasing her memories of these events.

The sentient *Schirron Dream* rescues its missing crew and destroys Bane's laboratory. With some sadness, Benny, Chris and Jason return young Roz to her native time, knowing she's destined to die in battle, then depart for home.

MEMORABLE MOMENTS Chris and Benny have an in-depth discussion about intra-dimensional mechanics that shows how far they've matured (previously, they needed the Doctor and five Brillo pads to work it out). Chris' researches conclude the Universe has 1.5 or two billion years left and Benny, without sarcasm, exclaims, "Is that all?"

Jason pilots the *Schirron Dream* while Benny bitches and asks about what his current "marriage" must be like. To reply and, just to be snide back, Jason revs the ship's acceleration and slams Benny into her seat. Throughout the book, Jason and Benny trade a beautiful number of verbal spars (Jason to Benny: "Blown the ink dry on your latest doctorate, yet?")

SEX AND SPIRITS Benny explains to a confused Sgloomi Po that she and Jason "haven't mated" in two years. That seems reasonable as the length of time since their divorce in *Eternity Weeps*, but overlooks their brief liaison in *Beyond the Sun*. Sgloomi Po observes Benny and Jason spend huge lumps of time simultaneously wanting to strangle each other and have sex.

Jason's associate Mira is a lesbian, ruling out a relationship between them. The *Schirron Dream* command crew—Nathan li Shao, Leetha and Kiru—evidently have a three-way relationship.

ASS-WHUPPINGS Young Roz beats the hell out of Chris, punches him in the balls and smacks his head into a bunk (trust us, we felt the blow from here). She goes for a killing blow, but Chris rolls and gets knocked out instead. Jason in turn uses martial arts to drive two fingers into Roz's throat and knock her out.

Simon Deed's mental assault supposedly blasts the *Schirron Dream* and its crew to atoms, but they're actually hit by an electrocution beam, then strung up on a rack (so much more civilized). Roz saves the day by dashing the Egg against the floor. Deed's incinerated corpse snaps Bane's neck an infinite number of times.

NOVEL TIE-INS Roslyn Forrester died overthrowing a corrupt Earth regime (*So Vile a Sin*).

Stone debuted the *Schirron Dream* crew in *Sky Pirates!*, the book where Sgloomi Po became the first shapeshifting Sloathe to attain true intelligence by exposure to Chris and Roz. *Oblivion*, in fact, forms the third part of Stone's "Clockwork

THE CRUCIAL BITS...

• **OBLIVION**—The *Schirron Dream* crew gets captured and, in obtaining help, the shapeshifting Sgloomi Po recovers the late Roz Forrester from another timeline. Roz helps defeat the power-mad Randolph Bane, but a power surge robs her memories and she's returned to her native time.

Trilogy," the first two parts being *Sky Pirates!* and *Death and Diplomacy* (truth be told, they're not very connected). The *Schirron Dream* hold a mosaic made from shards of Olabrian joy-luck crystal (Stone's *Ship of Fools*). Jason has unfinished business in the Catan Nebula (also *Ship of Fools*).

The Shadow Directory, the ultra-secret organization that held the Egg, played roles in *Christmas on a Rational Planet* and *The Death of Art*.

Oblivion hints that Chris Cwej works for the Time Lords (revealed in *Dead Romance*).

Benny ribs Jason for his marriage of convenience to ex-prisoner Charlene Conner (*Deadfall*), but Jason indicates it's anything but a marriage.

Sgloomi Po located Chris in spiritual contemplation at a monastery, a habit he picked up in *The Room With No Doors*. Sgloomi Po found Jason habitating one of the lower-level Habitats' seedier bars in the Proximan Chain-rifts (*Ship of Fools*).

CHARACTER DEVELOPMENT

Bernice Summerfield: Benny, dead broke, babysits rich kids on privately funded archaeological digs. A few years back, Benny lit up on a planet where not smoking would have instantly branded her an outsider. She doesn't smoke now, but understands addiction better.

When the Legion military drafted Benny, they used the Haze (See *Stuff You Need*) to break her down, but the treatment didn't take. The Haze inflicted on Benny the image of an alien soldier raping and bayoneting her mother to death, but Benny's memory of her mother's actual death at alien hands was too strong. The military didn't boot Benny out when the Haze failed, but it motivated her to escape.

Benny and Jason: If you'll recall, Benny and Jason's divorce in *Eternity Weeps* was accompanied by the scathing deaths of a good chunk of Earth's population. Benny now admits to Jason that she didn't handle their divorce very well, lashing out for the deaths even though it wasn't Jason's fault.

Jason admits he screwed up a short time-travel jaunt he took in that novel, but it broke him when Benny withdrew her love when he needed it most.

Jason concedes he didn't necessarily deserve her love, but he needed it anyway. In this, Jason's simply stating facts, not trying to dish out blame or ask for forgiveness. He even admits that Benny leaving him to preserve her happiness was likely the right thing to do. All in all, this forms what's possibly the most honest New Adventures discussion between Benny and Jason (you'll cry).

Fleeing from a squad of Dragan mechanics, intent on finding infiltration plan wafers that Benny had, Jason lost his pursuers by running through a Morlonia Prime burial ground, but as a consequence got him and Benny deported and barred for life. Benny's still smoldering over the event because it hurt her visa codes.

Chris Cwej: To find some inner peace after recent events, Chris visited the Beneficent Brothers of Saint Sidney over on Dragos, an inter-denominational sect that uses koan constructions as jokes. Chris was tending the Suspiciously Large Vegetable when the *Schirron Dream* arrived. His name's pronounced Schvey (Author's note: We're ill-spoken heretic geeks and still call him "Cwej," so feel free.)

Chris and Jason: Chris has superior skimmer and aircraft piloting skills, but Jason drives spaceships better.

Roz Forrester: Don't screw with Roz. She carries spare ammunition in her left biceps pouch, and a basic maintenance toolkit in her right. Her right thigh holds a snap-racked Multi-Function Gun. She's also equipped with an advanced police truncheon. Her belt-webbing pouches hold micro-grenades, comms and a sensor pack. A little zipped pocket holds a membrane-thin gas mask. And just for kicks, she's got a Bowie-like hunting knife. Stars, the woman should be a Klingon.

Roz and Fenn Martle: Roz's dead lover Fenn Martle declined promotion, claiming he could "do more good" on the street, but was more likely interested in protecting his bribes. Roz was fully ordained and squired to Martle when she was 19; he was 28. He "saved" her life a number of times, mostly to help villains who'd paid him off escape. The Adjudicators once sent Roz and Martle to investigate colonists on Zarjax, who were marketing a drug made from human pituitary extract.

Twenty-year-old Roz is considerably less hardened than the older Roz who partnered with Chris (presumably, the discovery of Martle's betrayal didn't help).

MISCELLANEOUS STUFF!

PERSONAL HELLS

Having captured Benny, Jason and Chris, Randolph Bane subjects them to an advanced form of the tortuous Haze (*See Stuff That You Need*) to wipe their personas and make them receptacles for the Egg's power. Each experience their worst personal nightmares. To wit:

Benny's Hell: The Army succeeds in brainwashing Benny, who becomes a concentration camp commandant directly responsible for the deaths of tens of millions. Brigadier-General Summerfield's convicted of crimes against sentient life, sentenced to constantly relive the deaths she caused via sensory immersion.
Where That Came From: Benny's brief military stint, first mentioned in *Love and War*.

Jason's Hell: Jason beats his wife Liora and kills their unborn child. Sentenced to life imprisonment, he loses an eye, three teeth and half an ear during his first 48 hours in prison due to a gang-rape incident—the first of many. He becomes HIV positive, but doesn't learn this for years (the prison doctor realizes it in four months).
Where That Came From: Jason's father routinely beat him and his sister, as revealed in *Death and Diplomacy*.

Chris' Hell: Chris evolves into a bribe-taking Adjudicator, rife with corruption. The New Reformation, led by incumbent High Justice Fenn Martle, finds him guilty of wholesale usury, extortion and several counts of homicide. As punishment, Chris gets excommunicated, branded, stripped and set loose without recourse in the Overcity's seedy Underlevels. Sadly for Chris, he lives.
Where That Came From: Chris' flight from a corrupt Adjudication system in *Original Sin*.

Sgloomi Po: Although he appears stupid at times, Sgloomi Po's quite intelligent and sympathetic—he's just incompatible with human beings and doesn't understand them.

ALIEN RACES Being asexual, *Sloathes* assume humans mate for life.

STUFF YOU NEED

The Haze: An offshoot of Bane Industries interactive virtual-reality rigs, the Haze uses long-term memory suppressants to make its subjects experience tortuous visions. The military uses the Haze to send its soldiers over the edge, making them more willing to kill (a treaty later banned the practice). Some resist the treatment, but few recover.

This book is not endorsed by the BBC. Doctor Who and TARDIS are trademarks of the BBC.

201

The Egg: A jeweled, duck-egg sized device that doesn't generate power itself, but serves as a control mechanism for directing extra-dimensional energies. Oddly enough, the Egg channels such forces through a specific kind of human being—those who lack an individual consciousness that would interfere with the process. Persona-wiped individuals, however, hold the precise electromagnetic impulse alignment that allows the Egg to affect the Universe's quantum processes. The Egg's much more useless for altering the laws of thermodynamics and biology, meaning you can't simply mindwipe someone with it and use their body.

ORGANIZATIONS *Adjudicators* have ID that're unique and unreproducable. Earth Adjudicators outrank nearly all other forms of law enforcement.

SHIPS *Schirron Dream*: Manta-shaped, sentient ship capable of vast space-time travel. The *Schirron Dream*'s command crew includes Nathan li Shao, Leetha t'Zhan, Kiru and (loosely) Sgloomi Po. The ship's also home to a great number of refugees from Dimension X (*Sky Pirates!*), including saurians from the planet Aneas, Fnarok-based albinos from icy Reklon, mostly humanoid nomads from the Shokesh deserts and frog-skinned amphibians from the water world of Elysium.

The ship's a compilation of different forms of alien technology and has evidently time traveled a great deal. It's stocked with foodstuffs and money for variety of alien races, but the armaments suck, limited to a couple of cannons designed to work only in an atmosphere.

The *Schirron Dream* destroys hundreds of thousands of miniature universes as it travels, but the effect's rather like consuming thousands of such realms along with your sandwich—you don't realize you're doing it. Jason therefore calls the realization that you're killing stuff a "Naked Lunch."

TIME TRAVEL If Sgloomi Po's to be believed, there wasn't much danger of young Roz learning something that would radically alter her timeline. Roz's morphic signal (*Lucifer Rising*) still resonates back and forth through the timeline, meaning her future's already locked and this adventure's merely an interval.

PHENOMENA *Parallel Universes:* The number of parallel universes is so enormous, it might as well be infinite. Fact is, we routinely cross inter-dimensionally into parallel realms simply by opening a letter or answering the door, writing off any inconsistencies we encounter as small lapses of memory. It's not stated, but we deduce from this that most parallel universes are dramatically similar

rather than being major deviations, a la "Inferno." Sometimes, a change in quantum state can even physically impose new structures on your memories, because the process of naturally crossing into parallel universes is one of the fundamental processes of the Universe. (The big question in all this, of course, is how do you really know who you're sleeping with?)

AT THE END OF THE DAY A mid-range novel that seeds decent enough dilemmas (young Roz, Bane's mad scheme for immortality), but annoyingly gets to the action with the plodding, syrupy speed of *Star Trek: The Motion Picture*. Fact is, the book's pretty schizophrenic, notably putting Benny, Chris and Jason through shocking Hells that're damnably telling to their characters, but wasting time on the *Schirron Dream* crew's hoaky unreality. The whole package ends much better than you'd expect and Stone nails the main Benny cast dead-on, but the book's convoluted scientific discussions and tendency toward Golden Age-style villains means *Oblivion*'s probably best skipped unless you're reading the majority of the Bennys.

THE MEDUSA EFFECT

By Justin Richards

Release Date: April 1998
Order: Benny New Adventure #12
(Who NA #73)

MAIN CHARACTERS Bernice Summerfield, Irving Braxiatel and Commander Skutloid.

TRAVEL LOG St. Oscar's University and the *Medusa*, 2594.

STORY SUMMARY St. Oscar's buries Maryann Decleiter, a member of the St. Oscar's Advanced Research Department (ARD) who died mysteriously. Consequently, Decleiter's boss, Taffeta Graize, asks Benny to take Decleiter's place on an expedition to the *Medusa*—a modified luxury spaceship that disappeared 20 years ago, but now is returning to Dellah. Benny agrees, but once onboard the *Medusa*, her team finds the original *Medusa* crew all brutally murdered, plus Stuart Stonley—a technician the ARD sent to service the *Medusa* for Benny's group.

Gradually, Benny's team experiences flashbacks of the murdered *Medusa* crew's memories. Worse, Benny's group assumes the personalities and characteristics of the original crew. Benny starts to act like the late *Medusa* passenger Anni Goranson, who asphyxiated in a chamber after she discovered two of her colleagues having an affair. Benny unwillingly endures a similar scenario and winds up in a chamber herself, but Stuart rescues her, shocking Goranson's personality out of Benny's mind. Sadly, Benny's colleagues re-enact the original *Medusa* slaughter, killing everyone save Benny and Stuart.

Benny concludes that the *Medusa* served as a military experiment to transfer mental engrams into telepathic synthoids, creating soldiers with vast information transfer abilities. Taffeta Graize appears onboard as a hologram, confirming both *Medusa* teams were implanted with false personalities in their medical injections in order to test how they'd interact in preparation for synthoid transfer. Benny, a last-minute replacement, didn't allow her personality graft to solidify, plus Benny's heavy drinking interfered with the injection. However, Stuart stands revealed as a *Medusa* synthoid who achieved independence and broke control.

Graize sends the *Medusa*'s prototype synthoids to kill Benny and Stuart, just as ARD Security Chief Styrus Kirk also docks with the *Medusa* to eliminate them. Benny and Stuart accidentally activate the *Medusa*'s self-destruct, then escape in Kirk's ship while the *Medusa* detonates, killing Kirk and the synthoids.

Back at St. Oscar's, Benny confronts ARD Director Silvera about the ARD's participation in the *Medusa* project. In exchange for their silence, Silvera arranges for Benny, Stuart and Irving Braxiatel to sneak into the ARD, then trick Graize into confessing her role in killing the *Medusa* Project members. To Benny's surprise, Stuart stabs Graize to death and they flee. With the *Medusa* project in ruins, Stuart leaves Dellah and assumes the identity of Jackson Hart, a *Medusa* stowaway.

MEMORABLE MOMENTS Benny cries for the deceased Maryann Decleiter, who was like Benny in spirit. The bizarre cover image of Benny dancing with a skeleton actually happens.

Stuart, imprinted with Jackson Hart's personality, says "You're standing in my chest" when Benny steps on Hart's corpse. After Stuart saves Benny from asphyxiating, he cradles her dead weight. (The affection-hating Benny weakly comments: "I'll give you just half an hour to stop that.")

As the synthoids approach, Benny grabs an "antique pistol," only to discover it's a lighter. She wrests a vodka bottle open and wonderfully takes a drink before lighting it afire.

SEX AND SPIRITS *The Medusa Effect* asks: "Is Benny a drunkard?" Certainly, Benny views her boozing as only a "habit," and here, drinking heavily counteracts the personality engrams in her sys-

tem. Yet, she drinks so often, it's possible she's an addict (*Dry Pilgrimage* also forwards this view). Benny supplies a urine sample in a beer bottle and comments, "[It's] probably more potent than what was in the bottle originally.]" Benny makes Thrascanian double-strength vodka bottles into flaming bombs.

ASS-WHUPPINGS Benny torches a synthoid with a pistol lighter and a bottle of alcohol-based perfume. Benny's crew re-creates the initial *Medusa* slaughter, with good doses of shootings, crushed heads, etc. As part of that, Benny's teammates drug her wine and stuff her into an airtight medical chamber. Like the late Anni Goranson, Benny claws up her face, throat and hands while trying to escape (thankfully, Stuart saves her).

ARD Security Chief Styrus Kirk killed Maryann Decleiter because she asked too many questions about the *Medusa* project. Stuart Stonley kills ARD member Taffeta Graize for her many sins. The *Medusa* explodes with ARD Security Chief Kirk aboard.

NOVEL TIE-INS The St. Oscar's Advanced Research Department, first mentioned in *Oh No It Isn't!*, tried to kill Benny in *Mean Streets*. ARD Director Silvera debuted there also. Styrus Kirk replaced Jarl Kendrick, murdered in that book, as ARD security chief. Kirk's mouth had a knife scar from a Dethak (also *Mean Streets*) battle. ARD member Taffeta Graize gained funding and experience by working on the DevCorps Project (*Mean Streets* again).

The Medusa Effect expands on Dellah's neutrality during the Earth war (*Oh No It Isn't!*). Benny started keeping diaries after her mother died (detailed in *Love and War*), probably to work out her aggression. She has replaced her destroyed bicycle (*Mean Streets*) with a new Mark 3.

It's possible Catan Nebula research (*Ship of Fools*) contributed to the ARD Personality Technique. Some octopods work in ARD surveillance (*Mean Streets*).

St. Oscar's Advanced Research Department has simularity technology, allowing planet-bound persons to project themselves into space as holograms and interact with events (*Lucifer Rising*).

CHARACTER DEVELOPMENT

Bernice Summerfield: Oddly enough, nobody's tried to kill Benny for several weeks (it must be a record). She hasn't dealt with strange alien menaces for at least a month (a Guinness for her, surely). Benny reads the St. Oscar's newspaper as a hard copy or onscreen, but never has the computer read it to her. She can't fly scout ships.

Irving Braxiatel: Braxiatel's search spiders collect massive amounts of online data. He quotes Sartre. Braxiatel suspected Stuart would kill Graize and allowed it to happen (becoming more like the manipulative seventh Doctor than ever), believing it would best end the *Medusa* Project.

Commander Skutloid: Head of the Institute of Strategic Studies at St. Oscar's, he's a 7-foot-tall Martian (*See Alien Races*). Skutloid wears armor, weapons and surveillance equipment grafted directly onto his body. An implant at the back of his brain holds the armor's central processor. Electrical impulses from his nervous system powers the armor's CPU and various systems. An artificial membrane in his throat filters air and supplies the nitrogen he requires. A red blast screen grants enhanced vision.

During the Earth war, Skutloid led several battalions into glory. Drexton and Garshal, formerly under his command, serve as trusted associates.

ALIEN RACES

Martians (a.k.a. Ice Warriors): Commander Skutloid's race long ago gave up wearing ceremonial helmets. They believe violent-death victims can't rest until atonement's made.

Synthoids: Artificial humans, perfected by the St. Oscar's ARD, designed to telepathically absorb and synthesize the personality, memories and skills of other beings. When the *Medusa* experiment failed, the onboard synthoids overgrew and became skeletal frames with large, putrefying, bulbous amounts of flesh and limbs jutting at odd angles (sounds like fun, doesn't it?).

PLACES TO GO

St. Oscar's University: The Gerondo Strait's near the University islands. The University Medical Center's an ugly red building.

St. Oscar's Advanced Research Department (ARD): The ARD lies on the University's main island. It's extremely closed and secretive, yet never lacks for sponsors. Most St. Oscar's residents don't even acknowledge the ARD's existence due to a clash of philosophies. During the war, the ARD protected scientists and thinkers who wanted to avoid the fighting and allegedly work on civilian projects (yeah, right).

Irving Braxiatel's study: It has 18th century France furnishings, plus an original Turner painting of ships in battle.

THE CRUCIAL BITS...

- **THE MEDUSA EFFECT**—First appearance of Commander Skutloid's associates Drexton and Garshal.

STUFF YOU NEED *Graduated Feedback:* The newspaper of St. Oscar's. The title narrowly beat out *Have A Banana*, largely because most students and staff didn't know what a banana was.

SHIPS The *Medusa* was a modified cruise liner, patterned on Jarrard luxury liners. Publicly, it was designed to perfect piloting ships by remote control. The *Medusa*'s power supply was a different phase from modern standards.

HISTORY As the Earth Empire fought a strenuous war (with the Daleks, but don't tell anyone), Dellah protected its neutrality by banning all military research. Weapons work continued in secret, though. Publicly, the *Medusa* prepared for launch as a prototype luxury liner, but *Medusa* team member Taffeta Graize, jealous of colleague Jackson Hart's talents (ironically, he loved her from afar), leaked information about the *Medusa* Project's military applications so the Project's sponsors would eliminate the team. Acting for the sponsors, Styrus Kirk (later ARD security chief) gunned the research team down. Hart survived and was framed for the crime—the largest mass murder in Dellah's history—but he smuggled himself aboard the *Medusa*.

Soon after, the ARD's personality experiment made the crew slaughter each other, their memories transferred to a group of incubating synthoids. However, the control synthoid (Stuart Stonley), gained independence by absorbing Hart's persona and killed in self-defense the ARD team sent to retrieve it. Stuart, barely cognizant, smashed the *Medusa*'s communications and navigations systems, forcing the ship to drift for 20 years.

- Dellah's neutrality was respected through blind luck. Had the Daleks won, Dellah would've been toast.

AT THE END OF THE DAY A vastly underrated book, alternating between the unnerving and the emotional. *The Medusa Effect* juggles a fairly ridiculous amount of secondary characters—some of which merely take up space—but throttles into high gear the second you realize Benny's becoming the asphyxiated Anni Goranson. It's grotesque in parts, but keeps the gore and violence in context, succeeding both as a good Benny story and good science fiction. Truth be told, it smartly *demanded* that I finish it.

DRY PILGRIMAGE

By Paul Leonard and Nick Walters

Release Date: May 1998
Order: Benny New Adventure #13
(Who NA #74)

MAIN CHARACTERS Bernice Summerfield.

TRAVEL LOG Planet Urtilaxia and the Silvasic Sea on Dellah, 2595. [Dating the Benny book's will never be a precise science, although *Beige Planet Mars'* conclusive date of June 2595 necessitates changing the calendar year at some point. To accommodate Virgin's sluggishness with changing the year—if they'd wanted us to know it was 2595 rather than 2594, they'd have said—leaves us erring on the side of caution and arbitrarily changing the date here.]

STORY SUMMARY Benny strikes up a friendship with Comparative Religions Professor Maeve Ruthven, who invites Benny on a sea cruise to study the alien Saraani, pilgrims fleeing their homeworld's religious oppression. Aboard the *Lady of Lorelei*, the Saraani will search Dellah for an island on which to settle. But as they set sail, Benny's horrified to learn the trip prohibits alcohol, while Maeve finds her ex-husband, engineer Brion Arvaile, aboard.

Suspicious of Brion, Maeve discovers him hiding dozens of military bioconstructs—vat-grown weapons of war—in the hold. Suddenly, one of the bioconstructs targets Maeve and kills her. But Brion compels a Saraani named Vilbian to perform the rite of "Holy Transference," a procedure used to reincarnate Saraani in their young, to draw Maeve's mind into Vilbian's own.

The Khulayn, leader of the hermaphroditic Saraani, grows incensed that Vilbian performed Holy Transference on an alien and aborts Vilbian's egg to prevent Maeve's mind from transferring to it. Vilbian instead transfers Maeve's consciousness into one of Brion's empty bioconstruct shells, but the bioconstruct's military programming overrides Maeve's personality.

Brion tells Benny that he's working for Czaritza Violaine, the exiled leader of his homeworld Visphok, to aid her alliance with the Khulayn. The Saraani will use Holy Transference to transfer the minds of Violaine's feeble veterans into the bioconstructs. In return, Violaine's promised to liberate her homeworld and Saraanis, but Violaine also plans to enslave the Saraani. Violaine's troops seize the *Lady of Lorelei*, allowing Brion to recog-

MISCELLANEOUS STUFF!

BENNY'S MANY LOVES

She's young, she's hot, and when Benny launched into her own novel line, it carried the expectation that she could romance any guy—or alien—she wanted in outrageously foreign locales. But as her final tally proves, Benny and her ex-husband Jason Kane sometimes had as much sex after their split as when they were married. Here's a rundown of Benny's conquests (and major non-conquests):

• **Student Michael Doran (Oh No It Isn't!)**—Benny amorally gives serious thought to seducing Michael Doran, one of her students, but settles for accidentally giving him a copy of *Make Dangerous Love to Me—The Erotic Poetry of Carla Tsampiras.*

• **Ex-hubby Jason Kane (Beyond the Sun)**—Divorcees Jason and Benny briefly re-unite for a sympathy screw.

• **Archaeologist John Lafayette (Walking to Babylon)**—On assignment to prevent war between the Time Lords and the People that will destroy Earth and numerous worlds, Benny encounters the time-lost John Lafayette in Babylon—and bangs him to relieve the stress.

• **London owner Marillian (The Sword of Forever)**—Benny marries the world's third richest man for political purposes (it's a bit complicated) but makes good on her threat not to sleep with him.

• **Ex-hubby Jason Kane (Beige Planet Mars)**—Unquestionably the Benny line's smuttiest book (Author's Note: I excused myself to "brush my hair"), topped off by an exceptionally racy scene in Jason's hotel room.

• **Ex-hubby Jason Kane (Tears of the Oracle)**—*Still more* sympathy sex (he's such a Samaritan, our Jason Kane).

• **Adventure hero Dent Harper (The Joy Device)**—Well, almost. Actually, Benny tries to...climax...an adventure holiday with danger seeker Dent Harper, but Jason and Clarence foil their attempts at the hot nookie.

• **Ex-hubby Jason Kane (Twilight of the Gods)**—Benny renews her pledge of love for Jason and declares they're meant to be together—so Jason naturally gets trapped in a parallel universe.

• **Scholar Porl (The Dead Men Diaries: "Step Back in Time")**—A young researcher names Porl pumps Benny with aphrodesic gas to have his way with her and steal a time ring.

• **Pilot Starl Stanmore (Gods of the Underworld)**—With Jason still missing, Benny probably (it's a bit vague) lays *New Dawn* pilot Stanmore.

nize Violaine's greed for power. The bioconstruct Maeve attempts to save Benny and Brion, but her robotic software loses control and she butchers Violaine, Violaine's men and Brion himself. Benny herds the Saraani to safety, but the Khulayn dies in the escape.

A horrified Maeve contemplates suicide, but her programming balks at self-inflicted pain. Benny therefore proposes letting Vilbian use Holy Transference to recover Maeve's mind from the armor, but the transfer fails to shift a mechanical-based mind to an organic host. Maeve's mind finally erases, leaving Benny to cry for her lost friend.

MEMORABLE MOMENTS The Saraani mistake Bernice's oath of "Bollocks!" as her calling on a human deity. Benny effectively becomes the Doctor at one point, taking people into giving up their guns ("Whatever is going on, it can't be worth any more people's lives.").

SEX AND SPIRITS This isn't the best book for Benny's lovelife. Eighteen-year-old xenobiology student Theo Tamlyn grows smitten with Benny and buys her beer. Unfortunately, he's converted into a bioconstruct and kicks it. Piss. Bugger.

Lady of Lorelei first officer Karl Donimo also dotes over Benny, graciously cleans up her puke when she's seasick (demonstrating true love is, in fact, cleaning up your lover's vomit) and pours her bath. They flirt a bit but nothing happens—a pity considering Donimo dies trying to release the *Lorelei*'s life raft. Benny, on vacation, struts about in a purple velvet bikini with gold tassels on the nipples and a big gold star on the crotch (regrettably, this isn't the book's cover image).

Benny drinks herself into a hangover in the Witch and Whirlwind bar, which sells Admiral's Old Antisocial beer. Benny's appalled when authorities confiscate her two bottles of Isle of Jura 45-year-old single malt and Chateau Yquatine. As further evidence Benny's a drunk, she guzzles Brettellian Potato Spirit, hanging on for dear life.

ASS-WHUPPINGS Maeve Ruthven endures a traumatic experience as a bioconstruct, but dies despite Benny's efforts. Before the end, Maeve lasers Violaine's soldiers. Maeve, under the bioconstruct's programming, crushes ex-hubby Brion to death.

The Khulayn aborts Vilbian's egg. The Khulayn also poisons the Saraani eggs to foster his military plan with Violaine and prevent the creation of alien-Saraani newborns. The crazed Khulayn also kills *Lady of Lorelei* Captain Dieter Fontana and the ship itself explodes.

Benny pukes and passes out from seasickness. Theo's spike embeds in Benny's left thigh, making her wheelchair-bound for a while.

NOVEL TIE-INS In a rare instance of the Virgin and BBC lines cross-pollinating, Professor Smith on page 77 mentions Krakenites (*Dreamstone Moon*), Xarax (*The Bodysnatchers*, *Deep Blue*), Tzun (*First Frontier*), Tractites (*Genocide*) and Valethske (*Superior Beings*). Benny and Maeve share Chateau Yquatine (*The Fall of Yquatine*).

CHARACTER DEVELOPMENT

Bernice Summerfield: Most important for male readers, Benny has trouble finding her little-used swimsuit. She's also an atheist. Benny takes Doc Shanley's Anti-Heave Pills for seasickness. Benny loans Menlove Stokes (*Oh No It Isn't!*) her bike while she's away. Student Jane Waspo sometimes babysits Wolsey.

Maeve Ruthven: Member of the St. Oscar's comparative religion department and the Marunianism faith. Maeve's red-haired and of Scottish ancestry. She's a couple of years younger than Benny, but hardly looks out of her teens. She liaisoned between the Saraani and St. Oscar's.

Benny and Maeve: Benny beats Maeve in armwrestling competitions.

ALIEN RACES

Saraani: Saraani have teardrop shaped heads, with pearly skin reflecting pinks, blues and yellow hues. Long, sharp horns sweep back from their crowns. They have large green eyes on either side of their snouts. Black slits, like gills, filter air. Saraani have broad chests and narrow waists, with clawed hands and feet. Their voices are typically quiet and musical. They can get drunk (but drinking booze warrants excommunication) and mainly eat insects.

Saraani (religion): Saraani religious factions worship the "GodUniverse," in which God and the Universe the same. The religious leaders, the Khulayns, wear blue robes, although the Council of Khulayns is now scattered. On Dellah, the more reasonable Saraani named Mirrium succeeded as the new Khulayn.

Saraani (reproduction): Saraani lack gender but lay eggs, fertilized by reproductive cells in their abdomens. As a Saraani's death approaches, it journeys to a special temple in its birth town called the "Temple of Ending." (The Saraani credit Zhylvlavian for founding the first of these.) Another Saraani performs "Holy Transference," extending a thick white protuberance from its mouth into the dying Saraani's brain steam, thus drawing the dying Saraani's mind into its own, an act that triggers fertilization. As the egg gestates, "Holy Instruction" erases the dead Saraani's personality while its knowledge and skills transfer to the egg. After birth, the Saraani ceremonially wash the newborn in holy water. It's forbidden to perform these rites on aliens.

Saraani (lifespan): Saraani live, on average, only 10 years. They enjoy healthy lives, but wither quickly at the end. They've eliminated most diseases and accidents, so old age kills most Saraani.

Bioconstructs: Humanoid-shaped suits of black body armor, armed with foot-long spikes attached to the gloves, neurotoxin-bearing spines, venom glands that kill by spitting, micro-grenades, a matter-dispersal beam, a Skailon flenser and an armor-piercing needle laser.

ALIEN PLANETS *Dellah:* Dellah's a watery planet, but has more air travel than sea transport. The Goll Navy owns most of the large seafaring ships. The Silvasic Sea, Dellah's largest body of water, occupies much of the southern hemisphere's temperate zone.

PLACES TO GO *St. Oscar's University:* Includes Goodyear College.

ORGANIZATIONS *"Renaissants":* Saraanis atheist faction that ousted the religious groups.

SHIPS *The Lady of Lorelei:* St. Oscar's only large seafaring vessel. It originally belonged to a defunct Earth-based leisure company. Until the Saraani pilgrimage, St. Oscar's used the ship to store cryogenic equipment and planned to scrap it. The Lorelei displayed an early 20th century Earth hotel design. It crewed 20, with St. Oscar's students composing the serving staff.

HISTORY About 200 years ago, the mainstream Protestant Church accepted all science, including genetic engineering. A Scottish Protestant, Marunia Lennox, opposed this move and deemed all science evil, forming the religion Marunianism. In time, Marunianism became more liberal until it only rejected genetics, vivisection and, just for the hell of it, experimentation.

• Slavs and Russians colonists on Visphok advocated genetic purity, the "Visphoi Ideal." For centuries, a succession of emperors and empresses ruled Visphok until the planet degenerated into a military dictatorship.

• Genetics eliminated all major human cancers and blood disorders—not to mention wisdom teeth. Genetic engineering also allows bodies to be repaired and granted new brains, if the original intelligence's somehow preserved (such as Knights of Jeneve founder Baygent in *Deadfall*). Cigarettes these days don't have harmful elements (and probably aren't much fun).

• Earth authorities arranged for Quinsidd and Verene to accept Saraani exiles.

AT THE END OF THE DAY Arguably stronger as the sum of its parts, *Dry Pilgrimage* comes across somewhat clunky because the first half smoothly focuses on Benny's trials on a no-booze cruise and her friendship with Maeve—however, the book's latter part plunges into a bloodbath, filled with talk of dirty alien biology. Benny's ever-rambling mouth wins some points and her misplaced guilt over Maeve makes for a potent end, but if you mix all this like a blender-made margarita, you wind up with a mid-level Benny book that's hard to read and feel good about yourself.

THE SWORD OF FOREVER

By Jim Mortimore

Release Date: June 1998
Order: Benny New Adventure #14
(Who NA #75)

TRAVEL LOG Antarctica, Egypt, London, Glasgow, Loch Ness, Arginy, Paris, Kampuchea and Dellah, all 2595. Also, Pangaia, 80 million years ago; the Orient, 4500 B.C.; Jerusalem, 3555 B.C. and Kampuchea, 150 A.D. (Benny gets around.)

STORY SUMMARY Benny researches a lost journal of Guillaime, a 14th-century Knights Templar member who constructed the trap-filled Castle Arginy to protect the Knights' greatest secrets. Years ago, Benny explored Castle Arginy to find the famed Finger of John the Baptist and win academic glory, but a snare killed her lover Daniel. But now, trying to return to Arginy and quell her guilt over Daniel's death, Benny chickens out and diverts to a stop over in Antarctica.

There, Benny discovers the mummified remains of a velociraptor, complete with human bone fragments in its stomach. Desperate to learn more, Benny asks for help from Marillian, a fantastically rich expedition leader who owns most of London. Unable to research the British Library's forbidden texts without a childbirth license, Benny marries Marillian out of convenience, then investigates the velociraptor's remains. To her horror, Benny finds bone fragments in the velociraptor's stomach match her DNA profile exactly—meaning the velociraptor fossil holds Benny's remains.

Benny and Marillian return to Castle Arginy, where Benny, older and wiser since her last visit, eludes Guillaime's traps and recovers the Finger of John the Baptist. Unexpectedly, Marillian takes the Finger, uses it to locate what's presumably the skull of Jesus Christ and abandons Benny. However, Freemason agents, the neo-successors to the Knights Templar, find Benny and explain that Marillian is actually a renegade Freemason collecting holy artifacts for his true master.

Twenty years ago, Marillian attempted to find the Ark of the Covenant but was executed by a mad Third World ruler named Gebmoses III. Resurrected by Gebmoses using the Ark's power, Marillian feared a second death and agreed to compile artifacts that composed the Sword of Forever—an immeasurably powerful device that can reshape space and time at the cost of its controller's life. After further research, Benny realizes that Gebmoses III seeks to use the Sword of Forever to retroactively create a master race with DNA from the alleged Christ skull.

Moreover, Benny and the Freemasons conclude that a botched use of the Sword flung Benny and the device back in time 60 million years, where a velociraptor ate Benny and the Sword destroyed Earth. Yet, further evidence suggests the Sword was paradoxically used again—by Benny—to retroactively re-create Earth's timeline.

Benny convinces Marillian the insane Gebmoses must be stopped. As Gebmoses' priests crucify him to trigger the Sword's power, Marillian withholds the Ark of the Covenant—the Sword's control device—until Gebmoses dies. Immediately afterward, Marillian and his allies crucify a willing Benny. By welcoming God into her heart as she dies, Benny activates the Sword and restores Earth's timeline as intended. The Ark then resurrects Benny into a new body, but she returns to Dellah without looking at her old body, denying the incident ever took place.

MEMORABLE MOMENTS As Benny makes a death-defying leap, she promises God on High she'll give up anything he wants—except booze, of course. Benny, upon discovering that her remains were found in a velociraptor's belly, asks for a drug-laced sugar cube. She loses a game of netball to a blind priest who supposedly sees on faith.

THE CRUCIAL BITS...

- **THE SWORD OF FOREVER**—Benny platonically marries the filthy rich Marillian to conduct research at the British Library. Benny sutures Earth's timeline using a powerful artifact named the Sword of Forever, but dies—and gets restored—in the process.

In the book's top moment, Benny breaks down before Marillian and argues she must have free will despite her apparent destiny to use the Sword.

SEX AND SPIRITS The lost Daniel loved Benny completely (*See Character Development*).

Benny trades sexy shots of herself on a camel, leg uncovered, for access to the Sphinx. She thinks Marillian attractive and marries him for convenience, but stresses they can't have sex. Benny gets information by undressing a couple of unconscious, drunken male Freemason agents, then entwining their arms together and putting a can of aerosol prophylactic between them. When the Freemasons wake up, Benny implies that her memories of their liaison varies according to how much information they give her.

ASS-WHUPPINGS Benny doesn't fare too well this book, dying not once but twice. It's omitted from the Story Summary to streamline the plot, but the Freemasons assassinate Benny. However, Marillian resurrects her—without Benny's knowledge—using the Ark of the Covenant. Benny dies a second time to activate the Sword of Forever but manages to restore herself. She also gets poisoned, but injects herself with anti-toxin. Ah yes, and a velociraptor gulps her like a rodent.

Benny's lover Daniel, believed dead, secretly survived the Castle Arginy trap (*See Character Development*).

Freemasons butcher Anson the talking pig, who befriended Bernice.

NOVEL TIE-INS *Dry Pilgrimage* stated Benny's an atheist, but this book says she's an agnostic, curious about religious issues.

The Library of Things that Never Were, first seen here, reappears in *The Taking of Planet Five*. Benny previously met dinosaurs in Mortimore's *Blood Heat*. Adolf Hitler (*Timewyrm: Exodus*, *The Shadow of the Glass*) suspected the Ark held great power but didn't harness it.

Benny trades the Doctor's antique Platinum American Express card (*Eternity Weeps*) as payment to trader Ikvor "Butterman" DeLongPre for rescuing her from a mutant sea lion.

CHARACTER DEVELOPMENT

Bernice Summerfield: Earth feels like Benny's second home. She's vegetarian when given the option. Trying to learn more about the Sword of Forever, Benny joins the Freemasons. Benny's use of the Sword of Forever makes her DNA compatible with various Freemason relics.

Bernice Summerfield and Daniel Beaujeu: Benny's lover Daniel was the eldest son of the Count of Arginy in France. When Benny was 22, they searched for the Holy Finger of John the Baptist, hoping to qualify Benny for a doctorate, plus an early fellowship, residency and cash. Within four weeks, Benny located Castle Arginy. She devised means to avoid the Castle's traps, but stones composing a water-based snare had eroded, meaning Daniel didn't know the correct stone combination to release the trap and apparently drowned.

After the incident, Benny ripped out her contact lenses, determined that she'd never again see the world through the "eyes" that had witnessed Daniel's death.

Unknown to Benny, Daniel survived but became infected with alien retroviruses that tainted Earth in the aftermath of the Dalek war ("The Dalek Invasion of Earth"). He joined a group of fellow victims and became decently happy, forgiving Benny for the Arginy accident.

Marillian: A second order Freemason who tried to seize the Ark of the Covenant from Emperor Gebmoses III by force. Sadly for Marillian, his archaic gun exploded and nearly tore him apart. Gebmoses III's military escort further blew Marillian's brains out, but Gebmoses III used the Ark to restore Marillian's life in return for his service.

Marillian, 46, is unofficially the third richest man in the world, director of the Future Foundation Research Group. He basically owns London, a Telecom Tower Penthouse and Greenwich.

Benny and Marillian: They got married at St. Paul's (Benny had never been there before), but she wore a black leather wedding dress.

PLACES TO GO

St. Oscar's University: Benny clones the velociraptor that ate her in an alternate timeline, hoping to learn more about the incident. Hailing from an intelligent civilization (*See History*), the raptor names itself Patience, learns sign language from Benny and joins the St. Oscar's teaching staff after being fitted with a voicecoder.

MISCELLANEOUS STUFF!

USING THE SWORD OF FOREVER

The Sword of Forever has four components: The Spear of Longinus that pierced Christ's side, Christ's Crown of Thorns, the Holy Grail and the Ark of the Covenant.

The Crown uses micromolecular protein chains (or 'thorns') to record memories and experiences from the prospective user's brain, assessing the "purity" of their request (Gebmoses wouldn't have succeeded in any instance, as his "master race" agenda isn't exactly wholesome). The Spear samples blood and body fluids to later clone a duplicate of the user. The Grail (a stone in this instance) serves as a storage mechanism by which the aforementioned materials are transported to the Ark, which carries the "laboratory mechanisms" to implement the user's last request and the cloning of any user deemed sufficiently pure.

Allegedly, the Sword of Forever guarded the gates of Eden after man and woman were cast out. If activated, the Sword can reshape the Universe by literally creating time and by extension rewriting matter. As such, the Sword presumably creates parallel timelines, overlaying the past with its new gush of time.

The Sword was presumably geared to be used by a higher power. Mortals can use the Sword, but must die to activate it. The operator must use the Sword as an act of faith, because it requires the sacrifice of the user's life. The operator needs only be killed, not crucified, although crucifixion (certainly in Benny's case) is a potent symbol for reshaping the world. The Sword doesn't require such metaphor, but recognizes such symbols as important and recognizes that Christ's resurrection changed the world.

HISTORY Eighty million years ago, some velociraptors developed intelligence (presumably offshoots of Silurian civilization) and a sophisticated culture. The Ruling Families shaped velociraptor policy, with differing views on pre-historic man. Unfortunately for the velociraptors, the extinction event ("Earthshock") annihilated them.

• In Egypt, 1287, a female Knights Templar agent kept the Sword of Forever secure in a secret chamber beneath the Sphinx but bequeathed it to Templar member Hughes de Chalons. In 1307, King Philip's agents captured de Chalons in a whore's bed and interrogated him. De Chalons had already passed the Sword along, but the King had him, plus Templar Grand Master Jacques de Molay and Order Preceptor Geoffrey de Charnay burnt to death. The Order effectively died, but their secrets remained hidden for more than 1,000 years. Afterward, Guillaime de Molay secured the Finger of John the Baptist in Castle Arginy. Following the Inquisition, the Freemasons rose from the defunct Knights' ashes.

• The Sphinx endured a variety of oddball menaces, including artist Heironymous Basquiat, who in 2234 tried to buy the monument and giftwrap it in Christmas paper. Authorities threw him out as a nut.

• The Leaning Tower perished when a half-ton asteroid decimated Pisa.

• Enemy missiles that pelted Europe during the Dalek war ("The Dalek Invasion of Earth") spread retroviruses that seeped into the food chain and atmosphere, tainting 68 percent of the terrestrial DNA across more than 40 percent of the globe. A number of countries fell apart and reformed. By 2577, some once-human mutants became tree-like, synthesizing sunlight and growing fruit.

• Coca-Cola drugged their beverages to insure the public's unswerving wartime allegiance.

• Internally torn Somalia finally gained some cohesiveness, but a virus-loaded Dalek missile turned the residents into bio-hybrids. By 2575, Kenya and Somalia remained sites of massive bio-infestation, with mutations ranging from Tanzania to the Ethiopian Plateau. A hybrid jungle overran the ex-Nairobi. Hybrids and a sanitizing force of Russian Conglomerate Military Red Cross set up a settlement in Adis Ababa.

• Farms in Glasgow and other areas use enhanced pigs, but their conversation's pretty much limited to "no," "yes" and "fuck you" (they're much like certain humans in that regard). Nike now makes infantry footwear (the boots are allegedly smarter than the soldiers).

POSSIBLE HISTORY Nearly 3,000 years ago, King Solomon's son—the Emperor Menelik I—stole the Ark of the Covenant from his father's temple and brought it into Debra Makeda, or Tana Kirkos as it was known. In 959 A.D., Queen Gudit burned many churches in Tigray and other parts of Ethiopia, overthrowing the Solomaic dynasty. The Ark of the Covenant's protectors, fearing Gudit would capture the relic, took it to Axum. An expedition led by Jennings-Bankhurst located the Ark just as the Red Cross nuked Axum to sterilize the area's retroviruses. Jennings-Bankhurst's translator, Ondemwu, stole the Ark and became its guardian. Five years later, Gebmoses III acquired the artifact.

AT THE END OF THE DAY Excellent, although *The Sword of Forever*'s tangled details will likely cleave your brain asunder. On the plus side: Benny's trauma from Daniel's loss, her impending death and Marillian's betrayal make this an intensely personal tale, seeped in a culture and force beyond humankind's understanding. On the down side: The book's jumping focus will damnably confuse many readers, and some religious people—myself included—will find its religious inferences hard to swallow. The final result: You'll probably walk away from the well-textured, underrated *The Sword of Forever* knowing you enjoyed yourself immensely—but unable to explain its details for love nor money.

ANOTHER GIRL, ANOTHER PLANET

By Martin Day and Len Beech

Release Date: August 1998
Order: Benny New Adventure #15
(Who NA #66)

MAIN CHARACTER Bernice Summerfield.

TRAVEL LOG Dimetos, 2595.

STORY SUMMARY Benny receives a troubled communiqué from her penpal of several months, fellow archaeologist Lizbeth Fugard, who worries that someone's stalking her on the colony planet Dimetos. The Dimetan government hired Lizbeth to validate the planet's heritage through industrial sites established by Eurogen Butler, the corporation that formerly owned Dimetos, but a saboteur has foiled Lizbeth's operations.

Sympathetic, Benny travels to Dimetos and finds that previous Dimetan administrations used inaccurate Eurogen Butler maps to build facilities, meaning several government installations are constructed atop discarded nuclear reactors and abandoned mine workings. Having discovered this politically damaging secret, Bantu Cooperative, a corrupt weapons manufacturer, appears to be ruining Lizbeth's digs to cover-up the government's past actions, curry favor with the current Dimetan regime and better entrench itself on Dimetos. But as Benny seeks to unravel the full truth, Lizbeth becomes unhelpful, dating Bantu operative Karl Csokor on the rebound and erroneously thinking her ex-boyfriend Alex Mphahlele's having a fling with Benny.

In a park, Csokor dissolves into a lethal gaseous

being and maniacally claims to be Assan, last of the Narayayan emperors. Worse, Csokor dubs Lizbeth the Shiga, an ancient evil that wiped out the Narayayans. Fearing bad publicity if the renegade Csokor goes too far, Bantu delegate Mastaba loans Benny an experimental warscarab vehicle. Benny rushes to the park and apparently kills Csokor with stun grenades, harmless to humans but fatal to Csokor's alien constitution. Before her control of the warscarab expires, Benny uses it to impulsively annihilate Bantu's automated research facility on Dimetos, seeking to stymie Bantu's rigid grip on the planet.

Mastaba's guards corner Benny and Lizbeth afterward, allowing Mastaba to explain that Eurogen Butler initially settled on Dimetos by wiping out the indigenous population. Csokor, whatever his personal dementia, is actually the last native Dimetan, mutually augmented by Eurogen Butler and Bantu as a shape-shifting assassin. However, the enhancements eventually degraded Csokor's personality and he latched onto similarities between the Shiga legend and Lizbeth, making him an unstable element that required termination.

Having decided Benny's destruction of the Bantu facility will expose the entire affair, Mastaba deems Benny and Lizbeth expendable and orders his cadre to kill them. Fortunately, the still-functional Csokor, having learned his true identity, uses his talents to vengefully butcher Mastaba and his men. Feeling desolate as the last of his species, Csokor allows his gaseous form to dissipate, killing himself.

The surviving Bantu delegates let Benny and Lizbeth live, desperate for political damage control, and ask Benny to watch for signs of the Shiga (presumably to modify it as a weapon). Lizbeth and Alex reconcile, allowing Benny to return to St. Oscar's troubled because she accidentally destroyed the largest Dimetan archaeological site when she leveled the Bantu research facility.

SEX AND SPIRITS Benny recalls making love to Jason a week or two after their wedding, despairing about how intimacy stepped aside and uninvolved humping took its place. While Jason was in his own little world, Benny felt unloved, uncherished and worthless (and isn't that a pleasant little memory).

Benny has a very strange and perplexing dream about attacking Jason with a blunt screwdriver. In turn, he charges at her with a gigantic erection.

Dr. Follett, Benny's boss, holds a soiree and Benny gets decently hammered. She feels attracted to Lizbeth's ex-boyfriend Alex Mphahlele, but doesn't want to get involved in such a triangle. Lizbeth broke up with Alex after she miscarried.

ASS-WHUPPINGS Benny catches the fringe of an explosion and cuts her head. Conversely, she orders the Bantu warscarab to self-destruct and destroy Bantu's main weapons testing facility (she ordered the warscarab to protect lives, but a few people surely died in the chaos). Csokor, last of the native Dimetans, kills Bantu delegate Mastaba and his guards, then dissipates himself.

NOVEL TIE-INS *Another Girl, Another Planet* marks the first appearance of John, Benny's trenchcoat-wearing, smoking informant who perishes in *Where Angels Fear*.

After this story, Lizbeth becomes a professor of Sidereal Mythology at Youkali University (*Return of the Living Dad*).

Eurogen Butler debuted as a corrupt Earth corporation in *Cat's Cradle: Warhead*. The Jauza race adapted morphic field technology (*Lucifer Rising*) for a profound range of military applications, but mostly used the result to create pretty lights.

Benny's got bootleg audio tapes from the early 2000s, including *Outta My Way Monkey-Boy* and *The Greytest Hips of Johnny Chess* (son of Ian Chesterton and Barbara Wright, who appears in *The King of Terror*).

CHARACTER DEVELOPMENT
Bernice Summerfield: Benny doesn't thrive as much on late nights and worries she's getting old (we know the feeling). She increasingly realizes she has no real home. She wrote a paper called *Propaganda and Myth*. Her classy wardrobe includes a "South Park" T-Shirt. Benny's more interested in societies that differ from our own (probably a facet of her escapism). She went swimming on the holiday planet of Alnasl in a purple-blue shallow sea with a young woman named Zavijava Akubens. A gathering of Midan zooplankton enchanted her, but they flew apart into itty-bitty bits and scared her. Benny learned a lesson about how beauty can be dangerous when she and Zavi crashed their skimmer through carelessness and the fish swam to eat blood pouring from Zavi's wound.

Dimetos' historical fraternity fondly regards Benny's articles and monographs. She wears drooping earrings. Her system absorbed a few million nanocules to pilot the Bantu warscarab, but they self-terminated.

Benny and Lizbeth Fugard: They've been corresponding for some months, regarding themselves as kindred female archaeologists. Unlike Benny, Lizbeth's got legitimate qualifications. She's in her mid-20s, and specializes in recent industry.

Karl Csokor: Eurogen Butler and Bantu Cooperative took Csokor—originally Assan, the last of the indigenous Dimetans—as a relic of his destroyed race and tested their morphic field technology on him. The transformed Csokor received an extended lifespan, shape-shifting talents and limited empathy. He was also embedded with a BioTek-designed hologen gas capable of turning sane opponents schizophrenic and delusional. Csokor himself suffered from amnesia and needed drugs to maintain his unstable biochemistry.

The Shiga: Allegedly the destroyer of the Narayayan people of Thuba Castelani, an evil from space that devastates planet after planet. The Shiga can reincarnate itself, but grows weaker with each rebirth.

Joseph: He's ordered not to disturb Benny while she "digests the wisdom of the greats" (i.e., sleeps).

ALIEN RACES *Dimetans (indigenous):* Could inherently manipulate the morphic fields (*Lucifer Rising*) that determined their genetic code. As such, the Dimetans were susceptible to the augmentations that made Csokor a shape-shifter.

ORGANIZATIONS *Bantu Cooperative* specializes in offensive and defensive systems, essentially serving as corporate arms dealers. Bantu's trying to get a foothold onto Dimetos, but likely serves as intermediaries for the unseen alien Jauzans.

HISTORY Eurogen Butler Corporation colonized Dimetos in 2142, and badly terraformed it, plundering the planet's mineral wealth. The corporation planned to ship the native Dimetans off-world, but the natives refused to cooperate, frightened of interstellar travel—so Eurogen Butler resorted to genocide. Still, the company had difficulties in taming Dimetos: An accident killed dozens in cave-in in 2147, and a riot and general strike were violently quelled in 2149. Eurogen Butler left Dimetos in 2151.

• The Bantu Independence Group (BIG) originated in 2011 as a political movement for the oppressed in southern Africa, purchasing land and helping to build model communities. By 2044, BIG existed only as a small holding company, but energy tycoon Olle Ahlin revitalized the BIG ruling council with funding in the 2060s and renewed the group with an emphasis on central Africa and Scandinavia. The group re-energized its political furor in the 2070s and 2080s, seeking out sub-light-speed vessels colonizing other worlds. Ahlin died in 2099.

• BIG become more militaristic in the 2200s and formed a loose alliance of dominated worlds, supported and governed by countless alien races. On Earth, Emah-ji-ji-Ke-gege became Bantu's first non-human leader circa 2397. Later, a chance diplomatic encounter with the Draconians (hundreds of years before "Frontier in Space") led to the Bantu co-funding a pre-emptive weapons initiative. Bantu worlds flourished until the early 2500s, then lost an unspecified war in 2511 and re-emerged as a purely commercial body—the Bantu Cooperative—in 2543.

AT THE END OF THE DAY Definitely a weak link in the Virgin Benny line, reading as a pulpy, ill-considered work that's loaded with filler. Sloppy implementation plagues *Another Girl, Another Planet*, making it terribly difficult to believe Benny could put her neck on the chop for someone she barely knows, then almost off-handedly outwit a planetary government and an arms-trading corporation. Not to mention how an irrelevant, supernatural Shiga plotline further tars the works. The back cover claims that Day (the glorious *Bunker Soldiers* and nimble *Menagerie*) and Beech have written or co-written 22 books between them—but you'd never know it from this story.

BEIGE PLANET MARS

By Lance Parkin and Mark Clapham

Release Date: October 1998
Order: Benny New Adventure #16
(Who NA #77)

MAIN CHARACTERS Bernice Summerfield, Jason Kane.

TRAVEL LOG Mars, June 21, 2595.

STORY SUMMARY At an academic conference on Mars, celebrating the 500th anniversary of its terraforming, Benny separately becomes acquaintances with fellow lecturer Elizabeth Trinity and elderly war veteran Isaac Deniken. But when Deniken gets murdered in the hotel room next to Benny—his heart literally cut out—she splits her time between procrastinating on her lecture and investigating Deniken's killing. As a further distraction, Benny's ex-husband Jason Kane arrives, now ludicrously wealthy from sales of his alien pornography book, and they have a torrid session in his hotel room.

Completely improvising her Martian history lecture onstage, Benny suddenly realizes that her friend Trinity is actually Tellassar, the ex-Mars

Minister of Defense, wanted because she failed to launch Mars' missiles against alien invaders 50 years ago. The newly informed public seethes for Tellassar's blood, but Benny helps Tellassar flee.

Tellassar explains that during her time as Mars' defense minister, authorities wanted those in charge of missile command codes to consider and re-consider the humanity and consequences of their actions. Thus, the command codes were sealed in the heart of a loved one—in Tellassar's case, her lover, Isaac Deniken. Tellassar, unable to cut out her Deniken's heart, even in the face of an alien invasion, fled into hiding, but Deniken's killer presumably took the missile codes.

At Tellassar's old missile base, Benny and Tellassar find the missiles intact. However, someone has used Deniken's command codes to steal CATCH, the advanced Artificial Intelligence that governed the base. Benny concludes that only Phillip and Christina York, the owners of York-Corp and sponsors of the conference, possess the resources to perform such a heist.

Benny, Jason and their various allies reach the Yorks' automated liner and find the Yorks have no interest in warfare. The Yorks, fearing a hostile takeover from Bantu Cooperative that would harm their employees, hope to use CATCH's advanced software to repel Bantu's efforts. However, CATCH misinterprets their instructions and prepares to launch the missiles, mistaking Bantu's "hostile takeover" is an alien invasion. The Yorks flee, even as Benny destroys CATCH's laptop and ends the threat to Mars.

Tellassar, out of guilt for her actions and inactions, puts her life at the mercies of Martian hero General Keele. Meanwhile, Jason and Benny leave the future open to a reconciliation, and Jason gives Benny his credit chit as a token of goodwill. Believing the chit only to be worth a few credits, Benny gives it to Jason's scruffy associates, Seez and Soaz, who become fabulously wealthy when the first royalty payment for Jason's pornography book appears on the chit. Whoops.

MEMORABLE MOMENTS *Beige Planet Mars* succeeds by its brazenness, starting when Benny, not realizing she's talking to Trinity, says about Trinity's work: "She treats her readers like morons." Graciously, Benny adds about herself: "She spends all her royalties on alcohol and Belgian chocolates and spends most of her time totally skint."

In a top comedy moment, an excerpt of Jason's pornography writing reads, "All he wanted was tentacle! Tentacle! Tentacle!" For that matter, the most steamy, downright trashy novel moment in the entire Benny line (or "Doctor Who") happens

TOP 5

BENNY TRIUMPHS

1) The Time Lord-People war averted (Tears of the Oracle)—Benny and Irving Braxiatel combine their talents to stymie the Dellan gods' power, preventing a Time Lord/People counter-strike that could've wasted creation.

2) Universal paradox popped (Ghost Devices)—Benny bursts a paradox involving a time travel device, Planetcracker missiles and quasars (confusing, isn't it?) that would've corrupted the Universe's timeline.

3) Earth's timeline saved (Walking to Babylon)—By closing down an illicit time portal, Benny prevents the People from atomizing ancient Babylon to cover their tracks.

4) Earth's timeline rewritten (The Sword of Forever)—Using the famed Sword of Forever (a combination of Christian holy relics), Benny retroactively restores Earth's past, present and future after a botched use of the Sword destroyed it.

5) Universe's philosophy preserved (Down)—MEPHISTO, a Universal archetype for doubt and uncertainty, uses the insane Person !X to attack Benny in hopes of manifesting a pain-filled philosophy throughout the Universe. Benny thwarts MEPHISTO's plans by shoving !X's gun up his ass (*See Top Comedy Moments*).

Honorable Mention: Benny cures her brain tumor (*Return to the Fractured Planet*)—A definite triumph, kept off the main list only because of the sheer number of times Benny's saved the Universe.

when Benny goes to Jason's hotel room and mercilessly straddles him (our glasses fogged over).

Benny and Jason's various wanted/unwanted crushes and dalliances (the ever insatiable Jason...how shall we say this politely?...lets the Pakhar Professor Scoblow live up to her name) ends with a brawl where Jason and Benny kiss, pausing only to bash opponents who come in range. In a top dramatic moment, Tellassar offers General Keele her life for failing Mars.

SEX AND SPIRITS *Beige Planet Mars* also proves to be one of the smuttiest Benny books (and we're not complaining). Benny's ex-hubby Jason argues that during their marriage, Benny wanted Jason to screw her as much as he did, but lacked the courage to say so. Benny basically agrees with him in a scene where they rut like bunnies just to vent some hormones. Jason asks Benny to marry him again, but they leave the future open.

All of that said, Jason also shamelessly shares a bed with the Pakhar Professor Scoblow. He admits that his sordid past as a male prostitute messed him up pretty bad—and we shouldn't find this as hilarious as we do—when he embarks on a career as a pornography writer.

The more conservative Benny turns down an offer from the much older Isaac Deniken to visit his hotel room. They don't get any further than Benny drunkenly revealing her life story to him, hazily using the word "clitoris" in some forgotten context. Deniken retires to his room to be murdered while Benny, sloshed from a combination of RedStar, Martian vodka and A Red Under the Bed, passes out in an armchair.

Benny flirts harmlessly with conference director Gerald Makhno, who's a decade younger than her. Makhno, perhaps a parody of science fiction convention types, sleeps with a copy of *Down Among The Dead Men* and envisions the ways he could pleasure Benny, given that they're at the height of their sexual powers (but nothing happens).

The last time Benny was on Mars, she was 24 and in love with a bloke named Tim (mentioned in *Lucifer Rising*). They spent most of their time uncovering tombs of Martian Lords at Mare Sirenum and sharing a sleeping bag.

ASS-WHUPPINGS Benny fails to recognize a cloaked Jason and knees him in the groin. Upon learning his identity, she knees him again. To reach the York's sea cruiser, Benny and Jason jury-rig a catapult that makes Jason hit the ship wrong and break his left leg.

Parkin and Clapham leave Tellassar's fate open, but General Keele likely cuts her heart out. Benny kills CATCH by destroying its host laptop.

TV TIE-INS The *Mona Lisa*—well, the fake *Mona Lisa* ("City of Death")—was destroyed in 2086 when Mars butchered Paris with an asteroid.

NOVEL TIE-INS *Lucifer Rising*, *GodEngine* and *The Dying Days* covered much of Mars' history and the Thousand Day War between Earth and Mars.

This is not, repeat, not canon, but the authors establish that two offworlders, an old man and a girl in her late teens, aided with the liberation of Mars (*See History*). It's never blatantly stated, but this is the apocryphal 42nd Doctor—yes, the 42nd Doctor—and his companion, used by Parkin and Clapham in various fan fiction pieces throughout the mid-1990s. The Doctor in this incarnation is modeled after actor Ian Richardson ("House of Cards," "The Magician's House"), with thin white hair, an aquiline face and a stylish blue business suit. He often travels with a plump companion

named Iphigenia "Iffy" Birmingham, who has a mass of curly black hair. Parkin slated the 42nd Doctor and Iffy to appear—married—in an epilogue to *The Dying Days*, but the scene went unused. The 42nd Doctor and Iffy also crop up in the apocryphal *Tales From the Solar System*: "Saturnalia" by Parkin.

Jason was always faithful to Benny, allaying her fears from *Happy Endings* and *Eternity Weeps*.

A humorous Chelonian cardboard cutout sports the words "One Bad Mother" (*The Highest Science*). Pakhars such as Professor Scoblow were introduced in *Legacy*.

At the conference, Professor Scoblow presents "The Ritual of Tuba: The Significance of Martial Brass Band Music in Human-Martian Relations"—obviously a parody on the Martian "Ritual of Tuburr" (*GodEngine*).

The fourth Doctor freed most of the Martians, frozen in suspended animation in the hollow moon of Phobos, in *Decalog 2*: "Crimson Dawn."

CHARACTER DEVELOPMENT
Bernice Summerfield: Benny here turns 35. 9Side Note: Parkin's *A History of the Universe* marks Benny's birth year as 2540, but TARDIS travel undoubtedly skewed her chronology.) At this age, Benny thinks her tiny breasts are an asset, but she's got a small beer belly.

She last visited Mars when she was 24. The St. Oscar's Archaeology department screwed up her ticket to Mars, meaning she woke up alone, surrounded by lots of bananas, in an automated hyperspace freighter's cargo hold.

Her conference lecture undergoes a dramatic name change—from "Untitled" to "The Martians." In a mere decade of interstellar travel, Benny's upset the Droge of Gabrielides by refusing to marry him, accidentally insulted the Master of the Fifth Galaxy and clashed with the Lord Herring on Sqakker's World.

During her brief army stint, Benny trained for zero-gee and has gone diving a couple of times.

Most importantly, Benny learns not to sleep with the TV on, variously dreaming about being in Tokyo during a giant chicken rampage and being turned into a Lego by a bearded villain.

Jason Kane: Fast living's prematurely aging Jason, giving him a receding hairline and a slight double chin. His hair's dyed with flecks of blond.

Karina Tellassar (a.k.a. Elizabeth K. Trinity): Tellassar, 80, is relatively spry. As Mars defense minister, she was exceptionally young for her position and gained special authority when Mars went to war alert. She lived at her sea command base for nine months before fleeing and crafting her Elizabeth K. Trinity identity, writing *A History of Mars* (*See Stuff That You Need*). She became the visiting professor of archaeology at King's College, Cambridge, and kept the knife she was supposed to kill her lover Isaac Deniken with.

Isaac Deniken: Born on Mars, Deniken was a young man during the second Dalek war in 2555. Afterward, he left Mars for 50 years, spending some time on Tyler's Folly (*Down*).

Phillip and Christina York: Trillionaire couple and founders of YorkCorp who owned the Hotel (*See Places to Go*) and Lake Jackson. Much of their resources came from Christina's inheritance. Before the deliberate bankruptcy of YorkCorp, the Yorks were the two most powerful people on Mars. Despite their ordering Deniken's murder, the Yorks were essentially goodwilled (adhering to the Christian faith) and kept YorkCorp operating at a loss because billions of lives relied on it.

Professor Megali Scoblow: Jason's lover hails from the Pakhar race and is essentially a meter-tall walking, talking hamster. Scoblow, a pollen fiend in her youth, serves as Emeritus Professor of Human History at the Santa Diana University on Mars. Scoblow (originally Sk'o'bel'ou) is a total humanophile, intellectually and sexually. Benny finds her views patronizing.

CATCH: An artificial intelligence system designed to run Mars' missile systems, CATCH came from an era before computers were installed with harsh limiters and safeguards, meaning the older CATCH was ironically more advanced.

ALIEN RACES

Xlanthi: Humanoid lizards with crests and large claws. They're superhumanly strong and agile, and master weaponsmiths, trading their weapons for powerful one-man warships. In appreciation for Xlanthi assistance during the Galactic Wars, the Earth Senate legally empowered them to hunt fugitives in Earthspace without recrimination.

A word to the wise: Do not piss off the Xlanthi. Better still, avoid all contact. Xlanthi culture bases itself around violently and with great ritual murdering all rivals, meaning virtually every offense of their law will net you a tortured death. For a list of lethal Xlanthi offenses, which include

"Knowing French," "Having Eaten Fruit" and "Fancying Scully Out Of The X-Files," consult *Beige Planet Mars* page 138. (Oh, how *The Hitchhiker's Guide to the Galaxy* would have a field day with this race.)

ALIEN PLANETS

Mars: Legendary as the second planet in humanspace (hope you figured out that Earth is the first). A million people arrive per day on Mars; only half that number depart. Mars seems ideal for retirees because its lower gravity puts less strain on the heart and improves arthritis symptoms. The fresher air also helps. Mars only gets 10,000 births a year because most young people depart for Earth, the Moon, the Asteroid Belt, the Jovian Archipelago or leave the solar system altogether.

The Martian economy tailors itself to pensioners, with multiple shops and two big arcades named for the first two men on Mars. The Grosvenor is rather exclusive, while the Guest market is more lower class.

The Martian Chronicle serves as the planet's native newspaper. The planet sometimes resembles a Wal-Mart in that it has 600 welcomers.

Mars has terraformed oceans at each pole, the greatest human engineering project since the pyramids. To the north, the freshwater Borealis Ocean supplies the entire planet with water via a canal network. The Southern Sea also has water, but more importantly, carbon dioxide to retain the Sun's heat and sustain the Martian forests.

Mars boasts a yachting lake in Utopia, a casino-plex in Deucalionis and vineyards in the Mare Sirenum. The Martian monorail runs hovertrains powered by atomic fusion, capable of speeds up to 2,000 miles per hour.

Noachis Spaceport handles about 60 percent of Mars' commercial flights. Mars apparently has a rugby team.

PLACES TO GO *Tellassar's Seabase:* Located at the bottom of Lake Jackson, Tellassar's seabase had 10 photon missiles and was the only missile base of its kind near a major population center. The Daleks left it intact because they needed Mars' residents as a human shield.

STUFF YOU NEED

Down Among the Dead Men: Benny's book on Martian culture is in its sixth printing. She earns 7.5 percent royalties for each sale. At this point, she's still naming the sequel *So Vast a Pile.*

Nights of the Perfumed Tentacle: Jason's book of smut, originally written as an autobiography. The publishers thankfully edited out all references to

Benny and marketed it as porn. The book sold 12 million copies, with Jason entitled to a Standard Currency Unit per copy. Jason marketed it under his real name, and the publishers want him to write a sequel.

A History of Mars: Published in 2555, Trinity's orthodox text argued the "noble" humans freed a magnificent planet from its backward ways, although Benny's generation reinterpreted the evidence to take in both sides.

ORGANIZATIONS

YorkCorp: Specialized in medical research and health care provision for the elderly. Bantu supplied most of its hardware.

HISTORY

Tellassar wasn't alone in her moral dilemma about killing her lover. Ever since Carter/Brezhnev, all nuclear codes were secured in someone the relevant military commander loved.

- In the waning years of the 20th century, alien powers watched mankind's affairs.
- In the late 20th century, a massive nuclear explosion in the Argyre crater on Mars completely wiped out the local clan. Water from the Southern Sea filled it.
- Between 2086 and 2089, humanity and the Martians fought the Thousand Day War (*See GodEngine for details*). Earth won the conflict and drove the Martians from Mars, colonizing it and founding the University of Mars in 2095.
- The Daleks invaded Mars as part of their scourge through the solar system in 2157 ("The Dalek Invasion of Earth," *GodEngine*).
- In June 2545, monitoring stations in the Oort cloud surrounding the Solar System registered hyperspace disturbances—300 Dalek battlesaucers, all heading for the Solar System. Nine hundred photon missiles protected Mars, concealed in undersea bases, but only Tellassar, Mars' Minister of Defense, was authorized to launch the defense. She never did. The Daleks destroyed the missile seabases with firestorm bombs, and only Tellassar's Missile Control survived.

The Daleks used Mars' three billion inhabitants, mostly pensioners, as a human shield, and pelted Earth with bioweapons. The Earth Senate narrowly voted not to nuke Mars. General Keele launched a counter-offensive that finally drove the invaders from Mars, although a few offworlders (presumably the 42nd Doctor and companion, *See Novel Tie-Ins*) aided him by downing a saucer at Argyre Dam and helping to coordinate the final attack. Mars, St. Oscar's, Berkeley and Loughborough universities all survived the conflict.

- Mars Central Plaza held a statue of Colonel Brusilov, the first UN soldier to hit a Martian soldier in 2086. In 2545, a Dalek energy blast melted the statue's head and right shoulder, but the people left the remains standing.
- YorkCorp's collapse was among the most spectacular ends in economic history. Before its demise, YorkCorp took out vast loans from banks and creditors with a reputation for ruthlessness, massacring them when YorkCorp declared bankruptcy. The greatest beneficiaries from YorkCorp's end were its employees, plus a wide range of charities and ethical support groups.

AT THE END OF THE DAY Hysterical, brave and lovingly trashy—a great example of Bernice being Bernice. *Beige Planet Mars* starts out with Benny acting like mystery detective Jessica Fletcher (wryly inquiring "Who's going to be the first guest to get murdered?"), then sails by with both its silliness (Benny's constant hot/cold relationship with her pornography writing ex-husband) and seriousness (Tellassar's moral choices). All in all, a story that's chock-full of meaty scenes, yet apparently about nothing, that handily wins as the funniest Benny book.

WHERE ANGELS FEAR

By Rebecca Levene
and Simon Winstone

> *Release Date: December 1998*
> *Order: Benny New Adventure #17*
> *(Virgin NA #78)*
> *"Dellan Gods Storyarc" begins*

MAIN CHARACTERS Bernice Summerfield, Irving Braxiatel, Emile Mars-Smith and Clarence.

TRAVEL LOG Dellah, 2595.

STORY SUMMARY When the People's supercomputer God starts withdrawing its agents from the Milky Way, a number of parties suspect impending danger and Clarence implores Benny to return to the safety of the Worldsphere. Not knowing the nature of the danger—or if any even exists— Benny opts to stay on Dellah.

Weeks later, reports say the god Maa'lon walks again on Dellah in the homeland of the Hut'eri race, so Benny investigates the rumors with a party of Grel. To Benny's horror, Maa'lon tests his followers by ordering them to war against the rival N'a'm'thuli race and encourages a pointless slaughter. When Benny refuses to follow Maa'lon's orders, he tries to kill Benny, but Clarence and his associate, the People Ship B-Aaron, rescue her.

During Benny's absence, Dellah experiences a surge of religious fanaticism, with the Sultan of Tashwari mandating all St. Oscar's students and staff adhere to a religion. Irving Braxiatel, having rebuffed the Time Lords' demands to return home, grows worried as religious-based acts of violence wrack the campus and the Sultan forms the militaristic "New Moral Army" from St. Oscar's personnel. Braxiatel manipulates his associate, musician Renée Thalia, into investigating the situation, but learns little and the threat of total chaos swells.

Running out of options, Braxiatel desperately leads the remaining campus academics to Dellah's spaceport and desperately tries to evacuate them. Simultaneously, student Emile Mars-Smith investigates the murder of 15 spaceship passengers on Benny's behalf and identifies the killer as a depressed policeman from Tyler's Folly. Unfortunately, Emile learns the killer plans to blow up the spaceport, stranding Dellah's residents as potential followers of his personal god. Emile and Braxiatel frantically herd people out of the spaceport as the policeman's bomb destroys it.

Clarence tells Benny that long ago, the former gods of the People were imprisoned within Dellah. Over time, however, the gods awakened enough to influence the people, finally gripping Dellah in a religious furor. With absolutely no choice, Benny and Clarence join Braxiatel's group at a Time Lord evacuation fleet, abandoning Dellah as explosions wrack St. Oscar's and more, quarantining the planet to contain the emerging gods.

MEMORABLE MOMENTS Benny's enigmatic contact John, pitting wits with Braxiatel, warns of events to come: "You dipped your toe in the current of the universe, and now you're in danger of getting swept away by the tide." The normally restrained Braxiatel pounds and pounds a desk at the University's madness. In a top dramatic moment, he finally leads a party of academics off-planet, unnervingly realizing, "There's nothing for me to stay for."

SEX AND SPIRITS Braxiatel's relationship with musician Renée Thalia drips with flirtation, but little comes of it. Renée regards Braxiatel as a mystery figure who challenges her. When she was away, Braxiatel missed her. When Renée unties a captive Braxiatel, her breasts squash softly against his naked chest and he feels human.

Emile Mars-Smith finds himself attracted to cult leader Adnan and even gets a small kiss, but on the whole turns down Adnan's advances.

TOP 5

BENNY DEFEATS

1) Jason Kane lost in a parallel universe (Twilight of the Gods)—Benny shunts Dellah to a parallel timeline, ending the threat of alternate Time Lords called the Ferutu, but her ex-husband Jason Kane remains captive.

2) Death of Clarence (Twilight of the Gods)—Benny's admirer Clarence catches a temporal blast and "youthens" to death.

3) St. Oscar's University leveled (Where Angels Fear)—The emergence of the Dellan gods forever wracks Benny's home, forcing her to become a space-time nomad.

4) Death of Commander Skutloid (Tears of the Oracle)—Irving Braxiatel's trusted associate, in one of the Benny books' most poignant passings, succumbs to his wounds, asking for a coin to pay the ferryman in the next life.

5) Death of Maeve Ruthven (Dry Pilgrimage)—Benny thwarts a dictator's ambitions but fails to save her friend and academic colleague Maeve.

Honorable Mention: The supercomputer God gives a Benny a brain tumor (*Tears of the Oracle*)—Worth noting, but unable to rank on the list because Benny gets better, whereas most of the people listed above kick it.

Clarence, a virgin, doesn't really know how sex works—believing it a final capitulation to his new biological form. Still, he keeps trying to get Benny's attention, and strives to rescue her because her death would cause him a long life of missing her.

ASS-WHUPPINGS *Where Angels Fear* butchers Dellah like no other novel, scorching St. Oscar's University with a green flame as the gods emerge, plus crumbling many university buildings to a dark red powder. A religiously fanatical cop from Tyler's Folly kills 15 starliner passengers, plus blows up the Dellah spaceport.

Benny observes a vicious Hut'eri and N'a'm'thuli massacre. The Grel Shemda blows off a N'a'm'thuli's head to save Benny's life. Conversely, the Hut'eri god Maa'lon literally turns the Grel Grenke and Benny's nefarious ally John (*See Novel Tie-Ins*) inside out. A skimmer crash gives Benny a shattered ankle and two crushed feet.

Professor Solomon Merrick, Fellow of All Souls and Chair of the University Cross-Cultural Council, is burnt to death for being a Jew who worked on Saturday.

NOVEL TIE-INS Benny abandons Dellah, but returns in *The Mary-Sue Extrusion* to search for Wolsey. That book also deals with student Emile Mars-Smith (*Beyond the Sun*), who here forges a deal with a demonic imp for information on the starliner murders and thereby gets possessed by one of the Dellan gods. The murderer, a depressed policeman, hails from Tyler's Folly (*Down*).

Tears of the Oracle reveals that Renée Thalia and Braxiatel had different ideas about what constituted a long-term relationship and she went off with the first officer of a heavy space hauler.

The mysterious "John," here killed by Maa'lon, first appeared in *Another Girl, Another Planet* as an homage to chain smoker John Constantine from DC Comics' *Hellblazer*. The Virgin editors intended that "John" would repeatedly show up from book to book to supply Benny with crucial information, but continual uncertainty about the Benny line's survival—or perhaps just a shift of emphasis—caused them to off the character.

God first approached Benny about being his agent in *Oh No It Isn't!*, likely using her as a means to monitor the sleeping Dellan gods without violating the Time Lord-People Treaty.

The Grel (*Oh No It Isn't!*) now regard Benny as a "fact catalyst." Grel data-axes can cauterize wounds. Benny reports not finding further information on the female Shiva (*Another Girl, Another Planet*), barring a link to Dellah.

The People Ship B-Aaron appeared in *Walking to Babylon* as a friend of the rogue People !Ci!ci-tel and WiRgo!xu. Sara!qava (*The Also People, Walking to Babylon*): Still keeps a house in iSanti Jeni.

CHARACTER DEVELOPMENT

Bernice Summerfield: Drives the university vehicles, although she's not qualified, tall enough or strong enough. She'll never forget the sound of the Hut'eri and N'a'm'thuli armies coming together. The Grel Shemda believes in her.

Irving Braxiatel: Braxiatel wonders how much he's missed by ignoring religion, yet reaffirms himself as a collector. ("That's what I've chosen to do with my life; everything else is just an accident of birth.") Then again, Braxiatel also discovers he's scared of dying, something he previously had a calm dispassion for.

Braxiatel physically looks in his 30s and never seems comfortable in The Witch and the Whirlwind bar, especially with a pint in his hands. He's spent too long honing his mysterious image to appreciate what it's done to him. Braxiatel drafted a cross-referencing sociology program, linked to a confiscated creative writing program, to write the

atrology advertising blurbs for him. He considers erotic mime, created by Professor Mordechai, to be a crime against sentience.

He has a master key to many St. Oscar's rooms and can deploy micro scanners (which John can deactivate). He's also got superior physical strength and can fake exit visas. Braxiatel helps lead 3,000 refugees to safety from Dellah, having never assumed a leadership role before.

Braxiatel and the Time Lords: Braxiatel hasn't lived on Gallifrey for centuries and didn't care for it much. Given the current crisis, the Time Lords order Braxiatel to return home but he refuses, feeling he's invested too much effort into Dellah to leave it behind. The Time Lords consequently confiscate Braxiatel's TARDIS.

Renée Thalia: As the Orchestral Attache to Braxiatel's Theatrology Department, Thalia plays cello, has a few extra pounds, curly blonde hair and dresses somewhat scantily. The Sultan of the Tashwari sponsors her. Braxiatel manipulated Renée to serving in the Sultan's New Moral Army, desperate to get information from an insider. With the Sultan's decree that all University staff and students must adhere to a religion, Renée even more feverishly pledged allegiance her faith—the independent-thinking Church of the Grey. She was promoted to Army Captain for converting so many members.

John: Benny's "deep throat" contact, John regards Bernice as too important to risk (claiming she's valued by a powerful, unnamed party) and thus dies saving her from Maa'lon. "John" isn't his real name. John apparently isn't a Time Lord but has two hearts. John's people, unlike the Time Lords, arrive at the first sign of trouble. John smokes and carries a black ovoid fusion bomb.

Braxiatel and John: Braxiatel can't dig up information on John, and John enjoys intellectually besting Braxiatel. They aren't old friends, although Braxiatel knows John's race.

Jason Kane: Has a friend (likely Mira) who can access police records.

Emile Mars-Smith: Benny asked him to investigate the cult-based passenger liner murders because Emile once belonged to a cult.

God: Portions of God's core intelligence on the plant Whynot (orbiting the sun at the Worldsphere's center) have sensor gaps. Information there gets rendered as a series of books. If you open one up, a virtual reality landscape appears, where various figures answer questions. God's been carefully watching events on Dellah—likely watching for the gods' return—using Bernice as an excuse to pry.

Clarence: His body needs to eat but proves immune to the gods' influence.

B-Aaron: Possibly the most hostile of the People's Very Aggressive Ships, having a wartime kill count second to none. Unlike other veterans from the War, B-Aaron had no visible guilt and the People invite him to many parties. He didn't know Clarence before Clarence's current incarnation.

B-Aaron's powerful shield can shroud conversations from everyone, including God (God is aware of this). B-Aaron's a member of the Apocalyptic Religions Interest Group, likes fighting and is terribly good at it. He can augment Clarence's lift and shielding, granting him enough power to carry Bernice and a Grel.

ALIEN RACES

The Time Lords: Fearing the gods' power, the Time Lords are isolating Gallifreyan society.

The People: Have a society based on the idea that there is no religious deity.

The Dellan Gods: Suggested to be the gods of the People, imprisoned by God on Dellah, where the population once believed in powerless gods. Yet over time, the gods' latent influence warped religion on the planet. A psi-gene found in humans enables the gods to draw power from eugenics, fueled by humanity's various beliefs (God diced the comparable psi-gene out of the People long ago, hedging its bets against the gods' return). The People's machines are immune to the gods' influence.

Hut'eri: Ochre colored, with scaly skin that protects against the elements. Hut'eri of the Great North Ridge are the most hardy.

Na'm'thuli: Blue-skinned, with barbed spikes.

ⓘ TOP 5

BENNY NOVELS

1) **Dead Romance (by Lawrence Miles)**—Highly disturbing with its mature discussions of sex, drugs and murder, *Dead Romance* proves the rule that the best "Doctor Who" books are outstanding science fiction novels in their own right. (We tested *Dead Romance* on non-"Doctor Who" readers and got little but ecstatic responses.) The absence of both the Doctor and Benny ironically aids this work, allowing Lawrence Miles more room to maneuver.

2) **Tears of the Oracle (by Justin Richards)**—The ultimate Benny season finale, to the extent of tying up plotlines and characters everyone forgot about. Our only regret for reading Tears of the Oracle is that it didn't end the Benny line outright.

3) **Beige Planet Mars (by Lance Parkin and Mark Clapham)**—Surprisingly fluid, *Beige Planet Mars* provides a hardcore drama plot (the potential extinction of Earth's colony on Mars) while making you laugh until your mate thinks you're demented (as if that's anything new).

4) **Where Angels Fear (by Rebecca Levene and Simon Winstone)**—A great ride, running roughshod over Benny with a new threat (the Dellan gods) and notching forward Irving Braxiatel's character.

5) **Walking to Babylon (by Kate Orman)**—Orman's clean prose wraps together Walking to Babylon as a time travel tour de force that makes Benny unique as a woman who parties with the People and saves Earth's history.

ALSO RECOMMENDED

Beyond the Sun (by Matt Jones)—A work that constantly strives to resonate with the reader, enthralling Benny (who loses Jason Kane—again) in a highly developed story about family and biological need.

Dragons' Wrath (by Justin Richards)—Not the most testosterone-filled book, but a novel that uses Benny first and foremost as an archaeologist.

They worship a nameless god linked with the deity of the Morkai.

ALIEN PLANETS

The People's Worldsphere: The Worldsphere's territory sector looks like emptiness from a distance, but an up-close examination reveals the Worldsphere's solar system. The Worldsphere globe was once seven planets and even more moons. At any given time, it shelters 80 percent of the People, plus a variety of species. The remainder of the People travel the local galaxy, but some

---

are returning from the Milky Way, their presence there a Treaty violation. The Worldsphere and Dellah are billions of light years apart.

Dellah: The supercomputer God likely chose Dellah to house the imprisoned Gods because Dellan religions originally worshiped an inanimate object to which very few powers were ascribed. God didn't foresee the imprisoned gods influencing the indigenous population.

Today, Dellan religions share a uniform belief that divinity is linked to the Earth and that paradise, the home of the gods, is beneath the Earth. They also feature sea-based elements that began 3,000 years ago, plus have elements of animal-spirit worship.

The Hut serves as Dellah's largest mountain range, with Maa'lon's Spear the planet's highest point at 3,524 meters above sea level. The area's locally known as "the roof of the world." The Grel geological formations on 8,734 other planets share this moniker.

Whynot: The small planet orbiting the Worldsphere's inner sun and containing the supercomputer God's intelligence, complete with a smelly market named Lefteye. God likes company and allows the People to live on Whynot's surface. The People there like unpredictability, so he redecorates at will.

STUFF YOU NEED *The Grimoire of Atheron the Mage* serves as a powerful artifact for a cult that respects people who're willing to die for the pursuit of knowledge. Cult leader Adnan owned the Grimoire, but gave it to Emile Mars-Smith to aid with his investigations. The Grimoire's spells can summon demon imps and project emotions, requiring only the caster's mind and a secondary, strong and centered mind as a focus. Emile and Braxiatel successfully used the Grimoire to evacuate the Dellah spaceport, but discovered the Grimoire also affects its casters.

ORGANIZATIONS

Worldsphere Interest Groups: Include Obscene Topiary Interest, Pointlessly Paranoid Worrying About God and Awfully Clever Hacking.

The Maa'lon Religion: Dellah-based religion that likely originated in the small town of Tal'een, a few hundred kilometers from the University. The Book of Maa'lon spawned from the Code that Maa'lon first gave his people (*See History*).

"Operation Ragnarok": Code-name for God's evacuation of the Milky Way.

PHENOMENA As the gods awakened, previously useless cult rituals became viable, with blood as the most useful currency.

HISTORY The *N'a'm'thuli Schism and the Dark Heart of the Hut'eri* by Jonaas Brenkler, professor of Ancient History, St. Oscar's, suggests the Hut'eri/Morkai conflict began 5,000 years ago on the Plain of Tumas, where the Morkai worshiped a being of darkness that demanded constant sacrifices. Fed up with sacrificing their own, the Morkai began sacrificing others, killing hundreds of nearby Hut'eri while thousands fled. When an old Hut'eri offered up *The Book of Blood* and swore that the god Maa'lon would protect them, the Hut'eri rushed to the counter-attack, decimating the Morkai and eating their hearts. Only the children were spared. The Hut'eri in turn built a new temple in their new capital, N'a'm'th ("vengeance" in the old tongue), and sacrificed the Morkai children to a god with no name.

• On Dellah, the early religions died out, replaced by new ones founded within 100 years of each other. The planet enjoyed a peaceful, multicultural pre-industrial society, then suffered 200 years of religious wars (*See Alien Planets*).

• Grel legend claims that when the paradise of Grellor was tamed, the Grel wondered about the cause of their good fortune. A Grel named Shenke said it was proof of the divine. *The First Book of Grel* says Shenke charged the people to build triangular buildings, but Melkan the Bold—the first Master of Facts—called the bluff, so the Grel abandoned building triangles and turned to fact instead. Subsequently, the Grel lost interest in gods and myths, deeming such catalogues as too difficult to access with a standard data-axe.

• On Dellah, the Great Act of Toleration of 2528 recognized 1,036 religions, including 512 indigenous groups.

AT THE END OF THE DAY Potent, emotional and unexpected—keeping Benny in the story while remarkably humanizing Braxiatel through his relationship with musician Renée. For continuity reasons, we don't recommend *Where Angels Fear* as your first Benny book (although it can be done) and certain scenes—largely during Benny's excursion to the Hut'eri homeland—admittedly drag a bit. Still, *Where Angels Fear* deserves credit for turbo-charging its characters and sparking the most compelling block of Benny reading, making us regret that schedule conflicts didn't allow Levene to write her slated "Who" novel *Freaks*.

THE MARY-SUE EXTRUSION

By Dave Stone

Release Date: February 1999
Order: Benny New Adventure #18
(Who NA #79)
"Dellan Gods Storyarc"

MAIN CHARACTERS A Stratum Seven agent, with Bernice Summerfield, Jason Kane, Emile Mars-Smith.

TRAVEL LOG Thanaxos and Proxima IV, 2595.

CHRONOLOGY Four months after *Where Angels Fear.*

STORY SUMMARY With the Dellan gods having leveled most of Dellah and threatening to enthrall other planets, Pseudopod Enterprises Corporation grows concerned about the gods' power and hires an unnamed, Stratum Seven-level Agent to investigate. Based on reports that Professor Bernice Summerfield might know what happened on Dellah, the Agent follows Benny's trail to Dellan refugee camps on Thanaxos.

There, a clone of Pseudopod director Volan, who works for the Thanaxan House Royal, separately hires the Agent to bodyguard the in-bred and rather stupid Prince Gjimbo. The Agent accepts, but takes Gjimbo with him to Dellah to find Bernice. Finding Benny's journals, the Agent concludes Benny revisited Dellah after the quarantine was established.

The Agent encounters Benny's ex-husband Jason Kane, who reads the journals and deduces that Benny submitted herself to a "Mary-Sue"—a mental procedure that overwrites one's memories with a new persona. From journal references to Benny's lover "Rebecca," Jason leads his associate Mira and the Agent to Benny's homeworld of Beta Caprisis. There, a shipwrecked, emaciated Benny at first claims to be "Rebecca," but her true personality finally reasserts itself.

Benny reveals she underwent the Mary-Sue to mentally block the influence of the Dellan gods, allowing her to return to Dellah and rescue Wolsey. Benny also concedes that recent events—including the loss of St. Oscar's—made her welcome the chance to live as someone other than herself.

On a deserted planet, Benny helps the Agent's group locate the self-exiled Emile Mars-Smith, who's possessed by one of the Dellan gods. With Jason's associate Mira telepathically helping

Emile restrain the god, Benny's party returns to Thanaxos and finds the planet gripped by the Dellan religious furor and preparing for holy jihad.

The Agent realizes the Thanaxan Volan clone has been embezzling from Pseudopod Enterprises. Meanwhile, the Dellan god in Emile emerges to combat a rival god hiding in Prince G"Jimbo. A fleeing Volan delays his pursuers with a "stupid bomb" that locks onto the stupidest person present, so Benny and her friends spontaneously spout philosophy and thereby cause the bomb to kill the dopey Gjimbo and the god possessing him. As the Thanaxan people return to normal, Benny's group returns Emile to his self-imposed exile with the Dellan god still possessing him and the heroes go their separate ways. Afterward, the Stratum Seven Agent writes of these events, tailoring the narrative to prevent anyone learning his identity.

MEMORABLE MOMENTS The funniest moment in *The Mary-Sue Extrusion* (and much of the Benny novel line) handily occurs when the Agent announces Volan's "stupid bomb" will lock onto the dumbest person present, so everyone turns intellectual to avoid it. Accordingly, Benny dissects the themes at work in *Finnegan's Wake*, Jason discusses the X-factor in the Special Theory of Relativity and Mira quotes from the wit and wisdom of Groucho Marx. ("Time flies like an arrow, fruit flies like a banana.") Fortunately, the hickish Prince Gjimbo wanders into the room, blathering about eggs and tea, and gets annihilated.

SEX AND SPIRITS The Agent has some homosexual tendencies, preferring masculine men to feminine ones (he can't see the point of feminine men). He's lovers with DataDay newscaster Sela Dane. Jason's pseudo-telepathic associate Mira has a girlfriend.

ASS-WHUPPINGS Wolsey and a Mary-Sued Benny crash on Beta Caprisis, both of them growing withered from lack of supplies.

In pursuing his duties, the efficient but messy Agent jabs the *Star of Afrique*'s captain's eyes out up to his knuckles. The Agent also strangles one attacker and kills another by smacking his head into a truncated conduit pipe. He cripples two T'-galk bravos by whacking their brain stems.

A stupid bomb (*See Memorable Moments, Stuff That You Need*) obliterates Prince G'jimo and the Dellan god within him.

NOVEL TIE-INS Benny learns in *Tears of the Oracle* that her Mary-Sue has caused a terminal brain tumor (although something else actually induced her illness). Stone's *Return to the*

Fractured Planet cures her of the disease. It also sees the return of the Stratum Seven Agent and the (here mentioned) villainous Sleed Corporation.

Emile Mars-Smith reappears, sans the possessing god, in *Twilight of the Gods*.

Stone's *Ship of Fools* first mentioned Jason Kane's colleague Mira. It also introduced the Catan Nebula, the region that produces synthetic personality constructs such as the Agent. Kimo Ani, mentioned here as Jason's associate, turns up in *More Short Trips*: "Moon Graffiti."

Love and War first mentioned Benny's doll Rebecca. In the Benny universe, the pulp story "Ship of Death" loosely chronicles her adventures aboard the *Titanium Queen* (*Ship of Fools*). Stone's sixth Doctor novel *Burning Heart* introduced the White Fire terrorist cell.

No official record exists of Benny and Jason's marriage (*Happy Endings*) or divorce (*Eternity Weeps*). Prince G'jimo's nickname is "Jimbo," perhaps a play on the name of novelist Jim Mortimore (*The Sword of Forever, Blood Heat*).

The Agent here visits Proxima IV; the eighth Doctor novel *The Face-Eater* leveled a colony on Proxima II.

CHARACTER DEVELOPMENT

The Agent: Synthoid manufacturers in the Catan Nebula originally imprinted the Agent's artificial personality as being a 20th century time traveler who disappeared from record at age 14 and reappeared "nine years ago" with Stratum Seven clearance and a physical age of 25. However, the Agent now believes Catan Nebula engineers constructed him in the 21st century, programming his personality with an amalgamation of scanned memories using a brain-etching device called Think Tank (*See Stuff That You Need*). The Agent stands unique as the only synthoid to break Think Tank's programming and assert his original core personality, dumping the others. As such, the Agent's more human than synthoid and is impossible to duplicate. He's got a massive healing factor and long life expectancy.

Today, the Agent acts as a broke but effective freelance agent, carrying a high-pressurized needle gun, a plasmatic flenser, three or four knives, a concussion detonator and a bunch of neuroptor grenades.

On Dramos, the Agent saved the half-niece of the Regent Elect from the Soldiers of Light and was awarded the unexceptional Keys to the Citadel. He once worked for El Diablo's, a fast-food division of the Matrox Incorporation.

He tried to fix a bad situation on Cantor Prime, but made it catastrophically worse. He also fared poorly on a disastrous retrieval operation on Golgotha, but claims his employers were incompetent, causing him to spend five months in a Skull Maze losing his mind. The Agent declined to seek revenge because his ex-employers are too powerful.

A few years back, DataDay hired him to retrieve newscaster Sela Dane and her crew from a collection of White Fire terrorists in the Cool Star Hegemony. He's saved her life a ridiculous number of times, but she occasionally saves him in return.

He despises the Benny-based "True Adventures of the New Frontier" series.

Bernice Summerfield: The Mary-Sue didn't destroy Benny's personality, but overwrote it with a new one ("Rebecca") designed to self-expire in a few months (certain keywords and mental mnemonics sped up the process). "Rebecca" can't land a spaceship.

Jason Kane: Jason's now in his mid-30s and exercises daily. His gene-modified skin withstands high ultraviolet and radiation intense sunlight. Traces of childhood gang tattoos remain on his shoulders and arms.

Mira: Mira has jet-black hair and a foxy looking face. She's moderately telepathic, enhanced by a super-conductive sensor system that runs parallel to her major ganglia. She can't read minds, but her keen insight helps compensate. If she mentally locks onto artificial minds such as the Agent, she can't focus on anyone else.

Mira can mentally shield herself and others from the Dellan gods' influence, or immobilize a single Dellan god. She can telepathically interrogate people in spacesuits by pulse pumping telepathic impulses through the suits and generating metal harmonics that scramble the wearer's gray matter.

Simonon Leviticus Sleed (Return to the Fractured Planet): Short founder of Sleed Corporation, burdened with a death-like face. Sleed was born on the fortified Squaxis Prime commune and has links to the human supremacist White Fire organization.

Box: Artificial Intelligence unit that aids the Agent. Box can transfer funds, plus detect body heat and movement.

ALIEN RACES

The Dellan gods: Benny suspects the gods twist the minds of their followers into a state of unquestioning belief, then feed off that belief. The hungrier a god gets, the more powerful it becomes. The gods have started warring with each other,

THE CRUCIAL BITS...

- **THE MARY-SUE EXTRUSION**—Benny undergoes a personality overwriting Mary-Sue procedure, rescuing Wolsey from Dellah but believing for a time that her name is Rebecca. First appearance of the unnamed Agent with Stratum Seven clearance.

fighting for the privilege of feasting on various followers. They're influencing worlds other than Dellah. They cannot influence synthetic creations such as the Agent.

Thanaxians: Basically humanoid, with slate-gray skin and a head crest.

ALIEN PLANETS

Dellah: Dellah's been reverting to desert since the destruction of the rain-giving Sky Pylon.

Thanaxos: The Earth-like Thanaxos seemingly accepted the majority of Dellan refugees, but rounded them into mass detention and buried official records of them. An opulent monarchy rules Thanaxos from the functional, advanced and diverse capital city of Rakath, very similar to the city of Aeon Flux on Mars. The Kings of Thanaxos have resided in the House Royal, located off the Rakath tourist quarter, for 473 years. The monarchy holds power, but a democratically elected Advisory Council carries out day-to-day administration.

Beta Caprisis: Nothing lives on Benny's former homeworld, where molten glass showers the detonation zones.

PLACES TO GO
Proximan Chain Habitats (Return to the Fractured Planet) formed from a hybrid of architectural concepts from space stations, colonies and planetary settlements. Mass-transit pods link the spread-out dwellings.

STUFF YOU NEED
Mary-Sue: Literary term denoting when an author puts himself or herself into a work of fiction. It also names a mindwipe-and-rebuild process that converts its subjects into new people, complete with memories and personality. Police and covert-observation and espionage agents use Mary-Sues to give them deep and unshakable covers. Mary-Sues aren't commonly used, restricted to power figures and the black market.

True Adventures of the New Frontier: Pulp adventures based on Benny's escapades, depicting "Berni" as a swashbuckling heroine sometimes aided by her dopey but loyal ex-husband Jason. "The Matrox Conundrum" details Berni's struggle against El Diablo and his assassin Moloch.

Down Among the Dead Men: Benny's book dissects how archaeologists often fail to ponder an artifact's historical context, over-focusing on its physicality and not considering the hows and whys of the object's existence. Various publishers have printed *Down Among the Dead Men*.

Stratum Seven clearance: A recognition of certain skills, contacts and standing. Stratum Seven-level personnel carry ID cards keyed to the their DNA and morphic pattern signature. The only people who could successfully duplicate the cards don't really have the need. The ID card doesn't mention where you're from, but tells people who you are and conveys certain privileges. There's no such thing as level One through Six clearance.

Interstellar Law: There basically isn't such a thing. For example, it's difficult to enforce anti-polygamy laws when some species require three genders or even a thousand to reproduce. Rules of hospitality often suspend murder laws. Be warned: A formal ID doesn't help much as you cross cultures.

Think Tank: High resolution holo-projector that functions on the subatomic level of the brain's consciousness. By scanning with high-powered lasers, Think Tank records its subjects' memories and personality, but destroys the brain in the process.

ORGANIZATIONS *EarthSec:* The basic peace-keeping force on the Moon, privately funded by a consortium of businessmen. The Adjudicators (*Burning Heart, Lucifer Rising*) are their rivals, but outright clashes with them are few.

HISTORY In this era, trans-galaxical travel is pretty easy for those with moolah—navigational computers are pretty expensive (time travel remains verboten). This era also features instant information transfer, and extensive psycho-testing and therapy for transsexuals to help them recover from waking in a different body.
- Benny dug up some begonia samples—long thought extinct—and the late Professor Sabron Jones raised them in an emergency DNA storage facility on Earth's Moon. Embryos there include ocelots and elephants, plus seeds and bulbs of plants long forgotten.

AT THE END OF THE DAY Some great ideas and twists finish off *The Mary-Sue Extrusion*, nicely complementing the brushfire lit by *Where Angels Fear*. Unfortunately, Mary-Sue takes too long to get there and the book's verboseness drags it down, not to mention some over-philosophizing interferes with the story. One has to wonder if a hurried production schedule—somewhat common in the Virgin line's last days—didn't force this book to be rushed, leaving *Mary-Sue* a work that smacks of an actor walking onstage, delivering lines ultra-fast and walking off without much retention of what happened.

DEAD ROMANCE

By Lawrence Miles

Release Date: April 1999
Order: Benny New Adventure #19
(Who NA #80)
"Dellan Gods Storyarc"

MAIN CHARACTERS Christine Summerfield and Chris Cwej.

TRAVEL LOG (The Universe-in-a-Bottle) The People's Worldsphere, a fortress on Simia KK98, markets on Cygni 8.6 and ruins on Gallifrey, 2595. (The Bottle-in-a-Bottle) London, September 27 to October 12, 1970.

STORY SUMMARY Two weeks before the world ends on October 12, 1970, London mourns for two slain women, their faces torn off by a killer whose modus operandi resembles Charles Manson. Meanwhile, policemen find 23-year-old supposed-art student Christine Summerfield at an abandoned building site—naked, near mute and evidently suffering from a drug overdose.

At a police station, Christine recovers and encounters Chris Cwej, who's questioned in connection with the Manson-like murders. Cwej takes Christine back to his flat and convinces her that he works for a time-active race named the Time Lords. Worse, Cwej details how Christine's Earth—indeed, her entire Universe—is self-contained in a dimensional Bottle and that Cwej hails from the reality surrounding it. Cwej stresses that the Time Lords, fearing defeat by an emerging power (the reality warping Dellan gods), are hedging their bets and preparing the Bottle Universe to house a small survival team, with Cwej serving as an advance scout.

As days go by, Cwej and Christine become lovers and he explains how the Bottle Universe's nature makes it susceptible to manipulation by certain rituals—particularly those involving human sacrifice. Unfortunately, "the Horror," the collective intelligence of hundreds of beings abandoned in the Time Vortex over millions of years, infiltrates the Bottle Universe through a dimensional gap left by crude Time Lord experiments.

Learning to manipulate the Bottle Universe's control protocols and rewrite its reality, the Horror lashes out in revenge for its inner despair and appears over London as a black void, gutting the city and heavily wounding Cwej. Out of options, Christine communes with the Horror and suggests it appease its inner pain by reincarnating itself as a human baby and learning to appreciate humanity. The Horror pauses and Christine desperately challenges it to a rock-scissors-paper match—with the fate of Bottle Earth in the balance. Christine thankfully wins, and the Horror honors Christine's proposal by dissipating itself to be reborn.

Over the next few days, Christine nurses Cwej to health. Finally, Cwej goes for a walk and Christine views a familiar photo that depicts a strange blonde girl standing in Christine's spot. Piecing together multiple clues that question her identity, Christine breaks into a private room in Cwej's flat and locates a cloning tank encoded with Christine's memories.

Fevered to know more, Christine races to the building site where the police first located her—and finds Cwej standing over the dead body of a Christine clone. Staring at her dead self, Christine confronts the truth: Cwej is the Manson-like murderer, and she was grown in the cloning tank as one of his intended victims.

Cwej sadly details how the Time Lords actually dispatched him to the Bottle Universe to open a gateway for them using a control ritual that required three human sacrifices. Unwilling to murder real people, Cwej grew identical clones and programmed them with a random blonde girl's memories, naming the clones after himself and his friend Bernice Summerfield. Unfortunately, the third of the clones—Christine—instinctively and blindly tore away from Cwej at the ritual site, achieving full awareness when the police recovered her. Cwej, hesitant to kill Christine once she was fully sentient, secretly grew (and murdered) another clone to fulfill the ritual's terms and grant the Time Lords full access.

As a giant portal opens above London, Christine realizes Cwej lied about a "survival team" and that the Time Lords intend to defensively move their civilization to Bottle Earth, retreating from the Dellan gods. Witnessing armageddon unfolding, the world's nations launch repeated nuclear strikes but fail to penetrate the Time Lords' shields and level Bottle Earth instead. Granted special status as one of Cwej's colleagues, Christine reaches the safety of a protective spire, but Cwej catches a lethal radiation dose. Effortlessly, the Time Lords reshape Bottle Earth to their needs and mutate the surviving humans into servants or surrogate next-generation Time Lords. As the last survivor of her world, Christine has a final, terse meeting with a dying Cwej and learns the Time Lords will likely regenerate him. Finally, Christine leaves her Bottle Universe, determined to keep living and someday find the real Bernice Summerfield.

MEMORABLE MOMENTS An "overdosed" Christine mumbles her name to the police, although later—when you learn her origins—you'll slap your head to realize she wasn't overdosed. Continuity freaks will laugh until they cry when people dream about the belief warping Dellan gods and wake up screaming, "No! Not the rectal probe!"

Christine challenges the Horror to rock-scissors-paper ("If I win, you go along with my plan. Otherwise, you kill me, and everybody else in the Universe, yeah?"). Playing best two out of three, Christine and the Horror split the first two games. For the third and final contest, Christine clenches up so tightly—unable to make the decision that could save or doom Bottle Earth—that she makes a stone and defeats the Horror's scissors.

Christine's confrontation with Cwej, covered in her clone's blood, carries as much gory detail as you can imagine. The Time Lord transformation of Bottle Earth ranks among the "Doctor Who" novel line's most intense "end of the world" scenarios.

Sitting in a ruin on Gallifrey, Christine writes journals on these events but tears out blank pages for use as toilet paper (she laughably speculates future archaeologists will suspect the missing pages hold some fearful secret).

SEX AND SPIRITS Virtually the whole damn book, it seems. Christine and Cwej first have sex on September 30, after a dragon boat ride. She wasn't on the pill, but he's apparently sterile (Christine's pregnancy tests confirm this).

Mind, Christine was hardly innocent, losing her virginity at age 15 to a hairy, muscular guy named Cal, pressed up against a wall in somebody's apartment. She's done a fair amount of drugs and men since. Even during her relationship with Cwej, Christine cheats and does the nasty with Time Lord agent Khiste (a stupid thing to do, she admits, given Cwej's responsibilities).

On one occasion, Cwej returns from a planet of machine people (almost certainly the Daleks) feel-

MISCELLANEOUS STUFF!

DEAD ROMANCE CANONICITY

One of the novel line's greatest Gordian Knots of continuity lies in the Universe-in-a-Bottle...errr, *Universes*-in-a-Bottle, as it were.

It was Miles' contention that the Virgin and BBC "Doctor Who" book universes were literally separate, with all the Virgin New and Missing Adventures events taking place in a Universe-in-a-Bottle created by I.M. Foreman in *Interference*. Miles notes: "I just read *The Eight Doctors*, which I thought couldn't exist in the same universe as *Blood Harvest*, and assumed that is was official policy to treat them as different universes. If I'd known that some of the other writers were planning on crossing things over, I honestly would never have done it. However, I'd still like to know how Romana can be President of Gallifrey in *Happy Endings* and again in *The Shadows of Avalon* but not even mentioned in *The Eight Doctors*."

Many readers inferred from this that every main "Doctor Who" character from TV had a Virgin and BBC counterpart. If you'll recall, the eighth Doctor peered into Foreman's Bottle Universe during *Interference* and commented, "Look under the glass. It's me. The way I was before. Only shorter."— referring to the New Adventures' seventh Doctor. However, the nature of the Bottles was never defined, so the splitting of characters between the Virgin/BBC universes was mostly the stuff of theory and never very clear-cut.

However, Miles established that unspecified beings in the Universe-in-a-Bottle had created another Bottle Universe—a Bottle-in-a-Bottle, as it were—in which most events in *Dead Romance* take place and which produced Christine Summerfield. The Bottle-in-a-Bottle's origins aren't specified, although Cwej speculates the sphinxes (*See Alien Races*) shat most of its space-time.

CONTINUED ON PAGE 227

ing so alien, so unnatural, he has sex with Christine to reassert his humanity.

Cwej likes to wear boots during sex—an homage to the TV show "EarthDoom XV" (*Sky Pirates!*). Christine can't stand going on top. Cwej struts about clad in Daffy Duck shorts (*The Room With No Doors*).

Cwej and Christine never had sex after October 7, probably because Cwej was steeling himself to murder the last Christine clone. Christine speculates Cwej might have seduced the unnamed blond girl to copy her brain patterns.

ASS-WHUPPINGS Not only does *Dead Romance* gut Bottle Earth in the most terrible of fashions (first the Horror, then the Time Lords), Cwej brutally murders three Christine clones to further the Time Lord agenda (the ritual required the victim's face and identity be stripped away). The ritual holds specific conditions, possibly because the public fear generated by such deaths is more potent than the slayings themselves.

A sphinx (*See Alien Races*) bites a hunk out of Christine's leg, scent-searching for Cwej. A battle between the sphinxes and Time Lord agents leaves many combatants smeared across space-time. Because the eventual Time Lord-sphinx treaty requires a blood signature, the Time Lords engineer a clone specifically for the event (a sphinx climbs inside the man and signs the document).

The Horror's assault near-fatally wounds Cwej, but a Time Lord healing fungus restores him. The newly humanized Horror presumably perished with Bottle Earth. Cwej gets a lethal dose of H-bomb radiation.

TV TIE-INS The Time Lords use chemicals to break down memory acids ("The War Games"), although dreams or paranoia might occur.

It's theorized that the Gallifreyan Matrix ("The Deadly Assassin") is so intelligent, it controls its users instead of vice versa (a leftover idea from Ben Aaronovtich's original *So Vile a Sin* storyline). The Matrix, coordinating a Time Lord defense when negotiations with the sphinxes (*See Alien Races*) go bad, thaws out prisoners on Shada (err, "Shada") and operates on them, rewriting their DNA and turning them into Time Lord weapons.

NOVEL TIE-INS Cwej's offer of employment by the Time Lords happens off-stage (he was last seen in *Oblivion*). Mortally wounded, Cwej regenerates in *Tears of the Oracle*.

The unnamed blonde girl that Cwej uses for Christine Summerfield's template shoots up at fortune teller Lady Diamond's bookshop on Henrietta Street in Covent Garden (Miles' *The Adventuress of Henrietta Street*).

Father Kreiner, lost to the Time Vortex in *Interference*, here appears as a one-armed man that speaks for the collective Horror intelligence. He later turns up (and kicks it) in *The Ancestor Cell*, which appears to contradict the Horror's fate here.

The Time Lords and People (*The Also People*) sign a treaty that allows the People time travel, but the supercomputer God (*Tears of the Oracle*) reports having trouble with time experiments.

THE CRUCIAL BITS...

- **DEAD ROMANCE**—Chris Cwej, brainwashed as a Time Lord agent, gets hit with a lethal radiation dose. The Time Lords, fearing the Dellan gods' power, dominate an Earth within a Universe-in-a-Bottle and reshape it to their needs. The Time Lords revise their treaty with the People, allowing the People to develop time travel.

The Dellan gods, freed in *Where Angels Fear*, have conquered Tyler's Folly (*Down*).

Time Lord agents submit themselves to machine gun fire, force-regenerating themselves into impervious warriors (Miles' *Alien Bodies*).

After leaving the Bottle Universe, Christine briefly stays on Ordifica (*Ghost Devices, Interference*). She leaves a voice mail for Benny in *Twilight of the Gods*.

The "central processing unit" that holds the Horror's intelligence together is the gestalt consciousness Pool, defeated by the Doctor and exiled to the Time Vortex in *Deceit*.

CHARACTER DEVELOPMENT

Christine Summerfield: Christine's falsified memories say she was born August 15, 1948 to a middle-class family that lives away from London. For four years, Christine's convinced her parents to send money for her "art school," but she's not enrolled (she hopes to milk them for 10 years). Mostly, she hangs out at a local bookshop and smokes a lot of drugs.

Through smell, the sphinxes know Christine was unnaturally made. Likely out of respect to Cwej's service, the Time Lords give Christine an unlimited credit card and one of Cwej's personal star charts.

Christine and Cwej: Cwej took Christine's genes from a standard human template, so it's impossible to trace her heredity. Christine calls him "Cwej" because, by her estimation, people from space don't have first names. As a defensive measure, Cwej taught Christine how to ward off the sphinxes, plus alter the Bottle Universe's reality (although this would require sacrifices).

Cwej variously gives Christine a paperweight carved like a sphinx, a watch that morphs to reflect the hour system on different planets, and a 26th century Mars bar-sized dictionary.

Chris Cwej: In preparing him for their service, the Time Lords brainwashed Cwej into thinking he got kidnapped by a rogue traveler named the "Evil Renegade," thus screwing up his remembrances of the Doctor. Cwej thinks the Evil Renegade experimented on him and originally possessed the Universe-in-a-Bottle, but the Time Lords saved Cwej's ass and put the Bottle under his protection.

The Time Lords enhanced Cwej with the Rassilon imprimature ("The Two Doctors"), a healing factor, improved senses and probably a good chunk of Time Lord DNA. A Time Lord mission before *Dead Romance* got Cwej tried as a war criminal (the Time Lords bailed him out).

Cwej has short, spiky hair and looks like he's in his early 30s. Having lived outside linear time for a couple of years, he's lost track of his real age. He wears a little gold earring stud and wards off the sphinxes with certain mantras and special electronic circuitry laid out in a pattern.

His cell phone communicates with alien beings. He likes plastic toys that come with cereal. Cwej helped forge Time Lord alliances with the People, the Machine People and a planet run by intelligent numbers—all between 17 and 18 (distinguishable by numbers after their decimal points). On Earth, he buys cigarettes to blend in. Most of his cooking involves peanut butter. At Christine's request, Cwej left the newly humanized Horror alone.

The Horror: An amalgamation of alien beings, humans, machines, a renegade 25th century supercomputer defeated by the Doctor (Pool from *Deceit*) and more—all of them dumped into the Time Vortex at various points and forgotten about. Empowered with only anger and loneliness for being abandoned, the Horror aches for destruction because it largely doesn't know what else to do.

The Time Lords, initially failing to understand the Bottle Universe's control rituals, forcibly drilled a path for Cwej to enter and accidentally punctured the Time Vortex, allowing the Horror access to the Bottle.

The Horror manifests as large as London and resists attempts to scan it. Physically, it's the living embodiment of a void. By manipulating the Bottle Universe's operating system, it can retroactively manifest objects (for example, producing a buried fossil that's existed for "millions of years" but didn't appear until this morning). Unfortunately, the Time Vortex stripped away the humanity and sense of self from the Horror's components, meaning it cannot rebuild its old bodies.

ALIEN RACES

Time Lords: They've known but didn't worry about the Dellan gods for years. The gods, who specialize in dominating cultural belief systems, could probably dominate Gallifreyan society.

MISCELLANEOUS STUFF!

DEAD ROMANCE CANONICITY CONTINUED FROM PAGE 225

Miles further suggested that the Time Lords of the BBC books, fleeing from the impending war with the future Enemy (*Alien Bodies, Interference*), escaped into the primary Bottle Universe and accidentally traveled back in time, eventually awakening with great powers as the Dellan gods. At least, that's what Christine Summerfield surmises. Meanwhile, the Virgin books' Time Lords, fearing the Dellan gods and completely unaware of their origins as Time Lords from another Universe, abandoned their Gallifrey and fled into their Bottle-in-a-Bottle.

But no author beyond Miles picked up the torch that the Virgin and BBC Universes were separate—or certainly, nobody else wrote about it, effectively scrapping the whole idea. *The Ancestor Cell* briefly paused to destroy Foreman's Universe-in-a-Bottle, but it certainly didn't validate different Universes for Virgin and the BBC. Moreover, *Twilight of the Gods* torpedoed Miles' idea about the dual races of Time Lords by unmasking the Dellan gods as alternate Time Lords named the Ferutu (*Cold Fusion*).

As a result, all the continuity just detailed pretty much ended with *Dead Romance*, leaving this book in its own self-contained realm, much like a Universe-in-a-Bottle.

The Time Lords' time travel control is genetically encoded, meaning they can't outright teach someone. When the Time Lords trade the sphinxes time technology for access to the Bottle Universe, the first time they've bargained away temporal secrets, they give the sphinxes clones encoded with the Rassilon imprimature.

Time Lords can bestow regenerative powers on non-Gallifreyans, but the unstable process causes side effects, including sterility (although the sex drive remains).

In conquering Bottle Earth, the Time Lords warp time, retroactively rewriting parts of the planet in their image. They chose Bottle Earth for its abundant resources and similarity in size to Gallifrey, dispatching Cwej to the 1970s because that time zone seemed receptive to manipulation.

An exceptionally nasty form of Time Lord interrogation involves giving limited regeneration prowess to a captive, then repeatedly killing the hapless victim and making them regenerate into misshapen forms.

227

This book is not endorsed by the BBC. Doctor Who and TARDIS are trademarks of the BBC.

The Sphinxes: The sphinxes' origins aren't clear (they aren't natural, and don't seem to evolve), but they're likely guardians fashioned by the Bottle Universe protocols to cleanse the system against invaders (the Horror overwhelmed them). However, some sphinxes exist outside the Bottle in the "real" universe.

Sphinxes have lumpy orange flesh, with spindly wings and bulbous heads (check out the book's cover—presuming you haven't eaten). The sphinxes feed on dimensional matter outside our normal five dimensions, excreting their waste as raw space-time (yes, they crap reality). They're fairly intelligent but act like utilities rather than independent beings, and can dimensionally stuff themselves into things such as the lions at Trafalgar Square, or even human bodies. Sphinxes track prey by scent and taste, and can amalgamate other beings' flesh into their own.

The sphinxes respond to certain control rituals, meaning persons with the right knowledge can capture them even by reciting poems in the correct ritual context. By warping space-time, sphinxes seriously screw up in-flight TARDISes. (Remember: Friends don't let friends drive space-time vehicles around sphinxes.)

The Kings of Space are two giant sphinxes, one black, one white, that rule sphinxkind and make judgements about sphinx law. It's implied they're related to the Dellan gods somehow. They've little interest in Dellan space. Only the Doctor's rumored to have visited sphinx homespace and lived.

The Time Lords and the People: The Time Lords revise their treaty and allow the People time travel—in exchange for their staying out of the Dellan god conflict.

Liquid Cats: Botched 26th century attempt to make liquid machines—it worked, but created devices with the intelligence of house pets.

ALIEN PLANETS *Gallifrey* is the same size as Earth (*The Infinity Doctors* and *Interference* say the two have the same rotational period and year-length), orbiting a supernova.

STUFF YOU NEED
Dead Romance: Title of Christine Summerfield's journals (she originally considered *Living Space* and *Real Life*).

The Gallifreyan Matrix ("The Deadly Assassin"): Hotwired into Time Lord bases across the Universe, always scanning for threats.

Gallifreyan Cloning Tanks: They're liquid, not solid, presumably held in place by a force field and directly encoding memories into the clones. Consequently, you might pick up stray memories simply by touching the tanks.

Cwej's Copycat Tissue: Healing fungus that seals over wounds and looks like a boiled potato.

PLACES TO GO
The Time Vortex: Objects adrift there cannot die.

Time Lord Space Station: Temporary outpost in Bottle Earth orbit, designed to organically reshape itself, sealing over wounds to preserve atmosphere. Long-term attacks exhaust its materials.

Simia KK98: A Time Lord base there includes an eight-armed statue of Rassilon holding a variety of rods, orbs, keys and sashes.

SHIPS
Time Lord Warships: Gold and spiky, armed with long-range weapons (possibly a throwback to Rassilon's Bowships, "State of Decay").

Time Lord Attack Spheres: Smaller vessels with monk-like crews moving through their walkways. Sphere pilots are linked to the control systems for life, pumped full of control-granting drugs.

HISTORY (The Universe-in-a-Bottle, i.e., Cwej's native Universe) By Cwej's account, the Time Lords were the first civilization to develop time travel. However, beings with god-like powers (the Great Old Ones, perhaps) pre-date them.

HISTORY (The Bottle-in-the-Bottle, i.e., Christine's native Universe) Humans, not aliens ("Pyramids of Mars") built the pyramids.
• The arrival of the Time Lords on October 12, 1970, ended the world, sparking a nuclear holocaust that made half the planet radioactive. Only Britain, protected by Time Lord force shields, went completely unscathed.

AT THE END OF THE DAY Years before *Fight Club*, Christine Summerfield wryly endures an identity revelation that minces your insides. As a world ends, Chris Cwej is unmasked as a heroic murderer. The Time Lords, devoid of morality, toy with other species' biology and emerge as the biggest bastards in all the Universes. This isn't a book for the meek—indeed, it's best suited for open-minded individuals who perceive all the layers between black and white. Lacking both the Doctor and Bernice, the story solidifies itself as a visceral, meaty and wry science fiction novel although it was spawned by "Doctor Who" mythology. As such, various sectors of fandom name *Dead Romance* as the absolute best novel among all the "Doctor Who" and "Doctor Who"-related books—Virgin and BBC combined. And so it is.

TEARS OF THE ORACLE

By Justin Richards

Release Date: June 1999
Order: Benny New Adventure #20
(Who NA #81)
"Dellan Gods Storyarc"

MAIN CHARACTERS Bernice Summerfield, Irving Braxiatel, Jason Kane, Chris Cwej, Divson Follett, Wolsey, Joseph, Commander Skutloid, Drexton, Garshal, Hayward Denson and God.

TRAVEL LOG Dellah and Asteroid KS-159, 2595.

STORY SUMMARY Benny agrees to help Irving Braxiatel find a location for his gigantic collection of universal artifacts, even as Braxiatel's trapped friend Commander Skutloid urgently requests an evacuation from the ravaged planet Dellah. Braxiatel and Benny reach Dellah, but seething mobs wound Skutloid and he later dies.

Back at Braxiatel's warehouses, Jason Kane announces he's located the mythical Oracle of the Lost—a fabled statue that can foretell the future—on asteroid KS-159. Braxiatel wins ownership of the asteroid from gambler and entrepreneur Hayward Denson, then sets out to find the statue with various allies that include Benny, Jason, ex-St. Oscar's professors Divson Follett and Emilia Winston and Denson himself.

On KS-159, the Oracle of the Lost predicts the emergence of the Dellan gods could spark Universal chaos and trigger a devastating war between the Time Lords and the People. On a more personal level, the Oracle reveals that Benny's recent Mary-Sue procedure has given her an inoperable, terminal brain tumor. Soon after, various expedition party members—including Divson Follett—are found dead, their corpses mummified. To prevent further deaths, Braxiatel requests help from the Time Lords, who force-regenerate their dying agent Chris Cwej to lend assistance.

Restored to life in a short, obese body, Chris finds evidence that decades ago, the famed archaeologist Edward Watkinson sought vengeance against the Oracle of the Lost for causing the death of his friend Oleg Mikelz (*See Sidebar*).

MISCELLANEOUS STUFF!

BRAXIATEL'S ORIGIN

When Braxiatel was young, he resisted the Time Lords' conformity and restraint. But Braxiatel continually succeeded at academics, merely pushing the envelope but never breaking through it. By the time his brother (read: the Doctor) was doing his exams, Braxiatel was off-world as an unofficial ambassador. Braxiatel believes the Doctor, his brother, was impatient and jealous, respecting Braxiatel and following his example, although the subconscious competition later caused resentment on both sides.

While Braxiatel thrived in his own arena, the Doctor achieved the same effect by deliberately drawing barely passing marks, then snubbing his nose at the Time Lords' ways. Because Braxiatel already held the post of off-world ambassador and there was no need for two, the Doctor left Gallifrey. Braxiatel misses him.

BENNY'S ILLNESS

Hayward Denson diagnoses Benny's brain tumor as stemming from her recent Mary-Sue and everyone involved seems to accept the explanation. But in truth, the People's supercomputer God secretly caused Benny's illness, knowing from the shapeshifter Kebara's visitation with the Oracle that Benny and Braxiatel would determine the outcome of the impending war. God make Benny terminally ill, attempting to distract Braxiatel and allow God to better impose its will upon events, hopefully expanding the People's political influence. However, Braxiatel thwarted the war by sending the parasite to Dellah (*Twilight of the Gods* withstanding), curtailing God from further power. Braxiatel knows God made Benny ill but chooses not to exact retribution (for which God is thankful), evidently deciding that a personal vendetta against a being as powerful as God isn't in anyone's interests.

Watkinson unearthed a mental parasite on the planet Paracletes, then infected the Oracle with it. But unable to consume the Oracle, the energy parasite burnt out the murdered expedition members for food before taking shelter in Benny.

Braxiatel and his allies fail to snare the creature and a distraught Benny tries to commit suicide. Although she fails, the parasite leaps into Benny's robotic porter Joseph to escape. However, Joseph is actually a drone of the People Ship J-Kibb, planted by the supercomputer God to monitor Benny's activities. Through Joseph's communications link, the mental parasite takes refuge in the J-Kibb's systems, allowing God to pilot the Ship by remote control and crash the parasite on Dellah. Because the Dellan gods feed on faith and the mental parasite feasts on uncertainty, God believes the two forces will cancel each other out and avert the Universal War.

As Benny's group recovers from their harrowing experience, Braxiatel suggests the mythical Fountain of Forever might cure Benny's brain tumor. With less than a month to live, Benny prepares for an expedition that could save her life.

MEMORABLE MOMENTS In the midst of death, we have life and hope: Benny realizes her friends' support is enough to get her through the destruction of St. Oscar's. Braxiatel wistfully stares in silence at the Theatrology Department building's broken facade, realizing one of his dreams lies in ruins. A dying Skutloid embraces his friend Braxiatel, asking for a coin to pay the Journeyman for entrance into the land of the dead.

Time Lord Braxiatel philosophically ponders the shortness of human lives and how an unstable humanity's just a stone's throw away from the abyss. Braxiatel's speech about his family will electro-shock those who realize the Doctor must be Braxiatel's brother. Formerly fit Chris Cwej hysterically registers shock at his regenerated, fat body. Most dramatic of all is Benny's attempted suicide—a recurring image foreshadowed from page one—which caps a ferocious amount of sacrifices and trials.

SEX AND SPIRITS A dying Benny, sensing her time in this Universe is running out, goes to bed with Jason. He proposes marriage again, but she pretends to be asleep. !Cin-ta!x of the People (*Walking to Babylon*) makes pancakes in the nude. Emilia Winston loved the doomed Divson Follett, but nothing came of it.

ASS-WHUPPINGS Attacked by the possessed shapeshifter Kebara—disguised as Jason Kane—Benny caves in his head with a lamp and thinks she's just murdered her ex-husband. A mentally possessed Benny shoots Braxiatel (fatally, she believes) with his anesthetic gun, then tries to commit suicide and blasting herself.

More than any other novel, *Tears of the Oracle* takes a number of Benny's secondary cast off the playing board. A crazed Dellan mob kills Commander Skutloid and his secondary Drexton. Braxiatel and Skutloid's assistant Garshal shoot down some of the masses to rescue their comrades. The mobs likely overrun St. Oscar's Advanced Research Department and kill Director Silvera. The

THE CRUCIAL BITS...

- **TEARS OF THE ORACLE**—The People's supercomputer God learns that Benny and Braxiatel will determine the outcome of an impending Universal war with the Dellan gods. In response, God infects Benny with a lethal brain tumor, hoping to distract Braxiatel and hopefully alter events to benefit the People. Braxiatel sends a mental parasite to Dellah, hampering the gods' power and thwarting the Universal war.

Braxiatel revealed as the Doctor's brother. Braxiatel gambles at Vega Station and wins Asteroid KS-159, the future home of the Braxiatel Collection.

The Time Lords regenerate a dying Chris Cwej into a shorter, black-haired body. Deaths of Commander Skutloid, Drexton, Garshal and St. Oscar's Archaeology Department Head Divson Follett. Destruction of St. Oscar's Advanced Research Department. Fate of famed archaeologist Edward Watkinson revealed.

mental parasite kills Garshal and Benny's head of department, Divson Follett. Tears also reveals the truth behind Edward Watkinson's last (and fatal) expedition (*See Sidebar*).

TV TIE-INS Braxiatel uses Time Lord message cubes ("The War Games," etc.). The Oracle numbers among the Great Wonders of the Universe, a system created by a man named Plackstead ("Death to the Daleks").

NOVEL TIE-INS Benny erroneously believes her Mary-Sue (*The Mary-Sue Extrusion*) has triggered a terminal brain tumor (*See Sidebar*). After Benny rescued Wolsey in *The Mary-Sue Extrusion*, the cat went into quarantine. The real Jason went off with his associate Mira after that book.

The Oracle drops the bomb that Clarence was formerly the rouge Ship !C-Mel (*The Also People*).

After *Where Angels Fear*, Braxiatel's potential romance partner, Renee Thalia, went off with a first officer of a heavy space hauler.

Oh No It Isn't! established that Benny held the Edward Watkinson Endowed Chair at St. Oscar's, and a smattering of books briefly mentioned him.

Theatre of War suggested Braxiatel won KS-159, the future location of the Braxiatel Collection (originally mentioned by Romana in "City of Death"), while playing cards. Braxiatel bests Hayward Denison on Vega Station, the famed casino featured in Richard's *Demontage*.

In *Happy Endings*, a future Braxiatel retroactively attempts to warn Benny of a shapeshifter usurping Jason's place by telling her: "The older he gets, the more interested in him you'll be."

Richards kills off a number of previously seen characters, including Commander Skutloid (Richards' *Dragons' Wrath*, *The Medusa Effect*), Skutloid's associates Garshal and Drexton (*The Medusa Effect*), the St. Oscar's Advanced Research Department (mentioned in *Oh No It Isn't!*, seen in *Mean Streets*, *The Medusa Effect*) and Divson Follett (first mentioned in *Oh No It Isn't!*).

After the destruction of St. Oscar's in *Where Angels Fear*, Follett spent months in the refugee camp on Thanaxos (*The Mary-Sue Extrusion*). Chris Cwej, terminally exposed to radiation in *Dead Romance*, here regenerates. The Time Lords forged a treaty with the People in that book, meaning !Cin-ta!x and the Temporal Interest Group (*Walking to Babylon*) are back in favor.

Braxiatel concluded Joseph was a remote drone in *Dragons' Wrath*, but failed to mention it. It's purely retcon, but Joseph relayed a message from God to Benny in *Walking to Babylon*—another clue to Joseph's true identity.

CHARACTER DEVELOPMENT

Bernice Summerfield: The St. Oscar's staff nicknamed Benny "Jonah." Denson estimates Benny's brain tumor started in an inactive part of her mind, but she'll notice symptoms in a week, likely dying in a month. The mental parasite momentarily ate Benny's greatest inner strength—her faith in her friendships.

Benny and Jason: God's simulation calculates they argue 93 percent of the time. Still, God also concludes that only Jason had a better than 80 percent chance of convincing Benny to search for the Oracle (*See Sidebar*).

Chris Cwej: A hooded Time Lord in dark monk's robes initiates a Chris' regeneration in return for his continued service. Blond-haired Chris changes into a stocky body that's shorter (he's not much taller than Benny) and fatter, with dark hair. His new voice sounds deeper and more mellow.

Irving Braxiatel: Braxiatel's collection of stuff (thankfully catalogued) occupies at least 17 warehouses. For a limited time, he can mentally shield himself and others against the Dellah religious furor. He's cash-poor at the moment, most of his capital tied up in long-term investments or frozen due to the Dellah crisis. The Time Lords owe Braxiatel a number of favors. Slipping a tracer on Braxiatel is virtually impossible. He has few friends but regards Benny as family. He pilots a medium range space chaser, collecting things for his enjoyment and to share with others.

MISCELLANEOUS STUFF!

WATKINSON VS. THE ORACLE

Eighty years ago (2515), Edward Watkinson encouraged his museum council to deny funding for Dr. Oleg Mikelz's rather fanciful expedition to find the Oracle of the Lost despite a personal friendship with Mikelz. Defiant, Mikelz mounted an expedition with his personal assistant Gregor and wife Louisa and located the Oracle anyway. Tired of its servile existence, the Oracle baited Mikelz by claiming he would become a murderer, then destroy the Oracle and die himself. The prediction made Mikelz increasingly paranoid until he mistakenly thought Louisa and Gregor were having an affair. Mikelz shot the two of them, falling into the Oracle's trap because he then had to destroy the Oracle or admit his murderous actions weren't predestined. Distraught, Mikelz crashed his cruiser to bury the Oracle but wound up killing himself.

Simultaneously, Watkinson's expedition to the planet Paracletes ended with a mental parasite possessing Watkinson and killing the rest of his team. On September 11, 2515, Watkinson returned home and deduced how the Oracle had manipulated his friend Mikelz. With some sense of the parasite possessing him, Watkinson traveled to Asteroid KS-159 to vengefully infect the Oracle with the parasite. When Watkinson died, the creature infected the Oracle and forced it to go dormant.

The creature starved until God sent the shapeshifter Kebara to see if Oracle technology could help the People develop time travel. Perhaps more important, God wanted information about the upcoming Time Lord-People War, but the parasite awakened and infected Kebara. When God learned Benny and Braxiatel (a Time Lord) would play key roles in the upcoming war, God sent Kebara disguised as Jason Kane to keep them occupied. Unfortunately, the creature blurred Kebara's sense of self, making him believe he was Jason Kane and approaching Benny about locating the Oracle of the Lost.

The Oracle of the Lost: Braxiatel speculated the sentient Oracle was telepathic, psionically deriving names and background from its questioners, then plugging that information into a social and behavioral model of the Universe and making predictions based on the result. The Oracle's accuracy increases if you ask a broad-based question, but the answer's probably less useful.

A limiter prevents the Oracle from directly lying, although it can use obfuscation and indirection. It cannot reveal what another questioner asks, although it can repeat its answer. It has difficulty conveying information if not asked.

Allegedly, leaders from Delfus-Clytaemnestra traveled to visit the Oracle in Delfus-Orestes. The Oracle supposedly slept for millennia. Apart from its size, the Oracle's incredibly lifelike.

The Oracle and Braxiatel: The Oracle instantly regarded Braxiatel as an old friend, willingly giving him information and actually conversing with him (it only answered questions for anyone else). The Oracle declined, with some sadness, to say if Braxiatel would ever return to his people.

Commander Skutloid: Considered the greatest strategist of his age. Braxiatel owes Skutloid his life several times over.

Divson Follett: Long-serving St. Oscar's archaeology chair who invested in off-shore trusts, plus owns a gold Cosmic Express card and an apartment on Kralinal Maxis. He wasn't very old by his race's standards.

Benny and Follett: Follett valued Benny highest of all his teaching staff. Conversely, Benny thought Follett dictatorial and someone who bullied her. Follett helped create the Watkinson Endowment Chair that Benny occupied.

God: Even with the revised Time Lord-People Treaty, God can't send its agents too far (Delfus-Orestes is out of bounds). The shapeshifter Kebara wasn't one of the People, so God deployed him with some flexibility. Despite improved relations with the Time Lords, God predicted (before this story) an 87 percent likelihood of the Dellah crisis triggering Universal War. Even with the revised treaty, God's time experiments fare poorly.

Professor Edward Watkinson: Considered the greatest archaeologist of the 26th century, Watkinson advocated a holistic approach to archaeological study, using various details to form an overall pattern. He was a prolific writer and thinker, touching virtually every area of archaeology.

Hayward Denson: Denson, who has steel-gray hair and a moustache, runs a diverse and comprehensive business empire. He's played gambling casinos that include New Holopia, Rick's, Tropsalon and Vega Station (*Demontage*). He's well-humored and trained in human medicine.

The mental parasite: Originating on Paracletes, the mental parasite could be unique or part of a species (it goes unstated). It enters through the optic nerve, using its host mind's innate telepathic powers to leap from victim to victim. The parasite absorbs energy, burning out its hosts very quickly. It mentally feeds on faith and belief, corroding the host's sense of self and trust.

J-Kibb: J-Kibb is sentient, but grows surprised when God takes direct control of its engines.

ALIEN RACES *Martians (a.k.a. Neo-Aretians):* Salute the dead with a right fist over the left breast. They move fast despite their bulk and gasping for breath. To humans, they all look the same. The Martians put coins in the mouths of their dead to pay the mythical Journeyman for the trip to Kinova, their equivalent of Heaven. Martians killed in battle are left where they drop.

ALIEN PLANETS
Dellah: After the emergence of the gods, various authorities froze Dellan funds.

Asteroid KS-159 (a.k.a. Delfus-Orestes, Delfestes, Cappa Nine Seven): Located in the Gamatra Sector, KS-159 has a number of names because naming conventions continually changed. It's not too large, but has above-average gravity.

PLACES TO GO *The Temple of the Lost:* The Oracle's temple has a Greco-Roman look, with coinage made with the Oracle's likeness.

STUFF YOU NEED
Braxiatel's Crate: An extra-dimensional box in one of Braxiatel's warehouses (possibly a TARDIS, but likely not) contains at least three bedrooms, each with an in-suite bathroom, plus a small study and fair-sized kitchen area.

Martian Armor: Protects Commander Skutloid and his men from the religious fervor. It also promotes advanced healing, grants invisibility and provides adrenaline and weapons systems.

The Fountain of Forever: The rare Reidel Manuscript (naturally, Braxiatel owns a copy) describes this Fountain, allegedly found by Magnus Reidel. It you stand under the Fountain's waters, you get eternal life or a cure of all ailments.

ORGANIZATIONS
St. Oscar's Advanced Research Department: Commander Skutloid and his men defended the Research Department, but it likely fell without

them to protect it. Director Silvera's devices briefly held off the Dellan religious mania.

Worldsphere Groups: Include Behavioral Analysis and Boring and Irrelevant Interest.

PHENOMENA Lack of telepathic ability hinders successful *time travel*.

ALTERNATE HISTORY The Oracle foresaw a future where the release of the Dellan gods would rip the Universe asunder, with the Time Lords blaming the People's supercomputer God and sparking temporal warfare.

HISTORY A series of wars destroyed many records relating to archaeologist Edward Watkinson.

AT THE END OF THE DAY Absolutely outstanding and a contender for the best Benny novel, the action-pumped *Tears of the Oracle* so ambitiously writes a conclusion for Benny's cast that it's a damn shame—as originally intended—this story didn't end the Virgin NA line. Skutloid's untimely death alone shows how much the Benny characters have grown, hurtling the book into a marbled series of graphic murders that dish out plot twist after plot twist. *Tears'* only downside is that its multiple threads will likely lose Benny NA newcomers, but that's hardly a crime, given its mandate of concluding the line. For everyone else, Richards unloads every bullet in his clip and gives Benny the "send-off" that she properly deserved.

RETURN TO THE FRACTURED PLANET

By Dave Stone

Release Date: August 1999
Order: Benny New Adventure #21
(Who NA #82)
"Dellan Gods Storyarc"

MAIN CHARACTERS A Stratum Seven Agent and Bernice Summerfield, with Irving Braxiatel and Chris Cwej.

TRAVEL LOG Proximan Chain, 2596. [Dating the Benny books is never an exact science, however *Beige Planet Mars* taking place in June 2595 and *Twilight of the Gods'* claim to take place "a year" after *Where Angels Fear* rather necessitates rolling the calendar at some point. As a number of weeks evidently pass between *Tears of the Oracle* and this book, this seems as good a point as any.]

STORY SUMMARY Irving Braxiatel and Benny recruit synthetic beings called Artificial Personality Embodiments (APEs), who can resist telepathic domination, to hunt down stray Dellan gods that elude the quarantine. But when freelance APE operative Kara Delbane is brutally murdered in her apartment, Benny and Braxiatel ask for help from Kara's lover—the unnamed Agent with Stratum Seven clearance who helped them during the Mary-Sue affair. Benny assists the Agent but worries about flawed mental protocols from her recent Mary-Sue that could activate and wipe her brain entirely at any time.

Together, Benny and the Agent find links between Kara's murder and the original mission for which the Agent was constructed. Shortly after coming online, the Agent and Kara worked for an APE mercenary group named the Oblivion Angels and investigated operations by the villainous Sleed Incorporated on the planet Sharabeth. The company's experiments to create mutagenic weapons were exposed, and aged company founder Absolam Sleed died at the Agent's hands.

Investigating Kara's murder further, the Agent determines she learned of a similar plan to slaughter the Proximan Chain populace with a mutagenic bomb. Sleed's operatives try to brainwash the Agent into murdering Benny and frame him for Kara's death, but the Agent resists and instead kills Kara's alleged murderer—a Sleed-hired assassin named Praetorian.

Benny and the Agent locate Absolam Sleed's base, discovering the madman's brain survived as a computer program after his "death." Having merged with a time-travelling Dellan god, Sleed now exists as a giant crystalline entity. Sleed unleashes a telepathic attack but the Agent's artificial brain protects him. Worse for Sleed, his psionics trigger the Mary-Sue protocols in Benny's mind, causing them to latch onto the most dominant personality present—Sleed's brain—and attempt to overwrite it. Sleed reels from the sudden mental attack, allowing Benny to smash his brain crystal and kill him.

Benny concludes that Sleed's merger with the Dellan god—a creature sustained by widespread belief—turned him into a caricature of a villain that sought power for its own sake. Restored to health, Benny suffers some memory loss and ponders whether to re-learn her experiences from her journals. Meanwhile, the Agent departs to grieve for Kara and resume his freelance existence.

MEMORABLE MOMENTS On Sharabeth, the Agent encounters a surgeon/torturer who can twist his subjects' intestines into three separate "balloon animals" before they die (the skill won him an award). The surgeon details his plans for the Agent (whipping off the "old meat and two veg first,"), so the Agent puts a finger in the surgeon's eyes and pulls his head apart (that'll teach 'im.)

The Agent orders an Olde Earth Traditional Burger made from Genuine Ground Beef, Three Kinds of Cheese, Choice Rashers of Crispy Creamery Butter-Fried Bacon, Fried Egg, French Fries and a Side Salad. A dying Benny decides, "What the hell. Me, too. You only live once."

While confronting mad industrialist Absolam Sleed, the Agent quips how he's not interested in the specifics of Sleed's sadistic agenda, which probably includes devices such as viewscreens that put out dirty-level radiation. To the Agent's frustration, Sleed scribbles a note because the idea hadn't occurred to him.

SEX AND SPIRITS After their days in the Oblivion Angels (*See Sidebar*), the Agent and Kara spent two weeks shagging and failing to live together in Aeon Flux on Mars. Later, infrequent meetings allowed them to develop a healthier relationship that worked toward being permanent. Telepathic probes from Jason Kane's associate Mira conclude the Agent felt an indescribable love for Kara.

The Agent and Benny platonically book into the Connaught Hotel pretending to be "Mr. and Mrs. Smith." The Agent inadvertently calls Mira while she's having sex but they still flirt over the phone a bit. Mira's not interested in the Agent sexually—which means he's uninterested in her. His pheromone system only reacts to people who're interested in him, meaning visual and aural stimuli don't help. His dealings with Benny, on the other hand, were clouded by the tiny possibility of seeing her underwear.

ASS-WHUPPINGS The Agent's killed 157 beings and has inexplicably "died once himself." On Sharabeth, the Agent slays a surgeon/torturer and impales several human mutants with the surgeon's scalpels. The Agent avenges himself on Khristoff Ramon Praetorian, the alleged murderer of Kara Delbane, with a single hand smack that basically pulps Praetorian's head. In battle with the Sleed monster, the Agent loses an arm but has it re-grafted.

An explosion momentarily puts Benny on a respirator. The brainwashed Agent twists a nerve cluster under Benny's earlobe and gives her shrieking agony. Benny's Mary-Sue protocols ravage Sleed's real mind and she smashes his brainglobe. Nanites (possibly a remnant from the TARDIS) somewhat suture her memory.

THE CRUCIAL BITS...

- **RETURN TO THE FRACTURED PLANET**—Benny's terminal brain tumor cured.

NOVEL TIE-INS Artificial Personality Embodiments, explored in detail here, and the computer system named ARVID first appeared in Stone's *Ship of Fools*. The Agent formerly searched for Benny in *The Mary-Sue Extrusion*, the novel where she received a Mary-Sue transplant. *Tears of the Oracle* (erroneously) suggested the procedure was terminal, but Benny's cured here.

After *Tears of the Oracle*, Braxiatel's tight money situation eased up. Mira got resentful at Benny for leaving Jason too soon and hurting him again. Benny's hunt for the Fountain of Forever, touted in *Tears of the Oracle* as having healing properties, isn't mentioned.

The Oblivion Angels are named for Stone's *Oblivion* and "Charlie's Angels," one supposes. The Thanaxon Council (*Mary-Sue Extrusion* again) voted to build a seven-ton monument on top of Prince Jimbo's coffin, probably fearing the Dellan god within him might awaken again.

Chris Cwej's latent telepathy (*Sleepy*) provides lots of mental shields.

CHARACTER DEVELOPMENT

Bernice Summerfield: Can make the Agent's computer Box run several hundred thousand cycles of self-diagnostics, gaining 45 minutes of time to work undetected. Braxiatel gave Benny an untraceable communication cube and a Suit of Lights, which grants its wearer near-invisibility. The new Chris Cwej sometimes annoys her because he's so attentive. Conversely, Benny finds Mira refreshing because she's candid and forgoes unnecessary politeness.

Benny and Jason Kane: Elanore Vita Hydrant Summerfield-Kane is allegedly their descendent and possesses Benny's journals, supplying the information to publishers.

Chris Cwej: He sometimes works undercover as "Roland Forrester," allegedly a member of the Sec-Serve Security Services.

Irving Braxiatel: Braxiatel employs a number of APEs as operatives and gives the Agent his complete confidence and support. Through hypnosis, Braxiatel makes people remember details their conscious mind ignores. As a Time Lord, he sometimes appears standoffish because he doesn't use human niceties.

The Stratum Seven Agent: The Agent grants his loyalty and services to employers such as Braxiatel, but demands a hefty fee and legal protection in return. He stringently honors his contracts—medical fees uncovered by his contract with Braxiatel wipe out his bank account. Thanks to his media contacts and Braxiatel's hacking, the Agent ends this story hailed as the savior of the Proximan Chain.

The Agent's undergoing something of an identity crisis, recognizing the original memories of his personality donors but having an artificial body. His synthetic form amplifies his emotional impulses and makes him somewhat moody.

He's got a taste for horrendously expensive antiques. The Agent has 412 associations of varying degrees, seven close associations and no intimate associations. He recognizes other APEs from their movement and musculature. He considers projectile weapons a liability, but carries a multi-functional one.

By internally shutting down his pain receptors, the Agent can extract an 85 mm-long polyceramic tube from inside his left arm that holds useful devices such as surgical adhesive, a mini-light and a little laser-cutter with enough charge for 20 seconds of use.

Kara Delbane: Fitted with "memories" to explain why she came online in a strange place, APE Kara at first believed she was a warrior princess in ancient Greece, sent to the future by her horny sidekick's hellspawn daughter (We hope this evokes "Xena: Warrior Princess" for you).

Kara served in the Oblivion Angels as an operative and pilot, but acquired more status than Angels leader ARVID. Before her death, a captured Kara tripped a mental fail-safe and completely razed her brain and personality, denying her torturers the information they sought (the Agent had a similar device but removed it).

The Agent and Kara: The Agent ends this book uncertain about Kara's death, recognizing Praetorian was involved but didn't necessarily kill her.

Mira: Mira doesn't have another name, effectively making her the "Cher" and "Madonna" of the Benny books. She can sometimes telepathically scan a freshly dead person's vestigial nerve impulses to reconstruct their last moments. The technique works better on APEs, but only gives a 25 to 35 percent success rate.

The Agent and Mira: She feels a natural affinity for him and offers her assistance.

MISCELLANEOUS STUFF!

THE AGENT'S ORIGIN

The Stratum Seven Agent's memories (and certainly his narration) can't fully be trusted, but here's a possible origin story:

The synthetic Agent was custom-made in the Catan Nebula for a special assignment and first came online in the company of fellow APE Kara Delbane. The Agent reported to the computer intelligence named ARVID, the leader of a mercenary group of enhanced APEs named the Oblivion Angels. Together, the Agent and Kara investigated the planet Sharabeth—a world in the grip of fractured time (*See Phenomena*). Sharabeth served its galactic sector as an industrial and commercial nexus point, so the Agent and Kara were assigned to investigate and see what could be salvaged.

On Sharabeth, the Agent and Kara found proof that Sleed Incorporated was killing people on an industrial basis, testing new types of ergotropic drugs, nanite technology and mutagenic chemicals. Sleed Incorporated's insane founder, Absolam Sleed, was developing ways to whittle down mass populations on a global scale. The Oblivion Angels seized control of Sharabeth and the Agent supposedly killed the aged Sleed. The Agent and Kara completed several more missions for the Oblivion Angels, but the group rebelled upon learning (something unexplained) their founders' true nature. Unspecified events that rocked half the galaxy tore the Angels apart, but the Agent and Kara survived as freelance agents.

Box: The Agent's computerized assistant—a customized cyberbiologics package that wraps around the Agent's forearm. Box automatically drops info blanket bombs and scrambles local GalNet systems if the Agent's out of contact for too long.

ALIEN RACES

Time Lords: Acting on Chris Cwej's data, the Time Lords retroactively deactivated Sleed's mutagenic Proximan Chain device (and no, they're not supposed to do that sort of thing).

Artificial Personality Embodiments (APEs): APEs are built for a number of purposes. Low-grade APEs carry out suicide missions. Mid-range ones are re-used for high-risk work. Top-of-the-range units might contain 35 or more subjective years of information and have stronger personality types. Some APEs recognize their artificial nature, achieving new levels of sentience. Each APE therefore has a different "Break Out" rating, denoting the likelihood of them doing this. Most buyers dispose of their APEs before this can happen. Broken-out APEs don't have much social status and are virtually unemployable. Sleed theorized that a magnesium suspension could saturate an APE's prefrontal lobes and effectively lobotomize him or her. The Agent resisted the process, perhaps because of his enhanced "Break Out" nature.

PLACES TO GO
The Braxiatel Collection: A photo-projecting dome there shows you the entire panoply of galactic history in 20 minutes. One of the garages contains a transmat.

Proximan Chain Habitats: An engineering hybrid of space stations, colonies and planetary settlements, the Proximan Chain Habitats provides rapid travel over a vast inhabited space. The area's a wide conglomeration of cultures and species, lacking a cohesive law.

STUFF YOU NEED
Mary-Sue Transplant: Benny's Mary-Sue went awry because the black market medic she used didn't properly encode the Mary-Sue's self-eradicating protocols.

Stratum Seven Clearance: Stratum Seven agents adhere to rigid codes of honor. They can willingly give loyalty and accept reasonable fees in exchange, but they can't be bribed. To insult a Stratum Seven agent, stick money into his or her bank account unauthorized.

PHENOMENA *Fractured Time:* A theory holds that the Universe doesn't travel through time at a rate of a second per second. Instead, it's accelerating at a second per second, falling toward some inconceivable end that'll demolish it. The superaccelerated Sharabeth somehow hit such an end, sending temporal shards throughout time.

AT THE END OF THE DAY It cross-pollinates continuity like mad, but *Return to the Fractured Planet* makes for surprisingly good reading, defining the Stratum Seven Agent from ground zero. While some fans bitch because it's not the strongest book about Benny, the work sports a science fiction foundation that makes it a more concrete novel overall and gives it a lively clarity. For that reason, *Return to the Fractured Planet* is among Dave Stone's better Benny novels, somewhat self-indulgent but delivering a tidy little futuristic mystery in the vein of Larry Niven's "Gil Hamilton" stories.

THE JOY DEVICE
By Justin Richards
Release Date: October 1999
Order: Benny New Adventure #22
(Who NA #83)

MAIN CHARACTERS　　Bernice Summerfield, Jason Kane and Clarence, with Irving Braxiatel.

TRAVEL LOG　　Asteroid KS-159, Cyrano Major, Virabilis, 2596.

STORY SUMMARY　　Benny makes plans for an adventure holiday in the cutthroat Rim frontier—with famed adventurer Dent Harper serving as her tour guide. But on Braxiatel's asteroid, Benny's friends quietly panic, fearing Benny will enjoy her newfound escapades too much and permanently leave their company. So before Benny meets Dent on the seedy planet Virabilis, Jason and Clarence get there first and work behind the scenes to prevent Benny from having a drop of excitement. Jason and Clarence variously bribe, cajole and trick a host of potential threats, ranging from muggers to hostile drug lords, largely convincing Benny that Dent's adventure stories are overrated.

Elsewhere on Virabilis, crimelord Rula Winther plots to steal a valuable artifact named Dorpfeld's Prism, but thief Miklos Frunt snitches it first. Winther's agents kill Frunt, but the Prism remains missing and curio dealer Jericko Klench, Frunt's employer, hires adventure-seekers Dent and Benny to help locate the relic. Upon learning of this, Jason contacts Braxiatel and discovers that the Prism, hailing from the defunct Smermashi civilization, silently modifies the alpha waves of anyone who touches it, granting them overwhelming feelings of joy and tranquility.

Meanwhile, Benny deduces Frunt hid the Prism in Klench's trash, variously trading the Prism's possession with Winther, Klench and Klench's associate Linn. As each person acquires the Prism, they become joyful and passive, happily giving it up to anyone who asks for it.

Finally, Winther's associates capture Jason and prepare to torture him, but a Prism-entranced Winter starts blathering about profit sharing and health insurance for Cartel members. In a struggle that follows, Winther and Jason accidentally fall off a balcony, but a flying Clarence saves Jason and the Prism, allowing Winther to plummet to her (extremely squished) demise. Immune to the Prism, Clarence pockets it while Winther's second-in-command Nikole becomes Cartel leader.

Still oblivious to anything that's happened, Benny tries to salvage her "adventure" holiday by bedding Dent. Realizing Benny's intent, Jason and Clarence unleash a myriad of delaying tactics—ripping out an escalator, sabotaging elevators, switching room numbers, rushing in as room service to dish out eggs and prunes, making scandalous phone calls and generally keeping Benny and Dent running ragged until they innocently fall asleep. Afterward, Benny and Dent blame each other's lack of stamina, forcing Benny to give up and return to Braxiatel's asteroid. As Jason and the others innocently look on, Benny resumes her "normal" life while Braxiatel has Clarence add Dorpfeld's Prism to the asteroid's archives.

MEMORABLE MOMENTS Benny declines to have wine at dinner and her friends ask if she's feeling okay. When Benny announces she's going on holiday to the Rim, they nearly crap themselves with worry that Benny might like it out there and not come back.

Benny and Dent travel to the cutthroat Prevoria City expecting a fight with hostile natives, but Jason gives up a fortune in fruit and vegetables to convince the tribe that Benny's a princess. When she shows up, the tribe marshals out banners saying, "Our Village Welcomes Bernice Summerfield."

Benny and Dent spend a solid 14 pages trying (and failing utterly) to have sex—easily the best farce of the Benny line.

SEX AND SPIRITS The aforementioned (and sadly unsuccessful) sex antics between Benny, Dent, Jason and Clarence are utterly hysterical. On an even more woeful note, Chris Cwej's new body doesn't tolerate alcohol as well as his old one.

ASS-WHUPPINGS Jason shoots a thug named Fronz in the head. Mrs. Winther, clutching the joy-giving Dorpfeld's Prism, falls to her death (a flying Clarence snatches the Prism, allowing Winther's laughter to turn to screams of horror.)

TV TIE-INS Braxiatel's study has several statues of Levithian Graffs ("The Ribos Operation").

NOVEL TIE-INS After losing some of her memories in *Return to the Fractured Planet*, Benny feels unsure if she should relive her old life and considers burning her diaries.

CHARACTER DEVELOPMENT

Bernice Summerfield: Benny's now "age 30 something—and a half." Domistos Tours handles her travel plans. She once found herself in the middle of a swamp surrounded by deadly shnorks,

but thanks to the Mary-Sue debacle, she doesn't remember how she escaped.

Jason Kane: Braxiatel gives Jason a small disc that clamps onto satellite relay boxes and allows the two of them to communicate via encrypted supralight microwave link—with a time delay of five seconds.

Chris Cwej: Chris new incarnation is slightly shorter and plumper than Jason. He's got dark, receding, slicked-back hair.

Clarence: He eats only for social reasons. He doesn't need sleep and proves immune to Dorpfeld's Prism.

Dent Harper: Barring only James Bond, Dent Harper's the ultimate man's man. He's got mucho muscles and a high IQ, plus trust fund income that equals the gross domestic product of several small planets. He's so handsome, Chris gets jealous.

Harper holds multiple degrees and is most legendary for his explorations of the Outer Limits while working for Madeleine, Duchess of Nimfette. Harper once returned from the Uncharted Isles with Matrik Ungeles, the famous cartographer.

He's written many best-selling travel documentaries, including *Adventures on the Rim* (Braxiatel has read Harper's work).

PLACES TO GO

Braxiatel's Study: Located at the future Braxiatel Collection on Asteroid KS-159, Braxiatel's study has inlaid marble walls and a mahogany writing desk in the center of the room. Alcoves line each wall. Other alcoves stand blank, intended for paintings of the grounds.

Braxiatel's Hall of Mirrors: The Hall features 17 large, arched and nearly identical windows. Richly colored oil paintings in Earth Classical style cover the ceiling. The Hall's mirrored alcoves and windows are ornamented with a round symbol, a disc with swirling embossed lines that designates the sun-and-lionskin emblem of Louis XIV in the original Hall of Mirrors at Versailles.

STUFF YOU NEED *Dorpfeld's Prism:* Smermashi crystal (*See History*) made from focusing stones that modulate the alpha and beta waves of anyone who touches it. Such people experience reality as being overly pleasant—rather like putting on "metaphorical rose-tinted spectacles." Lead neutralizes the prism's effects.

HISTORY The Smermashi homeworld endured ozone-layer depletion, pollution, mad-dodontrous disease and more. But sadly, the Smermashi's joy crystals made them think everything was nicey-nicey, so they kicked the bucket.

• Famed explorer Andreas Dorpfeld unearthed a multi-faceted Smermashi crystal in 2315, although it perverted Dorpfeld's value system and constantly made him happy. On his deathbed, Dorpfeld suspected the prism's taint on him and implored his friend Myerson to destroy the crystal, calling it, "My prison." Unfortunately, Myerson heard Dorpfeld's muttered words as "My prism" and named it after Dorpfeld. (Braxiatel was either present at Dorpfeld's death or certainly knew of Dorpfeld's true request.) Eventually, a Virabilis mining company came to own the prism.

AT THE END OF THE DAY Downright hysterical in parts—but hardly the sort of story that necessitated an entire book. The sweet premise of Jason sabotaging Benny's adventure holiday works at first, but eventually gets dull for the simple reason that while Benny's not experiencing any danger, we're not getting much excitement either. Also, there's a rushed feel, no doubt enhanced by a last-minute production schedule (Virgin often asked fast-writing authors Richards and Dave Stone to adhere to ridiculously stringent deadlines), although the Benny/Dent/Jason farce helps you walk away with a good feeling.

TWILIGHT OF THE GODS

By Mark Clapham
and Jon de Burgh Miller

Release Date: December 1999
Order: Benny New Adventure #23
(Who NA #84)
"Dellan Gods Storyarc" Conclusion

MAIN CHARACTERS Bernice Summerfield, Jason Kane, Chris Cwej, Clarence and Irving Braxiatel, with Emile Mars-Smith.

TRAVEL LOG Asteroid KS-159 and Dellah, circa June 2596 (nearly a year after *Where Angels Fear*).

STORY SUMMARY Braxiatel learns the Time Lords and the People have proposed to jointly deploy a Doomsday Probe that will eliminate the Dellan gods' threat—and by consequence, Dellah's entire sector of space. Fearful of massive casualties, Braxiatel summons Benny, Jason Kane, Chris Cwej and Clarence for a last-ditch mission.

Together, they plan to smuggle a dimensional transfer node onto Dellah, then warp the entire planet into the dying universe from which the gods originated and return home in the dimension-hopping ship *Revelation*. As part of the Time Lord-People treaty, the transfer node will only respond to neutral agents Benny and Jason.

On Dellah, the gods war amongst themselves for a dwindling number of followers and the god Tehke slays most of his fellows. With difficulty, Benny and Jason reach Casmov Power Station and install the node while Chris and Clarence cover them. Tehke's followers heavily wound Jason, but Benny activates the node and shifts Dellah into the gods' home dimension.

A number of the Dellan gods don't survive the experience and the rest lose their formidable abilities. In the gods' home dimension, Benny's group encounters the Ferutu, the race of alternate-reality Time Lords from which the Dellan gods originated. The Ferutu grow angry at their "godlike" fellows for usurping too much power, but simultaneously view the *Revelation* as the perfect opportunity to evacuate their dying universe.

The Ferutu attack Benny's group with temporal bolts, reverting Chris down his personal timeline and leaving him a 13-year-old version of his original blond-haired body. Worse, another temporal strike hits Clarence dead center, changing back into his original state as the People Ship !C-Mel. Unfortunately, !C-Mel's form proves incompatible with the physics of the Ferutu universe and fatally ruptures.

Benny and Chris reach for the *Revelation*, but the Ferutu capture Jason. Realizing she cannot allow the Ferutu to seize the ship and regain their god-like status in our Universe, Benny pledges her love for Jason and triggers the transfer node, warping the *Revelation* for home. Frustrated, the Ferutu pledge to study Jason's nature and find a way to conquer our Universe.

As the Time Lords and the People retreat into isolationism, life in Dellah's sector of space slowly returns to normal. Braxiatel helps establish a new university on the recovering planet Vremnya, then secures Benny a position there as head of the archaeology department. Reassured that her life will never be normal, Benny begins to recruit her staff and dreams of reuniting with Jason.

MEMORABLE MOMENTS Braxiatel advises Benny only hire archaeology professors similar to the Benny who went to Heaven in *Love and War*—a delicious way of bringing Benny's 74-novel arc full circle.

THE CRUCIAL BITS...

• **TWILIGHT OF THE GODS**—Death of Clarence. The Dellan gods revealed as a Ferutu splinter group and consigned, with Dellah, to their home universe. Jason Kane trapped as a Ferutu captive. A glancing Ferutu time blast de-ages Benny about five years. Chris Cwej returned into a blonde-haired body—as a 13-year-old (hello again, puberty). First full appearance and death of the Sultan of the Tashwari. Benny longs for Jason and becomes head of the Archaeology Department at Vremnya University.

Virgin New Adventures line ends after more than eight years.

SEX AND SPIRITS Benny ends this story determined to be with Jason, but only has time for a declaration of "I love you," before sending him off. Benny has a vision of being gray-haired and pregnant, married to Jason for years. Despite Jason's loss, Benny predicts her vision will come true.

She also realizes that although Clarence liked Chris and Jason as friends, he hung around to spend time with Benny. Jason went mountain climbing after his divorce from Charlene (*Deadfall*) because he fancied the instructor.

ASS-WHUPPINGS Aside from Jason, Benny also abandons the remaining Dellan survivors, including ex-St. Oscar's librarian Gruat. She guns down a group of Ferutu with the *Revelation*'s weaponry and cracks a spanner over a Ferutu's skull.

Dellan god Tehke kills enough of his fellows, including Maa'lon (*Where Angels Fear*), to become leader of the Dellan pantheon. The irked Ferutu in turn rub out Tehke and his followers. A number of other Dellan gods, including Mor'yuchi, perish in the transfer to their home universe.

Twilight of the Gods kills off the Dellah's famed Sultan of Tashwari, killed by a girl named Palma for abuses while under the gods' control.

Chris shoots down a pursuit ship. Jason guns down several of Tehke's followers, but takes a knife blow and gets beaten up for his efforts. Clarence torches Mor'yuchi with his sword, but Mor'yuchi's blade digs into Clarence's shoulder. A Ferutu time blast kills Clarence.

TV TIE-INS The Dellan god Tehke has a number of alter egos alter egos, including Urmungdasatra (*The Taking of Planet 5*), Liege Maximo (*Transformers: Generation 2* comics) and Dahak ("Hercules: The Legendary Journeys").

Archaeologist Heldov hails from Dellah's Iacon City, undoubtedly "Transformers" fan Miller (we suspect he's got a life-sized Optimus Prime model in his bedroom) having fun and naming it after an Autobot stronghold. Other "Transformers" references include planetary defenses being manned by Officer Witwicky, named after "Transformers" characters Buster and Spike Witwicky.

NOVEL TIE-INS *The Dead Men Diaries* (*See Sidebar*) picks up Benny's story some years after these events. Jason Kane briefly returns in *The Dead Men Diaries*: "The Door into Bedlam."

The Ferutu debuted in *Cold Fusion*. The seventh Doctor thought he'd destroyed the Ferutu timeline (barring a few odd survivors), but their magics delayed the end.

Oh No It Isn't! first mentioned the Sultan of Tashwari who appears (and dies) here.

The god Tehke decapitates rival god Maa'lon. Benny's friend Reverend Harker survived as one of Maa'lon's followers. Student Emile Mars-Smith here returns, freed from possession by a Dellan god and currently serving as Braxiatel's assistant (all *Where Angels Fear*).

Christine Summerfield (*Dead Romance*) leaves a message on Benny's answering machine. Chris Cwej's body contains healing nanites, either a result of his Time Lord service (*Dead Romance*) or his TARDIS days.

The mental parasite deposited on Dellah(*Tears of the Oracle*) caused massive amounts of disbelief, fracturing but not destroying the gods' power and leading to a civil war for the remaining followers. Despite summoning assistance in that story, outcast Braxiatel doesn't have much influence with the Time Lords.

Braxiatel summons the Stratum Seven Agent (*Return to the Fractured Planet*) to help with the Dellan mission, but only gets an obscene reply, then static in return. Benny has a dream sequence of her as a gray-haired, pregnant woman, a nod to *The Infinity Doctors* (Clapham and Miller are humorously—not seriously—suggesting that Benny is preggers with the Doctor's child).

CHARACTER DEVELOPMENT

Bernice Summerfield: Benny's office at Vremnya University is remarkably tidy because she lost everything on Dellah (Braxiatel gives her a selection of first-edition archaeology books). A glancing Ferutu temporal blast makes Benny about five years younger, removing a silver streak from her hair and taking off a few wrinkles.

Jason Kane: Jason strangely dreams of electric gerbils (we're concerned for the boy). He looks like crap even after a wash and a good night's sleep.

Chris Cwej: Chris' regenerated black-haired body doesn't handle junk food with the efficiency of his blond-haired one. His nuclei are no longer human, jury-rigged by the Time Lords for a number of purposes. Latently telepathic Chris can sense thousands of thoughts by simple touch, but the talent doesn't work in the Ferutu universe.

In this, Chris' last appearance to date, he finishes up a 13-year-old version of his blonde-haired self, having regained a number of the memories the Time Lords blocked off. Braxiatel theorizes the Ferutu's temporal effect might fade and return Chris to his black-haired body, or it could unpredictably return blond-haired Chris to his true age. More terrifying, it could age him to being a senior citizen overnight.

Chris carries a projectile gun and can hotwire certain vehicles. Young Chris' mother let him pretend he was driving a skimmer.

Irving Braxiatel: He's got thin, dark hair and more money than most governments. Braxiatel was born a mere lord but matured to make decisions that affected a number of cultures. He's one of human space's greatest sponsors of advanced research and a key negotiator. He left his decrypting kit on Dellah.

Braxiatel pledges to recover Jason, partly out of friendship and partly because Jason's technical knowledge must be kept away from the Ferutu.

Emile Mars-Smith: Emile's slimmer and more self-confident. He still suffers from blackouts, but knows how to use a low-level medical scanner. He helps Braxiatel set up Vremnya University.

Clarence: Clarence doesn't need to eat, but he's learning to appreciate life through pizza. A corporeal shield makes him look human. His wings fold into a battering ram. He can survive in space but cannot fly in the Ferutu universe. Clarence's internal power source could destroy an entire carrier if his outer shell were heavily breached.

Chris and Clarence: They're engineered to resist the gods' influence.

Tehke: Tehke was among the first Ferutu visitors to our Universe, taking his name from Tehke of Anapalas (a.k.a. the Burning One), the legendary outcast of the gods. He eventually returned home and fought a losing a civil war that led to his imprisonment on Dellah, but already had many human followers. Even before Tehke's release, St. Oscar's students protested in his name.

Sultan of the Tashwari: Tainted by the Dellan gods, the Sultan originally served Mor'yuchi (the so-called Tashwari god of abundance) but later claims allegiance to Tehke. The Sultan's become more delusional, talking to a golden bust (a golden head that is, not a golden...well, you know). He hears voices from a magic conch shell and keeps skins of infidels killed in his name.

Wolsey: He's due for his yearly check-up (circle your calendar, Benny—we're just trying to help).

ALIEN RACES

The Time Lords and the People: Agree that in a worst case scenario, the People's worldsphere will retreat into its dimensional pocket while the Time Lords stop up their Universe-in-a-Bottle (*Dead Romance*). Braxiatel makes vague threats to deploy the trans-dimensional bomb against the Time Lords and the People if they don't leave human space alone, but it's unlikely they had much interest anyway.

Ferutu: Are mostly bald, with near-transparent skin and Time Lord-ish tunics. They're forbidden from harming each other, but the Dellan gods break this rule. In their home universe, the Ferutu sport a number of magical abilities that include telepathy, memory retrieval, telekinesis, magical force bolts, time acceleration and reversal, super-speed and transporting energy spheres.

ALIEN PLANETS

Earth: Expansionist Earth doesn't have much interest in the Dellan sector, but Braxiatel convinced authorities to help against the gods.

Dellah: From space, Dellah looks like a sugar coated emerald. EGA 97 Proximity Detector satellites protected the planet from weapons smugglers and invasion fleets. The planet's icy region contains elephant-sized junlagi animals.

Vremnya: Planet built on gangsterism of the black market. That's changed with the war and subsequent peace treaty, but old tensions die hard.

STUFF YOU NEED

Doomsday Probe: Time Lord device equipped to release five seconds of accelerated entropy, ravaging time across an entire sector of space and killing every last cell.

Braxiatel's Alpha Wave Disrupters: Ear-fitted silver discs that protect Benny and Jason from the gods' influence by recalibrating their brains.

PLACES TO GO

Asteroid KS-159: Braxiatel's lacing the asteroid with monstrously expensive weather control systems to irrigate its desert areas. Among other things, he's planning to construct a lake and summerhouse named the Garden of Whispers. The asteroid's sky is light purple (*Theatre of War*).

Vremnya University: Situated in a string of aging redbrick houses, only a few minutes' walk from the sandstone Cathedral of Vremnya that tells the history of Vremnya's kings. The redbrick houses formerly belonged to bankrupt businesses. Braxiatel bought the entire street from the city council, providing funds that help rebuild the war-torn Vremnyan capital.

SHIPS The *Revelation*, a dimension-hopping ship created by Berkeley scientists, comes equipped with a scan-blocking shield and "vworp" engines (we can't fathom where that term came from).

ORGANIZATIONS *Berkeley researchers* are having some success with multiple dimension-transport techniques. Berkeley scientists helped Braxiatel locate the Ferutu's home dimension.

HISTORY Accomplished diplomat Terin Sevic helped negotiate an uneasy peace on the war-torn Vremnya, allowing a coalition of generous rich people — living Braxiatel among them — to create a university there.

AT THE END OF THE DAY Not the finale it should have been, likely cursed with being hastily written in the Virgin line's confusing last days. The book's overall plot isn't too bad, but the first half's saddled with a drawn-out expedition up a Dellan hill and Tehke's sadly put forth as a "hip" god who spouts some atrocious dialogue (after sculpting, Tehke concludes, "I just rock, don't I?"). For that matter, most of the characters have the same attitude (the Sultan sounds like he's about 15) and flat inflection (an archaeologist adds: "We're a strong bunch, us villagers."), leaving us with a book that's definitely competent in parts but lacks true fire in its belly.

THE DOOMSDAY MANUSCRIPT

By Justin Richards

Release Date: November 2000
Order: Big Finish Benny Adventure #1

MAIN CHARACTERS Bernice Summerfield, Irving Braxiatel, Joseph and Wolsey.

TRAVEL LOG Braxiatel Collection, plus planets Habadoss and Kasagrad, December 31, 2599 to January 6, 2600.

STORY SUMMARY A security system identifies one of the Braxiatel Collection's visitors as Kolonel Daglan Straklant of the Fifth Axis—a military organization dangerously expanding across the galaxy and subjugating multiple worlds. Already unhappy with Straklant's presence, Braxiatel and Benny investigate when Straklant happens upon research graduate Dale Pettit stealing an uncatalogued Collection holosphere and kills Pettit in self-defense.

In conference with Braxiatel and Benny, Straklant claims to lead an Axis relic restoration team, hoping to benignly catalog art treasures on Axis-dominated worlds and potentially return them to their true owners. Braxiatel, filled with contempt for the Axis' conquest-driven goals, identifies the holosphere Pettit strangely tried to steal as half of the Doomsday Manuscript—a chronicle by archaeologists Niall Goram and Matt Lacey of their expedition to the cursed tomb of Rablev, a royal engineer. Straklant offers to prove his goodwill by locating the Manuscript's other half. Benny, intrigued when a 400-year-old photograph shows the missing Jason Kane casually standing with Goram and Lacey, agrees to go with him.

Benny helps Straklant track the Manuscript's second half and recover it from the estate of aged film star Munroe Hennessy. But enroute to the tomb's homeworld of Kasagrad, a mysterious pursuit ship fires on them and apparently kills Straklant as Benny escapes to Kasagrad's surface. Benny finds Kasagrad, located in the heart of Axis territory, defiant to Axis rule and protected by a planetary defense barrier. Unfortunately, the Kasagrad government expects the intolerant Axis to shortly overrun the planet and becomes curious why the Axis would be looking for Rablev's tomb.

With help from a cybercracker named Georgia, Benny finds Braxiatel's half of the Doomsday Manuscript to be a somewhat-flawed copy, but compiles enough information to discover that the Tomb of Rablev lies directly under the Kasagrad citadel that controls the planetary defense grid. Benny concludes that Straklant, desperate for help in finding the Manuscript's second half, fooled Benny from the start by planting a copied Manuscript holosphere at the Braxiatel Collection, then killing Pettit when he blundered upon the crime. To further enflame Benny's curiosity, Straklant doctored Jason Kane into a photo of Goram and Lacey and included it with the holosphere.

Straklant, having faked his death, triangulates

the Tomb of Rablev's whereabouts from the Manuscript pieces. Intent on lowering the planetary defense screen—his mission from the beginning—Straklant sets out to use the tomb's ancient vents, drilled for the purpose of letting souls pass into the next world, to penetrate the Kasagrad citadel's security. Luckily, Braxiatel deduces Straklant's duplicity and tracks Benny to Kasagrad, then disguises himself as a Fifth Axis commander. Together, Benny and Braxiatel trick Straklant into revealing the Fifth Axis' command frequency, allowing Kasagrad authorities to decipher the Fifth Axis' battle strategy and rally their defense. As the Kasagrad government obliterates the approaching Axis warfleet, Benny and Braxiatel return to the Braxiatel Collection while Fifth Axis officials capture a fleeing Straklant and punish his failure.

MEMORABLE MOMENTS Benny implores cybercracker Georgia for aid in stopping Straklant, but Georgia, recognizing what's a long shot at best, says she must stay by her children during the Axis invasion. In a poignant, rip-out-your-gut moment, Georgia adds that the situation's easier for Benny because she's got nobody to care for. Benny, more than a little distraught for precisely that reason, adds: "Yeah, it's all right for me."

Benny and colleague Luci turn a corner, see a skeleton and practically shatter glass screaming. (Benny: "The old dust-to-dust skeleton routine gets me every time.")

Braxiatel and Benny masterfully deceive Straklant into revealing the Axis' command codes, a scene that concludes with Braxiatel feeling a mixture of sadness and anger toward his discompassionate foe. Benny and Braxiatel toast champagne and revel in the fun of being back (a touch of symbolism toward Big Finish picking up the Benny books' torch from Virgin Publishing).

SEX AND SPIRITS Benny still longs and lusts for Jason, crying to sleep while thinking of him.

ASS-WHUPPINGS Straklant wins Benny's confidence by breaking Wolsey's paw, then pretending to help the "wounded" critter home (when Benny discovers the truth, she snaps and launches herself at Straklant). Ms. Jones, head of administration for the Braxiatel Collection, fixes Wolsey's wound with genetic binding ointment.

Straklant led an Axis incursion of Frastus Minima, decimating the indigenous population.

Benny makes the mistake of dining on Vendolusian plankton, a dish that's poisonous until partly digested by the Vendolusian pond squwelch. Local farmers force their fingers down the pond squwelch's throats to induce vomit, meaning—you

THE CRUCIAL BITS...

- **THE DEAD MEN DIARIES**—Big Finish takes up the Bernice Summerfield torch and begins producing original Benny audios and books. Benny's story opens four years after *Twilight of the Gods* as she relocates to the Braxiatel Collection. First appearance of Braxiatel Collection groundskeeper Mister Crofton.

THE CRUCIAL BITS...

- **THE DOOMSDAY MANUSCRIPT**—Braxiatel gives Benny a replacement Joseph drone. First appearance of Braxiatel Collection architect Adrian Wall and administrative assistant Ms. Jones. First mention of Broderick Naismith, the Collection's chief public relations officer.

guessed it—Benny eats pond puke (and quickly hurls herself).

NOVEL TIE-INS The Oracle of the Lost (*Tears of the Oracle*) now resides in the Braxiatel Collection's Small Trianon, out of bounds to visitors. Braxiatel here replaces the previous Joseph, actually a monitoring drone for the People's supercomputer God (also *Tears of the Oracle*).

Skutloid's Glitter Glory, undoubtedly named for the late, great Commander Skutloid (killed in *Tears of the Oracle*) rings in the new millennium.

Benny's amazed by the newly constructed Garden of Whispers, where she first met Braxiatel in *Theatre of War* (due to the miracle of time travel, the event hasn't happened for Braxiatel yet).

CHARACTER DEVELOPMENT

Bernice Summerfield: Benny's birthday is June 21. She's overawed by parts of the Braxiatel Collection, including the Archaeology Department. She gets along well with groundskeeper Mister Crofton, who insists on calling her "Professor." Braxiatel greatly helped her credit situation.

Irving Braxiatel: He owns champagne glasses that were modeled on Marie Antoinette's breasts—the standard wide-bodied glasses rather than the flute (we shudder to think). Braxiatel's pen light flashes to indicate an intruder on the Collection grounds, with a small screen relaying text information. Like most Time Lords, Braxiatel doesn't need much sleep. He decries the Axis' methods. Braxiatel can disguise his features by wearing a hat with a miniature holo-projector in the brim.

Kolonel Daglan Straklant: Fifth Axis Security Elite member and secondary to Marshal Raul Kendrick. Straklant lost a hand to enemy firepower on Celestos and keeps an artificial one containing a poison-coated needle.

Joseph: Benny's new Joseph unit can organize Benny's diary, link into Braxiatel Collection mainframes and schedule her appointments. Upon realizing this, Benny asks: "Can you do anything useful?" A bit more practically, Joseph contains limited scanning systems and can patch himself into weak security systems to download video surveillance footage (although this clogs his memory). He can calibrate chronometers by synching into temporal satellites on civilized worlds. Joseph's programmed to tidy Benny's personal space while she sleeps, but Benny prefers to stuff him in a box.

Adrian Wall: Head of construction at the Braxiatel Collection and member of the Killoran race. Like other Killorans, Wall's real name is unpronounceable. A misunderstanding made him believe "Adrian Wall" was a great ancient Roman emperor responsible for defending England against the Scots. At eight-feet tall, Wall's big even for a Killoran. He has a grating voice.

Ms. Jones: Formidable head of administration for the Braxiatel Collection, complete with horn-rimmed spectacles, a gray hair bun and a generous bosom. Her sterile office makes even broom closets seem exciting, lacking any decoration or chairs for visitors. Ms. Jones, knowing Benny's tendency to lose ID discs, keeps a spare supply for her. She gives everyone the shivers (even Braxiatel appears leery of her), and only displays fondness for Wolsey.

Mister Crofton and Ms. Jones: Mister Crofton, the Collection's groundskeeper, doesn't think much of Ms. Jones. The sentiment's mutual.

ALIEN PLANETS *Kasagrad:* Planet located deep in Fifth Axis territory, continually embarrassing the Axis by resisting their rule. The planet's defense grid coordinates Kasagrad's space-based minefields and smartbombs. Until now, the Axis opted to strangle Kasagrad with trade sanctions.

PLACES TO GO
Braxiatel Collection (general): Still in its early years, the Collection includes extremely rare artifacts, literature, play scripts, recordings, geological specimens, software and hardware. It's rumored to devote an entire gallery to Deauxob of Glanatanus, and possesses Howard Carter's original notebooks from the Tutankhamen expedition.

The Collection's asteroid is only 10 miles in circumference. Braxiatel's devices regulate the as-

MISCELLANEOUS STUFF!

THE DEAD MEN DIARIES

Release Date: August 2000
Order: Big Finish Benny Anthology
Editor: Paul Cornell

After Virgin Publishing canceled the Benny New Adventures, Benny creator Paul Cornell authorized Big Finish to launch a new series of Benny audios and novels. Accordingly, the line debuted with *The Dead Men Diaries* anthology, featuring 10 short stories from professional writers and newcomers.

The Dead Men Diaries opens about three-and-a-half years after *Twilight of the Gods*, with Benny moving to the Braxiatel Collection to serve as one Braxiatel's teachers and researchers. When Benny's publisher sends bounty hunters to collect her autobiography on pain of assassination, Benny scours the Galaxy Wide Web and collects stories of herself written by others. Those tales compose *The Dead Men Diaries*, a couple of which, described below, have some bearing on continuity:

• **"Steal From the World" (by Kate Orman)**—Benny travels to Capella Four, a world she visited 20 years ago to find rock paintings left by the extinct Aurigan race. On that occasion, Benny fell off a cliff and broke her legs, spending days climbing back to her shuttle and eating nightcrawlers for to survive (first mentioned in *Parasite*). But now, Benny finds the Aurigan paintings and stones form an AI computer system—one that aided Benny by secretly resetting her legs and sending out a distress signal during her first visit. Having found another piece of history, Benny takes the Aurigan relics back to the Braxiatel Collection.

• **"The Door Into Bedlam" (by Dave Stone)**—Having escaped from the Ferutu (*Twilight of the Gods*), a wandering Jason Kane winds up in an infernal dimension where Agraxar Flatchlock, a demonic-looking travel agent, hires Jason to help calibrate a dimensional portal back to Jason's home universe, allowing Flatchlock's company to offer holidays there. Meanwhile, Benny researches a Goron IV "joining stone," capable of opening dimensional portals. Unfortunately, the Goron IV natives capture Benny and open a wormhole, offering her up as a sacrifice. Benny slides down the dimensional gateway just as Flatchlock's ship enters from the opposite direction. The two efforts cancel each other out, forever destroying the gateway but renewing Benny and Jason's quest to be together.

teroid's gravity to Earth normal. The Collection isn't open to the general public and issues privileged invites only (Straklant killed Dr Josiah Vanderbilt for his invitation). Plasti-discs, keyed to personal bio-emissions, serve as security passes.

A famous architect named Dupok designed the Collection's buildings. The Great and Small Stables are under construction.

Braxiatel Collection (Mansionhouse): The Mansionhouse serves as the Collection's central structure and Braxiatel's private dwelling, off-limits to all but Braxiatel, Benny and Braxiatel's staff. It's based on the Palace of Versailles and equidistant, north to south, from the Grand Trianon.

Braxiatel Collection (Hamlet): A small village, presumably to house Collection visitors, located on the banks of Great Trianon Lake, three miles north and seven miles southeast of the Mansionhouse.

Braxiatel Collection (Grounds and Gardens): Includes the Avenue of Fountains, with works labeled "Cherubs," "Angels" and "Future," plus a summerhouse in the Garden of Whispers.

ORGANIZATIONS

The Braxiatel Collection: The elusive Broderick Naismith serves as Chief Publicity Relations Officer. Benny has yet to meet him.

The Fifth Axis: A typical Nazi-like regime, expanding its territory without permission and looting assimilated territories with little regard for privacy or property (how rude). Rumors suggest the Axis indulges in racial atrocities, concentration camps and species cleansing. The Axis' Security Elite takes extremist views toward Axis policy.

Leery of enemies cracking their communications array, the Axis warfleets broadcast hundreds of false signals, with the true command code known only to the head of military operations and his second. The Kasagrad operation had a command frequency of 53 centibels.

Volf Gator serves as the Fifth Axis' ruling imperator. Marshal Raul Kendrick commands military operations, with Straklant as his second.

HISTORY Circa 400 B.C., a spaceship crashed in the Kasagrad region and Rablev, chief engineer of King-Emperor Hieronimes, attempted to harness its power. In all likelihood, Rablev hoped to seize Hieronimes' throne for himself, but the ship's atomic stacks overloaded and flooded the planet with radiation, killing thousands if not millions. The people, decreeing that Rablev's arrogance had

brought the gods' wrath upon them, sealed Rablev within the ship for eternity. A story persisted that to re-open the tomb would doom the world.

• Circa 2200 A.D., archaeologists Niall Goram and Matt Lacey opened the radioactive tomb and contracted a wasting disease they blamed on the curse. They re-sealed the tomb, but found themselves reluctant to fully destroy their work. Instead, they split their journal, later called "The Doomsday Manuscript," into halves for safekeeping (their estates variously sold off the documents for cash). Circa 2400, the Kasagrad spaceship's radiation dipped to non-lethal levels.

AT THE END OF THE DAY An entertaining yarn, tempered enough to keep its beginning and ending pumping. Unfortunately, the filler-loaded middle, including an irrelevant side plot involving an aged actor (trust us, you don't need to know) diminishes a sound Fifth Axis thread. Benny and Braxiatel seem a bit naïve to trust a Fifth Axis officer, however honorable, but Richards otherwise nails Benny's character (Georgia on the doctored Jason photo: "Anyone can spot is as a fake a mile off." Benny: "Absolutely. Anyone. I wasn't fooled. Not for a moment, not me. Hah!"). The final product succeeds at making Benny's adventures "fun" but at the cost of cut-throat drama.

THE SECRET OF CASSANDRA

By David Bailey

Release Date: December 2000
Order: Big Finish Benny Audio #1

MAIN CHARACTERS Bernice Summerfield.

TRAVEL LOG Sailing waters near nation of Calabraxia, unspecified Earth colony, likely 2600.

STORY SUMMARY On an unspecified Earth colony, warfare between the rival nations of Calabraxia and Pevena intensifies when a Calabraxian attack levels a Pevenan weapons research facility named Glory Hill. A Pevenan scientist named Cassandra Colley dies in the crossfire, but her father, Captain Damien Colley of the freelance sailing ship *Cassandra*, oddly continues working for both sides. Hired to shuttle Calabraxian General Hannah Brennan and her prisoner, a man named Sheen, back to Calabraxia, Colley sets out with his two passengers.

Meanwhile, Benny arrives on the colony world to vacation and goes sailing alone, unwisely falling asleep at the wheel and drifting into a Calabraxi-an/Pevenan warzone. Artillery fire sinks Benny's vessel, but Colley, sickened by the constant war-fare, spots Benny and brings her aboard despite General Brennan's orders to forge on.

Colley makes Benny feel welcome, explaining that his late daughter programmed the ship's com-puter with an AI personality, also named "Cas-sandra." However, the paranoid General Brennan, dubbing Benny a Pevenan spy, physically assaults her until a mysterious headache renders Brennan unconscious. Proclaiming Brennan overly tyran-nical, Benny frees the captive Sheen and radios a nearby Pevenan vessel to retrieve him.

Surprisingly, Sheen resists the idea of returning home, destroying the Pevenan ship with *Cassan-dra*'s deck cannons and killing hundreds of his countrymen. Appalled, Benny realizes that Colley and Sheen collaborated from the start to manipu-late Brennan and use her security clearance to reach Calabraxia. Brennan believes Sheen pos-sesses vital information on Glory Hill's weapons research, but Colley explains that Sheen is actu-ally a synthetic being, created for the sole purpose of housing a Glory Hill-made doomsday bomb. When Sheen reaches Calabraxia, he'll self-deto-nate, ending the war and revenging Colley for his daughter's death.

By scanning Brennan, the AI Cassandra real-izes Sheen placed chemical blocks on Brennan's memories to prevent her from remembering Sheen's true identity. AI Cassandra neutralizes the mental barrier, allowing Brennan to reveal, from her period as a Calabraxian spy, that the "late" Cassandra Colley downloaded her con-sciousness into Sheen's artificial frame before Glory Hill's destruction. In short, Sheen is the original Cassandra—hell-bent on destroying the nation that "killed" her.

Appalled at his daughter's hatred, Colley re-cants his plan to level Calabraxia. However, Cas-sandra/Sheen rebukes her father's pacifism, vowing to destroy every Calabraxian. Aghast, Col-ley shoots Cassandra/Sheen—inadvertently arm-ing the doomsday device, which is rigged to detonate upon termination of Cassandra/Sheen's vital signs. Realizing that the artificial Sheen and the AI Cassandra, both programmed by Cassan-dra Colley, likely have the same neural template, Benny urges the AI Cassandra to upload her con-sciousness into Sheen's body. The AI Cassandra complies, erasing Cassandra/Sheen's mental en-grams, stabilizing Sheen's synthoid body and dis-arming the doomsday weapon.

Brennan returns to Calabraxia, thanking Benny for saving her nation. Benny departs while a reformed Colley vows to keep the AI Cassan-dra—and the atomic device inside her—out of mil-itary hands, peacefully sailing southward.

MEMORABLE MOMENTS Stranded on a desert island with Tom Hanks (sorry…wrong story), Benny records in her journal that she's likely to die, "alone, unloved … and thoroughly annoyed." At dinner, purely to break the ice, Benny jokes that she's poisoned General Brennan's wine (the General's less than amused at the prank). In a moment sure to make gender-bender lovers shiv-er with delight, Sheen steps forward and confirms that he's really Cassandra Colley.

ASS-WHUPPINGS Benny's negligence while sail-ing (no, she wasn't drinking—perish the thought) gets her blown out of the water and trapped on a desert island for a few days. After Cassandra Colley's "death," her mother failed to recover from the loss and died soon after, fueling Cassandra/Sheen's hated for Calabraxia.

CHARACTER DEVELOPMENT

Cassandra/Sheen's super-strong artificial body is shielded from electronic detection. Chemicals that maintain the doomsday mechanism inside Sheen have clouded his vision with cataracts.

PLACES TO GO In addition to weapons develop-ment, *Glory Hill* specialized in neuro-technology that alters or enhances brain states.

SHIPS *Cassandra,* Captain Colley's vessel, looks like a 17th century Earth sailing ship with white sails. However, the period design masks a modern-day engine and automated computer system.

AT THE END OF THE DAY In the words of the sage Austin Powers: *"She's a man, baby!"* The entertaining "Secret of Cassandra" forges through the waters and fleshes out its characters—a com-mendable feat considering that the limitations of a single CD format constrict "Cassandra" to a pal-try 70 minutes and deny the work the complexity of a full-blown Big Finish audio. As a result, this audio's definitely worth listening to once—but sorely lacks the timber to hit A-level.

THE GODS OF THE UNDERWORLD

By Stephen Cole

Release Date: January 2001
Order: Big Finish Benny Adventure #2

MAIN CHARACTERS Bernice Summerfield.

TRAVEL LOG The Braxiatel Collection, Pan Leica spaceport and Venedel, March 12, 2600.

STORY SUMMARY Braxiatel finds evidence that the Argians, a long-extinct race of conquerors, hoarded their riches into a War Temple on the planet Venedel. Unfortunately, the Earthlink Federation, an allied group of worlds with Earth ties, has accused Venedel's ruling Thane of Mahel of human rights violations and blockaded the planet. Denied a request for an official expedition, Braxiatel proposes Benny covertly examine the War Temple because it supposedly contains a device known as the Argian Oracle, capable of locating anyone in the Universe. With the device, Benny hopes to find the still-missing Jason Kane.

At Pan Leica spaceport, Benny assembles a small archaeology team and hires the services of pilot Starl Stanmore. Benny's crew departs for Venedel, but Starl's space vessel, the *New Dawn*, takes heavy fire from Federation gunships and crashes into a Venedel swamp. Benny quickly discovers Venedel's primitive people are suffering from an infection of Ilijah lizards—hostile reptiles that use other species as hosts for their eggs. As Benny's group watches, multiple Ilijah burst newborn out of their hosts, ravenously tearing into the surviving primitives.

Benny learns that extortionists named the Boor once used the reptilian Ilijah to further a protection racket, seeding the monsters onto various worlds and charging exorbitant rates for an antidote. Although the Boor lost power 500 years ago, the mercenary Nishtubi, hoping to reclaim the Boor's glory days, have re-engineered an even deadlier Ilijah variant and used the isolated Venedel as a testing ground.

Furthermore, Benny discovers that when the Boor fell from favor, a deal was struck with the Federation to adapt the Venedel War Temple as a cryogenics chamber. The Federation put the Boor and the galaxy's greatest criminals into suspended animation, allowing them to dodge prosecution with the intent of awakening one day to start an unprecedented criminal empire—with Federation officials as silent partners. Unfortunately, the *New Dawn* holed the Federation's cryosleep facility when it crashed, leaving the sleepers vulnerable as potential Ilijah food.

Fleeing from the Ilijah, Benny locates the Argian Oracle's chamber and asks it to locate Jason Kane. Unfortunately, some of the cyrocenter's systems, heavily damaged by the *New Dawn*, detonate and destroy the Oracle. As the Ilijah pour through into the damaged Federation facility and feast upon the sleeping crimelords, High Boor Bantagel, awakened by the Nishtubi to aid with their extortion schemes, recognizes the Ilijah's threat and intensifies the cryosleep field with the help of Benny's team, freezing the Ilijah into immobility. In the process, Benny re-freezes Bantagel, blocking his plans for a criminal empire.

Actually a covert agent working for benevolent Federation officials, Starl pledges to use evidence from Venedel to purge the Federation's corrupt elements. As Starl helps the Federation cleanse Venedel of the Ilijah infection and the Braxiatel Collection gains formal permission for an expedition, Benny returns home broken-hearted for the Argian Oracle's destruction.

MEMORABLE MOMENTS Benny looks up at *The Supremacy of Venus* replica on the ceiling of Braxiatel's study and hurls "Bitch!" at Venus' apparent optimism.

SEX AND SPIRITS Benny and Federation agent Starl Stanmore share some flirtation. There's a suggestion that Benny, having three hours until her shuttle to the Braxiatel Collection arrives, boffs Starl. Ilijah sex woefully amounts to nothing but self-fertilization and a bunch of egg spitting.

ASS-WHUPPINGS The Thane of Mahel rounds up hundreds of his Ilijah-tainted people and orders them burnt with flame-throwers. The Ilijah kill the Thane and another good chunk of his people, clawing up their hosts' throats and bursting from their mouths.

NOVEL TIE-INS Jason Kane went missing in *Twilight of the Gods*. Braxiatel wanted the Argian Oracle partly to help Benny, but also to compliment his Oracle of the Lost (*Tears of the Oracle*).

The Earthlink Federation tolerates the Fifth Axis (*The Doomsday Manuscript*) so long as they restrict their overt activities to frontier worlds.

CHARACTER DEVELOPMENT

Bernice Summerfield: Her expedition members include Arko and Forno (two bear-like Waskas) and a human archaeologist named Shell.

Irving Braxiatel: Sponsored an excavation of the Argian Temple of Blood Messengers on Betheral.

Joseph: Benny's computerized assistant can see in the dark, but it drains his energy reserves. Because he's a computer, Joseph cannot see holograms. His levitation engines, designed to handle high-gravity worlds, can't support Benny's weight.

ALIEN RACES

Ilijah: Reptilian creatures that originated on an unspecified world inhabited only by animals. Ilijah sport cobra-like heads with thick, scaly bodies (somewhat akin to a rosebush branch covered in thorns). Ilijah self-fertilize their eggs, then spit them out via a watery jet onto potential hosts. The incubating Ilijah then mature and slip/tear themselves out of their host's mouth.

The Boor re-engineered the Ilijah for increased aggression and fertility at the cost of shorter lifespans. The Boor wisely added a degenerate gene into the Ilijah's make-up that immunized the Boor and Nishtubi from Ilijah eggs, also allowing for an antidote that ended their protection schemes when necessary. In the Boor's absence, the Nishtubi stupidly re-engineered an Ilijah variant that can use any species as a host. Ilijah are hardly invulnerable—a good shovel does them in.

Boor: Rather hideous creatures, with misshapen heads, scarred faces and squat, blubbery bodies. Not surprisingly, they're intimidating (a useful talent, given the Boor's penchant for racketeering.)

ALIEN PLANETS

Venedel: Earthlink Federation world, also among the poorest planets in the sector. The Thane of Mahel, ruling from his Throne of Solitude, oversees land from Venedel's Shadow Coast to the Fungus Mountains.

STUFF YOU NEED

Argian Oracle: Useful device capable of locating anyone in the Universe—it aided the war-like Argians in pinpointing the whereabouts of enemy leaders. The Argian Oracle looks like a huge bronze sphere nestling in a cobwebbed cauldron, with a myriad of whirling dots and lines showing the Universe's geometry.

PLACES TO GO

Argian War Temples: Off-world safehouses for Argian riches, which also serve to indoctrinate slaved peoples to the Argian war gods. After the Argians went extinct, most of the War Temples were plundered. Dozens exist in this sector of space. Argian war religion doesn't allow synthetic materials to be used in temple construction.

Temple of the Gods of the Underworld: Alternate name for the Venedel War Temple, symbolically denoting the "gods of the criminal underworld" sleeping within.

ORGANIZATIONS *Shadow Federation:* Overly fanciful nickname for corrupt elements within the Earthlink Federation. The Federation's Special Internal Investigations Unit (Starl Stanmore's a member), directly clashes with this group.

HISTORY The military minded Argians were damnably unstoppable during their heyday, fixated on their war gods and combining the mystical with the scientific. On Venedel, they burnt all knowledge. Eventually, arrogance led to the Argian empire waning over a millennium and falling apart.

• Circa 2100, Venedel raised itself back to the level of a primitive, feudal rut.

• About the same time, the alien Boor became masters at blackmail and extortion and furthered the Ilijah protection scheme on worlds such as Venedel. On Obvion, the Boor let the Ilijah consume the populace—while presumably focusing on other endeavors—but saved Obvion's criminal elements. Eventually, they helped fund (in order to heavily influence) the Earthlink Federation, an alliance designed to cement Earth's relations with other planets.

• In time, the stellar police fractured the Boor's power. The Boor then blackmailed corrupt Federation elements into participating with the Venedel cryosleep operation. Leaders of other criminal syndicates would join the Boor in cryosleep so that upon revival by the mercenary Nishtubi, the Boor could operate under Federation protection as heads of an unprecedented criminal empire. However, upstarts within the Federation eliminated members with ties to the Boor. The newly empowered Federation members, wanting power for themselves, paid off the Nishtubi to leave the Boor and crimelords in stasis.

• Venedel joined the Federation 30 years ago, but recently withdrew due to political squabbles.

AT THE END OF THE DAY A work that fails to tunnel to freedom, *The Gods of the Underworld* sacrifices character concerns to plot demands (Benny's archaeology teammates all blend together). It also manages to feel like two stories, not one (as if the chest-popping Ilijah reptiles weren't enough, unseen Federation forces irrelevantly try to nuke everyone's ass). Cole ("The Land of the Dead") is a much better writer than this, leading one to suspect *The Gods of the Underworld* was scripted in about five minutes.

THE BENNY AUDIO ADAPTATIONS

It's easy to forget, amid a mass of "Doctor Who" audios that's approaching two dozen strong, that Big Finish first produced official audio adaptations of the Bernice Summerfield New Adventures. Starring Lisa Bowerman ("Survival") as Benny and Stephen Fewell as her roguish ex-husband Jason Kane, these audios didn't impact the fan consciousness much, but they proved Big Finish's professionalism and convinced the BBC to fork over the "Doctor Who" audio license.

Assorted Notes:

• Big Finish's license with Virgin Publishing didn't allow use of "Doctor Who" related characters, meaning Jason Kane swaps for Ace in the audio "Birthright" and the Doctor in "Just War."

• "Walking to Babylon," "Birthright" and "Just War" compose what's called "The Time Ring Trilogy," a trio of stories where Benny and Jason are flung through time by use of their time rings (a wedding gift from the Doctor in *Happy Endings*).

• Aside from "Beyond the Sun" (written in all formats by Matt Jones), Jacqueline ("Jac") Rayner ("The Marian Conspiracy") adapted all of the following stories for audio.

• The "Novel/Audio Differences" sub-sections details major differences between the audio/novel formats.

At the End of the Day: Looking at the Benny adaptations collectively, they're remarkably consistent for quality, graced with a full cast, Big Finish's high standards and exceptional sound effects. Conversely, the audios don't present a wealth of information that the respective novels lack, meaning you're won't have a major epiphany, for example, from the "Walking to Babylon" audio if you've already ingested the book. The inspired, farcical "Oh No It Isn't" and the gritty "Just War" carry our highest recommendations, respectively serving as a frolicking comedy and a gripping Nazi story. Although slightly less outstanding, the remaining audios are worth your time, save for "Dragons' Wrath"—a story hamstrung by production difficulties and unable story-wise to endure shrinkage down to a single CD format.

1) "Oh No It Isn't!" (by Paul Cornell)

Novel/Audio Differences: None worth mentioning. Guest-star: Nicholas Courtney ("the Brigadier") as the humanoid Wolsey the cat.

2) "Beyond the Sun" (by Matt Jones)

Novel/Audio Differences: Ditto. Guest-stars: Anneke Wills ("Polly") as biologist Kitzinger, Sophie Aldred ("Ace") as villainess Miranda.

3) "Walking to Babylon" (by Kate Orman)

Novel/Audio Differences: Two members of the People, !Ci!ci-tel and WiRgo!xu, hire Jason Kane to steal Benny's time ring and forge an illicit time link (called "The Path") to ancient Babylon. !Ci!ci-tel and WiRgo!xu hope to spur warfare between the Time Lords and the People (*See Walking to Babylon*), but Benny tracks them with her time sensitive "Chrono-connetiscope" device and foils their scheme. In the process, time-lost archaeologist John Lafayette inadvertently acquires Benny's Chrono-Connetiscope and takes it back to his native 1901. Benny and Jason use their time rings to close down The Path, but get flung through history in the process.

Guest-star: Elizabeth Sladen ("Sarah Jane Smith") as Babylonian priestess Ninan.

4) "Birthright" (by Nigel Robinson)

Novel/Audio Differences: Benny and Jason's time rings lock onto "The Great Divide," an unstable wormhole through which the insectoid Charrl hope to abandon their dying homeworld and invade Earth. Landing on Earth in 1909, Benny finds a note from Lafayette, now married and on his honeymoon, saying he placed her Chrono-Connetiscope in a safety deposit box on his native isle of Guernsey. Benny convinces the Charrl Queen to avoid a destructive human-Charrl war. Together, Benny and Jason combine their time rings to re-route the Great Divide to the planet Anonyus Six, gaining the Charrl a home but again getting thrown through time.

Guest-star: Colin Baker ("the sixth Doctor") as Russian detective Popov.

5) "Just War" (by Lance Parkin)

Novel/Audio Differences: Jason materializes on Earth, 1936 and makes his way to Guernsey. Unable to find Benny, he forges a friendship with German engineer Emil Hartung and vaguely talks about the concept of radar. By the time Benny arrives in 1941, Hartung has found her Chrono-Connetiscope and used its material, along with his foreknowledge of radar, to create Hugin and Munin, radar resistance planes that could win the war. Having spent five years in the British military, Captain Jason Kane reunites with Benny on Guernsey. Hartung dies when a design flaw explodes Hugin (Benny retrieves her Chrono-Connetiscope from his charred body), and Jason and Benny blow up Munin before returning to the 26th century with their time rings.

6) "Dragons' Wrath" (by Justin Richards)

Novel/Audio Differences: None worth reporting. Guest-star: Richard Franklin ("Captain Yates") as warlord Romolo Nusek.

Apocrypha
Alterniverse Travels
in Time and Space

APOCRYPHA: THE SANDS OF TIME MISSING CHAPTER

Addendum

The Chronicler peered into the glowing embers of reality. Deep within the holosphere, a single quantum choice played itself out for him. He was at one with the world he watched, oblivious to the great hallway in which he worked, not seeing the shadows and patterns cast by the sunlight shining through the stained glass.

The holosphere cast its own lights for him to follow, tiny bit patterns blitted into a replay of reality. He stared into the depths of time, aware of nothing in his world apart from the scraping of his quill across the parchment as he noted the salient points and drew deductions.

As events reached their closure, he leaned back. The Doctor's solution was elegant. He had learned from his previous encounter with an Osiran. But while there was a certain symmetry and poetic justice in the events, there was also a niggling feeling that the Doctor had somehow cheated.

The Chronicler dipped his quill in the dark ink, and scratched a note in his book. Then he adjusted a pattern within the sphere and replayed the sequence.

Somewhere within the universal scheme, a tiny quantum choice was played out. A slight variation introduced into the mathematical and physical structure of Time, and another universe split from the first. Or rather the last. Or rather the latest. The patterns spun and resolved themselves into a new mosaic.

'I think we're a little late,' the Doctor said. His voice was quiet, but everyone turned to him. Even Vanessa swung her head slightly. 'I'm afraid your calculations were slightly off. As you can see, Nyssa has actually been awake for quite some time. Or at least, in a sort of waking sleep. Just enough to continue the ageing process while she dozed.'

'No,' breathed Vanessa, her voice an exhalation of disbelief.

'You know it's true,' the Doctor told her. 'You just scanned her mind, looking for the reasoning, calculating, intelligent part of your own self.'

'It is not there.' Vanessa's voice was low, despondent.

'So, even at the instinctive level on which you're operating you can tell that the rest of the mind of Nephthys no longer exists. It was freed when Nyssa awoke, and you weren't here. Now it's lost forever.'

'How long ago did she wake?' Atkins asked.

'She woke up in 1926.'

'Seventy years,' Atkins murmured.

The Doctor nodded. 'I like good round numbers,' he said.

'Doctor.' Tegan's voice was accusing, shaking with emotion. Her face was set and she was glaring at him.

'I'm sorry, Tegan. If there had been any other way.'

'How could you?' She was in tears now. 'How could you do this to Nyssa, after - after everything?'

The Doctor smiled sadly. 'Rassul knows. He asked if I could sacrifice a friend to save the universe, if I could make that choice.'

Tegan turned away. 'He didn't believe you could,' she said through her sobs. 'But I should have known better.'

Rassul too was shaking with anger. 'Doctor, I shall kill you for this.'

The Doctor returned his stare. 'I don't care,' he said levelly. 'The universe is safe now. All you have is a woman who hardly knows who she is and can't make a decision beyond the next instinctive moment. She can respond to circumstances, make impassioned speeches from the heart of the evil goddess she once was, but longer term than that she can never make up her mind.' He grinned suddenly. 'I hope you'll excuse the choice of phrase.'

'She will be whole,' Rassul insisted. 'We shall find a way.'

Vanessa stood watching them, listening to the exchange but taking no part. Her face was impassive.

The Doctor shook his head. 'Nephthys' reasoning intelligence is gone forever, evaporated into the ether when Nyssa woke up and you weren't there. There is no way you can recapture it.' He smiled thinly. 'None.'

Rassul's lip twitched, his face contorted in rage. 'There is,' he hissed. 'There has to be.' Behind him, Vanessa stood silent and still. A motionless mummy stood massively by her side. The other two mummies held the bandaged form of Nyssa, her ancient wizened face turned slightly so she could see the Doctor. He looked across at her for a moment, then returned his attention to Rassul.

'Well, apart from the odd conjuring trick,' the Doctor said quietly, 'like bringing the near-dead back to life, I don't see there's much mileage left in the power of Nephthys.'

Rassul frowned. He looked as if he might be about to say something in return, but then he turned away, stared at Vanessa.

'Doctor,' Tegan said again, 'what about Nyssa.' Her eyes were dark.

The Doctor's brow creased slightly. 'Not now, Tegan. Not now.'

'Not now?'

But before her anger could increase further, or the Doctor could reply, Atkins cleared his throat. 'Er, what will they do now, Doctor?'

'I'm not sure. There are a couple of possibilities.'

Rassul turned back to face them, and his voice rang across the tomb. 'Indeed there are, Doctor.'

'Ah. I take it from your tone of voice that you are not tending towards the let-us-all-go option.'

Rassul laughed. 'When you yourself suggested we could raise the dead?' He snorted his derision. 'Come now Doctor.'

The Doctor's eyes opened wide. 'Oh no. Not that. Even you can't be that desperate, Rassul.'

Rassul nodded to the mummies holding Nyssa. As one, they let go of her and lurched towards the door leading to the inner chamber.

'I suggest you join us, Doctor. You and your friends may witness one final miracle before your lives are snuffed out forever.' He gestured for them to follow the mummies.

Atkins went to Nyssa's aid, lifting her out of the sarcophagus. Tegan glared at the Doctor, then went to help Atkins as he pulled the bandages from her friend. Underneath, Nyssa was wearing a simple linen gown, crumpled and creased but surprisingly clean and well-preserved. Nyssa said nothing, but her eyes held the Doctor's.

Rassul shuffled impatiently as the Doctor led Atkins, Tegan and Nyssa after the mummies. Then Rassul, Vanessa and the third service robot followed.

'What does he intend, Doctor?' Atkins asked quietly. He had helped Tegan to support Nyssa, but she seemed well able now to manage on her own.

'There is a ceremony,' the Doctor replied, 'an ancient Osiran rite for raising the dead. I'm rather afraid he's going to try to awaken the pile of bones that was his daughter.'

Atkins stopped dead for a split second. Tegan and Nyssa both paused at the Doctor's words.

'Of course,' the Doctor continued, 'the mummified remains could never live again, could never walk or breath. The ceremony is for the recently deceased, not the long-departed.'

'You are quite right, Doctor,' Rassul said as they reached the doorway. 'But we do not need to reanimate the bones of Nephthys.' He reached out and placed his hand on the Doctor's shoulder, gripping it tightly. 'Her mind will be quite sufficient.'

'Why didn't you do that before, if it's so simple?' Tegan demanded.

MISCELLANEOUS STUFF!

'SANDS' ORIGINS

The Sands of Time author Justin Richards notes about the "lost" chapter that you hold in your hands: "All authors have times when they decide that everything they've written is absolute rubbish. I try to keep my own moments of self-doubt to a few minutes rather than hours or days. There was only one occasion really when I decided I'd got it all completely wrong and remained of that opinion for long enough to do it all again.

"One of the things I set out to do with *The Sands of Time* was to build on "Pyramids of Mars," but not to debase it. The worst form of debasement is inventing a convenient weakness in the enemy for the Doctor to exploit—so I was dead against that. Having him discover (or worse, simply remember) that the Osirans are allergic to gold, for example, would have rather punctured the whole thing.

"But this did give me a problem when devising an ending for the story. My decision was to use a variation on the ending of "Pyramids of Mars"—the Doctor uses the same inherent weakness but in a different and hopefully surprisingly imaginative way.

"Having sent my draft manuscript to Rebecca Levene, the editor at Virgin, I began to have my doubts. What if the readers weren't that impressed—if what I had written really was just a re-run of the end of "Pyramids"? So thought about whether I could change the ending while remaining true to my original intention and without having to rewrite the whole book.

"And I wrote a different ending.

"When Rebecca sent back her comments, she didn't seem to have any problem with the ending of the story as originally written. But I'd already got an alternative. Not wanting to waste it, I decided perhaps we could have both endings, leaving readers to decide which they preferred. So I added the chapter reproduced here to the end of the book. Then I sat back and waited to see if Rebecca would notice.

"She did notice. And—quite rightly—she suggested that having both endings was probably a tad self-indulgent and quite redundant. Which would I prefer to keep? I decided to keep the original, which I think is cleaner and more focused. But somewhere, in another quantum universe, people have read (and I hope enjoyed) the alternative instead. So here it is.

"One final comment—I'm glad Lars has decided to print the chapter and that you can (if you wish) finally read it. But read it as a curiosity. Because Rebecca was absolutely right—*The Sands of Time* is better focused and less fragmented without it."

'He's bluffing,' Atkins suggested. 'Isn't he, Doctor?'

'They didn't try it before, as there's no guarantee it will work,' the Doctor said. 'He's gambling that some vestige of the conscious side of Nephthys' mind is still buried in there somewhere - that Horus suppressed it totally rather than split it away entirely. Because of that, and for another very good reason, it was better to be patient and work through the foolproof plan that has just failed.' The Doctor stopped on the threshold of the inner chamber. He turned to face Rassul. 'It may just work. There may be just enough of the reasoning side of Nephthys character buried deep within the memories of the girl, even after the mind was ripped apart, to harness the forces held in the relics and release some semblance of her. But the real reason you never considered this before, is your own fear.'

Rassul stared at the Doctor for a second. Then he looked away. 'But now, Doctor, you leave us no choice.'

'What's he afraid of?'

'The same thing I am, Tegan. It's just so obvious a course of action that Horus would have thought of it.'

Atkins frowned. 'You think he wouldn't play fair?'

'He was an Osiran. They never play fair.' The Doctor broke into a smile. 'Like me, they play to win.' Then he stepped forward, over the threshold and into the inner chamber.

The mummies had positioned themselves either side of the coffin. The Doctor, Tegan, Nyssa and Atkins stopped just inside the door. The third mummy blocked the doorway behind them, and they waited quietly beside the twin Shabti figures who continued their endless vigil either side of the doorway.

Rassul and Vanessa approached the casket. The servicers beside it stepped back a pace as they approached and bowed their heads. Vanessa stood at the head of the coffin; Rassul stood at the foot. They looked down at the crumpled, decayed figure inside.

As Atkins watched, Rassul reached into his jacket pocket and took out an hourglass. He held it up, and Atkins could see the final few grains of sand in the upper bowl. Then Rassul placed the hourglass on the rim of the sarcophagus, and bowed to his goddess. The muffled sound of the organ filtered through the floor, swelling as if it were emanating from the stonework itself.

Rassul was chanting now, his voice adding to the discordant frenzy. As he spoke, he raised his arms

above his head, and the mummies beside the coffin mirrored his actions. Vanessa stood silent as the ceremony proceeded. But Atkins could see the edges of her mouth curling slightly upwards into the beginnings of a triumphant smile.

Atkins could sense the tension in the Doctor beside him. He was shaking his head slowly, clenching his fists by his sides. At last, as if unable to help himself any more, the Doctor shouted across the room: 'Stop this, Rassul. Stop it now before it's too late. Don't tempt Horus out of his lair or Osiris from the netherworld.'

'Be silent,' hissed Vanessa in reply. Her eyes were large and angry. As she raised her arm, and pointed accusingly at the Doctor, the two service robots also turned towards him. Atkins sensed the mummy behind them take a step forward. 'My time is now.' He could hear the power gathering behind Vanessa's words, could feel the tension in the stale air.

Then Rassul let out a piercing cry. His arms stretched up to their full extent, and his whole body went rigid for a second. Then he stepped back, arms open wide as if to welcome a friend. His voice was clear across the room as the chords of the organ died away. 'Nephthys, I conjure thee from the realm of the dead. Arise and do thy work.'

The reply was almost melodious. A female voice, musical and strong. It sounded to Atkins like a pair of supreme tenors chanting their twin response.

'Here am I. I answer. I awake.'

But what Atkins found most surprising was that the voices came from behind him.

And the two Shabti figures stepped forward from the back of the chamber, making their ponderous wooden way towards the sarcophagus.

Rassul shook his head in disbelief. 'This is not how it is written. What is your purpose here?'

'Doctor?' Tegan and Atkins both asked together.

The Doctor put his finger to his lips, then answered quietly. 'I think I told you, Shabti figures are provided to do the work of the deceased in the next life.'

'That's right,' Atkins said. 'Ushabti means answerer. They answer for the dead person.' He broke off. 'I see.'

'You mean all they've done is wake up the figures again? Terrific.'

'Oh no, Tegan,' the Doctor said. 'I'm afraid they may have done much more than that.'

The Shabti paused in front of the coffin. Twin statues, they stared across the casket at the woman they were carved to represent. She stared back in silence. When the figures spoke, it was in unison: 'We are the guardians. We protect the tomb of Nephthys from all who would enter. And we prevent the body of Nephthys from rising again. We answer for her.'

Rassul addressed them. 'You mean that the body cannot be restored?' There was a note of desperation, a dying cadence in his voice. 'But we were sent by Horus himself,' he was close to hysteria now. 'We will - we must - have Nephthys whole again, complete. It is the will of Horus.'

'We are her Shabti, as ordained and instructed by Horus. If you would wake Nephthys, then you must answer the question. If you truly act for Horus, you will know the answer.'

Rassul stepped up to the Shabti nearest him. 'Then ask your question,' he spat.

'If you act for Horus, you will know the secret of his power. Where is the focus for the eye of Horus?'

Rassul frowned for a moment. Then he threw his head back and let out a triumphant screech of laughter. 'The power of the Osirans devolves from the Great Sphinx in Egypt.' His face cracked into a smile.

'And the local focus point?'

The smile froze. Atkins could see the tracery of veins standing out on Rassul's bald scalp. 'Local?' He shook his head, and looked to Vanessa. 'Nephthys, where is the local focus?'

No reply.

'You draw energy from it, you must be able to tell where that energy comes from.'

Vanessa stared back. Her mouth was still curled into a half smile. But her face was empty.

It was the Doctor who answered. 'It's over, Rassul.'

'Never,' shouted Rassul. 'Nephthys can deduce the position of the local power source.'

'You're missing the point,' the Doctor all but shouted back. 'Nephthys is only half there - she can't deduce anything.'

Rassul flinched, as if he had been hit. Then he turned to Vanessa. The two Shabti figures followed his gaze. She stared blankly back at them.

'No,' Rassul said as the Shabti pushed past him. 'No!' he shouted as they approached Vanessa. 'She can answer. She knows the response. We are true servants of Horus.'

But the Shabti figures ignored him and continued their ponderous progress towards Vanessa. She stared into space, waiting for them.

She was still staring as Rassul screamed at the service robots to attack the Shabti figures. She was still staring as he tried to stand between the Shabti and his goddess, to halt their advance. She was still staring as they hurled him out of their way across the room. He collapsed senseless at the base of the wall.

Then, out of an instinctive recognition that something was wrong, Nephthys started to back away from them.

The mummies beside the casket lumbered after the Shabti. The mummy behind Atkins pushed past and made its massive way across the chamber to help its mistress. Rassul was picking himself up from the floor as the two closer mummies reached the Shabti. It seemed an extremely unequal match as the two massive bandaged robots reached out their huge hands for the delicate wooden carved women.

The Shabti continued their progress as if nothing was happening. They shrugged off the grip of the mummies without seeming to notice the hindrance. As the mummies tried again to grab them, the figures turned in unison. The movement was almost graceful, hand and arm describing a lazy curve through the air. The two mummies collapsed to their knees, one toppled backwards, its legs still working, as flames and smoke erupted from its chest. The other staggered back to its feet as the third mummy joined it.

Vanessa had reached the wall. There was nowhere else for her to go. Rassul was regaining his consciousness, shouting and screaming at her to run, but the Shabti were closing in too quickly. She faced them with fear but no understanding in her eyes.

The surviving mummies dragged at the Shabti, tried to hold them back. But the twin figures reached out, and took the arms of their flesh and blood sister. They drew the arms out, away from her body. The mummies continued to pull at the Shabti, and they in turn continued their grotesque tug of war with Vanessa. She screamed.

Rassul had staggered back to his feet, and had almost reached them when Vanessa's body gave way to the strain. The blood and tissue splashed across the room and caught him in the face. He coughed and fell. And cried.

Atkins felt sick and horrified, but he was unable to look away. Across the room, the mummies battered uselessly at the blood-red figures tearing at the remains of their image. Rassul skidded and slipped on the wet floor, his sobs adding to the unholy sounds.

Atkins felt the Doctor's hand on his shoulder, and allowed himself to be turned away. The door behind them was slowly swinging shut. They hurled themselves against it, pushing their way through. The Doctor pulled his fingers from the stonework just as the wall sealed itself into place with a grinding finality. Through the thickness of the stone they could hear Rassul's wails and cries.

'That's interesting,' the Doctor said.

Atkins frowned at the contrast between his light tone and what they had just witnessed. The Doc-

This book is not endorsed by the BBC. Doctor Who and TARDIS are trademarks of the BBC.

253

tor mistook his expression and pointed to the hieroglyphics carved into the hidden door. The Nephthys cartouche, the opening mechanism, was gone. In its place was a congealed volcanic mess, as if the stonework had been melted away.

'The sands of time wash us all clean,' the Doctor said quietly. 'No one will ever find their way through that. And if they do, I fancy they won't find much left the other side.' Then he brightened. 'Still, all's well that ends well, eh?' And with that he strode back across the room and slapped Tegan on the shoulder.

She pulled away. 'Is that it?' she asked. Her voice was vibrant with suppressed emotion.

The Doctor seemed not to notice. 'Yes, I think so. A pretty good result considering. All over -'

'Doctor!' Tegan screamed at him, her whole body tense with anger.

'- bar the shouting.' The Doctor frowned, his eyebrows knitting together as he leaned towards her. 'Yes?' he asked irritably.

Tegan turned away, arms folded.

'What is it?' The Doctor asked the group collectively. 'What's wrong with her now?'

'I think she might be worried about Nyssa,' Atkins suggested quietly.

'Nyssa? Oh yes, I nearly forgot.' The Doctor fumbled in his pocket and drew out the TARDIS key. 'Well, let's go and wake her up then.' The cries from behind the stone door had subsided into faint sobs now. The noise of the fight between Shabti and mummies had completely subsided.

The old woman who had woken in the sarcophagus followed the Doctor to the TARDIS. It was only after he had unlocked the door and ushered her in ahead of him that he seemed to realize that nobody else was following. They were standing open-mouthed, watching him from the other side of the dais.

'Well, are you coming or not?' he demanded.

From behind the sealed doorway came the faint sound of scratching. Fingernails scrabbling desperately on stone. Tegan and Atkins looked at each other in silence.

The Chronicler nodded slowly. So, when circumstances were varied, even by the tiniest of changes, the Doctor was still able to adapt and react. A point was made, and the Chronicler returned the holosphere's environment to its original settings.

Then he smiled, laid down his pen, and closed the book.

APOCRYPHA: THE MASTERS OF LUXOR

By Anthony Coburn

Release Date: October 1992
"Doctor Who: The Scripts" Series
Individual Episode Titles: The Cannibal Flower (Part 1); The Mockery of a Man (Part 2), A Light on the Dead Planet (Part 3), Tabon of Luxor (Part 4), An Infinity of Surprises (Part 5), The Flower Blooms (Part 6)

TARDIS CREW The first Doctor, Ian, Barbara and Susan.

TRAVEL LOG A moon of Luxor, time unknown.

CHRONOLOGY Intended as the second "Doctor Who" story, *The Masters of Luxor* follows on the heels of Coburn's "An Unearthly Child." Yet, it was eventually shelved in favor of "The Daleks." (Television producers changing their mind about a script? Never.) The following text hails from *The Master of Luxor* scriptbook, released in 1992 along with such canonized works as "The Crusades" and "The Daemons."

STORY SUMMARY On a remote moon orbiting the planet Luxor, a crystal structure drains the TARDIS of power and strands the Doctor and his friends in an empty complex with a banqueting hall. After a splendid meal, the Doctor's party greets the robotic Derivitrons but grows uneasy with their human-looking leader, the so-called "Perfect One." To their terror, the TARDIS crew discovers the complex actually serves as a Luxor prison—and worse, the Perfect One has illicitly atomized the prisoners and drained their life-forces, attempting to augment itself and become fully human.

Having only experimented on men, the Perfect One grows curious about Susan and Barbara's female bodies, and suspects they might contain superior forms of energy. Susan and Barbara fail to escape but momentarily damage one of the base's power coils, allowing the Doctor and Ian to flee outside the complex. On the moon's dark surface, they spot a flashing light and hope it belongs to potential allies that fled the Perfect One's wrath.

The Doctor and Ian track the flashing light to a mausoleum and discover a hermetically sealed coffin. Investigating further, Ian breaks the coffin seal and revives a Luxor scientist named Tabon from suspended animation. Guilt ridden, Tabon admits to using his own people as fodder to create the "superior" Derivitrons, but says the Derivitrons collectively grew stronger and in time developed the Perfect One to express their inner schizophrenia. Tabon, fearing the Perfect One's power, cowardly fled and entered suspended animation while the Perfect One butchered travelers from Luxor to augment his power.

Convincing Tabon to aid them, the Doctor and Ian return to the complex but learn the Perfect One has linked his life rhythms to the base's atomic reactor—meaning it'll explode if he's killed. As the Perfect One prepares Barbara and Susan for his transference process, the Doctor's trio intercedes and Tabon decries the Perfect One as a monstrosity of science.

Unhinged by his creator's rebuke, the Perfect One tells the Derivitrons to kill his enemies, but Tabon orders the robots to halt. Unsure which master to obey, the Derivitrons suffer a mental breakdown and flail about. Completely schizophrenic and unable to accept he's less-than-human, the Perfect One rants while an out-of-control Derivitron pounds on him.

The Doctor, Ian and Tabon rescue the wounded Perfect One—fearing an atomic explosion—but a second assault cracks the Perfect One's brain insulation. While a redeemed Tabon holds the Perfect One's head together and delays his death, the Doctor's team reaches the TARDIS and dematerializes just as the complex's systems falter and the Ship's power returns. Seconds later, the Perfect One expires and the atomic stacks rupture, destroying Tabon and the entire moon forever while the TARDIS crew presses on to new adventures.

MEMORABLE MOMENTS The Doctor ponders why Earth-written science fiction always paints unknown intelligences as hostile. The Derivitrons supply the TARDIS crew with new clothes, but the stubborn Doctor flushes his down the loo. Barbara and Susan momentarily disrupt a Derivitron's logic-based circuits by singing "Onward Christian Soldiers." The Perfect One, obviously mad, admits he just wants to be loved (Ian drives home the point that Tabon hates the Perfect One and is ashamed for building him).

Some great cliffhangers: The Perfect One acknowledging he's dead, but vowing to gain true life (Part 2). Mercury rising as an injury to the Perfect One threatens to blow the atomic stacks (Part 4). Ian tied in the Perfect One's death chair as the switch gets thrown (Part 5).

SEX AND SPIRITS The (unintentionally) double-entendre loaded *The Masters of Luxor* includes the Doctor trying to fix the TARDIS' ailing power supply and telling Barbara: "It's no use, Miss Wright.

MISCELLANEOUS STUFF!

LUXOR ORIGINS

Originally intended as the second "Doctor Who" TV story, *The Masters of Luxor* was ultimately rejected in favor of Terry Nation's "The Daleks." As such, this script at best represents a "parallel universe" view of events after "An Unearthly Child" and could only be considered canon with the greatest of difficulties (the TARDIS' flying like a helicopter and the probable scrapping of "Edge of Destruction" had *The Masters of Luxor* been filmed being just a couple of the problems).

Whereas the missing sixth Doctor stories (*The Nightmare Fair*, *The Ultimate Evil* and *Mission to Magnus*) effortlessly fit between "Revelation of the Daleks" and "Trial of a Time Lord" and are largely considered canon, *The Masters of Luxor* would give early "Doctor Who" a continuity aneurysm if it counted. The "Doctor Who" novelists indirectly concur—Gary Russell's *Divided Loyalties* incorporated elements of *Nightmare Fair*, whereas only Jim Mortimore's *Campaign*, also apocryphal, has included *The Masters of Luxor*.

The final judges of such things—fandom at large—mostly seem to dub *The Masters of Luxor* as apocrypha, leaving it a tasty little view of a might-have-been world.

It was being sucked out before I turned it on."

A Derivitron's perceptor coils dangerously vibrate upon seeing females Susan and Barbara, so Ian cheekily adds: "They're women, old mechanical chum...w-o-m-e-n. And if you think your perceptor coils are the only ones affected..."

Most of all, we grew moon-eyed to read Ian telling the incomplete Perfect One, "I could give you a man's life, Perfect One. A man's life."

ASS-WHUPPINGS The Doctor bangs his head as the TARDIS violently lands (between this and "Edge of Destruction," he's just got no luck). Barbara and Susan smash a Derivitron with a trolley. Per tradition for most companions, Ian twists an ankle (they shoot horses that can't run, you know).

The Perfect One likely murdered dozens of prisoners, and atomizes a prisoner, on-screen, in his torture chair. Tabon opts for suicide in the grand finale, which destroys the Perfect One and the entire moon in a ball of flame.

TV TIE-INS Susan and Ian are hungry, having skipped proper meals thanks to their detention by cavemen. The Doctor re-establishes that he and Susan don't hail from Earth ("An Unearthly Child"). The TARDIS' Fault Locator ("The Daleks") allows the Doctor to trace circuit flaws *and* direct the Ship to repair herself.

CHARACTER DEVELOPMENT

The Doctor: Has a photographic memory, but struggles to remember the name of rough cider. He learned strategy by reading memoirs of 20th century generals. His people have achieved suspended animation, but he doesn't know much about it.

The Doctor and Susan: The Doctor claims that Susan is all he has left, perhaps indicating his family's dead.

Ian Chesterton: Ian moves faster than the Derivitrons or the Perfect One, and knows a good rugby tackle.

Tabon (a.k.a. Exalted Lord of Urdanna, Warden of the High District, and Scientific Master of the Masters of Luxor): Tabon developed most of the equipment used by the Perfect One for experimenting on prisoners from Luxor and making the Derivitrons. He spent seven years in suspended animation, and renounces a time he burned a holy book in front of his students.

The Perfect One: The human-looking Perfect One has…well…perfect features and a shining face. The Derivitrons, limited in thought and action, collectively dreamed of the Perfect One as a means of escaping their slavery. However advanced he might seem, the Perfect One has a robotic design, lacking the ability to heal or experience pain. His mental engrams are patterned after Tabon's memories.

The Perfect One doesn't need to eat but enjoys food anyway. He's dangerous because "evil" holds no meaning for him. The Perfect One removes his captive's speech with a spray and has a uses a paralyzing drug. His personality center's a cerebrum cortex of liquefied Azzintium metal, which stores electrical and magnetic impulses almost to infinity. However, it quickly solidifies if exposed beyond an unspecified temperature.

The TARDIS: The solar-powered TARDIS falls lifeless on sunless worlds (the roof light glows as the Ship recharges). The Ship can fly about like a helicopter and has an altimeter. The scanner's fuzzy until it adjusts to the outside light. Any fault in the TARDIS systems puts the Ship into the safety of "free float" mode (presumably a means of suspending in the Time Vortex) via use of the hyper-dimensional neutralizer circuit. The Ship can't withstand an atomic explosion.

ALIEN RACES *Derivitrons:* Crafted as robotic servitors, the Derivitrons have some intelligence and engineering skill. Like the Daleks, they falter on stairs. One advanced Derivitron is named "Proto," but most are nameless. Derivitrons designate themselves as "Mark One" class or the slightly more advanced, talking "Mark Two."

ALIEN PLANETS *Luxor:* Located in the center of the Primiddion Galaxy, Luxor sports a whopping 700 dead satellites. The people heavily rely on machines, but Luxorian architects meld beauty and mechanical efficiency. Revolutionaries are sent to the prison moon.

Luxor has women (praise God), although it's alleged that female children who don't meet a certain standard are killed (men of all shapes and sizes are allowed). Before the Derivitrons went renegade, the Luxorians sent them disused atomic devices to deactivate. A God-based cemetery indicates Luxorites adhere to religion.

STUFF YOU NEED *The Perfect One's Chair* atomizes his hapless victims (come sit in my chair, little boy). No Luxorite has ever taken "50,000 lomotrons" and lived.

PLACES TO GO

The Milky Way Galaxy: Several million planets in the Milky Way look like Earth's moon.

The Perfect One's Fortress: Initially served as a prison, complete with a dome that looks like a giant menacing flower. A 500-year-old mountain tunnel allows secret access. A crystal globe monitoring system tracks people throughout the base, but you can tip out the globes' liquid to disable it. After the Perfect One's insurrection, ships from Luxor stopped visiting.

PHENOMENA The Doctor says *robot-human transference*, or the process of draining life from flesh to make robots human, is impossible.

AT THE END OF THE DAY Tragic, engaging and horrific in intent—rather like looking into the mirror and seeing a scarred half-face glaring back at you. *The Masters of Luxor* understandably skews its characterization from what we're familiar with, but the final product's nicely eerie, surprisingly brutal and highly reflective of its time period (the Perfect One singles out Susan and Barbara for special examination simply because they're women). Obviously, we're ecstatic the show's producers opted for "The Daleks," but can't help pondering if they could've scrapped "The Keys of Marinus" or "The Sensorites" and filmed *The Masters of Luxor* instead. Unless you're mortally opposed to black-and-white "Who," here's an oddity worth reading.

APOCRYHPHA: CAMPAIGN

By Jim Mortimore

Independent release, 2001, for the benefit of Bristol Area Down Syndrome Association

TARDIS CREW The first Doctor, Ian, Barbara, Susan and a heap of alternate companions.

TRAVEL LOG The in-flight TARDIS. At story's end, the Ship prepares to land at Pella during Alexander's reign.

CHRONOLOGY For the real TARDIS crew, likely between "Planet of Giants" and "The Dalek Invasion of Earth." Several alternate timelines appear, one involving *The Masters of Luxor*.

STORY SUMMARY Months after Barbara died from radiation poisoning on Skaro, the Doctor, Ian and Susan poorly acclimate to a nomadic life in time and space without her. But perhaps more disturbing, the Doctor reports that the Universe outside the TARDIS—literally the entirety of creation—has ceased to exist.

Suddenly, the "deceased" Barbara nonchalantly reappears in the TARDIS, staggering her Shipmates. Barbara fails to recall the Daleks—let alone her "death"—but insists she remembers Ian serving as one of Alexander the Great's soldiers and dying beneath a chariot's wheels.

Gradually, the TARDIS crew records their memories, searching for further discrepancies. With the Universe still vanished, the crew spends a number of decades in the TARDIS, variously experiencing (and usually failing to notice) a number of continuity shifts. In some versions, a young boy named Philip, the son of Susan and Alexander the Great, appears. In another timeline, a despair-riddled Ian commits suicide, opening the TARDIS doors and launching himself into a void. Even more bizarrely, the TARDIS crew sometimes shifts identities, becoming "companions" such as Cliff, Lola, Sue, Bridget and Mandy.

Eventually, the Doctor disappears from the TARDIS altogether, leaving a note that claims he unlocked the secret of something called the "Game of Me." Increasingly convinced that one moves

MISCELLANEOUS STUFF!

'CAMPAIGN' ORIGINS

The BBC originally commissioned Jim Mortimore (*Eye of Heaven*, *Blood Heat*), to write a first Doctor novel entitled *Campaign*, but later—from what we can piece together—Mortimore submitted a completed *Campaign* draft that barely, if at all, matched his approved proposal. The BBC, unwilling to accept a book it essentially hadn't commissioned, pulled *Campaign* from its release schedule.

Sometime later, Mortimore self-released *Campaign* and stipulated proceeds would go to the Bristol Area Down Syndrome Association. A number of *Campaign* softbacks were released, with most reports indicating that Mortimore successfully fulfilled his orders. However, as *I, Who 2* went to press, rumors circulated that BBC higher-ups had finally cited Mortimore with a cease-and-desist order, taking the book out of print over night and certainly scrapping a limited hardback edition sponsored by Ambrosia Books and Collectibles.

through "Game of Me" levels by dying, Ian and Ida (one of the random TARDIS companions) cut their own throats. Again reincarnated, Ian advances to the final level and "wins" when a game-generated version of the Doctor translates various languages and helps construct the Tower of Babel.

Soon after, a highly amused Ian wakes up in the TARDIS console room, greeted by an also-pleased Doctor, Susan and Barbara. Ian tells Susan he enjoyed playing the "Game of Me," an alien device that mentally links players into a computer-generated landscape full of challenges and shifting rules. Susan impishly offers her friends another round, but a weary Ian and Barbara toss cushions at her as the TARDIS continues onward.

MEMORABLE MOMENTS Ian faints upon seeing the "deceased" Barbara strut into the console room like nothing's happened. Barbara and Ian hysterically laugh over a time when the Doctor counteracted giant jellyfish stings with a sea cucumber concoction.

The Doctor claims, despite the TARDIS' extra-dimensional nature, that one can't put infinite space into a finite box—but one can put infinite meaning into such a space.

The top moment in *Campaign* (and indeed, a number of first Doctor books): The reserved Doctor affectionately tells an angered Barbara: "I care for you. Yes. Yes, of course, my dear Barbara. Of course I care for you. There are only the four of us now. We must care for each other."

SEX AND SPIRITS Susan bears Alexander's son (young Philip) in some "Game of Me" scenarios. In others, Alexander seems infatuated with Ian. The real Susan is looks only smitten with Alexander (after Barbara's history lessons).

Ian and Barbara have difficulty showing affection (older versions of Ian and Barbara probably sleep together). Cleopatra tried to revenge herself upon King Philip's infidelity by seducing Ian (he declined). Queen Olympia tried to seduce the variant Cliff Chesterton.

Among the alternate TARDIS companions, Lola's deeply in love with the violent tempered Cliff while siblings Alan and Ida, trapped in the TARDIS alone for several decades, resort to incest (and won't that make great Saturday viewing for the whole family).

ASS-WHUPPINGS The TARDIS crew dies a shocking amount—but rarely on-screen. Most striking, Ian commits suicide by opening the TARDIS doors and throwing himself out.

In one "Game" version, the Doctor's actions get Ian heavily shot by archers, then crushed beneath chariot wheels (you'd think one or the other would have been plenty). Alternatively, Ian drunkenly goads Kleitus the Black, one of Alexander's most trusted officers, and inadvertently spurs an assault on the city of Halikarnassos that kills thousands (Ian takes an arrow in the chest for his trouble). In a couple scenarios, Ian killed the Doctor. Pseudo-companion Lola, pining for years without her lover Cliff, goes berserk upon his sudden return and knifes him in the heart.

Ian's mother has passed away (for years, they only met at Christmas).

TV TIE-INS The Doctor still insists time travelers cannot change history ("The Aztecs"). There's mention of the Sensorites ("The Sensorites") and their giant spiders, plus the Menoptera ("The Web Planet") and the Zarbi Supremo (which sounds like a pizza).

NOVEL TIE-INS A heavy amount of alternate continuity hails from *The Masters of Luxor*. Alexander's war horse is named Bukephalas (the inspiration for the restaurant in *The Crystal Bucephalus*).

CHARACTER DEVELOPMENT

The Doctor: Has lived for centuries. He can sit in thought for days without eating or drinking (sounds artistic, doesn't it?).

The Doctor and Susan: Their similar movements sometimes appear choreographed.

Ian Chesterton: An Ian variant thinks he first encountered the TARDIS at Barnes Common while working as a mathematician at Cambridge University. He still can't read the TARDIS controls. The Doctor gave older Ian, who can't taste much, an ointment for depression (but it made his hair fall out). To find Ian's TARDIS room, leave the console room, walk along a short connecting corridor to a hallway and open the fifth door on left.

Cliff Chesterton: Ian variant who's a bit older than 30, 5'11" and starting to gray. He remembers the Ship landing on Luxor, encountering the Saxons in Britain around 408 A.D. and finding an Earth duplicate where everything was reversed and the enemy leader looked like the Doctor. As a child, he read H.G. Wells' *Lord of the Dynamos*.

Barbara Wright: In one Game version, Barbara's a secretary, teaching history and geography to make extra money. She lives in Barnes Common. In other scenarios, Barbara can't drive and was never a secretary, but teaches history at Coal Hill secondary modern. A Barbara who doesn't remember the Daleks recalls events from *The Masters of Luxor* and watched Alexander die with the remains of his army. She recollects the God-machines of Mechanistra and the amphibious fish people of Kandalinga—one of whom tried to eat the TARDIS.

Older Barbara needs bifocals to read (but the TARDIS can't manufacture them).

Susan (a.k.a. Susan English): Susan was present when Mark Twain wrote his draft outline for *Huckleberry Finn* (the Doctor spent time on Twain's riverboat as a gambler). Susan's several centuries older than she looks.

In one "Game" version, the Doctor abandoned Susan over some argument in the little town of Bespher. A 40-year-old woman named Anshar cared for Susan but died in a bandit raid. Later, Alexander discovered Bespher was peopled with Greeks descendants who collaborated with the Persian Xerxes' invasion of Macedonia. Alexander's soldiers, including Ian, slaughtered the town. Susan went on to live for many human lifetimes.

Alan and Ida: Two of the more notable alternate companions, siblings brought as children into the TARDIS by their parents during the Great Fire of London. Alan and Ida's parents soon died and years later, the Doctor vanished also. Afterward, Alan and Ida spent 40 years alone in the TARDIS.

Philip: Susan and Alexander's two-year-old son has calm, clear eyes and somewhat curly hair.

Aristotle: Depending on which "Game" version you prefer, Aristotle argued mathematics with the Doctor or helped him fix the TARDIS.

The TARDIS (a.k.a. Tardis, T.A.R.D.I.S.): The Ship is solar powered (*The Masters of Luxor*). The TARDIS' central power source can transmutate matter, turning lead into gold or frogs into children with relative ease. The TARDIS contains a Martian chess set. Its interior dimensions act like a mini-universe.

The Ship makes innumerable changes to its internal configuration, but sometimes forgets where it puts things (it once placed the swimming pool in the broom-cupboard). It regulates its internal gravity, as well as floor and wall hardness, for optimum comfort.

The TARDIS contains a Mediterranean rooftop courtyard, complete with clear blue sky and bright sunlight. It also houses a frigid polar observatory (you'd better wear a parka). Best of all, a horse lives in the TARDIS.

ALIEN RACES *The Doctor's People (The Time Lords, naturally)* have never encountered a void such as the "missing" Universe.

STUFF YOU NEED Susan acquired *"The Game of Me,"* a mechanical device, on an unspecified planet (not even the Doctor knows which one). Its objectives are always different, creating an interactive landscape for its players. Slaving it to the TARDIS console activates it.

PLACES TO GO *The TARDIS Library:* More of a forest grove, where trees encode book text as chemical patterns. The more appealing the scent, the better the book. To read, simply pluck a fruit and eat it. Spending too much time there results in a unique form of eyestrain.

AT THE END OF THE DAY Let's be crystal clear on one thing: However much as we support creators' rights, it *would not* be appropriate to paint the BBC as villains for rejecting *Campaign*. At the end of the day, business as business, and any writer who completes a text that wildly deviates from the approved outline must bear responsibility for it. Period.

That said, speaking purely on the book at hand, *Campaign* provides an enthralling march as a "Twilight Zone"-ish memory play, heavily favoring radical "Doctor Who" readers with its multiple continuity shifts. The opening and ending, while

devastatingly lucid, border an acid trip of a middle that verges from "utterly brilliant" to "virtually incomprehensible" (meaning you'd damn well better pay attention). Still, you'll get a lot from the effort, allowing *Campaign* to deserve praise as a grand experiment and a book we're glad we read.

APOCRYPHA: DEATH COMES TO TIME

By Dan Freedman and Colin Meake

Release Date: July 2001
Episode 1: "At the Temple of the Fourth"
NOTES: Intended as five-part radio broadcast for BBC Radio Four, "Death Comes to Time" failed to make it through the pilot stage, with only Episode One produced for broadcast. The official BBC "Doctor Who" website ran that single episode as a webcast in July 2001, generating (as of this writing) 1.5 million hits (the BBC expected a paltry 40,000 or 50,000).

TARDIS CREW The seventh Doctor, Ace and Antimony.

TRAVEL LOG Santiny and Micen Island in Orion, time unknown.

CHRONOLOGY Likely between *Cat's Cradle: Witchmark* and *Nightshade* (actually, there's no way of knowing, although Ace's slight maturing and the lack of Bernice suggests this takes place a short while into the New Adventures).

STORY SUMMARY Hostile Canisian battlefleets, led by the ruthless General Tannis, overrun the peaceful republic of Santiny and capture its central legislature. In the midst of the slaughter, the Doctor and his hard-hitting companion Antimony (Kevin Eldon) arrive, fearful that a permanent occupation of Santiny could cause further Canisian conquests. The Doctor and Antimony rescue the surviving Santiny senators, briefly shuttling them in the TARDIS to a safer location and encouraging them to incite rebellion. The Doctor pledges to help destabilize the Canisian military, but first departs to answer a Time Lord summons coming from the heart of Orion.

Meanwhile, Ace rots in a Canisian prison cell—having evidently failed in a secret mission for the Doctor—until a venerable Time Lord named Casmus rescues her. Casmus takes Ace back to Gallifrey, educating her about the nature of the Universe and preparing her for a greater task.

On Micen Island in Orion, the Doctor and Antimony find an ancient edifice called "The Temple of the Fourth," containing statues of long-departed Time Lords. There, a Time Lord named the Minister of Chance (Stephen Fry) nefariously informs the Doctor that two Time Lords, Antinor and Valentine, died recently under mysterious circumstances. The Doctor and the Minister of Chance agree that a greater game is afoot, but the Doctor intends to continue efforts against the Canisians.

Elsewhere, General Tannis discovers a third party has helped the Santiny senators to escape. Clearly possessing inside knowledge, Tannis vows to destroy anyone who opposes his secret agenda, declaring, "Even Time Lords die..."

ASS-WHUPPINGS General Tannis eradicates the Santiny city of Annet and its nine million inhabitants with a tectonic bomb. Santiny Admiral Letner orders her troops to suicide runs, but the Canisians mop the floor with them. It's reported that two Time Lords named Antinor and Valentine have snuffed it.

CHARACTER DEVELOPMENT

The Doctor: He knew some of the Time Lords represented in statues on Micen Island.

Antimony: Artwork accompanying the webcast (by longtime *Doctor Who Magazine* artist Lee Sullivan) depicts Antimony as having light purple skin, blonde hair and black eyes. He's a polite and curious newcomer to the TARDIS, but seems to have enhanced strength and likes hitting things.

The Minister of Chance: A flamboyant Time Lord and old friend of the Doctor's. His TARDIS is newer than the Doctor's Ship.

ALIEN RACES *Canisians:* Hailing from Alpha Canis, the Canisians thrive on money and evidently conquer for economic value.

PLACES TO GO *Micen Island:* During their interventionist days, the Time Lords wiped out the inhabitants of Micen Island, although the Temple of the Fourth remains as a memorial.

AT THE END OF THE DAY We're refraining from a solid review, given that it's unfair to make concrete statements when you've heard only Episode One of a story (rather like trying to evaluate *A Tale of Two Cities* after reading the first chapter). Yet, on pain of death, we'd have to admit that "Death Comes to Time" has a lot to overcome. The Canisians are largely your average gunslingers in space, there's a lot of weak dialogue and

the Doctor, despite his consultation with the Minister of Chance, has only a pindrop of subtlety. Still, this story prompted coverage from the Associated Press and *Entertainment Weekly*, so we're hoping for its completion—and the chance to reevaluate it.

APOCRYPHA: THE CURSE OF FATAL DEATH

By Steven Moffat

Release Date: Broadcast as a "Comic Relief" special on March 12, 1999.

TARDIS CREW The ninth, tenth, eleventh, twelfth and thirteenth Doctors and Emma.

TRAVEL LOG Terserus and Dalek spacecraft, time unknown.

STORY SUMMARY When the Doctor (Rowan Atkinson) mysteriously invites the Master (Jonathan Pryce) to a deserted castle on the planet Terserus, the Master travels even further back in time and bribes the castle architect, convincing him to incorporate fiendish traps into the castle's structure. Thankfully, the Doctor anticipates this and also bribes the architect, countering the Master's deadly "Spikes of Doom" snare with a "Sofa of Reasonable Comfort" escape route.

Weary of fighting and crawling through ventilation shafts, the Doctor announces his intention to retire and marry his companion Emma (Julia Sawalha). Undaunted, the Master threatens to retroactively bribe the castle architect again and make him build a trap door where the Doctor's standing. However, the Doctor has further expected this and bought the castle architect an elaborate dinner. As the Master throws a lever, intending to drop the Doctor and Emma into Terserus' 500-mile-long sewer system, a trap door unexpectedly opens under the Master's feet and he disappears.

The Master spends 312 years crawling through Terserus' sewers and travels back in his TARDIS, bursting in on the Doctor and Emma as an aged, feces-covered Time Lord. The Master attempts to throttle the Doctor, but misses and again falls through the open trap door, spending a further 312 years climbing through mountains of shit. Even more wizened and crap-covered, the Master allies himself with the nose-less Daleks, the only race in the Universe who will tolerate his ingrained stench. The Master and the Daleks return to Terserus, where a merry chase ensues and the

Master again falls into the sewers, but the Daleks capture the Doctor and Emma.

Aboard the Dalek spaceship, the Doctor and Emma find the Daleks have restored the Master to health and vigor, augmenting his chest with etheric beam locators that look disturbingly like firm, well-polished breasts. To the Doctor's dismay, the Master helps the Daleks build a Zentronic energy beam—one of the most powerful devices in the Universe. The Doctor realizes the nose-less Daleks will eventually dispose of the Master and decides to warn his old adversary using ancient Terseron—a means of communication that involves one deploying precisely attuned farts. However, the Daleks discover the Doctor's deception and unleash a fury of blasts, killing the Doctor and sending the Zentronic beam emitter out of control.

The Doctor regenerates into a strikingly handsome body (Richard E Grant) with a very talented tongue, but the Master declares that the damaged Zentronic beam emitter will soon explode and destroy them all. The Doctor attempts to repair the device, but a short circuit makes him regenerate into a shy incarnation (Jim Broadbent), then a hormone loaded sex muffin (Hugh Grant). The Doctor brings the Zentronic beam emitter under control, but a final Zentronic energy burst seems to permanently kill him.

To honor their fallen enemy, the Daleks and the Master both denounce their evil ways. However, the laws of physics, unable to imagine a Universe without the Doctor, bend a bit and regenerate the Doctor into a blonde-haired, firmly bosomed female body (Joanna Lumley). Disappointed, Emma breaks off her engagement to the Doctor. However, the female Doctor suddenly finds the reformed Master shockingly attractive and walks off with him, even as the Master promises to demonstrate *why* he's named "the Master."

MEMORABLE MOMENTS The utter hilarity of the Master promising to drop the Doctor and Emma into "Five hundred miles of fear and feces!" but repeatedly falling into the Terserus sewers himself. A cliffhanger ends with the running Doctor and Emma opening a door—and finding what looks like 4855 Daleks on the other side.

The Master brags to Emma that his tit-shaped Dalek bumps are "extremely firm." The oft-repeated "I'll explain later" joke (you'll have to watch the tape) nearly killed us. The dying Hugh Grant Doctor's last words are, "Look after the Universe for me...I've put a lot of work into it."

The newly born Joanna Lumley Doctor examines her mammaries, wondering if they can detect etheric beam emissions like the Master's Dalek bumps. She walks off with the Master at the story's climax, even as the Master's mad laughter fills the screen.

SEX AND SPIRITS The central columns in the Doctor and Master's TARDISes display more phallic thrusts than a jackhammer. The Doctor proposes to Emma, the only companion "he's ever had." Dung slugs keep the sewer-captive Master company on those "long, lonely nights."

The female Doctor grows ecstatic to learn her vibrating sonic screwdriver has a high-speed setting. Emma breaks her engagement by telling the female Doctor: "You're just the man I fell in love with." The Master and the female Doctor walk off arm in arm.

TV TIE-INS The Roger Delgado Master snuffed it on Terserus (*Legacy of the Daleks*), although Chancellor Goth later rescued him ("The Deadly Assassin"). Still, we doubt "The Curse of Fatal Death" has much to do with those stories.

CHARACTER DEVELOPMENT

The Doctor: By his calculation, the Doctor's saved every planet in the known Universe a minimum of 27 times.

The Master: As a further augmentation, the Master's replaced his right hand with a Dalek suction cup—and doesn't know what the hell to do with it. His TARDIS has a green interior. Dramatic license makes lightning flare in the Master's console room while he cackles.

HISTORY The Terserons, the most kind and peace-loving race the Doctor has ever encountered, became the most shunned species in the Universe because they could communicate only through precise breaking of wind. They tragically died out when they discovered fire.

AT THE END OF THE DAY Riotously funny—oh God, we laughed until we cried. Hell, even our girlfriends found it downright hysterical (the Part One cliffhanger involving dozens of Daleks did them in). What makes "The Curse of Fatal Death" beautiful is that it's done as a comedy, *not* as a string of banal inside jokes designed only to appease the fans. Even better, its intelligent wit makes this a glorious romp for adults, unburdened by a cheapening laugh track. Our only regret for "The Curse of Fatal Death" is that it's a mere 22 minutes long.

THE NEW
ADVENTURES
Doctor WHO

POSTER OFFER INSIDE

FIFTIETH NEW ADVENTURE

HAPPY ENDINGS

PAUL CORNELL

VII

Apocrypha:
Alternate Covers

HAPPY ENDINGS

A close-up shot of Bernice's wedding in *Happy Endings*, featuring (from left) Silurian musician Jacquilian, the Pakhar Keri, Benny, Jason Kane and adult Ace. The final cover, as you likely know, showed a sprawling wedding audience with two versions of the seventh Doctor. Please excuse that Sophie Aldred's signature (oh, the shame of it all) slightly obscures this piece of artwork.

VII

Apocrypha:
Alternate Covers

CHRISTMAS ON A RATIONAL PLANET

Unbelievable as it seems, Virgin planned an even *more* surreal cover for Lawrence Miles' debut *Christmas on a Rational Planet*. Virgin first publicized this version, but the editors later deemed it— and this is a technical term—sheer crap. It probably didn't help that the border and back cover sported an ungodly yellow hue that the black-and-white version at right mercifully spares you from. Again, pardon that Sylvester McCoy's autograph appears on this proof copy— it was the best we could get.

THE NEW
ADVENTURES
Doctor WHO

CHRISTMAS ON A
RATIONAL PLANET

LAWRENCE MILES